I0661412

# The Miriyanti Trilogy
## Omnibus

## by M J McBride

CR ୫ଠ
Quelle Press
CR ୫ଠ

The Miriyanti Trilogy Omnibus
Copyright © 2018 and 2021 by M J McBride

All rights reserved. This book or any portion thereof may not be
reproduced or used in any manner whatsoever without the express
written permission of the publisher except for the use of brief
quotations in a book review.

ISBN: 979-8-218-27937-0

References to historical events, real people, and real places are used
fictitiously. Names, characters, and places are products of the author's
imagination.

Front cover: Artwork by Dmitry Yakhovsky. Design by M J McBride.

*The board is clearing. The old game is almost played, and the pieces broken.*

– Dorothy Dunnett, *Checkmate*

# Nor Do the Stars Shine There

## The Wrong Path

"We're on the wrong path. I'm sure of it." Wil reined his horse around and waited for Ruarshi to come up beside him. "We ought to turn back."

"You don't seriously intend for us to go haring off down that game trail we passed, do you? I can't believe that boy back in town would describe that as a road."

"Maybe that was the closest German word for it he could find. I would imagine his Polish was more precise. We've come too far south and west."

"You're certain?"

"Yes."

Ruarshi tilted his head back and looked up into the thickly intertwined branches above them. Even though most of their leaves had fallen, brown and withered, to the forest floor, they and a layer of high clouds still made it difficult for him to locate the sun.

"We haven't got many hours before nightfall. We'll have to move faster." He urged his mount forward a few paces until he had room to turn her and then gestured for Wil to start back. "Lead on."

"I think we'd make better time if we carried our horses," the Welshman grumbled as they moved off.

"That's possible," Ruarshi said mildly, "but I don't think my back's up to it today. How's yours?"

"Thoroughly jolted. This nag's gait could churn butter."

"We could always try to steal better ones from that nobleman's army."

Wil glared back at him. "Thank you, no. My hair is quite gray enough already without—"

The Welshman gave a strangled cry and began to slide sideways from his saddle. Ruarshi, gasping with the pain that echoed through their link, half fell off his own horse in his rush to catch him before he could hit the ground. They both went down together, landing hard among the dead leaves that carpeted the trail.

Wil looked up at him with wide eyes. "Good lord," he said weakly.

Ruarshi was up on his knees, rolling the Welshman onto his back and ripping at his tunic in order to get a better look at the wound. The arrow had hit Wil in the abdomen and gone deep. He would almost certainly die unless Ruarshi healed him on the spot. A dangerous thing to do, given the circumstances. Not that he had any choice.

"We've got to leave. Whoever it is may try for you next. I can ride."

"Like hell you can. I'm going to heal you here."

"No. Go."

Ruarshi shook his head. "Don't be ridiculous." He quickly scanned the forest for any sign of movement but saw none beyond that caused by the light wind. If the archer intended to shoot him, too, he was certainly taking his time about it. He seized the Welshman's hand. "I'm going to put you to sleep now."

"No. Ruarshi—"

"Shut up."

He sat back and closed his eyes, sending his healer's power flowing into Wil's body. The last bit of his friend's resistance faded as Ruarshi pushed him into unconsciousness. He turned his attention then to the wound itself, staunching the flow of blood before easing the arrow free and tossing it aside. Settling into a deeper trance, he lost himself in the weave of his power as he worked to clean out the injury and knit the damaged organs back together. When he decided he'd done as much as he could, he shook himself back to full wakefulness and looked down at the Welshman.

The ugly, jagged tear in his abdomen had been transformed into a faint pink scar that puckered slightly at the edges, and Wil was resting peacefully, the lines of pain gone from around his eyes and mouth. Ruarshi sighed in relief. His *pir* would recover, given sufficient opportunity. Unless the healer was much mistaken about what was happening, it would now be up to him to ensure Wil had that opportunity.

Ruarshi raised his eyes. Three soldiers stood a few feet off the edge of the path, staring at him warily. The horses were nowhere in sight.

The healer forced himself to his feet, blinking in an effort to make the world stop spinning. He was only partially successful. It had been a long time since he'd carried out a healing without his *pir's* strength to support him, and he felt thoroughly drained.

The soldiers would be counting on that.

"Seen enough?" he asked.

"Not quite. I'd like to take a look at your familiar."

"His name is Wil, and he's right here. What's to look at?"

"The hole Anton put in him. I've never seen a Miriyanti healer's handiwork before. If I may?"

"It's a little late for polite behavior." Ruarshi watched in helpless fury as the speaker stepped forward and knelt next to the Welshman, pushing his bloodied tunic aside. The man whistled through his teeth and beckoned the other two over to gawk.

"I told you he was Miriyanti. White hair and black eyes. You're going to have to learn to have more faith in me." The man stood and nudged Wil with his boot. The prodding didn't wake him. "We've got a sick man in our camp. You're to come with us and heal him."

"No."

The soldier rolled his eyes. "I could carry you all the way back to camp one-handed. Wouldn't you prefer to walk? We'll put your man on a horse and bring him with us."

"I said no."

"Anton, shoot the familiar again."

"What?" The archer glanced up nervously at Ruarshi before returning his attention to his companion.

"Shoot him again. The healer's got too much energy for his own good. Another healing will take it right out of him."

"Who is it you want us to heal?" Ruarshi asked.

The soldier smiled. "You'll find out when you get to our camp. He's not one of the Black Crusaders, if that's what you're worried about."

"I'm worried about your methods. How will you be able to trust me after bringing us into your camp like this?"

"He's got a point, Sebastian," the archer said.

"No, he doesn't. All this dickering is simply for the sake of making himself feel better. Look at him. He can barely stand. Ready to go, healer?"

"Does it matter?" So this was all about saving face, was it? He wove his magic sloppily into three improvised garrotes and flung them at the men. They couldn't see or sense the weaves, but they felt them well enough when Ruarshi looped them around their throats and pulled them taut.

The archer and the silent soldier fell to their knees, clawing at their necks. Unfortunately Sebastian had greater presence of mind. He yanked his sword from its sheath, rested it against Wil's chest, and waited.

Ruarshi didn't dare try to knock the blade aside. He was quick, but the soldier might very well prove to be quicker. Instead he dropped his hold on the weaves, allowing them to disperse and disappear in the cool evening air.

A boot connected with the small of Ruarshi's back and he was flung forward onto the pathway. He struggled to rise but could no longer find his balance. The boot next smashed into his ribs and he curled into a ball, covering his head with his arms as the man continued to kick him. He needed to say something. If only he could catch his breath...

"Stop, damn it. He'll be of no use to anyone if you keep that up."

"He tried to choke me!"

"He tried it on all of us and he failed. Move off if you can't control yourself better."

"This was a stupid goddamn idea. What if he'd been one of their fighters?"

"You'd probably be dead by now. Quit your worrying."

Ruarshi swallowed and spoke. "We'll come with you to heal this man." His declaration was greeted by silence, so he repeated it. "We'll come with you."

"Good. That's good. We won't touch you or your familiar again as long as you cooperate with us."

"Agreed. We'll see to your man as soon as we're able."

✳ ✳ ✳

When Wil awoke, the first thing he noticed was the presence of a roof over his head, rather than the tangled branches and slate gray sky he'd been expecting. Although the notion that he'd slept inside didn't bother him at all, the fact that he couldn't remember how he'd gotten there worried him a little. He didn't have a hangover, so that couldn't account for it, and the only other possibility was that he and Ruarshi had spent a good half day or more on a particularly difficult healing. If that were the case, he should be able to recall something about it, like who the patient was and where they'd found him. Or her. A name would be nice.

He shifted on—his pallet?—and looked around. He was alone in a small room in a dilapidated farmhouse. Its one window had been boarded up. Outside the closed door he could hear the heavy tread of boots and masculine voices rising and falling in conversation. From farther away came the sound of someone hammering on metal.

He began to sit up, stiffened, and lay slowly back down again. With one hand he carefully explored the sore spot, stopping first at the blood-encrusted hole in his clothing and going on from there to the skin of his abdomen. He seemed to have developed a rather large scar sometime during those hours that had gone missing from his memory. Maybe he'd tripped and fallen onto a dagger blade. He doubted it.

The Welshman closed his eyes and tried the link that bound him to the healer. A few seconds later he was on his feet and moving in the general direction of the door, wondering if his legs were going to cooperate long enough to get him there. He would crawl if he had to, until he found the Miriyanti and figured out why their link had become so weak. If the feeble state of their bond was related to his own mysterious injury, that was one thing. If there were a different explanation for it, someone was going to pay for his lapse in judgment.

"… your idea of following orders?"

Wil was still a few steps away from the door when raised voices brought him up short.

"I told you I wouldn't touch him." Ruarshi sounded intensely annoyed. "He's awake now and I need to see him. The longer it takes him to get well, the more likely it is your man will die before we can do anything about it."

The Welshman held his breath during the pause that followed. It clearly hadn't been an accident that had brought them there.

"What do you think, Father?"

"As long as they are not allowed to come into physical contact, I believe we will be safe."

Safe from what?

The door opened. Ruarshi stood in the hallway, flanked by two soldiers. A priest in his middle years stood a short distance away, regarding the healer with distaste.

Wil took in at a glance the strain on the healer's face and the stiff way he was holding himself. So. "Been reading Montoya's manual, Father?" he asked. "He's a moron, you know. It's good to see you, Ruarshi. What's kept you?"

"Wil, meet Sebastian and Kristoph. Unfortunately Anton isn't here at present. He's the one who shot you from ambush. This is Father Rost. He's quite exercised about my lack of a soul. He's not too sure about yours, either." He stepped forward.

"Watch him!" the priest warned.

"You can watch me all you like. I'm sure you'll find it quite dull."

"We have to let him tend to his man, Father," Sebastian said laconically. "If this goes wrong, blame it on me."

"I've told you what he's capable of. If my instructions aren't followed, we'll all have to deal with the results." The priest faced Ruarshi. "Much as I hope for the Graf's survival, I do not wish him to owe it to you. And I do hope you're both still here when the Teutonic knights arrive." Rost opened a door onto dingy gray light and disappeared outside.

Wil felt a chill. They were with Graf Stahl's army, then, the one besieging Reuenberg. They'd been going out of their way to avoid the place, as he remembered it.

"Until you prove otherwise, I'll assume your word is good, healer," Sebastian said. "Even if it isn't, there will be little enough trouble you can cause. I stopped taking Rost seriously a long time ago. You can visit your familiar for as long as you want."

"Thank you." To the Welshman's ears, Ruarshi didn't sound particularly grateful. "Wil is recovering from a serious wound, as you know. If you'd have someone bring him some food, I'd appreciate it. Something with meat in it, if you please."

The soldier nodded. "We'll see to it."

Though he found the entire discussion fascinating, Wil wanted very badly to retreat to his pallet. The area around his scar was beginning to feel distinctly unpleasant, all the way through to his backbone.

Even through their attenuated link, the healer was aware of his discomfort. "He needs to sit down," Ruarshi said sharply. "One of you will have to assist him."

After a whispered exchange with the older soldier, Kristoph guided the Welshman back to his pallet and got him settled before heading out of the building. Ruarshi entered the room and sat a good yard away from the mattress.

"I'm going to leave this door open in case the priest comes back," Sebastian said, leaning through the doorway. "He's got a good imagination. No need to make it too easy for him to cause you trouble."

"Considerate of you," Ruarshi said, and switched to Welsh. "I'm gratified to see you looking so chipper this morning, Wil, but don't push it."

The Welshman waved that away. "Am I to understand that they shot me because they need you to heal Stahl for them?"

"That seems to be the situation, yes."

"It never occurred to them that they could simply *ask?*"

"They must have been concerned that I would simply refuse. Not without reason."

"The man does have a nasty reputation."

"Then we'll just have to hold our noses when the time comes."

"Maybe," Wil said. "If the time comes. I'd prefer that it didn't. What's the priest think we're going to do?"

"Summon demons to spread disease through the army or something along those lines. The Graf's physician is related to him. Herr Doctor Kramer visited me earlier this morning."

"Why?"

"To pick my brain. It would have been a more worthwhile meeting for both of us if he'd had something more interesting to say. It's hard to reach a diagnosis based on two symptoms. The Graf apparently went into convulsions three days ago, after which he fell into a coma. No improvement since."

"Did anyone check to see if the man had been hit in the head?"

"I asked. The good doctor perceived it as an unfriendly question."

The Welshman started to chuckle, but squelched it hastily. "That was a mistake. Has he had a fever recently? Could it have been a stroke?"

"No to the first question. I won't be able to answer to the second until I see him."

"And when is that going to happen?"

"I don't know. I'll try to put them off for a while on the basis of your condition. If I have to attempt the healing without you, though, I will. Contrary to the wishes of our good priest, I do *not* want to be in this camp when the Crusaders get here."

"It could be awkward," Wil agreed. "They're going to let us leave after we heal Stahl?"

"A nondescript nobleman by the name of Brant assures me we'll be released."

"Nice of them. I'd really like to meet that archer before we go."

"You're in no condition to do anything about him right now."

"Well. That's as may be. I—" He broke off as Kristoph returned carrying a bowl, a thick slice of bread, and a piece of hard cheese. He mumbled a grudging word of thanks to the man and dug in eagerly. He hadn't realized how hungry he was until the smell of the food awakened his appetite.

"He'll need something to drink—" Ruarshi began, but was overridden by the soldier.

"A boy is coming with some beer." A clattering at the door drew their attention. "That's him now." A lanky youth set an enormous mug down at Wil's left hand.

"That will do nicely," the healer said. Once the soldier had left, he resumed. "Don't drink any water while you're here. We're downstream of both the fortress and the army camp. I would mention the town, but they've already destroyed it."

"I thought the Graf intended to take possession of the place."

"He must suppose that all he really needs is the castle. He's probably right. Once the knights and the Polish king stop fighting over it, this should be a fairly prosperous area. The town will be rebuilt."

"Sown with bones. I'm sure it'll be lovely. This is good."

"The peasants around here must still have decent food to steal."

"Now you're making me feel bad for enjoying it."

"Sorry. I don't mean to."

The Welshman looked up from his meal, considering. "Sebastian and Kristoph. Is one of them responsible for your broken ribs?"

"I've said it once. You're in no condition—"

"What am I here for, then? I should have prevented you from being injured. Since I failed so miserably at that, I have to do the next best thing: retaliate. If you tell me I can't, you might as well break our link right now and stop calling me your *pir*."

"Oho, Wil. No you don't. You're not going to take responsibility for my error."

The Welshman took a long pull at his beer. Fortunately it was fairly weak stuff. "What are you talking about?"

"Shields. I know very good and well how to weave the damn things. I should have used them. That arrow would never have hit you."

"And if I'd figured out earlier that we were in the wrong place, the soldiers would never have been anywhere near us. We can probably play this game for hours."

"It's not a game, Wil. I've gotten careless and you're paying for it."

"Umm. The scar does hurt, yes. How many ribs did the soldiers break? It's a shame you can't heal yourself, and I don't blame you for not letting that physician touch you, though he may have been able to help a little. I'd say we're both paying for it. That being the case, can we call it a draw?"

"I just thought you should know that your pair-bonded partner has not lived up to his end of the bargain, in case you want to consider switching to a less hazardous occupation in the future."

"It'll take more than a mortal wound now and then to put me off the life of a wandering healer. There are people from Ireland to Cyprus who adore me. I've grown accustomed to that sort of thing and I don't intend to give it up. Now remind me: what are we arguing about?"

The healer gave a subdued snort. "Nothing, I suppose. But you do have to promise me that you'll forget about defending my honor until after you've recovered."

"By then we won't even be here."

"Exactly."

"I'll agree to that, if you'll find somebody you can trust to wrap your rib cage."

"I'll see what I can do."

Wil grinned into his beer. "It's a deal."

"I'd like you to go back to sleep for a while, unless you have pressing business around the camp. You lost a lot of blood yesterday."

"I feel about ready for a nap. You'll wake me up if anything interesting happens?"

"You'll be the first to know. Can you lie down without help?"

"Let's see. I—" The Welshman maneuvered himself away from the wall and fell precipitously backwards. The beer had gone straight to his head. "The answer to your question was no," he said, biting his lip against the groan he felt building in his chest. Ruarshi sent a trickle of power through their link and the pain faded slowly to a tolerable level. "Thank you."

"Don't thank me. Get some sleep. We'll be out of here soon enough."

The Welshman was happy to oblige. He slipped away into oblivion, distantly aware of the healer's steady presence at his side.

✳ ✳ ✳

Ruarshi sat in the lone chair in the room he'd been allotted, facing the boarded-over window and wishing there were something he could do about his aching chest. The constant pain caused by his two snapped ribs was starting to make him feel nauseous. Between that and his concern for Wil, he found it difficult to think clearly about their situation, a fact that struck him as both unfortunate and predictable. The enforced inactivity was further dulling his wits. He needed some sleep, but lying down was simply out of the question at this point. He'd think about rest only after he'd managed to put at least two coherent thoughts together.

He supposed he should expect another visit from Sebastian soon, a prospect that disgusted him. Ruarshi never wanted to set eyes on the man again. The soldier had made it very clear that he expected his captives to succeed in their attempt to heal the Graf. That was reasonable enough, since the man was apparently hoping for some sort of advancement as a result. What the healer couldn't stomach was the threat that had come after. If Sebastian so much as *looked* at the Welshman again in a way Ruarshi didn't like...

He stood abruptly and walked to the window, where he began to pull idly at one of the boards nailed over the opening. The atmosphere in the room was too close and he badly wanted a breath of fresh air. He wasn't worried about what would happen if his jailer caught him at it. Sebastian was sufficiently perceptive to realize he wouldn't try to leave the camp without his *pir*.

When the door opened some time later, Ruarshi didn't stop what he was doing. He'd almost finished working the nails from the board at the window's left edge, and he could see weak sunlight through the growing gap. The cool air flowed over his hands and into the room. He stood with his back to the door, breathing it in.

"Ruarshi Miriyanti?"

It was a new voice. The healer looked over his shoulder at his visitor, an older man with close-cropped gray hair and an angry red welt running along the left side of his jaw. "Yes?"

"My name is Friedrich Eisen. I've come to talk to you about Stahl."

"Are you a physician?"

"No."

Ruarshi pivoted and leaned back against the wall. "Are you a friend of his?"

"I've known him for years, but I wouldn't go so far as to say that."

The healer waited. Eisen gestured toward the chair. "May I?"

"Of course."

His visitor spent more time than was necessary getting settled, after which he glanced at the bed, the walls, and the ceiling before turning his attention once again to Ruarshi. "Not bad, for a prison. I saw you when they brought you in. I understand they damn near killed your familiar. How badly did they hurt you?"

"Don't trouble yourself about it. Miriyanti heal quickly."

"You saw Reuenberg?"

"What was left of it."

The man nodded. "The inhabitants were mostly Polish. They weren't happy to see us coming and they put up what resistance they could. Stahl's had his eye on the place ever since the knights lost it to King Wladislav a dozen years ago, and he was less than gratified by the reception. He ordered us to burn the town. I think he means to repopulate it with Germans once the castle falls."

"Why are you telling me this?" Ruarshi asked.

"I thought you might have an opinion about the slaughter of civilians."

"I do. How many did you kill?"

"I wasn't counting."

"You don't want me to heal the Graf. Why?"

"I just explained why."

"I have no way of knowing whether or not you're telling me the truth. All I can be certain of is your motivation."

"Ask Sebastian about it. He'll confirm the story. Ask Father Rost. Ask anyone in camp you care to. They'll tell you the same thing. Find someone who doesn't like Stahl, which would be easy enough, and they might tell you even more. You know Stahl beat his oldest son to death when the boy was three years old?"

"I'd heard the rumor. None of that explains why you're here."

Eisen crossed his arms and sat back. "I think it explains my presence rather well. The Graf is a brutal man. Heal him, and his subsequent brutality will be laid to your account. I'm aware that you don't believe in God, but the prospect of a fresh pile of corpses ought to trouble you a little."

"What will change if he dies? Anything?"

"There'll be one less commander who's inclined to give those kinds of orders to his men."

"Who will take over his command?"

"I will. I have an arrangement with the knights. Before you jump to any conclusions, remember that I didn't have to admit that to you. And it's not something you can find out quite so easily as the sordid details of Stahl's life."

"There can't be anything wrong with tying practical considerations to moral ones, surely," Ruarshi said. "You're a friend to the Teutonic Order?"

"Yes. Which doesn't mean I intend to try enslaving or converting you."

"What would the knights think of this conversation?"

Eisen laughed. "You're planning on telling them about it? They'd congratulate me, if you must know, for keeping a heathen sorcerer away from the Graf. I doubt any of them will be too upset if he dies. The knights and Stahl make for uncomfortable bedfellows. He's shown an unfortunate susceptibility in the past to the ideas of John Wycliffe."

"Stahl's a heretic?"

"Some would say so."

Ruarshi looked down at the narrow triangle of sunlight dancing on the floorboards. "Tell me something, Herr Eisen. What do you think is wrong with the Graf?"

"I'm not a doctor. One fever looks much the same as another to me."

"I've already spoken with Kramer. He told me Stahl went into convulsions and then fell into a coma. Can you add anything to that?"

"… No."

"There could be a number of reasons for his collapse. One possibility is poison."

Eisen went stiff as a statue. "I didn't poison him."

"I didn't say you did. Who else profits by his death?"

"He has plenty of personal enemies. Some of them might poison him out of sheer dislike. If that's really the cause of his illness."

"If he was poisoned, I'm surprised he's still alive after suffering that kind of reaction. Another dose of the poison, whatever it was, would almost certainly kill him."

Eisen regarded the healer speculatively and then rose from his chair to join him at the window. He jerked at the piece of wood Ruarshi had loosened and pulled it from the frame. The healer could now see the river out of the corner of his eye, flowing placidly through the brown autumn countryside.

"I find it interesting that you should tell me that, since you apparently think I may have tried once already to murder the man."

"That would explain your visit."

"So would a conscience. But I take your point. If it isn't disease he's suffering from, I make the most likely villain." He tossed the board onto the narrow bed. "If you were to accuse me of poisoning the

Graf, my position here would become awkward. It would be impossible for me to arrange for you and your familiar to leave. That was my main purpose in coming here, to discuss a way to get you out if you decide you'd rather not heal the hero of Reuenberg."

"I'll want to confirm your story."

"Please do." Eisen pointed out the window. "The nearest ford is about a half mile downstream. I can have a man there tonight to show you the place. Some confusion in the camp will cover your departure. Once you cross the river, follow the path leading west from the ford and take the right branch where it forks. In a few hours you'll come to a place called Hamlin. You shouldn't count on the villagers to hide you from any search parties that may be sent out. If you need something from the people there, let your familiar get it. I'll see to it that you have food to last you a few days."

"That sounds reasonable, but there's a problem. My *pir* isn't capable of taking an extended jaunt through the wilderness just now."

"So leave without him. Once you're gone, there'll be no reason for anyone to keep him here. He can catch up with you."

"You underestimate Sebastian."

"I can make sure your familiar's protected."

"I prefer not to risk it."

"Fine." Eisen drummed his fingers against the wall as he stared out at the river. "Can he make it as far as the ford?"

"Yes."

"There will be a boat waiting for you and a man to guide it. You'll be well downstream before anyone realizes you're not where you're supposed to be. He'll put you ashore after a few miles."

"We can manage from there."

"Good. You'll have to." The man headed for the door. "You won't see me again. When you hear the ruckus in camp, go. Or don't. It's entirely up to you. I wish you luck, whatever your decision."

Ruarshi watched him leave. As the sound of Eisen's footsteps faded down the hall, the healer lowered himself onto the edge of the bed and closed his eyes.

✳ ✳ ✳

Wil awoke and started to stretch, but a twinge in his abdomen caused him to think better of it. He didn't believe he'd slept very long, but in the uniform dimness of the room he couldn't be sure. After glancing around in search of something to drink and finding nothing, he arose carefully from his pallet to stumble toward the door.

"Hello," he said, pushing it open. Two soldiers stood in the hall, both of them strangers. "I could use some beer."

"So could we," one of the men replied, looking him over. "Water's easier to come by. The river's just a stone's throw to the south."

"That's revolting. I won't drink from a sewer. How about some wine then? Ale? Anything to get this taste out of my mouth." He spat on the floor at their feet. The man who'd spoken stepped hastily backward, while the other just glared. "It's pretty nasty."

"We're not your servants."

"Did anyone order you to make me as uncomfortable as possible? No? Then I need something to drink." Wil fiddled deliberately with the bloody rent in his clothing. "I'm a sick man."

"So go find something."

"Outside?"

"I don't see anything in here. Do you?"

Wil looked up and down the short hall. "No. I guess I'll take your advice, then." He walked carefully toward the front of the old house and let himself out.

The midday sun burned high in a faded blue sky. It had warmed the place up nicely. The Welshman paused for a moment to enjoy the light breeze swirling through the camp, which was welcome in spite of the various smells it brought along with it. Even the presence of the two soldiers a short distance behind him couldn't dampen his improved mood.

He made his way toward the nearest tent, taking brief note of the entrenchments that surrounded the fortress walls a short distance to the southeast. The siege had already fallen into a state of vaguely anticipatory boredom, for all that it couldn't have been more than a month or two old. All things considered, Wil preferred this idleness to the alternative. The quieter the war, the better.

Two older women sat outside the tent he'd chosen as his destination, busying themselves with the plucking of chickens. An iron pot full of water stood off to one side. The Welshman gestured toward it as they glanced up from their work.

"I don't suppose that water's been boiled?" A few of the women nearby stopped what they were doing to listen.

"Not yet. Why?"

"I dislike dysentery. Could you direct me toward the nearest source of beer?"

"How about wine?"

Wil started. He hadn't heard Ruarshi approaching.

"Good afternoon, ladies," the healer said. A buzz of conversation rose around them as the women took in Ruarshi's coloring and noticed the bloodstains on the Welshman's tunic.

"Here, Wil," Ruarshi continued softly. "Sebastian has his uses. He doesn't stint to provide me with what luxuries he can." The healer handed him his cup, making no effort to avoid contact as the Welshman took it from him. Their link hummed back to full life and the ache in Wil's side faded at once to an echo of its former intensity. He took a slow, deep breath as Ruarshi went on. "If Father Rost wants to cause us trouble he'll do it regardless, and the soldiers don't care."

The healer raised his voice then and introduced them both to their growing audience. "I'll be back later," he promised them. After offering them a slight bow, he headed off toward the river. Wil followed, sipping at the wine.

"I've had another interesting conversation you ought to know about."

"I seem to be sleeping through everything. You'll let me know how all this ends?"

Ruarshi smiled. "What's your opinion? Do we heal the Graf or not?"

The Welshman took a moment to grasp the implication of the question. "Are we in a position to refuse?"

"We might be in a position to escape."

"When?"

"Tonight."

"I'm all for it. Just point me in the right direction."

"This is the right direction. A man by the name of Friedrich Eisen has promised us a distraction and a boat."

"Why?"

"That's harder to say. He pleads a tender conscience."

"Stahl offends him that badly?"

"So he claims. The destruction of Reuenberg was apparently the final straw."

"I'm sure. What else did he say?"

"He'll assume command if Stahl dies."

Wil sat down by the side of the river, a little more quickly than he'd intended. "Say no more. I understand completely."

The healer sat next to him. "Since when have you been such a cynic?"

"You have to replace naiveté with something."

"I suppose you're right. If we get caught, we surrender. Immediately."

"Shouldn't we base that decision on whatever's happening at the time?"

"No. We're surrounded by over two thousand troops, neither of us is well, and I can't rule out the possibility that Eisen is setting us up to be killed."

"You're thinking too hard about this, I can tell."

"Probably. I should have kept my mouth shut. I brought up the subject of poison."

The Welshman had thought of that himself. "As the cause of the Graf's problem? Eisen thought you were accusing him of attempting to murder his commander?"

"Yes. How could he have thought otherwise? I *was* accusing him. I hoped to shake something loose. The man was impossible to read."

"Did it work?"

"No."

Wil felt like lying down for a few minutes, but the ground was too wet. He set the empty cup aside and leaned back, propping himself up with his arms. "So, on the word of a man you don't trust and who's nervous about your opinion of him, we're going to dash through an army encampment in the dark of night toward a boat that might or might not be there, in an effort to carry out an escape that may have been doomed from the beginning. Sounds reasonable to me. I don't care for the company here."

Ruarshi chuckled. "It's worth a try. Eisen may be sincere. And if we're going to attempt anything at all, it has to happen tonight."

"Why?"

"Sebastian tells me we're expected to heal Stahl tomorrow."

"I should have stayed in my room, clutching my side and groaning."

"That wouldn't have made any difference. Our jailer's getting nervous. The Graf must be fading quickly."

"I've half a mind to sneak into Reuenberg once we make it out of here."

"Use the other half to come up with something better, would you? I'm not dragging you into another siege. You'll remember how useful we were the last time, once we began starving along with everyone else."

"Yes, I remember. I just want a chance to take a few shots at our captors. I can't bring myself to abandon the notion."

"That's ambitious, coming from someone who's about to topple over in the mud."

Wil shook himself. "The sound of the water is very relaxing. Don't you think?"

"Definitely. Give me your hand."

"What? Why?"

The healer had risen to his feet. "We're attracting the wrong kind of attention. We should go back inside."

The Welshman blinked and looked around. He didn't have any trouble locating the cause of Ruarshi's concern: a group of ten soldiers was heading toward them. Wil was about to comply with the healer's request when one of them waved and hailed him in loud, profane, and unaccented Welsh. He grinned and subsided onto the damp earth.

"I do believe they're friendly," he said, and turned to face his countrymen. "What the devil are so many fine-looking Welshmen doing fighting for these backward Germans?"

"Nothing to keep us busy back home," one of the men replied, squatting on his haunches next to Wil. "The English are completely played out."

"Frightened of us," another added.

"You're the famous familiar," said a third. "We've been talking about nothing else all day. It's been a boring war lately. Introduce us."

The Welshman was only too happy to oblige. As the men rattled off their names one by one, he toyed with the idea of trying to enlist their aid in some way. Regretfully, he quashed the idea before he'd gotten very far with it. The fact that they were friendly didn't make them trustworthy. If he was going to be labeled a cynic, he'd at least try to get some good use out of the character flaw.

"Delighted to meet you. Would you object to sharing some of that cheese? Is that beer? Sorry, I'm ravenous. I've got this really impressive scar ..."

Wil realized he was grinning like a maniac. Ruarshi had relaxed and was once again sitting at his right hand, smiling up at the Welshmen in some bemusement.

It was going to be a much less tedious day than Wil had anticipated.

❊ ❊ ❊

The sun was almost touching the tops of the trees that defined the western horizon, sending golden and red rays through the tatters of cloud that scudded across the pale sky. Ruarshi was still among the camp followers, tending as well as he could to the sicknesses and injuries he found there. He was exhausted. It occurred to him that this might prove to be problematic later, but he didn't intend to stop what he was doing. There were too many who needed his help, those too stubborn or too sensible to go to the camp hospital, and the work kept his mind off his own discomfort, his discussions with Eisen and Sebastian, and the real possibility that he and Wil were about to walk into a disaster.

The Welshman at least would be alert, whatever happened. He hadn't managed to sustain the conversation with his countrymen for very long and was once again asleep, as he had been for most of the afternoon. Ruarshi could practically hear him snoring through their link.

He grinned and glanced down at the blond, dirty hair of the child tugging at his hand. Anna, an orphan of ten or eleven who apparently belonged to everyone and no one, had attached herself to him shortly after he'd shown up among the tents and had cheerfully become his guide. Though some of the women had lingered near him at first, asking him questions and taking him to see those they knew to be in need of healing, as the day wore on they'd all returned to their work. Now only the child remained.

"That's Rahel calling for me. See?" Anna pointed. "She must want to meet you. Her skirt caught on fire and she burned her leg. It happened a long time ago and I think she's almost well, but you could take a look at her anyway."

"Of course, yes. Take me to her." Anna ran ahead through the early evening bustle, weaving her way among steaming cookpots and drying laundry. At times she left Ruarshi so far behind that he could no longer see her, but he'd learned that was just part of the game. She always appeared again when he lagged too badly, impatiently waving him on.

Anna returned to him and claimed his hand as they neared their destination, pulling him forward into a small circle of tents where a solitary woman stood holding a torn pair of breeches.

"Rahel! I've brought the healer for your burns."

"Thank you, Anna."

The child gave her a quick hug as the woman's level gaze swept over the Miriyanti. He smiled and bowed. "Honored to meet you."

He thought he saw color rise in her cheeks but he couldn't be sure.

She gestured toward the packed earth next to the small campfire. "Sit, please. You too, Anna."

The child waited for Rahel to get settled and then happily complied. "Can I help with the sewing?"

"No. Just sit. Have you had any supper?"

"Yes. Every place we stopped they gave us food."

"Good." Rahel put an arm around Anna's waist and returned her full attention to the healer, who had lowered himself to the ground a few feet away.

"You seem a little stiff."

"It's been a long day."

"I've heard it wasn't your idea to come here."

It was a question he'd been answering for the past several hours, in one form or another. "Our arrival wasn't entirely voluntary, no."

"Tact must be an important skill for a physician. It will be mostly wasted around here, I'm afraid. I haven't asked yet if you'd like anything to eat."

Ruarshi shook his head. "Anna and I have been well taken care of, thank you. You have some burns that need tending?"

"So polite," Rahel remarked, smiling. "The burn has mostly mended itself, but I would be grateful if you could see to what's left."

"Is there still pain?"

"Not enough to worry about."

"There should be none when I've finished. If you'll give me your hand...?"

"This won't endanger my soul, will it?" she asked after a brief hesitation, though she deliberately placed her hand in his own even before she'd finished speaking.

"I'm the wrong person to ask."

Rahel laughed. "You don't look too concerned about it, so I guess I shouldn't be either."

"I'm going to close my eyes. It helps me concentrate on what I'm doing. You might feel some tingling in the area of the burn but that will be all. Are you ready?"

"Yes."

There had been no reluctance in her voice, but the tension in her fingers told a different story. Ruarshi squeezed her hand gently before descending into a light trance and seeking out her injury.

The burn was larger than he'd expected, covering most of Rahel's left leg below the knee. The pain must initially have been horrendous, but as she'd said, time and care had healed it almost as thoroughly as nature would allow. She would carry an ugly scar for the rest of her life, but he was able to minimize the disfigurement it would cause and restore the skin under the few small scabs that remained.

When Ruarshi emerged blinking into the sudden dusk, Rahel had become a dimly illuminated shadow, sitting just at the edge the circle of light cast by the fire.

Anna, who'd been feeding sticks to the small blaze, saw his eyes open and promptly abandoned her task. "Can I see your leg now, Rahel?"

"Later, Anna." The woman gave Ruarshi a questioning look which he answered with a nod. She withdrew her hand from his and ran it up and down her leg, exploring her calf through the thin fabric of her skirt.

"That wasn't what I was expecting."

"What were you expecting?"

"I… don't know. Thank you."

The healer smiled. "I have to go. I don't want my jailer wondering where I am now that night has fallen. I wish you good fortune. Anna, would you lead me back out of here?"

He started to push himself to his feet but was stayed by Rahel's hand on his arm. "Anna, go visit with Renate for a few minutes. I need to talk to the healer."

"I don't want to go."

"I'll call you before he leaves."

"Do you promise?"

"I promise. Go. I'll check with Renate later to make sure you got there."

"Damn it," the child mumbled.

"Anna," Rahel said warningly. "That's enough."

"I'm going," she said, and flounced out of the circle of tents.

Only when the child's small form had disappeared in the dimness did Rahel seem to realize she was still gripping the healer's wrist. She released him immediately. "I'm sorry. Friedrich has been to see you, hasn't he?"

Ruarshi struggled against a moment's disorientation. "Eisen?"

"Yes. That wasn't an honest question. I know he has and I know why. Don't do anything he suggests. Tell him you will, that's safer, but don't do it. You might not care for Stahl, but Eisen would be worse."

"Rahel—"

"Stahl has a few principles, at least. He can be as bloody as any of them when it comes to this war with the Polish king, but he's not as bad as you think. He leaves us alone. Eisen doesn't believe in anything greater than himself. And he's very hard on those of us he visits."

The healer chose his next words carefully. "I don't see how Stahl's survival would improve Eisen's behavior."

"Don't you? Every success makes him more confident. A defeat now and then might not make him any less sure of himself, but it would slow him down."

"I haven't even seen the Graf yet. I might not be able to do anything for him."

"But you will try?"

Ruarshi didn't reply.

"Is that why you came out here today? Because you know you're going to refuse help to a dying man, and you wanted to heal someone so you'd feel less guilty about that decision?"

Unfortunately Rahel's accusation was essentially true. "Would you like a detailed description of just how I and my *pir* were brought here? The soldiers very nearly killed him. If I heal Stahl, there will be other Miriyanti who will go through the same thing. I refuse to do that to them."

Rahel had gone still. "I will not have it. We will not have it." She gestured toward the low tents that surrounded them. "Friedrich wouldn't even pay Anna if we—that is, his favorites—didn't insist upon it. We do put up with a lot. Much more than we should have to. Eisen mustn't be allowed to win this time."

Christ. "You've guessed what Eisen's offered us?"

Rahel snorted. "It doesn't take a genius to figure it out. He's going to help you and your man escape."

"Explain to me what other choice I have. If they succeed in dragging me to Stahl's bedside and he turns out to be beyond my skill, Wil's going to die alongside him. That's another risk I can't take."

"Wil is your familiar?"

"Yes."

"I didn't know. I'm sorry." Rahel looked away from him. "I can't wish you luck but I do hope you're not hurt."

"I'm willing to take Anna with us if you think she's mature enough to stay quiet when we need her to."

"Take her where?"

"Away from here."

"To a... convent?"

"No. To a family that will look after her. Wil and I will find one sooner or later."

"You have a generous heart, but no. I won't have her put in danger."

"She's in danger here, I think."

"No."

Ruarshi stood. "May Nerthu preserve you. I do have to get back now."

"Nerthu?"

"The goddess of healers."

"Is she like the Virgin Mary?"

"Not really. 'The healers she created first, with a warm breath across a mountain's peak. Then did she create the warriors, with a cold breath through a flame's heart.' She seems never to have borne children in the usual way. Good night, Rahel."

She rose. "May Nerthu preserve you as well. Thank you again for healing my leg."

"No thanks are necessary."

"I disagree. Anna!"

They waited together in silence until the girl reappeared, her cheeks flushed from running through the chilly night air. "The healer—" Rahel looked at him, frowning. "I don't know your name."

"Ruarshi, clan Doshae."

Rahel accepted the information with a nod. "Ruarshi wants to go back now. Can you take him to the soldiers and then return to me?"

Anna nodded. "Will you come back tomorrow?"

"I don't think so. They expect me to heal the Graf in the morning."

"That leaves the entire rest of the day," the girl said stubbornly.

"The Graf is very sick, Anna, and Ruarshi will need to rest afterward. He'll come by again when he can."

"Okay." She held out her hand to him. "Come on."

He reached out to take it and Anna pulled him out of the circle of tents into the darkness.

❋ ❋ ❋

"Loose horses! Watch out!"

Wil peered through the knothole in one of the boards covering his window. In spite of the fact that the hole was now about three times the size it had been, a result of some determined work involving the spoon he'd been brought with his dinner, he still couldn't see a thing. It was almost pitch black outside and he was facing the wrong direction, southwest toward the river. The commotion, an interesting mixture of raised voices, hoofbeats, and assorted muffled thuds, was centered off to the east where the main encampment lay. He cursed in frustration but remained at the window and was rewarded a few minutes later with a peripheral view of torches bobbing through the darkness, surrounded by running forms.

The door to his room burst open. He whirled.

"Ready for some exercise?" Ruarshi asked.

"I've never been readier," Wil replied, rushing out the door and running together with the healer toward the back entrance of the house. He felt Ruarshi weave loose shields around each of them as they slipped out into the night, free for the first time since they'd arrived of the soldiers posted to guard them. The Welshman hadn't realized how oppressive their constant presence had been until this moment. Even breathing seemed easier.

"Sebastian and his minions out on a wild horse chase?"

"Let's hope so," the healer said.

They reached the river and turned downstream, jogging nimbly along its bank and staying under the cover of the trees as much as possible. Darting torches off to their right defined the centers of activity within the camp. Wil risked a glance over his shoulder, noting with glee a few larger sources of illumination too big to be campfires. The horses, or those chasing them, had set at least two tents ablaze. A good number of men were heading off to the northeast, still in pursuit of the animals. Even with the pain steadily growing in the area around his wound, it was all he could do to keep from laughing.

He looked back around just in time to watch his foot catch under the gnarled, iron-hard root of an oak. The Welshman fell forward heavily and lay against the cold earth, gulping for air.

Ruarshi was at his side in an instant, helping him to his feet. "It's not much farther. I'll dull the pain when we reach the boat."

"Okay," Wil gasped.

He thought he could see the small craft already, a spot of deeper darkness against the undulating surface of the river. It disappeared and then reappeared as they dodged through the trees. Its form grew gradually larger and better defined until at last the Welshman was sure he'd been correct. The boat was there and waiting for them, just as planned.

The healer slowed his pace and Wil very nearly collided with him.

"What is it?"

"There's supposed to be a man with the boat."

"He's hiding in the trees somewhere. That's what we're—"

"Shhh," Ruarshi said, coming to a halt. "Listen."

The Welshman wasn't sure what he was listening for but he complied. A moment later he understood.

There were men in the trees around them, many men. Try as they might to wait out their ambush in silence, a myriad of small sounds whispered their presence. Wil felt a quicksilver flash of fear, followed by a surge of pure belligerence.

Ruarshi took a step backwards, then another. A torch flared to life a short distance in front of them.

"It's the Miriyanti and his familiar, sure enough." Sebastian strode forward, followed by about a dozen others. Wil and the healer retreated toward the edge of the river. Three or four shadowy figures already stood along its bank, but if this ambush turned out to be lethal a quick dive would be their only chance. Ruarshi's shields could only protect them from so much.

"So you are a liar, after all."

"Not until the Graf dies or I disappear, I'm not. We'll heal Stahl in the morning, provided we're in any condition to manage it."

The soldiers were close to them now, standing above them on the gently sloping ground. "You'll be in no worse condition than you are now. But since you're here, you're going to have to help us with something else."

"What?"

"Did Eisen put you up to this?" Several seconds of silence ticked by. "Oh, for Christ's sake. It's a simple question."

"Yes," Ruarshi said.

At this admission, the stillness was broken by a spate of excited comment from the soldiers. Sebastian gestured for silence and the chatter subsided.

"Eisen has enemies of his own, healer. From this point onward, you'd best consider yourself one of them."

"*What* did he say?" Ruarshi asked, staring intently at one of their captors. "'She' who?"

"One of the camp—"

Sebastian cut the man off. "Stow it." He turned back toward the healer. "No good deed goes unpunished. Miriyanti live a long time, don't they? You should know that by now. We're not going to have to tie you two up to get you to come back with us, are we?"

Ruarshi didn't answer so Wil spoke up instead.

"No." He was aware they'd been betrayed but not terribly interested in the identity of the individual who'd done it. He'd worry about that later, after the healer was safe.

"Fine." The man gave him a withering look and gestured upstream with his torch. "Come along. There's been a slight change in plan. For your own safety, we're going to—"

Sebastian spotted the small party making its way along the riverbank at the same time the Welshman did. The soldier shoved his torch into another man's hand and barreled down the slope toward them.

"It's the goddamn knight. Feuchtwangen. Get back behind those trees." Sebastian grabbed Wil by the arm. He jerked free, staggering with the pain the sudden motion sent shooting through his abdomen. The soldier seized him again, shoved him between two massive trunks, and pushed the healer in beside him. "Don't fight me, you little shit. He *will* interfere with you if he gets so much as a glimpse of your friend's pretty white hair. Think either one of you would enjoy the life of a slave? You three, grab a couple others and watch them for me."

Sebastian moved to intercept the small group of men. Wil, who had a clear view of the spot where the two parties came together, let out a hoot of laughter. One of the soldiers raised a fist to strike him but Ruarshi blocked the blow. When the man then turned on the healer, the Welshman gleefully kicked him in the groin.

"Owain!"

"Eh? Wil? We had a man watching the farmhouse. Where are you, Brother?"

"Over here!" He dodged another fist and jumped away from the trees and the men encircling him. Ruarshi was only a step behind. "We're having some trouble!"

"Time for a swim?" the healer asked.

"I'd say so."

They turned in unison and dove, barely evading the grasping hands of the soldiers. Wil was shocked by the temperature of the water, but he set out strongly when his head broke the surface of the river. Ruarshi was slightly ahead of him, angling toward the boat. It was still their best bet and probably their only real chance given the way his fingers and toes were already going numb. He heard some splashing behind him, and had just enough time to wonder how many of the soldiers had been wearing chain mail before an enormous weight landed on his back and bore him under.

He struggled upward into the night air, clawing at the arm around his throat. It fell away and he kicked backward at the man with all his strength, trying to ignore the tearing sensation in his gut. The soldier grabbed his legs and yanked him back under, but Wil was already finished fighting. He was in fact dangerously close to passing out. When he could breathe again, he raised his hands out of the water in what he hoped would be understood as a gesture of surrender.

Apparently it was. His pursuer wrapped an arm around his chest and pulled him toward the bank. The next thing he knew he was lying in a patch of sparse grass and watching as a burly German hauled a drenched and furious Ruarshi up onto the dirt about twenty yards away.

The healer hurried toward him. "Lie still." Ruarshi's hand touched his brow and he felt himself becoming stronger and more alert with every second that passed. The healer was siphoning off his own strength through their link in order to get him moving again. Probably not a good idea. He wanted to protest, but rethought his position when he began to comprehend what Sebastian was saying.

"… on his own two feet, well and good. Otherwise we leave him here to live or die as he pleases."

Ruarshi swore and the pressure on Wil's forehead disappeared. He heard the sounds of renewed struggle.

"Gently, gently. He's a cousin of ours." That would be one of the Welshmen. "So's the other, honorarily, since he had the good sense to pick one of us as his partner. No need to be so rough."

"When I want advice from you, I'll ask for it. Get him on his feet. We're going."

Wil summoned every last scrap of energy he possessed and sat up. He looked for and found the healer a short distance away, in the grip of a man a good foot taller than he was.

"You see?" Ruarshi asked, his voice thin. "He'll make it with a little assistance. Get this idiot off me."

Several of his countrymen stepped forward to help Wil up. Sebastian extinguished the torch and they all headed back through the darkness to the encampment. To his surprise, the Welshman then found himself shoved into a sagging and grimy canvas tent. What was wrong with the farmhouse? Ruarshi joined him some time later.

"Twice in two days, Wil. Neither one of us can keep this up."

Wil remained awake through the entire healing. It felt distinctly odd but didn't take long. He must not have done as much actual damage as he'd thought. He remembered being quite sure that he'd killed himself.

"Where are we?"

"Among the soldiers." Ruarshi, lying next to him, paused to clear his throat. He sounded terrible. "Feuchtwangen has in fact arrived and they're trying to keep us out of his way. I'm sure the man must have been impressed with what he saw this evening. Horses running in all directions, fires…"

"We're going to have to heal that nobleman, aren't we?"

"I expect so."

"Damn."

"We can't win them all, Wil. Though we certainly gave it a good try, didn't we?"

The Welshman nodded and fell asleep.

*** *** ***

"Healer. Healer, wake up."

Someone was talking to him. Ruarshi didn't move, hoping whoever it was would go away. He hurt all over.

"Healer! The Graf needs your help. Now."

The sense of the words finally got through to him. "Why should that concern me?"

"Because it concerns me. Get up."

Ruarshi sat up slowly. His clothes were still damp. The flame of the oil lamp in Sebastian's hand flickered in the cold breeze.

"Why so early? It's still pitch black out there."

"Feuchtwangen is sleeping off a drunk. Do you know how hard it was to keep him from turning the entire camp upside down in an effort to find you? He won't let himself be put off twice. Heal the Graf and we'll have you out of here before dawn."

"Wil." The healer grasped the Welshman's shoulder and shook him. His eyes popped open and he looked at the Miriyanti in some confusion.

"Sebastian's here to take us to Stahl's tent." He knew that Wil had absorbed the sense of his words when the expression on his *pir's* face went from befuddlement to disgust. "I agree. Come on."

The Welshman had even more trouble forcing himself upright than Ruarshi had, but they were both soon trailing the soldier through the sleeping camp. It took very little time for them to reach the Graf's tent, a large and elaborate structure decorated with pennons of indeterminate color. They fluttered lightly as Sebastian lifted a section of canvas aside so the two of them could enter. The soldier himself remained outside, taking up a post next to one of the guards stationed there.

Of the five men who occupied the tent, Ruarshi had already met three. Father Rost and Doctor Kramer were hovering over a prone form lying on a narrow bed at the back of the enclosed space, Rost mumbling softly in Latin and Kramer, as far as the healer could tell, engaged in some form of pointless dithering. Konrad Brant was sitting on a camp stool at the foot of the bed. A young man rose from a heavy wooden chair and approached them.

"I am pleased finally to meet you," he said, extending a hand. Ruarshi and Wil took it in turn as he went on. "My name is Klaus. The Graf is my father. I apologize for awakening you at this unholy hour, but his condition is worsening quickly. Come, please."

The doctor gave way only reluctantly as Klaus escorted them forward for a closer look at the patient. The healer estimated Stahl's age at somewhat over sixty. He had the emaciated frame of ascetic, his skin had no color to it whatsoever, and he was barely breathing.

"He was stronger only an hour ago," Klaus said. "He's been taking beef broth and wine. The doctor fed him again last night but now he's incapable of swallowing anything."

"If I may?" Ruarshi asked. The Graf's son responded with a tight nod and the healer leaned forward to rest his palm against the older man's forehead.

What he sensed took his breath away. Stahl's entire body was rotten with poison. A single exposure to it four days previously couldn't even begin to account for the level of toxicity in his system. Some of his organs were already failing.

There was nothing Ruarshi could do for him.

He opened his eyes and stepped back, exchanging a quick glance with Wil. The Welshman knew what he'd found, but telling the others about the poison would only make things more difficult and dangerous than they already were. He settled on a different explanation. "It's a rare disease caused by an imbalance in the blood. I've encountered it before. I've never succeeded in healing it. No one who's been tending him is in any danger."

"Gibberish," the physician muttered, tossing a towel down by the pitcher at the Graf's bedside. "I've done all I can. I believe he'll survive. If he dies it's on your head, Miriyanti." Kramer stormed out of the tent.

Klaus, meanwhile, had gone as pale as his father. "You will at least attempt to heal him?"

"Yes," Ruarshi said. "But you shouldn't hold out much hope for his recovery."

"You see? It's just as I predicted." Rost looked from Klaus to the healer and back again. "Because the Miriyanti lack souls of their own, they hunger for those possessed by humans. This demon intends to take your father's soul when he dies."

"We've been through this, Father," Brant said, sitting forward. "We can rehash it again later if you insist, but for now you're going to surrender Annon to the healer's care. Or I will personally throw you off the bluffs and into the river. Understood?"

"Konrad," the Graf's son said chidingly. Ruarshi felt a hint of exhausted glee come whispering through his link to Wil. He shot the Welshman a warning look.

"No, Klaus," the nobleman said. "Your father is my oldest friend. Not to mention my fellow heretic. I've had enough of the priest's snide comments and condemnations. Get out, Rost. And don't even consider waking the knight until the Miriyanti has left the camp."

The priest stood frozen for a moment before finding his voice. "The Graf is a dear friend of mine as well. His theological errors distress me but they don't change that. I am simply trying to prevent a great evil from happening here."

"Are you really?" Ruarshi asked quietly. He didn't know if speaking up was a good idea or not, but at this point he was willing to seize on any opening that presented itself. "If the Graf dies in spite of my best efforts, I have been told that my *pir* will die as well. Does that qualify as a 'great evil' in your estimation? Because it does in mine."

"Who made this threat?" Klaus asked, rising.

"His name is Sebastian and he's standing outside this tent. He's one of the three who brought us into the camp. He's eager for a promotion, I believe." Ruarshi glanced toward the Welshman, who appeared both startled and indignant. With any luck he'd have plenty of opportunity later on to complain about having been kept in the dark.

"That is unacceptable," the Graf's son said. "Konrad, go find this man."

Brant disappeared through the tent flap. He ducked back in a few moments later with Sebastian following in his wake.

"Soldier," Klaus said, "The Miriyanti tells me that you have made threats against his familiar, in the event that he fails to heal my father.

Is this true?"

"No, my lord. I brought them here and helped guard them, but I never made any threats."

"You're quite sure about that?" The young man's voice was sardonic.

"Yes."

"So if I were to allow you to remain outside this tent, and the healer's efforts were to prove unsuccessful, you would not draw your weapon and strike the familiar down as he left?"

Klaus' eyes slid sideways to meet Ruarshi's own and only then did he finally understand the purpose of this exchange. He exhaled slowly. His gambit had backfired.

"Of course not, my lord." Sebastian wasn't quite grinning—both the priest and Brant were still present, and he couldn't afford to be so obvious—but it was apparent that he'd drawn the same meaning from Klaus's words that Ruarshi himself had. So the danger to Wil's life remained, and now Sebastian knew he'd have a noble's protection if he chose to go through with the murder.

"That's good news, soldier. You may leave."

Sebastian pivoted on his heel and ducked back outside.

Konrad was shaking his head. "I'm not sure you made the healer or his familiar any safer, Klaus. I'll send some men to see that one on his way."

"It will be fine." Klaus waved a hand dismissively. "We've wasted enough time on this."

Brant shrugged and returned to his seat. "As you say. You're still here, Father."

"I'd like him to remain," Klaus said. "I don't believe his tales of soul stealing, but another observer will do no harm."

The older man shrugged again.

"You caught what just happened?" Ruarshi asked in a low voice, speaking Welsh.

"Yes. This entire place is a nest of vipers."

"I'm going to try to goad them into doing… something. Throwing us out? Unless you have a better idea."

"No. I don't."

Ruarshi turned back to face the others. The priest was watching them narrowly.

"Is that your demon's language?" Rost asked.

Wil snorted. "It's Welsh."

"Tell me, Herr Stahl," the healer said, moving to stand once again by the bed, "what kind of man is your father?"

"Why do you ask?"

"This is not about souls. It makes it easier for me to heal someone, if I know something about them." It was all nonsense, of course.

"He's a stubborn man, I suppose. Resourceful. He—"

"Brutal, even?"

Klaus sat back in his chair. "His enemies would probably say so."

"Does he have a lot of them? Enemies, I mean?"

"Anyone who follows his own conscience is going to end up with enemies."

"I heard that he beat your older brother to death. Is this true?"

"I have heard the same story, healer, but I never believed it. Is this really relevant or are you just stalling? The longer this takes, the more likely it is that the knight will show up here. Is that what you want? He will certainly prevent you from healing my father, but you won't like his alternative."

The Graf's son was right about that. While Ruarshi was considering simply making a run for it, Klaus reached for the pitcher next to his chair and poured himself a cup of wine. For the first time the healer noticed that there were two such pitchers in the tent, the one by Stahl's sickbed evidently meant for his exclusive use.

That was interesting.

"I apologize if I've offended," Ruarshi said, bowing. "We can begin anytime. We'll need two stools brought over to the bed."

As Brant fetched them from a corner of the tent, the healer poured himself his own cupful of wine from the Graf's pitcher. He drank it quickly, noting that under its almost cloyingly sweet taste lay a strong bitterness that should not have been there. When he was finished he returned the cup to its tray and then pretended to stumble, knocking the pitcher to the floor where its remaining contents spilled out onto the threadbare carpet and into the dirt beneath.

"Clumsy of me," he murmured, righting the container and returning it to the low end table. He turned to find Wil sitting next to him, staring at him curiously. The healer settled onto the other stool and then looked past the Welshman toward their audience.

"When my *pir* and I close our eyes, it means we've begun with the healing. It will go more quickly and easily if you keep the tent relatively quiet, and for god's sake don't touch either one of us or the patient. When we come out of it, you'll know. The entire process could take hours. Given the seriousness of the Graf's condition, there is real danger to us as well, but we'll do everything we can. Do you have any questions?"

No one did. The priest scowled at them once more before grabbing another stool and sitting down next to the others.

"Ready?" Ruarshi asked, switching again to Welsh and holding out his hand.

Wil took it. "I will be, just as soon as you explain what you're doing."

The healer reached forward and grasped the Graf by the wrist. "Don't jump. I'm about to sever our link."

"Why?" Wil's voice remained quiet and reasonable, but Ruarshi clearly sensed the man's strong urge to strangle him just before he cut the flow of power that bound them together.

"Have I ever described for you the way a Miriyanti's body metabolizes poison?"

"You bastard. It was in the wine."

"Yes. Belladonna, I think. The murderers were taking no chances this time around. When I lose consciousness, act as though I'm dead. and get us out of here as quickly as possible. I'll wake up in a day or two."

"You're quite sure of that? Then restore our bond."

"If I do that, you'll probably be affected by the poison. I don't want you trying to stagger your way to safety." It was a half truth and Ruarshi was certain the Welshman knew it. There was no point in admitting to anything now.

"Damn you."

"We need to quit talking. We're supposed to be healing this man."

Feigning a trance state wasn't particularly easy, and it only became harder as the minutes ticked by and the poison progressed with its work. In spite of the cold air flowing into the tent, Ruarshi soon began to sweat. Shortly thereafter his hands started to shake, and try as he might he couldn't force them to stop. His growing unsteadiness was, he hoped, at least partially concealed by the Welshman's body and the poor lighting.

By the time a quarter of an hour had passed, Ruarshi had come to the unwelcome realization that this was going to be much worse than he had expected. But he couldn't move or make a sound or the charade would be over.

He prayed to a goddess he didn't believe in, silently but with increasing urgency, for the darkness to rise and swallow him.

Eventually it did.

❅ ❅ ❅

Wil sat on the cold wooden floor by the side of the bed, staring into the fire and wondering how long he'd wait before giving up. Ruarshi lay lifeless next to him, as still and pale and cold as marble, just as he'd been for the past eight days. The innkeeper thought he was crazy, sharing his quarters with a corpse, but he paid the man well enough that he kept his complaints to a minimum. All the Welshman wanted was to be left in peace until he decided what to do.

He knew he'd have more success planning his next move if he weren't so angry, but there seemed to be nothing he could do about that. The healer's desperate solution to their dilemma had worked like a charm, of course. Everyone had been thoroughly persuaded by Ruarshi's imitation of death, and Wil had been allowed to go on his way unmolested. The Welshman had suppressed his own fury at the time in the interest of bringing the healer to safety. Since it now seemed he hadn't even managed to do that, he was beginning to regret his earlier decision. If any of the Germans from the camp were to appear before him at this point he would gladly split the villain's skull.

He needed to go home to his family in Wales but he didn't dare. What was he supposed to do, saunter up to their door and casually announce that the Miriyanti healer he'd pledged to protect had died while he's sat frozen with dread and done nothing? Not that Ruarshi had given him any choice in the matter. The healer was like that, sometimes.

Had been like that.

Wil stood and began to pace, ignoring his fatigue. How long was he going to wait before making a decision? It was becoming impossible for him to continue to share space with the shell of a man he'd known most of his life and loved as a brother. He couldn't leave the room for very long at any one time, either, for fear that the innkeeper would have the healer's body thrown into a common grave while he was out.

He went to the window. Night had fallen while he sat by the fire in a stupor, night of the eighth day.

If nothing had changed by the tenth, he would leave and make his way north to Miriyan. It would be a hard trip, overland in the winter, but that meant less than nothing to him. It would keep his mind and hands occupied for a while, and that was the best he could hope for.

The Welshman threw a log on the fire and sat back down. He didn't think he would sleep, but when he looked up again the fireplace was filled with glowing embers and snow scraped lightly at the window.

He thought at first that it was the change in the weather that had awakened him. Then he heard something else and his heart froze.

"Wil?" A weak but recognizable voice, a feeble hint of movement. He surged to his feet.

"Ruarshi?"

"I feel like hell. Do you have any water?"

Wil swung around and filled a mug from the bowl he kept near the bed. "Here." He lifted Ruarshi's head and helped him to drink. The healer downed three full mugs before indicating he was finished.

"I thought you were dead."

"I'll have to tell you about my dreams sometime. How long's it been?"

"Eight days."

"... More than I expected."

"Should I get some food from the kitchen? I'll rouse the entire inn if—"

"Not just yet. Morning will be soon enough. So you made good on our escape?"

"Oh, yes. We didn't even have to get wet."

"I'm relieved to hear it. Mind if I do this?"

Their bond snapped back into existence. It was weak yet but it would do.

Wil closed his eyes so the healer wouldn't see his tears.

# Strong Right Arm

"That's Viterno," Ginevra said, pointing toward a dim gray smudge in the distance. "Ghiai is only a few hours' ride to the east. We've made almost a complete circle."

Wil peered through the drizzle, squinting. A few church steeples, a few red tile roofs that looked muddy brown in the murky light, and the broad dark expanse of the city wall were all he could make out. That, and the small assembly of tents to the west of the city.

Ruarshi had also spotted the encampment. "Well, well, well. Do you suppose we've cornered our quarry at last?"

"Erasmo's *condottieri?*" Ginevra shrugged. "Perhaps."

The Welshman stifled a sigh. He was tired, and his joints ached, and he didn't know what to do to cut the fine thread of tension that ran between his two companions. He'd been trying to manage that for the past eight months, and hadn't succeeded yet. Knowing he was the cause of the problem only exasperated him.

"Let's all go into town, get dried off, and leave the mercenaries until tomorrow morning," Wil said, in German. "They won't pack up and leave overnight." Even his choice of language was a question fraught with complications. Ruarshi preferred German, for the simple reason that he was more fluent in it than he was in Italian. Wil, who'd had Ginevra's constant help in learning her native tongue for the better part of a year now, was equally conversant in both. At least Ginevra understood German, even though she didn't speak it at all.

"They might," the healer replied, but made no move to alter the direction in which they were riding.

"Not a chance, if Roberti is here," the Welshman said. "Erasmo's going to have at least a couple weeks' worth of explaining to do."

"Or he might decide to bolt, depending on the offer he got from Bentivoglio."

"Even if he does, he can't move as fast as we can," Ginevra pointed out. "They've got wagonloads of supplies they have to drag around with them."

"True," Ruarshi conceded. "But if Slan's still with this troop, I intend to find her this evening."

"What would you do if I flat out told you I don't want you to go look for her tonight?" Up to this point, Wil had deliberately avoided provoking a confrontation over the issue of the mercenary. If he was ever going to abandon that strategy, though, now was the time. "This does involve me, too, you know, whether you think so or not."

"I know it does, Wil," the healer replied. "I know it does."

The Welshman waited, but Ruarshi didn't continue.

"Okay. Maybe you're right," Wil said. He wasn't going to let himself become angry. The important thing was to keep the healer talking until he'd given in. "Go, introduce yourself, reminisce about Miriyan. Whatever. Just don't commit to anything yet."

"She might not agree to teach me anything in any case. As you know. But I'll do as you ask: no business until tomorrow."

The Welshman considered pointing out that his original request, made over two years ago, had been that Ruarshi completely drop the idea of seeking out a Naishanti. He decided against it.

"I'd like to meet her," Ginevra said. "Not this evening, of course, but eventually. The two of you needn't look so startled. Female mercenaries are sufficiently rare as to be an object of curiosity."

"I don't want you in that camp," Wil said.

"But love, there's nothing you can do to keep me out of it. I would prefer not to wander through it alone. You'll come with me?"

Wil had never been one to pray, but he considered climbing off his horse and falling to his knees in that moment. Then he caught Ruarshi's expression out of the corner of his eye, and a horrible if unlikely suspicion sprang full grown into his mind.

"Are you two in on this together?" he demanded.

"Not at all," Ruarshi replied equably. "That was a sympathy smirk. I'd like to know what criteria you use when picking your friends."

"So would I," the Welshman muttered. He supposed he would have been amused had he not been so sore. The healer could dampen the pain, but only if he knew about it, and Wil wasn't going to mention it. Doing so would turn the conversation in a hazardous direction: Wil's age. Yet another reason the Welshman opposed Ruarshi's plan. He was going to be rendered obsolete even before he became incapable of carrying out his duties as a *pir*.

The healer, of course, still looked almost exactly the same as he had the day they'd met, over thirty years before.

"Will she look like you?" Ginevra asked, glancing at Ruarshi. "The coloring, I mean."

"Probably, though she may not." The healer had switched to Italian. Wil felt faintly relieved. "If one of her parents was European, she might have ended up with black hair and green eyes. There's no telling."

"Will she have the same magic as the male warriors? She'll be a match for Erasmo and the others?"

"Yes to your first question, no to your second. In Miriyan, she'd be able to hold her own against the men, but we've got a different style of fighting there. The hack-and-slash style used here, and the heavy swords, will put her at a disadvantage. I expect she excels at archery."

"What do you hope she'll teach you?"

"Whatever I'm capable of learning from her," the healer said coolly.

That did it. The wall that separated them was back up, possibly higher now than it had been earlier. It had been an unwise question, and Wil was sure Ginevra had known that before she asked it. He still resented the prickly pride that had caused Ruarshi to push her so firmly away from the topic of his magic, of those things that bound healer to *pir*.

Quite suddenly he was out of patience. "He hopes to learn how to use a warrior's magic. How to shatter things instead of weaving them back together."

Ruarshi glanced at him and then away again. "And how to use magic on myself, so I can move more quickly and surely in a dangerous situation, and possibly even heal myself."

"I thought that was impossible," Ginevra said neutrally.

"Maybe it is, maybe it isn't. I'd rather find out for myself than continue to take someone else's word for it."

"And if she refuses to help you?"

"Then I'll try again later with another warrior."

"I know I shouldn't meddle in this," Ginevra began, "but I have to." The Welshman listened in tired admiration as she went on. "Wil doesn't want you to do this. That much I've been able to figure out all on my own, from the few clues that have been dropped in my hearing. Why do you persist?"

"Ginevra, please—"

"He also doesn't want you to go seek out Slan in the mercenary camp. Why do *you* persist?" Ruarshi smiled to take some of the sting out of the question. "I'm sorry, but I don't like talking about this. Even with Wil, who shares in it."

"If I thought he cared as deeply about my presence among the mercenaries as he does about this, maybe I'd relent for his sake."

Wil must have made some sort of noise, because Ginevra swung around to scowl at him. "Thank you ever so much for undercutting me so effectively," she said wryly.

"Poor Wil. If and when I see her, I'll let Slan know that you're coming."

"Thank you."

"So we're not going to need rooms at separate ends of the hall tonight?" Wil asked, taking refuge in halfhearted sarcasm. "That's a relief." Nothing had really changed as a result of their latest exchange, but if Ruarshi and Ginevra were willing to call even a temporary truce on such an evening, that would be enough to make him happy. "Now, after all this wrangling, it will probably turn out that the Naishanti left the troop months ago to return home and visit her family."

"I hope not," Ginevra murmured.

✻ ✻ ✻

Ruarshi stood outside the tent, collecting his wits and trying to ignore the rain that was soaking through the hood of his cloak and plastering his hair to the sides of his head. Discomfort mattered much less than handling this correctly.

When he was ready, he stepped forward. "Hello? Slan Naishanti?"

"Come on in. I'm sure as hell not coming out in this weather."

The healer pulled back the tent flap and stepped inside, letting it fall shut behind him.

"Do I know you?" Slan had a slender sword lying across her lap. Ruarshi couldn't tell what she'd been doing with it before he came in.

"Not yet." He pulled back his hood. "Ruarshi Illyana, clan Doshae."

"I've heard of you. I didn't expect you to show up in my tent, however." She set her sword aside and stood to approach him. "None of the ritual formalities? Europe has made you rude."

Ruarshi considered bowing; the Naishanti was obviously quite a bit older than he was. Instead, he said, "It's had time enough. When I tell you why I've come, I think you'll agree that the usual forms are out of place."

"Is that so." Slan was standing face to face with him, uncomfortably close. The healer didn't step back, though he very much wanted to. "This sounds interesting. Have a seat." She motioned toward a folding camp stool in the corner of the tent and sat back down on her cot, taking up her blade once again. Her eyes followed him as he moved to set up the chair.

"Rumor has it that you managed to cure quite a number of people of the plague, right after you came down. Is that true?"

"I did what I could." He settled himself on the stool.

"You're younger than I thought you'd be."

The healer smiled faintly. "Which is the only reason I didn't realize at once that the plague years were unusually bad, even for Europe, and return home immediately."

Slan returned his smile. "I was here in Italy for most of that. I know what it was like. Would you like some wine or ale?"

"No, thank you. I've just come from dinner."

"Do you have a *pir*?"

"Yes."

"You left him in town? Her?"

"Yes, I left him at the inn."

"Well, I don't have one, so this is as private a conversation as you could wish for. My clan is Maelae, by the way."

"Honored to meet you, Slan Naishanti *stamm* Maelae." Ruarshi bowed ever so slightly.

"Old habits are hard to break, aren't they?" She bowed as well, even less deeply, though how she managed that the healer wasn't quite sure. "Honored. Now. What is it that brings an Illyana to my tent this rainy evening?"

"I've come to ask that you teach me how to introduce dissonance into a weave, and how to augment my own strength and speed."

Slan stared at him. "You've come to learn how to be a Naishanti, in other words."

"In essence, yes."

"You're a damn unnatural little Illyana, aren't you? How do you think one of these European nobles would react if one of his mud-grubbing peasants went to him and asked for lessons in lordship?"

"Badly."

"Test number one, failed miserably. No Naishanti would ever sit still and allow himself to be compared to a peasant. I'll teach you nothing. Is there anything else?"

"You forget, I've been healing these mud grubbers for fifty years. In general, they're far more decent than the landowners who ride roughshod over them. And I may have been sitting still, but I wasn't idle." With a quick yank on the shield he'd woven around Slan's sword, he jerked the weapon from her grasp. Then he threw himself sideways, barely dodging a flung dagger. It ripped through the back of the tent as he tossed the sword out the doorway. A startled oath issued from the darkness outside.

"That's my best blade, goddamn it." The Naishanti darted out into the night while Ruarshi picked himself up off the ground. He was back on the stool by the time Slan returned with her sword, dripping and cursing.

"Aren't you going after the dagger?"

"The hell with you, you freak. Get out."

"No."

"Will it be necessary for me to physically throw you out of my tent?"

"Probably. But before you do that, I'd like to ask you one more question. What did your mercenary friends say to you when you first arrived on the scene and asked to join their troop?"

Slan laughed. "I wouldn't want to repeat most of it. Don't think I don't see where you're going with this. Stand up."

"If this is preparatory to being flung outside, I'd rather—"

"This is preparatory to your first and last lesson."

Ruarshi stood slowly. "I promised my *pir* that I—"

"You've come to me for instruction. You will either accept my direction or you will leave." She stood with her arms crossed, one eyebrow raised in challenge.

The healer pondered. He could either break his word to Wil, or he could stand by helpless again if someone else chose to threaten the Welshman's life. There was no decision to be made, really, though he knew he'd regret his acquiescence later. "What is it you'd have me do?"

"Child's play. Decent warriors figure it out on their own by the age of twelve. I'm going to weave a weak shield, and you're going to break it into a million little pieces for me. After that we can move on to more mundane objects."

"I'll need guidance. I'm not a Naishanti by nature." Now that he'd finally gotten what he wanted, Ruarshi realized that he was terrified. He feared success much more than failure.

"Really." Slan placed her hands on either side of his head. Surprised, he flinched from the contact, and she lowered her arms. "You seem a little jumpy. Sure you want to do this?"

"Just tell me what to do," he grated.

"If you insist on doing it that way we'll be up all night. It'll be much easier for me to show you." She raised her hands again. "If I may?"

Ruarshi nodded and forced himself to remain still as her hands settled around the curve of his jaw.

"The magic that you Illyana and Chamani use is outward-focused, yes? It tickles over your skin when you draw on it. Our magic starts within us and flows outward from there. Imagine it emanating from your heart. That's the original source of the dissonance, the heartbeat. It's what young warriors first realize, that they can channel its rhythm into their magic, speed it up, and shake things apart. Proficient Naishanti and Diamyo can wield dozens of fast pulses at once and shatter objects instantly. I'm sure you've seen it done. Very impressive if executed properly. But it all begins with the slow pounding of your own heart."

The healer took a shaky breath. "It sounds like you're talking about a completely different approach to using the magic."

"Of course I am. Why do you think we make the distinction between warrior and healer?"

"One lesson won't be enough."

"This isn't a lesson so much as a proficiency test. Certainly you went through one of those yourself, before you were accepted at the healers' circle. Be quiet and pay attention."

Slan wove a small shield in the air between them. Ruarshi closed his eyes and concentrated on following what she was doing.

"You feel the shield?" the Naishanti asked.

"Yes."

"Good. Now, I'm going to start it pulsing."

In a lost, sardonic corner of his mind, Ruarshi made note of the fact that Slan wasn't a very good instructor. One instant her shield was as steady as one of his own, and the next it was fluttering like a pennon caught in a violent storm.

"Do that again, slowly."

"I don't know if I can," she muttered. "I'm struggling against all my best fighting instincts here. Okay."

The shield returned to its immobile state. Then a single, quick pulse began snaking its way along the weaves. The healer focused on it with his mind's eye, watched as it spun suddenly toward his throat, tore through the cloth of his cloak with only the faintest ripping sound, and vanished into the air.

He opened his eyes and glanced downward at the pile of dark cloth puddled at his feet. Slan was watching him and smiling.

"Think you can approximate that? If you've got any aptitude for warriors' magic at all, you ought to be able to make a shield vibrate with no more guidance than what I've just given you."

"I'll want to sit down first."

"Be my guest."

"I'd rather use the cot."

"What, are you planning on fainting or something? As you like."

The Naishanti moved aside and Ruarshi sat down gingerly on the edge of the cot. He extended his hand. "Would you care to watch?"

"I wouldn't miss it." Slan took his hand and crouched down in front of him. "There's your shield. Fire away, Illyana."

Ruarshi searched for and found her shield hovering slightly off to one side, about two feet off the ground. After memorizing its location, and hoping that the Naishanti wouldn't start moving it around as some kind of joke, he began trying to reproduce what he had sensed from her. Somehow, she had brought the magic coiling outward from within her own body. For him, magic had always been something to be snatched from the air and sent spiraling toward someone else, for the purpose of healing their hurts. That it could be made to originate from beneath his own skin was both a revelation and a challenge.

Ruarshi concentrated on his heartbeat, as she'd said he must, on the unusually fast rhythm of it. He tried to pull it outward, tried to force its beat into the separate strands of the shield.

Nothing happened.

He didn't intend to quit trying.

He had no idea how much time was ticking by, though he was dimly aware that he was going to have a pounding headache when he finally emerged into full wakefulness. Slan said something to him, but he couldn't make out the words. There was a hint of motion in the shield now, not the kind that resulted from fatigue, but something quite different, and new...

The dam burst. Slan's shield flew apart, blasted by a handful of drumming pulses shuddering through it all at once.

Ruarshi leaned over the edge of the bed, catching his breath and pressing his hands to his temples. The candlelight danced on the walls of the tent, casting strange shadows in his peripheral vision.

Through his link to Wil, attenuated with distance though it was, he felt dismay, and anger, and fear. Or perhaps those were echoes of his own emotions bounced back at him. He was disoriented and couldn't be sure.

"That was something I never thought I'd see."

The healer raised his head, still supporting it with his hands. As he'd anticipated, it hurt. Slan was watching him carefully.

"You've got a nosebleed. Here." The Naishanti opened a small wooden trunk and handed him a piece of linen. Only then did he notice the small puddle staining the deep green of his tunic. He pressed the cloth to his nose and leaned his head back.

"So. You'll teach me?"

"I'm not at all sure I should."

"What has 'should' got to do with anything that's happened since I came here?"

"Does this mean that I could learn to heal if I wanted to?"

"I don't know. Do you want to trade, lesson for lesson?"

"No. Healers' work doesn't appeal to me. I was just speculating."

Ruarshi stood. "You can tell me tomorrow what you've decided. I need to go."

"They've probably already closed the town gates."

"Then I'll climb over the wall. My *pir* and I have to talk."

Slan retrieved the healer's cloak and draped it over his shoulders. Then she grabbed one of her own. "I'll go with you as far as the wall. The guards there know me, and will let you in on my word."

"Thank you."

"Don't mention it."

❋ ❋ ❋

Wil stood before the fireplace in Ruarshi's room, waiting for the healer to return. Ginevra had wanted to stay with him, but he'd explained what he'd sensed through his link to the Miriyanti, and what it meant, and she had respected his desire to be alone. He would have been comforted by her nearness, but comfort was something he couldn't afford to indulge in right now. He wanted his anger burning white-hot when Ruarshi arrived.

The fact that he wasn't sure of what he wanted to say only increased his annoyance and agitation. He was being pulled with equal force in opposite directions. The past months with Ginevra had been a small slice of heaven, but that heaven would lose its charm without the healer at his side. A parting of the ways was imminent, so much was obvious. But he had no idea which direction he ought to go.

The Welshman bent down to warm his hands over the fire, not really seeing the flames. The door clicked open behind him.

"Hello, Wil. I thought you might still be up."

"Ruarshi." The healer looked terrible, positively green around the edges. Wil wasn't going to cut him any slack because of it. "Your first lesson went well, I take it."

"Not especially. Once I made it clear to Slan that I wasn't going to go away until she agreed to help me, she became rather insistent about doing things her way. Now or never, was how she put it."

"Never would have been a fine answer."

Ruarshi removed his cloak and threw it on the bed. Then he joined the Welshman by the fire, sitting down and leaning back against the warm stone at its edge.

"Say it, Wil. Whatever it is that's on your mind."

"All right. I signed on with you to travel around healing people. That's what Miriyanti healers do, right? I resent what you did tonight. I resent it like hell, your siphoning energy off me to do… that."

"I'm sorry."

"No you're not. You're so not sorry that you'd do it again."

The healer pulled a piece of cloth out of his tunic and started dabbing at his nose. "You're right."

"I think Ginevra intends to return to her home in Ghiai and settle down. If she asks me to stay here with her, I just might do that."

"You both have my blessing."

"Damn it, Illyana." Wil had never laid a hand on Ruarshi in anger. Never yet.

"You two do well together. I never meant back at the beginning to imply that you were stuck with me for the rest of your life. If you love her, stay with her."

"Stop squeezing the link."

"What?"

"You've got our link practically choked off. And your back is to the damn fire." Wil seized the healer by his shoulders and turned his face toward the flames. Ruarshi's expression told him nothing, but he noticed a dark stain on his clothing. "What's this? Blood? Did that Naishanti hurt you?"

"No. It's a nosebleed." The healer showed him the stained cloth. "That's what I get for trying to do too much too fast."

The Welshman hadn't let go of him. "Open our link or I swear I will hit you until you no longer have a choice."

"Allow me some privacy, Wil."

"No. Not now. I want to know what's going on with you, and you're clearly not going to tell me."

A minute dragged by. Two.

"I've already given in once tonight, against my better judgment." Ruarshi's voice was a rasp. "I won't do it again."

The Welshman released him and stepped back. His bluff had been called. "What I'm trying to find out," he said tightly, "is whether or not I *can* stay with you. God knows I don't want to leave Ginevra, but I don't want to leave you, either. So I need to know what's happened. You're a healer, and a good one. You reach into people with your magic and put them back together. Now you can just as easily reach in there and rip them to shreds. That scares the hell out of me, Ruarshi."

"So you have thought of that. I hope it doesn't occur to Slan."

Wil moved toward the door. "I can't talk to you now. We'll continue this some other time."

"I would only use that in self-defense, Wil, and only if I had no other options. Surely that much should be clear, without your needing to ask."

The Welshman paused in the doorway, facing out into the hall. "But that's what I'm here for. Admittedly, there have been a couple times I could have used reinforcements. But *this*?"

"This has nothing to do with any self-perceived failures on your part. Come back inside and shut the door."

Slowly, Wil did as he was asked. "Then what does it have to do with?"

"With betrayal and curiosity. Whether they knew they were doing it or not, my instructors cut me off from at least half of what I was born with. I'd always wondered why some Naishanti's shields were so strong; shielding is supposed to be a healer's particular talent. I wanted to know the truth. Unfortunately, experimenting on myself meant experimenting on you as well. I apologize for that, but it was unavoidable."

"So this had nothing to do with Reuenberg."

"That sped me up, but it didn't start me down the path."

The Welshman ran his hand through his hair. He felt as tired as Ruarshi looked. "You could have mentioned some of this before."

"There was no point, as long as it remained a theory."

"Sure there was a point. You don't need to make yourself opaque to everyone, all the time. It's irritating and unnecessary."

"Old habits are hard to break." Ruarshi smiled. "As was pointed out to me earlier this evening."

"Are you going in again tomorrow?"

"Yes. On the way back here, Slan was kind enough to tell me that I show potential. She's taken me on as her student for however long the arrangement remains convenient."

"I'd rather not go along."

"There's no reason for you to. Now that the initial breakthrough has been made, the excitement's over. I expect to face a lot of dull and repetitive drilling in the near future."

"I guess I'll go see if Ginevra's still awake." Wil hesitated at the threshold of the room. "Something important was lost tonight, Ruarshi." The words were awkward, but they were the best he could do to describe the emptiness he felt.

"Yes. But something was gained as well."

"Enough to make it worthwhile?"

"I don't know."

❋ ❋ ❋

Slan lowered her bow and stepped back from the line of archers as Ruarshi cantered up to her and swung out of the saddle.

"I didn't expect to see you here this early. You do look better. Are you sure you want to provoke another nosebleed so soon?"

"I feel fine."

The Naishanti snorted. "I thought healers had better sense about such things. You were puking up your guts last night."

"A little purging once in a while is good for the system."

"Right. I'll use that as my excuse the next time I swallow too much ale." She turned away from the practice field and began to walk toward her tent. "We seem to be attracting an audience."

The healer didn't move to follow her. "Why don't we give them a show? Arrows are as good an object as any to practice on, I assume. And it's too nice a day to go sit inside. Sorry about your sword, by the way."

"No, I asked for that maneuver. Besides, no harm done." She gazed out over the butts of hay set up across the field, the arrows slicing through the bright morning air, and the growing number of heads turned in their direction. "That's a truly inspired idea. Let's make their target practice a little more interesting than usual this morning, shall we?"

"With no more control than I've got at this point, it's sure to be interesting."

"It'll come with time, Illyana. Don't try to force it and you'll do fine."

They started by shattering more shields, these larger and more tightly woven than the one Ruarshi had already demolished. He was relieved to discover that his mild headache, all that was left of the pounding agony of the night before, was made no worse by the exercise. After the sun had climbed a handful of degrees toward the zenith, Slan abruptly ended that part of the lesson and pointed toward a short but powerfully built man emerging from the camp with a bow in one hand and a quiver in the other.

"See him?"

"Yes."

"That is the famous Erasmo di Nardi, come to demonstrate his prowess for the troops. I've always been curious about how he deals with professional embarrassment. Of which he's been suffering a lot lately. Did you hear he went looking for higher bidders behind Roberti's back?"

"Everyone in Italy has heard of that by now, I expect." Ruarshi could tell he was about to be dragged into some kind of messy mercenary rivalry, but he didn't particularly care. He had too many other things on his mind. "I would guess that you're going to have me practicing on his arrows."

"Very good. Follow me."

They left Ruarshi's horse contentedly cropping grass and made their way to the far end of the field, stopping just out of earshot of the men who'd gathered around Erasmo. The mercenary general glanced toward them once and then looked deliberately away again.

"The easiest way to frustrate an archer is to knock his shot off course with a shield. This method's got a serious drawback, however. You have to know the arrow's coming, or spot it while it's still some distance off, for your block to do you any good." Slan sat down in the damp grass and waved Ruarshi down beside her. "I'm sure you can figure the technique out yourself. We're going to try something a bit more complicated as a warm-up."

The healer sat watching in silence as Erasmo threaded his bow and gestured impatiently for the men near him to move back. He notched an arrow, pulled the bow taut, loosed… and the missile split in two just before it hit the target, the pieces flying harmlessly to the sides and spinning into the damp grass. Laughter erupted from among the assembled mercenaries, and a few pointed their way. Slan appeared oblivious to it all.

"If you break an arrow, rather than knocking it aside, you've got a little more time to play with. Give it a try. Wait as long as you dare before splitting it, but make sure the pieces miss the target entirely. Remember, that's you standing there, not a pile of straw."

Ruarshi smiled wryly. "This isn't going to be pretty."

"Aesthetics aren't important," the Naishanti replied. "Survival is. Do it."

The healer watched as Erasmo sent two more arrows whistling from his bow. Both struck the target within inches of its center. As the man selected a third and took aim, Ruarshi held his breath. The arrow arched out over the green field, over the blades of grass still glinting with dew in the slanting sunlight, and plunged toward its mark. The healer sent a thread of dissonance winging toward it. For an instant he thought he'd missed completely. Then the arrow's tail flew sideways, leaving the greater part of the missile to bounce harmlessly off the edge of the butt.

More laughter.

"Not bad for a first attempt. If that had been a friend of yours standing there, he'd be startled but still very much alive. Method number two: shatter the arrow completely. I don't expect you to be able to do this yet. It usually takes years to learn to do properly, and initial practice is carried out on unmoving objects. Rocks, for instance. Warriors in training spend a lot of time clearing rocks out of fields."

Erasmo continued practicing while Slan spoke, resolutely ignoring them. Some of the others weren't so reticent; Ruarshi caught more than one nod of approval and amusement from among the growing crowd. He glanced at his instructor as she readied herself for another demonstration on his behalf, curious as to just how far she intended to take this.

The general's next shot disappeared in a small explosion of sawdust just inches from the target. The healer was too far away to tell for certain, but he thought it likely that the arrowhead had also disappeared in a shower of iron slivers.

Ruarshi turned back to the Naishanti just in time to see the trailing edge of a delighted, malicious smile vanish from her face.

"There's one more good way of handling a hostile archer. It's more showy than the other techniques, and is advisable in situations that call for humiliating your opponent in addition to simply ruining his shot. It involves shaving one or two of the fletchings off the arrow. Very difficult to carry off, but oh so impressive when it works."

Erasmo's last few shots had flown wide of the target's center, one missing the butt entirely and embedding itself in the ground a few feet beyond. The man's anger was readily apparent in the stiffness of his shoulders, the jerky way he bent down to pull the arrows from the quiver.

"What are you doing?" the healer asked quietly.

"You mean you haven't puzzled it out? And here you had almost convinced me of your intelligence." Slan's attention remained focused on the general, predatory in its intensity. "Watch."

Another arrow was notched and sent flying. About halfway across the field, at the apex of its arc, it began to wobble. Then it went spiraling clumsily downward, coming to rest yards short of its intended destination.

This time a smattering of applause was intermixed with the laughter. Erasmo dropped his bow and turned to face them.

"A real life tutorial, Slan?"

"Something like that." She rose from her sitting position, and Ruarshi followed her lead. "He's a fool. He's got no business being in charge of a stable, much less a band of mercenaries."

So. He'd stumbled his way into the middle of a coup attempt. "They'll never accept a woman as their leader. No matter how good you are."

"No? Entire nations have followed queens in the past."

"Because they inherited the throne. Not because of their strong right arms."

"Slan Naishanti." Erasmo stopped a few feet in front of them, obviously furious and just as clearly having trouble controlling it. The healer edged closer to Slan, wishing he could get his back up against something solid.

"Admirable shooting, sir."

"I have heard that you take issue with my style of leadership."

"Not your style of leadership, sir. Your overall competence. You made us all look silly by flirting with Bentivoglio."

"Is that so, witch?"

"Yes, that's so. We need new leadership."

The general surveyed the faces surrounding them. "I'd like to know who put her up to this."

Slan hissed. "Nobody, you jackass."

"Nobody? You can be sure I'll find out." Again he turned to the others. "By admitting it now, you'll make your life easier. Anyone care to step forward and second her motion?"

"This is all beside the point, sir. In the way of my people, I challenge you for leadership of this troop."

Erasmo barked a laugh. "Are you serious?"

"Quite."

"I want you out of here by tomorrow. You're no longer welcome among my men."

"Don't tell me you're afraid to fight a woman?" The Naishanti's tone was derisive.

Ruarshi saw a shadow slip across the back of the general's eyes. He was afraid of her. He had good reason to be.

"I want you out, witch. Go or I'll turn you over to the Dominicans."

"I'm not so easily disposed of, sir. A challenge once issued can't be withdrawn. It is your privilege to designate the time and place. I'll be waiting to hear from you."

"Go to hell."

"After you, sir. After you." Slan bowed and turned away. The healer followed her out of the circle of spectators and down the slope of the hill toward her tent.

"You'd best be alert for treachery. I wouldn't be at all surprised if he sent somebody after you in the middle of the night with a stiletto."

"I've been sleeping with a tied-off shield around my tent for months now. I'm ready for whatever he cares to throw at me."

"Ruarshi. There you are." The healer looked up to see Wil and Ginevra thread their way past the last few tents at the edge of the camp, leading their horses. "We've come by to let you know that we're heading over to Ghiai this morning. We'll probably be there for a few days."

"Enjoy yourselves. Give my regards to Menocchio. Slan Naishanti, this is Wil, my *pir*, and his companion, Ginevra of Ghiai."

"Slan Naishanti, clan Maelae," the Miriyanti elaborated, bowing. "I'm honored to meet you."

The Welshman returned the bow with stiff grace. Ginevra essayed a small curtsey.

"Ruarshi tells me that you have been his *pir* for over thirty years. I congratulate you. Most such partnerships don't last so long."

"They don't?" Wil blinked.

"Almost never."

"Slan Naishanti? If it pleases you, I'd like to come visit you when we return from my village."

Slan looked Ginevra over. "You won't ask me to tutor you in the fine arts of murder and mayhem, I assume?"

"… No."

"Good. One student at a time is plenty. You're welcome to come anytime you like. But please don't talk to me as though I were one of your European lordlings."

"Done. Have you got a moment right now to talk?"

"I've got nothing but moments. I'm waiting for an answer to an invitation I just issued. Come inside the tent and we can sit for a while." Slan nodded back at Ruarshi. "We'll continue with your lesson presently." Then she inclined her head toward Wil and ushered Ginevra inside.

As the canvas flapped shut behind them, Wil gestured toward the group of men still milling about on the archery field. "I saw some of that. What was going on?"

"Slan's trying to take over command of the troop from Erasmo. She challenged him to a duel, his choice of weapons."

"You're kidding."

"Do I look amused?"

"He'll kill her."

"Only if he manages to surprise her first. What's more likely is that they'll end up seriously wounding each other. Putting them back together isn't a job I want."

"Is that why she decided to challenge him now, because you're here?"

"That hadn't occurred to me. Maybe. What's Ginevra want with her?"

"I'm not sure. She's being pretty close-mouthed about the whole thing. I know she finds the whole idea of Slan fascinating."

"I hope Slan takes to her. She can be hard on you if you rub her the wrong way."

✳ ✳ ✳

Wil took Ginevra's hand as they went down the stairs to the inn's common room. Neither of them had slept much, Ginevra because she was too upset and the Welshman because he was too angry on her behalf. He knew that Ruarshi was waiting for them below, and wondered how much of what had happened in Ghiai the day before the healer already understood, and how much would have to be explained.

They spotted the healer sitting at a small table in the corner and went to join him.

"I've asked the keeper to bring sufficient wine, bread, butter, and fruit for three."

"Thanks," Wil mumbled, sliding onto the bench after Ginevra.

It was her tale to tell, really, not his own. He didn't want to leave Ruarshi in the dark, but neither did he want to jump in with his own version of the story, perhaps including details she would rather keep private. So he waited for her to speak, allowing the silence to stretch through the meal and beyond.

"Ginevra," Ruarshi said finally, "what happens between you and your family is your concern. And Wil's. But not mine, unless you want me to know."

"If I could, I'd see to it that the whole world knew," she began slowly. "My brother Bastian is a snake. He's legally assumed ownership of my land and house, the house I shared for almost two decades with my husband, the house in which my children died. On the grounds that my running away with a sorcerer's familiar makes me unfit to own property. 'Mentally unsound and morally unfit.' That was the phrasing he used."

"I'm sorry. Can you challenge him in court?"

"Not without blackening Wil's name along with my own. I refuse to do that."

"Better that than to have me up on trial for murder," Wil said. "One way or another, I am going to make him hurt for this, even if it comes down to my having to wring his scrawny little—"

Ginevra seized his flailing hands and pressed them beneath hers onto the table. "Calm down. You're not to get yourself into trouble over this. I don't need the extra grief. If the Holy Mother chooses to answer my prayers and bring about Bastian's early demise, that's Her affair."

"I'd rather make sure of things."

"That's because you're a heathen. If you weren't, you'd trust justice to catch up with him eventually."

Wil grimaced. "After he lives to a ripe, happy old age on your stolen property? Not nearly good enough, my dear."

"Was he a pagan when you found him in Wales, or did you corrupt him?"

The Welshman's heart leapt in alarm. He couldn't tell if she was joking with Ruarshi or not.

"I corrupted him. Absolutely. When I first met him, he was suffering from chills he'd caught as a result of too many nights spent lying prostrate on the cold stone floor of a drafty old church. He had bruises from genuflecting too often. I knew right away I had to have him."

Ginevra laughed. "I'm feeling vulnerable at the moment. Before I lose the urge, there's something I'd like to say, but only if you'll both agree not to remind me of it later."

"Agreed," Ruarshi said at once. Wil nodded cautiously.

"Okay, here it is. It's not precisely a secret. I'm terribly jealous of your relationship. Your link. I've hoped in the past that Wil would break it for my sake. I won't say that today I'm suddenly glad that he hasn't, but I believe I can live with it."

The healer smiled. "I was thinking that the two of you ought to settle down. There's a difference between contentment and real happiness."

The Welshman was offended. "Meaning what?"

"I think you know."

"No, as a matter of fact, I don't."

"Yes, you do. And you've admitted as much to yourself. You're just afraid to admit it to me."

"I pledged that I would travel with you as your *pir*—"

"Is that what's getting in the way? For god's sake, thirty years is enough—"

"Let me finish. The pledge meant everything to me in the beginning, when I was homesick and cold all the time, but now I don't care a rat's ass for it. That is not why I'm still drifting all over Europe with you."

Ruarshi twisted his cup around and around on the table, watching the spiraling pattern of water rings it left behind.

"You don't have to choose between us. That was the whole point of my confession," Ginevra said impatiently. "The past eight months have been the best in my life. I'll gladly keep traveling with both of you. Especially as I have no land of my own to live on now."

"He does have to choose, I'm afraid." The healer was still gazing abstractedly at the table. "And I'd prefer he do so while he's still got enough time ahead of him to enjoy a more leisurely way of living, and the company of the woman he loves."

"Oh, now I'm too old, is that it?"

Quite suddenly Ruarshi's eyes met his, challenging. "Deny for me the pain you have to deal with every time you climb into the saddle."

Wil shifted uncomfortably, the mere mention of the soreness enough to cause it to flare up again on the spot. "It's insignificant."

"Pain is never insignificant. I can't heal the problem that causes it. All I can do is quell the ache for a while. Living as you do, riding around with me through all kinds of weather, will only make it worse."

"And I still say it's worth it."

"You are stubborn."

"You're both ridiculous," Ginevra said. "Have you ever heard the word 'compromise'? It's very simple. We all settle together somewhere, preferably in a big city so you'd never have to worry about running out of patients. Does that suit the need? Can we end this wrangle now?"

The Welshman and the healer looked at each other and Wil burst out laughing. When he could breathe again, he said, "I'm rather fond of Italy. It's warmer here. Rome is out. Florence?"

"Padua, maybe. Or Venice."

"There's no need to decide right this instant," Ginevra said acerbically. "And we needn't stay in Italy, either, if there's somewhere else you'd rather go. I've always been curious about Spain. Somewhere in Navarre?"

Ruarshi was smiling bemusedly. "When common sense hits you like a voice from on high... I feel like an idiot."

"Yes, well, you're not the only one," Wil admitted. "Though I'm not surprised you didn't think of it. Any solution that doesn't allow you to exercise your contrary instincts isn't likely to occur to you."

"You're a fine one to throw stones."

"Not for the first time, I find myself wondering how you two have survived this long," Ginevra said. She pivoted on the bench and stood. "I'm going to visit the hospital this morning. I assume you're both going out to see Slan?"

"Later. I'll come with you." Ruarshi drank the last of his wine, set his cup down, and rose from the table. "Wil?"

"Lead on."

"Don't look at me. I don't know where the hospital is. Ginevra?"

She rolled her eyes and led them out into the street.

"Should we take the horses?" Wil had to raise his voice to be heard above the clatter of rough wheels on cobblestones.

"It's not that far away."

"Who runs the hospital here?" Ruarshi asked.

"The Dominicans have about fifty beds. Their monastery is two streets ahead and around the corner to the right."

"Do you have any idea what kind of reception we should anticipate?"

Ginevra glanced at the healer and shrugged. "They haven't got any resident zealots here in Viterno, as far as I know. We should be all right."

"Alessandro! Hey!" A well-dressed man darted past them, waving his hands at the retreating back of another young aristocrat. "It's Erasmo di Nardi and the Miriyanti witch, some kind of duel. I'm going to…" The words faded as the man disappeared behind the lumbering mass of a farmer's cart.

"Erasmo certainly didn't waste any time." Ruarshi had already whirled and begun heading back to the inn at a jog. Wil and Ginevra were only a pace behind him.

Within minutes they'd mounted their horses and were on their way toward the western gates of the city.

✳ ✳ ✳

It took mere moments for Ruarshi to spot the Naishanti among the restless crowd in the mercenary camp. Picking his way through the press to her side took rather longer. He found her brushing a sturdy bay mare, quite alone amidst the tumult.

"I hear Erasmo decided to take you up on your challenge."

"In a manner of speaking, yes."

"What weapon did he choose?"

"This one." She smacked the horse's chest with an open palm. "He's trying to make a game of it. I'll see that he comes to repent his sense of humor."

"A horse race?"

"Yes. This way even if he loses it won't be much of a reflection on his abilities. It will mean a loss of face, but not so much that he'll be ashamed to look at his men afterward." Slan tugged vehemently at a tangle in the horse's mane. "Either way, I can't win the troop."

Wil and Ginevra arrived in the small bubble of empty space surrounding the Naishanti. Slan nodded a curt welcome.

"He didn't achieve his success through stupidity," Ruarshi said.

"No. That he won through luck and an unparalleled ability to bluster and a rudimentary knowledge of battlefield tactics. I would love to see him in action against a Miriyanti army."

"What's the course?"

"Down along the river. We'll start there at the flag." She pointed toward a pike with a crimson cloth tied to it. "Then it's downstream until we reach those trees, at which point we'll turn around and come back. About two miles overall."

"Does he have anything extra planned?"

"You mean, is he going to cheat? I hope so." She ducked under her horse's neck, straightened back up, and resumed her brushing. "That'll give me free rein to do whatever I like, such as tripping his horse or clotheslining him on a bit of weave. I'll probably go for the second option. I don't want to hurt the horse."

"You'd better make damn sure before you do that everyone knows he tried to pull something on you first."

"I've known you less than two days and already you're lecturing me? That's my role, Illyana."

"Yes, and I'd like to see my instructor in one piece at the end of the day."

"Travel in foreign lands makes for strange bedfellows. Excuse me." She slid past him and started working out the knots in the horse's tail.

"I don't believe a well-groomed tail will make a difference in her speed."

The Naishanti grinned. "You'd be surprised. She likes to look good when she runs."

"You've raced her before?"

"Of course. What do you suppose mercenaries do in their free time? Write epic poetry?"

"Possibly. This is Italy."

"Be quiet. You're distracting me and I need to concentrate."

"If you concentrate any harder this animal isn't going to have a tail left."

Ruarshi put a foot in his stirrup, hoisted himself up, and glanced over the camp. Erasmo and his hangers-on were in the process of throwing a saddle over the back of a gray stallion, down the hill closer to the pike with its scrap of rag.

Wil had followed his gaze. "That's a damn big horse," he murmured.

"Big and stupid, like his rider," Slan said.

"Call off this race. Why should you let him set the terms of your contest?" Ginevra asked.

The Naishanti set her brush down and lifted a saddle from the grass, throwing it easily into place and tightening it down. "Because those are the rules. To violate them would be to hand him a totally un-earned victory. Is he ready over there?"

"It looks like it," Wil replied. "He's up on his horse now, heading toward the river."

"Time to go." Slan leapt into the saddle. Ruarshi could practically feel the waves of magic radiating off her, increasing her strength and sharpening her senses. He raised his hand to her as she rode away.

"Best of luck."

"Luck is Erasmo's weapon. I rely on skill." The Naishanti returned the salute and trotted down to join the general by the edge of the water.

By common consent Ruarshi, Wil, and Ginevra edged forward, determined to have a clear view of the stretch of land on which the race was to be run. A few of the spectators seemed prepared to challenge their position, but relented when they got a good look at the healer.

Ruarshi wound his horse's reins tightly around his hand as they waited for the signal that would begin the match, and then nervously unwound them again. Soon he had red marks running across his fingers and palm. Ginevra noticed his fidgeting.

"Whatever rules it is she's playing by, they're stupid," she said.

"I couldn't agree with you more."

A whistle pierced the air and the horses leapt forward, their hooves digging into the soft dirt. The animals ran neck and neck along the bank of the river, their riders crouched low over their backs. As they neared the trees, Slan's bay began ever so slowly to edge ahead, the mare's lean power more than a match for the sheer size of Erasmo's mount over this initial stretch of the race. By the time the Naishanti's horse reached the halfway point of the course, she was a full two lengths ahead of the general's stallion.

Slan wheeled the bay around with a precise grace beautiful to watch and started her running back the way they'd come, toward the finish line and victory.

Something small and white, barely visible in the tall grass, came bounding out of the trees almost directly under the mare's hooves. The animal shied sideways and stumbled. Slan shouted as she flew from the bay's back, a wordless exclamation that expressed rage rather than fear.

Ruarshi was in the saddle instantly, though he didn't remember moving. Wil was right next to him. "Ginevra," the healer said, "try to find that animal. Better yet, find whoever it is that put it there."

She nodded once and heeled her mount forward. Ruarshi and the Welshman galloped ahead at a slightly different angle, toward the unmoving form of the Naishanti. In her fall, she'd tumbled partway down the river's shallow bank.

Several mercenaries were already leaning over Slan when the healer reached her. He pushed through them and got his first clear view of the damage that had been done.

"Someone please go inform Erasmo that I plan to see he's put on trial for murder if she dies," he said flatly. Then he was on his knees, lifting her head and searching delicately for the source of the blood spilling out in a black halo around her face.

He realized at once that this was more than he could handle on his own. He needed a Chamani's help, but doubted there was such a healer within a thousand miles of Viterno.

With Wil's assistance, he mended the more obvious aspects of the injury. When he finally resigned himself to the fact that he could do no more, Slan was no longer losing blood and her skull was back in one piece, but what he sensed inside that jigsaw shelter of bone made him wince.

He opened his eyes on late afternoon, and the sight of Ginevra crouched in the dirt at the Naishanti's feet, holding a dead rabbit. The Welshman stirred beside him and rubbed his eyes.

"Will she wake up?" Wil asked, fatigue slurring his words.

"I don't know. I'm not sure we want her to."

"This is the culprit," Ginevra said, lifting the rabbit by its ears. "I couldn't find the person responsible for loosing it in her path."

"We know who's responsible." Ruarshi shook his head to clear it and looked around. Their earlier audience had vanished entirely. "Wil, would you mind going for a blanket and some help? I want to get her moved into her tent."

"Consider it done." The Welshman stood and stumbled away.

"What did you mean about not wanting her to wake up?"

"Her brain was damaged. If she wakes up, she might not be Slan anymore. She might not be anyone."

"There's nothing that can be done for her?"

"There's nothing I can do," the healer amended. His eyes snagged on a bloodstained rock. He looked away again in disgust.

"How could she ever have willingly put herself under the command of that man?" Ginevra asked.

"Where is he?"

"I don't know."

"He returned to camp afterward?"

"I suppose. I wasn't paying attention."

Wil returned with a blanket slung under his arm, leading two subdued young men. Ruarshi supervised the process of transferring Slan onto the blanket and carrying her back to her cot. Then he dismissed the mercenaries and slumped down next to the Naishanti.

"Would you watch her for a few minutes, Wil?"

"Not a chance. I'm going with you."

"I need you here in case there's a change in her condition. I promise I'll do nothing but talk to him."

"She's not going to wake up anytime soon. And you're not going to see Erasmo without me."

"If you insist. Can I have that rabbit?"

Ginevra seemed surprised to realize that she'd carried it with her into the tent. "Take it."

Ruarshi plucked it out of her hand. "Would you mind staying here with her?"

"Not at all. But tell me before you go: is this a deathwatch?"

"Very possibly."

"I have experience with those."

"Thank you. We won't be gone long." The healer plunged outside and stood breathing deeply, waiting for Wil. Hushed voices rose and fell within the thin canvas shell of the tent, and then the Welshman emerged as well.

"Will Ginevra be all right?"

"Yes. What's the point of this?"

"There isn't one."

Wil seemed satisfied with that answer and they walked in silence to the general's tent, ducking through the entranceway without pausing.

They had interrupted a quiet conversation between Erasmo and a small group of his men. The mercenary leader set his mug of wine aside and rose to his feet.

Before Erasmo could speak, Ruarshi stepped forward and deposited the dead rabbit in the man's washbowl. "I just wanted to return the murder weapon. In case you have further need of it later."

"I had nothing to do with this. It was an unfortunate accident." The general paused. "She is dead?"

"For all practical purposes. One might even say that the state she's in now is worse than death. You can pay off the magistrates, of course, but they're going to hear from me. They're not the ones you really need to be concerned about, though."

Erasmo pulled his eyes away from the mangled remains of the rabbit. "Oh?"

"She's not without family. As you may know, Miriyanti have long lifespans. As you may not know, we have equally long memories and a penchant for carrying vendettas to ridiculous extremes. Her people will find you eventually. Don't settle down and have children. I would advise a quick and noble death in battle. That's certainly preferable to the alternative."

"Get him out of here, Erasmo," one of the mercenaries advised. "His prattle is irritating me."

Ruarshi shrugged and turned to go.

"I'm sorry for what happened to her, Miriyanti," the general said.

"Are you really?"

"Yes, I really am."

Erasmo was telling the truth. The healer was sure of it. "Unfortunately, it's much too late for that."

As he and Wil exited the tent, Ruarshi extended a pulsing weave of power and split several of the poles supporting its structure. The canvas collapsed onto the general's silver candelabra, and the evening stillness was broken by a rush of flame and shouting voices and a tumble of bodies diving outward to safety in the waving grass.

❋ ❋ ❋

It was long past midnight. Both Wil and Ruarshi had taken turns lying down on the floor of Slan's tent in an attempt to get some rest, an effort that had been mostly futile in spite of their exhaustion. Ginevra slept fitfully on a small cot they'd had brought in. The Naishanti never stirred.

"I'm taking her back to Miriyan," the healer said. "I'll start tomorrow, after I've talked with the local authorities. For all the good that will do."

The Welshman raised his head. He'd almost dozed off. "To turn her over to a Chamani?"

"Yes."

Wil wasn't surprised. "By ship?"

"Of course. Venice to one of the northern German ports, and from there to Tomir."

"Ginevra's brilliant compromise isn't going to work out, after all."

"No."

Silence descended again as the Welshman considered his alternatives. He was too tired to follow any given train of thought for very long.

"There's something you ought to know before you make up your mind," the healer said. The black eyes regarded him, steady and clear.

"What's that?"

"Ginevra's pregnant."

A rush of adrenaline jolted through the Welshman. "What?"

"I didn't think she'd told you."

"When?" Wil looked over at her. Her features, relaxed in sleep, had lost some of their daytime sharpness. His heart constricted.

"She's a little over a month along."

"How long have you known?"

"About a week."

"I wonder why she didn't say something earlier."

"She probably didn't want to use her pregnancy as a means of keeping you by her."

The Welshman swallowed. "That sounds about right." He stared at her. He was suddenly incapable of looking away.

"I can't do this, Ruarshi."

"I'll be back before a year has passed. Send letters to me at the healer's circle in Tomir, so I'll know where to find you when I return. Do you want to know the child's gender?"

"Uh, no. That should be a surprise, I think."

"Congratulations."

"Thanks." The dim candlelight in the tent blurred. "I wish you could be here when her time comes."

"I do, too, but don't worry about the practical side of things. Most midwives know what they're doing. Stay away from the university-trained physicians and both she and the baby will be fine. Ginevra's a very healthy woman. You've got enough coin and jewelry to buy a nice house somewhere?"

Wil felt absently for the lumps in the fabric of his belt, his portion of the wealth they'd earned over the years from their occasional rich patient. "Plenty."

"Here's a little more." Ruarshi leaned forward, a small pile of gaudy rings in his outstretched palm.

"No. I have more than we'll need as it is."

"You're not one man now; you're a family," the healer persisted. "I want you to spoil that child."

"I can't. You need at least—"

"Jewels won't get me very far in Miriyan, especially not these ugly things. You'll get a lot more value out of them."

Reluctantly, the Welshman accepted the gift. "Thank you."

"You're most welcome." Ruarshi sat back. "Now, one more choice to make."

"Can I beg off?"

"No. It concerns the link. I can leave it in place, and it will fade to what I've heard described as an annoying scratching sensation in the back of your mind, like someone constantly breathing down your neck. Or I can cut it, and save you the irritation."

"Leave it."

The healer inclined his head.

"I'm not quite sure what I'll do with myself," Wil said. "I don't know any trades, I've got no real skills …"

"That's about as unintentionally offensive as it's possible to be. Are you trying to say you've learned nothing from me in all this time?"

"Well, no, but I can't pass myself off as some kind of doctor. I've got no degree."

"If word gets out that you worked with a Miriyanti healer for three decades, people will come to you. Not the highest ranks of the nobility, maybe, but just about everyone else. Give it a try, if you're so inclined. You could always move into the countryside and become a sheep farmer."

"Return to my roots? I hate sheep. I always have. They stink."

"So buy some land and make wine. Or olive oil. Or help finance trading ventures to the East."

"You've made your point. I'll find a way to make a living. What are you planning to do when you get home?"

"I have no idea."

"Continue your lessons with another Naishanti?"

"That would be rather difficult to do in Miriyan itself. But perhaps not impossible."

"So you do intend to pursue this?"

"Yes."

"You be damn careful."

"I always am."

"Why am I not reassured?" Wil sighed. "I guess you'll be happy to see your family and friends again."

"Some of them."

"You've been away among the barbarians for a long time."

"Barbarians have a certain rough charm."

"That was meant as some kind of compliment? I hereby express my gratitude on behalf of charmingly barbaric Europeans everywhere."

The Welshman glanced again at the Naishanti. There was still no change in her condition. Under the circumstances, he supposed that was a good sign.

"Will she survive the trip?"

"I doubt it."

"I suspect her odds are better than you're willing to allow. She's under the care of the most capable healer on the continent."

Ruarshi laughed, a tired sound. "I appreciate your confidence. I wish I could share it."

✳ ✳ ✳

Ruarshi rode through Viterno's city gates and into the *condottieri* camp for the fourth time in as many days. The more important of his two errands hadn't gone well. He would have been startled if it had. None of the officials he'd talked to had wanted anything to do with the near murder of one of Erasmo's mercenaries, and the fact that the victim was a Miriyanti had only made them even less eager to get involved. One twitchy burgher after another had assured him that it had been an accident and his accusations were unfounded, and that Erasmo's troop wasn't under their jurisdiction in any case.

A pointless series of confrontations, carried out for dignity's sake alone. The harm was already done.

His second purpose for heading into town had met with more success. Strapped to his mount by a worn leather harness was a small wagon full of clean blankets. The ride would be rough, but it was the only way he'd be able to get Slan to Venice. He could only wish she were awake and alert enough to complain about her uncomfortable method of transportation.

He dismounted a short distance from the Naishanti's tent. Now that he and his *pir* had gotten some rest, they could carry her safely from her cot to the wagon. The rest of her possessions they would pile in around her, with the exception of the larger pieces of furniture, which would have to be left behind. And then it would be time for him to go.

Ginevra's and Wil's horses were standing by the tent when he arrived, saddles cinched and saddlebags strapped on. He stared at the animals for a moment, not sure why he hadn't realized earlier that his two erstwhile companions would also be leaving Viterno. They had no more cause than he did to remain in the city.

The tent's interior was dim, illuminated only by the light spilling through the front flaps and the small rip left behind by Slan's dagger. Ginevra was bent over the Naishanti, bathing her face with a damp cloth.

"Ginevra. Good morning."

"Good morning. How did it go in town?"

"The local authorities are no more conscientious than they should be. They're staying out of this."

"Cowards."

"I agree, but we've got no proof of Erasmo's guilt. Antagonizing mercenaries needlessly isn't a wise move from their point of view."

"I'm not interested in their side of it just now." Ginevra looked up at him from beneath her lashes. "So, is it going to be a boy or a girl?"

The healer grinned wryly. "I apologize for telling Wil. It wasn't my place, but I thought he needed to know."

"You're forgiven. Boy or girl?"

Ruarshi sat down on Slan's trunk. "Girl."

Ginevra's sudden smile was radiant. "This one is going to live past her fifth birthday. We're coming with you to Miriyan."

The healer was momentarily speechless. "When did you decide on this?"

"A few hours ago. I practically had to shout at Wil to convince him I'm not too fragile to get on a boat, but he did finally relent. Mostly. There's something else bothering him. He won't tell me what it is, but I don't intend to let it change my mind."

"Are you sure you want to travel so far from your home? Miriyan might strike you as an odd place."

"Home is the last place I want to be for this. Italy has taken all my other children. It's not getting this one."

"You'll be welcome there. My clan's a large one." Ruarshi stood, feeling lighter than he had in days. He extended his hand to her. Ginevra seized it, pulled him close, and gave him a quick hug.

"Tell me," she said, "at what age do most girls marry in Miriyan?"

"I... marriage isn't... Can we talk about this later? We'll have plenty of time."

"Yes, I guess I can wait. Wil's out collecting some water and wine for our journey. He should be back soon."

"Good. Has she moved at all?" Ruarshi stepped up to the cot and rested a hand on Slan's forehead. "Even so much as a twitch of an eyelid?"

"I haven't noticed anything."

The healer nodded. "I'm going out to find Wil. I'll need his help to move her. You two are ready to go?"

"Oh, yes."

He nodded again and pushed the tent flaps aside.

The Welshman had returned and was busily tying wineskins to his saddle. His frown deepened when he caught sight of the healer.

"Been talking to Ginevra?"

"Yes."

"So what do you think?"

"I think we should stop having important conversations that she's not involved in. Did you have any inkling last night that she wanted to go to Miriyan?"

"No."

"None?"

"You know she's always been curious about it. But it's one thing to wonder about a place and another to commit to going there. She surprised me. She still does that with some regularity."

"You don't sound entirely pleased."

"For myself, I couldn't be happier. For her, too, since it's what she wants. I'm concerned about the child."

Ruarshi saw a flicker of movement at the tent's entrance and realized Ginevra was listening in on their conversation. He took a step to one side, giving her a clear view of the Welshman.

"Why?"

"I was remembering something you told me once about some of the Miriyanti. The ones who dislike Europeans. I don't want our child to feel like I did, growing up hemmed in on all sides by English convinced of their own superiority. Children shouldn't have to put up with that." Wil glanced up from his work. "A comment of some kind would be helpful."

"I can't tell you your child won't have to deal with some harassment."

"I doubt it will be any worse than what she could expect here." Ginevra stepped out into the sunlight.

The Welshman blinked at her. "She?"

"Yes, she," Ginevra repeated, brushing past Ruarshi. "A bastard with a whore for a mother and a sorcerer's familiar for a father. How well do you suppose she'll get on, with that pedigree trailing her wherever she goes?"

"Ginevra, I've asked you at least half a dozen times to marry—"

"And the answer is still no. For now. That's got nothing to do with our girl. Slan told me the Miriyanti don't even have a word in their language for 'bastard.'" She looked to the healer for confirmation.

"True. We don't have a word for 'whore,' either."

"What's the worst she'd have to face?" Wil asked slowly.

"Taunts about her appearance. Some might make assumptions about her intelligence. A few would ridicule her for her lack of magic. It's a minority that feels this way, Wil. Most would treat her no differently than they would a Miriyanti child."

"Is this a loud minority we're talking about?"

"Use some sense, please," Ginevra said. "None of that sounds as bad to me as taking our child into church someday and subjecting her to a lecture about bastardy and lust. Sooner or later she'd learn that the priest was talking about her."

"Maybe you're right."

"Of course I am, but that doesn't matter. I'm going and our girl is going also."

"It would be rather difficult for you to go without her." A smile spread gradually over the Welshman's face. "I guess it's pretty cold up there?"

"Fairly," Ruarshi replied.

"Well, Ginevra and I can keep each other warm if we try hard enough, I imagine. You still haven't given me your opinion of the idea, though."

"I'm glad for it. Very glad."

Wil gave a final tug on the wineskins and, satisfied with his work, moved forward to give Ginevra a whirling hug that lifted her off the ground. She slapped him on the hip as he set her down. Then he turned to clasp Ruarshi firmly by the shoulder.

"So am I."

## A Dream of You

Wil regarded the table before him with satisfaction. A roast duck rested at the center of the modest oval expanse, stuffed with some kind of spicy mixture that smelled wonderful and reminded him vaguely of Italy. Several loaves of braided bread and a cheese wheel were also in evidence, as was a large bowl of sugared fruit. He rubbed his hands together in happy anticipation.

"Can we borrow your cook, Slan? We'll let her come back over here once a month or so, at least."

"Tired of sausages? No, you can't have her. Why don't you make yourself useful and fetch Lucia's chair from the corner? Lorion, get your hands out of the fruit. That's for dessert."

"Tyrant," Lorion muttered, dropping into the chair closest to the fruit bowl. Ruarshi settled in next to him, as Ginevra deposited a drowsy Lucia in her chair and sat down with Wil. Slan alone remained standing, surveying the little group assembled around her dining table. Her eyebrow quirked.

"How did I end up with you lot?"

"You invited us, Sister. I'm surprised you don't remember," Lorion said. "Would you sit down now so that we can eat? Wil's not the only one who's sick of sausages. I believe those Hanse merchants flooded the market with their pork as an act of warfare."

"Paranoia is one way to keep your life interesting," Slan said, "though it can be hard on others." She stepped forward, her limp barely perceptible, and took her seat.

"Not the Lions again. You don't really think I hassle them because I'm worried about them?" Lorion asked as he carved the duck into thick slices. "They thrive on harassment. I serve a valuable purpose in lending them a sense of mission and group coherence. Who wants duck?"

A brief silence descended as everyone filled their plates. After demolishing a significant percentage of the delightful food that had ended up in front of him, Wil took up the thread of the conversation. "Maybe if everyone just ignored them, their organization would dissolve on its own. I don't find them very funny."

"That's precisely why someone needs to laugh at them. They really hate that."

"Do they also hate having barrels of beer spilled on them?" Ginevra asked, spooning some softened food into Lucia's mouth.

"That was an accident, and a waste of good beer," Lorion said. "The Elders are making me pay for the damages, even though it was Dunthala who toppled the damn thing. It was only one barrel, by the way."

"Such language in front of the baby," Slan observed. "Shame. What language do the two of you speak at home?"

"Italian, mostly. A little Welsh, a little German, some Miriyanti," Wil said.

"Very little Welsh," Ginevra amended. "The language is impossible."

"Is any of it grammatically correct?" Lorion asked.

"They're confusing the poor child, that much is certain," Ruarshi said. "If Lucia's first word ends up as an incomprehensible hybrid, they've got only themselves to blame."

Lucia heard her name and began to wriggle and smack the sides of her chair in excitement. Wil reached over to take her hand and she subsided once more into the smiling, subdued infant she usually was during the daylight hours. The middle of the night was an entirely different story.

Ginevra spooned more duck into her waiting mouth.

"Babies," Slan said. "Perhaps I'll have one of my own someday."

"You, Sister?" Lorion looked at her. "You can't allow them to teethe on dagger blades, you realize. Sharp pointy things are right out until the child hits at least three or four years of age."

"Spoken like a true expert," Slan said. "I'll listen to your advice on the subject just as soon as I see a brood of yours running around the clan home."

"You never listen to my advice. So, have you got a father picked out?"

"Perhaps."

Wil, occupied as he was with his meal, didn't realize anything unusual was happening until he heard Ruarshi choke on his wine. He
looked up into the healer's red face and then over at Slan, who was staring at Ruarshi and smiling enigmatically. The Welshman dropped his
fork and started to laugh. When the healer threw him a hassled look, he
laughed harder. Lorion seemed nonplussed and Ginevra was staring
into her lap, one hand covering her mouth.

"There's time enough to talk this over later, I think," Slan said, sipping at her wine. "I do apologize sincerely to anyone I may have embarrassed." She was looking at Ruarshi again.

With effort, Wil was able to squelch his mirth. "I apologize, too. I
wasn't laughing at the idea, just its presentation. It wasn't, er, terribly
romantic."

"And I'm sorry I asked the question," Lorion muttered. "I didn't expect an answer, you realize."

"I may have to leave Miriyan soon," Ruarshi said quietly.

Slan's eyes narrowed. "Why?"

The healer sat back. "Someone has been talking. Ardan summoned
me this afternoon through an intermediary to meet with her tomorrow."

So that was it. Wil leaned back in his chair, unconsciously mimicking
Ruarshi's posture. He'd thought something was bothering the healer,
but the air in Tomir buzzed with so many pair-bond links that it required a real effort on his part to separate his and Ruarshi's from the
rest. And he'd been so tired for so long, what with Lucia to raise and
the translation work to be done...

"That could mean anything," Slan snapped.

"Not quite," Ruarshi said. "The use of a go-between is unusual for
her. She's my great aunt, for Christ's sake. And judging by the way some
of those in the circle were looking at me, she's not the only one who
knows."

"You think she will really ask you to leave Miriyan?" Ginevra asked.

"Maybe. The Sotarii Council may not have left her much choice.
Even if they have decided to rely on her judgment, I don't know that I
can convince her of anything. She may recommend exile regardless of
what I say."

"Perhaps one of us should have a talk with her beforehand."

Wil smiled wanly at his wife. "I think we'd best stay out of it. Ardan
can be inflexible, especially when pushed."

Ruarshi snorted. "That's putting it mildly."

"The Chamani Elders aren't the only ones with a voice before the Council," Lorion observed.

"No," Slan said. "A dispute over this is the last thing we want. The less that's said about it, the better."

"That's uncommonly defeatist of you, Sister."

"Not defeatist," Ruarshi countered, "wise. Neither she nor I wants the name Seggita brought up. By either side."

Lorion considered this for a moment. "But you can't just let her push you out. If you leave, I'll probably lose my one chance to become an uncle."

Slan scowled at him.

"Who's Seggita?" Wil asked.

"A Miriyanti demon," Lorion said slowly, "used to frighten little children. Only he wasn't really a demon. He was a Naishanti who learned how to heal. He used his skills poorly."

"After killing his family in Miriyan, he fled south and basically wiped a small French village off the map." Ruarshi still had a lot of food on his plate, which he had begin to push around idly with his fork. "It took six Diamyo to catch and execute him."

The weight of the accumulated months of weariness settled onto Wil's shoulders as he listened. He'd known since Ruarshi's lessons with Slan had resumed that they would become public knowledge eventually. He just wished the revelation could have been delayed by about ten or twenty years, or at least until Lucia stopped fussing every night.

"How does that story relate to you?"

The corner of Ruarshi's mouth curved up in a smile. "I'm obviously imbalanced, Wil, or I'd never have sought Slan out as an instructor. That much will be quite clear to everyone before I do so much as open my mouth. It was clear to you at the time, as I recall. And how far a distance is it, really, from imbalanced to dangerous?"

"That's ridiculous," Ginevra said indignantly.

"Yes, it is," Slan agreed. "You are most definitely not going to be exiled on the strength of an old horror story. Let Ardan rant, let her rave, and then go on about your life. You are one of the sanest people I have ever met. Lorion, pass that fruit around to the others before you eat it all."

The Naishanti obediently picked up the bowl and handed it to Ginevra. Wil watched curiously as Ruarshi pushed his chair back, stood up, and walked the length of the table until he stood in front of Slan.

The healer bent over and kissed her. It was not, Wil judged, an entirely chaste kiss.

"Thank you," the healer murmured, his hands still cradling her face. Then he left the room.

❋ ❋ ❋

The next morning Ruarshi took extra care as he dressed. He put on his best tunic, a deep green velvet of the shade traditionally associated with the Illyana, and cinched it tightly at his waist with a black leather belt. From the belt hung a dark brown sheath in which nestled the small throwing dagger Slan had given him, to commemorate the day he had first performed 'almost tolerably' as a Naishanti. He smiled, remembering the moment and wondering for about the thousandth time if Slan had been serious the evening before at dinner, when she'd mentioned babies.

He wanted desperately to forget that particular exchange but he couldn't. This wasn't a good situation. He needed to have his wits about him when he went to talk to Ardan.

He had just pivoted away from his mirror and was headed toward the door when a knock brought him up short. The intermediary of the day before stood at his threshold. The young man was obviously a novice, and just as obviously he was ill at ease. His eyes widened when he spotted the bone handle of Ruarshi's dagger.

"Uh, Ardan Chamani has asked that you meet her in the Chamber. I'm supposed to escort you there."

Ruarshi shut the door carefully behind him. "The Chamber? Has she called the Elders together, then?"

"No, sir, it's just her." The young man waited, fidgeting, and then gestured nervously toward the hallway. Only at that point did Ruarshi realize he was still standing just outside his room, his back to the wall. He smiled and started walking.

"What's your name?"

"Shey Illyanu, *stamm* Eloh."

"And how long have you been a novice here, Shey?"

"Just under three years, sir."

"Stop with the 'sir' business. My name's Ruarshi. What have you been told about me?"

"Umm…"

"Did it have anything to do with my taking instruction from a Naishanti?"

"... Yes."

"I have only one bit of advice for you: withhold judgment until you learn the whole story. And if you never learn the whole story, never judge. Think you can handle that?"

"I can do that, sir. But I'm not certain that I should."

The healer glanced again at the novice, who was still studiously avoiding his eyes. "Just so long as your conclusions are your own, and not imposed by someone else who you assume knows better."

They rounded a corner. Ruarshi slowed as he saw the guards stationed outside the Chamber. They were not Diamyo, but there were six of them.

Six, regarded throughout Miriyan as an unlucky number. Associated with murder and exile. Hardly accidental.

"I'm here now, Shey. You can go."

Was Ardan trying to make him angry before he even arrived? Of course she would remember what anger did to his concentration, having served as his instructor for close to thirty years before he left for Europe.

He knew the guards. Not well, but they were all older Illyana who had been living at the circle ever since he could remember. They had been present at the communal meal which had marked the official beginning of his journey south, over half a century ago. He looked straight ahead as he passed between them and pushed open the double doors to the Chamber.

Ardan stood waiting for him in the middle of the room, her arms crossed, encircled by the shafts of sunlight that streamed down from the thick windows at the top of the dome. The seven massive, imposing chairs used by the Elders loomed empty and dark behind her.

"Good morning, *Tai* Chamani," Ruarshi said, and bowed deeply from the waist. Since she apparently wanted fire, he would give her ice.

"Good morning, *Tai* Illyana. That's a very nice tunic you're wearing, though the color is somewhat inappropriate."

Ruarshi found that he could not stand still, so he began slowly circling his great aunt, outside the boundary marked by the sunlight. She did not move in response.

"Why is the color inappropriate, Aunt?" he asked, the hard soles of his boots ringing against the wood floor as he walked. "I am still the Illyana that you helped to create."

"That may still be a part of what you are but it is no longer the whole. If it ever was. What you have done is wrong, a misuse of your abilities, a perversion."

"What have I done?"

"You know what you have done."

"I have explored. I have learned new skills. I have exposed a lie, first taught to me by my early instructors and then reiterated by you. I have sought and found a means of protecting myself and those dear to me."

"You have transgressed boundaries. You have placed yourself and the entire community in danger. You have betrayed those closest to you."

"I have betrayed no one. I have placed no one in danger, except insofar as you wish to threaten us."

"You have betrayed me and your other teachers by twisting what we have taught you into something obscene. You have betrayed Slan, by making her your tool in this. You have betrayed your *pir* and his family, by making them subject to the same judgment that may one day fall on you. You will betray Miriyan, by bringing fear of past Miriyanti crimes back into the minds of our European allies. But what is most painful to me is the fact that you have betrayed yourself."

Silence, as his footsteps echoed off the walls of the Chamber. "We appear to have very different opinions of what I have done. I cannot convince myself I have acted in error. The 'boundaries' you speak of serve only to cripple us."

"Do you feel crippled in that you cannot fly, or live among the fish of the sea? Each creature is born with certain gifts. It is the individual's obligation to develop these gifts but not to grasp for more. I can hardly look at you, Ruarshi, knowing what you have become."

"And what is that? A healer who not only treats wounds, but is now perhaps able to prevent some of them from being inflicted?"

"I see a proud young man who is pulling himself and others over the edge of a precipice, because he cannot see it."

"I hope you're not alluding to Sotar. If you don't want your students to end up atheists, you should never let them travel to Europe."

"I am not alluding to Sotar, though if you ignore my words, you'll soon find yourself before the Sotarii Council. And they *will* exile you, and Slan, and your *pir*, and you'll never return to Miriyan again. They will also bar you from using your magic once in exile, even to do so much as heal a scratch on a child's arm. Do you think you could live with that?"

"No." Ruarshi felt chilled. For the first time, it occurred to him that perhaps he'd created more problems for himself than he'd be able to handle. "So that's what I'm playing with here. I thank you for the warning. Though I still don't understand the nature of the crime."

Ardan turned to face him and then began keeping pace with him by moving in smaller circles of her own within her border of light. "Clearly you are no longer receptive to arguments about social order and personal limits. So be it. Let me ask you a question: before you started taking lessons with the Naishanti, had you ever thought of ending someone's life using your power alone?"

"The ability to do a thing doesn't create the will to do it. Wil was worried about this too, in the beginning. He has since come to trust me. Can't you do the same?"

"This is not about me, Ruarshi. It's about the Sotarii and what they will *have* to do if you prove resistant to their authority. Now answer my question."

"No, because I knew it to be impossible. I used poppy overdoses in hopeless cases when the patient was in pain and pled for an end to it."

"Is it still impossible for you?"

"No."

"And why not?"

"Because when you combine the two types of magic, the constraint that prevents a healer from knowingly doing harm falls away. I may have tried it out on a rat. Once. The result was ghastly and left me with no desire to do it again. But really it wasn't all that different than what could happen if you set a novice healer to work on a difficult wound and they killed the patient accidentally." Ruarshi stopped his prowling and met Ardan's eyes. "Should I expect to be called before the Sotarii soon?"

"Only if you persist. If you agree to stop the lessons and never to use what you've learned from the Naishanti again, I will go to Simah and Ferenc today and that will be an end to the matter."

"You lost a *pir* once, didn't you, Aunt? In Russia at the hands of bandits."

"I will not discuss that with you."

"I'm not asking you to. I'm trying to explain why I'm going to continue my instruction with Slan."

"And willingly turn yourself into a powerless exile?"

"I'll throw myself on the Sotarii's mercy. And if they prove to have none, I'll leave before they have a chance to exile me."

"Really. How do you propose to escape from the prison under the Council Hall? Those cells were built to hold Diamyo."

Ruarshi shrugged. "I'll think of something."

His great aunt approached him then, coming to a halt about an arm's length away. She simply looked at him for a time before speaking.

"You are not expendable, Ruarshi," she said finally. "I will not allow you to do this to yourself." Ardan started toward the doors.

"Don't, Aunt. Please."

"I don't believe you've left me with any choice." She had almost reached the entrance to the Chamber.

"I came here knowing that there was only one way out of this room. And I can explain your rationale in using six old Illyana as guards. Throw me in one of those cells in an effort to change my mind and all you'll get from me eventually is a lie. Please don't do this."

She opened one of the doors and he lowered his head, defeated. His great aunt didn't know exactly what she was threatening him with. She'd learn soon enough, he supposed.

The silent seconds ticked by, uninterrupted by raised voices or footsteps. When a faint whisper of sound at last caught his attention, he looked up to find Ardan standing before him, her expression thoughtful and bleak at the same time. They were still alone.

"I do talk to Yael once in a while, Ruarshi. Your sister told me the story of the difficulty you had with the English lordling after his wife died. You spent a year in that cell?"

"Almost. It would have been longer had his mistress not fallen ill."

"She said it left you intensely claustrophobic."

Ruarshi remained silent.

"Tell me why you decided not to resist."

"As I said before, the ability to do a thing doesn't create the will to do it. I won't lay a hand on you or those others. I hope this wasn't a cynical test of my character. You know better."

"Of course it was a cynical test of your character. The results of which will be relayed to the High Sotarii."

"Does this mean that I'm safe?"

"For now. Ultimately, no. Walk carefully, Nephew. You're free to go."

"I don't understand. I thought you had declared me guilty of some kind of cosmically significant offense. Nothing that's happened in this room has changed any of that."

"You are guilty. I am still disappointed in you. But the Sotarii like to judge each man on his own merits. You are reprieved for the present. Go."

Ruarshi took a deep breath. He felt unaccountably stiff and sore.

"Next time let them do this themselves."

"They wanted to but I insisted that they leave it to me. I still love you, Nephew."

\* \* \*

Wil pinched the bridge of his nose and looked again at the last sentence of his translation. He was so weary and frazzled that he couldn't remember the proper Miriyanti word for 'eagle.' The one he'd written down, now that he thought on it, meant 'pelican.' It would have to do. The merchant he was currently working for was, for some unaccountable reason, more concerned with the clean appearance of a page than with the correctness of the text. For someone who was trying to learn Miriyanti, the man was going about it in an exceptionally sloppy fashion.

But that was his business. As long as Herr Hans Rodler wanted to pay him for his trouble, Wil would do his best, and make sure each page of parchment was a minor miracle of penmanship. And if the fellow later found himself talking to someone about the Romans and their pelican standards, there would be few enough in Miriyan who would bother to correct him.

He set his quill aside and leaned back, breathing deeply. Once he got this final chapter delivered he was going to take a few weeks off. Only when the upcoming midsummer festivities were over would he consider getting back to work.

Closing his eyes, the Welshman checked his link to Ruarshi. Thankfully he seemed fine. The healer had come out of his meeting with his great aunt a few days ago a bundle of nerves, saying little but asking for help in moving his few belongings from the healers' circle to the Doshae clan circle on the southeast side of town. Wil had helped him and made sure he was well settled in before getting back to his own home and family. Where he had pretty much remained ever since, translating. And helping with Lucia, who seemed at long last ready to relent and sleep through the entire night. Now it was his and Ginevra's turn to catch up on some sleep.

Starting tonight, after he got this manuscript delivered. He peered out the window. The odd twilight that characterized Miriyan's summers had already descended and the light coming through the uneven glass was taking on a deep bluish tinge. Sometimes it was greenish. More than once during an evening stroll with Ginevra the Welshman had felt

almost as though he were underwater. The perception was both comforting and eerie at the same time.

He pushed the latest pages of his translation into his leather satchel
and stood. On his way out of the house he stopped in the bedroom,
where Ginevra sat rocking Lucia and humming a lullaby.

"I'll be back soon, love."

She smiled tiredly. "If I'm asleep in the chair when you get back,
shake me, please."

He smiled in reply and jogged down the stairs.

The Rodlers' house was less than a half mile away so Wil decided to
walk. The streets through which he passed were unusually lively, even
for midsummer. The expected crush of Miriyanti coming into town for
the festival was complemented this year by a bevy of foreign merchants. Herr Hans was one of these new arrivals, in fact. Not for the
first time Wil wondered what they were all doing in Tomir at this particular juncture, other than importing offensive amounts of sausage. If
Rodler offered him another one, Wil intended to test it out as a weapon
and see what happened. No more Roman pelicans to contend with
probably.

He pounded on the merchant's door, smiled amiably at the elderly
servant who answered, and stepped inside.

"Herr Rodler's not at dinner presently, I take it."

"No, not for a while yet. Come in and have a seat. I'll let him know
you're here."

Wil settled into an inordinately comfortable chair and watched
hazily as the servant made his way up the steep staircase on the south
side of the room. A heartbeat later Hans had materialized before him
as though by magic.

The Welshman stood, blinking sleep out of his eyes. "Sorry about
that, Herr Rodler. I hope I wasn't snoring."

They shook hands and the merchant sat down opposite him. "You
were, but I'll wager you're no match for me. Assuming my long-suffering wife hasn't been exaggerating about the magnitude of the problem."

Wil smiled. "This is the final chapter of the book." He opened the
satchel and removed the manuscript, extending it toward the affable,
wiry German. Rodler flipped through the pages with even less attention than usual. When he reached the last one he set the work aside and
nodded.

"I'll have Paul deliver your payment in the morning. Plus a bonus for having finished the task so quickly."

"Thank you."

"It's fortunate that you stopped by this evening. I have some questions I need to ask you."

Wil groaned inwardly but managed to keep a polite expression on his face. "Relating to…?"

"I just realized the other week that you're pair-bonded with one of the Miriyanti."

The Welshman felt all his defenses snap into place. That wasn't the kind of thing Rodler could just 'realize.' Someone had told the merchant about his connection to Ruarshi, which he instinctively and fiercely resented.

"That's true."

"Tell me about them."

"Who?"

"The Miriyanti."

"You're surrounded by them. What can I tell you that you don't already know?"

The merchant was beginning to be annoyed but he concealed it well. "My business prevents me from socializing very much and my language skills are still very weak. I live among them, but I know almost nothing about them. I'd like to rectify this situation."

Wil relaxed somewhat. Since Rodler's questions involved all Miriyanti, not just himself and the healer, he was inclined to answer them. The merchant was after all showing a healthy if rather belated sense of curiosity about his hosts.

"It's a large subject. Is there anything in particular you want to start with?"

"Oh, general things. Since I already know a little about their homeland, what they wear, and the kinds of food they eat, let's move on to beliefs. What is their religion like, for example? I haven't seen a single church that's not owned by a foreign community."

"They don't build churches of their own. Except for their festivals, religious expression here tends to be private and spontaneous."

"What's their theology like?"

"I'm not sure that's the right word for it. They've got dozens of gods and goddesses, and each one has its own particular personality and set of duties. They're rather like the Roman deities." Wil nodded toward his manuscript, sitting on the small rosewood table where Rodler had deposited it.

"Do they really take any of that seriously?"

The Welshman's face went determinedly bland. "Do you take the Church seriously?"

"Yes, but ours is a sophisticated religion. This untidy paganism has no unifying theme or meaning."

"I suppose it's all in what you're used to. I've seen some amazing things here. Real magic. Real miracles. Not at all like a cloud assuming the shape of the Holy Mother, which was about as good as it got back in Wales."

The merchant shifted in his seat. "You've seen this Miriyanti magic work, then? It's real?"

"Oh, yes. If you were ever to fall seriously ill while here, you could literally bet your life on it. Tell me: is the Church still split between two Popes? I haven't heard anything about it lately."

"Yes, and it's a terrible situation. Everyone, except apparently the French, knows very well that Boniface is the true Pope."

"Maybe the French are correct and everybody else has it wrong."

Rodler laughed. "Maybe, though that would truly require a miracle. I have noticed that some of the Miriyanti have converted. Do you believe that any of their leaders would also be willing to do so?"

"That would depend on the individual. Why does the issue interest you? You're not a churchman."

"No, but I do have an abiding affection for my faith and I'm never sorry to see another accept it. Even Miriyan may have a role to play in reunifying the Church."

"Really?" The assertion made Wil deeply uneasy. "Conversions here are few and far between, Herr Rodler. The Lions are still a small group, though they make a lot of noise. Any plan for Miriyan that requires conversions should be regarded as unreliable at best."

"You're probably right, but it's a sin to abandon hope, so I shan't do so. Not yet." The merchant rose. "Thank you for the translation work. I'm sure I'll look you up again when I've made it as far as I can with the text."

Wil had gotten to his feet while Rodler spoke. "Good. I enjoy translating this type of thing." This wasn't entirely true but it sounded good. "I'll look for your runner in the morning."

The servant reappeared in the room as they made their way toward the foyer. Behind him stood a stooped Miriyanti whom the Welshman recognized as a healer, but to whom he couldn't assign a name.

"Welcome, Shadel Chamani," the merchant said cheerily. "Please make yourself comfortable. We'll get to your alien fire just as soon as I come back."

The old man glanced at Wil for a moment but his eyes skittered away when the Welshman returned the look. Wil followed Rodler to the door.

"Thank you again for coming by," the merchant said, seizing Wil's hand and shaking it vigorously. "Please give my regards to your lovely wife."

"Thank you, sir. I hope you'll do the same for Hannah on my behalf."

"Of course, of course. Safe trip home."

Wil stepped outside and the door closed behind him. He stood for a moment rubbing his eyes and shaking his head in bemusement. Then he set off for home, and Ginevra, and the baby, and a little bit of peace.

✳ ✳ ✳

"Our audience must be making you nervous," Lorion said, lowering his wooden sword and planting its point gently in the earth. "You haven't been this bad for months."

"Many thanks for that helpful critique of my performance," Ruarshi replied. He was winded but trying very hard to hide the fact. "I'll skewer you yet. Arrogance doesn't help your form any."

"Would you like a more detailed assessment?" Slan walked slowly over from the edge of the cliff, where she had been enjoying the wind off the gulf while watching them practice. Yael came with her, a strange expression on her face. Ruarshi didn't dare guess what the two of them had been talking about.

Closer to Tomir stood a small group of Miriyanti, the audience that Lorion had been referring to. It had formed gradually as they sparred with each other but hadn't bothered Ruarshi at all until he'd glimpsed Ferenc, one of the two High Sotarii, among its ranks. That was approximately when Lorion had decisively begun to get the better of him. All the same he couldn't complain. It had been his idea to move his lessons to such a public venue.

"You're stiff as a board," Slan said. "That's your primary problem. Number two, you're not paying enough attention to your magic and it's getting away from you. If it weren't, you wouldn't be breathing so hard. No more than you've done out here today, you ought to be breathing like a sleeper rather than a panicked reindeer. Number three, you're distracted. Ignore Ferenc. If he had anything to say to you he'd have said it by this time. He's just bored like the others. Now get up off your haunches and stop embarrassing me."

"Do all of her inspirational talks follow that format, or is it just me?" the healer asked. He was still on his haunches and had every intention of remaining there for a while.

"That's fairly standard," Lorion replied, grinning. "You're lucky, actually. She can't hit you with the 'disgrace to your line' criticism. I get it all the time."

"Usually for reasons that have nothing to do with your swordsmanship," Slan observed. "Are you going to enter any of the show bouts at the festival, Ruarshi?"

The thought had never even crossed his mind. "No. That's not something healers do."

"Still on about that, are you?" Lorion asked. "How about this. If I win our next little scuffle, you remove that green armband and never wear it to practice again. The color really doesn't suit you anymore."

"You'll be gratified to know you're not the only one who thinks so. Okay, you're on."

Ruarshi took a few deep breaths and surged to his feet. The power tingled through his body, lending him once again the sharpness of eye and quickness of arm that he needed when facing the Naishanti. Lorion jabbed at the healer's right shoulder with the thin ash blade, trying to disarm him with one quick, sharp cut. Ruarshi saw it coming and dodged aside, but not quickly enough to avoid a follow-up blow to his lower ribcage. He danced away from his opponent and intensified the Naishanti weave that flowed through his torso. That seemed to help block the pain, though it did nothing to lessen the bruising that would appear later.

The warrior, sensing his advantage, pursued him across the cliff top. Another flurry of blows, a matching number of successful parries. Ruarshi then initiated an attack of his own, only to be sent reeling backward moments later with a thin trickle of blood issuing from his side.

He and the Naishanti spent the next several seconds circling each other warily. Ruarshi knew very well that he was going to have to cheat if he wanted to win this. That had presumably been clear to everyone from the beginning. He'd never won a straight sword fight against Lorion. It was only when he got tricky that the fights actually became interesting...

The healer wove a fist-sized, spherical shield and hurtled it toward Lorion's stomach. The Naishanti realized at the last moment that it was coming but couldn't act quickly enough to protect himself. The shield slammed into him, doubling him over. As Ruarshi stepped forward to press his advantage, he found himself suddenly on his back, having had his legs jerked out from under him by a thin loop of Lorion's making. He rolled away, barely in time to avoid the blade that was plunging toward his neck.

Ruarshi surged back up onto his feet and an instant later Lorion's sword shattered like glass. The Naishanti released the handle at once, but none of the glinting splinters came close to him, hurtling instead over their heads to fall harmlessly to the ground. Ruarshi, guessing what was coming, tossed his own blade into the air and watched as the warrior repeated the trick. Lorion guided the resulting splinters to land in a small, neat pile by the healer's feet.

The Naishanti smiled then and lunged at him. Ruarshi went down under the larger man, only to push the warrior off a moment later with the help of another shield. The healer slapped the porous weave over Lorion's mouth and nose, hoping to cut off just enough of his air to take the fight out of him.

No such luck. One more disorienting roll later and he found himself lying on his back with the Naishanti's knee in his gut. Lorion increased the pressure just enough to make it clear that he had sufficient weight and leverage on his side to rupture something important if he really wanted to. Before he could lean even farther forward, Ruarshi spoke.

"I yield." Suddenly he could breathe again. He released the power he'd been holding, letting it flow out of his body to disperse in the air.

He stayed where he was, looking over at his opponent. Lorion was crouched beside him, also catching his breath. When the warrior became aware of Ruarshi's scrutiny, he chuckled, reached over the healer's prone form, and untied the scrap of green cloth from Ruarshi's arm.

"Mine," he asserted, stuffing it under his belt.

"You bastard," the healer said.

"Nope. You took the bet."

"Well, so I'm a bastard too. That doesn't exonerate you."

"That was better," Slan said. Ruarshi tilted his head back until he could see her, noting idly to himself that she was just as lovely upside-down as she was from any other angle. "Though there was really no need to destroy two perfectly good practice swords in an effort to defend Illyana honor."

The healer sat up. "I only destroyed one of them."

"Knowing perfectly well that my brother would respond in kind."

"True. I'll see if I can convince my woodshaper cousin to replace them." Ruarshi brushed the grass from his chest and arms and stood. "Would you two like to come to the Doshae circle for some lunch? Danai arrived last night so the food will be several hundred times better than it was before."

"We really—" Slan began, only to be cut off by Lorion.

"Don't you dare refuse. I'm hungry and I want a taste of this food. All you've been doing is sitting there for the past hour while I've been working."

"Only if you agree to come with me to the Maelae circle afterward. Neglecting one's clan before the festival is rude, little brother, and I'll not have that said of you."

"Not by anyone other than yourself, you mean."

Slan extended a hand to Lorion to help him up. When he took it and began to rise, she jerked him around and pinned his arm against his back, applying a steadily increasing pressure to the shoulder joint until he stopped trying to wriggle away. "No sass from you, Brother. I am still your senior. I shouldn't have to remind you of family obligations."

Ruarshi realized with some surprise that Slan was only half joking. For the first time he wondered what it must have been like growing up as part of a family that had produced two Naishanti in the same generation. And what her injury and continuing convalescence had done to her relationship with her brother.

"Relax, Slan. I've never done otherwise than to defer to your seniority. As you well know. Let go."

She released him.

"Thank you," Lorion said. He turned, smiling, and without warning grabbed Slan up and slung her over his shoulder. Before she could even do so much as yelp, he was off, running down the hill.

"We'll meet you there," Lorion called back, still running.

"Stop," Slan protested, though she was laughing too hard to put any force behind the command. "This is uncomfortable, you idiot. You're too bony for this. I refuse to enter town backwards…"

Ruarshi smiled as he watched them recede in the distance. When he could no longer make out Slan's face, he looked over at his sister, walking silently by his side.

"You've been very quiet today."

"Yes," she conceded. "I've been trying to figure out how to reintroduce you to Mother and Father. They won't understand. They were so proud of you. Mother sang for an entire month after you left for the healers' circle."

"Are they here now?" The prospect distressed him. At least they'd had a chance at a few weeks' worth of amiable companionship, right after he'd returned to Miriyan.

"No, but I expect them by evening. Aethel came in this morning."

"Aethel. Born to be a thorn in everyone's side. I don't suppose that the past fifty years have mellowed him?"

"Not at all."

"I'll avoid him, Yael."

"Wise of you. Mother will help."

"I appreciate the fact that you don't look at me as though I had two heads. I've been getting a lot of that lately."

"You've changed but I still recognize you as my brother. You ought to know that some of those odd looks have concealed a sneaking admiration for you, especially among the younger Doshae."

"Who are still enamored of the idea of bucking tradition. Wonderful. I do not want to become a magnet for the disaffected."

Yael laughed. "Such a development would certainly get Aethel's goat."

"I don't want his goat."

"Slan was telling me some interesting things."

Ruarshi blinked. "Really."

"Are you in love with her?"

"I don't know how to answer that question."

Yael made an exasperated sound. "A simple yes or no would do."

"Nothing simple would cover the subject. She's a mercenary. My co-conspirator. A woman who's recovered almost completely from a horrific head wound that I thought was going to kill her. She refuses to admit she still has bad days, when her whole left side stiffens up and she can hardly climb out of bed. I can tell when she's had a day like that, and she knows I can tell, and she resents me for it."

"You respect each other, at least. It's something to build on."

"What about you, Yael?"

"No prospects yet, which is fine. Starting a family is the last thing on my mind."

"What's the first thing on your mind?"

"The festival. Enjoying myself for a while."

"How are things going at the Beguinage?"

"Fairly well. We're having a bit of trouble with the Hanse. A few wives and daughters have jumped ship on their male relatives since arriving. A few widows too, but nobody gets very worked up when they disappear."

"Any threats lately?"

"There are always threats, Ruarshi. You learn to live with them."

The healer put his arm around Yael as they entered the outskirts of Tomir. "My ferocious little sister. Just be careful."

"You too, Brother."

※ ※ ※

Wil clasped Ginevra's hand tightly and took a deep breath of the cool evening air. The meadow east of Tomir in which they stood was a kaleidoscope of color and movement, as the Miriyanti came together to celebrate the start of the midsummer festival. Ruarshi's people, dressed as brightly as birds and some with their animal familiars by their sides, flowed through the open space as they hurried toward the seven Sotarii who would lead the procession to the cliffs north of town. The ostensible purpose of the ritualized walk was to bless the fertility of Miriyan's fields and waters, but this first night of celebration was more about drunken, riotous joy than anything else. Wil could relate. The Rogation Days in Europe weren't much different.

The Welshman caught a glimpse of Ruarshi, wearing startlingly bright red clothes that he must have borrowed from someone, walking with Slan, who was dressed in an equally bright blue. He was about to point them out when he heard Ginevra gasp.

"What is it?"

She pointed toward the north edge of the meadow. "Is that a bear?"

"Looks like one. It's probably a hunter's familiar."

"I've already seen several wolves. And some kind of very large cat, walking next to three very small children."

"Nothing to worry about. These animals are all about half human anyway."

"I understand now why you came back from this last year with that glassy look in your eye."

Wil sniffed. "Good. Are you going to drop the 'odorless alcohol' theory now?"

Ginevra chuckled. "Shall we go say hello to Ruarshi?"

"Where'd he go? There he is."

They headed off toward the middle part of the double line that was forming, following the flashes of red that betrayed the healer's location. Wil was glad for the twilight; in the full glare of midday he doubted he'd be able to look at that particular outfit without squinting. They made their way around several pockets of foreigners, gathered to stare, and were brought up short once by the darting form of a fox. By the time they made it to Ruarshi's side the procession was almost ready to move out.

"Hello, Wil. Hello, Ginevra. Why don't you jump into line here behind us?"

The Welshman started and then stared. The healer was drunk, no doubt about it. The smell of *keth* wasn't exactly overwhelming, but it wasn't subtle either. He looked at Slan. She wasn't any steadier.

When Wil didn't respond immediately, Ruarshi grabbed his and Ginevra's hands and pulled them into the procession. "You won't be the only foreigners here, and besides there are no rules against it. Shhhh."

Simah, the First among the Sotarii, was speaking. The Welshman couldn't understand the words any better than he had at the previous midsummer festival, which he found disheartening. He had thought his knowledge of Miriyanti was fairly thorough by now.

"Don't look so glum," Slan admonished. "The language she's using is archaic. The only reason we understand it is that we've memorized it."

"She's asking Sotar to watch over us, you know, blah blah blah," Ruarshi whispered. "The good part comes next."

Wil remembered the good part. The Sotarii began humming a wordless melody, sometimes harmonious and sometimes dissonant, and as they hit the final note a purple flame erupted upward from the short iron rod held at shoulder height by Simah and Ferenc. The flame was at least fifteen feet tall and it scarcely wavered, even in the gusts of wind that skimmed over the surface of the meadow.

"How do they do that?" Ginevra asked quietly.

"I have no idea," Ruarshi replied.

"It's fortunate the flame doesn't actually give off any heat," Slan commented. "They'd burn themselves."

The lines moved forward at a stately pace and the Miriyanti before and behind Wil and Ginevra started singing. It was a solemn song, probably some kind of prayer, but it hadn't been going on for five minutes before it morphed into a different sort of tune altogether, one that seemed to contain numerous words of a startlingly explicit and even vulgar nature.

The Welshman poked Ruarshi in the shoulder. "Did you just say what I think you just said?"

"Yes. Come on, you've heard worse."

"But the Sotarii are singing this too!"

"Why shouldn't they? They're not ascetics. I've heard that Bren can drink any three Naishanti under the table."

"That's not true," Slan said. "He's tried, but the best he's been able to do is two Naishanti. And one of them was a novice."

Wil exchanged an owlish glance with Ginevra. "I can't stand it. Would you like to go get roaring drunk once this is over?"

"Absolutely," she said.

"That's the spirit!" Slan leaned over to give Wil a kiss on the cheek. Then she turned to Ruarshi and did the same, only she somehow missed his cheek.

The uproarious singing continued until the Sotarii reached the cliffs that overlooked the city. When the purple fire winked out, the entire assembly went silent and the double lines dissolved as the Miriyanti crowded forward toward the edge.

The Welshman followed in the wake of Ruarshi and Slan, who snaked their way effortlessly through the press until they were all looking down into the tossing waters of the gulf. Wil shivered and stepped back a pace, away from the strongest gusts of wind, and wondered what was coming next. The year before he'd remained in the meadow.

"Time to wake up, fish." Ruarshi patted the Welshman's back. "This is the other good part."

The Sotarii were singing again, a more mournful melody than before. The water in the gulf, as far out as Wil could see, gradually turned the same deep shade of purple as the flame, the same shade as the wide stripe that ran down the back of each individual Sotari's white cloak. It was one of the most wonderful things he had ever seen.

"They're asking the sea to be kind to our fishermen."

The song continued for ten minutes, twenty, plaintive and slow. The Welshman watched the Sotarii for a time, wondering how it was that people so old could sing with such clear voices.

As the music faded so did the glow, and the Miriyanti were once again standing in the pale illumination of a normal twilight. The silence remained absolute until first one torch was kindled, then another, and then others throughout the crowd. That must have been part of the ritual too, Wil decided, since there was no practical need for them at this time of year. Gradually at first, and then with greater momentum, the Miriyanti began pouring back toward Tomir. Intent on getting drunk, or more drunk? The Welshman hoped so.

He grasped Ginevra's hand again and they hurried down the incline, leaving Ruarshi and Slan behind. He did not intend to make them ask for their privacy.

In the glare of a nearby torch Wil could see that his wife's skin was flushed, her eyes sparkling. More beautiful even than the purple waves. He hoped that Lucia would grow up to look just like her mother.

He felt like an idiot.

He felt as though his heart might burst.

✳ ✳ ✳

The fourth time Wil shot him that questioning look, Ruarshi started to laugh. The pair-bonded Miriyanti standing around them shushed him impatiently but he couldn't stop. Clapping a hand over his mouth to stifle some of the noise, the healer laughed until his sides ached and he could no longer breathe properly. Then he scraped the richly embroidered sleeve of his dark green jacket over his watering eyes. The stiff new fabric did nothing to soak up the moisture, instead smearing it all over his face, and Ruarshi was once again doubled over by uncontrollable laughter.

The Welshman grabbed him by the shoulders. "You're scandalizing people," he whispered in mock ferocity. "This is supposed to be solemn."

"I've been scandalizing people for at least a week now. Sorry." Ruarshi put his hands on his hips and breathed deeply for several minutes, until he felt he was back under control. "If you have a question, Wil, just ask it."

"It's, er, personal. About you and... you know."

"No, I don't know. What?"

"The other night... ah... you know. Don't play stupid."

"The answer is no. Do you really think I'd try that after five mugs of *keth*? I don't believe she'd be impressed by alcohol-induced impotence. What did you and Ginevra do afterward?"

Wil choked slightly and didn't respond.

The pair next to them, a Naishanti and her Sotari stoneshaper partner, were chuckling now. "Hush, Illyana," the warrior said. "Otherwise we won't be able to hear our names."

"It could take another two or three hours—" Ruarshi stopped when he heard his own name called along with Wil's. "We're up," he muttered, and then raised his eyebrows at the surprised expressions on the faces of the couple he'd been talking to.

"What?" he asked obnoxiously. Straightening his jacket one final time, he stepped forward with the Welshman.

The distance to the low dais on which Simah and Ferenc sat was actually quite short, but the walk to it always seemed to take an inordinate amount of time. This year was no different in that respect. He looked for and found Yael in the audience, waving from her perch on the roof of a building that bordered the square. He knew better than to search for his parents, as they'd made it clear that they didn't plan to attend. And if Aethel showed up in the front ranks somewhere, Ruarshi thought it likely he would hit the man with whatever large heavy object was closest to hand.

They stopped in front of the High Sotarii and bowed. Simah was the first to address them.

"Ruarshi Illyana, *stamm* Doshae, and Wil *Pirtai* ap Davydd, do you come before us this day prepared to renew your pair-bond for another cycle of seasons?"

"Yes," Ruarshi said.

"Yes," Wil echoed.

The next question came from Ferenc. "Does either of you have any objection to lodge against the behavior of your pair-bonded partner over this past year?"

"No, I do not," Wil said loudly.

The healer shot him an amused glance. "No."

Simah again. "Do you wish to change the terms of your pledge in any way?"

"No."

"No."

And then the final question. "Do you plan to set out on any journeys outside Miriyan over the coming year?" Ferenc asked.

"No." In unison.

Ruarshi lowered his head and waited for the traditional blessing. When a sudden murmur swept through the crowd, he looked back up.

Oh, god. What were Ardan and Jair, the First of the Diamyo Elders, doing up there? He bit his lip to keep himself from swearing.

"Ardan Chamani and Jair Diamyo have asked to speak," Simah declared.

"Ruarshi Illyana," Ardan began, stepping forward, "have you over this past year learned the basic skills taught to all Naishanti and Diamyo, under the tutelage of Slan Naishanti, *stamm* Maelae?"

Ardan should have warned him about this. "...Yes."

"Did you ever request permission from the Diamyo Elders to do so?"

"No."

"Any why did you not do this?"

"Permission would not have been granted."

"Would you like to rectify that omission at this time?"

Ruarshi looked to Wil, who simply shook his head, at a loss.

"On what legal basis is an Illyana allowed to request Naishanti training?" he asked.

"The Sotarii Council has discussed your case and granted you a dispensation. I ask again: would you like to rectify your omission?"

It was a trap, of course. To take a warrior's oath would bring him under the watchful authority of the Diamyo Elders, who would tell him exactly what he could study and when. On the other hand, it would also lend sanction to his and Wil's currently anomalous position. He could hardly afford to turn down that sort of legitimacy.

Ruarshi smiled up at his great aunt. "Yes," he said.

"Do you consent to this, Wil *Pirtai*?"

"Yes," the Welshman replied.

Ardan surrendered her place at the front of the dais to Jair. The Diamyo drew his sword, flipped it over, and extended its hilt toward the healer. Ruarshi accepted it and immediately drove its point deep into the hard ground, ignoring the gasps of surprise that greeted his action. It was customary to take the warrior's oath while holding the blade horizontally at chest level, but the healer had no intention of doing this in the traditional way. He was the least martial Naishanti they would ever swear in and the Diamyo and his cohorts needed to know that from the outset. He didn't want anybody making unreasonable demands on him later.

Jair would probably be annoyed about the dirt. It couldn't be helped.

Ruarshi wrapped his hand lightly around the sword's hilt and inclined his head slightly, indicating his readiness to go on.

The Diamyo, lips pursed, tore his eyes away from his sword and began.

"Do you, Ruarshi *stamm* Doshae, pledge yourself on this day to submit to the training required of all Naishanti and Diamyo, for the purpose of becoming proficient in their skills and adding thereby to the honor and strength of your people?"

A modified oath, with nothing in it about having to assume the title Naishanti one day. The healer wondered how long Ardan had spent arguing with Jair about that.

"Yes," he said. He was still having a hard time believing the Sotarii wanted to set a precedent like this, but his conscience felt lighter already.

"It is understood," Jair went on, "that your title shall remain Illyana throughout this training and thereafter. Is this acceptable to you?"

The healer's grin widened. "That is my preference." He pulled the sword from the ground and tossed it back to the Diamyo. Ruarshi then bowed deeply to everyone on the dais, at the same time touching his forehead in an added gesture of respect.

"I thank you for your trust."

Simah nodded once in acknowledgment. "May you continue to be worthy of it."

And that, after Ferenc had finished reciting the blessing, was all.

Ruarshi and Wil retreated down the aisle until they met and merged with the crowd gathered at its far end. It gave slightly at their approach, allowing them a quick exit from the center of the square. When they finally managed to reach a less densely packed side street, the healer threw his arm around his *pir's* shoulders and drew him into a quick, fierce, exhilarated hug.

"Was that what I think it was?" the Welshman asked, still rattled.

"Yes."

"You had led me to believe that was impossible."

"It is impossible."

"Ardan?"

"No doubt. And the Sotarii. Whom I would otherwise never have suspected of such flexibility. Stop analyzing."

"I can't. I was just beginning to get used to the attention."

"That will last for a few more weeks yet. Then we'll fade into the background and become objects of merely idle curiosity, like any other village idiot."

Wil snorted. "I presume I can stop worrying about exile now?"

"Probably." Ruarshi's smile grew lopsided. "For at least a month or two."

"Are you going to go get drunk again?"

"Not a chance. I plan to go see Slan this evening. How about you?"

"Why would I want to see Slan?"

"Funny."

"No, no *keth* for me either. That stuff has a way of burning a hole in your stomach."

"Yes, it does." Ruarshi sobered somewhat. "Come with me to the market and help me find something Ginevra would like. I need to thank her properly for this jacket."

"You'll just embarrass her."

"She'll recover. Sometimes it's necessary to embarrass people for their own good."

✳ ✳ ✳

Wil scanned the faces around him. In the flickering light cast by the multiple bonfires scattered throughout the meadow, it was difficult to make out anyone's features clearly.

"This could take a while," he observed. "I'm not sure I'd recognize my own mother in a mess like this."

"So listen for his voice instead," Ruarshi said. "Only remember to take into account the possible effects of a drunken slur."

"Ginevra won't want him at our celebratory meal if he's going to slobber on the dishes. Let's go back. I've had more than enough excitement for one day."

"Give it five more minutes. Lorion ought to be there, assuming he wants to come."

"Okay."

The Welshman trudged on in Ruarshi's wake, halfheartedly searching the crowd for Slan's brother. He would be glad enough to find the man, but what he most wanted at that moment was to be back at home, sitting in a padded armchair with a sleeping Lucia on his lap. That's exactly where he had been, in fact, until Ginevra and Slan had all but pushed the two of them out the door. Wil suspected they had ulterior motives for removing all masculine presence from the house, that even now they were deeply engrossed in the kind of women's conversation that must never, under any circumstances, be overheard by a male. He blinked at the healer's back. Maybe there was more going on between Ruarshi and Slan than the Illyana had yet admitted to. Unfortunately the healer didn't seem inclined to clear up that particular question for him.

A burst of laughter to his right caught Wil's attention. He spotted Dunthala, the rather dissolute Naishanti in whose company Lorion could often be found, and reached out to grab Ruarshi's sleeve.

The healer responded to his tugging and turned toward the commotion. "That looks like him, lying there on that bench," Ruarshi said, pointing.

The Welshman squinted in the direction indicated. All he could see from his vantage point was part of a split log and a shock of silver-white hair. He shrugged. "Let's go see."

As they wove their way amongst the revelers, the man lying next to the bonfire sat up and Wil recognized Lorion. The Naishanti had a small cup in his hand and a glint in his eye, and he was turning to face a fairly sizeable group of… uh oh.

"Lions," Ruarshi said and darted forward.

The Welshman was right behind him. He arrived just in time to hear Lorion ask one of them to take off his breeches.

"And why should I do that?" the Lion asked sardonically. It was a Naishanti Wil didn't know.

"Word has it that the Christian priests castrate you fellows and that's why you can't use your magic anymore. For the sake of your own reputations, you really ought to refute that kind of thing. If you can."

In response the Lions spread out a little farther to each side of the fire. All eight of them.

Lorion took due note of this and laughed. He opened his mouth to speak but closed it again when Ruarshi bent down to whisper urgently into his ear. The Welshman watched the Lions, ready to jump in whichever direction seemed wisest, very glad for the law that forbade the carrying of weapons during festivals. Even if the situation did get out of hand, bystanders would be able to pull the combatants apart before anyone was seriously injured. He hoped.

"Gentlemen," Lorion said, standing up shakily from his log, "I have been invited to a celebration, from which you are regretfully excluded. We will have to continue this fascinating conversation later if you don't mind. I still have some questions relating to ritual cannibalism."

"We'd like to continue the conversation now," another Lion replied. This one had a stone in his hand and, if Wil remembered correctly, a well-deserved reputation for violence.

So much for the prohibition on weapons.

The Welshman felt Ruarshi pull upon his power to weave a small, tight shield around the two of them. A moment later several rocks went flying through the air. In the next heartbeat Lorion, Dunthala, and at least half of the Lions were holding burning brands.

People on all sides had begun shouting and running toward them. Wil couldn't tell whether they wanted to stop the fight or join it. He skipped sideways, intending to pull Ruarshi away from the fray, only to realize that the healer had already circled around behind him. The Welshman pivoted and was greeted by an unwelcome but not entirely unexpected sight.

Three novice Naishanti had stepped out of the crowd to close in on the healer. Wil wasn't close enough to hear what they and Ruarshi were talking about, but he did catch the single word 'freak.' Which really told him everything he needed to know.

The healer had dropped into a crouch, moving with the alacrity lent him by the Naishanti magic that now flowed through their link. The novice on Ruarshi's opposite side carried something that glinted silver in the erratic firelight, probably a dagger. Since he already had that to deal with, Wil didn't believe the Illyana would object to being relieved of his other two opponents.

They'd forgotten that Ruarshi had a *pir*, shame on them. The Welshman came up behind the other novices and, grabbing up two solid fistfuls of hair, jerked their heads down and inward until they collided with a satisfying crack. Dropping the one on the left, he wrenched his right wrist over and flung the other one onto his back, where the youngster seemed content to stay after the Welshman hit him once, neatly breaking his nose.

Wil glanced upward just in time to see the second Naishanti come barreling toward him. He rolled to the side and allowed the man to barrel by. When the novice reappeared he was carrying a torch, which he swung in the Welshman's face. Wil got a hand on it and then kneed the man in the groin, at which point the fight seemed to go out of him, too.

Panting, the Welshman walked over to Ruarshi, who was leaning over the prone, still form of the third novice.

"What happened here?"

"It's still happening. Yon idiot has been given to know that the shield currently pinching off his windpipe will be released just as soon as he's ready to apologize. He seems to be turning blue."

"He is. The shade doesn't suit him at all."

"No," Ruarshi agreed.

The expression in the Naishanti's eyes had been growing increasingly desperate. He nodded vigorously.

"Does this mean you're ready to give this up?"

The nodding increased in tempo.

"Very well." The healer released the weave and stood. The novice sat up slowly.

"Let me tell you what you're thinking," Ruarshi said. He crossed his arms and regarded the young warrior. "You're thinking that there's no longer any point in becoming a Naishanti, since the title has now been hopelessly soiled. By me. You're thinking that the only way you can win back your honor and that of your fellow warriors is to remove this stain. This necessarily involves attacking me. You're welcome to your opinion, of course, but you'd best get used to the idea that this stain is indelible. The precedent has been set. There will be others besides myself. Now. Apologize."

The Naishanti pushed himself upright, bowed stiffly, and stalked away.

"Look at that," Wil observed. "He's not even going to check on his friends."

Ruarshi turned to look at them, and the Welshman saw the shallow cut on his cheek for the first time.

"How did he manage that?"

"What? Oh." Ruarshi rubbed at the cut with the back of his hand and brought it away bloody. "I did that when I shattered that little toy of his. One of the shards got away from me. What did you do to those two?"

"The one who's holding his face has a broken nose. The one who's still on the ground will be a severe disappointment to his girlfriend for the next week or so."

"Ah."

"Why Ruarshi, you look almost amused."

"I am almost amused. This reminds me of the bad old days. It seems as though the other brawl has also come to an end. Shall we fetch Lorion?"

"By all means. I'd hate to go back empty-handed with nothing but cuts and bruises to show for our trouble."

They wandered toward the log bench, now toppled over into the ashes of the bonfire, where they'd first spotted Lorion. An amazing amount of woody debris littered the ground, as did a number of groaning Naishanti. They finally found Slan's brother lying alone almost twenty yards from the place the fight had started.

"You are not nearly drunk enough to justify any of that," Ruarshi said by way of greeting.

"What makes you think I'm interested in justifying anything?" Lorion's voice was dreamy. He was staring at the stars.

The healer sat down in the grass next to the Naishanti. "Are you hurt?"

"No. Well, my face stings a little. I'd see to it that it stung a lot more if I thought that would keep even one more of us from joining the Lions."

"You're worried about nothing. They're a handful only and a handful they'll remain."

"Until some kind of religious fever sweeps through Miriyan, after which there'll be nobody left who hasn't forsworn the power needed to keep the Europeans out. They're killing us."

"Maybe he is drunker than you thought," Wil said.

"Scoff if you like. Those priests are going to destroy all of us eventually. I've been having the most vivid nightmares about them. They're like a great black wave, lapping at our shores."

"Nerthu save us, he's waxing poetic," Ruarshi said. "Get up. We're already late for dinner, I'm quite sure."

"I hope Ginevra and my sister have cooked up something soft," Lorion said, pushing himself upward on his elbows. "I'd hate to leave teeth behind on my plate."

✳ ✳ ✳

"Slan, that is *enough*," Ruarshi said emphatically. "The limp will disappear in its own good time. Or else it won't. You're not helping matters by doing this."

"Physically, maybe not," Slan replied breathlessly, "but this is very good for my morale. Either give me space or get out."

Ruarshi stood fuming at the bottom of the stairs as Slan continued with the self-torture she liked to call therapy. Five hundred repetitions. She'd told him she didn't intend to quit for the day until she'd made it up and down that staircase five hundred times.

It was ridiculous.

"Slan—"

"No, Illyana. I will not be coddled. You should have seen the sorts of things I used to do every day back in Italy."

"I did see some of those things. I watched you beat your head against a wall, figuratively of course, trying to change the world overnight by sheer force of will. I was duly impressed."

"Go to hell, my dear."

Ruarshi turned his back, found a chair that faced away from the stairs, and sat in it. "Tell me when you're done."

He had told himself that he would take a nap, let her do whatever it was she had to do, and then check on her before he left. Sleeping proved to be impossible, however. He couldn't block out the sound of her labored breathing any more than he could ignore the occasional sound of her left foot colliding with a step, whenever she couldn't lift her leg quite high enough to clear it. Those collisions grew more frequent as the minutes lengthened into hours.

When silence finally descended on the room, Ruarshi lifted his head and rose from the chair.

"That was five hundred fifty, by my count."

Slan smiled at him tiredly from the foot of the stairs, where she had come to rest. "Your presence was an inspiration. Or a goad. Take your pick."

"Do you need something to drink?"

"No. My stomach's too unsettled. Later. Right now I just want to sleep."

"The bedroom is at the top of the stairs."

"So it is. I think you'll have to carry me up there. And if you use anything I've taught you in order to do it, I'll kill you myself. You're strong enough to manage it on your own, healer."

"Do you think so."

"Oh yes. You're not the flabby fellow I first met."

"Flabby?"

"And pale. You'd been spending too much time in sickrooms."

"That much is certainly true." He bent, slipped one arm around her shoulders and another under her knees, and lifted her. She was in fact surprisingly light.

"I see I shall have to increase the amount of food in your daily diet. You weigh no more than a feather."

"Don't I wish. In that case I could simply fly around the room."

"But only on windy days. The rest of the time you'd be at the mercy of whatever pillow maker happened to come along."

Slan giggled, a sound so shocking coming from her that Ruarshi very nearly missed the top step.

"Clumsy, aren't you?"

"Apparently."

Ruarshi pushed open the door to Slan's bedroom with his shoulder and deposited her gently on the bed. The mattress was supported by a monstrous Italian hardwood frame. He began to trace the ornate carvings on the bed's footboard with a forefinger.

"Grapes, pomegranates, some animal I couldn't possibly identify..."

"What are you doing?"

"Examining this thing."

"It was payment for an assassination I helped with."

Ruarshi lost interest in the bed and stared. "Really?"

"Oh, Christ," Slan muttered. "You're much easier to hold a conversation with when you're not so jumpy. Come here."

"What?"

"I plan to get some sleep now. I would prefer to have you in here with me. You're warmer and more comfortable than the blankets. And you're very handsome when you blush like that."

"It does cut down on the paleness problem," Ruarshi observed. "Should I come in with or without these dirty boots?"

"Please yourself. If you're not here when I wake up, I might have to lodge a complaint with the Chamani Elders."

"I'd love to read it." By the time Ruarshi had pulled his boots off, Slan was asleep. He crawled into the bed beside her and snuggled up against her back, laying one hand on her hip so that he could ease the stiffness and ache he found there. Afterward he left his hand resting there, because he rather liked the way her hip felt.

When the healer next opened his eyes it was evening, and Slan had rolled over onto her back to look at him. Ruarshi blinked at her.

"I'm glad to see you had sense enough to take your boots off."

"I learned a smattering of social graces as a child."

"May I bring up a delicate subject?"

"By all means."

"It relates to mortality, I'm afraid."

"Whose?"

"Wil's."

The healer felt something freeze within him. "It will be a few years yet."

"I hope he lasts another fifty years. He's one of the most decent male Europeans I've ever met. But when the mourning period is over and you're free to pair-bond, I want to partner you."

"You?" Ruarshi sat up. "Why?"

"So much for those social graces. Because you are interesting, Illyana. You're already taking the Sotarii Council and the Elders in directions they never meant to go, and you're what, barely over two hundred? And because you managed to disarm me the first time we met. That still annoys me, you know."

"No, I didn't know. You very nearly skewered me, if you recall." The healer was having a hard time getting his thoughts together. They kept skittering in all directions, like a nervous flock of birds.

"I realize the proposal is sudden. But I want some kind of answer now."

"I think you do me too much honor. You should find someone more senior."

"No one more senior interests me, healer," Slan growled. "Hence the question. And I don't want to hear the word 'honor' ever again in this context. It's inappropriate. Stop being so damn polite. You use politeness like a wall."

"You're right, of course." Ruarshi leaned in to give her a kiss, and his world changed.

✳ ✳ ✳

"Wil." Ginevra gently removed the mangled quill from his fingers and laid it on the writing table before him. "Is something wrong?"

"No, not exactly. I don't know. Maybe."

"I'm glad to have that clarified."

The Welshman smiled faintly. "I wish there were some way I could find out. I've been worrying for a while now at something Herr Rodler said. Lorion lent the question some added urgency the other evening."

"Before or after he got the two of you involved in that fight?"

"After, after." Wil waved his hands absently.

Ginevra swung a chair around and sat facing him. "What is it?"

"The foreign merchants are up to something. Specifically the Hanseatic merchants. Doesn't it strike you as odd that there are so many of them here right now?"

"It's unusual. I'm not convinced it's odd. What is it you suspect them of?"

"Some scheme involving conversion of Miriyanti. Rodler said something about Miriyan helping Pope Boniface to triumph over the other Pope. Benedict? I forget. And Lorion's been having nightmares about priests."

Ginevra chuckled. "He's a fanciful man. He's just scaring himself. Did Rodler say anything else?"

"Not really. He asked some questions about how attached the Miriyanti really are to Sotar and Nerthu and the others. All of which brings us back to conversion. I can't see how a few souls this far north are expected to swing the balance of papal power in Europe."

"Since it involves merchants it will involve money as well. And that's always of interest to Popes, beleaguered and otherwise." Ginevra stood. "Come on."

"Where?"

"To see Marion Cohen. She's a merchant in her own right, and a friend of mine, and if your suspicions have any basis at all she'll know what it is."

Wil stood and followed his wife toward the front of the house. "Do I know her? I don't think I've met her."

"I don't believe you've been introduced. I ran into her at the Beguinage."

"Oh."

"Quit with the 'oh'. I'm going to take you there sometime. I have yet to meet one of those women who's actually worthy of the reputation the priests are trying to foist off on them. They're perfectly normal people, no more wicked than I am."

Wil chuckled. "You just undercut your own argument, love."

"Which is it, then? Did my coming here with you make me other than normal, or wicked?"

"A little bit of both, I think. Is Sophia still...?"

"Yes, she's already agreed to watch Lucia for a little longer tonight." Ginevra opened the door. "Stop dawdling. I don't want you fretting all evening, but if we arrive too late at Marion's I'll be too embarrassed to knock."

They obtained horses at a nearby stable and set off through town, heading south and west. This particular twilight was taking on a greenish tinge, Wil noticed, and he felt another stab of longing for that amazing purple shade the Sotarii had conjured up the week before. It would be another year before he saw that again, he supposed. The midsummer festival was set to end the next day with a flash of multicolored fire dancing across the sky.

After about a quarter hour of riding, Ginevra swung down from her horse in front of a small but sturdy stone house. She looped the animal's reins through an iron ring set into the front wall of the building and Wil followed suit.

"All the windows are dark," the Welshman observed. "Do you think she's gone to bed?"

"I suspect she's studying. She does that of an evening."

"Should we interrupt her?"

His wife considered him. "How worried are you?"

"Now that you mention it, very."

Ginevra stepped up to the front door. It swung open before she could even raise her hand and Wil found himself looking into the dark eyes of a small, middle-aged woman who was carrying an oil lamp in one hand and holding a deep blue shawl around her shoulders with the other.

"Ginevra," she said warmly. "I heard your voices. Wil *Pirtai*? I'm glad I finally get to meet you. Come in, please."

"Thank you. We're so sorry to bother you this late, Marion."

They trailed the woman inside, to a room at the back of the house that was filled with books. The Welshman glanced at their spines and realized with some relief that he couldn't read any of them. There was no chance his translator's reflexes would kick in and distract him.

"Are you hungry? I can fetch some cheese from the pantry…"

"Oh, no, we've just eaten," Ginevra replied. Her eyes fell on a large tome that rested open on Marion's desk. "You *were* studying. What is it?"

"A tractate from the Talmud. *Niddah*. It's fortunate you came by, as it was beginning to give me a headache. For several different reasons." She must have noticed Wil's startled expression, for she turned to him then and ushered him into a chair. "There is no one here who dares to tell me I am forbidden such study. I saw you and your Illyana at the ceremony the other day. Miriyanti law is nicely flexible, don't you think?"

The Welshman chuckled and reached over to take his wife's hand as she sat down next to him. "Rather too much so, sometimes. It can be disconcerting when someone changes the ground rules on you without warning."

"So," Marion said as she also took a seat, "tell me why you've come."

Wil and Ginevra exchanged a look. "It relates to the Hanseatic merchants," his wife began. "Wil has been doing a translation job for Herr Rodler, who implied that Miriyanti conversions are being sought. As a way of resolving the papal dispute, apparently, though Rodler never made the connection clear."

"If Europe has plans for Miriyan, I want to know about them," Wil added. "I rather like this place the way it is."

Marion had steepled her fingers and was staring into her lap. "So do I. You're right to be concerned. The Hanse's grandiose fantasy has a lot of determination behind it."

"What fantasy?" the Welshman asked. "What on earth does Miriyan have to do with the Pope?"

"Very little at this point, though that could change at any time." Their hostess raised her eyes and regarded them steadily. "Boniface's supporters, both within and outside the Church, have been putting a great deal of pressure on the Sotarii lately. Especially the High Sotarii. They're hoping to convince Simah and Ferenc, at minimum, to convert. If they agree to do this, Boniface will lift the ban on commerce in Miriyanti goods and Christians living in his sphere of influence will be allowed to trade even those items obviously created by means of magic. The beautiful Miriyanti woodwork, stonework, and metalwork. Their blades and bows. The list goes on."

"I see," Wil said. "This trade enriches the Hanse and the Hanse enriches Boniface. Who then uses the money to field an army, whose goal will be to chase Benedict to Ethiopia?"

"Something like that. The trade would also enrich Miriyan. The plan has supporters everywhere."

"What about Benedict's followers?" Ginevra asked.

"They're not well represented here," Marion said. "If the Sotarii choose to convert, I don't believe there's anything Benedict's people can do to prevent the other from profiting disproportionately. They would end up with some fraction of the money, I suppose, as it wouldn't take long for Benedict to follow his rival in legalizing trade with Miriyan.

"If this has satisfied your curiosity," she went on, "I'd now like you to satisfy mine."

"Certainly," Ginevra said, subdued, "if we can."

"How likely are the Sotarii to convert?"

Wil realized belatedly that both women were looking at him. He'd been staring at the wall and hadn't noticed their scrutiny. "Simah and Ferenc? The chances are nil. They're the living Peter and Paul of Miriyan. The others... no. They wouldn't either, I don't think."

"How old are the High Sotarii?" Marion persisted.

"Around a millennium each. They've both got a handful of centuries left."

"And if they were to meet with untimely deaths?"

Wil shook his head emphatically. "That wouldn't work. If they were killed, the clan chiefs would meet to elect their successors. The chiefs aren't incorruptible, but most of them live off in the countryside and would have little use for bags of gold coins. They also tend to be prickly about matters of national pride. They would name novices to the office of High Sotarii if they had to, to keep that position out of the hands of converts."

Their hostess seemed to relax a little. "There's something to be said for certain kinds of provincialism."

Wil laughed at that, though he still felt rather bleak. "Amen."

Ginevra squeezed his hand and shifted forward in her chair. "We appreciate your help, Marion. The next time an urgent question comes up we'll try to arrange for a daytime visit."

"Your company is always welcome, night or day."

"If you hear anything new, please let us know. We'll do the same for you."

Marion smiled and rose. "I'm sure I'll see you soon at the Beguinage. Give my love to Lucia."

✳ ✳ ✳

"This is your second move in, what, two weeks?" Yael asked. She was leaning lazily against the windowpane in Ruarshi's room at the Doshae clan circle, scowling in an unsuccessful attempt to make him believe she disapproved of his plans. She disapproved so little, in fact, that she could scarcely contain her excitement. The healer knew her well enough to recognize that much without even looking at her closely.

"Yes, it is. Why don't you make yourself useful and stuff some of my clothes in here?" He tossed her a worn leather sack, which she caught and stared at disdainfully.

"You've already convinced one poor woman to look after you, and even to open her house to you. You definitely don't need another."

"Since when does putting clothes in a bag constitute looking after someone? Just do it."

"I suppose if I wad up your new green jacket, it might fit in here," Yael mused, wandering toward Ruarshi's bed where the item in question lay.

"No. No. Sit." The healer relieved her of the sack and pointed toward a low stool. His sister sat obediently. Ruarshi glanced at her suspiciously out of the corner of his eye and then went on with his packing.

He had just about gotten his sparse belongings gathered into manageable bundles when Yael laughed, making him jump. His distraction was so complete that he'd forgotten she was there.

"I hope I run into Lorion later today. Will he be at Slan's? There's a new rumor floating around that will feed those nightmares of his."

"You're a cruel woman. What is it?"

"Somebody spotted Shadel Chamani with a crucifix hanging around his neck. A Chamani Elder, of all people."

A shiver ran up Ruarshi's spine and he stopped what he was doing. "You're quite sure of that name?" He'd had a conversation with Wil that very morning in which the Chamani's name had come up, and another discussion some time earlier dealing with the same man. He remembered a strange short phrase in Miriyanti that Wil had mentioned, one which had caught the Welshman's attention because it sounded odd to his ears and because it had been dropped into the middle of an otherwise unremarkable German sentence. Ruarshi thought he'd heard the phrase once or twice before in a specific context but had never bothered trying to place it. Now if he could just recall what that context had been…

"Yes. He was never your instructor, was he?"

"No."

Alien fire. The phrase came from the European holy book. Someone had offered alien fire to their god and had been destroyed by fire as a result.

The fire that the Sotarii Council was going to offer to the heavens that afternoon was nothing if not alien.

What would happen if the entire Council disappeared at once? Chaos, certainly. Civil war, possibly, as the Miriyanti with close ties to Europe fought to retain those ties, and the lucrative trade deals that suddenly went with them, in the face of opposition from the traditionalists and rural Miriyanti.

Was Boniface perhaps tired of waiting? In the absence of a unified voice to contend such a declaration, would he simply announce that Miriyan was now Christianized and therefore acceptable as a trading partner?

Why shouldn't he?

"What's wrong, Brother? You look worried."

"I am worried. Would you do something for me? Go find Ardan

and ask her to meet me at the Renewal Ceremony."

"I'll need to tell her why."

"Tell her I'm concerned about what might happen. I'm probably wrong but if not her presence there would be helpful."

"Are you sure she'll listen to that? That's pretty vague."

"It's meant to be. I'll feel like an idiot if I get too specific and then... Okay. Tell her I'm worried about a possible assassination attempt. That should get her attention."

"Assassination? Whose? Wait!"

"Go, Sister, please."

By the time Ruarshi reached the clan circle's yard he was running, and he didn't waste time putting a saddle on the wiry gray mare he found in the stable's first stall.

He urged the horse into a quick canter and guided her toward the center of town. When he arrived at the edge of the familiar square, the closing ceremony was already half over. The seven members of the So-tarii Council stood chanting in a circle next to the ornate stone well that bore the statue of their primary god. The unsmiling Sotar held a lightning bolt in his right fist, while his other hand, the crippled hand, hung lifeless and atrophied by his naked thigh.

There were hundreds of Miriyanti and a few foreigners present to watch as the wildfire was kindled, but the square wasn't so crowded that a horse couldn't pick its way along the perimeter. Ignoring the handful of outraged glares that this subtle profanation of the ritual won him, Ruarshi prodded the horse forward. He kept close track of the progress of the invocation even as he searched among the multi-tude for anyone or anything that looked out of place.

Not that he would necessarily recognize such a thing if he saw it.

He did, however, know exactly what Shadel looked like, and unless he was very much mistaken...

Ruarshi slid off his horse and wound his way through the mass of onlookers toward the well. As long as Shadel didn't change direction, he ought to run into the man before he got particularly close to the So-tarii, at which point he could ask the old healer a few questions.

Movement, off to his left. He'd missed Shadel by about ten feet. He snaked his way through the crowd to the Chamani's side and linked arms with him. The man's head whipped around and he blinked at Ru-arshi in surprise.

"Shadel Chamani, good to see you," the healer said. "Would you mind coming with me for a moment?"

Shadel tried in vain to slide his arm from Ruarshi's grasp. "What is this about? I'm trying to watch the ritual."

"It's nothing to be alarmed about. But I need to know what's in the pouch."

The Chamani glared. "It's a gift for my wife, if you must know. I'd like to find her before the ceremony ends."

"Does your wife have a preference for perfume that smells like caustic chemicals, then?"

"Let go, Naishanti."

Shadel's struggles were now obvious to those standing near them but Ruarshi had no intention of letting him go. Instead he tightened his grip on the old healer's forearm and began dragging him slowly away from the well and the sound of chanting.

Someone collided with him from behind, hard, and he felt a dagger slip neatly between his ribs and then out again. The Chamani twisted away from him and gave his arm a final jerk, freeing himself.

Ruarshi lunged for the man and caught the edge of his cloak. He yanked it backwards and wove a quick loop around Shadel's ankles, giving the old Chamani no choice but to fall right onto the pouch that held the chemicals.

The man erupted into a screaming ball of flame and acrid black smoke began pouring skyward. Ruarshi stumbled back in an effort to avoid the searing heat and fell to his knees. Only then did he realize that his right lung was filling with blood and that he was actually in quite a bit of trouble.

Shadel was still screaming, a sound that was growing increasingly ghastly as the seconds ticked by. Ruarshi couldn't stand the noise any longer. He reached outward and stopped the man's frenetically pounding heart.

Silence, blessed silence as the wildfire shot upward from the square to bathe the low clouds in a rainbow of swirling light.

The healer lay on his back watching the play of color and gathering his magic to start working on his stab wound. He would have to heal it from the inside out. This meant tackling the lung tissue first. That was always tricky to knit back together. In a kind of half-trance, his gaze still fixed on the lights in the sky, he began.

❋ ❋ ❋

Wil arrived at the square ten minutes later and jumped from his winded mount. The first person he saw was Ardan, pacing back and forth next to a charred corpse, tossing a small glass ball from hand to hand. His gaze slipped past her and came to rest on Simah and a healer he'd met once or twice, both of them with their backs to him, bent over a third figure. A third very familiar figure, lying in a pool of blood.

He started in that direction but was intercepted by Ardan.

"He was stabbed. They tell me it's not going to prove fatal. It's about time you damn well got here."

"Is he conscious?"

"Not any more. See this?" Ardan pulled a small bloody knife from her belt.

"That's a Naishanti's knife."

"Exactly. Here, take it. And what do you make of this?"

Wil took the glass ball from her outstretched hand, noting the thin partition that separated its hemispheres. He sniffed gently at one of the two resin stoppers and then handed it back to her.

"One of the alchemists. I assume…" He gestured toward the corpse.

"Yes. That was Shadel. Ruarshi knocked him over onto his collection of these, which he just happened to be carrying with him today when he came to watch the ceremony. I want you to take that knife to the Doshae clan Seer, Michel, and have him tell you who it belongs to. I'll track down the alchemist who made these clever little things. If we move fast we can get these people before they find their way aboard one of the Hanse's ships. Are you up to it?"

Something about Ardan's predatory expression was contagious and Wil found himself mirroring it effortlessly.

"Oh, yes."

"Go, then. I'll meet you at the healers' circle later."

"I'll be there."

❋ ❋ ❋

Ruarshi lay resting in Slan's bed, staring upward at the parallel wooden beams that supported the roof of her house. While he'd been recovering, the world had changed again. About half of the Church's representatives had gone home, as had a majority of the recently arrived Hanseatic merchants. A few of the Miriyanti who'd chosen to ally themselves with European interests had also left and would likely be exiled in absentia. Everyone else was busy distancing themselves from past connections with known conspirators and church attendance had gone down sharply.

He wondered idly if the European who had stabbed him in the back was among those who'd gone. All Michel had been able to tell them about the dagger was that it hadn't been wielded by a Miriyanti. As long as the individual in question didn't decide to have another go at him, Ruarshi supposed he could live with that. He didn't have much choice.

Surprisingly, not one of the Lions had been implicated in the conspiracy. Ruarshi hoped that this would mellow Lorion's attitude toward them somewhat, or that it would at least cut down on his bad dreams.

Speaking of which. The healer remembered one dream of his own, mixed in among the febrile unpleasantness of his unconscious imaginings, which still intrigued him. It had been uncommonly vivid and the only actor in it had been Slan. Ruarshi wanted to ask her about it just as soon as he could find her.

He sat up slowly in the bed and maneuvered his legs over the side. Standing wasn't as easy as it should have been but he managed it. His loose robe was adequate clothing for his purposes and he didn't need shoes.

So. He was ready.

Ruarshi went out the door and hobbled his way down the stairs. It was amazing to him that such simple acts could pull so painfully at the tender scar that covered his wound. Even though he'd been under Ardan's extremely competent care ever since the injury had been inflicted, it still hurt. He thought he might submit to some poppy in his wine a bit later.

In the meantime he needed to rest for a minute. He lowered himself onto the bottom step and leaned into the railing, making sure his breathing remained slow, measured, and as shallow as he could manage. Deep breaths were simply out of the question.

About a quarter hour later Slan found him sitting there, half asleep.

"Ruarshi! What the devil are you thinking?"

"I thought I'd ask you to carry me up the stairs. One good turn deserves another."

She stared at him, her hands on her hips, clearly exasperated. "I can't carry you, and you know it. I'll help you walk it yourself when you're ready."

"No hurry. I came down because I have a question to ask you."

"What?"

"I recall a dream of you. Did I imagine it or was it real?"

Slan's smile was brilliant. "What dream was that?"

"You said we'd have a son by spring. Is it true?"

"Nerthu willing, yes."

Ruarshi laughed, weakly, because he could not shout or twirl her around in his arms. Those things he would also do, later.

# Blue Tattoos

Ruarshi glanced up from the study of his interlaced fingers to see Mikha standing beside him, looking into the healer's half-empty mug of *keth* in bemusement.

"I think you've been spending too much time with your goodbrother. Isn't that the fourth mug of that stuff you've had tonight?"

Ruarshi quirked an eyebrow at his cousin. "Lorion isn't nearly the lout he pretends to be. Haven't you ever noticed how much more people will confess to a drunk than they will to a sober person? My goodbrother is simply one of the world's greatest natural spies."

"You shouldn't worry so much about this thing with your parents," Mikha continued, resting a hand tentatively on the healer's shoulder. "They don't mean it. This is all just something Aethel cooked up."

"Do you think so. They seem to be serious enough to have traveled seventy miles through a blizzard to be here. Have they arrived yet?"

"Not that I've heard about. I did spot your brother a few minutes ago, though. He's over by the hearth."

"Perhaps I should go and say hello to him," Ruarshi said. He had been well aware of his brother's presence since Aethel had first entered the clan circle's hall a half hour before. The healer rose carefully from the bench, testing his balance, and started moving slowly toward the fire. "We've hardly spoken since I returned from Europe after all."

"Uh, Ruarshi…" Mikha seized a handful of the healer's sleeve, only to relinquish it again when his cousin turned to glare at him.

"Yes, Mikha, I appreciate what you're trying to do. And you are right, I'm quite drunk. If I'm going to get my head smashed against a wall by my own brother I prefer to do it in this state. You have my permission to nurse me back to health afterwards."

Ruarshi resumed his interrupted progress toward the hearth, aware that he was being unfair to his terribly earnest and well-meaning cousin, and not in the least troubled about it. His attention, though rendered somewhat less than focused by the alcohol, was wholly directed toward the figure of his elder brother. Aethel stood talking animatedly with a group of older men, most of whom Ruarshi couldn't identify at this distance, all of them backlit by the enormous fire that kept most but not all of the night's chill at bay.

His brother's back was to him, but another of the men must have warned him of Ruarshi's approach. Aethel swung around, smiling broadly as the healer drew near.

"Ruarshi! My dear little brother. Have you finally come to offer your older brother a bow? I notice you've been avoiding that obligation since your return."

The healer considered Aethel's indolent face for a moment. Then without a word he sketched an ostentatious, courtly, European bow, totally different from the rigid gesture conventional among the Miriyanti. As he reached the climax of what even Aethel had come to recognize by then as an elaborate insult, Ruarshi extended a delicate tendril of power toward his brother and, with an inspiration that could only have been born of inebriation, cut the cords that held up Aethel's breeches. The heavy cloth fell of its own accord to the floor. The healer straightened swiftly and hit his brother with all the force he could muster across the jaw.

A small, shocked silence ensued, one that soon spread throughout the hall. Ruarshi, looking down on the bewildered, half-naked spectacle of his brother, spared himself an instant to wonder how he felt about what he'd just done. Then his brother was up and moving and the time for reflection was over.

It took Aethel some few seconds to get his clothing back in order, which he did wordlessly. Ruarshi was aware that those closest to them had moved back, giving the brothers room for the fight whose sudden imminence should have surprised no one. He fully expected Aethel to pound him bloody. Instead of dread, he felt only the kind of wild exhilaration he used to experience when, as a child, he crept out of his family's cottage in the summer to stand for hours amidst the buffeting wind and rain of a northern gale. He usually got sick as a result but it was always worth it.

Ruarshi dodged Aethel's first two blows. Only after the third had sent him reeling, ears ringing, into the giant trestle table that dominated the hall did it occur to him that he was no longer at a disadvantage in this kind of confrontation. His drunken imagination supplied him unbidden with a vivid picture of his brother sprawled once again on the floor of the hall, this time broken and bloody and begging him to stop. The healer blinked and the vision disappeared, to be replaced by the all too real sight of Aethel rushing toward him again, his face distorted in fury.

Because he didn't particularly care for either image, because he didn't have any good ideas about how to stop what he'd started, and because he was drunk, Ruarshi began to laugh. He was still laughing when a small group of spectators, disturbed by what they were witnessing, pulled his enraged brother off of him some time later. Mikha and a few others hurried over with a warm bowl of water and were attempting to clean him up when his parents, Rori and Leisha, walked through the door.

His father spotted him at once and froze. It took his mother a bit longer to realize that the bloody and rather limp individual sitting on the wooden floorboards in the middle of the hall was her younger son. They both located Aethel, who had returned to the hearth and was to all appearances unharmed, before they started toward the healer. Their small retinue, composed of an uncle, a first cousin, and a few others, assessed the situation and drifted away in another direction.

His father spoke first. "Aethel did this?"

"We conspired," Ruarshi replied after some thought. "I started it by yanking his pants down in public. He just supplied the required rejoinder."

It was an impertinent and wildly inappropriate answer to give to one's parents, Ruarshi knew. Under the circumstances it seemed to be the best he could do.

His mother and father exchanged a look that seemed composed of equal parts pain and anger. The healer glanced away, did what he could to steady himself, and rose to his feet. After executing a very proper and formal bow to each of his parents, Ruarshi requested their permission to leave the hall.

"I need to find someplace quiet to heal my face," he added. His mother flinched, and he shrugged. "I'd prefer that this cut under my eye not turn into a scar. I'm quite vain, as you know."

For an instant Ruarshi was afraid that his father intended to hit him, too, but instead Rori nodded tightly and turned away. Leisha had already wandered farther into the hall. The healer was quite sure she was weeping.

Ruarshi pivoted on his heel and plunged out into the snowstorm. The torches in the courtyard of the clan circle hardly illuminated anything other than themselves, but he was still able to make his way quickly to the door that led to the clan's living quarters. He didn't suppose Mikha would mind if he borrowed his room for an hour or so. The poor boy had been much more upset than Ruarshi himself was.

The room was very cold and pitch black, as of course he should have known it would be. He considered going back to the hall for a candle but dismissed the notion almost as soon as it occurred to him. Instead he stumbled around in the darkness until he'd located Mikha's flint and oil lamp, and kindled his own small flame. What he saw when he looked into the mirror over the washbasin was no more than he had expected, but bad enough for all that. He was defiantly, angrily gratified that he could heal most of the damage himself. There was no need for anyone who hadn't been in that hall to see what brotherly love could, when distorted sufficiently, come to mean.

Ruarshi was initially surprised to find that he had a fractured eye socket, and then decided that he was probably lucky to have come through the scuffle with damage no worse than that. The shield he'd been using to dampen the force of Aethel's blows had become dangerously weak there at the end when he'd been on the verge of passing out.

Ruarshi wasn't sure how long he spent tending to his wounds, but by the end of it he looked somewhat better and felt a great deal more sober. He would still have bruises to explain to Slan, Wil, Yael, Ginevra, Lorion, his students...

He only became aware that someone was standing in the doorway of Mikha's quarters when he heard the soft scuff of shoe leather against wood.

"I owe you an apology, *Tai* Nerthi. I've actually been here for some time, watching you at your work. My name is Piotyr, also *stamm* Doshae."

The healer stared at the man, wondering if he had understood him correctly. He took in Piotyr's tattered European clothes, his black hair growing in white at the roots, the old sword at his hip with a single ruby set into the pommel.

"Nerthi," Ruarshi repeated flatly.

"You're fully clever enough to have guessed that already. May I come in?"

The healer stood and gestured toward the low bed on which he'd been sitting. "This isn't even my room."

"Thank you." Piotyr made his way to Mikha's bed and settled himself on it, moving with a slight limp and obvious discomfort. "I'm not staying with the clan, either. I came this evening because I thought you might be here. And yes, before you ask, I saw what happened in the hall."

Ruarshi remained standing. He was not going to talk with this man about his family. He doubted there would be any need for him to. "You're an exile."

"I knew you were clever." Piotyr smiled and leaned back against the wall. "Your reputation very much precedes you. I was living in Danzig until this past summer, posing as a merchant of modest means. Actually I'd been at it so long that it was no longer really a pose. You have heard what happened there after word of midsummer's events reached us?"

"No."

"The story was garbled, of course, quite intentionally in some ways to protect the guilty. You, Ruarshi Illyana or Ruarshi Naishanti—no one could quite decide on the correct designation—have developed the mysterious power to set people afire. Using this devilish gift, you helped to destroy a plan to bring the benefits of Hanseatic trade to Miriyan by immolating a Christianized member of your own people. You probably shouldn't travel in Hanseatic regions anytime soon using your own name, incidentally. This account led to an entirely predictable and entirely regrettable surge of hostility toward Miriyanti. There was some rioting in the streets, some rocks thrown, daggers brandished. Three Miriyanti were murdered. A few dozen blond Poles also perished. I hadn't kept my origins quite secret enough, hence the limp. That sort of thing did not spread far or last long, but many of the Miriyanti living in Europe have now decided to settle in France. There we are heroes."

Ruarshi studied Piotyr's sardonic expression and considered what he'd just been told. It was almost inconceivable that such a tale, if true, shouldn't have made its way to him at some point during the past eight months. Then again, he had largely restricted himself to the company of his friends while he recuperated and hadn't widened his circle of contacts very much since he'd recovered.

It was just possible.

"I see," he said. "In how many cities was this a problem?"

"Oh, not many. There has been some ecclesiastical gnashing of teeth that may create problems for us in the future, but for the present the situation is stable. Now. I told you this for a very specific reason. You should no longer regard yourself as quite the private individual you once were. You should have been exiled as I was exiled. Instead you are a national hero, even if most Miriyanti don't like to admit it. You have taken a very old idea, *Tai* Nerthi, one that has been in eclipse for generations, and have made it very nearly acceptable again. I am not the only exile who has returned. You have given us some hope. Or rather, the way you've been treated has done so."

The healer realized that the last of the *keth* had worn off, that he was in pain, and that he wasn't following Piotyr's words very well. His healing of himself, as always, had been only moderately successful. He lowered himself to the floor.

"You don't believe this will last, do you?"

Piotyr grimaced. "It could go either way. The stories you have heard regarding the Nerthii are largely true. We were useful in the days of the ice, when the Miriyanti lived in the south and came into conflict with the slope-skulled Europeans who could crush us with their bare hands. We were not so useful afterward, when the internecine squabbling got started. Being able to kill someone with a thought is an unfair advantage. The Sotarii didn't like it. The Seers especially didn't care for it. So the rebellious Nerthii, after what was apparently a vicious confrontation with some of their own, were clapped in those old cells here in Tomir where they died of something other than old age. Subsequently the Nerthii disappeared, as those with the old capabilities were shunted in one direction or another, healer or warrior but never again both. We remain uncommon. Your Slan, for instance, is likely just a warrior and nothing more."

"How do you know this?"

"The Seers keep good records. But you have to be a Seer to get into their library. Unless you're just lucky, like me." The bitterness in his tone was unmistakable.

Ruarshi had been sitting with his knees up, his head resting on his crossed arms. When Piotyr fell silent he looked up to find the man standing right in front of him. He jerked, startled, and began to rise.

"Stay." Piotyr put a hand on his arm to reinforce the request. "I have to go soon. One more thing before I do: don't you ever allow anyone do violence like that to you again. I don't care what your reasons were. Never again.

"Now, would you like me to heal what you couldn't?"

Wil sat in the kitchen of the house he shared with Ginevra and their daughter, watching as the fire slowly burned itself down to ashes. It was very late. Ruarshi's earlier crisis, the nature of which he thought he could guess, seemed to have passed. Somewhere, he had found a healer to tend to him and he was now sleeping, but probably not very peacefully. There wasn't much that had been peaceful about the Illyana's life recently, what with Slan weeks away from delivery and his parents pushing for the Doshae clan to disown him. The original impetus for those legal maneuverings had come from the warriors' enclave, according to Lorion, with Aethel's role limited to that of go-between. In Wil's mind that made him no less responsible, and he wished Ruarshi had made his brother regret his poor judgment. The Welshman knew, though, that something quite different had happened. He would have gone to the clan circle hours ago if the healer hadn't forbidden him to show up there this evening, on pain of some kind of nameless but no doubt terrifying consequence. He'd warned off the rest of his friends and allies as well.

Sighing, Wil leaned forward and removed the cooling teapot from its trivet. He set it down next to an old, chipped mug he'd retrieved from the cabinet. He wasn't ready to try out his first batch of willow bark tea, not just yet. First he needed to break his link to Ruarshi. This was proving more difficult to do than he had anticipated, though he'd never supposed it would be easy.

There were two very good reasons why it had to be done. The first involved his and Ginevra's plans: they had decided to leave Miriyan soon after Slan's child was born. Neither one of them could tolerate living under a sun that scarcely showed itself for months on end, lending little enough light and no warmth whatsoever to the world. To Wil it felt disconcertingly like being trapped under some kind of massive blanket which could fall to earth at any moment and smother him. He knew he was being irrational, but he nevertheless found himself hunching his shoulders every time he went outside. For Ginevra he suspected it was even worse. He'd grown up with the frequent Welsh mists, but she'd known nothing other than Italian sun all her life. Lucia had nothing to which to compare Miriyan but she could sense her parents' moods well enough. They needed to go.

They would live at Wil's home in Gwynedd and make what summer visits to Miriyan they could. The Welshman's accumulated wealth was sufficient to maintain them in comfort and eventually to supply Lucia with a dowry. He'd been surprised by how much he'd accumulated, both as *pir* to Ruarshi and as a translator, when he'd finally sat down to go through it all with his banker. He thought the healer had somehow contrived to add to his total when he wasn't looking, but that wasn't the kind of question Ruarshi would answer so there was no point in his asking.

The other reason the link had to be broken was more urgent. It explained Wil's presence, and that of the tea, in his darkened kitchen in the middle of the night. The pain in his joints was getting worse. Ruarshi had told him back in Italy that the condition could not be cured, but indicated that it would require very little effort on his part to use their link to block most of the Welshman's pain. He had believed it because he had wanted to. Two weeks ago he'd finally worked up the courage to ask Ardan about it. Everything Ruarshi had told him had been true, naturally enough, with the possible exception of the way he'd characterized the amount of strain it was costing him to keep Wil comfortable. The Welshman had thanked Ruarshi's great aunt for the information and had stopped by an apothecary's shop on his way home. He supposed the healer would be angry with him for making this decision on his own, and probably even angrier that Wil had chosen to take this step on the same night he'd been beaten up by his brother. But the healer was exhausted, sleeping off a drunk, helpfully distracted by his family problems, and there would never be a good time for this anyway.

Wil prodded at the link that bound him to the Illyana. In three decades it had only been broken once. He wondered if it would feel like an amputated limb when it was gone for good, buzzing and throbbing with the pain of phantom nerve endings. He certainly hoped not.

Irritably, after checking once more to make sure the healer was still asleep, Wil seized their link and with clumsy mental fingers tore it in two.

Afterward there was only absence, and silence, and the increasingly acute protests of his joints. Wil poured himself a cup of the tea, drank it quickly, and then poured another. He didn't know of anything more efficacious than willow bark. If the tea didn't start working soon, he'd make a pill from the bark and try swallowing that. Then he'd just have to learn to live with whatever aches remained, intolerable as the prospect seemed to him at the moment.

Wil was still sitting in the kitchen, nursing a cup of tea, when Ginevra wandered downstairs in the pitch blackness of a Miriyan winter's morning.

❋ ❋ ❋

Ruarshi couldn't tell, as his seven students filed out the front door of his home, whether they had believed a word of the story he'd presented to them or not. He wasn't sure he believed a word of it himself. Even if the tale Piotyr told him had been nonsense, he still wanted it circulated as widely as possible. By tying what Ruarshi and his students were doing to the mythic past of the Miriyanti, Piotyr may have hit on the one thing that would finally render their efforts acceptable to the public imagination. At the very least it couldn't hurt them. He hoped.

He leaned back and ran his hands over his face, checking the sore spots. He needed to go visit Wil. It had been four days since the Welshman had broken their link, and Ruarshi had been trying to show respect for that decision by leaving him alone with it for a while, but the healer could no longer stand the silence that now occupied the place where Wil used to be. He intended to ask for an explanation and possibly to offer one.

Ruarshi stood and went into the kitchen, where Slan sat reading next to the oven. She was round as an egg, not very mobile, and irritable with it.

"Your disciples have gone? How did they like your story?"

"I don't care whether they liked it or not, as long as they spread it."

"I'd guess they were considerably more interested in the origin of your bruises."

The healer snorted. "Probably. Fortunately none of them asked."

"Good discipline," Slan remarked.

Ruarshi bent over the back of her chair and planted a kiss on her forehead. "I'm going to see Wil."

That captured Slan's attention and she closed her book. "I've already invited him over for lunch. Catharin came in and prepared it for us while you were regaling your students with fairy tales. I invited Ginevra too, of course. And Yael. I tactfully hinted that Lucia's screaming presence isn't required. As long as I'm moody I may as well get some good use out of it."

"I always knew you were brilliant. I hope our son takes after you."

Slan smiled and went back to her reading. Ruarshi lay down on the bench next to her and closed his eyes. When he opened them again their guests were already there and had apparently had time to make it halfway through the food. He rolled over and stood up, suddenly self-conscious in his former *pir's* presence.

"Well, that was rude of me. And uncommonly quiet of you."

"You looked... good, lying there," Yael said. "I shushed them."

"Um." Ruarshi sat in the remaining vacant chair, between Wil and Slan. "How's your chronicle coming?"

"I've finished it," the Welshman said. He was staring at his plate. The healer had the distinct impression they must have been talking about him before he awoke. He glanced toward his sister and was sure of it.

"Yael, Wil, Ginevra. Slan." He wanted to look at all of them while he spoke, but found his gaze glued to the floor instead. "I'm sorry..."

"You shut up, Brother," Yael said, slamming her knife down onto the table for emphasis. "Just shut up. I've only got one brother who needs to apologize and it isn't you."

"It was intentional, Yael," Wil said. "Wasn't it?"

"What? That's ridiculous." Her protest died when she saw the expression on her brother's face.

Even Slan was shocked. "Ruarshi?"

The healer shrugged, his face red beneath the bruising. "Aethel had cause. This hasn't been easy on my parents. I thought..."

"He thought," the Welshman continued for him, "to submit himself to his family's judgment, in the person of its most violent and resentful member. He hopes they'll now be able to begin reconciling themselves to what he's doing. Pretty accurate?"

"Christ, Wil," Ruarshi mumbled. He stood up and went to the doorway. "Will the rest of you excuse us for a moment?" The healer looked at Wil and inclined his head slightly, motioning toward the front of the house. When the Welshman rose to follow him, he led him up the stairs and into the room that was to be his son's. As his former *pir* crossed the threshold, Ruarshi grasped him by the wrist. Wil gasped and tried to free himself but the healer didn't let him go.

"You're in a lot of pain. Why did you break our link?"

"If you'll stop squeezing my wrist I might tell you."

The healer loosened his grip but didn't release him. "Well?"

"Ginevra and I have decided to leave Miriyan after your son is born. We're going to live in Wales. I wanted to start getting ready for that now."

Ruarshi wandered over to the window and looked out, though there was little enough to see. "Why suffer later when you can suffer today, Wil? Even at that distance, our link would be worth something. This is only going to get worse."

"I know."

"Who's treating you?"

"Ardan."

"Ah. How often?"

"Every other day. She's teaching me how to use willow bark, poultices, things that will help me when I don't have access to Miriyanti magic."

"And what specifically did she say about the link?"

Wil regarded him warily. "She told me that as the pain worsened, it would take more and more out of you to hold it at bay. She said she could already see the toll it was taking. If I'd known that earlier, I'd have never—"

"Watch out for Ardan, Wil. Her advice is seldom disinterested. Blocking your pain wasn't a burden. Give yourself a few more months without it. You can still learn from Ardan what you'll need to know in Wales, but in the meantime—"

"Stop, please, or I'll start listening to you. I want to do this here, where I know I can get help if it ever becomes more than I can handle. I need to know how bad it's likely to get."

Ruarshi regarded the Welshman for a time in silence. Then, quite simply, he surrendered. "In Wales, you will rest, yes? Enjoy your wife and Lucia and future children? Stop trying to save the world?"

"Just as soon as you do."

"That is hardly—"

"*Slan!*"

The shout was accompanied by the slamming of their front door and a gust of cold air that Ruarshi could feel where he stood. He knew the voice.

"I guess we'll have to continue this later. Shall we?"

He and the Welshman left the room and made their way back down the stairs. Lorion was in the kitchen, regaling his sister and her guests with the latest news.

"... fantastic. Literally. Everyone I talked to is practically quivering with excitement over it."

"I'm sure they are," Slan said. "Sit, you two. He's got something earth-shattering for us."

"Don't mock. A dead man's come back to life. Guess who's been spotted in town?"

"Caligula?" Yael suggested.

Lorion shot her a withering look. "What would he be doing up here? Besides, he's dead. It's Seggita."

Slan laughed. "Really."

"Who saw him?" Yael asked. "Is Dunthala on one of his benders?"

"I don't know who saw him, but whoever it is has a lot of credibility with the Sotarii. I ran across a dozen patrols out looking for him, just between our clan circle and here. Every one had an Adept in tow."

"They think he's out floundering through the snow?" Ginevra asked, puzzled.

"Did you get a description of him?" Ruarshi asked.

"Tall guy, hair dyed black. Supposedly he's even got that sword they mention in the stories."

"Well, damn," the healer muttered. Only Slan heard him.

"What does that mean?" she asked him sharply.

He had quite abruptly become the focus of all eyes. "I believe he helped me heal my face the other night."

✳ ✳ ✳

Wil made his way toward the healers' circle at his usual time the next day, glad he would be able to see Ardan right away without having to deviate from his accustomed schedule. He hadn't noticed anyone watching him, but this was Miriyan and he was quite sure that some of Ruarshi's countrymen had unconventional methods of keeping track of him if they wanted to.

He was terrified, in the gut-churning manner he thought he'd left behind for good. On reflection he'd realized that Ardan had actually encouraged him to drop his link to Ruarshi when he'd spoken to her about it. Now the Illyana was receiving visits from the most famous lunatic in Miriyan's history. The Welshman felt himself oddly responsible for the entire situation. True, he hadn't been in on the planning that had left him lying flat on his back in the German underbrush with an arrow in his guts, but it had been that incident that had led Ruarshi to go chasing through Italy after Slan. And to start taking lessons with her. And to continue those lessons here, where such behavior had been absolutely forbidden until the previous summer.

Ruarshi had assumed that the Sotarii Council was behind his provisional acceptance back into respectable society. Wil was no longer so sure about that. Before he'd started writing his account of his adventures with the healer, which he hoped would counteract the effects of the paranoid trash about the Miriyanti being circulated in Europe, he'd studied some of the country's history. He was now convinced that much of the real power in Miriyan lay out at Mirror Lake, home of the Seers. The Sotarii Council's records didn't exactly emphasize the role their occasional tattooed visitors played in shaping policy, but the influence was there and had on occasion been decisive. Even more interesting to Wil was the fact that most Miriyanti seemed unaware of this aspect of the Seers' activities. They were generally thought of as harmless dreamers, obsessed with their scrying and their opium. Maybe that's all they really were but Wil doubted it.

His torch almost blew out as he pushed open the gates to the healers' circle. A novice relieved him of its sputtering stub and took him inside, ushering him to Ardan's door and announcing him in a voice slightly muffled by a head cold. The old healer came to the door and let him in, greeting him with a nod before returning to her green velvet perch by the heavily draped window.

"Ardan Chamani." Wil sketched a perfunctory bow.

"How do you feel today, Wil?" she asked him. She gestured for him to take a seat on the couch closest to the fire, which he did.

"Frightened, actually. Is Seggita still alive?"

"Why do you ask?"

"Because Ruarshi got a visit the other night from a man with a ruby in his sword. At his clan circle."

"What happened?"

Ardan appeared to be as calm as ever but Wil wasn't buying it. And the stabbing pains in his knees and hips weren't improving his temper any.

"Talk to me, Ardan. Please. I can guess why Seggita might have a personal interest in Ruarshi. But what do the Seers have to do with it?"

The Chamani sighed and stood. "What did Seggita say about the Seers?"

"He implied that he'd had a lot of contact with them. Why did you want me to cut our link?"

Ardan was in the corner of her room, belting her heaviest cloak around her slight frame. "Because it really wasn't helping either one of you anymore. I assume Ruarshi was not harmed?"

"No. In fact, his visitor healed him."

She paused before pulling her hood up over her face. "That's interesting. Ruarshi trusted him so far, knowing nothing of him?"

"I doubt he was thinking all that clearly at the time."

"Probably true. I'm going to speak with Ferenc. I would like you to come with me."

Wil was surprised by the invitation but he did his best not to show it. "Of course."

Within minutes they were both mounted and headed toward Tomir's central plaza, at the edge of which the members of the Sotarii Council kept their quarters. Wil was Ardan's sole escort. He wondered about the wisdom of that, but if she wasn't concerned he decided he wouldn't worry about it either. A short time later they were out of the rising wind, standing in Ferenc Sotari's elegant parlor over the Council Hall. Wil shed his coat and handed it to the young woman who had answered to Ardan's knock, and then drifted idly toward a large painting depicting a scene of battlefield parley. Both sides at the negotiating table were composed entirely of Miriyanti.

When their attendant had left he turned to Ardan, who seemed to be staring abstractedly at nothing.

"How long do you think...?"

Before he could even finish the question, Ferenc entered the room.

"Ardan, it's good to see you. I know you, young man, but I cannot remember...?"

"Wil ap Davydd." He managed another bow, his second of the day and probably the last he would be capable of for a while, young man or not.

"Former *pir* of Ruarshi Illyana. Ruarshi recently spent some time in the company of the long-lost Seggita," Ardan said. "You will forgive us if we get right to the matter that brought us here?"

Ferenc held up his index finger, asking them to wait. He disappeared back through the door and returned a few seconds later, carrying a jug of hot spiced wine and three long-stemmed silver goblets.

"Please." He waved the hand holding the goblets toward a neat semicircle of chairs before the fire. "I've taken the liberty of watering the wine fairly liberally. No one objects, I hope?"

The Welshman hadn't expected quite this level of informality from the Sotari, and he waited until the others were settled before choosing a spot for himself.

"Have you seen Seggita?" Ferenc asked him, pouring the wine with quick, economical gestures.

"No," Wil said. "I can't even tell you for sure that's who it was."

"He's a troublesome man, for a ghost. I wish he would come say hello to us." The Sotari handed a goblet to each of his guests and then sat back, rolling his half-filled cup back and forth between his palms. "You knew him slightly, didn't you, Ardan?"

"Very slightly. I think I met him all of three times, back when he was nosing around our circle. I have no idea how he feels about Casimir now or if the other side will attempt to exploit their rift. I am inclined to believe that he will renew old ties, or at worst remain neutral. Ruarshi is charismatic and in very much the same position that Seggita once occupied, and is the first and thus far only person we know for certain he's spoken with."

Ferenc met Wil's eyes and smiled. "Are you following all this?"

"Not really."

"I've had no opportunity to explain anything to him, Ferenc. That's why he's here. It's time and past time that some of this became common knowledge. Secrecy isn't going to help our cause."

Ferenc leaned forward to rest his elbows on his knees. Wil had always thought of the entire Sotarii Council as ancient. At this distance Ferenc didn't look to be all that much older than Slan, in spite of the weight of his many centuries.

"I haven't had to rely on rumor to get information for quite some time now," the Sotari said. "Particularly when events move quickly, it tends to obscure more than it illuminates. Tell me what you do know."

Wil glanced over at Ardan, who gave him an encouraging nod. He took a deep breath. "I can only tell you how the situation looks from where I'm standing. My political interests are identical to Ruarshi's and to those of the Nerthii more generally. I'm no longer his *pir* but that makes no difference.

"The warriors are harassing Ruarshi by stirring up his clan. If there's anyone over at their enclave who feels the least bit of sympathy for the Nerthii, I haven't heard of them. You and the other Sotarii aren't hostile—Ardan wouldn't have brought me here if you were—but you're also not inclined to intervene at present. I'm not asking for help; I'm just telling you what I've noticed. The healers aren't interested in a conflict but will oppose whatever the warriors do. That's what they've always done and it's become a reflex with them. The Seers... well. I know very little about them. They were behind last year's shift in policy on the Nerthii. Someone knew Ruarshi was going to play a role in saving all of you and so they protected him. Now? I'm inclined to think they've split but that's just a guess."

Ferenc's eyebrows had climbed up into his hairline while Wil spoke. When he went silent the Sotari exchanged a look with Ardan, who was smiling.

"You're a savvy observer," she remarked.

Wil shrugged, embarrassed. He didn't know what to say to that.

"I have no corrections to offer," Ferenc said, "but I can help a little. You're right about the Seers. The worst of them have made common cause with the worst of the warriors, which never makes for a happy combination. No one wanted the Europeans to succeed last summer but the fallout from that event has led to some difficulties. There is a small but determined faction that wants the Sotarii deposed in favor of those Diamyo who wish to retaliate. Take the fight to Europe, as it were, to show them that Miriyanti aren't to be trifled with in order to further their internal game-playing. Others among the Seers are convinced that any such initiative will lead us to disaster. As for the Sotarii, we're just trying to ride this out and ensure that the disagreement won't end in bloodshed."

"What odds do you give yourselves on that?" Wil asked.

"About eighty-twenty."

"Eighty percent that it doesn't end in fighting?"

"Eighty that it does."

Ardan looked as appalled as he felt at that answer. "Where does Jair stand?"

"He stands with us and I'm confident that won't change. But his adversaries inside the enclave are promising their followers the chance to shed European blood, which means he's fighting an uphill battle."

"I don't suppose any of the Seers have spoken with you about the Nerthii specifically?" Wil asked.

"Their fate is tied up with ours. Most started out as healers so I'm not concerned about which way they'll jump."

"And Seggita?"

"Is just one person," Ferenc replied.

"What is he doing, I mean? Why the visit to Ruarshi? Is he a threat?"

The Sotari considered his answer, still rolling his cup between his hands. "He and Casimir have a history. Casimir's the Seer in charge out at Mirror Lake, were you aware of that?" When Wil nodded, Ferenc went on. "To say their last meeting didn't go well would be something of an understatement. It's possible that Seggita might oppose him for that reason alone. Sotar knows he has cause to feel aggrieved. But if you've heard that he's an indiscriminate murderer, you should know that this isn't true. Casimir himself doesn't know what the old Nerthi intends. Or that's what he tells me, at any rate."

Wil was beginning to have the uncomfortable intuition that he knew at least part of what had happened to Seggita. "He sounds like someone Ruarshi would do best to avoid."

Ferenc tilted his head from one side to the other in a gesture of equivocation. "Should he decide to ally with the other Nerthii, he could be a great help to them. I'm afraid that when the Seers wish us to remain blind about possible outcomes, that's exactly what we do. When it comes to Seggita we're fumbling about in the dark like everyone else."

"Is there a strategy at work here?" Wil asked. "Something you'd like for the Nerthii to do?"

"If they could continue to keep their heads down, that would be welcome. You might caution them about being careful around warriors they don't know. Or even those they do," the Sotari added sourly. "We've already passed word to the foreign communities in Tomir about possible threats from that quarter. If violence can be avoided we can probably keep them talking. What we don't want to do is give the warriors any pretext to take action."

"Tomir isn't that big. You're asking them to put themselves under what amounts to house arrest until this is over."

"That would be ideal, yes."

Ardan chuckled. "I know, Wil. I've already advised the Sotarii that Ruarshi would dismiss any such request out of hand. The same is likely true of any of the young hopefuls he may have influenced."

"I... don't think that's quite right. When I tell Ruarshi about this conversation, I suspect that he'll turn right around and insist that his students stay home until this blows over."

"Is there not then a chance that he'll do the exact same to you and your family?" Ferenc asked. "If some of the warriors wish for a confrontation with him, harming you would be an excellent means of bringing that about."

The Sotari was correct, which irritated Wil to no end. "He and I know each other very well. He won't ask it of me but I'll do what I can to see that everyone else stays off the streets. Including you, Ardan."

The old healer waved that away. "I'll arrange some bodyguards from among the Doshae warriors currently staying at the clan circle. Depending on their numbers we may be able to get out and about well enough. This situation could drag on for months."

"Sotar willing it won't take so long," Ferenc said. "The Sotarii Council is working on something that may give us an appropriate task for some of our more belligerent warriors. I can't go into details just yet, but there are few enough in that particular group who would turn down a bodyguard assignment in Europe. Though they'd have to be chosen carefully to separate the duty-oriented from the dangerous. We don't want to solve one problem by creating another."

The Welshman judged from Ardan's expression that she knew what Ferenc was talking about. He was just heartened to hear that the Sotarii had a plan to pursue. Wil took a sip of his wine, the first of the evening, and tried to relax a little while he got to know Ferenc better. It never hurt to have friends in high places.

❄ ❄ ❄

Ruarshi glanced around the brightly lit hall, blinking in the smoke from the oil lamps and candles. The room was nearly full. To his surprise there were almost as many people assembled on his side of the hall as there were on the other. He had already spotted five of his students, sitting in the back and attempting to be inconspicuous. There were some young healers a few rows farther up, a rambunctious lot that included in their number a newly initiated Illyana named Shey. Some of the Doshae, including Mikha, had also chosen to take his part in this dispute, as well as a good number of people he didn't recognize.

Wil sat at his right hand, a position he'd scarcely vacated since his little chat a few days before with Ferenc and Ardan. Yael sat at his left, silent and rather withdrawn. Lorion was expected but probably wouldn't show up until the proceedings were half over, if then, and in what state Nerthu alone knew. Slan had mercifully agreed to stay at home with Ginevra and the toddler. Before he'd left, she had remarked with some acerbity that having to share space with Ruarshi's idiot family would be bad for the baby. For his part, the healer was simply relieved that he wouldn't be treated to the spectacle of Slan clambering over the benches in an effort to get at his brother.

It was time to start. The Doshae clan chief, Ciarn, rose to his feet at the front of the hall and asked for silence. When the room had become reasonably quiet, he went through the preliminaries, reciting the standard blessing to Voitan and explaining the nature of the petition that

Ruarshi's parents had submitted to the Clan Council. They had requested that the Doshae make a formal declaration, to be read aloud on the next market day in Tomir's central plaza, stating that the clan would no longer be held responsible for the half of his maintenance they currently paid. The other half, as was conventional, was paid by the Chamani Elders. As a practical matter, the clan's acceptance of the petition would merely mean that Ruarshi would have to offer his healing services to Tomir's foreign population for a fee. Such an arrangement wasn't unheard of. It was the meaning of the petition that mattered. If it was approved he would have no clan. That would be inconvenient but tolerable. As to his family...

It was hypocritical for him to be too concerned about them now, he supposed. He'd known what he was doing all along.

The petitioner was required to speak first. Ruarshi watched his father stand up from the bench, but looked away as he began to present his case.

"I haven't got much to say to you today. It's all in the petition. My second son, Ruarshi Illyana, has been taking warriors' training for two years now. He's been asked to stop, by us and by his older brother, but he refuses. I know the Sotarii Council has accepted what he's doing. We do not. His first duty is to us and to his clan, and he's shown no regard for either. If he wants to go his own way he's free to, but he should do it without expecting our help. The clan has enough others to support."

Leisha stood next and turned to face her son. "Ruarshi. Feeling at the clan home has been running high against you since we heard about your lessons with Slan. This petition is about our duty to our clan. And that's all it's about."

Ruarshi looked up at that but his mother was already seated again, shaking her head in response to something Rori had said.

Yael squeezed Ruarshi's hand, hard. "I knew it. Father's going to be stubborn, but we've already got Mom."

Ciarn had once again taken the floor and motioned for stillness. The surge of comment that had greeted Leisha's statement subsided.

"Ruarshi Illyana, it is your turn to speak."

The healer rose. "As is my right, I would like to name a second to speak for me."

The clan chief nodded. "That is your right. Whom do you name?"

"Aethel Sotaru, my brother."

He heard Yael gasp at this announcement. Wil started coughing in what Ruarshi suspected was an effort to suppress an outburst of laughter. Meanwhile the rest of the hall seemed to be experiencing a mild eruption.

It was a dirty trick for him to play on his brother. If Aethel didn't do an honest job of presenting Ruarshi's side of the question, the Doshae clan would have to defend itself against accusations of unfair dealing with its own. Still, it seemed to the healer to be a fine response to the situation his brother had put him in. It had been Aethel's own decision to act as a messenger boy for that faction of warriors who'd made Ruarshi their target.

"Aethel Sotaru, your brother has named you his second. Please rise and address this assembly."

For a moment both brothers were standing. Aethel's eyes met his, but all Ruarshi could read in them before he subsided onto his bench was a kind of puzzled wariness. The healer crossed his arms and waited.

"Our father has already made the only point that needs to be made," Aethel said slowly into the hush that had fallen over the hall. "The Sotarii Council has recognized Ruarshi's right to learn the skills of a Naishanti. Even the First of the Diamyo Elders has been persuaded of the wisdom of this. We as a clan should not second-guess their decisions."

Which was a nice and tidy way of undermining his own argument, as Aethel well knew. No clan liked to be told it should defer to any Council but its own, and the Doshae's first inclination would be to respond to this claim with a knee-jerk assertion of its own independence.

Yael rose to her feet but was forestalled by an ironic voice from the back of the room.

"Bravo, Aethel. You couldn't have done worse if you'd rehearsed for hours."

Ruarshi jumped up off the bench as though stung. The speaker had found the only shadowy spot in the hall to stand in, but the healer knew very well who it was.

"I take it the floor is now open to questions?" Seggita went on.

"Wil, stay here," Ruarshi said.

The Welshman grabbed his arm and yanked him back down, speaking in a furious whisper. "You cannot trust this man."

"I'm going to talk to him."

"Why?"

"To find out why he's here. Come with me if you must."

At that Wil set him free.

In the meantime Seggita's questioning of his brother continued.

"Pray tell us, Aethel Sotaru, what you said to your parents about the part of Ruarshi's maintenance that will no longer be paid by the Doshae." Aethel didn't reply and Seggita went on. "Did you not suggest to them that the Diamyo Elders had already agreed to make up the difference? Even though you knew that to be a lie? Is it your purpose to beggar your brother?"

"Seggita." Ruarshi stood in front of him now, speaking in a low voice he hoped wouldn't be overheard and blocking his view of Aethel. "What are you doing?"

"Trying to prevent an injustice. I'm not referring to the petition. Would you care to leave this place? I'm certainly not staying."

"Why should he go anywhere with you?" Wil asked.

"The warriors have sent—"

The door burst open and Lorion tumbled in. Several of his friends were with him.

"Sorry to be so late," he said. "Did anyone here ask for a rather sizeable escort of Naishanti? There are dozens of them out there and they seem to be headed in this direction."

"Mary Mother," Wil said.

"Quite," Seggita agreed. He turned to Ruarshi. "You really don't want them to find you. You needn't worry about your family."

"Wil, would you see to them?"

The Welshman glanced from Ruarshi to Seggita and back again. "Yes. Go."

"Thank you."

The healer gestured reassuringly toward Yael, his parents, even Aethel. He looked back once more to see Wil deep in conversation with Lorion as he ducked out the door.

He and Seggita ran through the darkness to the clan circle's arched entrance. The torchlight that heralded the Naishanti's approach was clearly visible to their left.

"Right it is, then," Seggita murmured. They darted through the streets of Tomir, dodging the occasional evening passersby, the cold damping the sound of their passage. Both of them were good runners, Seggita moving quickly in spite of his limp, but Ruarshi knew it wouldn't make any difference in the end. The Naishanti were on horseback and everywhere he and Seggita went, they left an obvious trail. He began steering them toward the river. It was the only place he could think of where they wouldn't leave tracks, since the Sotarii kept it flowing through the winter. It would be very cold, however.

"Not that way," Seggita said. "In here." He pulled him into a wood-shed and banged the door shut.

"They'll find us," Ruarshi said, speaking to the darkness.

"Of course they will. They'll do that anyway. They've got three Adepts. I don't believe either one of us will evade them this time."

"Then what the hell was the point of—"

"Shut up. There's something I've got to show you. Figuratively speaking." Seggita laughed breathily. "Where are you?"

"Right here. What…?"

"Take my hand. Okay. Now, try to put a bond on me."

"Why would—"

"If you keep asking stupid questions, Nerthi, you're going to render all my best efforts worthless. Try to put a bond on me and pay close attention to what I do."

"Now?"

"Now."

Ruarshi extended a pair-bond weave toward the man, fighting to ignore the sense of urgency that was trying to push him back out the door. When his power had almost reached the point at which it would fuse with the other man's consciousness, Seggita scooped it up and slammed it back toward him. The healer staggered but the other man steadied him before he could fall.

"Were you able to tell what I did?"

"No. Sort of. I—"

"Try it again."

Ruarshi had observed the trick five times before he understood what the Nerthi was teaching him. It was brilliant and quite odd, as its sole purpose seemed to be to avoid an unwanted bond. There were easier ways to do that.

"Did you get it that time?"

"Yes."

"Good. We're leaving this damn woodshed now. I'm going to go one way and you're going to go another. Believe me when I tell you I know exactly what's about to happen, because I made sure it would. The alternatives were worse. You'll understand eventually."

Seggita pushed his way outside and ran back the way they'd come, right into the Naishanti.

He had just enough time to throw his arms wide in an expansive, almost welcoming gesture before he was transfixed by a shower of arrows. Ruarshi watched from the door of the shed as Seggita collapsed forward into a black and steaming pool of his own blood. In the flurry of excitement that ensued he stayed where he was, wondering if the chase would continue or if the Nerthi's death had marked the end of it.

He felt curiously empty. He continued to feel that way until the Naishanti started up once again on his trail, at which point the emptiness was replaced by a fear so intense it took his breath away.

He had to get to his house and to Slan before they did. Whether she was among their quarry or not, they'd go there sooner or later. Unless they caught him first.

And he'd left her alone with Ginevra and a two-year old.

He crept farther down the alley and waited for the first of the Naishanti to draw even with its mouth. Murmuring a brief prayer to Nerthu, he threw the strongest weave he could fashion into the interior of the woodshed. Between one breath and the next he shattered everything it touched, and then pushed the resulting mass of splintered wood with all his force into the street.

The sound of screaming, both animal and human, was all that pursued him as he turned and ran toward home.

※ ※ ※

Wil rested his knee in the window embrasure and pressed his forehead against the cold glass. He was exhausted but there was little chance he'd be able to rest anytime soon.

"See anything?" Lorion asked.

"Three riders on horses. Do you have any notion what time it is?"

"Early morning. Almost time to feed the chickens."

"I wish my life were so bucolic." The Welshman moved back into the room and lay down for roughly the tenth time on the lavish bed in one corner of their temporary prison. He had no real reason to complain. It would have been much worse if the Sotarii hadn't taken an interest in events and interceded to keep them out of the belowground cells. As it was they were physically comfortable, warm, and behind doors that locked from the inside. The only important thing they lacked was news.

"They're not going to let us languish in here all day. Someone will show up sooner or later. Hopefully with food."

Lorion was sprawled indolently in a high-backed chair, his ankles crossed before him, apparently unconcerned about the smears of ash and grime he was leaving on the yellow silk. That was about all that remained of the Doshae clan hall.

Their plan had been merely to delay the Naishanti for a time. Ruarshi's students and some young healers had started up an enthusiastic snowball fight that had already obliterated the first thirty or forty yards of the Nerthii's tracks before the patrols arrived. Once the commanders had fought their way through the bombardment to the door of the hall, they were confronted by a shouting chaos that made interrogation difficult. They hadn't yet managed to extract any useful information from anyone when Lorion, in an apparent drunken swoon, had set one of their cloaks on fire. The man had immediately yanked the garment off and that would have been the end of it if he hadn't dropped it under a wall hanging. Soon most of the Naishanti were helping the Doshae fight the blaze that resulted, though Wil saw about twenty of the warriors leave the clan circle to continue their hunt. When it was all over the circle had been saved, but the hall was reduced to a smoldering ruin.

At least no one had been hurt, beyond a few superficial burns and some bruises.

"Quit worrying, would you," Lorion said. "Slan, even in her hugely pregnant state, is quite capable of taking care of Ginevra and Lucia. And Ruarshi can take care of himself. I wouldn't want to be chasing him through town even if he didn't have that maniac in tow."

Wil sighed. The tacit agreement that had kept them from speculating about the night's events had just been dealt its *coup de grâce*.

"I know. But I'd like some confirmation. Suppose anyone would mind if we left?"

Lorion eyed him doubtfully. "Count on it. And whatever happened with the others was over with long before those idiot Naishanti strongarmed us up here. When I leave I'd like to know where to go."

"And whether or not we'll be brought back?"

The Naishanti grimaced. "I've been thinking about that. I'm very glad that you had that talk with Ferenc. If he's smart, and he is, he'll use this. Against the warriors and the Seers supporting them, I mean."

Wil just shook his head. He wasn't up to analyzing Miriyanti politics, not at this hour when he'd had no sleep. He laid his arm over his eyes and tried to relax.

He was still staring sleeplessly at the inside of his eyelids when there was a knock on the door some time later. He pushed himself stiffly to a sitting position while Lorion went to answer it.

It was one of the ubiquitous Sotari novices, bearing a tray of food and drink. Behind her stood Simah, Ferenc's counterpart.

"Good morning, gentlemen. Tiel, you can set that there. Thank you."

Wil and Lorion made their bows while the novice slid the tray onto a table and quietly vacated the room.

"Please, you must be hungry."

Actually the Welshman didn't feel hungry at all, but he was thirsty. He poured himself a mug of water and drank half of it before sitting back down. Lorion, for all his talk of food, also left the cheese and sweetmeats untouched.

"First let me put your worries to rest," Simah said as she took a seat. "Slan and Ginevra were not molested by the warriors. They and the child have taken shelter at the Maelae clan circle. I would expect that Ruarshi has also made his way there by this time. His family is safe and still residing at the Doshae circle. What's left of it."

She looked consideringly at Lorion, who maintained her gaze steadily. Then her focus shifted to the Naishanti's arm.

"You were burned. You should have told someone."

Lorion waved his hand in a dismissive gesture. "Later. It's not as bad as it looks."

"It looks quite bad enough. It will be treated before you're allowed to leave. You will be released once the patrols have all been brought in. You should know that the Seers are no longer in command of a military force. Their Naishanti have been detached from service at Mirror Lake, pending an investigation into their role in last night's events. It has been alleged that the Seers attempted to burn down the Doshae clan circle. It has further been alleged that they murdered a man who had never been tried nor sentenced for his crimes. Seggita is dead. If he threatened the Naishanti that is one thing. If the Seers ordered this murder the ramifications will be quite other."

Lorion was smiling faintly. Wil wasn't the least bit amused.

"Ruarshi wasn't hurt?"

"No." Simah pursed her lips and shifted in her chair to face him. "The matter is complicated. He escaped the patrols but in the course of doing so he killed three Naishanti and injured ten."

The Welshman winced. "How?"

"The conventional way, Wil. Any strong warrior could have done the same. Two of the survivors' injuries are serious and the healers are not sure they can save them. We need to talk to him, to find out why this happened. You no longer share a link with him, is this correct?"

"Yes," Wil said. "Are you going to arrest him?"

"We may have to. And Ruarshi might be safer in our custody than anywhere else."

"The law of refusal," Lorion said. "If it's proven that the Naishanti were ordered to kill Seggita, and they went along with this because of the man's reputation or for whatever godforsaken reason…"

"Yes, Ruarshi can use that if need be."

"Use what?" Wil asked.

"Every Miriyanti who places himself under the command of another has the obligation to refuse illegal orders. This law is relaxed a bit in times of war, but we're not at war yet. It is well known that Seggita was never put on trial. His murderers are therefore subject to prosecution, even if they were only doing as they'd been told.

"There's something I'd like to ask you to do for us."

"'Us' being the Sotarii?" Lorion asked.

"The entire Council, yes. And the Chamani Elders. We are all equally implicated in these moves against the Seers."

"What is it?" the Welshman asked.

"Take this document," she pulled a yellowed scroll from her belt, "and display it somewhere prominent during Seggita's funeral. I take it you will both attend?"

Lorion accepted the scroll and unrolled it carefully. He scanned the first several lines of spidery handwriting and then stopped abruptly, his eyes darting upward to meet Simah's placid gaze. "He put this in *writing?*"

He passed the document on to Wil, who took rather longer to decipher the old-fashioned script. When he'd finished reading he passed it back to Lorion, feeling wearier than ever.

"One of the happier errors of our history," Simah observed. "That is the order, as you gentlemen will have observed, which sent a number of warriors to Seggita's clan home in the year 953. Thank goodness the Seers employ a competent archivist."

"Nobody has ever come right out and admitted it," the Welshman said. "He wasn't actually the one responsible for the murder of his family?"

"No. At Casimir's behest, a group of Naishanti were trying to find him. His clan, the Sylvae, lives in the far north. A fight broke out when the warriors arrived and several members of Seggita's family died. The Sylvae have always known the truth but they don't maintain a clan circle here, and tend to associate only with other northern clans. Casimir was free to make up any story he wanted."

"And those of you who knew what had happened didn't say anything?" Wil asked.

"Two years before that incident, Miriyan was attacked by the Danes," Simah replied. "The Seers were the only reason we knew the invasion was coming. We owed Casimir the benefit of the doubt. He was a very different man then."

"Why is a funeral being held here?" Lorion asked. "Or can I guess?"

"The Sotarii Council wishes to honor him with a state ceremony. As a way of recognizing the courage he displayed in Miriyan's service."

"Members of the Sylvae clan will be here to retrieve the body."

"Naturally. Word has already gone out."

"It's going to be a riot," Lorion said. "Are you sure you should be using a dead man this way?"

"I feel confident that Seggita, could he only see it, would approve our purpose. We don't want a riot. Right now what we want is that the people of Miriyan should learn of the role the Seers played in Seggita's life and death. They will then be free to come to their own conclusions."

"And he's much more sympathetic as a corpse than he ever was as a patricidal, matricidal, fratricidal madman, wrongly accused or not," the Naishanti observed.

Simah said nothing and Wil found himself wondering with uncharacteristic cynicism how many Seggitas of their own the Sotarii had misused over the years.

"When's the funeral?" Lorion asked.

✳ ✳ ✳

"I timed this wrong," Slan said, looking down with some exasperation at her swollen belly. "Or else you did. Could you delay having any further crises for two or three weeks?"

"I'll try to arrange it," Ruarshi said wryly, brushing both her and their unborn son with a feather of power, as he often did of late. There had been some question in his mind at the beginning of her pregnancy whether it was wise for her to have a child just yet. Her head injury hadn't caused her any problems, though, and both she and their son were strong and healthy.

"If the Sotarii come to arrest you, they're going to find themselves saddled with me as well. I'll see to it we're assigned a nice cozy cell in which to rot. You've done them a service, little as they may be inclined to admit it."

"What I did served no purpose, Slan. I panicked."

"We've had this conversation already, my dear," she said, stretching like a cat and smiling at him. "A more effective response to panic I've never seen. You're quite sure they would have handled you nicely if you'd surrendered instead?"

"... No."

"Then you were under no obligation to do so, were you? It had to be one or the other. They were too close to you by then."

Ruarshi lay back against the pillows and regarded his bedmate. She was doing her best to conceal it but the strain of the past several days was taking its toll on her. Though she had no qualms about what he'd done in the alley, the waiting game that had ensued was setting her teeth on edge, largely because there was nothing she could do about it. Being caught in the middle of a round of vicious political maneuvering appealed to her no more than it did to him.

"A fourth Naishanti died last night. I suppose you heard."

"Yes, and her name was Neyth. I knew her. I even liked her. She died following a stupid, criminal order, and has no one to blame for it but herself. Unless you have something new to add, that is the end of this conversation."

The healer sighed and got up out of the bed they shared. He retrieved his clothes from the back of a chair and pulled them on, though he had no idea what he would do with his day. Sitting around the Maelae clan circle held no appeal but if he tried to leave he was sure he'd suddenly acquire a bodyguard of about a dozen of Slan's closest Naishanti friends. He could do without that.

Ruarshi walked around to the other side of the bed and sat down next to the woman he couldn't help regarding, as a result of his half century spent in Europe, as his wife. He hadn't admitted as much to her and didn't plan to. She would be touched by the sentiment and then would cheerfully break all his fingers.

He pushed her hair back out of her face, hooking it behind her ears with a gentle touch. "This will end. And when it does, I'd like to go visit your clan home. Do you think they'd object?"

"Let them try," Slan replied, resting her hand against his chest. "I'll force every one of them to read that." She nodded toward a stack of pages lying on the small table by the side of the bed.

"What is it?"

"Wil's account of your mutual adventures in Europe."

"Oh, good lord. What does it say?"

"Nothing that isn't true, I trust. He portrays you in quite a sympathetic light."

"I'm... relieved? I think. I'll bring you some breakfast."

He lit a candle from their oil lamp and, throwing his cloak around his shoulders, headed out the door.

The hall was nearly deserted when he got there. It was older and smaller than the hall at his own clan circle had been, with a low ceiling deeply stained by centuries of greasy smoke. He was filling up a tray with food for himself and Slan when a young Maelae approached him.

"She said you'd be in here. Three of your students have arrived and are asking to see you."

Ruarshi set the tray down. "At this hour? Who?"

"Brion was the only name I caught, sir."

"Did they say what they wanted?"

"No."

"Where are they?"

"I took them to the rooms above the kitchen. They looked pretty cold."

"That was thoughtful of you. Would you take this in to Slan while I talk to them?"

"Yes, sir." The boy picked up the tray and hurried off.

Ruarshi went back out into the yard and started up the outside staircase that led to the small apartment the youngster had specified, wondering what could have persuaded Brion and the others to get out of bed so early. Perhaps one of them had had a breakthrough. Or perhaps their regular instructors had told them, yet again, to stop taking lessons from that unnatural Illyana. He hoped that whatever it was it wouldn't take long.

Brion opened the door before the healer had even made it to the landing. It was clear he was terrified.

Ruarshi's steps slowed. "Good morning, Brion. What brings you here?"

"We just wanted to ask you about something you showed us the other day," the Naishanti replied. He raised a finger to his face and drew a sinuous line along one cheek as he spoke.

A Seer, come to visit him. How flattering.

"Well, we can hardly discuss it standing out here in the cold. May I come in?"

Brion remained where he was for a moment, blocking the doorway. Then he moved aside and Ruarshi brushed past him into the room.

A hand clasped his forearm. The healer had just enough time to register that its owner was a Miriyanti woman, and old, when he felt a bond very unlike the ones he knew slam into his mind. He moved to counter it, using the maneuver Seggita had shown him. An instant later he realized that he was lying on the floor and that something was very wrong.

He blinked. The woman was sprawled next to him, staring into his face. She looked like she wanted to scream.

"That was interesting." The Seer, his face half covered in winding blue tattoos, squatted down to get a better view. "I take it you were successful, Inge?"

"Yes." She raised herself shakily onto her elbows. "The bond has been set."

Ruarshi closed his eyes, trying to figure out what she had done. He discovered part of a bond, splintered and lodged deep within that place where his link to Wil used to be. He pushed at it tentatively.

Brion was kneeling next to him, looking utterly miserable, and the Seer was holding a candle near his eyes. Ruarshi flinched away from the brightness. His skull felt like it was about to split open. He had evidently blacked out.

"I had to, Ruarshi," Brion was saying, over and over. "My sister is a Seer and they told me—"

"Hush, boy," the Seer interrupted finally. "I'm sure he's not at all interested in your excuses just now. How do you feel?"

The healer hissed in reply.

"Have you discovered yet what happens when you try to use your power? Impossible, yes? Inge may remove the bond at a later date if you stop interfering in matters that don't concern you. Or she may not."

The woman meanwhile had regained her feet, her face still set in a rictus of horror. How could the Seer look at her and believe that her attempt to set the bond had really gone as planned? Ruarshi remembered how it had felt when his countermove had gone wrong, breaking the bond rather than turning it back on itself as he'd intended, and guessed that she was in no better condition that he was. She wouldn't be removing the bond today or at any other time.

"I think you chose the wrong faction," Ruarshi said, his voice hoarse. He pushed himself to his hands and knees. Brion helped him to stand from there.

"That has yet to be determined," the Seer said, "but who are you to judge? The Sotarii Council exiled her. They'll exile you too, if you become inconvenient to them."

"It's their prerogative."

"Not for much longer. You should pray for our success, Illyana, if you're a praying man. Once things settle down your role should become clearer and we may decide to set you free."

"My role in what?"

The Seer gestured airily at nothing. He was enjoying himself. "The future, of course. You're one of a handful of people who tend to throw off our predictive ability, has anyone told you? No? Inge here has just fixed that for us, which will be helpful to our cause one way or the other. I am sorry about the headache. I understand that it will fade in a few hours."

Given the way he felt at this moment Ruarshi doubted this would prove to be true. Then again, the Seer had been given bad information. He glanced at Inge, wondering when or if she intended to say anything about her failure.

"Don't worry at it or the pain will get worse," the Seer went on. "We'll send Brion to find you when we're ready for the bond to come off. In the meantime please return to whatever it was you were doing with your evening. It's been a pleasure. Inge, come with me."

The man set the candle back in its holder and went out the door. Inge hesitated on the threshold before following him.

"I lived in Europe for nine hundred years, healer. I'm tired of exile. I'm sorry for what I just did but I believe my punishment has already begun." Then she too was gone.

Ruarshi lowered himself into a chair and sat looking at his student. "What's your sister's name?"

"Nemayne."

"Would you object if the Sotarii were to remove her from Mirror Lake?"

"No! She might not like it, but she doesn't know about the threats. Those will change her mind."

"I want you to help me get on a horse. Then I want you to talk to Slan. Tell her that my parents sent me an urgent summons to the clan circle. Tell her I'll be back later. Make whatever apologies are necessary. Afterward talk to Lorion. I'm sure he'll be able to get word to the Sotarii about your sister. Clear?"

"Yes. Thank you. I'm sorry, I didn't know what—"

"You knew enough. Next time ask somebody for help, for Christ's sake."

"Where will you be?"

"That," Ruarshi said, "is my own concern."

❋ ❋ ❋

Wil stood near the west windows of the Council Hall, soaking up the wan light of midday. The room was enormous though low-ceilinged, made of stone that almost seemed to glow when he looked at it out of the corner of his eye. He was searching the room for Lorion but hadn't found him yet. The Naishanti had disappeared from the clan circle shortly after Ruarshi had, and the Welshman wanted to ask him certain questions about the coincidence. Something about the message Ruarshi had left with Slan didn't sound quite right to him.

The hall was already packed with Tomirans come to get a glimpse of Seggita's body. Behind the Nerthi's coffin stood seven chairs in a semi-circle, which Wil presumed would soon be filled by the Sotarii Council. Some roughly dressed Miriyanti stood near the bier. Wil started toward them, unsure of what he meant to say. As he wove his way through the crowd he spotted Lorion approaching them from the other direction.

"… my deepest condolences. I did not know him but he was trying to help a friend of mine when he was killed," the Naishanti was saying when Wil arrived. "This is Wil *Pirtai*. He met Seggita the same evening I did. Wil, these are Olaf, Hilde, and Ceolfrid, Seggita's uncle, sister, and nephew."

Wil bowed to them, ignoring the protests in his hip joints and trying to do the same with the look Olaf was giving him. It was composed of three parts hauteur and one part mild disgust and the Welshman had seen it before. Olaf was clearly one of those more traditional Miriyanti who didn't care much for Europeans.

"I'm honored to meet you," he said politely. The three bowed slightly in return.

"I have something for you," Lorion went on. He handed Olaf a small metal tube. "It's a gift from the Seers, one that they did not intend to give. Please open it."

The eldest of the Sylvae would be a handsome man, Wil decided, if only he could get rid of the suspicious squint that narrowed his eyes to slits and made him look as though he had a perpetual headache. As the three bent over the scroll, the Welshman traded a look with Lorion, his eyebrows raised. The Naishanti mouthed a single word at him, *Later*.

"This is no news to us," Ceolfrid said.

"Not to you, no, but very possibly to almost everyone else here."

"They're using him." Hilde nodded toward the half circle of chairs.

"Yes," Lorion said. "But the truth still has value. How would you like Seggita to be remembered?"

"These people are fools," Olaf said. "Let them believe what they want. It makes no difference to us."

"Perhaps that wasn't quite the right question." Wil glanced toward the yellowed parchment, half crushed in the old man's hand. "How would Seggita himself like to be remembered? As the man who killed his family and was rightly punished for it?"

Ceolfrid's lip curled. "We'll do nothing to help the Sotarii. They did nothing to help him." He jerked his head toward the coffin and its silent occupant.

"As you wish," Lorion said. "You remember that friend of mine I mentioned, the one Seggita was trying to help? He's my good-brother. His name's Ruarshi and you may have heard of him. What you decide to do with that," he pointed toward the scroll, "could determine what kind of life he's going to be allowed to have. Feel free to burn it if you like."

The Naishanti stalked away. Wil followed after a brief and ironic nod to Seggita's family. He caught up to Lorion within a few long strides.

"You're going to leave that with them?"

"I don't see what choice we have. I wanted to tack it to Seggita's coffin but I can't really do that without the consent of his family. Let them burn it. If Simah didn't have several copies made before handing it off to me, I'll eat my cloak pin."

"What about—"

"One moment."

Lorion led him to a corner of the hall, where in spite of the considerable crowd they might hope to hold a conversation in relative privacy.

"I don't think he's at his clan circle. One of his students came to me and asked me to take a message to the Sotarii. Brion."

"The same one who talked to Slan. Do you know where he lives?"

"Not yet." The Naishanti smiled. "But I will soon."

"What was the message?"

"He wanted his sister removed from Mirror Lake. She's a Seer. And a more ungrateful, spiteful little chit you're not likely to meet."

The Welshman stood for a moment in thought. "Did she have anything useful to say?"

"Other than several accurate criticisms regarding my personal hygiene, no."

"You raided the fortress?"

Lorion laughed. "No. She's a novice. We just waited until they'd sent her to Tomir on an errand."

Wil sighed. "I had hoped he would be here."

"Me too. Slan is losing her mind over this. Ruarshi—"

"Yes, where is that brother of mine?"

The Welshman found himself looking into Aethel's narrow face. Without thinking he pulled his fist back and started to swing.

Lorion grabbed him from behind, pinning his arms to his sides.

"Brawling at a funeral," he said quietly, "is considered very bad form." He waited until he felt the Welshman relax a fraction and then released him.

"What do you want, Aethel?" the Naishanti asked.

"The same thing you do. I'm trying to find my brother."

"So you can beat him again?" Wil's pent-up fury had finally found a target. He was having a surprising amount of difficulty controlling himself.

Aethel flushed. "To apologize to him, among other things. Where is he?"

"We don't know," Lorion said. "If you find him be good enough to tell us about it, will you?"

Ruarshi's brother appeared troubled for the first time in Wil's memory. "I've been hearing some strange rumors..."

"They're probably all true," Lorion said, "but of course we can't confirm anything. If there's nothing else...?"

"No, there's nothing else." Aethel glared at both of them before disappearing back into the crowd.

"At least he has Yael," Lorion muttered.

"This isn't getting—" Wil began impatiently, only to realize that the groups around them were going silent one by one. As stillness settled over the assembled Tomirans, he heard Hilde's voice, though he couldn't see her over the heads of those in he crowd.

"... a lament for my brother, Seggita Nerthi, *stamm* Sylvae. You know him as a murderer. You know nothing. You rely on rumor to tell you the story of what I saw with my own eyes. For what my brother did in Europe, his soul will now answer. For what he was forced to do in Miriyan, all of us will one day answer. I believe this. I ask Nerthu to stand as witness to the truth of my words.

"The day was cold. I, a child still, was asleep when the six Naishanti arrived. Striving voices soon woke me. They had come for Seggita at the Seers' behest, to make him messenger of their masters' blood-dreams. My youngest of brothers, he knew their errand and true to himself he defied their commands. The Naishanti lifted their swords and advanced, no more to convince but to kill.

"Beorhtic my father he picked up his axe and died first, his foe falling with him. My eldest brother Karl, a bear of a man, he could not resist the combined might of two. Valmaren my brother, quick as a fox, he wove his way through the battle. Before he was able to reach me he fell, his tunic soaked through with blood. Langewhilde my mother, archer of renown, she brought swift death to two of her foes. Her bow then broken, she yet stood her ground till a third found her heart with his blade. My youngest of brothers slew those who remained and then fled, fearing reprisal. From that time to this, he lived as an exile, and only today do I see him again: a proud son of the Sylvae, now dead."

Wil stood holding his breath in the silence that followed Hilde's eerily sing-song account of her family's murder. There was something about the rhythm of it that had made the hair rise on the back of his neck.

Olaf spoke next. "That is the story of the man who lies dead before you. This," he held the scroll up over his head so everyone could see it, "means less than nothing to the Sylvae but it may mean something to you. Read it as you pay honor to my nephew."

The Naishanti whistled softly. "That was all they could have wished for and more."

"Where are they?" the Welshman asked.

"Right there." Lorion couldn't quite keep his opinion of what the Sotarii Council was doing out of his tone. "As though on cue."

Wil stretched until he could see what was happening. As Lorion had said, the Sotarii were even then filing into the Council Hall to start the official ceremony in recognition of Seggita's diverse and noble deeds.

At least none of them were smiling.

Ruarshi sat in the dark in what was intended to be his unborn son's bedroom. He had lost track of the time that had passed since his meeting with the Seer. It could have happened the day before or a week ago. When he could he thought about Slan. He believed he might still know the moment she went into labor, if by chance his self-immurement went on so long. He waited for that even as he struggled to rid himself of the bond placed on him by the old exile.

He had made some progress, but not nearly enough. Even wielding the smallest trickle of power left him with a pounding headache that didn't subside for hours. It was still worse when he tampered with the bond itself. And at random, unpredictable moments the disjointed weave sent shocks of pain through his body. Sometimes those were followed by what could best be characterized as a moderate seizure. Experienced from the inside it didn't feel all that moderate, but fortunately that hadn't happened recently.

The healer succeeded in teasing another strand out of the jagged tangle that composed the block and then sank down on the bed, waiting for the pain to commence. When it had come and gone, he would think about going downstairs for some food. He hadn't been eating well and the oversight was beginning to catch up with him.

Once again Ruarshi considered going to the healers' circle for help. He wasn't ready to do that yet. He wouldn't face Ardan's sorrowful, accusatory gaze until he had no other choice. The mess he'd gotten himself into was too embarrassing for that. And it was just too much trouble.

He drifted for a while in a half-sleep, only coming fully awake when he saw reflected firelight dancing against the wall opposite the bed. His brother came into the room carrying a candle and Ruarshi surged upward.

"What are you doing here?"

Aethel gasped and staggered backward a few steps, then caught himself and brought the light forward.

"Sotar have mercy, Ruarshi. What's wrong?"

"This has got nothing to do with you."

"I've been looking for you for the better part of a week. I came here hoping to find some kind of clue… When was the last time you ate something? Or slept?"

The healer leaned against the bed, regarding his brother. "Your sudden concern for my physical state is a welcome change, Aethel, but not something I care to deal with just now. I'm sure you can find your way back out."

"I'm not leaving until you talk to me. I've never seen—"

"You can leave under your own power, or I can throw you out the window. Which will it be?"

Unfortunately it was all bluff at this point and Aethel knew it.

"No, I don't think so." His brother moved even closer. "You're going to eat, and you're going to tell me what happened and why you're hiding here."

"No. I'm not."

"I hear rumors, Ruarshi. And then you disappear. Are the Seers responsible for this?"

"Some of them. I really don't care to keep up with all the factions. There will be more of them tomorrow anyway so what's the point?"

"What did they do to you?"

Ruarshi tapped the side of his head. "Destroyed me, I think. Will you go now? I need to rest."

"I'll go but you're coming with me. We'll find you a more comfortable place to sleep. Can you stand?"

Ruarshi studied his brother, trying to gauge how serious he was about this. Serious enough to drag him out of here, it appeared. He sighed. "I think so. Help me up."

Aethel set the candle on the floor and hauled his brother awkwardly to his feet. Ruarshi wasn't able to give him as much assistance as he'd thought he could. Once they were both upright, Aethel pulled the healer's arm across his shoulders and wrapped his other hand around his brother's waist.

"Will this work?"

"It will if we go slowly," Ruarshi said.

Aethel snuffed the candle with his boot and they made their way out to the stairs and down, proceeding cautiously in the darkness. As they shuffled toward the front door Ruarshi spoke again.

"I will not go to the healers."

"That's not where I'm taking you. The Maelae circle will be better, more private. We can summon a healer in." Aethel struggled briefly with the latch and guided Ruarshi out the door and into the snow. A horse waited there, chewing patiently at its bit.

"You're going to have to help me here," Aethel said.

Ruarshi dragged himself up into the horse's saddle. Then his brother was with him and they were moving.

"Everyone is all right?"

"Physically sound if that's what you mean. Very worried about you."

His brother paused for a heartbeat. "I'm sorry for what I did at the clan circle. For all of it. Our parents have dropped their petition."

"And everyone lived happily ever after."

"You make it hard to apologize."

"Then don't try."

"Ruarshi…"

"I have a favor to ask."

"What is it?"

"When we get to the clan circle, I don't want Slan or Wil or the others to be told I'm there. Not until a healer's been in to see me."

"That might be difficult."

"But not impossible. I need to know what to say to them. I might come out of this unable to heal or do much of anything else. I can't tell yet."

Aethel swore and his arm tightened around Ruarshi's waist. The next few minutes passed in silence.

"I would be honored if you would accept my help, Ruarshi," his brother said.

"I would be delighted to have your support for once, Brother, but not if you're doing it out of pity. If by some chance I recover from this, I don't want you switching sides."

Aethel's voice was subdued when he replied. "I've resented you for years, and yes, your talent had something to do with that. Mother and Yael had something to do with it. And even you have to admit you can be pretty damn insufferable…"

"True. But I won't apologize again."

"I don't want you to. I'd smack you if you tried."

"Would you."

"I might, damn it. I can't say I know what's going on, but I have the general outlines. I'm not going to let them kill you."

"Nobody actually wants me dead, as far as I know," Ruarshi said. He felt light-headed.

Aethel was slapping at his cheeks. "Come on, come on, wake up, we're almost there, wake up, I don't want you falling off this horse—"

"I'm awake."

His brother took several deep breaths. "Don't do that again."

Ruarshi discovered he was laughing. "Do what? Die?"

"I don't find that funny."

"I don't either. You'd probably be blamed for it."

Aethel didn't comment and a short time later they arrived at the clan circle.

"We're here. Keep your head down. Which room is yours?"

"Help me off. I can walk. What time is it?"

"Around midnight."

"Good."

Ruarshi's knees almost gave way when his feet hit the packed snow of the courtyard. He held onto the saddle until he felt slightly better. When he let go Aethel was there at his elbow.

"Follow me."

He led his brother inside and down to a room far from the one he shared with Slan. It had been unoccupied when he'd left and he hoped it still was.

The door opened onto a musty stillness. Ruarshi went inside, feeling along the wall until he came to the headboard of the bed. He lowered himself onto the mattress, pulled off his boots with hands that shook, and lay back.

"I can't see a damn thing. Where are you?" Aethel asked.

"Here. Where I plan to stay."

"I'm going to find something for you to eat. And drink. Then I'll go for a healer. You will be all right?"

"Of course."

Aethel hesitated as though he would say something more, then turned and left.

As the door closed behind him, Ruarshi murmured into the stillness.

"Thank you, Brother."

※ ※ ※

Wil leaned his shoulder against the front wall of his room, keeping one eye on the hallway outside Slan's door and the other on Ruarshi, who sat near the window, his eyes closed. The sun's tentative rays bathed the Illyana's face in late winter light, accentuating his sharpened cheekbones and deeply shadowed eyes. The Welshman found it difficult to look at him for long. He knew the nature of the battle Ruarshi was fighting and most of the details of the encounter that had made it necessary. Once located, Brion had been much more forthcoming about what had happened in that room over the kitchen than the healer had been.

The young Naishanti had also brought word the day before that the woman responsible for Ruarshi's condition had been found dead at her clan home, an apparent suicide. Wil had felt no regret at the news. The healer's expression had remained typically unreadable.

Since his return to the Maelae clan circle in the entirely unexpected company of his brother, Ruarshi had spent most of his time closeted with Slan. She had come running out of their room once, her eyes wild, after the healer experienced one of his seizures, but since that incident a sort of artificial calm had descended over them all. They were waiting, though for what Wil scarcely knew.

Then again that wasn't completely true. He glanced out into the hall again, wishing that Yael or Ginevra would come and update them on Slan's progress. She had gone into labor early that morning and neither Ruarshi nor her brother had been allowed in to see her since. The last they'd heard everything had been going well, but the Welshman understood how quickly that could change. To the healer, who had expected to be able to monitor and even participate in the birth using his magic, the hours of silence were no doubt becoming intolerable.

"I'm sure she's fine, Ruarshi," Wil said, though he was not at all certain he should speak.

"She is," the Illyana said, not opening his eyes. "I am… watching, insofar as I'm able. She's also terribly unamused by the whole process. I expect the midwives' ears are burning."

The Welshman laughed, startled.

"What's funny?" Lorion, whose approach neither of them had heard, stuck his head through their open doorway. "Is there news?"

"Ruarshi tells me that your sister is in there swearing like a sailor."

"I'm not surprised. I don't imagine she's enjoying herself very much. Would either of you like some *keth*? They've got plenty in the hall in anticipation of the event."

The healer shook his head, smiling. Wil also turned down the offer.

"Where'd you go?" the Welshman asked.

"Took a walk. It's not warm out there exactly, but it's just far enough to this side of frigid to be better than sitting in here. I don't possess the patience of women."

"Neither does your sister," Ruarshi said. "How's the arm?"

Lorion placed his hand over his right forearm and gave it a gentle squeeze. "Improving. They've got the Naishanti rebuilding your clan hall, by the way. It's keeping them out of trouble."

"Have you seen my brother lately?"

"He's here, skulking in the hall."

"Why?"

"Why's he here, or why's he skulking? Never mind, I don't know the answer in either case though I could make some pretty good guesses. You'll have to ask him yourself."

Wil, who was having trouble supporting the Naishanti's mood, considered shoving the man back out into the snow. Before he could decide how best to go about it, the door to Slan's room swung open and Yael came out.

"Out of the way, oaf," she said, pushing Lorion aside.

"Oaf?"

"Ruarshi!" The healer's beaming sister flung herself to her knees beside his chair, and took up his hands in her own. "The baby is on his way. In a few minutes you and Slan will be *chesid* and *chesida*. And I'll be an aunt."

*Chesid* and *chesida*, the Miriyanti terms for a couple who'd had a child together. The words could mean as much or as little as the parents wanted them to mean. Wil thought he had some idea of what they signified to the healer.

"You already knew that, didn't you?" Yael asked, then visibly restrained herself from continuing with the obvious question. Instead she put her arms around her brother.

"And I'll be an uncle," Lorion mused. "An innocent child to corrupt. I'll bring him sweets at every opportunity. And of course he must have a toy drum as soon as he's old enough to beat on it."

"Slan will appreciate that," Wil said.

Ginevra drifted in next, heralded by the energetic crying of an infant. She held a damp cloth and was still wiping blood from her hands. "Congratulations, Ruarshi. You have a son. The midwives will come get you when Slan is ready."

She moved into Wil's embrace as the healer stood and went out into the hall. When the door to his *chesida's* room opened again and the two midwife-healers emerged, gesturing, Ruarshi smiled and went in to meet his son.

# Reckoning

Wil slipped on a patch of ice and cursed as his right foot sank into a shallow but muddy pool of water. He jerked his foot out and swore again in three languages while he watched the water drip from the leather of his boot onto the soggy earth of Tomir's foreign quarter. Sighing, he stepped back out onto the ice and snow and continued up the street. Better to walk carefully the rest of the way to the priest's house than to track mud all over the man's floor. He hoped he'd catch Father Villalobos at home. The little Spaniard wasn't expecting him.

He tapped the front of his coat, reassuring himself that the parchment pages folded against his chest were still there. They were the coda to his chronicle of the years he'd spent with Ruarshi, and the last words he expected to write on the subject. If his account of the healer's actions and those of his people ended up having no effect on European opinion, he wouldn't be surprised, but the hope that it might had compelled him to be thorough. Up to a point. There were things about the Miriyanti and the Welshman's own increasing anger and disgust with their leadership that the Europeans didn't need to know.

Wil considered the interview he'd just left and smiled thinly. It would have gone better, he supposed, if he had been able to keep that particular attitude from becoming apparent. He was afraid his frustration had been all too clear. He'd expected to be talking only to Simon Flavel, the French fur merchant for whom he'd once done some translation work, but instead had found himself addressing almost an entire roomful of anxious traders. He'd told them what he could about the situation in Tomir and explained the intentions of the clans who'd seized control of the city's central market in the aftermath of Seggita's funeral. The merchants were understandably more concerned about that aspect of the current political mess than most others, even though the clans in question hadn't done anything as of yet to disrupt their business.

The German and Polish traders' chief worry involved the possible existence of an anti-Hanseatic treaty between Miriyan and Margaret of Denmark, which Wil knew nothing about. Such an agreement would be sensible enough from the Sotarii Council's point of view but the Welshman refrained from pointing that out, as the offended merchants were already doing a fine job of working themselves into a lather over it without his help. How such a treaty fit into the larger picture Wil couldn't say, though he thought Ferenc might have alluded to it during their little chat. The issue of how deeply Miriyan should mix itself in European affairs was a divisive one, he was coming to understand, and tended to split the Miriyanti along lines of clan, magical talent, and even social standing.

Wil slipped again, caught himself against the side of a building, and then sprinted the remaining handful of yards to the priest's front door. Margot opened it to his knock.

The Welshman bowed formally to her, as he always did. He'd never had a problem with the notion of a priest's mistress. "Good afternoon, Margot. You're looking lovely today as usual. Is Emilio in?"

"Come in, Wil," she replied, answering his Miriyanti with Welsh. He had taught her the phrase and it was about all of his language that she knew. She continued in Spanish. "I will go get him. He's out back in the garden." Margot rolled her eyes at him, expressing her opinion of the kind of garden that could be grown in such cold northern soil. "Sit there by the fire and help yourself to some hot wine."

"Thank you," Wil said, switching to Italian since his Spanish was basically nonexistent. He moved into the room and dropped into a chair, unbuttoning his coat as he went. "I've just been to Flavel's."

"Unpleasant man," Margot observed. "Is he worrying about his furs?"

"He's worrying about civil war. As are many others."

Margot paused at the threshold of the room. "And what is your opinion?"

He could be honest with her, as he could not in the presence of so many prickly merchants. "It's possible."

She nodded slowly. "And what will you do if it comes?"

"Throw everyone I care about into a large sack and drag it with me onto the first ship that sails."

"You will need more than one sack."

"Yes," Wil said bleakly. "What will you do?"

"We will leave when the ice melts in any case," Margot replied, to the Welshman's surprise. "I see you have more pages for Emilio. He intends to take them all to Rome."

"What?"

Margot bit her lip and glanced over her shoulder toward the back of the house. "I see Emilio has not told you. That is not right of him. Here." She poured some wine into a mug and pushed it into his hands. "Pope Boniface intends to make a decision in the fall. About the Miriyanti. He has asked all those with knowledge and interest to come to Rome this summer."

"A decision about what?"

"About whether the Miriyanti are human or not."

Wil jumped to his feet. "Human? But... Pope Gregory..." He couldn't seem to catch his breath.

"Yes, Pope Gregory decided they were. Are. It may be that Boniface is just looking for a reason to authorize trade, looking for a way around what happened last summer. Or it could be that he is influenced by the wrong people. We do not know. Emilio intends that the Pope should read your work."

"Margot," the priest said reprovingly. He was standing in the doorway behind her, his hands clean but his trousers covered in mud up to his knees. "You have terrified our guest."

"You should have told him earlier, Emilio."

"I did not want knowledge of his eventual audience to influence his writing. I see you have more for me." The man swept into the room and snapped up the loose pages from the chair next to Wil's. "It relates to midsummer. Good. This may be of more use to us than all the rest combined. I do not want a council of theologians deciding I have spent my life ministering among demons. That would be hard on me and even harder on the demons."

Wil finally found his tongue. "You've been aware of this for the better part of a year."

"Yes. Forgive me, Wil *Pirtai*. I simply did not want to scare you away."

"Scare me away...? What happens if Boniface decides they're not human?" He knew the answer to that question and decided that he didn't want to hear it said aloud. "I will go with you to Rome, if you think I'll be of some use." Ginevra would understand. She had to.

Emilio looked taken aback. Margot spoke for him. "Your work will be enough on its own, Wil, or it will not. Your being there would not... The enemies of the Miriyanti would only twist your words. If you are not there to question, you are not there to be tricked into muddying your own portrayal of these people."

"It will be a cold day in hell before I let those—"

Emilio laid a hand on his shoulder, forestalling the rest of his outburst. "Wil. The story you tell is all we need." The priest inclined his head toward the pages he still held. "Go home to your wife and your daughter. Let us pious churchmen rip at each other in private. I will send you word of the outcome. Will that suffice?"

Wil set his mug of wine on a side table, untouched. "Yes, Emilio, it will. Thank you. Thank you for the wine, Margot. I would like to see both of you again before you go."

"You will," Margot said. "We will invite you and Ginevra over for dinner, along with your elusive Ruarshi and his *chesida*."

The Welshman nodded and began buttoning his coat back up. His suddenly clumsy fingers were making the task difficult. "Having any trouble translating any of that into Latin?"

The priest smiled. "I had not realized how challenging your occupation was until I turned my own hand to it. The task was not good for my patience. But I think Boniface will be satisfied."

"Good, good. I'll wait for your invitation." Wil couldn't come up with anything further to say beyond some rather meaningless pleasantries, and he made a hasty exit from the house. When he turned the corner and could no longer feel Emilio's eyes on his back, he stopped and took several deep breaths before going on.

The *Pope*. One of them anyway. Would what he had written really convince the man of anything? Or was Boniface's invitation a sham, the outcome of the discussion already determined? He was relieved that Emilio and Margot had rejected his offer to accompany them to Rome, but if it turned out they needed him then by god he would find a way to get there...

He dodged a sledge and continued toward the Beguinage, wondering what he would tell Ruarshi and the others about this. They certainly didn't need the extra worry. Neither did he for that matter.

"Wil?"

The Welshman nearly jumped when the young Naishanti appeared at his side. He hadn't seen the man in almost a month. "Yes, Brion?"

"I need to talk to Ruarshi."

"Why?"

"He's my instructor."

"He's not giving any lessons right now."

"I know you're all at that convent. Just help me get through the gates. All I want is a word with him."

"I can relay a message for you," Wil said.

"This is private."

"Then it will have to wait."

Brion grabbed the Welshman's arm and spun him to a halt. "This can't wait. Get me in there, foreigner." The Naishanti's grasp tightened.

"Or what? You'll break my arm?" Wil stared at the man until he relinquished his grip.

"This isn't a social call. I have—"

"I don't trust you, Naishanti," Wil broke in. "Shall I tell you exactly why? You lured Ruarshi into an ambush. That tale you told him about threats to you sister was very affecting but there's no way of confirming it, is there? I think you were doing exactly what your Diamyo masters were telling you to. Slan agrees with me. So does Lorion."

Brion's face had lost color as the Welshman spoke. Wil was both gratified and sorry to see it.

"And Ruarshi?"

"He's trying very hard not to have an opinion about your motives. I'm not at all sure he's succeeding, but then it can be hard to tell."

The Naishanti was staring downward at the snow, his arms crossed tightly over his chest. "How is he?"

"He's crippled. Permanently. And you don't look nearly as surprised by that as you should."

"Inge said something before she died about Ruarshi breaking the block. Do you know what happened?"

"Yes, he broke it before she could get the vile thing in place. I expect it did to her the same thing it did to him. What did she tell you?"

"She wasn't talking to me. It was her cousin. She couldn't use her power anymore. Any of it. It was still there, she could still sense it, but there was too much pain..."

"Accurate enough."

"Has he seen a healer?"

"Yes." Technically that was true, though the timid Illyana that Aethel had taken in to see Ruarshi had been worse than useless.

"And?"

"And there's nothing they can damn well do about it. He'll be giving no more lessons to you or to anyone else, ever."

Brion had turned away from him. "Would you take him a message?"

"That depends on what it is."

"Tell him that I'm sorry. And that his students are well. Lynesse shattered a shield of mine last week and has been scared to death ever since."

"As well she should be. Are you going to turn on her too?"

"May I be twice blessed by the left hand of Sotar if I do. She needs to see him, regardless of his condition." The Naishanti was silent for a moment. "That's all. That's the message. If you could pass it on to him I would be grateful."

Wil studied the young man. Odd that he could think of the Miriyanti as young, even though Brion had lived for two to three times his own span of years.

"I'll let him know."

"Thank you." The Naishanti walked away from him, his back to the setting sun.

※ ※ ※

Ruarshi's face was still burning as he rode away from the clerk's office, heading toward his clan circle. He'd stuffed the document the man had written up for him into his boot, where it scratched uncomfortably against his ankle. He could simply have held onto it but he didn't want to look at it again until he had to. If he accidentally splashed slush or mud onto it in the interim, so much the better. The copy the clerk had made would stay clean and safe in the Sotarii archives to be consulted at need. Assuming there would be a need. That would depend upon the outcome of his talk with Ciarn.

He pulled the hood of his cloak farther down over his face as he got closer to the Doshae circle, though doing so made him feel more than a little ridiculous. He felt even sillier when he thought of how he'd had to slip out of the Beguinage earlier that morning while Slan, Wil, and the rest were still busy with their breakfast. Dodging potential enemies was one thing but dodging friends was quite another. He hoped it wouldn't become necessary again. He could already hear the lecture he'd receive when he returned. It would be worth it if he succeeded. Or possibly even if he didn't. He'd fallen into a kind of timelessness since Davyt's birth, and he needed to shake himself out of it before someone else did it for him. The standoff between the northern clans and the Seers couldn't last forever. Nor was it likely to end well.

And Lynesse, along with all his other students, needed him to do something other than hide and hope that the trouble would simply disappear with the melting snow. He was responsible for their safety, both now and in the years to come. It was up to him to find a niche in which the Nerthii could survive. Exile was not a solution which he would accept, not now. He had a son to raise and a cantankerous *chesida* from whom he refused to be separated. He had no desire to drag her back to Europe with him, though he was certain she would go if it came to that. So he couldn't allow it to.

As he rode through the gates of his clan circle he surveyed the new hall curiously. He hadn't been back since Lorion's fire had destroyed the old one. It looked like the Naishanti had done a good, solid job of it, even though they'd undoubtedly resented the work. Ruarshi smiled when he saw that the roof of the building was at least ten feet higher than that of its predecessor. The Doshae were a not insignificant clan, to be sure, but he didn't see how making the place that much harder to keep warm in the winter could be considered a reasonable way to express status.

Ruarshi swung out of the saddle and looped his horse's reins through an iron ring attached to the stable wall. He didn't anticipate his visit with Ciarn lasting too long and it was a warm day for April. The mare would probably enjoy a bit of sunshine. He patted her muzzle absently before making his way to the clan hall.

Once inside he threw back his hood and pulled the rolled document from his boot. It was somewhat crushed and damp but beyond that had taken no damage. A pity. He stood tapping it against his palm while he waited for his eyes to adjust to the dimness.

Those inside could see him quite clearly, of course. He was already attracting attention. He approached an older man standing close to the door and bowed.

"Can you tell me where I might find Ciarn?"

The man looked him over and shrugged. "In his rooms, I'd guess. What's your business with him?"

"Thank you." Ruarshi bowed again and jogged across the circle to the living quarters, relieved that Ciarn hadn't been in the hall. Trying to explain why privacy was required for their conversation in front of a dozen clan members would have been excruciating and quite possibly futile.

His relief evaporated when, in response to Ciarn's spoken invitation, he lifted the latch on the clan chief's door and stepped into his room. Liam was with him, the chief of the Taanor, known for his hidebound attitudes regarding just about everything.

Ciarn rose from his seat by the open window. "Ruarshi. I didn't think to see you today. Did your parents make it to the clan home safely?"

"Yes, Ciarn. Aethel tells me they are well." He bowed stiffly, first to his own chief and then to Liam, who'd remained in his chair.

"You have met Liam?"

"Yes."

"What brings you here?"

Ciarn was friendly enough but wary. Ruarshi wished he knew if the guardedness reflected Ciarn's own attitude, or was based on concern over Liam's opinion of him. With a mental shrug the healer stepped forward and handed the rolled parchment to his chief.

"A proposal, Ciarn."

The man accepted the document with raised eyebrows. "What sort of proposal?"

"I ask that you read it first, sir."

Ruarshi stared determinedly out the window as Ciarn unrolled and scanned the sheet. At the chief's initial startled exclamation, Liam unfolded his lanky frame from his chair and started reading over the shorter man's shoulder.

"This is what I think it is? A Writ of Submission to the Clan Council?"

"It is." The healer was quite sure his face had gone red again. He hated this.

Ciarn was momentarily speechless. Liam wasn't, however.

"You are a manipulator, sir."

"No, sir. I am desperate." There was little enough harm in admitting to it, Ruarshi thought, as the piece of paper Ciarn held made that fact clear enough all on its own.

"And you expect us to rescue you from your predicament?"

"Again, no. I expect to provide the Council with a service and to be offered your protection in exchange."

"You had this written up of your own volition?" Ciarn asked. "No one encouraged it?"

"No one."

"I am not... unaware of recent events. And if you do not object to the observation, I would say that you do not look well. But I do not understand why you are offering this."

Ruarshi glanced toward his clan chief and took a deep breath. "I'm trying to remove myself from the power struggle. I have played a role in it against my will and I need a way out that doesn't require me to leave Miriyan. The healers, the warriors, the Sotarii, and the Seers are all involved. The Clan Council, unless I am very much mistaken, remains neutral. And you have the authority to accept that Writ."

"So we win by virtue of the process of elimination? I am insulted."

"I suppose I could present the same offer to the Stoneshapers' Guild, Liam, and hope that the prospect of having their houses melted around their ears would be a sufficient deterrent to those who wish me and my family ill." The healer stopped himself, returned his attention to Ciarn, and went on. "You must know that the Clan Council has less authority in Miriyan than it could, as a result of the way chiefs rotate in and out of it, depending upon who is in Tomir at any given time. I could provide a constant presence for you here."

"To what end?" Ciarn seemed genuinely puzzled.

"To supply you with accurate and current information, if nothing else. I could also speak for you in situations where it might be impolitic for you to intercede directly."

"What kind of information could you give us?" Liam asked, returning to his seat.

Ruarshi looked at the Taanor chief, considering. The man was interested in spite of himself. He had to be careful.

"There must be something about the current situation that doesn't make sense to you."

"And you can enlighten us?"

"Possibly."

"But you will refrain from doing so until we sign your Writ."

"Wrong again, Liam. You're not terribly perceptive, are you?"

"Ciarn, I don't like your clansman."

The chief waved that away. "Why did all those Naishanti from Mirror Lake come looking for you here?"

Ruarshi leaned back against the wall and let the cold air coming in the window wash across his face. He should have known Ciarn would start with that. "The correct but unhelpful answer is that they knew I would be here. One of the Seers wanted to... talk with me."

"Why?" Ciarn prompted.

"They wanted to take me off the chessboard. Not by murdering me, no. Something that extreme would have attracted attention."

The Doshae clan chief regarded him curiously. "Yet here you are, asking us to do that very thing by accepting this Writ. The Seers failed?"

"They did, but they believe they succeeded. For my safety and that of my family I need them to continue to believe that for as long as possible. Forever by preference. Otherwise the Writ might not be enough."

Liam snorted. "I hardly think you're much of a threat to the Seers or their allies at the warriors' enclave."

"I agree with you. Unfortunately the man I spoke with was imprecise in explaining the reasons for his animosity. Someone must have had a vision they didn't like in which I was involved."

Ciarn didn't respond to that and silence stretched between them until Ruarshi began to feel uncomfortable. He forced himself to remain still and wait.

The clan chief cleared his throat and asked mildly, "You have reconciled with your brother?"

Ruarshi blinked, wondering where that question had come from. "Yes."

"You've been gone from Miriyan so long that you may have forgotten it is an important part of a chief's duties to watch out for the welfare of his clan members."

The healer briefly considered letting off a string of oaths that would have made Slan proud. "You spoke with Aethel." It was just like his brother to jump into this with both feet without looking first to see if it was safe.

"I did. I always start with questions I already know the answer to. Either you're lying to everybody or you're lying to nobody. And you wouldn't be living at the Beguinage if you weren't worried about something."

"Does *everyone* know where we are?" Ruarshi asked, irritated.

Ciarn smiled. "I say we take his offer to the Council, Liam."

"If you wish. I for one will argue against accepting it. We've no need for his enemies to become ours as well. We must not be seen to favor one faction over another. And the Taanor will not stand for it. Neither will your own Doshae or most of the other clans. He is a perversion."

Now they came to it. "A perversion you can either keep an eye on or leave running around loose."

"The Sotarii Council will exile you eventually. They'll have no choice once the situation settles down. I think we can survive your depredations until then."

"Maybe the Sotarii Council doesn't intend to exile me at all. The Seers interceded to keep me here until midsummer had come and gone. But after that what use was I? It's been ten months and you're not rid of me yet. What if you're wrong?"

"The Sotarii keep our society in balance. You disturb that balance. They will send you away."

Ruarshi left the window and moved into the room toward Liam. "We disturb nothing. It's the way others react to us that causes problems. And that's changing. How many people were sitting on my side of the hall during the petition hearing, Ciarn? What might the Sotarii Council's handling of Seggita's funeral mean for Miriyan's future? I will still be here in ten years. Wouldn't you prefer to exercise some control over me during that time?"

"You said 'we'," Liam noted. "How many of you are there?"

"I also said 'some control,'" Ruarshi replied. "You'll notice that the subject of the other Nerthii is one of the two exceptions I had included in the Writ. I won't answer questions about them."

"Even if it means your gambit fails?"

"Even if it means my gambit fails. Their secrets are their own. Though the exiles who've returned must be staying with someone, presumably someone who knows they're Nerthii. Not everyone is disgusted by us."

"I have always maintained that there are a lot of fools in the world."

"You're right about that."

"The other exception," Ciarn said, "states that you'll use your power only at your own discretion regardless of any request the Clan Council might make. That's redundant, Ruarshi. No one can ask you to use Nerthu's gifts in a way that conflicts with your own conscience."

"I thought the point worth reiterating." The healer was still focused on Liam, who was clearly beginning to find the scrutiny unnerving. "So what do you say, Liam? Either the Clan Council convinces us that there's someone worth dealing with in Tomir, or we all go underground and you don't know who or where we are. One of us could be standing right next to you at the May Day festival. And you wouldn't like that at all, would you?"

As Ruarshi spoke he continued to approach the clan chief's chair. Liam hadn't moved an inch to avoid him but his entire body was rigid. The man's revulsion was palpable.

"Were you Seggita's catamite, too?"

"What?"

Liam could move quickly for such a tall man. Ruarshi narrowly dodged the blow the clan chief aimed at the side of his head, stumbling backward into the wall as Ciarn jumped between them.

"No, Liam," the Doshae chief said. "Go to the hall and get yourself a mug of ale. Ruarshi will be gone when you come back."

The Taanor chief stood glaring at Ruarshi for a moment more before turning and very nearly fleeing the room. After the door slammed shut behind him, Ciarn turned to face the healer.

"What's wrong with you? You were practically begging him to hit you. Has this become a habit?"

"No," Ruarshi replied quietly, holding himself as still as possible until he was sure the slight jar to his head wasn't going to have any adverse consequences. Then he pushed himself away from the wall and sighed. "And now I'm not even sure on what account he despises me. You can reassure him about Seggita if you think it will do any good." He knew that what Liam had implied about the Nerthi was true, though it almost always went unmentioned.

Ciarn shook his head. "You may have found the one argument that will convince Liam and those like him to work with you. But proud men don't like doing things out of fear or having their noses rubbed in it. You've done yourself no favors here today. You'd best go."

Ruarshi nodded, bowed, and left. He'd been prepared to make specific and bloody-minded threats in order to persuade Liam, had that been necessary. Fortunately the mere prospect of proximity seemed to have been enough. He hoped Ciarn's estimation was correct. He doubted he'd ever again have the heart to argue so persuasively for his own indenture. But perhaps the day's errand had served its purpose.

Liam stood scowling at him from the door of the clan hall as he mounted his horse and swung her toward the gates. He considered blowing the man a kiss but instead contented himself with a brief salute. Then he pulled up his hood and rode away.

✳ ✳ ✳

"I've been waiting over half a year for this," Wil said, lying back against the rough wooden boards of the brewery's roof and heaving an enormous sigh. It seemed like it had been much longer since he'd felt so warm. The sun rode in a cloudless sky overhead, forcing him to squint but at the same time soothing every one of his aching joints. If not for the risk of a ten-foot fall he thought he might try sleeping up here. He closed his eyes.

"I do believe you have the right idea," Lorion commented, "but shouldn't we at least look at the rotten spot first? Our gracious hostess is going to expect us to return with some notion of what will be required to repair the leak." He nudged the Welshman's leg with his boot.

Wil swatted at him, eyes still closed. "How long until the sun goes down?"

"Oh, hours." Lorion settled in beside him. "I suppose we could rest a while before getting to work. The climb up that ladder was rather strenuous."

"Just as I thought." Ruarshi's voice floated over to them from the edge of the roof. "You never were good for anything after a meal."

"Which one of us is he insulting?" Lorion asked.

"Me, I think," Wil replied. He tracked the healer's progress across the sloping wooden expanse and opened an eye when the healer's shadow fell across his face. "Quit looming. Now that you're up here you may as well fall in with the consensus."

"May as well," Ruarshi conceded. He sat down on the Welshman's other side and looked out over the muddy yard of the Beguinage. Wil watched him.

"All's well with Davyt?"

"Yes. Slan was feeding him when I left. And Lucia was resisting the notion of taking a nap. Vocally. She has inherited her father's talent for language. I almost found myself persuaded."

Wil laughed. "Then it's a good thing Ginevra's in charge."

"What did Joanna send you two up here for?"

"The roof sprang a leak this morning," Lorion said. "She apparently felt the need for some male wisdom in regard to fixing it. We were most unfortunately the nearest sources of such wisdom."

"Does either of you know the first thing about it?"

"No," Lorion admitted.

"Not really," Wil said. "Building styles up here aren't the same as they are in Wales. I might be able to make a reasonable suggestion."

"They could just call in a woodshaper," the Naishanti said. "That would be the easiest solution. Europeans can be an illogical bunch."

The Welshman caught the gleam in Ruarshi's eye and realized that the afternoon's relaxed mood was about to be interrupted. He closed his eyes in resignation and waited.

"Exactly how logical was it for you to go to the warriors' enclave last night?"

"It made perfect sense to me or I wouldn't have gone, brother mine," Lorion said. "I don't plan to go back anytime in the near future. The place is rather tense."

"Your foray nearly drove Slan to distraction."

"We've been taking turns at that, haven't we?"

The healer didn't reply. Wil was beginning to wonder whether he should say something when Ruarshi laughed.

"Yes, we have. So what's going on over there?"

"Umm. My overall impression was of a place where everyone is spending three-quarters of their time whispering in corners. I never did actually see anyone doing that, you understand, but that's the atmosphere. It gave me the vapors."

Wil chuckled. "I'll just bet it did."

"It's the simple truth. I—"

Whatever else the Naishanti had intended to say was cut off by a shriek from the courtyard. Wil sat up just in time to see Lucia dart into the shadow of the brewery, followed at an only slightly more sedate pace by Ginevra.

"Maybe she doesn't need a nap today," he called down to her.

Wil's wife stopped at the sight of the three of them, her skirts hiked up out of the mud and her feet bare. "What are you doing up there?"

"Working," the Welshman said.

"I can tell," she said. "If one of you would please help me round up my child before she disappears completely in this quagmire?"

Wil rose, and saw Slan and Yael emerging from a doorway farther back in the Beguinage. "Reinforcements are on the way."

He climbed down the ladder, catching sight of his daughter peering around the corner of the building at him as he neared the bottom. With a roar he dropped the last few feet to the ground and gave chase to the little girl, who had resumed her shrieking. He caught her before she had gone ten yards and swung her up onto his shoulders, where she sat laughing, her fists knotted in his hair and her muddy heels drumming against his chest.

When he emerged around the opposite end of the brewery, all three women were looking toward Ruarshi and Lorion, who were for some reason standing with their backs to the courtyard. Wil's steps slowed. Ginevra and the others weren't looking at the men, after all, but past them at a thin column of black smoke that rose lazily into the sapphire sky.

"It's coming from the market square," Lorion said, hurrying toward the ladder with Ruarshi right behind him.

"War?" Ginevra asked faintly.

Wil plucked Lucia off his shoulders and handed her to her mother. "I'm going to ask you to do something for me. I'm going to ask you to stay here while we go find out what's happened."

"Mama?" Lucia asked anxiously. Ginevra tightened her grip on her daughter and looked levelly at her husband.

"I expect Slan will go too. I will look after the children. I want you back by midday tomorrow, and if you are not here I will go find you. This is not your fight."

"I won't be fighting. Ruarshi and I will see to the injured." What exactly that would entail Wil wasn't sure. The Illyana still couldn't heal.

A number of Beguines had come into the courtyard. Slan was handing off a screaming Davyt to one of them, a slight Englishwoman named Kate, her efforts to hush the infant distracted and ineffective. Ruarshi laid a hand on the baby's back and his crying subsided almost immediately. In spite of everything Wil grinned. The healer found his effortless ability to soothe his son's tempers to be a constant source of amazement. Slan's view of the matter was much more complex, Wil knew, and involved a large measure of exasperation.

The Welshman kissed his wife and daughter and hurried into the stable, where Lorion and Yael were already throwing saddles on horses. Ruarshi followed him in.

"The Sylvae should never have loaded up the Seers' supply sledges with rocks," Lorion observed. "It was bad enough when they sent them a week's worth of rotten pork, and *keth* spiked with senna."

"I've been holding my breath for a while now. It's almost a relief that Jair's finally done something." Wil ducked under his horse's chest to gather up a dangling strap and cinched up his saddle.

"Almost," Lorion agreed.

"Most of the northern clans fight with axes," Slan said. "Even against Naishanti they'll do a lot of damage."

"It's going to be a delightful day," Lorion said. "Everybody ready?"

They filed out of the stable and mounted up in the courtyard. Wil waved to Ginevra and Lucia as he rode out of the Beguinage's gates, pretending a nonchalance he didn't feel. His wife could probably see right through it but it might have some effect on their little girl. He trusted they would be safe there, because Ruarshi and the others had assured him they would be, and because he needed so desperately for it to be true. For his own part, he couldn't see how it would benefit any Miriyanti faction to attack a group of foreign religious women. A handful of hostages wouldn't be enough to offset the damage such an action would cause to Miriyan's reputation.

Slan and Lorion rode ahead and he followed with Ruarshi and Yael. The scene that greeted them when they arrived at the market square was no worse than he had expected. What did surprise him was the absence of combatants. Clearly it had become a running battle at some point and there would be more devastation wrought elsewhere in Tomir before the day was over.

Slan and her brother had wheeled around and were headed back toward them.

"We're going to ride after them," she said. "We'll meet you at the healers' circle later." Ruarshi nudged his horse forward and spoke quietly with his *chesida*.

Wil threw a warning look at Lorion. "Try not to get the vapors. And see to it that you don't leave us wondering for too long."

The Naishanti shrugged but remained silent as he waited for his sister. When the pair had galloped from the square, Ruarshi rejoined them.

"Find me some sledges while I identify those with the worst injuries, would you, Wil? Yael, you don't have to stay here."

"Miriyan is falling apart, Ruarshi. There's no better place to be."

The healer nodded and he and Yael moved away into the chaos of shattered market stalls. The blackened ruin of a section of booths could be seen on the other side of the square, but the fire appeared to have burnt itself out. A body lay in the mud next to it. Wil could see others scattered around the open space. Somewhere a woman was groaning with pain, and he thought he heard a man's voice mumbling a name over and over. There would be more of that sort of thing soon as the shock wore off.

The Welshman reined his horse around and headed toward a small group of Miriyanti that had gathered at the mouth of an alleyway. Hopefully one of them would know where he could get the sledges. He suspected they would need a lot of them.

Ruarshi stumbled out of the flickering lamplight and bustle of the hall and emptied the basin of bloody water over a patch of ice on the building's north side. He stood for a moment watching the packed snow absorb the darker color, black in the thin light of the moon. He couldn't have said what time it was. He thought it was probably past midnight but he wasn't sure. Not that it mattered. The day had been one of those in which time very quickly ceased to have any meaning, beyond the increased difficulties associated with the disappearance of the sun. He'd spent the entirety of the daylight hours binding up wounds and shuttling the injured to the healers' circle. They were still coming in, though now at a much slower rate, carried by pale Tomirans who sometimes turned around and left but just as often stayed, huddled by the fireplace in the hall. The healers were working around them, having abandoned their efforts to chase them back out into the night.

Wil had left a short while before to return to the Beguinage. Ruarshi had been glad to see him go. As the former *pir* of a crippled healer there hadn't been much for him to do, other than mutter occasionally about the strange looks Ruarshi received as he went about the fetch-and-carry work typically assigned to the most inexperienced of novices. It was all he was currently capable of.

He filled the basin with clean water from the well and carried it back inside, setting it on the floor next to one of those most recently brought in. The man was conscious but silent, and he followed Ruarshi's movements with light blue eyes dulled by pain. The healer wondered if anyone had yet checked the man for internal injuries. That should have been done immediately upon his arrival, but Ruarshi knew that collective fatigue would take its toll sooner or later and that some of the injured would suffer unnecessarily as a result. It was inevitable.

He decided to do a quick scan, just to make sure the man's wounds weren't critical. He wouldn't even try to heal what he found. It should be simple enough.

Ruarshi closed his eyes and dropped into a trance. Nothing life-threatening, no, though one of the bones in the man's lower left leg was broken and the splintered end had very nearly pushed its way out through the skin. He would bring the clansman some wine or *keth* if he could find any. An imperfect solution, but better than letting him lie there in that kind of pain until someone could see to him.

The healer opened his eyes and stood. The prickling along his scalp started almost at once. He tried taking some deep, steady breaths, but the sensation only grew in intensity.

Ruarshi whirled and jogged toward the door. As he stepped into the night air a hand wrapped itself around his forearm. Feminine. And old.

An instant later he was face-to-face with the woman, his right forearm across her throat, his left hand pressing his knife against her ribs. He had apparently slammed her against the front wall of the hall. She stared up at him with frightened eyes.

It was Ardan.

Shaking, Ruarshi stepped backward and dropped his knife into the ice-encrusted mud. He understood his reaction all too well. Ardan would not.

"Forgive me," he whispered. The expression on her face did not change. He turned away from her and continued toward the circle's living quarters.

Once inside he knocked on the first door he came to. When there was no answer, he pushed it open and stepped inside, carefully closing the door behind him and sitting down on the floor with his back against it.

His seizures were no longer quite as devastating as they had been in the beginning, and it seemed he had developed some limited ability to stave them off or at least delay them. It had been ten days or so since his last one. He had begun to hope that they were a part of his past. He bit his lip to keep from moaning as the first jolt of pain flashed through his body.

When he came to himself some time later, shuddering and nauseous, he was lying on his side. Along with the lessening of the pain had come an increase in the exhaustion that followed. The last thing he wanted to do was drag himself to his feet and leave the room but he thought he probably should. The occupant of this room would want to go to bed eventually. A short walk would certainly be preferable to explaining his presence here.

Ruarshi forced himself up, stumbled into the wall, and managed to get his hand on the door latch. His trip back across the circle was hazy but he was fairly sure that Ardan was nowhere in sight.

The situation was ridiculous. He'd carried his stubbornness more than far enough. Miriyan was at war and here he was, staggering around in the darkness like a drunk.

Once inside the hall he located a novice and gestured her aside.

"The next time you run into Mecheta, would you ask him to come to me? I'll be over there." He pointed toward the cold end of the hall opposite the fireplace.

"Yes, *Tai* Illyana." She was looking at him strangely, he thought. He ignored it and wove his way through the press of healers, refugees, and wounded toward the back corner of the building. He settled in next to a sleeping woman, resting his head against her shoulder where she sat on one of the low benches built into the wall. He doubted she would mind.

Someone was shaking his shoulder.

"Ruarshi?"

Mecheta was crouched in front of him. With some difficulty Ruarshi sat up. He had fallen asleep and ended up back over on his side.

The Chamani looked exhausted. "It took me quite a while to wake you. Elspeth said you'd asked for me and that you were slurring your words. Oddly, you don't smell like alcohol."

As Mecheta spoke, Ruarshi glanced toward the door of the hall and saw that the first gray tinge of dawn had replaced the flat blackness of night. The Chamani had likely not been to bed yet.

"I'm sorry," Ruarshi said. This was the man who had healed Slan's head wound, and the Illyana respected his character every bit as much as he did his talent. "It was nothing. I should not have pulled you from your work."

"There's no one waiting for me and I'm far too tired to sleep right now. Perhaps you should talk to me. Unless giving up on healing was really your own idea."

"I… There's no—"

"You've also got blood all over your chin," Mecheta observed. "Did you have a seizure, boy?"

Ruarshi rubbed at his chin, knocking away the dried blood. The man made him feel like an infant for reasons that had nothing to do with the difference in their ages.

"Yes. If you could take a look…" He tapped the side of his head.

"Certainly." Mecheta rested his hand against the back of Ruarshi's neck and closed his eyes.

When the Chamani brushed the remains of Inge's broken block with his power, Ruarshi gasped and began to shiver again. Mecheta lifted his hand away and sat regarding him.

"It's been a long time since I've seen one of those. I was probably about your age when I last ran across one, a complete bond, not the mess you've got in there. You've been picking it apart?"

"Trying to."

"Do you know what it is?"

"No. I know what it does. Or what it was intended to do."

"It's called a slave-bond. The exclusive preserve of the Nerthii. Very, very nasty. Did Seggita put it there?"

"No."

The Chamani stood. "It's going to take me the better part of a day to get the rest of that out of there and to undo what I can of the damage your clumsy fumbling has caused. Do you have anywhere you need to be before sundown? I believe I will have a nap before I get started."

Ruarshi thought of Slan, and then told himself that in his current state he would be of no use to her, even in the unlikely event she ended up getting herself into more trouble than she could handle. She was probably asleep.

"No, there's nowhere I need to go."

"Come with me."

Mecheta helped him up and led him to his chambers, where he directed Ruarshi toward the bed.

"While I'm resting, I want you resting. You clearly haven't been taking care of yourself. That will only complicate my task."

Ruarshi stripped down to his shirt and climbed into the Chamani's bed, too tired to argue. He hoped he would slip into sleep and wake up as he'd been before he'd ever met the old exile, but he knew that outcome was impossible. Mecheta had been right about his attempts at self-healing. But they'd been as compulsively necessary as they had been unwise.

He settled in under the blanket and thought of his son, and of Wil, who would probably be leaving Miriyan sooner rather than later...

For the second time that day, Ruarshi found himself looking up into Mecheta's concerned face.

"How do you feel?"

The Illyana thought about it. "Better, I think." His head felt clearer. Almost normal. Almost...

"Oh, Nerthu," he whispered. A cursory examination told him everything he needed to know. The place where the slave-bond had been lodged had a curiously flat aspect to it, and was completely unresponsive to the touch of his magic. He couldn't share a bond with anyone now. He was completely alone inside his head and would remain so.

He made an attempt to rise but the Chamani's hand was on his shoulder, pressing him back down into the pillows. "I know, Ruarshi. I know. Don't try to get up. Slan is here."

Ruarshi turned his head. His *chesida* was sitting next to the bed. She was trying to keep her expression neutral but he could see the dismay in her eyes.

"I came rushing here a few hours ago when I was told you'd had another seizure. Mecheta told me what he did and what he couldn't do. I'm so sorry. If it had been any other healer who'd said those things to me, I believe I would have hit him." Though the sentiment behind her words was quite sincere, she couldn't keep the real affection she felt for the Chamani from her voice.

"I'm pleased to see how well you've recovered, Slan," Mecheta said, smiling. "Ruarshi will also recover, though not as completely. I am sorry that my healing has taken away your ability to bond but I had little choice. Once I had removed the Nerthi's handiwork you started to bleed power. If I had allowed it to go on, it would have killed you."

"Is there any chance I could—"

"No, absolutely not. You stay out of your head. And everyone else's, unless you want to take lessons with me."

"Maybe later."

"Do you have any trace of a headache?"

"... No."

"Good. I'll go now. You stay here until tomorrow morning and sleep as much as possible. I'll have some food brought in." The Chamani inclined his head and left his chambers.

Ruarshi closed his eyes, trying to get used to the silence. His connection to Davyt was gone. It had always been faint and would have disappeared on its own by late summer, but that didn't make it any easier to have it taken away so abruptly.

"Ruarshi. Open your eyes."

He did as Slan asked. She left her chair and sat down on the edge of the bed. "This changes nothing. Yes, I wanted to share a bond with you one day, but even without one you are and will remain the better half of my soul. I'm simply glad that you're free of that thing."

He smiled up at her and drew her into his embrace. She curled up within the circle of his arms and nuzzled his neck. They lay peacefully, without speaking, until a knock came at the door.

Slan disentangled herself and sat up. "Come in."

A young man entered carrying a tray of food. He set it on the bed at Slan's direction and left. Ruarshi laughed when his *chesida* interrupted her slow crawl across his prone form to prop him up with pillows, straddling him in a way that was absolutely intended to be suggestive in spite of the fact that she was fully clothed. And muddy to boot. When she was finally satisfied with the arrangement, she lowered herself to the bed next to him and pulled the tray over.

"It looks edible at least," she observed. "Do you mind if I feed you? While you eat, I'll tell you what's been happening."

✳ ✳ ✳

Wil tugged gently at his horse's reins as the mare again pranced sideways, fretful about the unaccustomed weight of the small sledge she was pulling. Once he'd gotten her settled back down he glanced at the load lashed to the sledge to make sure it hadn't been jostled too badly. The ten crocks of honey still rode securely where he'd tied them. Satisfied that nothing was broken he turned his attention once again to the streets of Tomir, which had been covered overnight with a fresh and rather thick layer of snow. It was an improvement over the mud but it was already turning to slush around the edges as the day warmed, a situation that would only get worse if the sun ever broke free of the thin layer of cloud that floated low over the city like a pall of smoke.

He hoped that his gift, which constituted all of the honey the French merchant community could be persuaded to part with, would have some effect on the morale at the healers' circle. The place had become something of an armed encampment since the attack on the northerners, as their uninjured clansmen and Tomirans opposed to the Diamyo's bloodletting gathered there with the wounded. The number of those coming in had dwindled to a trickle until the previous evening, when the worrisome rumor that Jair had ordered the High Sotarii placed under house arrest at his clan circle began making the rounds. That had led to another surge in Miriyanti coming through the circle's gates and the consequent overcrowding had done nothing to lessen the level of tension within the walls. Add to that the healers' general annoyance at having their residence turned into a mustering ground for a badly disciplined and restless ad hoc army, and the resulting mix was fairly miserable, at times bordering on the explosive.

Wil trusted the Chamani to keep a lid on things, out of enlightened self-interest if for no other reason. What concerned him more was the possibility that the Diamyo were adopting the clansmens' tactics. The food supplies that were coming in were not particularly fresh, which one could excuse at this time of the year, but neither were they of sufficient quantity to feed even the usual inhabitants of the circle. Thus far the difference had been made up by sympathetic Tomirans who lived nearby, but that source would exhaust itself soon enough. The

Welshman had lived through two sieges with Ruarshi while they were in Europe and he had no desire to experience another.

This consideration had driven him out of bed early that morning and to the home of Henri Mende, the unofficial leader of the French merchant delegation in Tomir, who fortunately had proven to possess more political acuity than his countryman Flavel. The man was understandably dubious about the prospects facing the Miriyanti assembled at the healers' circle, but Wil believed he had convinced him that a direct attack by the warriors was unlikely. When the Welshman threw in what he knew about the Sotarii's negotiations with Denmark and the news of Ferenc and Simah's arrest, the Frenchman had quickly come to see the light. A little support for the healers' faction now, combined with the High Sotarii's dislike for the Hanseatic regions, could lead to lucrative trade deals for him later. Potentially. At the very least, Wil had continued, it couldn't hurt for the French to deal with both sides of the conflict. He knew that they had wrested partial control of Miriyan's opium imports from the Italians a few decades back. Compared to that, a few shipments of food to the northerners and their allies wouldn't weigh too heavily. If their side ultimately lost, the French could credibly claim to have maintained neutrality and should suffer no more than any other foreign group under isolationist Diamyo rule.

The Welshman had used the words 'isolationist Diamyo' as often as he could, just to make sure Mende understood what he might be dealing with if the reactionaries among the warriors won their little war. Wil wasn't actually certain of their opinions on the matter but had decided it couldn't hurt to dangle the prospect of a precipitous drop in profits before the Frenchman. Diplomacy could be a cruel business.

The Welshman had ended his meeting with Mende by slipping some gold into the man's hand, which had brightened his mood considerably. Wil had originally meant to use the money to set himself up in Wales but there was more where that came from and this need wouldn't wait. The unlikely group that had come together at the healers' circle couldn't be allowed to disintegrate for lack of food, not if there was any means at hand to prevent it. The Frenchman had agreed that deliveries would start that night, probably very late, and would continue regularly unless and until they were prevented from making it across town by the warriors. At which point they'd need to discuss alternative methods of getting supplies through to the circle. Wil had smiled and bowed Miriyanti-style, and had turned to go before a sudden inspiration led him to ask about honey.

Though he was trying to ignore the fact, he felt a good deal less satisfied with himself now than he had earlier. It was entirely possible that his uninformed intervention could cause problems with plans the High Sotarii had already laid, though he didn't see how the slow starvation of their friends could help them. And he didn't intend to apologize for his efforts, either, if it came to that. He could only act on the information he had, not on secrets that others might choose to withhold from him.

He rode into the healers' circle and skirted the edge of the courtyard, currently milling with people, until he came to the kitchens. The hassled cooking staff merely looked irritated when he interrupted them but they very nearly managed to smile when he came back through the door carrying a crock of honey under each arm. That won him a brief audience with Danai, who actually did smile when he told her about his arrangement with the foreign merchant.

Somewhat happier with himself than he had been, Wil returned to the courtyard and unhitched his mare from the sledge. He returned her to the stable and took his time brushing her down, wondering what, if anything, he needed to do next. He badly wanted to sneak back to Villalobos' house and stay there with his wife and daughter for a day or two, though he knew he would not. The same concern for secrecy kept Ruarshi and Slan from returning to Davyt, who was being cared for by Ginevra and a wet nurse from the Beguinage. The less coming and going they did from the priest's house, the less likely it was that their families' new location would be discovered by those who didn't need to know it.

The stakes had been raised when the bloodshed had started, as they were all too aware. Ruarshi's very existence was an affront to some of the warriors and there was still the matter of those four Naishanti he had killed. The Sotarii Council had so far refused to deal with that issue but the Diamyo might not be so reticent. Slan was viewed as a traitor by her fellow Naishanti. And now Wil was himself taking steps that could win him the unfavorable attention of the warriors, even though as a general rule foreigners were of little concern to them.

So Wil would remain among the healers and continue making himself useful. Somehow.

The Welshman left the stable and headed toward the hall, intending to grab something to eat while he thought about how best to continue aggravating his enemies. He spotted Ruarshi standing near the gates and changed direction. As he drew closer and the intervening crowd thinned, he saw that the healer was in close conversation with four

Miriyanti he'd never met before. Ruarshi saw him coming but didn't wave him off. Just as well, Wil decided. He'd have kept right on going anyway.

"… dead. Both of them had talked to you. You *must* know more than that."

The woman who'd been speaking turned to stare at the Welshman when he stopped at Ruarshi's side.

"Why don't you introduce us?" Wil suggested helpfully.

The healer took a deep breath. "Wil, these are Mara, Aurel, Coewyn, and Niklas. They are exiles, finally come to call. *Tai* Nerthii, this is Wil, my former *pir*. You're only forcing me to repeat myself, Mara. I have no good theories about the reasons for Seggita's suicide. Inge's death I have already explained."

"We should have come to talk to you earlier. Point taken." That was Niklas, the only man among the four. "But we're here now and offering our help, which is something."

"You said seven had returned. That leaves three who didn't come with you. Where are they?"

"They want no part of this," Coewyn said. "They're all over eight centuries old and have earned some rest."

"I hope they're at their clan homes, then," Wil muttered. "They'll get precious little rest in Tomir." That earned him four sidewise glances but no requests that he find something else to do. He supposed he shouldn't be surprised by that, as all of the Miriyanti in the group had spent a good long time in Europe. He could stop being obnoxious now, apparently.

"Perhaps you can tell me something," Ruarshi said. "How did Seggita come to know so much about the Nerthii? Was he involved with someone at Mirror Lake?"

Aurel laughed. "You could say so. He and Casimir were lovers for decades."

"Oh." Ruarshi was silent a moment. "What was his attitude toward Casimir the last time one of you spoke with him?"

"He never told any of us what his attitude was," Niklas said. "His references to the old spider were rarely complimentary, though."

"His references to Miriyan were rarely complimentary," Aurel observed, "yet he still came back here as soon as he could."

"True," the man conceded.

"I've been told that there is dissension among the Seers," Ruarshi said. "Can we turn that to our advantage?"

"I don't see how we could," Mara said, shaking her head. "Not without help from the Sotarii, who have their own troubles at the moment. And the Seers have no strength beyond that loaned to them by the warriors. I'm more concerned by what they're doing."

"They're bickering among themselves, as usual," Aurel said. "The enclave has never been big enough to contain the ambitions of all the warriors living there."

"Jair did have the right to enforce the Seers' access to edible food," Coewyn said. "I always found him to be reasonable, even under pressure. There are others on the Diamyo Council of whom that can't be said."

"Beorn?" Ruarshi asked.

"Elyon," Wil added. Lorion seemed to think those two were the most dangerous and extreme of the Elders.

Aurel and Coewyn exchanged a look.

"I'd be happy to kill either one of them," Coewyn said, "but I'd want to take care of Aerik first. He's a sadist in addition to his other faults."

"Assassination isn't a bad idea, if you take the larger view," Aurel said. "But if part of our purpose is to ensure that we'll be able to remain here, we'd best think of something else."

"No assassinations," Wil said. "At least none that can be traced back to any of you," he amended a moment later. The comment earned him a considering glance from Niklas.

"There's another possibility," Ruarshi said reluctantly.

The Welshman perceived that the Illyana was very determinedly not looking in his direction. He crossed his arms. "What would that be?" He was half afraid of the answer.

"How do you feel about the Clan Council?" Ruarshi addressed his question to the exiles.

"They're backward, narrow-minded, and just as likely to spit on us as talk to us. Why?" Mara asked.

"I presented a Writ of Submission to my clan chief, Ciarn, a while ago. The Taanor chief was there too. They did not turn me down or throw me out. I haven't heard yet if the Council has made a decision about accepting it."

"I won't do that," Niklas said.

Coewyn's expression was one of profound distaste. "Nor I."

"What," Wil asked, "is a Writ of Submission?"

"A piece of paper," Ruarshi said. "I agree to do what the Clan

Council tells me for the next ten years if they'll keep Beorn, Elyon, and Aerik from killing me in the interim. I plan to be their spy."

"Liam was there?" Aurel appeared intrigued. "I haven't gone back to my clan home for fear of that man recognizing me."

"Yes, he was. He liked the idea of using me to acquire more power. Then he tried to hit me before I left."

The Welshman scowled at the healer. It had no effect.

"If they accept your Writ, I will consider giving them one of my own." When Coewyn scoffed, Aurel went on, her voice heated. "We can't expect to be accepted back into Tomiran society without some expression of goodwill. Or even submission if need be. Don't tell me you haven't put some thought into this."

"I won't submit to people who harbor nothing but disgust for me," Coewyn said. "They won't even let the word 'Nerthi' pass their lips."

"So if Ruarshi does, and I do, you'll try to ride into everyone's good graces on our backs? What do you think, Mara?"

The question held more weight in Miriyanti society than it would have in Europe. Mara was the oldest member of the group by two centuries at least.

"It... could work," she said. "But I am concerned that it will look to our countrymen like part of another punishment, since that's how such writs are typically used. We didn't return here in order to be punished again."

"I know that," Ruarshi said, "yet you could be anyway. The Sotarii could have all of you executed tomorrow for coming back to Miriyan without their leave. If you place yourself under the authority of the chiefs, the Sotarii lose their jurisdiction over you. Isn't ten years of bowing your head to the Clan Council the better alternative?"

"We'll see," Mara said. "Let's find out first how they answer you."

Ruarshi nodded and turned his attention to Niklas, changing the subject.

"I've met you before. Do you remember?"

"... No."

"I arrived here right before you left. The story was that you had been expelled for disobedience and went home."

Niklas chuckled. "The truth was that I had been found by my instructor pulling metal shards out of the wall of my room. I suppose that was disobedience of a sort. Unpleasant questioning followed. They dealt with me very quickly. My family knew what had really happened, but they were too ashamed of me to contradict the less damaging tale floating around the circle."

"Only you and Seggita were allowed to remain in Miriyan after your activities had become known," Mara said, her gaze on Ruarshi's face. "And from the sound of it, Casimir likely had a hand in your reprieve, too."

Wil wished she hadn't linked the three of them together like that. It seemed an ill-omened combination.

"You might as well come into the hall and eat something," Ruarshi said. "Let the Chamani glare at us if they must. You do plan to stay?"

✳ ✳ ✳

"I'm glad you're on our side, Wil," Ruarshi remarked as he settled into the saddle of the stocky white mare he'd borrowed from the circle's stable. "You've been playing merry hell with the warriors' plans for us and I doubt they even know it."

"I've always preferred stealth," the Welshman replied, making a final adjustment to one of his stirrups before climbing up onto his own mount. The healer watched him critically, looking for signs of the joint pain that had sent his former *pir* to bed early the night before. Other than moving rather more slowly than he once did, Wil gave no indication that he hurt. Unless his vacant facial expression was meant to conceal something.

Ruarshi frowned, wondering if he should try again to convince him to remain at the circle. His brother spoke up and saved him the trouble.

"If that were true you wouldn't be on that horse," Aethel said. "There's no reason why the two of you need to go. We don't exactly lack for volunteers." He gestured agitatedly toward the courtyard, where a dozen other small groups like their own were readying to leave. "You've got northerners, healers, Tomirans, Sotarii, even a couple of walking wounded Naishanti willing to post those things. You ought to stay here."

"And miss the fun?" Ruarshi asked.

"Not a chance," Wil said. "This was my idea, remember."

Though his words were ostensibly meant for Aethel, the Welshman was watching Ruarshi as he spoke. The healer met his eyes and nodded, once. Wil was every bit as restless as he was and Ruarshi thought he knew why. It couldn't be coincidence that their destination was directly adjacent to the foreign quarter.

Aethel threw up his hands in exasperation. "I promised our parents

I would take care of you, little brother."

The healer supposed that explained why Aethel had been such a nuisance since returning from their clan home a few days before. "Then watch our backs. And feel free to take an arrow for me if it comes to that."

His brother growled and put his heels to his horse, preceding them out of the circle's gates. They followed him at a quick trot, making their way northwest through Miriyan's capital city with the fruits of Wil's most recent labors concealed in their saddlebags.

Ruarshi was still a bit surprised when he thought about it. Wil's talent for intrigue, though never exactly what he would have called negligible, had positively blossomed over the past week.

For his part, the Illyana had been spending much of his time in a largely unsuccessful attempt to teach the few receptive healers at the circle how to defend themselves from Naishanti. He probably would have had more luck with his lessons if he'd been able to use his magic to show them what he meant, rather than just describing the techniques to them, but that was out of the question. Unless and until Liam betrayed him by passing on word of the Seer's failure, he had to continue to conceal all evidence of his partial recovery, however much he disliked maintaining the lie. Even his brother and sister didn't know the truth. And he would have to keep this up until the crisis had passed and he had somehow wended his way to a place of safety.

Wil, on the other hand, had been making good use of his days. Not only had he seen to it that everyone at the circle would be fed, but he'd also struck up a tentative friendship with the Danish ambassador. So much so that the man had passed on to him a copy of the treaty he'd been working on with the Sotarii. Ruarshi had looked it over, as had many of those staying at the circle, and almost everyone agreed that the document was inoffensive. It was a simple anti-Hanseatic mutual defense treaty and involved only minimal trade concessions on each side. While those might irritate a few clans, the more important question had been resolved in an entirely satisfactory manner. Miriyan would not be treated as part of the Danish state, as Queen Margaret had insisted with regard to Sweden and Norway. There was nothing about the agreement that could be used to justify the continued imprisonment of Ferenc and Simah, in spite of the secrecy they'd maintained while negotiating its terms.

Which was where their current errand came in. Wil, Ruarshi, and a handful of others had spent most of the previous evening and that morning making copies of the treaty. They intended to post them at every public gathering place in town. With any luck public pressure would compel Jair to release the High Sotarii by the end of the day. Ardan had remained firm in her contention that the Diamyo First was actually on their side in this, suggesting at one point that he might have taken the Sotarii into custody at the Tirae circle in order to ensure they'd be safe, but even if that turned out to be true she agreed that it was time they were set free to take action. Now that blood had been shed Ruarshi wasn't sure how the two of them could intercede to slow the conflict's momentum, but any effort they chose to make would be welcome.

The healer's musings came to a halt when Aethel stopped next to a large stone well in the middle of a square and turned back to wait for them.

"This is as good a place to start as any," his brother said, and held out a hand toward Wil as they reined in next to him. "Give me one of those and I'll put it up over there." He jerked his head toward the northern edge of the square.

The Welshman handed him a copy of the treaty and they watched as he moved off to nail it to the outer wall of some unsuspecting Miriyanti's house.

"After this we should circle a bit east, and then back around—"

Ruarshi broke off, startled, as Aethel rose in his stirrups and began to bellow at the few people occupying the square.

"Fellow Tomirans! For the sake of a lie, the Diamyo are destroying Miriyan! Come read the truth of the treaty that the High Sotarii have negotiated with Margaret of Denmark! Ferenc and Simah must be freed at once!"

"Good lord," Ruarshi muttered.

"It did get their attention," Wil commented. "I didn't know your brother had such a flair for the dramatic."

"I did. I just never expected it to be turned to good use."

"Good use? What happened to stealth?"

Aethel had heard the Welshman's question and answered it as they all swung around to leave the square. "No point in that if we want as many people as possible to read the treaty before the warriors catch on to what we're doing. Shall we pick up the pace?"

Wil echoed Ruarshi's grin. Together the three of them urged their horses to a canter and wove their way through their assigned section of the city. Before too long, they were all shouting Aethel's message in unison and getting a lot of attention from the startled populace. It was midafternoon when they finally ran out of copies of the treaty, at which point they slipped into the foreign neighborhoods and called a halt at a small tavern to eat. After swallowing some bland but solid English food they decided to part ways. Ruarshi knew Wil had decided to go to his family before he'd even so much as opened his mouth to say so.

"Go, Wil. There was no one following us. You'll be safe enough. Give my regards to everyone."

The Welshman rode wearily off, no longer able to conceal the fact of his discomfort. Ruarshi watched him go and then glanced toward his brother, eyeing the older man speculatively. He'd had more fun with Aethel in the past hours than he'd had since they were boys. He wondered if his brother felt the same way.

"Since when did you become so political?"

"Since my brother got himself in over his head."

"Is that what you think?"

"Am I wrong?"

Ruarshi laughed. "God, sometimes talking to you is like talking to myself. Do our parents answer questions with more questions? Is that where we got it?"

"I don't think so," Aethel said, considering. "I think this is all ours. Even Yael doesn't do it."

"How would you like to go take a look at the warriors' enclave?"

"What? Oh." His brother understood him very well. Almost as well sometimes as Wil did. "Dying to find out if there's any truth to the tale?"

"That rumor can't be true."

"It's no more unlikely than any of the others currently making the rounds, is it? I guess I would like to see if the Sotarii really are attacking the warriors with vegetation."

"Five *taeler* says they're not."

"You're on. Though I didn't realize you had any money."

"I don't have any with me. That's different. It doesn't matter since I'm going to win the bet anyway."

"Sure of that?"

Their journey to the warriors' enclave ended up as a race, complicated by the need not to run over anyone along their route. They both succeeded in dodging the obstacles thrown in their way, with only one close call that almost sent Ruarshi tumbling off his horse. They pulled up in unison when they emerged into the clear area beside the enclave's gates.

Ruarshi had forgotten how big the place was, easily four times the size of the healers' circle and with log walls high and thick enough to withstand an attack. But that wasn't what compelled his attention. No, that distinction belonged to the gigantic oak tree that had grown up apparently overnight, directly under the right side of the gatehouse. It had completely broken the enclave's defensive wall at that point, leaving gaps so large the healer could see parts of the muddy interior yard beyond its massive trunk. The leafy tops of at least four more sizable trees rose into the sky at various points along the enclave's perimeter.

Ruarshi whooped with laughter, not at all concerned to have lost the bet. Beside him Aethel was having equal trouble getting sufficient air into his lungs.

"It just doesn't pay to annoy the Sotarii, does it?" his brother asked, his expression gleeful.

"I'd say not." The healer caught his breath. "And I'd also say we both just got exactly the kind of trouble we were looking for."

Ruarshi's good humor had left him when he realized that the three Naishanti coming out of the gates had recognized him. Not only recognized him, but shouted a name at him: Andrej. One of the warriors he had killed on the night Seggita died. He wished for a fleeting instant that he'd bothered to disguise or conceal himself in some way, and then was fiercely glad he had not.

The healer dug his heels into his horse's flanks, trusting Aethel to follow his lead. Before his brother's horse could make it around the corner it was tripped up by a hastily-woven shield and Aethel flew off into the mud, landing hard on his side. Ruarshi pulled up and reined around desperately to offer Aethel his arm. His brother clasped it and swung up onto the little mare's back.

The animal wasn't big enough to carry two. The healer swerved right at the next intersection, hoping she wouldn't stumble. They needed to stay out of sight of the Naishanti at all costs. If the warriors couldn't see them they couldn't throw any more shields in their way.

After the fifth turn it was clear that they wouldn't get much farther on horseback. Ruarshi stopped and both he and Aethel slid to the ground. The healer smacked the mare on her rump but she only stumbled forward a few steps before coming to a halt again, utterly spent. His brother meanwhile had dashed to the side of the alley and leaped atop a low fence.

*Up,* he gestured.

The healer understood him then. He didn't like the idea, but unless his ears were playing tricks on him at least two of their pursuers were now mounted,and gaining on them quickly. They couldn't outrun the Naishanti on foot. And Ruarshi had no desire to use his magic until all other possibilities had been exhausted.

Aethel scrabbled up onto the gently pitched eave of the building and pulled his brother up after him. They ran lightly over the apex of the roof and down the other side, where they jogged along close to the edge until they reached the end of what turned out to be a long and winding row of houses. Then it was time to get down. Ruarshi clung for a moment to the eave before letting himself drop, thankful for the slushy snow and mud that met him when he hit the ground. His brother came down next to him, landing badly.

"Are you hurt?" the healer asked urgently.

"No. Bruised. *Damn* this weather. They're going to have no trouble following us."

"Wait." Ruarshi pulled Aethel into the center of the street, running a small shield over the ground behind them to obscure their tracks as they went.

His brother gasped. "I thought—"

The healer put a finger to his lips. "Shhhh. Don't tell anyone what I just did. I think we can blend in with traffic now."

They headed south into a small square, the location of a minor market that sold primarily metal goods. Fortunately the point at which they'd left the roof hadn't been visible from any of the booths so there were no witnesses to worry about. They gradually sped up as they went and were halfway down another alley by the time hoof beats again became audible behind them.

"I don't know Tomir like you do. How much farther to the circle?" Aethel asked.

"A good distance. Let's just keep walking. I doubt they'll be able to separate our tracks from any of the others leaving the market. I wasn't serious about the arrow, you know."

The sun was almost touching the western horizon when they finally turned the last corner and came in sight of the healers' circle. Home, for now.

"Sotar be blessed," Aethel said. "I wasn't sure, back there—"

Two Naishanti rode out of a side street in front of them, blocking their way forward.

Ruarshi regarded them, unsurprised. Nerthu, but he was an idiot. Now he would have to do something that would betray the improving state of his health.

The healer felt a shield wrap itself around his throat and start pulling him toward the warriors. He went to his knees, plunged his hands down into the wet earth, and held on. They wouldn't be able to kill him this way. Knock him out, yes, but that was preferable to allowing himself to be dragged over to them like some kind of disobedient dog.

"Shoot them! Shoot them! For the love of—"

Ruarshi had just enough time to wonder who Aethel was shouting at before the pressure on his neck subsided and disappeared. He sagged into the snow, blinking, until he could see properly again.

His brother was kneeling in front of him. "Can you breathe?"

"Yes." The healer got to his feet and looked up. The warriors were sprawled face down in the snow, several arrows embedded in each of their backs.

"They shot them from the walls of the circle," Aethel said. "Has that ever happened before?"

"I'm sure it has. Just not lately. The Naishanti certainly didn't expect it."

Ruarshi's sense of relief evaporated when he saw Lynesse striding toward them, still clutching a bow. He nevertheless forced himself to smile, for her sake.

✳ ✳ ✳

"A few of the Chamani had a fair-sized conniption over it, but what could they do?" Ruarshi plunked discordantly at the *klaviat* he held, a pear-shaped stringed instrument native to Miriyan and popular with Tomirans when played properly. The healer had quite clearly never been taught what to do with one. Wil considered yanking it out of Ruarshi's hands and sending it flying over the circle's outer wall.

"Ardan was surprisingly helpful in getting them calmed down. Johav might actually have tossed us all out but the rest of them were prepared to be sensible. No point in throwing out your collection of tame Nerthii, especially not now that we've got Naishanti loitering about the neighborhood. Did they give you any trouble coming in?"

Ruarshi smelled vaguely of *keth*, as did almost everyone else sitting out in the courtyard on this unusually warm spring evening, but the

Welshman was convinced he wasn't drunk. Nowhere near it, in fact.

"No, of course not. I'm a harmless foreigner."

"A foreigner you are but harmless you have never been. Aurel, I cannot play this instrument. You may as well take it before I mangle it."

The Miriyanti thus addressed wandered over from the next table and took the *klaviat* from Ruarshi's hands.

"Your *chesida* tells me you can sing. Is that so?"

The healer leaned back and regarded the woman owlishly in the odd mix of torch- and twilight. "I'm sure there are differing opinions on the subject. What did you have in mind?"

"A series of dirty German drinking songs. Know any?"

"Of course. Could we throw in one or two about Til Eulenspiegel? I prefer those. Will you excuse me, Wil? I promise I'll come back."

The Welshman shrugged in frustration and watched as Ruarshi moved off with the exile. When he began singing a minute or two later, Wil rose from the bench and scanned the crowd. Though the healer had a good voice it was only rarely that he agreed to sing solo in public. Something was clearly going on here, something that went beyond the escapade with the warriors. With Ruarshi in his current fey mood he knew he'd get nothing sensible out of the man for the next several hours.

He hadn't come pelting back from the priest's house a day late in order to settle for the healer's nonsense. And he could have sworn, when he'd first arrived, that the look in the Illyana's eyes had been one of pure relief. A discussion with someone of slightly more level temperament was obviously required.

Wil's searching eyes came to rest on Lorion, sitting in a group with Yael, Aethel, Slan, and Niklas. They would have information, complete with commentary, he was sure. He started in their direction, giving the northerners at the next table a wide berth. They were arguing loudly about something in a heavy dialect. In spite of the volume and general air of boisterousness in the courtyard, the Welshman would have been willing to swear that no one had swallowed more than a single mug of *keth* all evening. Celebrating the change of season was all very well but everyone at the circle knew they were part of an army now, one that was arguably under siege.

Lorion hailed him as he approached their table. "Smile, friend Welshman, and join us. The weather is fine, is it not? You're up to your knees in mud."

Wil groaned inwardly. The Naishanti was in a mood, too. What was wrong with everyone? He nodded toward the others as he took a seat next to Slan.

"I don't know much German. That was a particularly vile verse, wasn't it?" Slan asked him.

The Welshman nodded, one ear still tuned to the musical entertainment in the background. "Yes."

"How is Ginevra?"

"Safe. Restless. Worried. Davyt is looking well. He and Lucia seem to have formed an attachment."

Slan stared down into her mug. Still full, Wil noted.

"You can come with us to Wales if you like," the Welshman said gently.

The Naishanti smiled wistfully. "Not for at least ten years we can't."

Wil took a moment to process that. "The Clan Council...?"

"Has accepted Ruarshi's Writ, yes. Ciarn sent him a message today. Thirty-five of the fifty-two chiefs are in town now, drawn in by word that the High Sotarii were arrested. That was plenty for them to take a binding vote. I could have killed him when he told me what he'd done but that would have defeated the whole purpose."

Yael made a face at him. "It's good news, actually. There should be no more scenes like the one yesterday. Nobody goes up against the chiefs, not if they value having a clan home to go back to."

Ruarshi didn't seem to be celebrating, not as far as Wil could tell. Then again, looked at from the healer's point of view this was probably a classic lose-lose situation even though the outcome was the one he had wanted. The Welshman felt himself start to relax a bit.

"What exactly happened?"

Aethel looked guilty. "He had a bad idea and I went along with it."

"What bad idea?"

A devilish grin worked its way onto the Sotaru's face and for an instant he looked startlingly like his brother. "Let's just say that we obtained visual confirmation of the fact that the Sotarii are tearing down the walls of the warriors' enclave with trees."

Lorion smacked the table with his fist. "And I wasn't there. Damn it. The group I went out with mucked around for a while and then came straight back here."

So. Wil glanced in Ruarshi's direction and was just able to catch glimpses of the man where he sat next to Aurel, still singing. The old Chamani had healed him of the block and very nearly his first thought had been to go out and do something monumentally stupid.

"If we hadn't been screeching like banshees I don't think they'd have taken any notice of us. Neither of us really expected to see anything remotely like that."

The Welshman turned to Niklas. "Will you submit a Writ?"

The man grimaced and shook his head. "I don't know. It wouldn't be my first choice but Aurel has been persuasive. It's not a bad solution. I believe Lynesse plans to submit one tomorrow."

"Ruarshi's new bodyguard," Yael said, laughing. "She's sticking to him like glue and he's doing his best to be gracious about it."

"Sooner or later I'll have to rescue him," Slan said. "But not just yet. He deserves to have his patience tried for a while, just so he'll remember what it feels like."

Wil snorted. "Are the copies of the treaty having any effect?"

"They're starting to," Lorion said happily. "People are beginning to ask some very pointed questions about what the Diamyo are doing and why. Poor Jair. All that hard work for nothing."

"I still don't see how you manage to come and go as you please," Yael said. "The warriors must know by now that you're not the idiot you pretend to be."

"It's part of the Warrior Code. You never interfere with a drinking buddy unless he's actually in the process of slitting your throat."

That got a laugh from Slan. "It's more complicated than that but there is actually a kernel of truth in what my brother just said. Not a large enough kernel to keep several residents of the enclave from turning him into a sieve at their first opportunity, however."

"I'm staying out of there for the nonce, Sister. I told you."

The Welshman had been looking at Yael while Lorion spoke. A fleeting but very interesting expression crossed her face and Wil had to swallow a burst of surprised laughter. Ruarshi's sister became aware of his regard and flushed.

Mary Mother. The girl was in love with Lorion. He wondered if the Naishanti knew.

A hand descended on Wil's shoulder, making him jump. Ruarshi slid onto the bench beside him.

"Broken string. And our audience had grown thoroughly tired of being spat upon. There's just no way to say some of those words without spitting, I'm afraid."

The Welshman considered remonstrating with him about his behavior the day before but decided to hold his peace. It would do no good with the healer in his present state of mind.

"Where's your shadow?" he asked instead.

"Tired and convinced that I'll be safe enough for the evening. I believe she has gone to bed. How's she coming along?"

"Pretty quickly," Niklas replied. "Though her control is still shaky. No longer than she's been at the circle, that's to be expected."

"Congratulations, by the way," Wil said. Ruarshi raised an eyebrow at him so he went on. "Your Writ. You must have been unusually persuasive to get through so quickly to the chiefs."

"Must have been," the healer agreed. "I'm certain I'll enjoy my next decade. I'll write you long letters about all of it, full of detail and idle gossip. Are you going to spend your fortune on sheep or on fomenting rebellion against the English?"

Wil gave up completely at that point. "Rebellion has fallen out of fashion. But I don't want sheep, either. Maybe I'll try goats."

"That would probably be easiest on your neighbors." Ruarshi cocked his head. "Or will you even have neighbors? I suppose you could build out in the middle of a marsh somewhere. Or a bog. Does Wales have bogs? I can't remember."

"I expect I'll stay on my family's land if they'll have me. I haven't asked them yet."

"Well, wherever you end up, you'll be damp all the time. What miserable weather you Welshmen have. You have warned Lucia that she'll grow up resembling a raisin?"

Lorion choked and began coughing into his sleeve. Yael pounded helpfully on his back until he recovered.

"I think they squeezed your neck a little too hard yesterday," Slan said. "I'll want to check you later for bruises. Remind me."

"That sounds delightful but I don't know what you're talking about. Spring always does this to me. Unless I'm in Wales, in which case it doesn't. Tell her, Wil."

The Welshman chuckled. "Check his neck anyway. It couldn't do any harm. It might even stall his chatter for five minutes. He's trying to drive us crazy, you know."

"I'm *trying* to improve morale around here. Just look at you somber lot…"

Wil closed his eyes, still chuckling, and pressed wearily at the bridge of his nose. In his weaker moments, such as this one, he was quite sure he'd never be able to leave this place and these people. Why had he wanted to? He couldn't quite remember.

At least the choice of when he would go wasn't entirely in his hands. He and Ginevra had agreed that they would stay until Miriyan's current troubles were over, even if that meant remaining where they were for another winter. Or two.

But he wasn't fool enough to believe that it would take so long.

* * *

Ruarshi sighed and looked away from the expression on Wil's face. After his argument with Slan, just ended, he wasn't sure he could deal with another. "This isn't some sadistic ploy of Liam's though I know that's what it looks like. It's a legitimate request, well within the rights of the Clan Council to make, and it's something I need to do if I ever want them to take me seriously."

"I'm sure they'll feel obligated to take your corpse seriously, Ruarshi, but how exactly will that help you?"

"Jair won't let the warriors so much as touch me. He can't afford to. He's having enough trouble maintaining his authority as it is. Antagonizing the clan chiefs will not be high on his list of priorities right now."

They paused in their conversation as a young healer darted by them, nodding to Ruarshi as he passed, and disappeared through the door of the stable. It was early in the morning yet, the sun only just having cleared the line of the horizon, but the Illyana could already tell it was going to be another unseasonably warm day.

"I understand that you don't want to jeopardize the protection the Clan Council has offered by refusing to do what they ask of you," Wil said, his arms crossed as he stared off over the muddy expanse of the courtyard. "Can they withdraw their acceptance of your Writ?"

"At this juncture, yes. Once I've taken an order from them, no."

"So there's no way for you to get out of this without abandoning the whole scheme. Who could you turn to then? The Chamani?"

The healer grimaced. "That would be a waste of my time."

"In other words the chiefs have got you backed into a corner and they know it. They're exploiting the fact. Are you going to let them?"

"Yes."

The Welshman leaned back against the stable wall and just looked at him for the space of several heartbeats. "Why? What kind of allies do you really suppose they'll be to you, if their first thought is to demand that you do something so dangerous?"

"I think that's exactly the point, Wil. This is similar to what the chiefs themselves go through. Before they're selected to lead their clans, they're required to run a gauntlet made up of clan members armed with stone weapons. It's a final test of their physical courage and willingness to suffer injury for the sake of their people. The purpose of the exercise isn't to hurt them."

"But I'm sure they come out of it pretty bloodied up anyway," Wil observed.

"As I said, Jair will never allow it to go so far."

"I'm sure the discipline at the enclave is good, Ruarshi, but I doubt that it's perfect. Are you taking anyone to watch your back?"

"I'm relying on the chiefs for that. They'll feel honor bound to jump in if things get out of hand."

"Slan's not going?" The Welshman was incredulous.

"No." Ruarshi paused to clear his throat. "She wanted to. I was... unkind. Look after her today, will you?"

Wil snorted. "I can try. It would probably be wiser for me to stay out of her way."

The healer smiled wanly. "Probably. If Lorion shows up let him know his presence isn't required, either. There's no reason why we should offer the warriors a unified target."

"They don't know about Mecheta...?"

"I certainly haven't told them. My recovery will no doubt come as a surprise."

"Christ, Ruarshi. Are you looking forward to this?"

"That would be overstating the case. Though I will enjoy the sensation of riding into the enclave and then back out of it with the warriors watching me do it. I hope the sight sticks in their collective craw for a good long time. I don't intend to continue slinking around Tomir."

"Like you did with Aethel?"

The healer laughed, a genuine outburst of mirth. "I wondered when you were going to get around to mentioning that. You'll have to forgive me."

"I already have. Any particular reason you're wearing the jacket Ginevra gave you?"

"I like the color. I still think it suits me better than any other. Mara told me what the traditional color of the Nerthii is. Care to take a guess?"

"Black?"

"Of course. Horrible, isn't it? We're going to have to do something about it once things get back to normal."

The young man who'd run by them earlier emerged from the stable leading a rangy bay gelding. Ruarshi took the reins from the youngster with a word of thanks. The boy bowed rather more deeply than was necessary and walked away.

"You're leaving now?"

"Soon. Ciarn is already here, presumably eating as much of Danai's cooking as he can put his hands on. You might want to hurry over there and get something for yourself before he cleans out the kitchens."

"How long is this little parley going to take?"

"Subjectively, forever. The Clan Council likes formalities. The meeting will be bracketed on both ends with chatter sufficient to wear out the Holy Roman Emperor and both Popes combined. We'll finish toward midafternoon at a guess."

The Doshae chief appeared in the doorway of the hall, still brushing crumbs from his tunic. Ruarshi waved to him. The man mirrored the gesture, ambled over to a shaggy black horse tethered at the edge of the courtyard, and mounted.

"It looks like your escort is ready," Wil said.

"You've gotten it backwards. I'm supposed to be his escort. He does look impatient."

"You be damn careful."

"I will be."

"See to it. I'll be here when you get back."

Ruarshi smiled, climbed up onto the bay's back, and bowed to the Welshman from the saddle. Then he put his heels to his horse and accompanied Ciarn through the gates of the circle.

After offering him an initial greeting the Doshae chief seemed content to ride in silence. Ruarshi was satisfied to leave it at that. His nerves had gotten the better of him the night before and he'd spent most of the dark hours sleepless, listening to Slan's even breathing. The mix of fatigue and adrenaline that had resulted this morning had given him a headache and made it very nearly impossible for him to eat anything. All in all he didn't consider these to be the best of conditions under which to ride into the warriors' enclave at the Clan Council's back, but there was nothing he could do about the situation now.

He wondered yet again what the chiefs hoped to accomplish with this meeting. They'd been forced by Ferenc and Simah's arrest to abandon their course of watchful inaction, that much was clear, but how they envisioned their future role Ruarshi wasn't sure. Ciarn would know but the healer decided not to ask him. He'd learn soon enough what the chiefs wanted from the Diamyo Elders.

When they arrived at Tomir's central square they found most of the other members of the Clan Council already there, along with their occasional small retinues of senior advisers. Ciarn rode forward to mingle with them but Ruarshi hung back, responding with only brief nods to the occasional glances cast his way. He felt conspicuous and out of place, more so than he had at almost any time since midsummer. It would only be worse inside the enclave, he knew. He was more than ready to go by the time Charis, leader of the Aesir clan, finally rode into the square.

Because he'd taken his place toward the end of the line that formed up in Charis' wake, he was one of the last to come in sight of the enclave's monstrous walls. As he rounded the final corner a wave of laughter and amused comment reached him, obviously prompted by the gaping hole next to the enclave's gates. The tree that had created the gap was gone, as were the others he and Aethel had seen, but the warriors hadn't yet had time to repair any of the damage the Sotarii had wrought. The chiefs hardly bothered to tone down their merriment as they rode through a double rank of silent Naishanti and passed into the shadow of the somewhat lopsided gatehouse. Ruarshi found himself wishing they'd made more of an effort to be quiet. The warriors were quite humiliated enough already, he was sure.

Once inside the gates Ruarshi dismounted, handed his reins off to a novice warrior, and was ushered along with the others into the enclave's Council Chamber. He'd been there once before to watch the initiation ceremony of his Doshae cousin Sabella, and the place hadn't changed at all in the intervening seventy or so years. Nor would he have expected it to. Ten tiers of stone benches divided into three sections rose in a semicircle around a rough wood-paneled floor on which sat seven chairs. Six of these were currently occupied by members of the Diamyo Council. Jair sat in the slightly larger chair in the middle, watching the chiefs and smiling placidly as they sorted themselves out and took their places. The Diamyo's gaze met Ruarshi's but didn't linger there, instead passing on to those few entering the chamber behind him.

The healer released a breath he hadn't been aware he was holding and moved forward to sit in the fifth row, where the most junior chiefs were settling in. That would leave his back exposed to a roomful of warriors, some of whose expressions were far less benevolent than

Jair's, but the fact that no one seemed surprised to see him was oddly reassuring. Anyone who wished him ill would have had plenty of time to plan, which rather ruled out the need for an overexcited youngster to attack him in full view of the Elders. All bets would be off once the meeting was adjourned, though. He would have to keep his wits about him when he left the Chamber.

Once the room had filled, the doors were closed and Jair stood to welcome the chiefs to the enclave. During the rote recitation of archaic language that followed, Ruarshi took the opportunity to glance around the room. The atmosphere was tense but didn't seem to be unduly so given the reason for the Clan Council's visit. None of the warriors would enjoy watching their chiefs challenging their Diamyo superiors. Such scenes tended to strain the loyalties of even the least punctilious Miriyanti.

Ruarshi turned back toward the floor, resigning himself to an uncomfortable wait. After Charis and Jair had finished reassuring each other of how glad they were to meet at such an auspicious time, and all the chiefs and Diamyo Elders had risen individually to add their sentiments to the already cloying air inside the Chamber, the actual business of the assembly got underway.

Charis began with a tactfully phrased demand that Jair release the High Sotarii before the day's end. The Diamyo First refused, but gently, noting that a delegation of healers was being allowed in to see them regularly where they were being held at the Tirae clan circle and that they'd had no complaints as of yet about the conditions of their captivity. The old Aesir then suggested that the Clan Council take charge of any trial that might be conducted regarding the 'Danish treaty,' a request that Jair chose to dodge, not responding to it definitively one way or the other. Charis had slightly better luck with her third sally, which involved the Clan Council acting as an arbitrator in order to settle the current disagreements between the warriors, the Sotarii, and the Seers. The Diamyo First stated that he wanted to meet with the seven most senior chiefs two days hence to discuss that possibility, if such an arrangement were to prove agreeable to his honored guests. After a brief colloquy with those sitting around her, Charis acceded to Jair's proposal. And that was the end of that. A few more formalities and they would be done.

Elyon rose from his seat just before Charis could begin the concluding invocations.

"One more minor matter, honored Aesir, if you will allow. There is one among your party, Ruarshi *stamm* Doshae, whom we would like to ask to stay behind. We are aware of the Writ he submitted to you. We wish to question him. As you must know, he has recently been involved in the deaths of six Naishanti."

The Diamyo had to speak louder and louder as he went on in order to be heard over the growing noise of competing voices. By the time he'd finished most of the warriors were on their feet. Some looked angry, others jubilant.

Ruarshi had remained seated, his fingers curled tightly around the edge of the bench, quite sure he couldn't have risen just then even if he'd wanted to. He kept his eyes on Jair and saw a flash of something very like fear cross the man's face.

Nerthu have mercy. He was witnessing a mutiny.

The doors to the Chamber burst open and the room began to dissolve into chaos. No weapons had been allowed into the meeting but Ruarshi suspected that the lack would be remedied soon enough. He heard running footsteps outside in the yard.

"We have no right to make such a request." Jair stood facing Elyon. His powerful voice was easily audible over the din. "The Clan Council's jurisdiction over Ruarshi Illyana is absolute. Only they can question him regarding those deaths."

"Only they can punish him," Elyon countered. "The matter of questioning is a much grayer area. By your leave, Charis."

Without waiting for the chief's assent, the Diamyo gestured to someone in the back of the room. Ruarshi stood and managed somehow not to flinch when two Naishanti grasped him by the upper arms and pulled him roughly out into the aisle.

"Indeed, you do not have my leave, *Tai* Diamyo," Charis said, her posture rigid as she looked back at the healer.

"Nor do you have mine," Jair added.

"We do not require yours." Elyon stood smiling as Beorn, Aerik, and Cyrin moved to flank him. "You are deposed. Honored Aesir, I apologize for overriding your will in this but the six dead are *ours*, not yours. I would ask that you and the rest of the Clan Council leave now. I will send you a message shortly regarding the requests you made here today."

Ruarshi was dimly aware that Ciarn was shouting his name but he had no attention to spare for it, his concentration being focused instead on the need to keep the Naishanti from breaking his wrist or arm as they forced him up the stairs and out of the Chamber. The courtyard

was a swirl of frenetic activity, some of it bloody, and the sheer number of warriors milling about precluded any thoughts of escape. He'd
have at least a dozen of them on him before he made it to one of the
broken sections of the wall, and even a Nerthi's magic wouldn't enable
him to hold off so many.

His attempt to lessen the pressure on his right arm was countered
by a blow to the stomach that left him weak-kneed and gasping. He
hadn't yet recovered when the warriors shoved him into a small, cold
room and slammed the door behind him.

Once he could sit up properly, Ruarshi took stock of his surroundings. A tiny window that admitted a narrow shaft of diffuse sunlight. A
broken bench along one wall. A chamber pot in the corner. And a
dense, thick magical weave that covered every square inch of the walls
and ceiling, one that he couldn't hope to get through if he had a month
to work on it.

A cell, in short. He wouldn't be leaving it until they let him.

✴ ✴ ✴

Slan applauded politely as Wil's arrow once again missed its target and
ended up embedded in the wall behind it. He turned to look at her
sourly.

"It's this rotten bow, I'm telling you," he said, only half joking. "It
was made for Miriyanti and you're the only ones who can use it. Give
me a good Welsh bow and—"

"And you'll probably clear out the entire courtyard instead of only
half of it." Aethel was sitting nearby on an empty barrel. It had been
his vantage point throughout the match as he kept up an accurate, if
tactless, running commentary on their poor performance. Both Wil and
Slan felt an identical need to shoot things but neither of them had been
worth a damn at it all afternoon.

"I think you should join us," Slan said, pulling an arrow from the
mud at her feet and cleaning its point against her thigh. She held it out
to him along with her bow. "You must be good at it or else you
wouldn't feel so free to criticize."

"Uh—"

"Well, come on. My ten-year-old second cousin could outshoot me
today."

Aethel slid off the barrel and took the bow from her with apparent
reluctance. She handed him the arrow and stood back, arms crossed, as

he stepped up to the mark and took aim.

A red hawk chose that moment to dive screeching into the circle. Ruarshi's brother lowered the bow, swearing, and glared at the bird until it settled onto the arch above the gates.

"What's wrong with that thing?" he asked.

"Mites?" Slan suggested.

One of the northerners, probably a Geroni to judge by his clothing, left the circle's living quarters and strode over toward the hawk. It rose in an agitated loop before subsiding once again onto its perch.

"What's he doing?" Wil asked.

"Trying to calm his familiar, I hope. They must be useful for hunting but I can't imagine anyone wanting to bond themselves to a bird. Shoot, good-brother." Slan pointed imperiously toward the target.

"All right. Stand back."

Aethel's expression changed ever so subtly right before he let the arrow fly. Wil knew without having to look that he and Slan had just been taken. Sometimes the man was almost painfully easy for him to read, especially in comparison to his brother.

The Sotaru laughed when he caught Slan's scowl and gestured airily toward the target. His arrow hadn't hit it quite dead center but it hadn't missed it by much, either.

"Not as badly out of practice as I thought. Shall I go retrieve the arrow? I wouldn't want your next shot to split it."

Wil was relieved to see that Slan chose to be amused rather than offended by Aethel's remark. It could have gone either way. He wandered out into the middle of the courtyard, intending to put a stop to the contest for the time being, when he heard a voice he knew.

"Open the goddamn gates! Open them! *Now!*"

It was Lorion, coming in at a gallop. Wil dove forward but the Geroni was both closer to the gates and faster than he was. The clansman pulled the bar off and swung the left door inward just in time to admit the Naishanti. The man was as wild-eyed as his lathered horse. He pulled up so hard that the animal was very nearly forced back onto its haunches.

Slan was at her brother's side instantly. "What is it?"

"Elyon, Aerik, Beorn. And Cyrin." Lorion clearly needed time to catch his breath, but he just as obviously didn't intend to slow the flow of words. "They've taken over. While Ruarshi was there. Jair—I think they've taken him, too—is trying to scuttle the whole thing. The Tirae clan circle. He needs as many of us as possible. Now. To free the High

Sotarii."

Slan was off, running toward the stables and shouting at the top of
her lungs toward those in the yard who hadn't been within earshot of
Lorion's report. Aethel and the northerner were headed toward the living quarters. Wil stayed where he was, looking up at the Naishanti.
There was blood on the man's tunic.

"Is he still alive?"

Lorion knew he wasn't talking about Jair. "I don't know. Go there.
Find him and stay with him. They won't stop you. We're too busy
killing each other to worry about lesser distractions. Once we release
Ferenc and Simah they'll get him out of there." The warrior wheeled
his exhausted horse around. "Tell Sister I've gone ahead. It's a blood-
bath, Wil. Nerthu help us." He drove his heels viciously into his
mount's sides and plunged back through the gate.

The Welshman found that he could move again. He darted into the
stable and threw a saddle on the horse closest to hand. Slan and a
dozen other Miriyanti were already doing the same.

"Lorion's on his way to the Tirae circle. I'm going to find Ruarshi,"
he told her. She threw him a pale glance and nodded. "I'll expect to see
you all there by sundown."

"You will," she said.

He led his horse out into the yard and jumped onto its back, the
pain in his hips hardly an impediment at this point. The hall and living
quarters were emptying rapidly as word of the mutiny spread. He cut
his way impatiently through the growing crowd and urged the mare
into a gallop as soon as he'd left the confines of the circle.

Wil hardly noticed the streets through which he rode. Only when
he'd arrived at the perimeter of the warriors' enclave did he again take
real note of his surroundings. He'd come to the place from the east
rather than the south but it didn't appear that he'd have to circle around
it to get in. There was a rather large hole right in front of him that
would suit his purposes nicely.

He dismounted and approached the wall, maneuvering his way with
some caution through the splintered gap. What he saw on the other
side of it horrified him. At least two dozen bodies lay scattered in the
mud of the enclave's yard, some of them with terrible wounds that far
exceeded what was necessary to separate one's soul from one's body.
Why had he ever thought the Miriyanti were less brutal than the Europeans?

It was Ruarshi's pernicious influence, of course. He'd made the mistake of thinking the healer's people must be like him in all the ways that truly mattered. What an idiot he was.

As he picked his way carefully through the carnage, a Naishanti ducked out of a low building to his right and approached him.

"What do you want here?" the man asked without preamble.

"I'm looking for Ruarshi Illyana."

"Why?"

"No particular reason. I'm his former *pir*."

"Are you?" The Naishanti looked him up and down, smiling. "No harm in a visit then, is there? Come with me."

Wil wanted to collapse with relief. Ruarshi had survived the initial slaughter. What he did instead was follow the warrior back through the doorway from which the man had originally emerged, into what he thought must be some sort of barracks. His opinion changed when his eyes adjusted to the dim light and he noticed the substantial locks on each of the eight doors that lined one side of the hall. The Naishanti led him to stand before the door at the far end.

"You've a visitor. He tells me he used to be your *pir*. I'm going to open the door and let him in. If you so much as move while it's open I'll slit his throat. Do you understand?"

"... Yes." Ruarshi's voice sounded oddly muffled.

Wil barely had time to register the pressure of a knife against his neck before the warrior had the door unlocked and opened.

Ruarshi sat motionless on the stone floor of the room, his legs crossed and his hands in his lap.

"Was this fellow really your *pir*?"

"Yes."

The tip of the knife pricked the Welshman's skin and he felt a thin line of blood trickle down into the collar of his shirt.

"Careful, healer. You have to move in order to speak. What would you do, I wonder, if I were to push the blade in a little farther? Could you do anything at all to stop me?"

Silence and stillness. Wil was considering how best to extricate himself from the situation when the Naishanti gave him a sudden push.

"Enjoy your visit."

The door closed and the Welshman dropped to his knees in front of his friend.

"Ruarshi?" Wil reached out hesitantly and took the healer's chin in his hand.

The Illyana drew in a shuddering breath before he spoke.

"I won't ask why you came here because I know the answer. If I didn't love you I'd tell you what a fool you are."

The Welshman jerked his hand away as though Ruarshi's skin had burned him. "Don't. Just... don't." They were speaking to each other in Welsh. If the guard were listening in he'd glean no information from this conversation. "Our friends have gone to release the two who are supposed to be in charge of this country. The whole rebellion will be over once they find their way here."

The healer's eyes widened. Wil chuckled and sat back on his heels. "Quite the antidote to a sour mood, isn't it? The whole ruckus interrupted the most fascinating archery match. I had no idea that your brother was a marksman."

"He used to be our family's chief source of rabbit meat. What's it like out there?"

The Welshman grimaced. "Ugly. The yard is... a mess. How much of it did you see?"

"Enough." The ghost of a smile flitted across Ruarshi's face. "There's something strangely familiar about all this, isn't there? If only Sebastian were to hand, I'd ask for a glass of wine."

Wil nodded. "Being locked in small rooms is highly overrated."

The healer stood and stretched. "I would simply blast my way out but they've got the entire room shielded."

"Too bad. There's a nice big hole in the outer wall not thirty yards away."

"I noticed. You missed quite a meeting. The chiefs are trying to get themselves deeply involved in the politics of our capital city for the first time in about a millennium. I will be curious to hear our erstwhile leaders' comments on the development."

The Welshman rose from his crouch and sat on the small part of the built-in bench that was still intact.

"Ruarshi..." The topic could prove to be a touchy one but he decided to broach it anyway. "I want you to come with us to Wales."

"You know I—"

"Have obligations here. Yes. After today the Clan Council can stick those up their honored backsides, as far as I'm concerned. Come back to Miriyan later to serve out your ten years. After I'm dead."

The healer's voice was soft. "Do you have any idea how tempting that is?"

Wil's heart leapt. This was the first crack he'd detected in Ruarshi's resolve when it came to this particular issue. But it had, after all, been an extraordinary day. "It's meant to be. This country of yours is too damn cold, too damn dark, and too damn dangerous. We were together thirty years in Europe, which is not exactly a peaceful place, but nobody actually managed to stab you until we got back here. Doesn't that strike you as a sign from on high?"

Ruarshi chuckled. "And how do you see me and my small family fitting into your little Welsh backwater? I assume you would like it to remain a backwater. It might not if three Miriyanti show up there."

"The locals will manage. My people are nothing if not resilient. We all adapt quickly to sudden unexpected changes. Did I never tell you that when I first spotted you lying on that rock, I thought you were a woman?"

"... No."

"Yes. The illusion lasted until you started trying to cough up your lungs. Then I realized my mistake."

"And came rushing over in a fortunately futile attempt to catch the plague yourself."

"No self-respecting Welshman would have let himself be put off by your feeble protestations. And it was exposure that was doing you in at that point, not the disease."

"I know." The healer paused for a moment and then went on, still speaking quietly. "I'll have to ask Slan about it first."

The Welshman felt a tight knot deep inside himself begin to dissolve. He hadn't even known it was there. "You'll come?"

"I rather think I will. After making the chiefs feel as guilty as is humanly possible about the way their meeting ended. They'll grant me a stay."

"Okay. Good. Now that we've got that settled, help me decide: do we live in a marsh or a bog?"

Wil was still steering their discussion from one bit of nonsense to another when, about an hour later, they were interrupted by a distant hubbub that gradually resolved itself into the sounds of celebration. Men and women were shouting and laughing; some were even singing. Their conversation limped to a halt as they listened and a few minutes later the door to Ruarshi's cell flew open.

Brion came in first followed by four more young Naishanti, all of them at least half drunk. The healer rose to face his former student. Only belatedly did Wil see the dagger in the boy's hand. The Welshman surged up off the bench, too late to prevent Brion from bringing the blade up and using it, augmented by magic, to slice cleanly through Ruarshi's hair just above the strip of leather that bound it at the nape of his neck.

Wil wasn't sure what he was witnessing, but for a moment he was certain that the healer was going to faint. Then Brion leaned in and whispered something to him and the stricken look on his face eased a little. A very little. The warriors piled out of the room a few seconds later, Brion holding Ruarshi's hair up over his head like some kind of trophy.

The Welshman thought he might be sick. "What the hell was that?"

Ruarshi had his back pressed tightly against the wall. None of the color had yet returned to his face. "An insult. It's what one does to a man who can't protect his *chesida*."

"Christ, what—"

"Our side lost, Wil. We lost. Brion doesn't think Slan's injury is fatal. I suppose that's something."

The blood was pounding in Wil's ears. "I'd say it's past time we got you out of here. The next time that door opens—"

"Whatever it is you've got in mind, it won't work. Don't try it." They could already hear more footsteps coming down the hall. "We're outnumbered, you see."

Elyon was part of this next delegation. As was Aerik. Wil planted himself between Ruarshi and the Diamyo, his hands on his hips.

"No, Wil." The healer pushed him gently aside and stepped forward. "What is it, Elyon?" He sounded more tired than anything else.

The Diamyo slapped Ruarshi hard across the face, addressing him by one of the vilest epithets in the Miriyanti language. "You're to come with us."

The healer recovered himself quickly and nodded. "I'm at your disposal." He turned to Wil. "Take my family with you when you go. Please. It's not going to be safe for them here for a very long time."

Elyon gestured impatiently toward one of the men with him. The warrior stepped forward, grabbed Ruarshi by the arm, and pulled him out the door.

The Welshman stumbled into the hall after them and kept following as they forced the healer out into the courtyard. Wil noted with a disengaged part of his mind that the bodies were now gone and twilight had fallen. Ruarshi turned to look back at him once more before disappearing through another doorway. What was waiting for him there, Wil didn't know.

He never actually decided to stay at the enclave. It was more a matter of never convincing himself, or even trying to, of the need to leave. The evening went on without him. He ignored those who came and went and even those who spoke to him directly. They hardly existed as far as he was concerned.

He was shivering in the full darkness of night when Brion finally staggered out of the building carrying the healer in his arms. Wil rushed over to them, sparing barely a glance for the young man's desolate face.

"They didn't kill him," the Naishanti said hoarsely. "Not quite."

The Welshman laid a trembling hand on Ruarshi's arm. He couldn't see what damage the warriors had done but he could smell it. Blood. And burned flesh.

Wil moved two paces away and vomited into the mud. Then he wiped his mouth on his sleeve and turned back to the Naishanti.

"Bring him."

The three of them left the enclave through the front gates. None of the warriors they encountered made any effort to stop them.

Ardan was waiting for them outside with a sledge. The Welshman was far too tired to ask questions about how she'd known she would be needed. He and Brion settled Ruarshi into it and waited while the Chamani climbed in beside him. When she declared herself ready, Wil took up the reins, extended a hand to help the Naishanti onto the seat next to him, and drove them through the stillness of night to the healers' circle.

✳ ✳ ✳

Ruarshi woke up lying on his stomach. He was in a dark room with only the uncertain light of single candle flickering against his closed eyelids. Someone was there with him. The memory of a soft voice told him who it was even before she spoke again.

"Ruarshi?"

He opened his eyes and found her sitting in a narrow wooden chair by the head of the bed. She looked much older than she had the day before.

"Ardan." His voice was a rasp. His great aunt leaned forward with a mug of water and helped him up on his elbows to drink it. He finished that one and a second before he was satisfied. Only then did it occur to him that there was anything incongruous about what he'd just done.

He lowered his upper body carefully back onto the bed, his arms already shaking with the strain of supporting his own weight. "Why am I not in pain?"

"Because Mecheta is a very talented man. And because we need you. Here." She lifted a small object off a low table to her left and held it out to him. "You dropped this. I believe you should take it back now."

It was the knife Slan had given him. He hadn't expected to see it again. "No."

"Take it. And sit up."

His shortened hair tickled his cheek as he shifted to look at the Chamani more directly. A pulse of pain rippled down his back, all the way from his shoulders to his thighs. He gasped and blinked back tears, then angrily shoved himself up into a sitting position.

"And just what do you expect me to do with it?"

"Come with us to rescue your *chesida*. What else? Elyon clapped the warriors who opposed him into the cells under the Council Hall. The High Sotarii and exiles, too, as far as we know. He has granted permission for eight of us to visit the prisoners. We're going tonight. Now." Ardan rose, lifted one of his hands, and pressed the hilt of the knife into it. "I am truly sorry to ask this of you, but Mara is the only other Nerthi we have and she's in worse shape than you are. She may not survive."

Ruarshi stared down at the blade. "Do you have any notion how many guards there will be?"

"I don't know. It may not be as bad as you fear. Elyon doesn't expect resistance from healers."

"I had best eat something first."

"Mecheta is coming with food and loose clothing. He'll help you dress. We're taking a number of sledges with us so that we can transport the wounded back here. You and I will go in first."

The healer didn't look up when Ardan went to the door in response to a quiet knock. She slipped out as a somber Mecheta entered, carrying a tray and with a matching set of tunic and trousers thrown over one shoulder. Ruarshi thought he saw a cloak as well. The tunic looked mercifully soft and much too large. When the older man moved closer to the light of the candle, the Illyana realized that all the clothing was a deep healer's green. The choice of color would have been Ardan's, of course. He felt only indifference toward whatever meaning it was she'd intended to convey.

Mecheta offered him the bowl of stew with a small bow. The Illyana reached forward to take it but was brought up short by another wave of pain. This one was rather more all-encompassing than the last, touching even on the faint pink marks on his wrists, all that remained of the rope burns. The Chamani took his hand and held it tightly as his shivering subsided.

"If I may?" the older man asked diffidently. After a brief hesitation Ruarshi nodded. Mecheta shut his eyes and a blessed numbness swept through the healer's body.

"Numbing a person's nerves is a tricky business and not a skill I use very often," the Chamani said. "Eat. I will need to do this once more before we leave and then again when we arrive at the Council Hall. The effect doesn't last long."

"You could show me how to do it."

"One day I will. It's complicated. I doubt you could even retain it now. Eat, I said. If we delay too long we'll have the Diamyo breathing down our necks again."

Ruarshi lifted the bowl and began drinking the stew, hardly tasting it. When he came to the first small chunk of cooked meat he gagged, and was only barely able to keep what he'd already eaten in his stomach. He set the bowl carefully down on the pillow and turned away from it, swinging his legs over the edge of the bed.

Mecheta had been watching him. He took the remainder of the stew, well over half of it, out into the hall and set it on the floor while Ruarshi plucked the undershirt that someone had brought for him off of the bedpost. He was about to slip it on when he had a sudden thought.

"Is there a mirror in here?"

"Yes."

He dropped the linen garment onto the bed sheets and stood, holding onto the mattress until he found his balance. "Where is it?"

"Behind you. In the corner."

Ruarshi picked up the candle and made his way over to the mirror. It wasn't full-length but it told him what he needed to know.

Many of the scars would never disappear in spite of the prompt healing he had received. The marks left by the whip would fade with time but burned skin could never be restored to its former appearance. He didn't know who'd come up with the idea of pressing the heated iron bar to his back. He supposed he ought to be glad Miriyan produced such clumsy torturers. If they'd utilized some of the refinements he'd heard of in Europe, he'd have been unable to maintain the wall of silence that had been his last and only defense against them. It had been a close enough thing as it was.

Which jogged another memory. "Where's Wil?"

"He's here at the circle. Asleep, I hope. He sat in here with you all day. He wanted to be here when you awoke but Ardan opposed it. I believe she gave him something unusually strong to drink."

"He wasn't hurt?"

"No."

Ruarshi nodded and began donning his clothes. It took much longer than it should have. He was miserably weak. Pulling his boots on was a particular challenge. When he had finished, he picked the knife up off the bed and returned it to the side table. Without a belt he had no way to wear it. He didn't think he wanted it back anyway.

Mecheta supported him unobtrusively by the elbow as they left the room, made their way down the narrow hall, and went out into the night. There were dozens of healers mounted and waiting for them, with more outside the walls tending to the sledges Ardan had mentioned. Ruarshi wondered if he had misunderstood something.

"I thought that Elyon had specified eight...?"

"Which is all they'll see when we first go in. We're cheating."

"I don't think I should try to sit a horse."

"Not until you have to. Come on."

At a soft word from an old Illyana whose name Ruarshi couldn't recall, most of the healers turned and rode out through the gates. The sledges ghosted along with them, all save the one sitting closest to the walls. Only eight Miriyanti now remained in the yard. Ardan was there along with two other members of the Chamani Council. Mecheta and three other healers of very nearly equal strength and skill rounded out their number. It was not the sort of company in which, under normal circumstances, Ruarshi would ever have found himself.

As they walked slowly across the courtyard, Mecheta pointed to the unoccupied sledge. "You'll be riding in that until we reach the square. How are you holding up?"

"Not well." The old Chamani's technique for alleviating pain was, as he'd said, a temporary measure. It had been at most twenty minutes since he'd last sent his power coursing through Ruarshi's body and already the nerves in the Illyana's back felt raw again. The friction caused by his clothing wasn't helping matters.

Mecheta assisted him in getting up onto the back of the sledge, after which he muted Ruarshi's pain once more. The relief was not quite so complete this time. The Illyana opened his mouth to call attention to that fact but the older man spoke first.

"That's why I don't use this skill unless there's no other choice. The next time I do it there will be even less effect."

Ruarshi let his head fall back into the folds of the blanket on which he rested. "Then for god's sake let's get this over with."

"I'd like nothing better," Mecheta said, and with a flick of the reins the sledge lurched into motion.

The healer closed his eyes and lay still, enjoying the sensation of cool air drifting across his face. He realized very quickly, now that he was alone with his thoughts, that he wasn't able to concentrate on any one thing for more than a few spare seconds at a time. Slan's face came and went in his mind's eye, as did Wil's, Aethel's, Yael's, Lorion's. All interrupted by persistent flashes of scenes from the night before. Try as he might he couldn't seem to block those out. He could still see the whip in Aerik's hands, dripping with blood, and feel the heat of the room.

When Mecheta stopped the sledge at the edge of Tomir's central square, Ruarshi climbed off it as quickly as he could. He slipped on a patch of ice and fell, and was only narrowly able to avoid striking his head on a nearby wall. He stumbled again when he tried to rise and went back down to his knees. He remained in that position until Mecheta and Ardan appeared at his side. They took his arms and gently helped him up.

"I can't do what you've asked of me," he said, once he'd gotten himself propped up against the wall and the world had stopped spinning. "It's going to be a disaster."

"It already is a disaster," Ardan said. She still held his arm, though doing so served no practical purpose at this point. "Even if you cannot help us, Ruarshi, we will still make an attempt to free the prisoners. Elyon has left us with no choice. The Miriyan that he's creating is not a place we wish to live."

Ruarshi allowed his head to fall back until he was looking up at the stars. "I can probably make it through the door and fall on them. Is that what you had in mind?" He had intended the words as a joke but he felt his throat tightening as he said them.

"That will do, as long as you take care to fall on *all* of them," Ardan replied.

The healer attempted a smile. "I plan to afflict them with strokes. Sever an artery in their brains. Easy enough to heal and with no lasting ill effects, assuming someone can get to them quickly. I understand we

M J McBRIDE

have other priorities. I'll leave that decision to you."

His great aunt took a moment to respond and when she did it was only to suggest that he mount up. The guards at the door needed to see them all riding in. She moved off and Mecheta stepped forward to help him into the saddle of one of the smallest horses Ruarshi thought he had ever seen. She was a placid little mare, unlikely to shake him off, and probably chosen for him for that very reason.

Before Mecheta took up the reins of his own mount he clasped Ruarshi's hand again. A wave of warmth swept through him. It left a fair amount of pain behind but the healer nevertheless found himself sagging in the saddle in relief. He hadn't realized just how bad it had become.

The ride across the square went all too quickly. From within the folds of his hood, which he had pulled up over his head only after a sharp reminder from Ardan, he could see two warriors waiting for them, one to each side of the iron-banded door that offered the only access to the cells beneath the Hall. His heart was beating much too fast as they reined in about ten yards from the Naishanti. Blood loss could account for some of that, he supposed.

Ardan dismounted and began speaking with the warriors. Ruarshi waited until the rest of the Chamani were moving before he slid off his horse, hoping their activity would make his clumsiness less noticeable. The tactic apparently worked; the Naishanti were spending no more time looking at him than they were at any of the others. Good.

One of the guards knocked on the door and called to someone inside. Ruarshi heard an answering hail and then, startlingly loud, the sound of the bolt being thrown back.

Time to go. Ruarshi stepped carefully forward over the icy ground until he stood at Ardan's side. As the door began to swing open he reached out to touch the two guards and dropped them simultaneously without a sound. He then reached into the growing gap and yanked the third warrior forward, pulling her partway out onto the ice even as she spasmed and collapsed beneath his hand. Several of the Chamani helped him move her out of the way as he pushed the door wide and looked down at the worn stone staircase that awaited them. Fortunately it was empty.

Ardan strode forward without hesitation, pulling Ruarshi with her. They descended side by side and had made it halfway to the turn in the stair when another Naishanti appeared below them. His great aunt greeted the man with a smile.

"We're with the healers' delegation. Could you tell me how many you've got down here?"

"Plenty," the man grumbled, continuing up toward them. "Most will need your attention. Where—?"

The instant the warrior came within reach Ruarshi had him. He fell as easily and silently as the others. The healer, his right hand still tangled in the man's clothes, almost went down with him. By the time he'd regained his balance he was shaking again.

"How many more?" he whispered.

"I don't know," Ardan said. "Let's find out."

They pushed the Naishanti's twitching body to the side of the stairway and went on, turning right at the landing and proceeding slowly down the remaining ten steps until they stood on the cold stone floor of the prison. A wide corridor stretched before them, fitfully illuminated by an occasional torch and lined on the right side by a row of cells. Narrower perpendicular hallways branched off to their left at regular intervals. The one they could see was also lined with cells and presumably all the others were as well. Ruarshi took a deep breath as they went forward. He'd had no idea the place was so large. The warriors could easily be holding hundreds of prisoners.

The soft tread of footsteps warned them of the presence of a fifth guard. They saw her as they drew even with the third hallway.

"Hello," Ardan said. "We're here with the healers."

The Naishanti was frowning as she approached them, her hand hovering over her sword hilt. "Laszo should be with you. What's keeping him?"

"I have no idea. I would suppose he's following with the rest of the Chamani."

The woman seemed disinclined to trust Ardan's guileless expression. "He knows better. You two, come with me." She motioned for them to precede her. Ruarshi turned as if to obey, waited until she drew near enough, and then pivoted back around. The warrior had her sword half out of its sheath before his hand brushed her cheek. She stumbled and went down.

Ruarshi heard movement off to his right. He whirled to find himself confronted by a sixth guard, a big Naishanti who must have seen what he'd just done. The man's sword was drawn and ready. The healer sent out a pulse of power to snap it off at the hilt and leaped sideways into the main corridor, trying to put as much distance as he could between himself and Ardan. The warrior wrapped him in a shield, using

Ruarshi's own momentum against him in an attempt to slam his back
into the opposite wall. So much for his anonymity.

The healer wrenched himself around at the last moment and his
right shoulder collided with the stone. His field of vision went white.
When he could see again he was on his knees and the Naishanti was
standing in front of him, a small curved dagger in his hand and blood
running down his chest. Its point of origin was low on the man's
throat, where a small triangle of silver protruded from the flesh beneath his larynx. Ruarshi was only barely able to get himself out of the
way as the warrior toppled forward.

His fall exposed Ardan, who was standing in the hallway looking at
the body with a disgusted expression on her face. Only then did Ruarshi understand that the knife in the Naishanti's neck was hers.

"That's a key, isn't it? They always underestimate healers." His great
aunt bent down and began fiddling with the iron ring that held the key.
When it became clear that she'd have to unbuckle the man's belt to remove it, she pulled her knife from the bloody wound and used it to cut
through the stiff leather. She rose again with the key in her hand.

"Stay here, Ruarshi. Certainly some of the Naishanti in these cells
must be uninjured and will be able to help you. I'll tell them where you
are."

Ardan walked back the way they had come, shouting for the healers
waiting on the stairs. As they hurried down into the prison Ruarshi
rose, utilizing the wall as support. Though he'd never had proper Naishanti training, he'd had Slan. He knew the passive defensive was never
a good strategy. He kept going, deeper into the maze of cells.

He ran across no more guards. What he found instead was a small
dark doorway in the left wall at the end of the corridor. He thought he
knew what was behind it. The French would call it an oubliette. To
most Miriyanti it was simply the Pit.

He pushed at the warped wood of the door and it swung inward
with only minimal resistance. A torch burned somewhere down below,
emitting light just sufficient to enable him to navigate the narrow, steep
stairway in safety.

The first thing Ruarshi noticed was the hole in the floor. Its iron
cover had been thrown back and lay off to one side. His eyes next
came to rest on the man crouched at the edge of the small room, directly under the only torch. He was about Seggita's age, the healer
thought. The face under the thick fall of long white hair was a mask of
blue tattoos. The greater part of the man's neck was also decorated

with the sinuous lines of ink. His eyes were as black as Ruarshi's own and they followed him as he stepped into the room and approached the mouth of the pit.

"How many of the Nerthii are in there?"

"Mara escaped with injuries, as you must know. Aurel remains unaccounted for. As for the rest…" The man rose and lifted the torch from its bracket, holding it out to him. "You won't be satisfied until you see it for yourself."

Ruarshi took the torch and bent down over the hole in the floor, his movements far from graceful. Soon the pain in his back would be more than he could bear.

Yes, they were dead. Everyone who'd studied with him along with Niklas and Coewyn.

Ruarshi jerked away from the pit and dropped the torch. It sputtered against the stone but continued to burn.

"You're a Seer. You should have prevented this."

"I would very much have liked to. I wanted them to live. Miriyan needed them to live. I will have to see what can be accomplished with only four of you remaining." The Seer retrieved the torch and returned it to its bracket. "You might be interested to know that in many of the futures I foresaw, both you and Seggita ended up down there as well. I made the mistake half a millennium ago of telling him that I'd witnessed his death and describing the manner of it." He tilted his head toward the pit's mouth before returning his gaze to Ruarshi's face. "We were having an argument at the time. I'm not usually so stupid. So he chose a different time and place to die and did everything he could to ensure that you in particular would survive. He always did have a wicked sense of humor."

"None of that explains why you allowed this to happen."

"Elyon moved sooner than I had anticipated, along with Mirror Lake's own little group of rebels. They won't be troubling us any longer but I and my allies were too busy yesterday to make it to Tomir, and our agents also number among the dead. Frightened Seers who don't understand what they're looking at tend to make grave mistakes. Are you still following what I'm telling you?"

Ruarshi thought he was, in spite of the pain and everything else. "Yes."

"Good. I know you're about to leave Miriyan for a time. It will make no difference in the long run. Go to Wales. Recover yourself. Say your goodbyes to your *pir*. And when all that is done, come back to us. Bring your good-brother with you. We will need you to help bind Europe more closely to Miriyan even while with our left hand we further its disintegration. If we do not do this, our country will cease to exist before you reach your middle years."

Ruarshi stared up at the Seer. He thought he should probably be alarmed about what he was hearing, but only one part of what Casimir had just said held his attention.

"My good-brother?"

"Yes." Casimir smiled. "You Nerthii have a way of finding each other. It's one of the mysteries about which our archives remain silent."

The Seer continued speaking but Ruarshi could no longer follow him or even hear more than every third word. There was a rushing noise in his ears that seemed to be steadily increasing in volume. He lowered himself carefully to the floor and closed his eyes. When he opened them again he was lying on his side and Casimir was kneeling over him. Then Ardan was there, talking with the Seer. The two seemed not unfamiliar with each other. Ruarshi tucked that thought away for later examination as he felt himself being lifted up off the floor and carried up the stairs. He forced his eyes open once more and was eventually able to focus on Casimir's narrow face. His ears cleared long enough for him to overhear a snippet of their conversation.

"It's over?" That was Ardan.

"Yes," the Seer replied. "It's over. For now."

✳ ✳ ✳

Wil leaned back against the sloping convex surface of the oven, enjoying the comfortable warmth it retained even at this hour of the night. He expected Ruarshi back soon. His farewell dinner with his parents and siblings would surely be over before too long if it hadn't ended already. The Welshman doubted that the Nerthi would be in any mood to embark on a conversation with his erstwhile *pir* when he returned, which was exactly why Wil was sitting up in his kitchen rather than sleeping. He'd chosen his moment with some care.

He thought it might be a bit early yet to attempt this, but Slan didn't agree and he'd decided to defer to her judgment. She spent far more time with Ruarshi than did anyone else, in spite of the fact that they'd all been sharing space in Wil and Ginevra's house for well over a month now. Slan and Ruarshi hadn't been able to return to their own home in the wake of the rebellion's suppression. It had been too thoroughly vandalized in their absence and they had salvaged very little.

Wil winced and shifted, trying to lessen the pain in his hips and knees. It seemed to be growing worse by the day but he thought that was probably an illusion caused by stress and anxiety and other emotions traditionally thought of as inappropriate to the aftermath of a victory. The near total elimination of their enemies, begun during the bloody attack on the warriors' enclave and continued under the meticulous direction of Casimir, the High Sotarii, and a vengeful Jair, hadn't done much to bring relief to any of them. Though the hurt and fury in Slan's eyes had abated somewhat, she still had a painful chest wound to deal with while at the same time she worked to renew her lapsed bond to her infant son. She continued to insist that she would never again wear warrior's blue. Ginevra watched them all worriedly and tried to deflect Lucia's questions about the bodies she'd seen laid out to one side of the marketplace the previous week. The Welshman for his part felt that he truly would suffocate if they didn't leave Miriyan soon. The intensity of his anger with the country's leaders, deceased and yet living, was just as strong as it had ever been and now it had a new and unexpected target: Ardan. Even if it had been necessary for her to use Ruarshi the way she had, Wil couldn't forgive her for it. He hoped he'd never see the old woman again in his life.

Ruarshi himself was of particular concern, not because of what he did but because of what he didn't do. Since the night the Diamyo had whipped and scorched the skin from his back, he had been unfailingly polite and gentle with everyone, when he wasn't simply silent and blank. He didn't complain. He didn't joke. Wil and Slan both knew him quite well enough to realize that he wasn't simply maintaining his usual inscrutable façade. This was something different and vastly worse.

Even the extraordinary ceremony that had taken place on the third day of the midsummer festival, two days ago now, had provoked no reaction from him beyond the prescribed choreography of bows. In the presence of Casimir and the entire Sotarii Council, as well as a good number of clan chiefs and spectators, he had been released from his Writ of Submission. Both copies of the document had been ritually burned. Afterward Simah had proclaimed that henceforth all Nerthii were to be recognized as such and addressed by that title, and had taken Ruarshi under the joint protection of the Sotarii Council and the Seers. Casimir had repeated that pledge on behalf of Mirror Lake. Ruarshi, the others, and any Nerthii who might come forward in the future were now as safe as any power in Miriyan could make them. The move came a bit later than it could have, though, and the man Wil knew would have wasted little time in pointing that out to anyone who would listen.

The Welshman's task on this night was to find that man and cajole, goad, or bully him back into existence. If Ruarshi proved recalcitrant he didn't know that he'd have the heart to push him too hard. He felt that he'd lost the right to do that somewhere along the line.

Wil sat up straighter when he heard the back door swing open. The light in the kitchen wasn't good, consisting only of the watery bluish illumination coming in the small window and the dull glow given off by the banked embers in the fireplace, but Ruarshi saw him the moment he entered the room.

"Good evening, Wil."

"How was dinner?"

The former healer shrugged and sat down next to the Welshman. "Interesting. Father was civil. Mother gave me a kiss. Yael and Aethel informed me that they plan to visit us in Wales. They may even stay the winter."

"Why Aethel?"

Ruarshi looked at him, a glint in his eye. "He doesn't want to feel left out. Who told Yael that Lorion was going?"

"Lorion?" Wil guessed.

"Did he? I hope he doesn't suppose this will make me go easier on him as an instructor. I remember the bruises he gave me. Why aren't you asleep?"

"I'm feeling restless. Ready to be gone."

"I can help you get to sleep if you like."

"No, thank you. Not yet. I'm enjoying the peace and quiet. I regret Lucia's having passed on to Davyt her enthusiasm for screaming."

The Nerthi rose and walked slowly to the fireplace. "Was he very loud tonight?"

The Welshman smiled tiredly. "Yes. Shortly after you left he started fussing. Slan was asleep so Ginevra and I tried to quiet him but we didn't have much success. Slan woke up and took over."

"That was my doing, I'm afraid."

The statement made no sense. "What?"

"Mecheta's grim prognosis regarding my recovery was only partially correct, at best."

"Your link to Davyt...?"

"Seems to coming back. In fits and starts. And what he's getting through it is upsetting him."

That was an opening. Not much of one but Wil decided he could use it. "What can be done about it?" he asked carefully.

"I could cut him off."

"Is that what you want to do?"

"No."

"And what are the alternatives?"

"I could ask Mecheta if it's possible to make the bond function in one direction only. Being completely alone in my own head is unnerving."

"That may be worth looking into. Does Slan know about this?"

"No. I wasn't even sure until late yesterday of what was happening."

"What cleared it up for you?"

Ruarshi laughed, a ghastly sound. "Do you really want to know?"

"Of course. I wouldn't have asked otherwise."

"I fell asleep over a book in the front room. I didn't rest long, maybe five minutes. For the entire duration of the nap I felt content, satisfied with my life because I was warm and my stomach was full. Not a normal thought for an adult."

"It sounds normal enough to me, Ruarshi. I feel that way a lot when I'm in warm climates. I even feel that way here when I sit close enough to a fire."

The Nerthi was silent for a long time. Wil waited, watching him, unwilling to break the stillness with any further comment of his own. His only fear was that Ruarshi would cut their conversation off there and bury himself in a book until sunrise, his usual routine of late.

He did not. "I should have fought them, Wil."

"Would you be talking to me now if you had?"

"I don't know. It hardly matters."

"It matters to me. Seven of them came to get you. Were there ever any fewer than that with you?"

"Not that I can remember. I've already had this argument with myself so often..."

"Then do me the courtesy of repeating it one more time. Could you have gotten away from seven at once?"

"Not without the personal intervention of Nerthu."

"You're going to have to explain your mistake to me, then, because I don't understand it."

"I survived. My students did not. If I'd done something... Why have I spent all this time studying with warriors if I intended to do nothing with what they taught me? Can you answer that? I can't. All I did was lure the other Nerthii into a disaster."

"Say you had gotten yourself killed by making it clear that you can still use your power. Would this have changed anything about what happened to the others?"

"It might have created some chaos, given them more time. I'll never know. No one will ever know. I am certain, though, that I valued my personal survival too highly while I was in that room."

"Ruarshi…" Wil paused, swallowed, and continued. "If Brion had come out that door carrying your dead body, I wouldn't have left the enclave either. So the decisions you made did save at least one life in addition to your own. And I don't believe you went into that prison the very next night because your highest concern was preserving yourself."

The healer had turned to look at him. "The prison. Yes. The people I actually tried to murder were the unlucky Naishanti who'd pulled guard duty that night. There was nothing redemptive about any of that. What do you mean you wouldn't have left the enclave?"

"You know what I meant, and don't change the subject. If you hadn't been there, do you really think the healers would have succeeded? That they would have been able to walk through all those guards, set everyone free, and send Elyon running? I don't. You used what Slan taught you in exactly the right ways, so what's the real problem?"

Ruarshi watched him for a moment more before returning his gaze to the flames. "What you just said. It helps. Thank you. But I still want out of this skin."

Something in his former *pir's* tone caused the hair to rise on the back of Wil's neck. "Explain."

"I've wondered lately, Wil, if the Europeans sentenced to die by immolation don't end up welcoming their punishment. As a means of burning away the filth of having been misused."

"I don't know why they would. None of the filth is theirs. Or yours."

"You're wrong, Wil. I wasn't faultless before this happened and I'd never argue otherwise, but now I contaminate everything I touch. It's not a matter of feeling unclean. That isn't the right word. There's a sort of poison that you absorb from people like Aerik. I don't know if I'll ever be rid of it. Sometimes—right now, in fact—I think I can smell it on my breath, and that if you were too close to me I'd kill you with it."

A statement like that couldn't be allowed to stand. Wil rose and approached the healer, who shook his head and backed away, his hands held out in front of him to ward the Welshman off.

"Christ, I didn't mean it literally. *Don't.*"

Wil stopped moving. A heartbeat later so did Ruarshi. "It just occurred to me that I haven't seen you touch anyone in days. I'd like to fix that. I'm not suggesting a wrestling match. A hug, maybe?"

"Best not."

They stood staring at each other in the dimly lit kitchen. "I will do whatever you need me to do, Ruarshi, whenever you need it. So will Slan and Yael. Probably Lorion too, along with your worthless brother. Let us help."

The former healer took a deep, shuddering breath. "You're a better friend than I deserve."

"I'd say that people tend to end up with exactly the friends they deserve. I want you to make me a promise."

"I'll do my best. What is it?"

"When you start feeling like your breath is poison, you find your son and you hold him until that idea fades from your mind. Let him remind you that you're not what you think you are during your worst moments."

"He'll just cry if I do that."

"He's a baby! Of course he'll cry. That's normal. Let your life be normal for a while."

Ruarshi raised a hand to cover his eyes. He scarcely moved but his breathing was quick and uneven. It was all Wil could do to remain still and watch him struggle.

Eventually the hand came down and Ruarshi met his gaze. "I'll try," he said.

The Welshman nodded once, emphatically. "Good."

❋ ❋ ❋

The glint of sunlight on water forced Ruarshi to turn away from the sight of Miriyan's receding coastline before he was entirely ready to do so. He leaned his hip against the starboard rail of the ship and looked out over the gently heaving deck, holding his son to his chest and keeping one hand wrapped protectively around the sleeping infant's tiny head. Though he had lost his earlier mysterious talent for pacifying Davyt with a touch, he was now able to soothe the baby with a bit of rocking and humming. It was a vast improvement over the infant's prior tendency to fret and wail whenever he was in his father's presence, and would no doubt make it much easier for them all to sleep in the cramped quarters that they'd been allotted in the ship's stern.

Wil, standing next to him, snorted and nodded toward their captain. The Englishman had an exasperated expression on his face, not surprising given the fact that Lorion had been interrogating him ever since the newly minted Nerthi had stepped aboard a half hour before. The two shared no common language and their discussion was proceeding largely by means of gestures, which made it fairly easy for their audience to discern the gist of the current line of questioning.

"He can't be serious," the Welshman said.

"I'd be willing to bet he is," Ruarshi countered. "It's the same way he approaches his lessons. Only when he's convinced that he understands a task inside and out will he move, but then he throws everything he's got at it."

"Sounds dangerous."

"It's a style much better suited to breaking things than to putting them back together. Slan just laughs at my efforts to teach him caution. She tells me he'll never learn it and that I know nothing about it, anyway."

His *chesida* chose that moment to emerge from the low doorway to their left that gave access to their quarters. She was followed by Ginevra with an excited Lucia in tow.

Wil raised an eyebrow at his wife as she approached. "Tolerable?" he asked.

"Yes, of course," she replied, over her daughter's chatter. "We'll have more space than we did coming here. The bedding is cleaner than last time, too."

"I'll have to take your word for it," Slan said. "Everything smells strongly of wool and whale fat. How is Davyt?"

"Still asleep," the former healer said. "Is it possible for infants to suffer from seasickness?" Ruarshi himself never had.

Slan took the baby gently from his arms. He didn't stir. "I don't know. I'll trust you to take care of it if it is." The ship's sails snapped in the rising wind and she turned. It took her a few seconds to locate her brother. "Oh, no."

Lorion was halfway up the mainmast, clinging to a spar. He stopped and waved cheerily down to them when he became aware of their regard. The captain, who was bellowing and pointing emphatically down at the deck, he ignored. The rest of the crew seemed about evenly divided between irritation and amusement. One or two called up to him with incomprehensible advice.

"I'm not sure if I paid the captain enough for this," the Welshman said. "He might charge extra for a madman clambering around in his rigging."

"How much for two madmen?" Ruarshi asked, looking forward along the railing. He'd want to use warriors' magic, as Lorion had, to get himself up onto the ratlines. Once he'd managed that the rest of the climb shouldn't be too difficult. His good-brother had already made it very nearly to the top.

He darted forward before either Wil or Slan had time to object, dodged a crewman, and was twenty feet off the deck before he paused to look down. The captain's face was now quite red. Those who knew him better seemed resigned. Lorion shouted words of encouragement from above.

The Naishanti was nimbler than he was. Ruarshi had to stop twice on the way up to untangle himself and figure out the best way to proceed. The skin at his hips and shoulders pulled uncomfortably as he climbed but never crossed the threshold into actual pain. He put the still unfamiliar sensation out of his mind and glanced upward to see Lorion sitting on one of the ship's crosstrees, clutching the rope that supported the mast. It appeared to Ruarshi to be a rather precarious choice of vantage points but as the ship had no crow's nest it was probably the best they were going to do. With a last burst of effort and a little help from his good-brother, the former healer found himself straddling the opposite crosstree and grinning over at the man he now called his student.

"Windy, isn't it?" Lorion observed.

Ruarshi nodded in agreement, turning his head until the gusts blew the hair out of his eyes. "See anything interesting?"

"A lot of water. Some very small people."

"Some very small, angry people."

"It's not as though we're in the way up here. I intend to come up every day as long as the weather holds. Our quarters smell terrible."

"You'll want to do some carpentry work if you mean to make this a habit. It would likely be even more fun up here in a storm."

The Naishanti grinned. "Then tonight's lesson probably ought to cover the treatment for lightning strikes."

"There isn't one. You're either dead or you're not."

Lorion laughed and used his hold on the rope to pull himself to his feet. "This is really quite something. Are you going to go back?"

The change of subject was so abrupt that it took Ruarshi several seconds to understand what his good-brother was asking him.

"To Miriyan?"

"Right."

"Of course. When the time comes."

Lorion shook his head. "What if you'd rather do something else?"

"That's very nearly a certainty, but it won't change my answer."

"Then we're both out of our minds."

Ruarshi couldn't improve on that observation so he didn't try. Instead he looked out over the water, toward the southwest and Wales. Consideration of the future would wait. It would have to. There was plenty of the present to keep him occupied.

He rose, wrapped his arm around the mast and then leaned into it, closing his eyes. The sun on his face was warm and his stomach was full. He smiled. The thought was not his own, but in that moment it could have been.

**Nor Rises the Moon**

# Arrival

Ruarshi jerked his hat from his head and regarded the sodden blue velvet sullenly, cursing Haarnan and the wet weather under his breath. He pivoted in his saddle and shoved the cap impatiently under the strap that held his saddlebags, not really caring if it stayed put or not. Taking the overland route back to Miriyan hadn't been his idea, though it did coincide neatly with his own aims. If it hadn't, he'd gladly have left Haarnan—the seasickness-prone putative leader of their little group— staring after him from the quayside in Genoa as he sailed away for Gibraltar and points north.

He squinted back through the rain at the other members of his party. Etienne, directly behind him, looked to be as disgusted by the rain as Ruarshi was, scowling toward the sheer rock wall before them. Haarnan, coming up third, was staring upward and appeared to be paying no attention whatsoever to the rain streaming into his collar, or to the river rushing through the gorge beneath them. Javri's head was down and he couldn't see her face at all, couldn't tell what her opinion of their current situation was, but he thought he could guess well enough. The four mules carrying their baggage trailed behind Javri, their ears twitching in the downpour.

He was just about to turn away when he saw Haarnan's horse slip on the slick stones of the bridge. It struggled to regain its footing and failed, falling forward hard onto its knees.

Haarnan had already jumped away from his thrashing, squealing mount by the time Ruarshi reined in beside him. A quick once-over of the old Sotari told him the man hadn't been hurt in the accident, though he was growing more frightened by the moment as he realized how close he'd come to the edge of the bridge.

The condition of the mare was a different matter entirely.

Ruarshi got off his horse and went to the old man, drawing him with Javri's help firmly back toward the center of the stone expanse. The Naishanti raised her eyebrows at him in inquiry. Ruarshi shook his head.

"He's fine."

"Fine?" Haarnan yanked his arms from their grasp. "This animal damn near kills me and you think I'm *fine?*"

"Yes, I do," Ruarshi said. "And as I'm the senior healer here, my diagnosis stands. Why don't you sit down before you fall down. We'll walk the horses across the rest of the bridge."

"I will get my saddlebags first, thank you."

Haarnan must have been more rattled than Ruarshi had believed, to have given in with such minimal complaint to his direction. "Wait for Etienne to calm the animal first," he said, noting without surprise that the boy was already doing what he could to ease the mare's panic.

They stood in the rain in silence until Etienne raised his head and nodded. The Sotari bent forward to cut his bags from their lashings and then stalked toward the far side of the bridge. When Ruarshi was satisfied that Haarnan's stride was steady enough to get him there without further incident—the wooden railing the bridge had once possessed had long since rotted away—he squatted down beside his student.

The white of splintered bone, liberally streaked with blood, met his eyes when he looked at the horse's front legs. Even under the best of conditions, it would be impossible for him or any other healer to save the animal.

"Nothing we can do," Etienne said.

"No."

"The two of you stand back," Javri said. "I'll cut her throat, we'll push her over the side, and that'll be the end of it."

Ruarshi shook his head. "It's a question of pain. We can see to it that this poor animal suffers a great deal more of it or none at all. If you use that thing to saw through her throat, it'll take her, what, four or five minutes to die? Not a nice fate, even for a horse." Etienne and Javri exchanged a glance. He ignored it. "I'd appreciate it, Javri, if you'd go see to Haarnan. And block his view while you're at it."

The warrior stared at him for a long moment, shrugged, and left. Etienne, who also knew better than to say anything, stood up. Ruarshi scooted forward and put his hands to either side of the horse's head, stilling its renewed thrashing before he went to work.

It didn't take long. Just enough time for him to wreak havoc within the mare's brain, starting with the pain centers. He stayed with her as she exhaled for the last time, and then pulled quickly away.

The worst part of the whole process, from Ruarshi's point of view, was how little effort it took to do such a thing. He was a healer, after all.

Or he had been.

Ruarshi opened his eyes. "She's rather heavy. How do you suppose Javri meant us to get her off the bridge?"

"I don't know. We'll have to ask her." Etienne whistled and gestured toward their companions. "I suppose if all four of us pitch in, we may be able to move her."

"For purposes of physical labor, there are only three of us present. Haarnan will only sniff and give instructions."

"Here they come."

"Yes, I had noticed." Ruarshi stood, ran a hand over his face, and waited.

The Sotari glanced from the horse to Ruarshi and pursed his lips in distaste, but he kept his mouth shut. Small mercies.

As it turned out Javri was the one who gave the instructions, and they tipped the mare into the gorge a few minutes later. Ruarshi emerged from the procedure liberally smeared in horse blood in spite of his best efforts to avoid the worst of it. He supposed it was appropriate that his clothes should be ruined, given the role he'd played, but he had to admit he was now anxious to be rid of them.

"Haarnan, you take Etienne's mount," Javri said, before any sort of conversation could resume. "The healers will ride together on Ruarshi's horse. We've got about six miles to go yet before we reach the first inn. We stop there regardless of how much sunlight we've got left."

"Pay some attention to where your horse is putting its feet this time," Ruarshi said, to Haarnan's back. "It would be a pity if you killed two in one day."

"Ruarshi," Javri said sharply. "Don't make it worse than it is."

"He is as Nerthu made him," the Sotari said, taking the reins of Etienne's bay. "An unpleasant human being, certainly, but also a useful tool. Thank you for putting my horse out of her misery. I will be more careful in future."

Which left Ruarshi with absolutely no good target upon which to vent his irritation. And reminded him, though he didn't need it, of why

Haarnan was such an effective diplomat.

"You're welcome."

☽○☾

Ruarshi was shivering by the time they reached the hostel. He had known this was going to happen, and there was no possibility of concealing it from Etienne, who was riding pillion. The incident with the horse marked the first time on this particular embassy that he'd found it necessary to do what he'd done, to use that part of his talents which had caused him so much trouble in the past. There was no physical reason for his reaction to it and never had been. This was a problem he made for himself. It was a serious nuisance, was linked somehow to his inability to bond, and he didn't intend to talk about it. Not even with Etienne, who deserved better.

He darted up to his room once the arrangements had been made, ignoring the small crowd in the common room and the feeble protestations of his stomach. Food was not high on the list of things he wanted right now.

A bath was, however. Which should be obtainable, as this route through the Alps was traversed all summer by prosperous European merchants, at least some of whom would want a wash now and then. Getting one would require leaving the room, though. And talking to someone. And possibly running into a member of his party. Not that Etienne wouldn't be up later anyway, since this was his room, too.

Ruarshi pulled his boots off and sat down on the bed. He caught a glimpse of blood on his sleeve and remembered how filthy his clothes were. Without bothering to get back up, he pulled his doublet off and threw it onto the floor. The height of Italian fashion, reduced to ruination. The pants would have to wait to come off. Eventually he was going to go out there and ask for that bath, and he couldn't very well manage it in his underwear.

He was still sitting in that same position with no real idea of how much time had passed when Etienne came in. The sky outside the window was black.

"Um," Etienne said. Ruarshi could see him standing in the doorway, backlit by the illumination from the common room, a curl of smoke rising from the taper in his hand. He was probably wondering what Ruarshi was doing and trying to decide how safe it was to start a conversation.

Ruarshi chuckled, fumbled around on the table by his elbow, and slid the candle he found there forward. "Come in and light this thing, would you?"

Etienne did as he asked and dropped the taper into the cold hearth. "You're still shaking," he said after a moment.

"Yes. It will last a few more hours and then it will stop. Nothing to be alarmed about."

"You will let me make sure…?"

"If it will make you feel better. Shutting the door might be advisable."

"Oh, yes." The Illyana made sure it was latched before he turned, businesslike, to sit down next to his teacher. "Your hand, please, sir."

Ruarshi extended his right hand, curious about the sudden formality. He hoped, he really hoped, it wasn't fear causing the stiffness in the Illyana's manner. He thinned the shield that protected the place where his bond to Wil had once been anchored, trying to figure out what it was his student was feeling.

A mistake.

Etienne chose that moment to run his healer's senses across that very spot. Without asking first, as he should have. *Knowing* that Ruarshi had suffered an injury there, but not having the faintest idea of what he'd done to himself after Wil had died, because no one knew about that…

The pain caused by that nearly unshielded contact erupted behind his eyes like a thousand flames, scaring him just as the initial wound had, bringing him back to that cold room in Tomir and the flickering candlelight just inches from his face.

He blinked and realized he was sitting on the floor with his back to the wall, his heels digging into the rough wooden boards next to his muddy boots. The pain in his head was ebbing away with remarkable and welcome speed. Etienne was staring at him in dismay.

And Ruarshi's shaking had stopped.

"I'm sorry," the Illyana breathed. "Really sorry. I was told to take a look at that. You're so damnably healthy I never had a chance before this. You should know. I talked with Mecheta before I left Tomir."

"You waited five years for this? You ought to be a better card player than you are, in that case." Ruarshi checked his shield before trying to stand, to make sure it hadn't been affected. It was right where it should be, if a little thicker than usual. Good. Nothing wrong with that self-taught reflex.

"He said the area around your bond was covered in scar tissue. Thick scar tissue. If that were still true you wouldn't need a shield. You did that, didn't you?"

On the one hand, Ruarshi reflected, he ought to be angry. Under normal circumstances, what Etienne had just done would be enough to get him kicked out of the healer's circle. Perhaps permanently. On the other hand, the boy was clearly upset and Ruarshi would probably have done the exact same thing if he'd been in the Illyana's position. So.

Ruarshi went to the window, pushed open the shutters, and leaned out into the night air. At this altitude the breeze was cool even though it was the middle of summer. It felt good on his face. When he thought he could speak without raising his voice, he turned back toward his student, leaning against the windowsill and crossing his arms.

"Since you've chosen to interfere in my life in this way, I'm going to ask two things of you. One, that you listen closely to what I'm about to say. Two, that you promise not to tell anyone what you know. If you can't promise me that, I'll be gone before you and the others get up in the morning."

Etienne nodded. "Okay."

"I'll start with a question: do you have any idea what it's like not to be able to bond with anyone? Of course not. Miriyanti don't. Even when we don't have an exclusive bond with someone, we're always connecting on a lesser level with other people, listening to them breathe from inside their own heads, watching them laugh and almost understanding the reasons for it without even making a conscious effort to find out. It's what you've been doing in Florence ever since I met you."

The Illyana nodded again.

"What would it do to you if you lost that ability? Do I even have to tell you what it did to me? The Miriyanti who end up in my company always seem to be remarkably well informed about my history."

"You left your clan home," Etienne said hesitantly. "They had to go find you."

"You're leaving out the most important part," Ruarshi said. "*Why* did I ride out into the middle of nowhere with no food, and then chase my horse off? The answer is obvious."

"I thought you'd gotten lost. No one ever said…"

"Suicide is the word you're looking for. I admit I wasn't thinking clearly and my plan wasn't a good one. Then someone got Simah involved, and she backtracked three-week old hoof prints until she found me. Casimir was annoyed. He fattened me up and sent me out on my first embassy, as though that would fix everything. It didn't. So I locked myself away in my room for a week and did what I could with the unresponsive scar Mecheta left behind. You just saw the results for yourself. The important thing is that I can sense others again. Not the way I used to, but it's something." An inadequate something, but the boy didn't need to know what other crutches he used. Especially since Etienne himself, as his student, was one of them.

"Now," Ruarshi said, "I want your oath. No one—not even Mecheta —learns any part of what I just told you. Not ever."

"You have my promise." Etienne met his eyes. "I shouldn't have done it. I expected to find what he told me I would. If he suspected you'd done something, he should have said so. You've been a considerate teacher, better than I expected, and this was no way to repay that."

"As you say, you didn't know that would happen. And welcome to the world of Miriyanti politics. Our country is filled with meddlers, of whom Mecheta is one. I'd be willing to wager he's already spoken with half the healers' circle about his suspicions. The rumors were probably what tipped him off, incidentally."

"Rumors?" The Illyana thought about it. "Oh. *Those* rumors. Are they true?"

"Keep thinking. You're tolerably good at it. Why had I allowed the shield to become so transparent?"

"You were trying to read my thoughts?" Rather than sounding outraged, as one might reasonably have expected, Etienne sounded intrigued. Excited, even.

"Not exactly. I'm not able to pick up thoughts as such. Emotions, yes. Sometimes those are just as good. I wanted to know if you were afraid of me."

"… No. Why would I be?"

"Because the other half of those same rumors label me a madman. And you found me sitting in a dark room staring at the walls, after killing a horse."

That elicited an uncomfortable laugh. "I wasn't worried about myself."

Ruarshi uncrossed his arms, closed the shutters, and made a decision. "When we get to Basle, I'm splitting off from the others. More Miriyanti politics. Or possibly a gigantic waste of time, since I'm running rather late. Interested?"

Etienne was watching him closely. "You mean I might be able to help you?"

"Yes."

"Then you've got me. What will we be doing?"

"I'll explain it after I've had a bath."

)O(

Etienne was fiddling with his cup of heavily watered wine and darting nervous glances toward Ruarshi whenever he thought Haarnan wasn't looking. It was an improvement over being stared at by the boy, but not much of one. The tale Ruarshi had told Etienne that night in the mountains had, for him, been so far in the past that it could almost have happened to someone else; it no longer affected him at all. The news had apparently hit his student somewhat harder. The strength of his reaction was something Ruarshi hadn't expected and didn't know what to do with. He supposed Etienne's anxiety would fade with time. Right now it was a much more immediate concern that accounted for his fidgeting.

Ruarshi decided to go ahead and get it over with. He was tired this morning, having slept poorly, and didn't really feel up to a fight. Though that's probably what he'd get.

"Haarnan." The old man turned to him, a look of polite inquiry on his face. "Etienne and I aren't coming home just yet. We'll be heading off on our own from here."

"Oh really?"

Ruarshi exhaled heavily. "Really. Etienne needs more experience. We'll be back in Miriyan soon. We've both written letters to our families and would appreciate it if you would pass them along when you get there."

"What will Casimir think of this?" Javri asked warily.

"That doesn't concern me. His right to give us orders ended with our embassy."

"The Seer would disagree with you about that," Haarnan said. "He wants us all back in Tomir as soon as possible. His letter couldn't have been clearer on that point."

Ruarshi shrugged. "He's wanted other things he hasn't gotten. He'll live."

"As you wish," Haarnan said, to Ruarshi's vast surprise. "I know there's no way I can force you to do anything. Casimir knows that, too. He did ask me to tell you, should you ever balk at doing your duty, that your son's position at the healer's circle could be jeopardized."

Ruarshi's chest constricted. "Repeat that."

"I take it he meant he'll have your son expelled. He never said so explicitly."

"That's disgusting," Etienne said. He was halfway out of his chair, gripping the table like he wanted to rip it in two. "How dare he do that? Since when have Miriyanti treated each other like hostages?"

"Sit down," Javri said. "And lower your voice."

Etienne glared at her, not moving.

"Do what she says, please," Ruarshi said mildly, and waited until the boy sat before continuing. "When did Casimir tell you this?" The timing did matter. Not more than the rest of it, no, but he had to start somewhere.

"When he assigned you to me," Haarnan said. "Why?"

That was the answer Ruarshi needed to hear. It meant the Seer might not be aware of his current plans, which was incredibly important to his prospects for success. "Just curious. That old bastard. He's likely been holding that threat in reserve the entire time I've been doing this. I've never been naïve enough to think he trusted me, however, so I can't really complain about heartbreak and betrayal."

"What are you going to do?" Javri looked like she was ready to throttle something, Haarnan by preference.

"I'm going to go on my merry way. How could Casimir doubt that? I have a few friends left at the circle who will make the going rough for him. If he's serious." The odds that it was a bluff weren't good. The Seer didn't operate that way. Ruarshi pushed his chair back and left the inn's front room, stepping out onto the streets of Basle with no destination in mind. Which was just as well, since he didn't know his way around.

Davyt, his long-suffering son, would forgive him. Slan wouldn't. She knew him better and would recognize his latest maneuver as another instance of him putting his own interests before those of his family. He'd been doing that consistently for decades. In some ways he'd become completely predictable.

He heard determined footsteps approaching him from behind, and recognized the tread. "Hello, Javri."

"Ruarshi." She drew even with him and matched his pace. "If you give me your letter home, I'll see to it that no one reads it. Other than the intended recipients, I mean. And if there's anything you want to add to it, given this morning's news, I'll sit on Haarnan until you get it done."

"I have nothing to add. What could I say? That my keen desire to avoid Tomir is more important than my son's training?"

Javri had always had a good understanding of his situation. She'd been friends with Lorion before Ruarshi had hauled him off to Wales. "You could say that but no one would believe it. Why aren't you coming back with us?"

"How are things in the capital these days?"

"That's not an answer."

"Oh, but it is."

Several minutes passed before she spoke. "You'd be perfectly safe there. In spite of the... extreme dislike some of the warriors and their families still feel for you. I think you should come home, whether Etienne is fully trained or not. You're better loved than you know."

"And I'm a bigger coward than *you* know. I've never been able to figure out what to say to people who think I helped Casimir decide whom to execute in the wake of the rebellion."

"How about the truth?"

Ruarshi shook his head. "They don't want to hear it."

"If you can't convince them, stop trying."

"I have."

"Okay." They detoured around a cart and she went on. "But you're only delaying the inevitable. I'll expect a visit shortly after you come back. Are you listening to me?"

"Yes."

"Good. If I run into Slan, is there anything you want me to say to her?"

"Tell her I'm in Mainz. I'll be there for a few months. Tell Davyt I'm sorry."

Javri nodded. "Anything else?"

"No. It's all in the letter."

"I need to go. Would you like to come with me or can you find your own way?"

Ruarshi's sense of direction was generally excellent, but he'd been paying no attention to where he was going when he left the inn. If he decided to be stubborn about it, finding the Golden Plough—or the Yellow Contraption, as Etienne called it—could prove to be a problem.

"I'm coming."

)O(

Being alone with Etienne was an enormous relief, and riding through the south German countryside—even hot and bug-infested as it was—had finally settled Ruarshi's nerves. He even felt cheerful. No longer did he have to monitor his surroundings every moment for someone who might want to stick a knife into the Miriyanti ambassador. He decided, as he waved a small buzzing insect away from his ear, that he could easily live this way forever.

The Illyana had picked up on his mood and was chatting away amiably about women, magic, Italian sculpture, and women. Ruarshi listened, contributing once in a while but more than content to let his student talk all day if that was his inclination. Mainz was waiting for them over the horizon, but they would get there when they got there and Ruarshi was in no hurry.

He halted his mare and reached for his wineskin. It was filled mostly with water, there being just enough alcohol in it to kill off the less savory beings that inhabited European wells and rivers. It was all he'd been drinking lately, and all he would let Etienne drink except on the rarest of occasions. One of which was coming up soon, if he remembered correctly.

"Your birthday," he said abruptly, interrupting a long-winded description of a party they'd both attended. "It's next month, isn't it?"

"Yes. I will be one hundred seventy-one years of age. An Illyana in his early prime. Are there any courtesans in Mainz?"

Ruarshi laughed. "I'm sure there are. It's a city full of highly-educated gentlemen with tastes they would no doubt describe as 'refined.' How the women would describe them is anyone's guess."

"Will you, uh, do the same thing you did in Florence?"

"What is it you're asking me?" He understood the question but wanted to make Etienne come out and say it.

"You know. Moira."

Yes, he knew. Another of his crutches. "I suppose I will," he said. "They're very pleasant company. And setting such a woman up in conditions approaching opulence earns a man a lot of respect, snide comments notwithstanding."

"Is that why you do it?"

Now that was a bit much. "No. You did meet her, didn't you?"

"A time or two."

"Then you know why."

"Mmmm. I guess so. Is there any reason I couldn't do that?"

"No reason I'd impose on you. Not here. But do you have the

money for it?"

"Of course not. Casimir's miserly stipend barely keeps me fed."

"You stretch the truth so far sometimes that it begs for mercy."

Etienne snorted. "It still isn't enough."

"I didn't think it would be." With him, on the other hand, Casimir had been quite generous with the proceeds of Miriyan's burgeoning foreign trade. It was a form of bribery. And he wouldn't be receiving any more of it now that he'd slipped his leash, but he had enough saved that this didn't worry him.

"I predict that you will find a group of young men to run with, that they will introduce you to the best establishment in town, and that you and they will all have a fine time. Even given your meager wages. You do have some left over, don't you?"

"Not a lot."

Ruarshi rolled his eyes, making sure Etienne noticed. "You'll receive from me whatever it was Casimir was paying you."

"You're not Casimir. I won't accept it from you."

"Defiance, is it? I don't think so. You're still my student. Speaking of which."

"What?"

They were on an obscure track in the middle of a vineyard. Perfect. He pulled power from the bond-shield until only wisps of it remained, so he'd be able to tell if anyone approached. Then he gestured toward the ground. "Dismount." He did the same, plucked a large bunch of grapes from the nearest vine, and faced the Illyana.

"Suppose you're surrounded by a howling pack of filthy friars, throwing rocks at you."

"Is this likely? I thought you said..."

"Shut up. This is a Lesson. And this grape," he held one up, "is a stone. I, playing the role of the ignorant unwashed, throw it. Like so." It bounced harmlessly off Etienne's shoulder. "Don't just stand there, for Christ's sake."

"Should I scream?"

"If that's the best response you can think of, then yes." He threw another, which caromed off Etienne's chest. Fortunately for him the grapes weren't ripe enough yet to burst and stain his clothes.

"I get it. Okay. Here."

The third grape hit a shield and fell to the ground a good half-foot in front of the Illyana. "Better." Ruarshi threw the grapes faster, one after another, until he again got through.

"Dammit." Etienne clapped a hand to his cheek. "That stings. You've made your point."

Ruarshi lowered his hand. "The only point I've made is that I'm a miserable teacher. I have sadly neglected this part of your education. Tell me what a shield is good for."

"Appeasing one's instructor."

"Besides that."

"Repelling rocks. It's of some use with arrows, unless you're too close to the person holding the bow. It's no help at all against someone with a gunpowder weapon. It also won't save you from a collapsing wall, or a rolling boulder, or anything else over a certain weight."

"There's nothing wrong with your practical knowledge. How big a shield can you make?"

"Nothing larger than about four by four. As you just found out."

"If you can't box yourself in with shields, you'd better not resort to them in the first place. Someone can kill you from behind just as easily as they can when they're facing you."

"When you invited me along on this adventure, you didn't say we'd be targets."

"I didn't need to, did I? If the Seer who sent me that note is correct and we're about to stumble into the middle of something Casimir's been trying to keep quiet, he could be looking at us in his nasty little water bowl right this moment."

"He wouldn't kill us for it."

"That depends. Do you have any idea how many Miriyanti he had executed after Elyon's revolt went sour?"

"Two or three dozen? I don't know."

"Those were the murders he committed in public. There were others, four hundred forty-two in Miriyan itself, fifty or so in Europe after they fled. Most of them warriors, the rest Seers. Then there are the thirty-one Naishanti who just disappeared, one of whom may be living somewhere near Mainz. What's one or two more, on top of all that? Having second thoughts?"

"No. Though you might have told me all that earlier." Etienne seized his own handful of grapes. "How wide an area can you protect?"

"Let's find out." Ruarshi stepped into the center of the path and raised a shield. The Illyana proceeded to assault it from all directions for the next several minutes. No matter how high or far to the side he threw the grapes, they collided with the weave of Ruarshi's power and tumbled into the dust.

Etienne dropped his denuded section of vine onto the track and raised his hands in surrender.

"Finished?" Ruarshi asked. "Good. That's what you're going to learn to do. Starting today. Two hours in the morning, two in the afternoon. The exercise will give you headaches and I'll get rid of them for you. In the time you have left over, you can dream about courtesans."

The Illyana hardly seemed to be listening. "That's a hell of a lot of dead bodies, Ruarshi. Are you sure you've got the numbers right?"

"Yes."

"So he went after everyone involved, not just the leaders. No wonder they're holding a grudge. Why hadn't I heard anything?"

"What would it have done to your opinion of the revolt if you had?"

Etienne nodded slowly. "No sympathy for the wicked. Casimir fights dirty. How did he end up in charge?"

"You answer your own question."

"Then why have you been doing what he wants you to all these years?"

"Because I agree with his goals in this instance. Either the Europeans get to know us and like us, or they keep wondering what their pale northern neighbors are doing up there with all that sorcery. Ignorance doesn't usually breed friendship. Shall we go?"

As they headed off again, Etienne said, "I'm not so sure about that. I felt a lot friendlier toward Casimir fifteen minutes ago."

"He's the exception that proves the rule."

"What will you do, if you find out he's doing something you don't like with the ones who are missing?"

"What would you suggest?"

Ruarshi meant the question seriously and was glad to see that Etienne had taken it that way. "The first thing I'd do? I'd write it down, three or four copies of it, and send it to people I trusted. Using reliable couriers."

"As plans go I've heard worse. Much worse. You'll become a master of intrigue yet."

"No, thanks."

)O(

They stopped about a mile from Mainz' southern gate to change clothes, a process which drew curious looks from the occasional passersby and a muttered string of complaints from Etienne.

"Oh, hush," Ruarshi said, pulling on the cuffs of his shirt until they emerged from the sleeves of his dark green coat. "I know it's heavy, but you've worn it in hotter weather than this."

"It's faded," Etienne said. He rubbed at the somewhat lighter green wool of his own coat in dissatisfaction. "And some of the buttons are loose. I'd have had it repaired if I'd known I'd be wearing it again."

"It likely wouldn't need repair if you hadn't gone carousing in it. Now that I think on it, I'm rather surprised that one or more buttons didn't end up in the possession of nice young Italian ladies."

Etienne looked away and began wrapping his wide linen belt around his waist. He mumbled something Ruarshi didn't quite catch.

"What was that?"

"Just remarking. It's a good thing you don't intend for us to change into the pants, too."

"You didn't."

"No buttons left on those at all. Keepsakes, you know."

Ruarshi smiled. "You're lucky Haarnan never found out. Let me look at you."

Etienne turned to face him and he tugged at the young man's clothing until it hung straight. The coats they both now wore were cut and decorated in the formal Miriyanti style, with swirling patterns in cloth of silver that ran from their shoulders to their calves. It was meant to be an abstract rendering of water flowing over a mossy riverbed, and Ruarshi supposed the approximation succeeded well enough if one didn't look at it too closely. A line of tiny silver buttons started at their necks and ended just beneath their ribcages, where the cloth parted in order to reveal their belts. Etienne, as a healer-in-training, wore a gray belt. Ruarshi's was black. He'd decided they would forego the pants that went with the outfit, as their bagginess made it hard to get on and off a horse without snagging on something.

"Very good. Now this." He stepped around behind his student and pulled the thong from his hair. "Civilized and barbaric at the same time. Forget the hat. I don't want any shadows on our faces. People need to see us."

"People already see us," Etienne said, nodding toward a small group of children who had paused to watch their transformation. "My hair's not going to be much of a clue, though."

"True," Ruarshi said. The Illyana had inherited his French mother's black hair. "But the contrast between the two of us will attract attention."

He slipped the leather tie from his own hair. It shone white in the afternoon sunlight and hung rather longer than he usually kept it, reaching nearly to the middle of his back. He would have to get it cut soon. For today's purposes it would do nicely.

"Everything in the right place?"

Ruarshi submitted to some tugging in his turn, and then Etienne clapped him on the back. "You'll do."

"Thanks. Well. It's time. Remember to keep your head up and look as arrogant as possible."

Etienne chuckled. "I'll do my best."

They climbed back onto their horses and resumed their journey north. A short while later they rode into Mainz, being only briefly delayed at the gate by the usual bottleneck of people coming and going. There were no guards posted there, which Ruarshi appreciated.

He thinned the bond-shield as soon as they emerged from the shadow of the gatehouse, just enough to enable him to read some of the stronger emotions coming from the Europeans closest to them. The extra time he'd taken with their appearance seemed to be having its intended effect. Almost no one they passed was unaware of them; many stared openly as they rode by. He sensed some hostility, but not much. Most people were curious or a little alarmed, and here and there he even felt a hint of excitement as some of the younger Mainzers realized they were seeing something new. Once Ruarshi even picked up a surge of what he'd learned to recognize as pure predatory lust, but he didn't turn to find the source of it. He couldn't tell whether it was directed toward himself or Etienne, and he felt a surge of protectiveness toward the boy. Misplaced in all likelihood. The Illyana had never had any trouble dealing with his admirers.

He glanced at Etienne and shook his head. If his student had been European, Ruarshi would have placed his age at no more than sixteen. And rather than looking arrogant, as he'd been told to, he reminded Ruarshi of a child who'd just been given a new toy. Which was pretty close to the truth, he supposed.

Ruarshi, on the other hand, looked older than he thought he ought to. He hadn't yet hit three hundred but he could easily pass for a Mainzer in his mid-thirties. A short Mainzer, with unusually sharp features and the black eyes common to Miriyanti.

He turned right at the next intersection, startling Etienne.

"Aren't we headed for an inn?"

"Eventually, yes. There's no need to go there directly."

"Ah."

When they reached the wharf that ran alongside the Rhine River, Ruarshi pulled his horse to a halt. It was a busy place in spite of the fact that Mainz wasn't a large city.

"You've been here before, right?" Etienne asked.

"Yes. A bit less than a century ago. The atmosphere is much the same."

"How long are we staying? You've never said."

"No more than a year. Hopefully quite a bit less. It doesn't look like anyone's about to be crushed by anything, does it?"

"Uh... no. Why?"

"I can't think of a better way to advertise our presence. A healing, performed here in front of all these people who could spread the word upriver and down. It would be perfect."

"That's a bit creepy, Ruarshi."

"Is it? I guess you're right. But the injured party would probably bless the coincidence."

Etienne considered that. "You have a point. Do you plan on coming down here a lot?"

"No. This detour is all about being seen. We could go to the river's edge and recite the blessing over water..."

"And have everyone believe we're trying to poison them? That's really not a useful sort of attention."

"True. Too bad." Ruarshi sat up straighter, stretching out the muscles in his back. He was uncomfortably warm. Etienne was pink-cheeked as well.

"Time to shed these coats for a while. We can stroll around town again later, after the sun goes down."

"Haarnan and Javri must be halfway home by now," Etienne said.

Ruarshi nodded and heeled his horse into motion, swinging its head around toward the center of the city. "Do you wish you'd gone with them?"

"No. I wouldn't mind seeing my friends, but a year more or less won't make any difference."

Ruarshi hoped he was right. His student still hadn't quite thought through everything he'd been told. If he had, the shield he'd woven for the day would have been quite a bit sturdier than it was. Ruarshi doubted it could protect Etienne from a determined barrage of pebbles, much less against whatever an irate Naishanti, sent into exile by Casimir, might be likely to throw at the Seer's oh-so-well-known ally.

No matter. Ruarshi's own shields were strong enough to keep them both relatively safe, if it came to that.

He put the subject out of his mind and set off to find the best inn Mainz had to offer.

# The Fountain

Several days of boredom followed, during which Ruarshi took the steps necessary to obtain permission to live in the city and to work as a healer while he did. This involved a tedious visit with two separate notaries, who assisted him with a petition to the city council and an obsequious letter to the overseer of the local physicians' guild. The bribes to the barbers' and bathers' guilds would come later, after he'd gotten word that he could stay. He had little doubt that he'd be allowed to. A Miriyanti healer meant increased traffic through the city, and not just in the form of suffering peasants. Everyone would make money off his presence. Only jealousy on the part of the city's more prominent doctors could bar his way, and he hoped the tone of his letter would take care of that.

To Etienne he delegated the more interesting task of finding them a suitable house to rent. There were extra living quarters to be had in Mainz, the Illyana explained to him on their second evening in town, because all of the city's Jews had been expelled two years previously.

"That's got to be the third or fourth time they've done that," Ruarshi said. "The city will soon decide it made a mistake, and the sons and daughters of Abraham will return. Try to rent something else. I don't want to be in the way of a family getting its home back when the city fathers come to their senses."

So Etienne had gone out again the next day and located a place Ruarshi thought would do: a narrow, three-story structure on the corner of a fashionable street four blocks from the city center. The monthly rate was high, but he would be able to set up his shop on the bottom floor without causing too much upset to the neighbors. And it came with a private well in its tiny courtyard, which was both convenient and unusual.

"How long will it take the city to give us a yes or no?" Etienne asked. He had demolished his dinner with his usual energy, and was leaning back in his chair near the inn's front door with a satisfied look on his face.

"A week? A month? I haven't a clue. Somebody will send for us, we'll have a polite discussion, and then we'll know. What do you think of the place?"

"It's tidier than most cities I've lived in. Fewer beggars and whatnot. Why is that?"

Ruarshi shrugged. "I had noticed a large percentage of churchmen."

"They're everywhere. There's an archbishop somewhere around here, too. Albrecht. Someone said he's ailing."

Ruarshi had a vague memory of hearing about some trouble involving the man, some years back, but he couldn't place it. "I hope he has a speedy recovery. How have you been received?"

"Well enough. People have no idea who I am until I tell them I'm with you. I met a journeyman printer today. Only he's not really journeying. He's working for his older brother, who owns the shop. Printing involves quite a racket, did you know? I went over to investigate and was invited in by the fellow. His name is Tobias. And he has a sister."

"Whom, as you know, you cannot touch."

"I know. They were printing missals. I found a misspelling and Tobias swore for ten minutes."

"Tell him to relax. No one else will notice."

"Don't be so pessimistic. There have to be a few Germans who know how to read Latin."

"A very few. I was thinking that tomorrow we could—"

The door slammed open behind Etienne and a young man stumbled in, looking wildly around the room until his eyes settled on them. Ruarshi stood as the stranger approached, gesturing for his student to do the same.

The man pulled off his shapeless hat when he reached their table. "You're the healers, right?"

"Yes."

"Can you come with me, please? My brother, he fell out the window, third floor, landed on a crate we were moving out of the house. He's broken his legs, he's bleeding, please…"

"We'll come. Show us."

The man hesitated, looking back and forth between them. "Don't you need to get anything? Instruments?"

"No," Ruarshi said. He held up his hands. "That's what these are."

"Okay." The man nodded apprehensively. "Follow me." He very nearly ran back out the door and the healers hurried to catch up.

"I guess this was inevitable," Etienne said, striding along through the twilight at Ruarshi's side.

"Unfortunately yes. Assuming the patient doesn't die on us, this should speed things along nicely."

His student gave him a sour look. "This is certainly the time to be worrying about our progress with the city council."

Ruarshi didn't even glance at him. "It's as good a time as any other. Would it make you happier if I started wringing my hands and sobbing? Yon youngster seems to be speeding up."

The home to which the young man led them turned out to be across the street and just a few yards down from the building they hoped to rent. A middle-aged woman stood silhouetted in the doorway, waiting for them.

"Johann." She turned furiously on their guide as they drew near. "I sent you for the doctor."

"And I've found two of them. Come in, please."

Ruarshi stepped forward. "Good evening, my lady. I am Ruarshi Nerthi, and this is my assistant Etienne Illyana. We will leave if you would prefer. But it sounds as though your son has been injured...?" He waited, giving the woman time to decide if she was going to allow her fear of them to override her concern for her son. He didn't think she would, not now that he had spoken to her.

And he was right. She moved back and motioned for them to enter. "Johann. You will go back out now and fetch Father Ulrich."

"Mother," the young man protested, "I want to be here."

"Then I suggest you hurry."

He ducked his head and left, and his mother closed the door gently behind him.

When she turned to face them, Ruarshi bowed. Out of the corner of his eye, he saw Etienne mirroring the gesture. "Johann told us his brother had fallen. Without seeing the boy I cannot be sure, but I doubt we should wait for the priest."

"I don't mean for you to wait. He's up here."

She led them up the stairs without another word. They trailed her into a small room overlooking the street. A young boy, perhaps eight years of age, lay sprawled unconscious on the bed there, attended by a nervous maid. She backed away and flattened herself against the wall by the window when she saw them.

"Liesl, that is enough of that. Bring in another chair for these gentlemen."

The maid hurried out of the room, but Ruarshi barely noticed. The boy's legs were broken and he had a few bloody scratches here and there, but that was hardly the worst of it. He was bleeding internally, and his spine had been damaged. Both problems needed immediate attention. He traded a glance with Etienne.

"Your son—"

"His name is Peter."

"Peter has a broken back, and he's bleeding inside. Saving his life and his ability to walk is going to require that both of us work on him. With your permission?"

The woman's eyes welled with tears. She attempted to blink them away with only partial success. "What you do... will it hurt him?"

"No. It's important that no one touch us or your son until we're finished. This will take several hours."

She nodded tightly. "Please begin. No one will disturb you." She leaned out into the hall. "Liesl? We need that chair."

The maid appeared a few moments later. She placed a low wooden chair by the side of the bed, next to the one she'd been sitting in earlier, and fled.

"May I watch?" the woman asked.

"Of course. I would prefer it." Ruarshi settled in, as did Etienne. He switched from German to Miriyanti and addressed his student. "I'll see what I can do with his back. You get that bleeding stopped and repair the damage to his abdomen. The legs we'll tend to last."

"Okay."

Working together on the same patient at the same time was not an easy thing to do. The weaves tended to get tangled unless the healers involved were very careful and well accustomed to each other's healing styles. Fortunately, both were true of Ruarshi and Etienne, who'd had five years together to perfect their technique.

Ruarshi nevertheless found himself tiring quickly. Spinal damage was by no means his area of expertise, which seemed to lie more in the realm of infectious disease, and he wished there were a Chamani nearby to consult. Which of course there wasn't, and wouldn't be, with Casimir pulling Miriyanti out of Europe as fast as he could manage it.

After Ruarshi finished knitting together the torn nerves in the boy's back, he moved on to the smashed vertebrae. Reassembling those was tedious business, something akin to gluing a shattered vase back together, and then there were still the ruptured discs to be mended. By the time he'd healed it all to his satisfaction, Etienne was finished with the boy's internal injuries and was doing a nice job of repairing his broken legs.

Ruarshi monitored his student for a few minutes, then surrendered to fatigue and pulled out of the healing trance. The room was darker than it had been with only a single candle burning behind them. He waited until Etienne started blinking to turn in his chair.

"He will be fine, with one exception." The boy's mother, Johann, and a gray-haired priest sat watching him solemnly. "He may find it difficult to walk. Or even impossible, though I think that's unlikely. Time will tell. He'll probably sleep until morning. When he does wake up, he'll be in some pain. That's normal and it shouldn't concern you unless it's too intense."

The woman was crying openly at this point. The priest clasped her hand.

"Will it disturb him if I apply some holy water to his forehead?" he asked.

"No, Father, not if you're careful about it. Would you like to sit?" Ruarshi stood, wavered, and put a hand on the wall to steady himself. His student hadn't moved, and he was gratified to note that Etienne looked every bit as tired as he felt. They both needed more practice than they'd been getting lately, that much was obvious.

"Sit back down, please. You look exhausted. I'll go around to the other side of the bed."

The priest did so, bent over the boy, and began speaking softly in Latin. Then he reached out and sketched a cross on Peter's forehead, leaving a faint gleam of holy water behind. Ruarshi watched without speaking. Magic versus magic, the usual story, the only difference being that Christian magic didn't actually do a damn thing. Proving that there was, in fact, something of a distinction to be made between real magic and religious superstition, to the chagrin of a few of the more radical Italian humanists he'd met.

His mind was wandering. He needed to go to bed.

"We should get back to our inn." He rose once again, more slowly this time, and held out a hand for Etienne. The boy took it gratefully and hauled himself to his feet.

"I must pay you for what you have done," the boy's mother said.

Ruarshi shook his head. "Tomorrow is early enough. Your son knows where to find us."

"I didn't introduce myself earlier. My name is Margaret Ross. If you need to stay here while you recuperate, you are welcome."

"That's kind of you, but no. We're hardy enough to walk a few blocks."

"Johann will go with you. Thank you."

Father Ulrich extended a hand. Ruarshi took it by reflex, feeling somewhat bemused by the offer until he realized the man's fingers were wet. More holy water. Damn the old priest, anyway.

Ruarshi smiled, or bared his teeth in something like a smile. "You'd better shake Etienne's hand, too."

The priest flushed and withdrew his hand. "I'm sorry. I had to know. To have done any less…"

Ruarshi turned his back on the old man, bowing again to Margaret. "I'd like to look in on Peter tomorrow afternoon. We can settle accounts then."

"Certainly," she replied, shooting a half-defiant look at Ulrich. "Johann, take a lamp with you."

Moments later they were outside in the muggy late night air. Or early morning air, depending on one's perspective. The city was silent and still with only the faintest of breezes winding its way through the streets.

"That was awkward," Etienne commented finally.

"It's a hazard of living north of the Alps," Ruarshi said, his voice flat. "I'm glad you came and got us, Johann. Your brother's injuries were beyond what a doctor or barber-surgeon could have helped with."

"I know. Father died in an accident. Or *after* an accident, I should say. Three weeks after, and he didn't look as bad as Peter." Ruarshi opened his mouth to express his condolences, but Johann apparently knew what was coming and waved it away. "It was years ago. But you never really forget the feeling you get when you realize the so-called experts are as helpless as you are. If either of you ever needs anything, just let me know. Are you staying in town for a while?"

"If we get permission, yes."

"City council dragging its feet? It's what they do best. I'll ask Mother to write them a letter on your behalf."

"That would be appreciated."

They'd reached their inn. Johann held the lantern up toward it, as though they needed to see the sign out front in order to identify the place. "Here we are," he said. "Thank you, sirs. Mother will pay you well but it won't ever be enough." The young man nodded to them both. "I'll see you tomorrow."

Ruarshi and Etienne watched his lantern bob through the darkness until he turned a corner and its glow faded from sight. Then they pushed open the front door of the inn and went up to their room.

☽○☾

When they went to visit the boy the next day, the first words out of his mouth were, "You're short!"

Ruarshi paused in the doorway to look him over while Margaret gave her son a mild tongue-lashing. Peter was propped up on several pillows, his pain level was about what it should be, and no further injury-related problems had developed overnight. Good.

"Had someone told you Miriyanti were giants?" Ruarshi asked, moving to the window and glancing out. "Is this the one you fell out of?"

The boy was bright red by this time. Etienne took pity on him. "Were you trying to climb onto the roof?"

Johann laughed. "If that was the only way he could get a look at Mechthild in her nightdress."

"That's not so," Peter said weakly.

"A child after my own heart," Etienne murmured.

"We'll talk about this later," his mother declared, before turning her attention back to the healers. "Is he well?"

"It seems so," Ruarshi said. "How much did he eat this morning?"

"About twice what he usually does."

Ruarshi smiled. "Then you've got nothing to worry about. Peter, would you move your legs for me?"

"Like this?" He slid them back and forth under his blankets.

"That will do. Now your toes."

Peter obligingly stuck his feet out from under the covers and did as he'd been asked. "I can wiggle my fingers, too. See?"

"So you can. Do you feel like you fell three stories?"

"Not really. More like I rolled downhill in a barrel."

"Do you do that often?"

The boy shook his head.

"I'm relieved," Ruarshi said. "I want you to remain in bed for three days. Then for the next month, and I do mean month, you're going to stay here at home, you're going to sleep whenever you need to, and you're going to eat as much as possible. And you're not to pick up anything heavier than a chicken. Your mother and brother are going to see to it that you do what I say."

"Yes, sir." Peter had perked up while Ruarshi was talking. He felt almost sorry for the boy's mother.

"Frau Ross," he said, "can I speak with you for a minute?" Ruarshi gestured toward the hallway.

"Certainly. I'll be right back, Peter. Be polite to our guests. And your brother." She rose from the edge of her son's bed and headed toward the door.

Johann took a step in the same direction.

"I have to ask your mother about a… matter of faith," Ruarshi said, forestalling him. "We'll be right outside."

"Who is this Mechthild?" Etienne asked. "Is she worthy of this sort of sacrifice, Johann, do you think?"

Johann nodded at Ruarshi and went back to leaning against the side of the large wardrobe in the corner.

Ruarshi slipped out of the room and closed the door behind him. Margaret was waiting for him in the murk of the hall, a square of sunlight from a westward-facing window painting the floorboards golden in the bedroom opposite. He had to blink the brilliance from his eyes before he could see the woman properly.

"Yes?" she prompted.

"I have a question about Father Ulrich. Did you ask him to do what he did last night or was that his own idea?"

"I must apologize for that. I had requested…" She trailed off. "I guess you would call it reassurance. I saw nothing that made me uneasy —I saw nothing at all, really, can you believe that I almost fell asleep, waiting…"

"So he wouldn't have done it otherwise?"

"I don't know. He didn't object to the notion. Should he have?"

"A few years ago I would have said yes. Then the pope muddied the waters again. What I need you to tell me—are you aware of any particular prejudice against Miriyanti on the part of the local clergy?"

Margaret watched him while she thought about it. "I have never heard a sermon from Father Ulrich or from any other priest that would suggest such an attitude. The subject doesn't come up."

"It will now."

"Yes."

"And what will Father Ulrich say, Frau Ross? Are Etienne and I safe here?"

"He is a gentle man. And last night he was quite overwhelmed when he left. He'll cause you no trouble."

"Is there anyone here who will? I couldn't help noticing that the Jews are gone."

"Oh, that. It wasn't a religious dispute. There were some members of prominent families who'd gotten in over their heads in a trading venture that collapsed, and then—"

"Say no more. I understand. Odd, isn't it, that certain kinds of despicable behavior can actually be reassuring in the right context?"

Margaret was looking at him quizzically.

Ruarshi shook his head. "Never mind. I feel much more at ease than I did when we began this conversation. You will let me know if you start hearing negative opinions about myself or my student?"

"I will do you better than that. I'll counter them with my own opinions. Here." She reached into a pocket of her skirt and pulled out a small, heavy bag. "This is payment for your services. And I've already composed a letter for the city council. It will be delivered today."

Ruarshi accepted the bag. "Are you sure? I see you have only one maid."

"By preference. One maid, an agent in Cologne, and a full tenth of the sugar trade in this part of the country. Not to mention interests in wool and wine. My husband was energetic and I've been no less so since his death."

"Thank you."

"You've got nothing to thank me for."

"You won't mind if we check in on your son from time to time?"

"No. In fact, I insist upon it."

)O(

*My Dearest Ruarshi,*

*I believe I have finally deciphered that cryptic passage in your latest letter. If I were in an uncharitable mood, I would point out that anything which causes you such embarrassment to relate is probably not worth doing in the first place. But I am not feeling uncharitable today, so I will simply tell you that I am not surprised. You made your wishes quite clear years ago when you de-*

*clined to ask Casimir to assign me to your first embassy. I'm sure you're aware he would have done that for you. He grants you anything you request, to the eternal vexation of those in Miriyan who are eager to ingratiate themselves with the new regime. It is no wonder that so many of them still believe you and he are lovers. But I know better, don't I, since you have taken the trouble to acquaint me with the form and location, if not the name, of the individual now fulfilling that role. I hope at the very least that she is intelligent.*

*You never did take me at my word when I told you that love can exist, and thrive, even in the absence of a pair-bond. You instead took upon yourself the tiresome mantle of martyrdom and made a decision for both of us, and based on what? Self-pity, I tell myself when I am angry. When I am able to be more honest with myself, I can admit that you thought you were doing me a kindness, though it is one I will never thank you for. I do not like being patronized, as you know, and I thought you were more pragmatic than that. You have idealized our relationship so thoroughly that you have destroyed it. Or tried to. When Casimir is done with you, you and I will come face-to-face again and we will talk. In the meantime I will take your letter as a formal renunciation, as you no doubt intended it, and will pursue my own amorous inclinations. As a nation the English do not interest me greatly, but there are a number of young men reckless and clever enough to have caught my eye. I will spare you the stilted letter once it is done.*

*I hear that Davyt is doing well at the healers' circle and I can only presume you have heard the same. Ardan continues in the position of guard dog, and I don't think your efforts to pry her from our son's side are at all likely to succeed…*

Ruarshi set the yellowed parchment back in its box and rose from his chair, cursing himself halfheartedly. Because it was Etienne's birthday, he'd shared a bottle of wine and a few glasses of something stronger with the young man earlier over dinner, and then he'd gone straight for that stack of letters. Even though he'd told himself repeatedly that he wouldn't. He ought to burn every last one of them, and if there'd been a fire in the grate he would have given the idea serious consideration. For about the hundredth time. There was a candle at hand, but getting it safely from one side of the inn's small room to the other seemed too complicated a procedure to risk just now.

He closed the box and stuffed it back into his pack underneath his somewhat rumpled clothing, and then stood looking out the window wondering where Etienne was. Surely he was fine; he'd only gone out a few hours ago to celebrate with Johann and Tobias and a few other young sons of the city's merchant class. Someone would already have come to find him if his student were in trouble. Or were causing trouble.

Ruarshi could hardly go in search of the boy, but if he stayed in this room any longer he knew he'd end up crawling into the bed and falling asleep. That was what alcohol did to him these days: first it made him maudlin and then it rendered him unconscious.

With a last longing glance at the bed, he turned on his heel and headed out the door and down the inn's front stairs. When he stepped outside, the first thing that caught his eye was the fountain in the middle of the square. He decided that was as good a place to wait as any and headed toward it in the slightly eerie light of the half moon.

The lighting conditions did not improve the thing's appearance. The sculpture at the fountain's center was evidently meant to be some sort of tribute to creatures aquatic; it depicted several different types of fish in various tortured attitudes, staring out in mute and desperate appeal at passersby. Ruarshi had never seen anyone actually drinking the water that pooled at the fountain's base, or in fact using it in any way whatsoever. No one should mind if he stuck his hands in it and splashed a little onto his face. It probably wouldn't help clear his head but it was something to do.

He wet his face and hair and sat on the fountain's rim for a few minutes, only gradually becoming aware that he was quite uncomfortably hot. The alcohol again, he supposed, combined with the late summer weather. He pulled off his boots, stepped into the fountain, and sat in the water with his legs crossed, leaning back against the least distressed fish he could find.

That was much better.

He realized he was being watched when a sense of wary amusement brushed against his bond-shield. That wasn't the kind of emotion he would expect from someone who intended to do him harm so he remained where he was. If whoever was hiding out there wanted to talk, he or she knew where to find him.

"You're drunk." He heard the voice before he saw its source. It was the innkeeper's oldest boy, lurking by the side of the building.

"Of course I'm drunk. I wouldn't be sitting here if I were sober. Please come closer. We shouldn't be shouting at this time of night."

The boy began sidling slowly in his direction. "Do you remember my name?"

Ruarshi did not, though he knew he'd heard it more than once. "I have forgotten. I forget a lot of things when I'm drunk."

"It's Gerhard. You're Ruarshi? I've been spying on you and your friend."

"You have been underfoot a lot. I'd thought you were shirking your chores."

Gerhard arrived at the rim of the fountain and started tapping at it nervously. "You've been my main chore since a couple of days after you got here. Somebody asked dad to keep an eye on you. He asked me to help him."

"'Somebody'? Who is 'somebody'?"

"You're not mad?"

"Not a bit. Sorcerers can be dangerous and should be watched."

"I don't know who it was. He has money, though. We're to report suspicious behavior."

"Does sitting in a fountain count?"

The boy chewed at his lip. "That would depend on why you're doing it."

"Because I'm hot."

"That doesn't sound suspicious to me." Gerhard sat down. "Are you as old as they say?"

"I have no idea. How old is that?"

"Five or six hundred, at least."

Ruarshi snorted. "Not hardly. I was born in 1198, which I understand was a bad year for the papacy. That makes me two hundred seventy-seven."

The boy hesitated. He seemed to be thinking over what he'd just been told. "How come Miriyanti live so long?"

"That's just the way the world works." The healer shifted, gesturing toward the water. "If you want to join me, feel free. I can't see how you'd get in trouble for it, since you're only doing as your father asked."

"I'd better not. I'm not really supposed to be talking to you at all."

"If it makes you feel better, I knew we'd be watched. Your 'somebody' probably sits on the city council or works for someone who does. We're hoping to be allowed to live here for a while."

"I know. Dad told me. Do you have a family?"

"Yes."

"Where are they?"

"At home in Miriyan."

"Then why are you clear down here? Wouldn't you rather be with them?"

"Yes. And no. It's complicated. Are you this forward with everyone or just the people you're spying on?"

"Just you. Dad is getting frustrated. He says you'll hardly talk to him."

"So you're trying to improve his mood by learning what he couldn't?"

"He's got a nasty mouth when he's mad about something." Gerhard shifted so he could dangle his feet in the fountain.

"What's the main thing he wants to find out?"

"I dunno. Mostly what kind of person you are, whether or not you're honest. There are bigger cities to train your assistant in."

"That is true. It may ease their minds if you tell them I was here once before, late in the last century. I didn't stay long but there might be something in the city's records about it. The year would have been... around 1390. I don't remember exactly. I caused no trouble that time around."

The boy's face had brightened. "I think that *will* help. Why are you drunk tonight? You never drank much before."

"It's Etienne's birthday."

"Oh. Do you two really work miracles like Father Ulrich has been saying?"

"What?"

"Father Ulrich, he was there when you—"

"I know who he is. *What* did he say?"

"That you worked a miracle when you healed the widow's boy."

"Shit," Ruarshi murmured. In spite of the alcoholic haze that blanketed his thoughts, he knew this wasn't good news. "I'll have to tell him to put a sock in it."

Gerhard giggled. "How come?"

"Because only Christian saints do miracles. Miriyanti do magic. If people start thinking we've converted, then we're not allowed to do magic. That would make us heretics and we'd be in all kinds of trouble. Here's something else for you to pass on: Etienne and I worship Nerthu. She's the goddess who gave us our magic. Tell everyone you know."

"Okay. Can I ask you one more thing?"

"Why stop now?"

The boy looked at him dubiously. "I can't tell if that was a yes or a no."

"It was a yes."

"When that old peasant came up to you today, why did you refuse to help him?"

"You're a decent boy," Ruarshi said after a moment. "I hope your parents tell you that from time to time. I didn't refuse. I told him I couldn't see his wife until I was given permission to practice here."

"But you healed the boy."

"Because it was an emergency. No one can object to that. If it's not..."

"But he traveled two days to get here."

"I'm not disagreeing with you. But if I'd seen his wife, the guilds could have had us tossed out of town. Then I'd have to start the whole process over somewhere else."

"The city shouldn't be getting in your way like that."

"That's my point exactly." Ruarshi cupped his hand and splashed water onto Gerhard's legs. "You should go to bed. It's the middle of the night and you need your sleep."

"You need—" The boy's eyes widened as a new thought occurred to him. "Do Miriyanti sleep?"

"Yes, of course we sleep. Don't be ridiculous."

"You're waiting up for your apprentice?" Gerhard stood and put his shoes back on.

"Yes."

"Dad never waits up for *me*. He's asleep right now."

"Then you'd best be quiet and not wake him."

Gerhard nodded. "Thanks for talking to me. I know you didn't have to."

"Anytime." Ruarshi latched onto the mouth of a fish and pulled himself upright, watching the boy as he returned to the inn. The conversation had woken him up and cleared out the better part of the muddle in his brain. He should be able to stay awake now until Etienne returned, with a little bit of help from Virgil.

Ruarshi stepped out of the fountain, picked up his boots, and went back to his room.

# Steel Cobwebs

The letter from the overseer of the physicians' guild, one Friedrich Bebel, came for Ruarshi two days later. He left Etienne behind at the inn, still groaning over the remnants of a truly impressive hangover. A hangover Ruarshi stubbornly declined to do anything about. It was all part of another Lesson, he'd told his student, and had received a suitably black look in reply.

He was wearing his formal Miriyanti outfit again, this time complete with the slightly baggy pants since he was walking to his destination. The doctor lived about ten minutes away in what turned out to be a sizeable red and white home set back several yards from the street. Ruarshi mounted the stairs, knocked on the front door, and waited.

An older man, obviously not a servant, opened the door.

"I am Ruarshi Nerthi of the clan Doshae, here to meet with Herr Doctor Bebel." He put a hint of a Miriyanti accent into his words.

"You hardly need to introduce yourself. Your fame has preceded you. I am Doctor Bebel, but I would prefer it if you would call me Friedrich. Please come in."

"Then you must return the favor and call me Ruarshi. Thank you."

The entryway was wide enough that he and the doctor didn't have to sidestep each other in order to get the door closed. When that was done, Bebel showed him into the house.

"I would have liked to take you out back to the garden, but as the heat is so oppressive today I have asked that the servants bring wine to us inside. Unless you have an objection...?"

"This is more than adequate. I trust that I and my student will have the opportunity to see your garden later on."

"Indeed." The doctor gestured him into a chair next to a large window that looked out onto greenery. Bebel took a seat opposite.

"I do look forward to meeting your student. Is he also Miriyanti?"

"He is."

"You must be aware that the story of Peter Ross' miraculous recovery has already spread to all quarters of the city. It was kind of you to heal him."

Ruarshi shrugged slightly. "It is what we do. There is a word I wanted to say about that."

"Yes?"

"I learned the other day that the priest is claiming he witnessed a miracle. This is untrue. Miriyanti have never claimed the god of the Europeans as our source of power."

Bebel waved his protestations away. "The priest is clearly an excitable sort. His superiors will take him to task and we'll hear no more about it. Please don't concern yourself. I understand you were recently in attendance upon the Medici in Florence?"

"I was part of our embassy there, yes. It is customary for our ambassadors to take a healer and a warrior along, and sometimes students as well."

"Ah. Here is our wine. Leave it on the table, Wolter." There was a pause in the conversation while Bebel poured wine for them both. Ruarshi accepted his glass and took a sip.

"This is very good," he remarked. As it happened he found the wine to be far too sour. But certain forms had to be upheld.

"Thank you. It's from my family's vineyards. I am a noble's second son who escaped the clutches of the church and went into medicine instead. I've never regretted it."

"Did you study in Italy?"

"Salerno. Galen and all the rest of it. What do you think of Galen?"

That was a tricky sort of question. If he told the doctor his real opinion of some of that worthy ancient's more beloved writings, the man would probably never speak to him again. "He was invaluable when engaged in the direct treatment of patients."

"And what of his theories?"

Ruarshi spread his hands. "Because of the way I heal, I have never had much use for theories."

"May I ask...?"

"How we heal?"

Bebel nodded.

"It is almost impossible to explain. Believe me, I have tried. Italians are nothing if not curious."

The doctor smiled. "I hope we Germans can match them in that. Has Mainz been treating you well?"

"Very much so. I find it to be less crowded and altogether more pleasant than most European cities."

"You must have traveled widely."

"I have."

Bebel hesitated and then smiled again in a way Ruarshi did not like. His reaction was hypocritical, he knew, as he'd been just as false since arriving on the doctor's front step.

"I may as well be frank with you," the man said. "I think the city fathers have set me an impossible task. They expect me to judge whether or not you are a healer. Rumor tells me you are, but I see our approaches to medicine are so different that no conversation can give me the information I need. What do you suggest?"

A few ideas leapt to mind, most of them unmentionable in polite company. But what had he expected? A warm welcome from a man whose own practice would suffer during the entirety of Ruarshi's stay? It fell to him to soothe the man's pride. Bebel didn't seem as venal as others he'd dealt with, so he obviously couldn't start off with talk of income and percentages.

"A demonstration might be best. Is there anyone in your household with a recent injury?"

"Oh, certainly. Wolter!"

The servant reappeared.

"The Miriyanti here would like to do you a favor. Take off your shirt."

Ruarshi watched with growing dread as the man—another youngster, probably no older than Johann—pulled his shirt over his head. Wolter paused and looked a question at his master.

"Turn around. It's not your front we're interested in."

The servant's back was covered in bloody welts, the result of a whipping administered within the past day or two. Ruarshi was so caught up in his own disgust that he missed some of Bebel's next words.

"… is a fool, but unfortunately she is also my only child. And the hired help is most definitely not to take that sort of interest in her, whether it is reciprocated or not. Wolter proved immune to verbal admonishment so I had to take sterner measures. Is something wrong?"

Ruarshi took control of his facial expression, smoothing it out until he was sure it was as flat and unrevealing as glass. He'd probably just ruined his chances of remaining in Mainz. Stupid. It wasn't as though he'd never heard of servants being beaten before, or seen results a good deal worse than this.

"You startled me. I apologize. If you will permit...?"

Bebel gestured for him to go ahead and sat back in his chair.

Ruarshi rose and approached the young man. Wolter stared back at him, terrified. "I'll not do this without your permission."

"I'm giving you permission," the doctor said.

"I understand that, but it has to come from him," the healer said. "I can heal your back. Not without scarring, but I can take most of the pain away. If you'll allow it."

Wolter's eyes left Ruarshi's face as he looked once more at the doctor. Whatever cues Bebel was giving him were apparently persuasive, because he stepped forward abruptly and nodded. "You can do it."

"Have a seat." Once Wolter was settled in the chair Ruarshi had been using, the healer pulled another up beside it and sat down. "This shouldn't take very long. While I'm in the trance, Herr Bebel, please do not touch either of us. It could be dangerous."

And yet he knew that the doctor was going to do exactly what he'd just been told not to. There was something coming through the bond-shield that gave the man's intentions away, something that Ruarshi didn't care to examine too closely. He didn't really have to. Eagerness to do the forbidden, to do harm, was easy to read.

So be it. He fell into a light trance and let his magic flow into the boy's back, while at the same time sparing as much attention for Bebel as he could. The doctor had already risen, he thought, and was even now stepping closer, reaching toward Wolter's arm...

Ruarshi sent a surge of power into the healing just as the doctor made contact, steering the greater part of the backlash down Wolter's arm and up through Bebel's fingers. Inevitably, he also had to absorb some of the shock.

He emerged from the broken trance gasping in pain. The servant seemed to have come through the incident all right; he looked to be more surprised than hurt. The doctor, on the other hand, was lying on the floor. His entire body was curled protectively around his right arm.

Ruarshi leaned toward Wolter. "Are you well?"

The boy nodded, pointed toward Bebel, and found his voice. "He needs... you have to..."

"I'll see to it." Ruarshi remained seated until he'd caught his breath and then knelt next to the doctor. "Herr Bebel? Take deep breaths. The pain will fade and you'll see you've suffered no permanent harm. That's it. Again. Try to sit up."

"Damnation," Bebel said, flexing his arm but not yet attempting to push himself upright. "Damnation. When you talk, Miriyanti, people had better listen to you. I—what are you doing here?"

A woman stood in the doorway to the room, watching them. Ruarshi flinched when he saw her. He hadn't known she was there.

"I'm observing your atrocious treatment of our guest. He did tell you not to touch them." She stepped inside and pushed the door shut. "I already see a difference in Wolter's back. You will let him finish?"

"Yes, Helene." Bebel levered his way into his chair. "I was merely trying to find out what it feels like to be on the receiving end of Miriyanti magic. Can't let the Italians outdo us."

Ruarshi was still on his knees on the floor. This woman felt… protective, and he was fairly certain the emotion was not directed toward her husband. A sense of relief ran through him, so strong and unexpected that he lowered his head in case any of it showed on his face.

There was a sudden warmth on his shoulder, where the woman's hand rested. "Do you need anything?"

He shook his head. "No."

"Then perhaps you'd like to return to your seat?"

"Oh. Yes." Helene helped him up. When her fingers slipped from his arm, some of the comfort she'd brought into the room went with them, and a deep coldness suffused his chest.

The doctor would let him stay. Of that he was now sure. Bebel was the sort of man who would view everything that had just happened as a challenge to his authority, and he'd want to keep the Miriyanti around until he was satisfied that they understood where the balance of power lay. Ruarshi had hoped for better but this would do. All he needed was sufficient time.

"If you're ready, Wolter."

"I am."

Because Ruarshi could now work without fear of interruption, the healing went more quickly than before. He opened his eyes a short time later and saw the results of his efforts, a pale swath of skin crisscrossed with pink.

"Flex your shoulders for me. How does it feel?"

Wolter's thin face broke into a grin. "It hardly hurts at all."

"Very impressive," the doctor said. "Very impressive indeed. You can pick up your shirt and go now, boy."

The servant obeyed with alacrity, hesitating at the threshold of the room where his master couldn't see him to smile at Ruarshi one more time. The healer inclined his head toward him and then turned back to Bebel.

"I wouldn't have thought a healer of your experience would be so squeamish. But no matter. I will recommend to the guild that you be granted permission to stay. The city council will not be an obstacle once the guild makes its wishes known. Would you concur, Helene?"

The question was sharp and addressed to the woman's back. She slipped out the door with a quiet, "Of course."

Bebel shook his head ruefully. "That woman. A trial to me since I met her. But she has a well-connected family, so what is a man to do? You are aware that there is a fee you must pay to the guild since you're not a member?"

The negotiations didn't last long. The doctor responded well to bribery, now that he thought he'd taken the measure of his opponent.

Ruarshi left as soon as they had finished, declining Bebel's offer of more wine. As he walked down the front steps and out into the street, he realized he was wiping his hands on his coat and he forced himself to stop. It wouldn't make him feel any cleaner.

## ☽○☾

"I don't care if the Holy Roman Emperor himself is there, and is suffering a heart attack and a stroke at the same time. With indigestion and cholera on top of it. You will not go to that house unless I'm with you. Let the Emperor die."

"Please, Ruarshi," Etienne said, "quit slamming around, will you? He sounds like a complete horror. I promise I won't go there alone, though I'm not sure why you're so insistent. You don't think he'd try to rape me?"

"Would you please pull your mind from the subject of sex for two minutes?" Ruarshi reached up to remove his coat and stumbled. His shoulder collided with the wall, hard enough to bruise. "Goddammit."

"What's wrong?" Etienne asked, rising. "What is it you haven't told me?"

"It's nothing." Which wasn't entirely true; it felt like his chest was being slowly crushed by a steel cobweb. "Just a bit of backlash. I saw to it that Bebel took most of it. His arm will be throbbing for a week.

Hands off, I'm sure it's not as bad as your headache."

"Okay, okay." Etienne backed away and leaned against the edge of the bed. "A week? That's a long time. You must have been pushing a lot of power around. More than you probably needed to heal flesh wounds."

"Damn right." On his second attempt Ruarshi got the coat off and hung it over the nearest chair. "I hope he has to use a sling."

"You knew he was going to touch one of you."

"Wolter. Not me. The good doctor never laid a finger on me. In retrospect I am grateful." Because the warmth of the sunlight seemed to help, Ruarshi remained standing near the room's one small window while he concentrated on his breathing. Etienne kept his mouth shut and let him do it, for a wonder. When he decided his lungs were functioning more or less properly again, he glanced at his student. The Illyana was looking at him strangely.

"What?" Ruarshi asked tiredly.

"That whole story about your forest sojourn," Etienne said. "You told me all that to help persuade me to come here with you, didn't you?"

It took Ruarshi several confused seconds to figure out what his student meant by 'forest sojourn.' When he finally did, his lips quirked. Not because what Etienne had said was all that funny, but because the Illyana still had the ability to surprise him. He hadn't thought the boy possessed sufficient insight to have put it all together.

"Yes, in part. I apologize for that."

"What was the other reason?"

"A warning, I suppose. Something along the lines of, 'Be careful, he's got a history of lunatic behavior.'"

"Oh, yes, that worked. I'm deeply frightened of you. Did you really take on six warriors single-handedly that night in Tomir?"

Etienne had caught him off balance yet again. Where was all this coming from, and why now? "No. Ardan was with me."

The Illyana rolled his eyes. "I'm sure she was a great help."

"She saved my life. That seemed like help enough."

"And all this happened the night after they, uh—"

"Yes." It had been inevitable that Etienne would get a good look at his back sooner or later. After years of close living that sort of thing happened, no matter how careful Ruarshi was. But his student had never commented on it or asked about it, not until today.

"And this afternoon you see a servant whose back has been cut up.

So to punish the man who did it, you set *yourself* up for days of un—"

"What's your point, Etienne?" Ruarshi was unnerved. He didn't have conversations like this anymore, not for decades could he remember having one like this, and he should have put a stop to it immediately.

"My *point* is that you don't have to manipulate me to get me to follow you. If you asked, I think I might follow you to hell."

Which was so eerily similar to something Wil had once said to him that Ruarshi felt his throat closing up. At the same moment the cobweb encircled him again, more fiercely this time, and he dropped the idea of leaving the room. Instead he leaned back against the wall, trying to give his lungs a little extra room to expand. To his intense annoyance he soon found himself struggling to keep his legs from giving out beneath him.

The effects of backlash were always unpredictable but rarely dangerous. He didn't think this instance would be different in either regard, though he couldn't recall ever having experienced anything quite so debilitating before. It looked like he'd have to take it easy until the reaction had passed. And if what had just happened also meant he needed to avoid aggravation, he thought he might have to send Etienne away for the duration. The boy was nothing if not aggravating. Perhaps there was a salt mine somewhere nearby that would take him in.

He looked up to see Etienne standing next to him, his face dark against the backdrop of afternoon sunshine.

"Stop glaring." His student sounded far too smug for Ruarshi's liking. "If it was me standing there, you'd tell me I'd gotten exactly what I deserved. If I could lecture my instructor I'd tell you the same thing. Since I can't I'll move on to the next step, which is getting you some food and making you eat it. Would you like to come down with me or shall I bring something up?"

Ruarshi growled at him.

"I didn't quite catch that."

"The room is delightful. I'll stay." He was quite suddenly ashamed of himself. "I may already have dragged you to hell, you know. We, you and I, are bait. Did you realize? What do I have to say to get it through your thick head? And what do I tell your family if the warrior kills you?"

"Now you're just being dramatic. I'm not the one with the fearsome reputation, and no one's out to get me that I know of. If I may be permitted to follow your thought process, I'd say you decided the Naishanti you're hunting may be able to get some blows in before you're ready, and you wanted a healer around to put you back together in case he does. That's a hell of a lot more sensible than doing this alone, and so I'm supposed to hold it against you?"

"That's reasonable but untrue. I'm not concerned about a single Naishanti. If I were to find out they were running in packs, that would be different."

"Then why am I here?" Etienne asked. The smile had vanished from his voice.

Ruarshi replayed his words in his head and discovered that he'd just told his student that he was useless. That he was here on a whim at best. Wonderful. Now he had to tell Etienne the truth. Didn't he?

Could he?

Maybe. He could at least try.

"If I'm anything at all, Etienne, I'm a healer."

"I know."

"Because of this," Ruarshi went on, tapping a finger against his temple, "it's happened that... from time to time I've been unable to heal. Flat out unable. Nothing's there because my connection to other people is gone, and skimming over their emotions just doesn't help. Am I making sense?"

"Yes. But what's that got to do with me?"

"I've found that there are two things I need to keep myself level. You're one of them."

"You mean you need a student," the Illyana ventured.

"Basically, yes. But I'm sure you're aware that I've sent other students away."

"You need a student you find agreeable."

"I'm not sure that's the right word, but it doesn't matter. I've never even thanked you for coming with me, have I?"

"I don't think so."

"I'll do it now. Thank you."

"Does this mean you're going to stop giving me orders and pelting me with grapes?"

"Of course not."

Etienne chuckled. "Good. That would just confuse me. I should mention that I wouldn't have missed out on any of this for all the *keth* in Miriyan."

Ruarshi's chest was loosening up again. Sort of. He took a careful step away from the wall. "I suppose I should take that as a compliment," he muttered.

"What's the other thing you need?"

Ruarshi's sigh turned into a cough. He took a few deep breaths before he spoke. "Can't you guess?"

"Courtesans?"

"Exactly. Physical contact."

"Well. Are you ready to wobble your way downstairs now?"

"Yes. You go ahead. I'll catch up."

"Not a chance. That wouldn't be very agreeable of me and I'd hate to be sent packing at this point. I'll go first, so if you trip on the stairs I can allow myself to be heroically mashed while saving you from a nasty tumble."

Ruarshi watched, exasperated, as his student preceded him out of the room.

)O(

Ruarshi stood on the second floor of the house they'd rented, staring at the massive four-poster bed near the front window in dismay. It was dark, squat, and ugly, like all of the pieces the owner had furnished the place with. And the mattress was inhabited. Lice. That would have to go—they'd donate it to one of the local monastery hospitals and let the monks figure out what to do with it—but he supposed he'd learn to live with the frame. Fortunately he'd spend most of his time in it with his eyes shut.

"Yecch," Etienne commented. "Why do Europeans put up with parasites? They're revolting. They're in this other mattress as well."

"We have advantages they don't," Ruarshi said. "Have you ever watched a family try to rid their home of them? Unless all their neighbors are doing the same thing at the same time, it doesn't work."

"It would still be worth the effort just for a few days of lice-free living. We've got to brighten up this room."

"I'll leave the decorating to you, if you don't mind. Start making a list of what we need. I've got an interview to conduct."

"Are they the wandering couple Margaret was talking about?" Etienne had come to stand beside him at the window.

"I assume so. They look rustic enough to be just in from the countryside. I'll be back."

He clapped a hand on his student's shoulder and ran down the stairs. By the time he made it to the front door, the pair had arrived.

Ruarshi swung it open before they could knock and was pleasantly surprised that neither of them jumped backward or cowered in terror. They had potential.

"I am Ruarshi. I expect you already knew that. You're looking for a position?"

"Yes, my lord," the male half of the pair said. "I'm Kilian Bonne and this is my wife Charitas. We were told you might need servants."

"Of course I need servants. Come in. We can go sit in the kitchen. Careful, it's dusty. We only got the keys this morning. Where are you from?"

"We're from a village near Wertheim, my lord."

"Sit. And quit calling me 'lord'. I'm not a member of your European nobility and I have a perfectly adequate name."

Ruarshi was in a good mood. He had been for days. He knew the root of it lay in the entirely unexpected talk he'd had with Etienne, and that the progress they'd made lately had only strengthened it. They'd finally gotten their permit from the city, Bebel was leaving them alone, and now they had a home. Soon they'd have servants to help them get moved in, and then he and Etienne could concentrate on healing. He wanted that in the same way he wanted air to breathe. But first things first.

"Sit, I said. I don't have to plant my own exalted ass in a chair before you do." He remained standing as they settled in at the table, every slow move reflecting the reluctance and discomfort they felt. What he was doing wasn't fair but he didn't intend to let up, not yet.

"You're both at least twenty pounds underweight. Is that why you're here?"

Kilian nodded. "We had a bad harvest last year, sir. It's looking better this year but our plot of land is just too small. We have to try something new or starve."

"So you have imagination. That's good. What can you do?"

"Sir?"

"What can you do, now that you're in a city?"

"I... can mend equipment. Repair this place if it needs it. Take care of animals and butcher them. I can split wood. I can run errands..."

"What about you, Charitas?"

She cleared her throat before speaking. "I can cook. I can make clothes, but I expect you'll use a city tailor for that. I know how to press laundry so you'll look nice. I can dry meat for the winter, and—"

"Is your food good?"

"I... um, I have been told it is."

"What do you think of it?"

Charitas was confused and on the verge of upset, but she hid it well. "I like it."

"Then I'm sure it's fine. Now the hard part: can the both of you live with two Miriyanti healers?"

"Yes."

"You answer quickly. Is that confidence talking, Kilian, or hunger?"

"We can do without a lot of things but food isn't one of them. We'll do what you ask us to. If we don't already know how, we'll learn."

"You'd never be asked to assist with magic. Etienne and I can handle that on our own. You're going to be close to the working of it, though, day after day. The front room is where we plan to receive our patients. Does that make you nervous?"

"There'd be something wrong with us if it didn't. But I've never heard that Miriyanti have aught to do with demons, so we'll be all right."

Ruarshi looked at the woman. "Do you agree?"

She nodded.

"People you run into will want to know what goes on in this house. And behind your backs, the Mainzers will ridicule you because you're from the country. How will you handle that? Charitas first this time."

"These city folk would already have starved if they tried to live our lives. They can laugh if it makes them feel better."

"And the other?" Ruarshi prompted gently.

"They don't need to know what happens here."

"You can talk about what you see when we're with patients. But we are not Christians and we've both lived a long time. Some of the things we say would not be well understood by others, and could impede our ability to make a living here if they got out. You will have to distinguish between what it's safe to say and what it isn't. When in doubt, ask. Does that sound reasonable?"

"Yes, sir," Kilian replied.

"Now, living arrangements. I don't particularly care, but tongues do wag, so I have to ask: are you are legally married?"

"Yes. Been married two years."

"You can set up a bed here in the kitchen if you prefer. The third floor is also available but it will be the coldest place in the house this winter. It's up to you. If you stay down here, you'll have to use something that can be folded or easily moved aside, so you're not constantly running into it. As to wages—"

"Are we hired, then?" The man had thoroughly mashed his hat, which had been mostly shapeless to start with.

"Yes. Unless there's something objectionable about the two of you that you haven't confessed to. Is there anything? Revolting personal habits? A secret dislike of foreigners?"

"Uh, no."

"So you're hired. I'll have you something stitched up in green and silver. Livery. Etienne—that horrible clattering is probably his fault—will get a tailor working on it soon. In the meantime, there will be a few items to move in and a few to move out. And the well ought to be looked at; the crank is jammed. Charitas, your first task will be to stock the pantry. We seem to have pots and cooking utensils, but of course there's no food in the house. Actually you'd better both see to that today. It's the most pressing need. That and mattresses. Ah, I forgot to tell you about your wages..."

By the time Ruarshi had finished, the couple seemed overwhelmed. But they were beginning to loosen up, which made him happy. Once Charitas even smiled at him.

They would do.

$$\text{)O(}$$

The old peasant Gerhard had asked about showed up at their house early one morning the week after they'd moved in. The weather had turned and they were all still huddled in the kitchen, bleary-eyed, when they heard the knock on the door. Ruarshi hastily tucked his shirt into his pants and nodded for Kilian to go see who it was.

The young man returned a few seconds later, bringing a wave of cold air with him. "It's an old man. There's a woman outside. He says she's sick."

"Ask him to give us a moment. Show them both in." Ruarshi set his mug aside and went up to the room he and Etienne shared, where he pulled on a coat and a heavy pair of boots. His student did the same, more slowly.

"You're moving like you're underwater. Would that have anything to do with beer?"

"Don't talk about beer. Please." The Illyana patted his stomach gingerly. "I'm going to stay away from the boys for a while. They're a bad influence on me."

"I don't care whether you keep to their company or not, but if you swallow that much alcohol again I'm locking you in this room. Is that quite clear?"

"Quite."

"If you're worried about throwing up, stay here by the fire until you feel better. The sight of vomit isn't going to improve the condition of my patients."

"I'm coming. Go on."

Ruarshi went back down to the front room, where he found Kilian standing nervously next to an old man.

"You," Ruarshi said. "I recognize you. Where's your wife?"

"Outside. Says she hurts too much to move. Can you come out and see her?"

He followed the man, who muttered the name "Henneke" when asked, out to the woman's side. She was lying in a pile of dirty straw in a rickety cart that looked to be on the verge of collapse.

"Would you wake her?"

"She's awake. Hilde!" The woman opened her eyes. "I've brought the healer."

"Thank you," she breathed.

"Christ," Ruarshi whispered. The old couple didn't hear him but Kilian did.

"What is it?"

"Go in and get the bottle on the right end of the second shelf up, would you?"

"Yes, sir."

Henneke looked a question at him.

"He's gone to get something for your wife to take. It will help her pain." He took a deep breath. "Hilde. You're dying and there's nothing I or anyone else can do for you." A blink was her only reaction. The old man was swearing at him but he ignored it. "You've got tumors in your brain, your lungs, your stomach. What I can do is give you something that will make you hurt less. Be careful with the dosage. Too much poppy taken at once will kill you."

Kilian approached and handed him the bottle. Henneke swatted at it, but missed.

"Take that back in," the old man said angrily. "We don't want it. I'll go find a barber."

"Who, if he is very stupid, will cut your wife open and she'll die that much sooner." Ruarshi clasped one of Hilde's thin hands and set the bottle in it. "Do you want this?"

"Yes. How much do I take?"

"Two pinches in a cup of water. There's plenty in there to last you." She'd grasped what he wasn't quite saying, he could tell. If she weren't exhausted she'd have been screaming loudly enough to wake the entire neighborhood.

Henneke was already reaching for the bottle. Ruarshi seized his wrist and held it until the man quit his halfhearted struggling. "Pain alone can kill a person if it's bad enough. You deny your wife the use of that, and I'll have you arrested for murder when she dies. She takes what she needs whenever she asks for it. Do you hear me?"

"I hear you."

Ruarshi let him go.

"How much will this cost us?" the old man asked, staring at the ground.

"Nothing. Kilian, fetch her a cup of milk. And a spoon." He took the bottle back, broke the seal, and stirred a large but nonlethal dose of poppy into the thick liquid. Even though he was more than a little afraid to, he looked up at Hilde before giving her the mug. What did she want him to do?

The woman met his eyes and shook her head, ever so slightly. Ruarshi watched, infinitely relieved, while she drank the concoction. When she was finished she clutched the bottle tightly to her chest.

"Thank you again. God bless."

He reached out to give her hand a final squeeze while Henneke climbed into the driver's seat. "Go in peace. You take care of her."

The man's only reply was a disgusted snort. Ruarshi and Kilian went back inside as the cart lurched away.

Etienne was waiting for them in the doorway.

"I saw the end of that," he said. "How long has she got?"

"Two to three weeks, at best."

His student nodded mutely. They'd handled similar situations in identical fashion in the past. "It took a week for someone to bring us a case we couldn't handle," he remarked, once they'd all returned to the warmth of the kitchen. "That's not so bad."

"No," Ruarshi conceded. "It could have been worse." He looked at Charitas, who was silently kneading bread in the corner by the oven. "You pray, right?"

She stopped what she was doing and nodded.

"Her name's Hilde. You might spare a thought for her the next time you're in church."

## Scores to be Settled

Ruarshi and Etienne were experiencing a late afternoon lull in business, and Charitas was in tears. After fetching a bucket of water for her, Kilian had retreated to the front room. Ruarshi raised his eyebrows at the man.

"She won't tell me what's wrong. She's bruising the vegetables. I hope you can stomach a mushy dinner."

"Think it's something to do with us?" Etienne asked.

Kilian shrugged helplessly.

"Shall we beard the lion in its den?" Ruarshi rose and stretched. "Well?"

"After you," his student replied.

"I'll watch, but I'll be keeping my mouth shut."

They traipsed one after the other into the kitchen, where Ruarshi sat at the table so he could watch Charitas in profile. She had a big knife in her hand and had gone from bruising the vegetables to slicing them. It seemed a hopeful sign.

"Charitas," he said sternly, "if you keep dabbing at your eyes like that, you're going to put one of them out. Then Etienne and I will have to clean up the mess you've made and dinner will be ruined. Tell me what happened."

"Miserable old bats," she muttered.

"Beg pardon?"

"They were only saying it because they saw me standing there. These city people are just as awful as you said they'd be."

"Saying what?"

"Nasty things about you." When she realized no one was going to interrupt, she went on. "How you're not a healer at all. They said you killed people instead of healing them. That you're not even a Christian, which you told us, but it sounded worse coming from them."

"Sounds like that old man's been complaining about you," Etienne said.

"Probably. Our spectacular failures sometimes come back to bite us. There's not a doctor on earth, or a hedge witch for that matter, who doesn't get accused of intentionally hurting people from time to time. It's how some people grieve. Nothing will come of it in the end."

"I don't know what to say to them to make them stop lying."

"It's not your obligation to defend us," Ruarshi said.

She waggled the knife at him. "You've harmed no one here. I'll not have it said I work for a murderer."

"You could tell 'em he'd be in jail if he'd done what they said," Kilian suggested. He'd been inching farther into the room as the conversation progressed, and now leaned against the counter opposite his wife.

Ruarshi grimaced. "No, I wouldn't be."

"Really? Why not?"

"We're *reichsunmittelbar,*" Etienne said with relish. "Untouchable unless the Emperor himself gives permission. We could literally burn the city down and run naked and screeching through the ashes, and no one could—"

"Etienne," Ruarshi said repressively. "Is your imagination always so vivid? Do you dream about this sort of thing?"

"Of course not."

"No pretending that you're offended, student."

"That's something else they said," Charitas remarked, shaking her head. "That you once set a man on fire."

A prickle ran down Ruarshi's back. "Quote them for me, if you would."

Something in his voice caught her full attention. "I don't remember it word for word."

"Do your best."

"'I was told he set one of his own afire, up in Miriyan.' That's as close as I can get."

"Fair enough." Ruarshi sat back and looked at Etienne, who was frowning at him. "Sound familiar?"

"... Yes?" The Illyana gestured vaguely. "I can't—"

"As it happens I was once responsible for a man going up in flames. For whatever it's worth, Charitas, magic had nothing to do with it, and he was trying to assassinate rather a large group of people when I intervened." He glanced once again at his student. "Someone is saying hello."

Etienne was grinning widely. "The Naishanti's here."

"He's here and he's rumor mongering, the bastard. What's he going to come up with next?" Ruarshi could think of several more tales the warrior could spread. None of them would make his life easier, and the one about homosexuality in particular could do him real harm. On the other hand, nothing Charitas had relayed to him had been that clear-cut a falsehood. Maybe the Naishanti had a sense of humor and was determined to hurt him with the truth.

He caught Charitas and Kilian exchanging an alarmed look. "Calm down, calm down. There's nothing amiss. I had thought there might be another Miriyanti living in the area, and we've been trying to attract his attention. Or hers. A word of caution: if you see someone around town with my coloring, or just with features that don't look quite European to you, let us know. And if such a person shows up here, don't even think of getting in their way. It's a warrior we're dealing with."

Etienne was smirking at him. Ruarshi didn't know what was behind it, but he was fairly sure he wouldn't like it. "What?"

"Nothing, nothing. Do you really think the Naishanti's going to come knocking?"

"Since I am not acquainted with this individual, I have no idea."

"But he—or she—is dangerous?" Kilian asked.

"Certainly. So is Etienne. So am I. The odds that the Naishanti would intentionally harm either of you are very low. To a warrior, attacking an unarmed servant would be like..." He wanted to say, *like kicking a puppy,* but that would be insulting. "Like backhanding a baby. It's not done."

The young couple still looked uncertain and Ruarshi didn't blame them. "If you want to be let go, I—"

"No," Kilian said emphatically. "But if this warrior found out we lived here, and wanted to ask questions...?"

"Tell the Naishanti whatever he wants to know. Do try to warn us if that happens. If we're out, put something unusual in the front window. If *you're* out, get back here before the warrior does."

"I don't like it."

"Nor should you. But you're part of my household and that means you're under my protection. The Naishanti will know that and it's worth more than you might think."

"I trust you," Charitas said, and went back to her vegetables. "Do you remember Dierk?" she asked Kilian quietly. "Got his hand mangled in an accident and died of it? We're as safe here as we are anywhere. Safer, probably. We'll just have to keep an eye out."

"Is this person going to attack *you*? Why are you trying to find him?"

"We want to talk to him," Ruarshi said. "That's all." Charitas said she trusted him, and not a minute later he was lying to her husband. It figured. "If the Naishanti attacks us here, leave the house."

)O(

Etienne shut the door to their room with a bang that rattled the shutters. "I keep meaning to say, and I keep forgetting," he gasped, his next words dissolving into tired laughter. He began again. "The other night when you told Kilian to leave if the Naishanti were to show up with mayhem in mind, you looked absolutely frightful. If he hadn't known you, I think he might have wet himself."

Ruarshi closed his book. He hadn't been enjoying it anyway. He was too preoccupied to concentrate on it, and it seemed to him that Boccaccio was vastly overrated. "What reminded you of this little gem?"

"I bumped into their bed on my way to the stairs and he jumped like a startled cat. I think his entire body left the mattress. Maybe he should rig up a curtain, to give them a little privacy."

"As long as it can be managed without the edge of it ending up in the fireplace."

"You should get out more. You're looking pasty. And the more I think about it, the more I become convinced that your reaction to what happened at Bebel's was peculiar. You're not getting sick, are you?"

"I'm not pasty." Ruarshi glanced at the back of his hand, just to make sure. It seemed normal to him. "And I'm not sick. The problem with your diagnoses is that you compare everyone to yourself, not making allowance for the fact that you've got ten times the energy of the rest of humanity. How are the boys?"

"They're as usual. They complain a lot. We were over at Kersten's tonight. You haven't met him; he's a carpenter. Wood shavings everywhere."

"Is Tobias still part of your group?"

"Yes. You should compare my energy level to his sometime and count your blessings. He could stay up all night and not even feel it the next day." Etienne sat down abruptly on his bed, which lay nearer to the door than Ruarshi's, and pulled off his boots. "Why?"

"After you left this evening I took a walk around the neighborhood. I found this." He pulled a piece of paper from under his book and held it out to the Illyana. Etienne leaned forward and took it from him. "Woodcuts, obviously printed here. The question is, which print shop is responsible?"

"Our Archbishop Albrecht, I assume," his student observed, holding the sheet closer to the fire. "Swallowing the city whole, and, um, excreting it? Along with a pile of corpses? Tobias and the others don't seem exactly friendly to Albrecht, but this…"

"Once I'd taken a good look at it, I cornered our neighbor for clarification. He wasn't happy to see it. Most of the townspeople, nobility excluded, opposed Albrecht when he was made archbishop. There was an attack on the town and a lot of people were killed. Now that it appears Albrecht is drawing his last breaths, there could be trouble. Especially since his likely successor is a man named Dieter, the same man most of the population supported in the first place."

"Scores to be settled. How long ago did all that happen? If everybody who wants revenge is eighty years old and incontinent—"

"No such luck. This was only thirteen years ago. Even if it had occurred decades before that, there would still be children and grandchildren to deal with."

"I'll ask Tobias when I see him again. If he or his brother had anything to do with it, he'll tell me."

"I can't make the decision for you," Ruarshi said, "but I would suggest that you stay away from Tobias' shop until after Albrecht is safely buried. Or until someone steps forward to take responsibility for that thing."

"Whoever did it has real talent. Not just anyone could carve out something so disgusting."

"Be sure to tell him that, if you meet him."

"I will." Etienne set the paper aside. "I wouldn't even ask, but it's become part of my evening routine. Any new developments with the Naishanti?"

"No. Unless you found him."

"If I had he'd be trussed up like a chicken and slung over my shoulder. Tell me what you think of this."

Ruarshi waited, puzzled, until a faint hum that he felt rather than heard began to emanate from the space between them. A shield. He traced it to its edges, only to find that it extended all the way from floor to ceiling, as well as to both walls. He grinned in delight.

"Very good."

Etienne's expression mirrored his own. "I practice when I'm out in the evenings. The boys think I'm absentminded. I know you don't like it that I'm staying out so late, what with god-knows-who creeping through the alleys. I hope this reassures you."

"A little."

"It was starting to snow when I came in. We'll have tracks to follow from now on."

"I wasn't aware that Naishanti had distinctive footprints."

"Hah. Cloven-hoofed, you mean? It's a pity they don't. Will you show me tomorrow how you tie off the shields around the windows and doors? I thought for a while I had the trick of it, but mine fall apart after a day or two."

"Of course."

"I'm for bed." Etienne stripped efficiently down to his hip-wrap, went to the nightstand to splash his face with water, and then eeled his way under the blankets. "Read as long as you want. Good night."

"Night."

Less than a minute later the Illyana was snoring. Ruarshi smiled again and went back to his book.

## ☽○☾

'Despicable' wasn't quite the right word to describe how he felt about himself, Ruarshi decided, but neither was it far from the truth. He shook his head in resignation and studied the chessboard sitting on the table in front of him, abandoned by its most recent players in the middle of a game. Whoever had been in charge of the black pieces was winning but it was a close thing, and he could see how the match could go either way. He reached out and moved a white rook a few squares forward, just to confuse the issue.

A whisper of sound from the hallway brought his head up, but no one appeared. His attempt to distract himself wasn't working.

Etienne had told him weeks ago how to find this place, reporting mournfully at the same time that the category of courtesan did not in fact exist in Mainz. Prostitutes kept to their particular houses and weren't allowed to go it alone. Nor were any of them well-educated. Ruarshi thought he might try to do something about that state of affairs, here in the next few months, but for today's purposes it didn't really matter.

He'd come early in the day, hoping to avoid other customers. So far he'd been successful in that. Unfortunately he'd also startled the house's staff, though their flustered reaction to his sudden appearance at their front door could just as easily have been caused by his identity. They probably weren't accustomed to hosting sorcerers.

Another noise from the hall. Ruarshi stood as a young woman in a pale yellow dress came into the room.

"You're the Miriyanti? Ruarshi Illyana?" she asked, looking him over in a way Etienne would have found hilarious.

The title she gave him was incorrect but there no was no need for him to explain that to her. "Yes. And you are?"

"A prostitute, naturally. You—"

"Isabel." The aggrieved voice belonged to a gray-haired woman wearing an exceptionally low-cut bodice who swept in and planted herself firmly between the two of them. "Is that any way to greet a customer?" She turned to Ruarshi. "My lord Miriyanti. I apologize. My name is Barbara and I own this establishment. You're very welcome here."

"Thank you. My name is Ruarshi."

"I know. I've been thinking of coming to see you ever since I learned you were in town. The barber who looks after my girls is a miserable hack. But that's not why you've come and we can talk about it some other time. I see Isabel has already introduced herself."

"After a fashion." Ruarshi glanced at the younger woman. She was still staring at him, a strange half-smile tugging at her lips.

"Shall I leave you two alone or would you prefer to see the other girls?"

"I think I'll let Isabel answer that."

Her smile widened. "Come with me," she said, extending a hand.

He reached out and felt her fingers fold over his. She began pulling him gently toward the doorway.

"Enjoy yourself, my lord," Barbara said. "Have someone fetch me when you're ready to go."

"I will."

Ruarshi followed Isabel in silence up some worn wooden stairs into a small but tidy room. She closed the door behind them and then leaned back against it. He sat down on the foot of her bed facing her and crossed his arms, carefully thinning his bond-shield as he did so.

Anger, resignation, and embarrassment. If that was how she felt about being alone with him, why had she been so aggressive just minutes earlier?

"Isabel," he said, "if you're having second thoughts, just tell me so."

"I'm not. Would you like some wine?"

"No."

"I'm going to have some, if it's all the same to you." She lifted a pitcher from a low table and poured herself a generous glass, then drank the better part of it down in a few quick swallows.

Ruarshi was becoming increasingly disconcerted by her behavior. "Are you always so determined to numb yourself up beforehand?"

"I like the taste of wine, that's all." She smiled over her shoulder at him and started pulling at the laces of her dress.

"Isabel, please stop."

Her hands froze in place. "Isn't this why you're here?"

He couldn't really say 'no' to that, now could he? "Yes. But not like this."

She snorted softly before turning again to face him. "Do you remember a little girl named Gisela Amrhein? You cured her of smallpox when she was eight. Unless it was a different Ruarshi who passed through here all those years ago."

"It was me, but I don't remember her."

"She was my grandmother. I owe my existence to you, you see. She told me you looked like an angel but I always thought she was exaggerating."

Ruarshi uncrossed his arms and stood to go. "You don't owe me anything, Isabel. I'm sorry my coming here has upset you. I'll find another house."

"Don't. I'm sorry. I didn't mean to make you think I felt beholden. I just wanted you to know why I was so quick to fetch you up here. I'm glad to finally meet you."

He hesitated. "I've been glad to meet people before, too. It rarely led me to want to sleep with them."

"If you go somewhere else, I'll just be jealous. I don't often wonder what grandmother would think of me if she was still alive…"

"But today, because I'm here, you are. Hmm. I hope she'd be pleased to see that you haven't starved to death or lost your teeth. Or become a nun."

She breathed a laugh. "You're right, she wouldn't have wanted me to disappear inside a convent."

"I see you've also managed not to die of the plague or be carried away by pirates. So you've done fairly well for yourself so far. How old are you?"

"Twenty-two."

"How old was your grandmother when she died?"

"Over seventy."

"So you may have a good fifty years ahead of you. What are you planning to do with all that time?" Ruarshi settled himself into a plush chair along one wall. He thought he might be able to salvage the situation after all.

"That's not something I think about much. How old are you?"

"Almost three hundred."

"And you've been able to keep yourself busy that whole time?"

"More or less."

"Doing what?"

"Healing people."

"Do you ever get bored?"

Ruarshi smiled. "Sometimes. Do you?"

"Yes. Why've you come back?"

"What do you mean?"

"To Mainz."

"I'm training an apprentice. He's fairly hopeless so it's taking longer than it should."

"His name's Etienne, right?"

"Yes."

"And he has black hair."

"This is true."

"I thought all Miriyanti had white hair."

"That depends. Etienne's mother was a Frenchwoman and he inherited her coloring. We've all got Europeans somewhere in our ancestry. Mine's just far enough back that you can't tell by looking at me, the way you can with him."

"Is that why he's so hard to teach?"

"No, no," Ruarshi replied, chuckling. "His problem has nothing to do with his abilities. It's his personality that gets in his way."

"How so?"

"I suppose you could say he enjoys life too much. Why spend time studying when there's so much else to do?"

"But you don't feel that way?"

"No, I suppose not."

Isabel sat down on the bed in front of him and smiled suggestively. "Care to join me?"

"In a moment. I was serious when I asked you what your plans are."

She lay back on the mattress and stared up at the ceiling. "Obviously I can't do this forever. That's as far ahead as I care to think."

"If you could read and write, you'd have more options."

"But I can't."

"Would you like to learn?"

Isabel shrugged. "Even if I could, no respectable merchant would hire me."

"You may be right. You may not. It's something to think about."

"What's Miriyan like?"

"Cold."

She waited for more. When no further information proved to be forthcoming, Isabel turned her head and blinked up at him. "That's it?"

"It's also full of Miriyanti."

"Why don't you like to talk about it?"

"There are too many people I dislike there."

"What people?"

"Warriors. A lot of warriors."

"Why do you dislike them?"

"Mostly because they dislike me."

One corner of her mouth quirked upward. "And why do they not like you?"

"I refuse to say," Ruarshi said, still smiling. "It must be my turn to ask questions again. Do you have any family?"

"Just a brother. He's a servant in a fuller's household. That's the kind of work I was looking for when I came here."

"You're not from Mainz?"

"A village nearby. How about you? Do you have a family?"

"Oh, yes. Rather a large one. If you count all my cousins, you'll end up with a figure somewhere in the low hundreds."

"Are you married?"

"... No."

"But you were?"

"There was a woman I was involved with. We stopped communicating with each other some time ago. By European standards we were never married."

"Do you have children?"

"One. A son. His name is Davyt."

"Is he a healer, too?"

"Yes."

"Does he look like you?"

"That's hard to say. We don't mature as fast as Europeans, and it's been thirty years or so since I saw him last."

"So long?"

It was Ruarshi's turn to shrug.

"I'm asking too many questions, aren't I?"

"I wouldn't say so. It seems to me we're having a normal conversation."

"I don't get a lot of that these days."

"I suspected not. Were you ever married?"

"No."

"Children?"

"No."

"I didn't think so."

"Why not?"

"You have an infection and it's made you barren."

Isabel sat up and gestured uncertainly toward herself. "You mean you've been...?"

"Checking people's health has become a habit with me. I hardly know I'm doing it anymore. The infection's not all that dangerous, but you'd be better off without it. Shall I get rid of it for you?"

"The surgeon told me I was clean."

"Is this the same one Barbara called a hack? That's not really fair of me, though. There are generally no symptoms for a surgeon to spot. Come over here and sit down."

She rose from the bed and approached him but remained standing.

"Give me your hand. And you really ought to sit. You could fall down if you don't."

"I'll be fine."

"If you insist." Ruarshi interlaced his fingers with hers, did what needed to be done, and looked up to find Isabel staring at him, wide-eyed.

"You did more than just cure me." Her cheeks were flushed.

"Which brings me to my next question." He hadn't let go of her hand. "Do you find the sensation enjoyable? Or would you rather I stopped?"

"God, no. Keep doing whatever it is you're doing. Was there really something wrong with me?"

"Cross my heart."

"Magic can do this?"

"It can when there's a healer behind it."

"I never wanted children anyway," she said distractedly. "And I think I like you." She gently extricated her hand from his and started unbuttoning his coat. "Is the rest of you as beautiful as your face?"

"No."

"No? Can I see?"

"Yes."

When she'd gotten his shirt off she spent some time examining his back, running her fingers over the scar tissue there. He could hardly feel it.

"Who did this to you?"

"More people who disliked me."

She started kissing the scars then, working her way upward to his neck. When she reached his nape he shuddered and turned to face her, slipping her dress off over her head.

Isabel giggled as she tugged at his pants. Once those had fallen to the floor along with the rest of their clothing, neither of them had breath enough for laughter.

$$\mathcal{D}\mathcal{O}\mathcal{C}$$

Ruarshi was still with Isabel when the sun rose the next morning. He lay back against the pillows, watching her dress in the thin gray light of dawn. Light snow pattered against the window.

"I'm going to have a talk with Barbara before I leave," he said.

She glanced over at him. "About what?"

"You. I'm going to make her an offer."

"What kind of offer?"

"I intend to bargain for your time. I'll agree to become the house doctor and sweeten the deal with some coin."

"Meaning... what? That you'll be my only visitor from now on?"

"Only if that's the way you want it. I understand that you'll still be living here long after I've left, and that there may be men in town you won't want to insult by turning them away. All I'll be paying for is your right to make that decision yourself."

"Barbara is bad-tempered when she first wakes up. You'd better stay here a while longer." Isabel sat down next to him and began running her fingers lightly through his hair. "The others aren't going to like it. Maybe you should leave it alone."

"That would certainly be the safest thing to do. But is it what you'd really prefer?"

"I don't know."

"Tell them I frighten you."

Isabel hesitated and then shook her head. "There are enough stories about you already. I don't think it would help you any to add that sort of thing to the rest of them."

Ruarshi stilled her hand by enclosing it in his own. He raised it to his lips and pressed a kiss into her palm. "You're lovely, Isabel. Don't tell me you've never dealt with jealous women before. Let me do this. Your life will get no worse and you may decide you like having time to yourself."

"That's what I'm afraid of," she said softly. "It'd be easy to get used to. And then I'd have to go back to what I've got now."

"If someone offered you an orange, would you turn it down because you knew it was the only one you'd ever get?"

"No."

"Then I don't understand your argument."

"Because you're making it sound silly. Why does it matter to you, what I do here when you're not around?"

"I want you to know that I mean you well. That's all."

"I believe you. Oma's stories…" Isabel's voice trailed off and she leaned forward to kiss Ruarshi on the forehead. "Barbara will start out by asking for twice what she'll settle for. Keep that in mind and you'll save yourself a lot of money. The cheaper I am, the less trouble I'll have."

"I wish you wouldn't phrase it that way," Ruarshi said, "but I'll point that out to her. She probably appreciates domestic harmony as much as anyone. Thank you."

"What for?"

"For granting me this sop to my conscience. There was a time when I didn't patronize prostitutes."

"You feel guilty about this?" she asked incredulously.

"I'll get over it. But I won't pretend it was really your idea."

"I hope all Miriyanti aren't so strange as you." Isabel stood and went over to her wardrobe, one door of which hung ajar. She elbowed it open the rest of the way and pulled out a heavy gray woolen dress, well-made but fraying around the hem and cuffs. "Have you ever laced up one of these?"

"I didn't mean to insult you, Isabel."

She draped the garment impatiently over one arm. "You didn't. But you're not sticking to the standard nonsense, either. I'm not awake enough to keep up with this."

"Then why put on that dress and run outside in this weather? Barbara should be making no more demands on your time."

"There's a little book I'd like to take another look at. It's got nice woodcuts that might help me learn to read it. Maybe. If I decide to go to the trouble."

"Ah. In that case, yes, I do know how to tie a woman's laces. If you'll let me put my pants back on first...?" Ruarshi threw aside the blankets and plucked his trousers from the floor. As he pulled them up, he asked her, "Is it always so cold in here?"

"Usually. Here's your shirt. Your coat looks like a litter of puppies slept in it."

"So it does. Set it there; it can wait. Let's get you into this dress. Arms up."

The fabric slipped easily over Isabel's slim body. Once it had settled into place, Ruarshi gently extricated her hair from the garment's high collar and asked her for her brush. She lifted it from the washstand and handed it to him wordlessly.

"Have you ever had a man braid your hair before?"

"No. I've never met a man I thought could do it without making a mess."

"So I'll be your first. Hold still."

Because his complaint about the temperature of the room had been anything but idle, Ruarshi tucked the brush under his arm and rubbed his hands together vigorously for several seconds before he got started. The stiffness in his fingers abated as he worked, and when he was finished he stepped back to get a good look at the result.

"It's perfect. You'll be pleased. Barbara does keep a mirror in the building somewhere, I presume?"

"It's at the bottom of the staircase. We passed it yesterday on the way up. Laces?"

"Patience, patience. How tight do you want it?"

"Keep pulling. There, that's it. Snug. I like snug."

"Snug it is." Ruarshi nuzzled her hair and she slapped at him ineffectually over her shoulders.

"Quit that. Are you done yet? I'll help you with your coat."

He smiled at her in silence while she buttoned it up. She grinned back at him.

"When should I expect you back?" Isabel asked.

"Soon, Nerthu willing and barring any disasters. You'll find I'm no satyr, I hope. Take good care, Isabel."

"I will. Barbara should be in a better mood by now. Good luck."

## Die Geschichte des Zauberers von Miriyan

"It's precisely *because* Bebel has left us alone that we have to go," Ruarshi said, gazing doubtfully into his mirror. He didn't really care for German clothing styles. In fact, he felt like he was wearing a well-tailored sack. "If he'd offered us insult, we could have begged off and everyone would have understood why. As it is we'll be the ones in the wrong if we refuse his invitation. And you understand all of this already, so why am I explaining it to you?"

"Because you mistook my surly, rhetorical question for something else?" Etienne ventured. "Or maybe because constant chatter helps to calm your nerves?"

His student's dark blue tunic, Ruarshi's birthday present to him, didn't seem to hang quite as oddly as his own did. Ruarshi squinted, trying to figure out where the difference lay, and decided it wasn't just a trick of the light.

"I think that tailor Charitas found has done me a disservice. I feel like a child in a grownup's clothing. Too late to do anything about it now. There's nothing wrong with my nerves."

"So I'm alone in dreading this? That doesn't make me feel better. Will you hold my hand?"

"No. And you might want to keep your sense of humor under wraps this evening."

"I could pretend to be a deaf mute."

"That's exactly what I was referring to. Are you ready?"

"I've been ready. I've spent the last five minutes doing nothing but watch you scowl at yourself. I hope your face doesn't freeze like that."

"If it did perhaps you'd be more inclined to show me some respect. Put on your coat and let's go."

They went downstairs, said their farewells to Kilian and Charitas—who were also bundling up to leave—and headed out the front door. Even though it was only late October, the weather was already miserably cold and four inches of fresh snow crunched under their boots as they made their way toward Bebel's house. It was a *Festtag* in Mainz and the streets were unusually crowded for that time of day, as people from all ranks of society walked, rode, and staggered to friends' houses and communal halls to celebrate. A few of the revelers waved at them as they went by. They waved back.

A small crowd of lesser nobles was gathered on Bebel's front walk when they arrived, filing slowly through the doctor's front door, their cheeks and noses red from the cold. Ruarshi hadn't met any of them. He didn't know whether to attribute that to their relative prosperity and the better health that went along with it, or to the rumors about him that were still floating around town. They'd had zero effect on the number of laborers and artisans coming to see him, as far as he could tell, but he wasn't so sure the same was true of the wealthier merchants and nobility.

Ruarshi smiled brilliantly at all of them and introduced himself and Etienne while they waited. If some of Bebel's guests were obviously uncomfortable in their presence, all the better. That sort of reaction, assuming it proved to be widespread enough, would enable them to leave even earlier than he'd planned without giving offense to the good doctor or anyone else.

He handed his coat over to the servant posted in the entryway and followed the others into Bebel's home, emerging into a parlor with a blazing fireplace along the back wall. A long room with a single massive table running down the middle of it could be seen through an open doorway to the right. It was as yet empty of food.

"No point in delaying the inevitable," Ruarshi said. "You go win them over while I scare them."

"One of these days," Etienne said wistfully, "I'd like to play the Great and Powerful Sorcerer. Charming Young Man is getting old."

"Just try not to get caught staring at bosoms. And drink as little of the wine as possible."

"Yes, yes, I know. What else would you expect me to do at a wine festival? Is that Bebel sliding ponderously through the doorway?"

"Yes. Oh, god, he's seen us. Brace yourself."

The doctor started in their direction, his wife on his arm, nodding and exchanging greetings with every guest he passed. There was no mistaking his destination, however, and it didn't take him long to reach them.

"Ruarshi," he boomed, "it is good to see you again. You remember my wife Helene? This must be your student."

"It is. Etienne Illyana, this is Herr Doctor Bebel. Herr Doctor, my assistant Etienne."

"Honored to meet you," the doctor said.

"As I am honored to be invited to your home," Etienne replied. "Thank you for making me feel so welcome in your city." He bowed formally, to a depth that made Ruarshi want to kick him.

Bebel was oblivious to the mockery. "It is the least I can do for a fellow physician. I trust your business is thriving?"

"We have no complaints," Ruarshi said. "The people here seem very open to our somewhat unorthodox methods."

"Good, good. Though I do have a bit of bad news in that regard, I'm afraid."

"Oh?"

"It's most regrettable. I heard from Helene's brother—you do know that her family is close to our Archbishop?—that Albrecht was considering calling you in to attempt a cure. Then he got wind of those unfortunate rumors, and, well… I believe the good Archbishop may have changed his mind. I am truly sorry. Do you have any idea where those vile tales may have originated?"

Ruarshi had some difficulty maintaining a somber expression. "I… regret that I may have lost the opportunity to consult on the Archbishop's case," he lied. "I'm sure I would have learned from it. As to the rumors, their origin is unknown. Probably a superstitious peasant in his cups."

"No doubt you're right. I hope you'll enjoy yourself here tonight, and will allow this gesture of hospitality to make up for your disappointment."

"You're a gracious host, Herr Doctor."

Bebel and his silent wife nodded and moved on. Ruarshi waited until he was out of earshot before turning back to his student.

"Sweet Nerthu preserve," he said quietly in Miriyanti. "I believe that man may have done me an actual favor."

Etienne was nodding. "Malicious idiots can be useful. I'll bet he pulled a muscle or two in his hurry to pass those stories along."

"Probably. If I act humbled and resentful all evening, maybe he'll consider that he's won our contest. Though I'm always suspicious of easy solutions." Ruarshi was still struggling to keep the relief from his face. Bebel could have no idea how much he'd dreaded a summons from the Archbishop, who was likely suffering from nothing more than old age and would therefore be quite incurable. He didn't need any entanglements involving dead clerics.

"Don't even try. You're not that good an actor. 'Brittle' might work."

Ruarshi snorted. "Remind me to put a spider in your bed. We'd better start talking to other people now. Please don't bow to anyone."

"There's no room left for that anyway. If Bebel's invited anyone else, somebody's going to have to start punching out windows."

Etienne arched an eyebrow and waded into the little gathering, Ruarshi following more slowly. He expected to have an interminable time, as he almost always did at such soirées, and tedious hours went by with no sign that his apprehensions would be proven wrong. Talk at the table swirled endlessly around the Archbishop's condition, the year's grape harvest, and the financial tribulations of those nobles not present. When someone directed a question at him, he kept his answers as brief and uninteresting as he could manage. Etienne was mercifully subdued. Only once did a guest bring up a topic that couldn't be deflected with banalities.

"I have read some of Ficino's work on the subject of magic," said a nobleman whose name Ruarshi had already forgotten. "Did you have the good fortune to meet him?"

"I did."

"I hope you do not find this to be an inappropriate suggestion, but could you work some magic for us?"

"I'd be happy to," Ruarshi replied. He'd learned decades ago how to deal with such a request when it came up in a social setting. "But as I'm a guest in this house, and our host is also an expert in the healing arts, it would be rude of me to exhibit my skills without asking that Herr Doctor Bebel be given a similar opportunity. What do you say, Doctor?"

At which point Ruarshi had the satisfaction of watching Bebel decline the invitation on behalf of them both. Even someone a good deal cruder than the doctor would have balked at the prospect of exhibiting a jar of urine, or something equally vile, at a dinner party.

Ruarshi pushed back his chair when the meal was over with an inward sigh of relief. Not much longer now and he and Etienne would be free to go, having fulfilled their social obligations. He didn't suppose he'd made any friends, but that hadn't been his purpose in coming and he didn't think he'd made any enemies, either. So all in all the party would end up on the positive side of his mental ledger, in spite of the excruciating boredom of the whole thing.

The guests had already separated themselves by gender when Bebel called for the masculine attendees to follow him into his library for a continuation of the dinner discussion, which would doubtless be livened up by drinks rather stronger than whatever was offered to the ladies.

"I miss Tobias," Etienne muttered as they trailed their host up a short staircase. "I cannot imagine what kinds of fun he must be having right now."

"Would you believe that I miss Ficino's badgering? You haven't seen a servant fitting Wolter's description, have you? I haven't spotted him anywhere."

"I've seen the same servants you've seen. Unless there was one hiding in your stuffed sausage?"

"No. There was no one in my pigeon pie either."

"How about your rat tart?"

"I must not have been served that. If you start laughing, Bebel will think we're making fun of him and we'll be back at square one. Swallow it."

"I… can't. I'm already too full." Etienne was gasping softly in an effort to suppress his mirth. "Rat tart… very rich."

"It's a good thing you enjoy your own sense of humor so well. Keeps it from going completely unappreciated. Give me another half hour, Etienne, and we'll make our excuses and go."

Bebel's library was bigger than Ruarshi had supposed it would be. One of the walls was completely covered in bookshelves containing what must have been upward of two hundred volumes, some of them obviously very old. He was impressed in spite of himself.

The doctor chose that moment to glance at him and a gratified smile spread across his face. "Quite a collection, isn't it? You're a man who appreciates the written word, I see. I own a number of books that have come off the printing press, but most of these were collected by my father and grandfather. Feel free to look through them. Come join us when you're done."

"Thank you," Ruarshi said.

He and Etienne weren't the only ones who eschewed the semicircle of chairs around the fireplace in favor of the books. A taciturn old man who'd come to the gathering unaccompanied followed them over.

"You did a good job back there," he commented, softly enough that the group by the fire wouldn't overhear him.

"Pardon?" Ruarshi paused in the process of pulling a water-damaged volume from the shelves to look over his shoulder at the man. Merten Something-or-other, he thought.

"You refused to entertain us. I've been acquainted with Bebel for so long I know what he's thinking before he does. Those men with him, they're all connected to Dieter von Isenburg. As such they've got no reason to care for our host. Yet here they are. How do you think he drew them in?" The old man stepped between Ruarshi and Etienne and began squinting at the mostly blank spines of the books arrayed in front of him.

"He could have hired tumblers," Ruarshi said mildly. The man was only confirming something he'd already begun to suspect, but he wasn't in the mood for this particular conversation. Especially as the information was coming from someone whose motives he understood not at all.

"Yes, well. He'll know better in the future. He wasn't alone in his miscalculation; I myself expected more of you. You have such wide experience of the world. Why don't you speak of it?"

"Dancing bears don't know how to talk," Ruarshi replied, thumbing carefully through a Latin treatise on surgical techniques. He'd finally mastered the language while living in Italy. "And if they did, no one would be interested in what they had to say."

"No reason to waste your cleverness on me. Here, take a look at this." The old man was smiling and holding a book out to him.

"What is it?"

"History. Read the title page." Merten obligingly swung back the book's cover.

*Die Geschichte des Zauberers von Miriyan.* Ruarshi read the title again in sheer disbelief. *The History of the Sorcerer from Miriyan.* A German translation of Wil's book, here, in this house. He set the Latin text aside, reached forward, and took the smaller volume from the man's outstretched hands.

"Bebel doesn't even know he has it. As far as he's concerned, this library is meant to impress rather than educate. But I am familiar with the book's contents and so are a few others. Berthold was simply too polite to mention it during dinner. So you see, there's no need for you to hide your light under a bushel. I'd like to invite both of you to our club next week. We meet for dinner on Thursdays at the Golden Tor.

It's by the city's northern gate."

Etienne had moved to stand behind his instructor and was peering at the book over Ruarshi's shoulder. "How does it compare to the Cock and Bull?"

Merten chuckled. "Much more elegant, suited to old men rather than young. It's the only place in town where you can find decent conversation. Trust me. I'm old enough to have tried them all."

Ruarshi shut the book and placed it gently back on the shelf. "Thank you for letting me know that's here. Does Doctor Bebel ever sell his books?"

"It's like trying to separate a dragon from his gold. In a word, no."

"That's unfortunate," Ruarshi said. He nodded thoughtfully. "What time do you meet?"

"Along about sundown. The proprietor holds a table for us in the back. You'll be there?"

"We will."

"Good."

The old man clapped him on the shoulder and went to sit with the others. Ruarshi and Etienne exchanged a glance and trailed after him.

## )O(

Ruarshi launched into a string of creative curses once they'd turned the corner and left Bebel's house behind. When he finally slowed down a little, Etienne interrupted his flow of words.

"So I guess we're left with the disgruntled old man theory? Fleshed out with the lip-flapping scholar theory?"

"I'm afraid so," Ruarshi said. "Those damn rumors don't necessarily mean anything, not with that book floating around town. I'd have a better idea of what to expect next if only I'd ever read it."

"You mean you haven't?"

"No. I tried once. After three pages I had to stop."

"Why?"

"Bad timing. That was right after Wil died."

"Oh." They walked in silence for several minutes before the Illyana spoke up again. "If you'd rather, I can stay home tonight. Tobias and the others will—"

"No, you may as well go ahead. I'm too aggravated to be good company and I need time to think. I'm no longer sure that staying on in Mainz will be worth our while. Not that I'd like to travel in this weather." It was snowing lightly again, the flakes landing delicately on their hats and shoulders.

"I won't be out long. If the boys aren't at the first few taverns I try, I'll give up. It's too cold for me to go chasing around after them for an hour."

"Is there really a tavern here called the Cock and Bull?"

"Yes. It's a rowdy place. I think livestock used to be sold near there."

"Enjoy yourself. And button your coat, would you?"

Etienne obliged, smiling, as he quickened his pace. "Yes, Mother."

Ruarshi hurried him on his way with a snowball and lapsed back into his reverie. He was more upset than he'd let on about seeing Wil's book in Bebel's house. Leaving it there when they'd said their goodbyes had felt to him like abandoning a holy relic to a pigsty, and he didn't intend to let the matter rest. Stealing the book was always an option, though he'd avoid going that route if he could. His method of getting into places he wasn't supposed to be made quite a bit of noise, and the servants would probably catch him even if the doctor and his family weren't home.

Under no circumstances could Bebel be allowed to learn that he had something Ruarshi wanted. Perhaps his wife would be more willing to negotiate, but going at the problem from that angle presumed that she had enough decision-making authority in that household to dispose of property on her own. Based on what little he'd seen, he doubted that was the case. Maybe he could just borrow the book one day, hidden amongst medical texts, and then forget to return it...

Ruarshi's head snapped around to his left, toward the street, before he quite realized what had alerted him. Someone was focusing on him so intensely that he could feel it from yards away; he'd experienced this before a time or two, and he knew what it meant.

He reacted instantly, raising a shield between himself and the source of that uncanny focus and pushing it outward, away from his body.

A pair of shutters on the wall behind him shattered, exploding outward with terrific force. Ruarshi pivoted, working frantically to strengthen his shield on that side as he threw up his arm to protect his head from the tumbling shards of wood. A large piece struck his forearm, breaking it with a snap he could hear even through the cold and his own concentration, and cutting a gouge along the side of his head. His second shield was in place a moment later, just a moment too late to be of any use.

The Naishanti was obviously good at what he did.

Ruarshi shoved his right fist between the buttons on his coat, giving his broken arm what stability he could, and started following the elusive mental traces of the man who'd attacked him. The focus was already gone from the Naishanti's mind. It had been replaced by a lazy satisfaction that heightened Ruarshi's fury and made him that much more determined to catch him.

The healer flooded his body with warrior's magic and broke into a run, ignoring the shocked looks of the people he passed. He supposed he must look frightful. He could feel the blood from his head wound soaking into his collar, and the entire right side of his face was wet. Without breaking stride he lifted his left arm and rubbed at his eye and cheek with the cuff of his sleeve.

Finally he turned a corner and spotted the man, who was smart enough to be keeping to the center of the street. The number of townspeople between him and the warrior had been dwindling throughout the chase, but there were still a good number present to witness whatever he did next.

Ruarshi wrapped a shield around the Naishanti's legs and the man tumbled to the ground, sliding several paces in the well-trodden snow. A heartbeat later the warrior broke through the shield, climbed to his feet, and once again took off running like a rabbit.

He had three choices. He could do something that would quickly and messily end the Naishanti's flight, while at the same time making it quite clear to a number of people in town that he was no healer. He could continue with his pursuit until pain and blood loss brought him to an unwilling but inevitable halt. Or he could let the man go.

Even though he'd never made it through Wil's book, Ruarshi was familiar with its contents. Most importantly, he knew what it *didn't* say.

There was really no decision to be made.

The healer stopped, leaned up against the nearest wall, and watched his opponent disappear into the darkness and distance. He hadn't even gotten a look at the man's face. But at least now he could be entirely certain that his quarry was nearby, and all too aware of his presence in Mainz. One had to find one's consolation somewhere.

Ruarshi had an unpleasant walk home through a city that seemed much less lively than it had just a short time earlier. No one was there to greet him when he finally staggered through the front door, leading him to conclude that his miserable luck was holding. He'd hoped that Kilian and Charitas would be in the kitchen, tending a blessedly warm fire, but it seemed that if he wanted one of those in the near future he'd have to see to it himself.

He climbed the stairs to his bedroom and sat down in front of the fireplace, where after poking halfheartedly at the embers he threw some kindling and a few small sticks onto the pile and watched, blinking with weariness, until all of it started to burn. Ruarshi then tossed in some larger pieces of wood and pulled off his boots one-handed, settling to the floor as close to the flames as he felt was safe.

His healing trance on this evening was a pathetic thing, constantly disrupted by the pain radiating from his arm and head. The gash on his scalp had already ceased bleeding, and though it was a clotted uncomfortable mess all it needed at this point was a good cleaning. It could wait.

Ruarshi turned next to his arm, examining the damage to it with as much dispassion as he could muster. The break was clean, though his wild run afterward had done quite a bit of damage to the surrounding tissue. He lay down and began knitting his own bone back together, working as carefully as he could, feeling his power pour out of him like water through a failing dam. Though his skills had improved over the years, he didn't have the same sort of raw strength he'd once had. Part of that he could attribute to the fact he had no *pir*. Wil had been an enormous help to him, back when they'd wandered the length and breadth of Europe together like gypsies. The rest of his decrease in strength he wasn't sure how to account for. Maybe his use of so much warrior magic had in some irreversible way diverted some of his power from his healing abilities. The notion made no sense, but it was all he'd ever been able to come up with.

Ruarshi had known he would faint before he was even half finished with his arm. He didn't fight the rising wave of darkness when it came.

## ☽○☾

The next thing he heard was the door slamming open and an appalled, "Oh, *fuck*," in Etienne's low voice, followed by a terse, "Fetch me a basin of warm water. And a jug of wine. That first. He'll be thirsty."

Ruarshi opened his eyes when he felt his student's presence at his side. "I'm glad to see you well."

"Good for you. As it happens, I am *not* very fucking glad. The story I heard made it sound like somebody'd shot you."

"No."

"Was it the Naishanti?"

"It was *a* Naishanti. I don't know if he was one of our exiles or not."

"Here's some wine."

Ruarshi could see Johann standing behind Etienne, and he had the vague conviction that there were other young men clustered near the doorway. He took the cup away from his student before the boy could commence treating him like an invalid, raised his head, and drank. When he was finished he handed it back and sat up.

Etienne glared at him before turning to the others. "Wait downstairs for me, would you? You can see he's alive. I'll be down in a minute."

The wide-eyed youngsters disappeared quickly and quietly, and the Illyana shut the door behind them.

"So what happened?" Etienne asked, lowering himself into a chair. His hands were shaking.

"My shields went one way, he went another. Busted up somebody's shutters and aimed them at me. I'll be angry about it again when I'm not so tired."

"You tried to catch him afterward?"

"Yes. Had there not been so many people out tonight, I would have succeeded."

"I shouldn't have left you."

"We'd just decided there *was* no Naishanti, remember?"

"I remember. Why in hell are you sitting up?"

"I don't receive guests in the horizontal, Etienne."

"They were worried about you. They wanted to come with me, and to be honest I think I'd have collapsed on the stairs if I hadn't been surrounded. There's a nice bloody handprint of yours on the wall there. Can I help you to bed?"

"That might be a good idea."

Ruarshi considered falling asleep on the way across the room, but he managed to stay on his feet for the required period of time. His bed was comfortable but cold.

"Warming this damn thing up is going to take me all night."

"After I heal you, I'll fetch Isabel."

"No."

"Then you're stuck with me burying you in blankets and overloading the fireplace. Ready?"

"Yes."

Ruarshi watched from the inside as Etienne mended the bones in his arm and the cut on his head, pausing only long enough to bring in some warm water to clean up the gore. It was a quick, efficient process that nevertheless took the better part of an hour. He was still in almost as much pain at the end of it as he had been when the Illyana came through the door.

"Now I'm going to mix something up for you and you're going to swallow it without arguing, like a good patient."

"No."

"Ruarshi…"

"If the Naishanti knew where to wait for us, he must know where we live."

"There will be six of us downstairs. Eight when the Bonnes get here. Do you really think you can outdo that in your current state?"

Ruarshi sighed. "I don't want my wits addled. But I'll have some more wine."

Etienne poured him another cup and sat without speaking while he drank it.

"I'm sorry I didn't take your warnings more seriously. I couldn't believe…" The Illyana's voice trailed off.

"It's shocking when someone directs violence at you. Always. It doesn't even matter that it's happened before."

"Let me bring Isabel here. Please."

Ruarshi shook his head and set the cup aside. "I want you indoors for the rest of the night."

Etienne pursed his lips but didn't argue. "You need to sleep."

"I assure you I will. If the Naishanti shows up, tell him I want to talk to him."

"I'm not letting him anywhere near you."

"There are some questions I need to ask him. The closer he is to me while I do that, the better. Proximity is the best deterrent I've got."

He knew the Illyana understood him. Perhaps he was thinking about the horse. "I should just invite him up here?"

"If he knocks, yes. If he destroys the door to get in, you probably shouldn't bother."

Etienne stood abruptly, disappeared around the corner, and returned carrying two heavy blankets he'd pulled off his own bed. "I won't be needing these," he said, bundling them carefully over Ruarshi's prone form and tucking them up under his chin until he was thoroughly immobilized. Not that he had any intention of moving.

"Thank you," he murmured. The agony in his arm was finally flattening out, and his head no longer throbbed in time with his heartbeat.

The light seemed to fade and when he opened his eyes again the fire was blazing and Etienne had disappeared.

It was several hours later, in the middle of that restless night, before Ruarshi realized that there was someone else in the bed with him, lending him a warmth that his own injured body couldn't sustain on its own. He felt a flash of anger, thinking Etienne had disobeyed him, and then he heard a familiar snore. A *very* familiar snore.

He relaxed and went back to sleep.

$$\mathcal{DOC}$$

The visits began early the next morning, but Ruarshi wasn't awake for any of them until well after noon. Former patients, neighbors, and assorted well-wishers, concerned about the tale they were hearing of a Miriyanti having been assaulted in their city, stopped by bearing gifts of food and promises of assistance. Bebel sent a servant to inquire after his health, a runner from Isabel's establishment appeared on the front step, and an official from the magistrate's office interviewed an uncommunicative Etienne about the particulars of the incident. He left unsatisfied, pledging to return at a later date.

By the time Ruarshi had gotten himself stripped, bathed, and reclothed, the sun was already plunging toward the western horizon. He tottered down the stairs and into the anxious, welcoming arms of Charitas. She pulled back immediately.

"I'm sorry, sir, I shouldn't have done that, but I was so worried… People have been bringing food. Are you hungry?"

"Don't apologize. People?" Ruarshi asked, nodding to Kilian, who'd helped him earlier with the tub and bathwater.

"Dozens of them," Charitas said. "Almost anything you might want to eat, we have."

"Warm up whatever sounds good. Where's Etienne?"

"Here." He was leaning against the door frame, smiling wryly. "Civic pride is a funny thing. And we must have become enormously popular when we weren't looking. Sweet old ladies have been kissing my cheeks all day."

"Huh," Ruarshi said. He pulled out a chair and sat down. "Thank you for receiving them."

"There've been a few who weren't quite so old. And Peter's on his way over, carrying something in a basket that looks to be heavier than a chicken."

"At this point he could carry an ox."

Margaret's younger son had been a regular visitor of theirs for some time now. Their front room, complete with its mysterious bottled contents and its regular stream of interestingly afflicted visitors, had become a favorite haunt of his since his recovery. They tolerated his presence and taught him not to stare at the less fortunate, or make rude comments.

As anticipated, Peter began banging on their door a few seconds later. When Etienne opened it, Margaret and Johann had caught up with the boy. He ushered the entire family into the light and heat of the kitchen.

"No, no, please don't stand up," Margaret said quickly when she saw that Ruarshi had started to rise. He nodded to her gratefully and sat back.

Peter stepped forward and set the basket on the table with all the gentleness one would expect from an excited eight year-old. His mother winced.

"Those are peach preserves. They probably survived that."

"Thank you, Margaret."

She was looking at him critically. "I'm not here to ask what happened. I know you've been getting that question all day. I'm just relieved to see that the story I heard was an exaggeration."

"Assault by harquebus," Etienne said. "No, I'm not kidding."

"No firearms involved," Ruarshi said. "An accident of some kind, I'm sure." He was watching Johann as he spoke. He knew that some part of his conversation with Etienne the night before had been overheard, but the details of the scene had vanished from his memory. He couldn't even recall what language the two of them had used.

The young man glanced at the Illyana's bland face before responding to Ruarshi's implicit question. "Must have been." To his credit, Johann appeared only mildly puzzled.

"Well, that's good," Margaret said. "I'd hate to think it was anything else. Let me know if you enjoy these. I'd be happy to give you more."

"We will."

"Come on, boys. The healer needs his rest." Her eyes lingered on the gash that marred Ruarshi's temple before she turned away, clearly still worried in spite of his reassurances.

Etienne ushered them out the door and returned to his earlier position.

"How much did you tell Johann?" Ruarshi asked, rubbing his forehead.

"Nothing, but you don't bar the doors and ask five of your friends to stay overnight because there's been an accident."

"So that's five families who will know we're lying. They'll talk to their friends and neighbors… God. I'm going to have to pretend I don't remember any of it. With this head wound I might even be believed."

Etienne was nodding. "That would be safest."

"But it was the warrior?" Kilian asked. He was perched on the edge of the bed he shared with his wife, while Charitas silently stirred at a pot hanging over the fire.

"Oh, yes. The bastard. I'd give you a description of him if I could."

"I could rig something up, over the doors. Something heavy that would fall on him if he came in at night."

Etienne's face had lit up at the idea but Ruarshi was already shaking his head. "He and I need to chat. Giving him a concussion won't really make that any easier."

The Illyana turned and strode away, shutting the door behind him more firmly than was necessary. Ruarshi sat staring after him until Charitas spoke.

"You've got to let him help you, sir," she said gently.

"He has. He does."

"Beyond the healing, I mean. He's got himself back together now, but I was watching him this morning when he looked in the mirror and saw a smear of your blood on his cheek."

"What did he do?" Ruarshi asked reluctantly.

"Nothing. But the look on his face… it was like he'd just taken a beating and thought he'd deserved it."

So it was worse than he'd supposed. "What would you suggest?"

"Tell him the rest of it, Chari," Kilian interjected.

"But that's the only important part," she said stubbornly.

Ruarshi waited, eyebrows raised, for her to continue. With an aggrieved sigh, she did.

"He swore a little, afterward."

"He said you were a piss-poor excuse for a healer and that if you meant to let yourself be killed, he wasn't going to fucking wait around to see it," Kilian said.

All of which did sound a lot like Etienne venting his frustrations, if a bit more emphatically than usual.

"What do you think I should do?" he asked again.

"Take him seriously," Charitas said.

Ruarshi's chin came up. "I do."

"You care for him, that's clear enough, but you don't listen to a word he says once you've made up your mind."

To which his only honest response would be, *That's how I am with everyone, so Etienne's got no reason to feel particularly put-upon.*

Ruarshi placed his left hand on the tabletop and pushed himself to his feet. "You're right." He couldn't bring his student here, issue dire warnings, and then attempt to shut him out of any of it. Even though they now knew for certain that the Naishanti was a danger to them. Even though he'd lost one group of students already, in circumstances that still gave him the occasional blood-soaked nightmare.

Etienne knew him well enough to have guessed what he'd so far left unspoken—that he'd intended to meet with the warrior in private. If he brought the Illyana into that conversation it would force him to be more cautious, which wouldn't necessarily be a bad thing and was probably all his student wanted from him. That and the chance to see how it would all turn out. Etienne was as bad as Lorion when it came to jumping into dicey situations out of sheer curiosity.

Allowing his student to put himself in harm's way went against all his best and deepest instincts, and making the offer was going to be difficult. None of which meant he could let it wait.

Ruarshi left the warmth of the kitchen and went into the front room, where Etienne sat staring at the front cover of an unopened book.

$$) O ($$

Neither Ruarshi nor Etienne left the house during the next five days except to run the quickest and simplest of errands in each other's company. Patients continued coming to their door, at first in a tentative trickle but soon in a renewed torrent. Ruarshi was of very little help to the Illyana in treating them. As the pain in his arm subsided it was replaced by a persistent lassitude that left him unable to perform more than two or three healings each morning, after which he retired to the bedroom to rest. It didn't take Etienne long to see through his feeble excuses and insist on another examination. In spite of its thoroughness, it revealed nothing out of the ordinary. Charitas ascribed his exhaustion to their diet and started adding more meat to their meals.

Ruarshi refused to speculate about what might be wrong, or to give in to his growing irritation with himself. Most of his waking hours were spent concentrating on the emotions coming to him through his bond-shield, which he kept deliberately thin. He could detect no traces of the Naishanti's presence in their neighborhood.

The exercise was good for him, though, involving as it did a sustained but not excessive use of his power. It also enabled him to keep track of his returning strength. When he was once again able to monitor everyone within about a hundred-yard radius, he decided he was mostly recovered and could return to a more normal schedule. Etienne was less sanguine about his intentions.

"Merten?" his student asked incredulously, blocking the doorway of their room like a recalcitrant ox. "That desiccated old husk can wait. I'm sure he doesn't expect to see you there, not after what's happened."

"So we'll surprise him. I want to know why he's so interested in us."

"Because we're fascinating people. Put him off for a week."

"I can't stay cooped up in here forever, Etienne. Nor should I. If the Naishanti is still in town, and paying attention to our movements, I've already given him more gratification than he deserves. As you've noted, I have a fearsome reputation to uphold." He finished buttoning his coat and went to slip past the Illyana. Etienne's arm shot out to bar his way.

"Yes?" Ruarshi asked, as patiently as he could. "You have something else on your mind?"

"I'm remembering a conversation we had the other day. I believe you said something about paying more attention to my concerns. I was under the impression that you intended to start doing that right away. Did I misunderstand you?"

"You did not."

"Good. Didn't think so." Etienne glanced quickly around the room, then shook his head in frustration. "Wait here."

He clattered down the stairs, and a moment later Ruarshi heard Charitas' voice raised in complaint.

"Come back here with that!"

"Soon, love," the Illyana replied cheerfully. "I promise."

A determined thumping started up at the base of the staircase. Shaking off his bemusement, Ruarshi went out onto the landing and saw Etienne struggling up the stairs with a heavy iron cook pot. Some of Charitas' latest creation slopped out onto the steps and the Illyana's boots as he watched.

"Damnation," his student muttered, but he didn't pause or even slow down. Etienne was breathing heavily by the time he ascended the final step and set the pot down next to Ruarshi's feet.

He grinned triumphantly at his instructor. "If you can lift that with your right arm, you can go talk to Merten this evening. If you can't, the arm's not sufficiently healed and you have to stay here. Deal?"

Ruarshi felt himself flushing. "And how long would you have me hold it up?"

A flash of alarm crossed Etienne's face, leaving a much more uncertain smile in its wake. "Until I count to ten."

"Very well." Ruarshi considered the pot. There was no way he could pick it up without reinjuring himself and both of them knew it. Still, the Illyana had made it possible for him to win this little battle of wills if he really wanted to, and there was clearly quite a bit more at stake here than his dinner plans. To back down would mean surrendering some of his independence to a man significantly younger than himself, a man whose experience of the world, if not necessarily his judgment, couldn't hope to match Ruarshi's own.

On the other hand, it would also mean that his word, once given, could actually be trusted. Or had he just been lying to the boy to make himself feel better?

Without a word he unbuttoned his coat and went back into their room to hang it up. When he returned to the landing, Etienne was still there waiting for him.

"You thought about that a lot harder than you should have had to," the Illyana said.

"True. But try to see it from my point of view. A decision I made may have ruined my son's opportunity to become a healer. What's another bad decision that results in a temporary inconvenience, compared to that?"

"We haven't got so many healers that we can afford to waste any. He'll be fine, one way or another."

Unexpected tears stung Ruarshi's eyes. He turned his head and blinked them quickly away. "I hope you're right."

"About this, I am. Sometimes it helps not to be personally involved."

Ruarshi nodded. "I think we'd better get that pot back to the kitchen before Charitas comes to get it."

"Probably. I brought it up here, I can—"

"There's nothing wrong with my left arm. Here."

Between the two of them, they managed to carry the pot back down to the first floor with no further spills. Charitas scowled at them but, perhaps sensing their mood, said nothing.

## The Print Shop

Ruarshi was even jumpier than his student by the time they reached the Golden Tor a week later. Nothing of note had occurred in the interim, a fact which made him more uneasy rather than less. He wanted the warrior out in the open where he could see him. Or at least sense him. The man obviously wasn't eager to oblige.

They found Merten after a brief search, sitting with three other men in a separate room at the back of the tavern. What followed was an entirely amiable if bland dinner, during which he and Etienne fielded questions about their personal histories and studiously avoided speculating about current events, even when pressed to do so. They'd both had plenty of practice avoiding political controversies while working for Casimir, and neither of them particularly liked being cast in the role of oracle in any case. Merten responded to their evasions with aggravated amusement, but the others seemed willing to let them pass. At no point did Ruarshi sense any hidden malice, and he decided he could put the issue of the rumors to rest once and for all. Even if some of the damaging information about his past had come from one or more of these men, their motive clearly wasn't ill will. All of which left him dwelling on the Naishanti again and worrying.

When the dinner had ended and the others had excused themselves, it was still fairly early in the evening. Ruarshi was turning toward home when Etienne snagged him by the elbow.

"Want to run by the Cock and Bull first?"

Somewhat to his surprise, Ruarshi found himself nodding. "Why not?"

His student's smile broadened and he pointed down an alley to their left. "This way."

He followed the Illyana southeast through the city, going by such a torturous route that Ruarshi was sure Etienne was trying to get him lost. For whatever perverse reason.

"I know where we are, you realize. Approximately."

"Good. You never know when you might end up in another foot chase."

"That's not in my plans. No, I'm not going that way. Has your nose stopped working altogether?"

"Come on. That's part of my purpose. Nobody who goes to the Cock and Bull ever washes. You'll thank me when we get there."

Ruarshi snorted but gave in. A few twists and turns later they'd emerged onto a much wider street, and he could just make out the tavern's sign by the light spilling through the building's closed shutters. They practically dove through the door, eager to escape the frigid autumn air.

It was much warmer inside, though that had less to do with the feeble fire in the corner than with the sheer number of bodies pressed into that small space. Ruarshi started scanning faces and clothing, noting sons of the merchant class shoulder-to-shoulder with the more ambitious sort of artisan. He could guess which of the two groups had moved outside its usual territory, but everyone seemed comfortable enough with the situation. Interesting, and very much the sort of place where Etienne always seemed most at home.

Ruarshi followed his student toward the fire, slipping carefully through the crowd. Etienne was hailed several times as they crossed the room, and a space was already being cleared for them by a dark-haired young man before they'd made it halfway to their destination.

"That's Kersten," Etienne said over his shoulder. "I've mentioned him, right? And there's Albert. Which ought to mean that Michel is here somewhere, too."

They took their seats at the bench amid a welter of introductions. Ruarshi clasped hands with at least a dozen men before Etienne leaned back, satisfied.

"Fair warning: Max, the burly one with the beard, is convinced he has some sort of obscure disease. He may pester you about it. I've come to the conclusion that he's not very handy with the barmaids and wants something to blame it on. Jasper suffers from an obsession with demons and thinks we must know more about them than we're admitting to. I'd recommend pretending you can't hear him."

"That shouldn't be a problem," Ruarshi said, raising his voice to

make himself audible over the general commotion. He was beginning
to be sorry that he'd come. The room was too loud and full of too
many people, and only the fact that he was sitting at the end of a bench
was making it possible for him to hold his claustrophobia at bay.

The Illyana smiled and hailed a harried-looking waiter, who brought
over two sizeable mugs of dark beer. Ruarshi took an obligatory swallow amid cries of *"Prosit!"* from all sides and then settled in, determined to enjoy himself.

Fortunately that turned out to be less difficult than he'd feared. After he'd responded to an initial flurry of curious questions from Etienne's little group, they stopped focusing on his presence among them
and settled back into what was clearly their more usual rhythm of interaction, which consisted almost entirely of crude jokes made at each
other's expense and stories about women. The Illyana was unusually
reticent when it came to the latter subject, and Ruarshi wasn't the only
one to notice.

"No new tales of conquest for us, Etienne?" Albert asked with a
smirk.

"I was just saving the best for last," the Illyana drawled, tapping at
the rim of his mug. Though he'd been sipping steadily at the beer since
he'd gotten it, Ruarshi could see that very little had actually disappeared.

"A likely story," Max said. "Go ahead and spill it."

"Can't. I'm right in the middle of putting the whole thing into verse,
you see, to do it justice, and German is such a nonpoetic sort of language that it's taking me longer than it should."

Which opened up a whole new bag of insults and completely
changed the subject, as Etienne had no doubt intended. Ruarshi
frowned down at his beer. Under different circumstances he would
have found a reason to head home so his student could speak more
freely, but that wasn't an option this evening. A quick trip outside to relieve himself would have to suffice.

He rose, clapping a hand onto Etienne's shoulder. "I'll be right
back." He waved vaguely toward the back of the tavern. "Have to answer nature's call."

The Illyana looked annoyed but responded only with a mumbled,
"All right."

Ruarshi made his way out to the building's noisome yard, took care
of his personal needs, and then loitered in the vicinity of the kitchen
door for a while. He'd never heard about Etienne's sex life in any detail,

and he definitely didn't want to end up back at that table in time to
learn anything that would embarrass them both. He cupped his cold
hands over his mouth and breathed into them, counting the minutes.

When he decided he'd probably waited long enough he ducked back
inside. He emerged a few moments later from the narrow hallway into
the main room and came to a startled halt. There was a thin, roughly-
dressed man, a peasant by the looks of him, standing in the now open
doorway and addressing the eerily quiet crowd. He was talking about
someone he called the Drummer, and though Ruarshi would have liked
to have the chance to make some sense of his harangue, he instead
found himself focusing on a small table off to his right. Waves of hostility, bordering on violence, were coming from three of the men seated
there.

Ruarshi abandoned his attempt to catch Etienne's eye and was already moving toward the door when one of the men jumped to his feet
and started pushing his way through the crowd. He was quickly followed by his two friends. They were shouting now, the peasant was
shouting back, damn him, and Ruarshi was paying very little attention
to any of it.

He reached the exit first, grabbed the startled peasant by the arm,
and pulled him out into the street. "Those men intend to do you serious harm. I suggest you leave. Now."

One of the voices from inside the tavern rose about an octave in
pitch, as though its owner had been surprised by something. If Etienne
had gotten himself mixed up in this...

The wiry little man nodded and pressed a small object into his hand,
murmuring, "Blessings of the Virgin be upon you." Then he turned
and walked hastily away.

Ruarshi shoved the item—it was made of leather, whatever it was—
into the front of his coat and headed back toward the tavern. Someone
came hurtling out of it and very nearly collided with him.

It was the ringleader, with his friends right behind him. Dozens
more trailed after them. Etienne was among the first few out the door.
Ruarshi shot him a warning look which the Illyana pretended not to
see.

The man glanced up and down the empty street before rounding on
Ruarshi, his face livid with anger. "I don't guess you're going to tell me
which way he went?"

"No," Ruarshi replied mildly. If the man came after him, he thought
he'd incapacitate the fellow with a particularly devastating bout of nau-

sea and vomiting. The amount of alcohol in the man's system would make it easy to do. It would just take a bit of tweaking here and there once he got close enough.

"Those people are thieves and heretics. They're not even supposed to be in the city, but where you see one, you know there'll be others. They're like rats that way."

"Let it go, Nyclas," one of the onlookers said. "It's not worth fighting about."

"I think it is," the man said, looking back at Ruarshi. "But not with you. You're a foreigner and I guess you don't know any better."

"We can find him on our own if we start now," one of his friends said, brushing past Ruarshi and starting off down the street in the wrong direction. "Let us keep our town clean, Miriyanti. It'll mean less work for you later."

The trio moved off into the night. Ruarshi watched them go, wondering if he should have put them all into a nice deep sleep when he'd had the opportunity.

"Don't even bother saying it," Etienne remarked, coming up beside him as their audience dispersed and throwing an arm around his shoulders. "I'm not the one who hurled himself between that big German and his target."

"So what exactly did you do?"

"Tripped him. One of his buddies fell over on top of him, which was probably the only reason that stupid farmer had time to get away. He thought it was an honest stumble, too."

"Since you didn't get caught, I have no complaints."

"Good. I thought the whole thing was pretty exciting."

"You would. I should have collapsed the table onto them before they could even stand up."

"But that would have left nothing for me to do."

"A great tragedy, I'm sure," Ruarshi said, "but it would have made our role in this quite invisible, which I would have preferred. Never let anyone know that you're up to something unless there's no way to avoid it. But that's really not the sort of thing I brought you here to learn."

"Of course it is. Miriyan's my home, too."

Ruarshi shrugged out from under the Illyana's arm. "Enough of that. Let's go find out who that farmer was."

)O(

As it turned out, the man apparently belonged to a small but growing sect of heterodox Christians who'd been swept up in the enthusiasm created by an eloquent young preacher named Hans. He was a swineherd, or a cowherd, or a festival drummer, or an unlikely prophet of God, depending upon whom one was talking to. It was immediately obvious to both Ruarshi and Etienne that their poorer patients held much more favorable opinions of the man than did their wealthier customers, which was only to be expected since part of Hans' message involved robbing from the rich to give to the poor. With God's blessing, no less, as He'd never meant for the world to divide itself into social classes in the first place.

It was a dangerous doctrine, and Ruarshi professed ignorance of it all when the magistrate's man came by a few days later to ask again about what had happened the night of Bebel's party. He was annoyed by the city's interest in the incident at the Cock and Bull, but not greatly troubled by it. The preacher's people had nothing to do with him. Nevertheless, he held onto the piece of leather he'd been given, upon one surface of which someone had stamped the crude outline of a drum.

He and the Illyana were tidying up the front room of their house late the next afternoon and had just succeeded in chasing Peter out the door when a single church bell in the northern part of the city began to ring. It was soon joined by all the others, creating a discordant and vaguely alarming effect. Since it was neither a Sunday nor a holiday, the meaning of the unexpected noise had to be sought elsewhere. Ruarshi was wondering uneasily about the Archbishop's health when Etienne looked up at him from the row of bottles he'd been putting back in order.

"Tobias never did tell me whether or not his shop was responsible for printing that woodcut."

"Let's not get ahead of ourselves." Ruarshi tossed a pillow back where it belonged and went into the kitchen. Charitas was kneading dough, sitting with her back to the oven. A clattering sound from the yard explained Kilian's momentary absence.

"Any idea what that's all about?" he asked her.

She shrugged. "Probably the Archbishop. Word is he's doing poorly."

"Any other sick nobility you've heard of?"

"No."

"Are you sure? I'd rather not have to go out in this."

"Why would you be doing that?" Kilian asked, coming through the back door with an impossibly large load of wood. "It's cold enough to freeze spit out there." He knelt to drop the wood next to the fireplace in a sort of controlled avalanche.

"Because I have an idiot for a friend," Etienne said, pushing past Ruarshi to sit next to Charitas. "Will there be trouble if it's the Archbishop who's died?"

"Maybe," Kilian said. "I imagine it'll be short-lived. Nobody in their right mind is going to be up for much troublemaking on a night like this."

"I more or less told Tobias I'd be there to help him when this happened." The Illyana pushed himself back to his feet. "No point in trying to warm up first. Want me to get your coat?"

"Yes, if you would."

Charitas dusted the flour off her hands and stood. "The two of you aren't leaving here until you've eaten. If you're in that big a hurry, you'll just have to chew faster."

"Yes, ma'am."

"No lip from you. Give me the time it takes to heal a broken finger and I'll have you fed."

Ruarshi smiled and sat down, content to delay his foray into the unpleasant December evening for a while. In his limited experience, urban unrest was generally a lot less spontaneous than it looked, and he doubted the delay would cause them to miss anything of importance.

Etienne, on the other hand, tore through his dinner with more than his usual alacrity, ignoring Charitas' dark looks. Ruarshi surrendered to his student's urgency and they were bundled up and out the door before the sun had disappeared over the horizon.

"You're sure he'll be at the shop?" Ruarshi asked. Tiny ice crystals were already forming on his scarf, pricking at his lips.

"Absolutely. Him, his brother, and twenty of their closest friends. They're not about to let anybody smash their equipment. The windows aren't big enough for people to climb through, but someone could throw a torch in. There are only two doors."

"So if our dreaded mob of restless nobility blocks both of them, we'll be trapped?"

"I suppose so. How hard is it for you to blow a hole in the wall?"

Ruarshi cuffed his student gently on the side of the head. "Hard enough. And what am I supposed to do with the debris, hmmm? If anybody does show up, we'll have to meet them outside."

"Or Tobias could sing out the window to them. He sounds like a monk crossed with a frog. They'll take fright and leave."

"Let's hope so."

They walked the rest of the distance in hurried silence. When they arrived, they were met at the door by Tobias' brother Ruprecht.

"Thanks for coming," he said, gesturing them in and barring the door behind them. He nodded to Ruarshi. "Honored to meet you."

He waved that away. "So it is Albrecht who's died?"

"Yes. Word is he died this morning but they delayed the announcement until later. They're counting on the weather to keep a lid on things."

"I don't think anything's going to happen," Tobias said, coming over from the door in the opposite wall. A number of young men followed him, one of whom Ruarshi thought he recognized from the night he'd been hurt. "The nobles will all be too busy warming their dainty feet in front of the fire to bother with the likes of us."

"They won't even have to," someone else chimed in. "Dieter will just be more of the same, so what do they have to worry about?"

"The optimist speaks. Somebody paid you off to ruin our morale."

"Yea, exactly. I'm going to open the postern gate for them and laugh while they impale you like a bunch of unlucky Turks. You'd better tie me to something."

"Can we gag you, too?"

A knock on the door silenced the group. Four more youngsters were admitted, one of them carrying a burlap sack that smelled strongly of butter and almonds.

"Blasius' mother is trying to poison us!" one of the young men yelled, pointing an accusatory finger. "Treachery! You'd better let me eat all of those, whatever they are, just in case I'm right."

This suggestion was greeted with loud booing and an inelegant rush on the sack that reminded Ruarshi of horses converging on a bag of oats. Etienne slipped in and came away effortlessly with two rolls, one of which he handed to his instructor.

"Could be a long night," the Illyana said around mouthfuls of sugar. "Have to be prepared."

Ruarshi nodded agreeably and wandered over toward the printing equipment as he chewed. A page of religious material in mirror-image Latin was laid out under the press waiting to be inked. Stacks of paper of various sizes lined the shelves along the back wall. He found the finished sheets on some lower shelving in a murky corner of the room. After making sure he'd gotten every last bit of sticky residue off his fingers, Ruarshi began paging idly through them.

He stopped and looked up when the others fell silent again. They were all listening intently to some barely audible shouting in the distance. Tobias leaped to one of the windows and pushed it open a crack, but Ruarshi still couldn't understand what was being said. It seemed that none of the others were having any success, either. A few minutes later the voices died away.

"Think somebody should go try to find out what that was?" Tobias asked.

"No, I don't," his brother responded. "We'll just sit tight here. If it comes our way, we'll deal with it."

Ruarshi sat back, reduced his bond-shield to almost nothing, and extended his senses as far as he could to the southwest. He was fairly certain that was the direction the noise had come from, and that there was no way in hell he'd be able to read anything from his current position. He'd never tried to push his perceptions so far, however, at least not while sober, and thought the effort was worth making by way of experiment.

He quit in frustration a little while later. He'd sensed a lot of uselessly generalized anxiety but that was all. If there was serious trouble somewhere in the city, the emotional echoes of it were well beyond his reach.

Etienne was watching him, his entire expression a question mark. Ruarshi shook his head, stood, and went to rejoin the others.

Their brief scare had left the youngsters subdued, and their conversation soon took on a darker tone that Ruarshi found unwarranted and faintly ridiculous.

"Douse the lights," he suggested, butting rudely into a desultory dialogue on the subject of a man's obligation to sacrifice himself for the honor of his family. "The moon's come up. It'll be to our advantage if we can get a look at the mob before it can get a look at us."

"Plus that'll make it creepy in here," Etienne added, "which will hopefully cheer you lot up. You're depressing me."

"We don't want that," Tobias said sarcastically, but he was grinning. He began a slow circuit of the room, blowing out the candles and lamps as he went. By the time he'd finished, leaving them all blinking uncertainly in the wan light of the quarter moon, Ruarshi had come up with an idea. It wasn't all that benevolent a notion, but he liked it anyway.

He wove a few small shields, wispy little insubstantial things, up near the window closest to him and then asked, "Have any of you ever seen a ghost?"

Three of Tobias' guests answered yes right away. Each of them jumped up howling an instant later as icy shields slithered down the backs of their necks. The others, unaware of what had alarmed their friends, were also rising to their feet while looking around wildly in the darkness.

Etienne, having recognized the game from his own childhood spent in the healers' circle, joined in with him and before long everyone in the room with the exception of the Miriyanti had cold fingers tickling them beneath their clothes. The swatting and shouting had reached a truly satisfactory crescendo when the Illyana spoiled the effect by bursting into gales of laughter.

Shortly thereafter Ruarshi and Etienne found themselves pinned against the wall by a dozen half angry, half relieved young men. A few more were relighting the candles.

"You all... should have seen that... from my point of view," Etienne wheezed. "Funniest thing... I've seen... in months."

"What was it?" Tobias rasped. He seemed to be having trouble relinquishing his death grip on the front of Ruarshi's coat.

"Shields," Ruarshi replied, brushing another one across the young man's cheek as he spoke. Tobias flinched away from the contact. "They'll come in handy if anyone starts throwing things at your shop."

"Sweet Mary Mother of Jesus, don't do that again."

"Or warn us beforehand. Shit, Etienne, now I see where you get it."

Ruarshi raised his eyebrows. That particular young man had the situation exactly backward. He glanced toward the Illyana, who was doubled over again, laughing helplessly.

"Oh, hell," Ruarshi muttered. Ruprecht helped him to his feet. "We'll stay as long as you need us. No more tricks."

"That's a relief."

"I'll keep an ear out for trouble. And you should probably know, someone's been at your spare letters. They all spell out profanities or names of body parts. I hope your mother and sister can't read."

## ☽ ◯ ☾

Midnight had come and gone before Tobias and his brother decided it was safe for them to send their allies home. The printers gave a small bottle of liquor to each group as it left, in thanks and in the vain hope that the alcohol would keep all of them warm on the way back to their own hearths. Ruarshi stuffed the bottle in his pocket and set off at a slow trot, Etienne keeping pace to his left. His throat and ears were aching before they'd gone ten steps.

When they came in sight of their house, a huddled figure detached itself from the shadows of the porch and headed in their direction. Ruarshi had woven thick shields around both himself and the Illyana before he realized it was Charitas.

"What's wrong?" he asked, striding forward to meet her. She was frightened and confused, but not hurt.

"There's a Miriyanti in your house. But I don't think it's the one who attacked you."

"Why not?"

"He seems more leery of us than we are of him. Kilian's with him now, keeping him company, even though we can't understand a word he says. He disarmed himself, gave his knife right to me. Here it is."

She held a sheathed dagger out to him. Ruarshi reached out to take it with a strange, lightheaded feeling of inevitability. He couldn't see the blade but the hilt was made of bone and was almost painful in its familiarity.

"It's a man who's come, you say?"

"A boy, really. I think he was trying to tell us his name is David."

Etienne gasped. "Your son is here?"

Ruarshi shook himself. "It's either him, or someone with the ability to burgle Slan's house. Thank you, Charitas. We can go in now."

He walked as calmly as he could toward the door, trying to ignore the pounding of the blood in his ears. Once through it and into the front room, he heard the scraping of chair legs against the kitchen floor and then the inner door was pushed back to reveal a face he hadn't seen in more than three decades.

He resembled Slan, Ruarshi thought. His face was rounder than Ruarshi's own, even with the thinning that had accompanied his transition to young adulthood, and something in the set of his jaw mirrored his mother's well-remembered determination. The expression Davyt wore, a mixture of relief, exhaustion, and affection, made Ruarshi's eyes burn.

"Father?"

# Davyt

Ruarshi couldn't speak. He stood frozen, blinking quickly, until he saw the shy smile on his son's face begin to shade into something more tentative. At that he threw open his arms, the dagger still clutched tightly in his fist, and waited as the boy abandoned the formal bow he'd already begun and hurried forward to embrace him.

"Welcome to my home," Ruarshi managed finally, through a mouthful of his son's silver-white hair. Davyt was every bit as tall as he was. "When did you arrive? Who came with you?"

"I got here this afternoon. It took me a while to find your house. I came alone."

Ruarshi pulled back and stared at his son incredulously, noting that they now had the room to themselves. A hasty but thorough check of the boy revealed no recent signs of injury or illness.

Davyt, though certainly aware of the scrutiny, made no move to break the physical contact between them. That sort of intrusion was a father's prerogative.

"It wasn't the smartest thing I've ever done," his son said, "but it wasn't as bad as I thought it'd be, either."

"How bad was it?"

"It was more awkward than bad. Hand signs tend to make people laugh, even when your meaning is perfectly obvious, and they're no good at all in the dark. But I'm here."

"So you are," Ruarshi said shakily, still half terrified by the thought of Davyt traveling alone through Europe. The fact that his son was here with him now didn't mitigate the feeling at all. He gestured to a chair by the fire and took one himself. When the boy was settled, he continued. "Who gave you permission to leave Miriyan?"

"My uncle."

"Aethel?"

"No. Lorion."

"Christ. I'm going to flay him alive."

"Why? He gave me good advice."

"What sort of advice?"

"'Dress well, but not too well,'" Davyt said, his voice a passable imitation of Lorion's own, "'and always travel in groups with old merchants who suffer from gout, move slowly, and make better targets than you do.'"

Ruarshi chuckled. "And that was sufficient?"

The shy smile returned. "Not quite. But it was better than nothing."

"Was it his idea that you come here?"

"No, it was mine."

"But he supported it." Ruarshi found it profoundly unsettling that Lorion had been the one to send his son away. His good-brother and fellow Nerthi always seemed to know what was coming before anyone else did; why had he decided that Davyt would be better off taking his chances in Europe than he would be staying at home?

"Yes."

"Does your mother know where you went?"

"She should. Uncle promised he'd tell her once I was well away."

"I'm sure that was a pleasant conversation. A surfeit of nerve and a dearth of brain, that's your uncle. I'll write Slan a letter tomorrow so she'll know you've gotten here safely. Though getting it delivered at this time of year might be impossible."

"It probably will be. Europeans don't seem to be all that handy with sledges. Maybe we can hand deliver the letter next spring?"

"Maybe. But that wouldn't be my preference."

"... So I can stay the winter?"

Ruarshi blinked in surprise. "Good lord, Son, there's no way you're leaving Mainz in anyone's company but my own."

Davyt smiled and nodded, staring distractedly at the fresh scar on Ruarshi's temple. "Thank you. How did that happen?"

"A misjudgment on my part."

"May I take a look? I haven't had much practice lately."

Ruarshi wanted to say no but checked himself before he could. In light of his own prior rudeness in that regard, he couldn't reasonably refuse Davyt's request. Not without falling back on the worst sort of familial privilege and giving further cause for grievance to a son who already had precious little reason to think of him as a father. He held out his hand in assent and Davyt took it between his own.

Ruarshi watched the boy as he slipped easily into a light trance and sent tendrils of power out along their physical connection, his weaves as light as gossamer and as minimally invasive as a healer could create. Davyt went immediately to the puckered flesh near his father's right eye, letting his magic linger there for a time before moving onward. He was using the same sort of superficial examination technique that Ruarshi had employed, which was to be expected, but doing it with such grace and consideration for his patient that the older healer felt suddenly embarrassed. Ashamed, even. His magic had become a blunt, unsubtle instrument over the years; why had he ever allowed that to happen?

Davyt's frown of concentration deepened as he came to the recent break in his father's arm. Ruarshi was waiting patiently for the boy to finish his exploration of the injury, relieved that the entire procedure would soon be over, when his vision grayed at the edges and he was overwhelmed by a sense of confusion and outrage.

He blinked and shook his head, wondering what had gone wrong. Certainly it couldn't have been the same thing that had happened with Etienne; he'd done nothing to alter his bond-shield, he wasn't in pain, and the boy would never have *dared*...

But his shield was in fact in tatters and Davyt had dropped his hand. His son was staring at him now, his face an unhealthy white.

"That... I don't... Father?"

The outrage was coming from Davyt, Ruarshi realized, as was the confusion, along with the leading edges of what felt like hurt, or fear, or both. The baffled fury—that was all Ruarshi's own, mixed together with everything else and being reflected back and forth between the two of them, increasing in intensity with each pass, even though they were no longer touching each other...

Christ. What had he done?

Ruarshi slammed his bond-shield back into place and was rewarded with an instant emotional silence, to go along with the very real silence in the room, and with the expression on his son's face.

What an idiot he was to have mistaken those first emotions for his own. His uncertain sense of violation could never have explained the love, faint but unmistakable, that underlay Davyt's reaction to his father's broken arm. Why hadn't he recognized that at once?

"I'm sorry, Son," Ruarshi said, sitting back carefully in his chair. He wanted to reach out to the boy but wasn't sure it would be safe to do so. "That was my fault. I overreacted because I misread the situation. Are you all right?"

"Yes."

His studied his son. Color was returning to Davyt's face, but not as quickly as Ruarshi would have liked. "No, you're not. Stoicism is an admirable character trait, but you must know as well as I do that it's generally wasted on healers." When the boy said nothing to that, he went on. "I've been able to read people's emotions for a while now. Usually it's an advantage. No one has ever gotten caught up in it like that before."

"But that... I'm not following you. A lot of that wasn't me. It works both ways, like a bond?"

"No, it doesn't." But it had. "Or not usually. I use it on strangers, to gauge their mood. Rarely on friends. Never on family. That was a mistake, an intrusion. I won't do that to you again."

"I apologize if I—"

"Son." Ruarshi waited until the boy looked up at him before continuing. "You didn't do anything wrong. I'm not angry. I certainly was, but not at you, although I know it felt that way. I was disoriented by what happened and responded badly. Okay?"

After a tense few moments Davyt nodded. "Okay. But how do you do it?"

"I'm not sure. It's related somehow to the difficulties I have with pair bonding. Surely your mother has told you some of this?"

"Not in any great detail. But Lorion told me that the Seers opposing Casimir tried to put a chain-bond on you, and you were able to break it."

"That's true. You know what a chain-bond is?"

"Of course. Everyone does."

"Everyone?"

"Everyone who lives in Tomir. Maybe not the more remote clans."

"I... would not have guessed." Ruarshi was startled, though he suspected he shouldn't be. With Nerthii living openly in Miriyan now, it was only to be expected that people would know more about them than he did while growing up.

"If I may ask, Father. Are you and Casimir still allies?"

"Your presence here makes it unlikely I'll ever work with him again. I regret that you're suffering as a result of our disagreement."

Davyt shrugged and glanced away. "I'm glad you're not doing what he says."

"Really? Tell me, how was your expulsion handled?"

"Ardan took care of it. When she came into my room, she was so red in the face that I thought she had a medical problem. She told me what had happened. She made sure that I knew from the beginning that I hadn't failed my classes."

There was something in the timbre of the boy's voice that Ruarshi didn't like. "So that was the official story? I assume there were some people who actually believed that, or pretended to."

"Yes," Davyt said. "Mostly the usual jerks. They're a small group but they make a lot of noise."

"I would guess that they come from clans that produce a lot of warriors."

"They do. I'd thought you were staying away from Miriyan because of them. Now I'm not so sure. Are you even safe here?" Davyt's eyes flicked toward Ruarshi's arm and away again.

"Yes. I know what I'm dealing with now. I'll explain it all, but not tonight. How angry are you about what's happened?"

"I'm not angry. I just don't care for Casimir and the others."

"If you like, I can take over as your instructor until we're back in Tomir. Longer than that if necessary."

"I'd like that, yes."

"What were you working on when you left?"

"I'd been studying with Mecheta for about six months."

"*Mecheta?*"

Davyt nodded. "Ardan seemed to think I had a talent for neurological work. I'm not sure where she got that idea, but it was a good opportunity and I took it."

Ruarshi shook his head in bemusement. "Illyana your age are never, *never* apprenticed to people like Mecheta. He's one of the most powerful Chamani of his generation. A healer twice my age and talent would be lucky to get an assignment like that."

"That's what I thought. Maybe it has something to do with Mother's injury?"

"Possible. Is Mecheta well?"

"He moves more slowly than he used to, but he always gets where he's going. He said he wanted me around because I remind him of his youth."

"A qualification certain to enrage everyone with seniority. I can't exactly pick up where he left off. The brain is by far the most difficult organ to work on, and I'm no good at it myself. How are you with garden-variety injuries and infectious diseases?"

"Fairly good."

"You'll have plenty of time to improve while you're here. Most of our patients have jabbed, crushed, or caught something."

"If I do something wrong to a European patient, will we be in trouble?"

"I'll be supervising you, or Etienne will. And of course not everyone can be cured. Europeans are much more accepting of that idea than Miriyanti are. You'll do fine."

"I hope so. Europeans are big."

"But we're scarier. You must have noticed the way they tend to step aside to let you pass."

"When they see me, they do. I think I must blend in. Do you always wear your hair that long now?"

"No."

"Maybe if I grow mine out like that I'll have better luck getting through crowds."

Ruarshi smiled. "Maybe. But it's a nuisance."

"Were you with a patient all evening?"

"No. The old archbishop died today, and that could have meant trouble for some friends of ours. We were helping to defend their print shop."

"Was it attacked?"

"Nerthu help us if it had been. There was no good way to defend it."

"You must have had a plan."

"The same way you had a plan when you left Tomir?" Ruarshi asked. "That's what I thought. You're as wild as your mother. I don't know whether to be pleased about that or not."

"I heard her say something about you before I left," Davyt said. "She said that you're still a thorn in her side and she doesn't think she'll sleep well until you're home again."

"Did she?" Ruarshi asked. "I hope she wasn't serious. She gets cranky when she's fatigued." He started to run a hand through his hair, realizing only then that he still held Slan's dagger. He stared at it, and then extended the weapon hilt-first toward his son. "You should take this back. It's a handy thing to have and a decent indicator of rank. Perhaps we should have some sort of gem attached to it."

Davyt accepted the blade and slipped it back onto his belt. "It should be an emerald. Or green glass. That way it will match all my green outfits."

"Your Doshae grandparents?"

"Them and Aunt Yael. They won't stop giving me clothes."

"I doubt that will change until you're well into your third century. Have you been fed?"

"Overfed. Your servants are very kind."

"Let's go attend to proper introductions," Ruarshi said, rising. Davyt stood as well, still finishing with his adjustments to his belt. "And you need to meet Etienne. Three-quarters of what he says is nonsense, but he's steady enough and an excellent healer. He'll be helping you with your shields."

"Shields?"

"Yes. But not until tomorrow. Come."

## ☽○☾

Ruarshi sat motionless in the bedroom he now shared with his son as well as his student, resting his forehead against steepled fingers. The embers smoldering in the fireplace cast a faint red glow throughout the room, providing him with just enough light to make out Davyt's sleeping profile. For want of any other option, the boy had agreed to share his father's bed for the duration of their stay in Mainz, though the prospect clearly made his son uncomfortable. Having been raised as a proper Miriyanti child, Davyt had obviously thought that he should sleep on the floor and leave the bed to his father. Ruarshi was quite sure the boy would have done just that if he hadn't insisted on the current arrangement, and Etienne's exaggerated eye-rolling during the argument hadn't helped matters any.

He was very tired, but there was something he needed to know before he joined his son in bed.

Ruarshi thinned his bond-shield, hoping to feel nothing as he peeled away successive layers of the delicate weave. As it happened, only about half of the shield had been removed before a wisp of well-being and contentment, shot through with a trace of anxiety, insinuated itself into Ruarshi's awareness. At the same time Davyt stirred ever so slightly in his sleep, as though someone had whispered his name. In a way, someone had.

So there was his answer.

Ruarshi restored his shield to its usual strength and straightened up wearily in his chair. For whatever reason, his son was still entangled with the part of his mind that had given him his oddest, most unexpected talent. Maybe it had something to do with the fact that Davyt was the last person he'd shared a bond with, back when his son was still an infant. Maybe it was just bad luck, a fluke caused by the boy's all-too emotional response to his father's broken arm. In either case, simply cutting Davyt off hadn't solved the problem. Which meant that Ruarshi was going to have to pay closer attention to what he was doing with his bond-shield, and give up on trying to read people whenever his son was around. Such a measure would protect his own privacy as well as Davyt's, sparing him any further unintended revelations about what an ass his father could be.

Giving up his emotional eavesdropping could also prove to be incredibly dangerous, in the wrong sort of situation.

He'd have plenty of time to worry about that later, however. For tonight he was just glad that Davyt was here and safe, and that he'd have a chance to get to know his son while they were both well beyond the reach of Tomir's poisonous atmosphere.

"Was he elbowing you in his sleep? Or is flatulence the problem?" Etienne asked quietly.

"Neither. I thought you were asleep."

"I was. Then I wasn't, and I saw you sitting there. Are you planning on skipping sleep tonight?"

"No."

"Then you might want to get to it. Some idiot churchman is bound to start ringing a bell in a couple of hours."

"That's what wax earplugs are for. Those are even effective against your snoring."

"If you could just get to sleep before me, you wouldn't have to listen to it. I don't know how many times I've suggested that. How much are you going to tell Davyt about the Naishanti?"

"All of it."

"Really?"

"Yes."

"Huh."

"Oh, don't look at me like that. It's your malign influence as much as anything else that's convinced me to handle it this way."

"What, you screw it up with me and then do it right for the next guy? That's worrisome. What's next? Trying experimental healing procedures out on me first, just to see what will happen?"

"You've read my mind, and I hope you have detailed nightmares about that very thing. Shut up and go back to sleep."

After several welcome minutes of silence, Etienne spoke up again. "He's terrified of you, you realize."

"He is not. Believe me, I'd know."

"Maybe I used the wrong word. Not 'terrified.' More like 'petrified by the prospect of failing in front of dad.' We should close the shop tomorrow, turn it into a holiday. Take the boy Christmas shopping."

Ruarshi cocked his head, considering the idea. "We'll take a handful of patients in the morning and then do as you suggest. He was just expelled from the circle. I don't know if he has Slan's temperament, or mine, or one that's all his own, but I would be very surprised if he's not anxious to prove that he's still a healer."

"All right. But I should be the one to supervise him while you fiddle with the bottles or something. Otherwise he'll die of nervous tension. When you were out of the room, he asked what sort of healing we'd done together."

"And you said?"

"I told him about the cholera outbreak in that overly damp little village near Florence."

"What about it?" Ruarshi's own memories of that episode were hazy, disjointed, and mostly unpleasant.

"That you were awake for basically five days straight. That I had to get the priest to lock you inside the sacristy to make you stop."

"You told him to do that?" Ruarshi wondered if he ought to be angry, remembered how close he'd come during that time to losing his bond-shield completely as a result of exhaustion, and decided to let it be.

"You think it would have occurred to him to imprison a Miriyanti if I hadn't? I think I had to threaten him a little bit. There was no chance I was going to tell you about it; I'd only known you for about a month. Anyway. Davyt was impressed. In retrospect I think I might have laid it on a little thick. I know you noticed his look of awe when you got back, because you asked him about it."

"I leave the room for ten minutes and you're poisoning my relationship with my son?"

"Poisoning, my ass. Laying it on thick isn't the same as lying, which I didn't do. You're just going to have to tolerate his opinion of you. You could probably moderate the worship aspect of it by burping a lot at breakfast, or tripping over the chamber pot. It won't last long regardless."

"You're insufferable when someone interrupts your sleep."

"Yes, unless the person doing it is good looking and in a state of undress."

"I'm going to bed now."

"Bless you. I like your son, by the way."

Ruarshi paused in the process of pulling off his tunic. "So do I."

)O(

In spite of Etienne's advice, it was Ruarshi who the next morning stood at Davyt's shoulder as half a dozen shivering patients were admitted to their front room. Ruarshi summoned forward a young couple from the countryside who had brought in their young daughter, while Etienne busied himself with an older man who was complaining loudly of a sore tooth. One of the two patients left waiting, a middle-aged man whose clothes marked him as a townsman of moderate prosperity, began to protest the arrangement but subsided without further argument after Ruarshi suggested mildly that he be quiet and take a seat. Etienne winked at Davyt as the man sat down, but Ruarshi's quick glance at his son revealed nothing but attentiveness in the young man's expression.

"We tend to those who are in pain, young patients, and pregnant women first," Ruarshi murmured in soft Miriyanti. "It's much the same procedure as that used back at the circle, with occasional complications caused by the European class system. As you just saw." Switching to German, he addressed the parents of the little girl, still resting half-asleep in the clasp of her father's thin arms.

"I am Ruarshi Nerthi of clan Doshae, and this is my son Davyt. How old is your daughter?"

"She's four, sir," the man said.

"I'm guessing she cries a lot and is hungry all the time, even after she's eaten enough to fill her?"

"That's true, sir." Both the man and his wife were staring warily at the two of them. "Is it magic told you that, sir?"

"No," Ruarshi replied, shaking his head. "It's her size and her hair." He gestured Davyt forward for a closer look. "Do you see the bands of gray that have started to grow in?" He repeated the question in Miriyanti and his son nodded.

"What's wrong with her?" the woman asked.

"The same thing that's wrong with both of you. It's hitting her harder because she's young. How long has it been since any of you have eaten meat or eggs?"

"A... while, sir."

"How about milk or cheese?"

"We thought she was old enough that she didn't need—"

"I'm not blaming you for her condition. I want all three of you to start drinking milk every other day, if you can manage it. Keep some of your meat and eggs. Lie to creditors; the bad harvests won't last forever and I'd prefer that you live to see the weather improve. Sit down. You've got lung infections. We're going to cure those and then Charitas will feed you breakfast before you leave. Eat less than you'd like to or else you'll just vomit it all back up. You can take some with you for the trip home. Sit, I said."

As they did so Ruarshi turned back to Davyt. "Have you treated this kind of infection before?"

"Yes, a few times. I'll heal all three of them, if you'll permit, but I'd like you to monitor me the first time through."

"Start with the man. He's the healthiest and will be the easiest to heal. I'll explain the procedure to them while you tell Charitas what's required. The news won't surprise her. Go."

Etienne had long finished with the others, and two more who came in besides, before the small family disappeared back out the door. The older Illyana watched with interest as they left.

"What was wrong with them?" Etienne asked.

"The usual: starvation. What did you get?"

"Abscessed tooth. Cataracts. A liver that's been destroyed by alcohol. Two minor cases of frostbite. How was it?" he asked Davyt, looking over Ruarshi's shoulder at the boy.

"It was harder than I'd expected."

"Their immune systems were all but destroyed," Ruarshi observed. "That always makes our job more difficult. No one else?"

"Not that I saw," Etienne replied. "Shall I take the sign down?"

"Yes."

"That's it for the day?" Davyt asked, startled.

"For us it is," Ruarshi said. "People come by whether we're here or not. When we're out Kilian sends them to a surgeon a few blocks away named Deynhard. He's competent for a European, which admittedly isn't saying much, but I've been able to influence his practice in small ways."

"What happens if there's an emergency?"

"Faithful Kilian comes to get us. Or failing that, to get Deynhard or his assistant. The arrangement is usually adequate. You did well this morning. Go get your coat; we're going out. I need to buy some gifts and you need to learn some German."

They were out the door and trudging toward one of the larger Christmas markets a short time later. The bitter cold of the night before had yielded grudgingly to the warming power of the sun, hanging low in the southern sky as the winter solstice drew near. A good number of townspeople were taking advantage of the slight warm-up, and the streets leading into the market square were crowded.

"German lesson number one," Ruarshi said as they reached the first row of brightly decorated booths. "They use two different words for 'you.' This is among the more evil of European linguistic conventions. Don't respond to anyone who calls you *du,* unless you think it might be the Emperor or someone of that ilk. Because our exact rank has never been specified here, insisting upon *Sie* from everyone except the highest of nobles will work and will make people less inclined to try badmouthing us for religious or other reasons. You, on the other hand, should use *du* with anyone not of the nobility. They won't resent it, even though they probably should."

"Which do I use with you?" Davyt asked.

"Uh, *Sie.* But only in public. No need to be formal in private." Ruarshi was aware that this statement contradicted Davyt's entire upbringing, and he watched as his son absorbed the request and apparently resigned himself to abide by it.

"You wouldn't happen to have a girl back home, would you?" Etienne asked.

"No. Why?"

"I see some bright-colored objects of the type usually favored by females. I should get a closer look. I'll catch up with the two of you in a little while. If you decide it's time to go and I haven't found you yet, just start bellowing."

Ruarshi considered going after his student, who was already vanishing around a corner, on the off chance the Naishanti was somewhere nearby. He had no way of checking the crowd for the man's presence, not with Davyt at his side, and letting the Illyana out of his sight made him uneasy. Then he shook his head and decided to allow Etienne some freedom. His abrupt departure had been kindly intended, after all. And he probably did have a number of women in town to whom he owed tokens of regard for putting up with him.

"What was that?" Davyt asked.

"Etienne's version of tact. He's still bad at it, but you should have seen what his attempts at social delicacy looked like five years ago."

"He's been your student that long?"

"Yes."

"Who are you buying gifts for?"

"The servants and a few friends in town. I have no confidence in my ability to pick out appropriate presents, though. Were you ever in the foreign quarter of Tomir during the Christmas season?"

"No. But there are a few Christians at the circle now and they're constantly throwing holiday parties. I went to some of them."

Why did changes like this still shock him? "What does the old guard think of that?"

"Depends. Most of them try to ignore it. Ardan lights candles to Sotar's Darkness. I don't think she used to do that."

"No, she didn't. What do you think of it?"

"I… don't know. It's done no harm that I can see, but some of my instructors seem to think it will sooner or later."

"Let's hope they're wrong."

"Can we go into the churches here? The size of some of them, and the way they're decorated…"

"No, Son. I'm sorry. It isn't safe."

"Why not?"

"It might give the church authorities the idea they have some kind of jurisdiction over us. We can't allow that."

"What if I were to sneak in when no one's there?"

"Don't try it. One, someone's always watching, and two, I'll wring your neck."

Davyt laughed. "No, you wouldn't. But I'll stay out of them."

"Good. Have you seen anything here that you need?"

"I haven't really been looking. Should I?"

"By all means. Your baggage struck me as rather light. That's commendable while traveling but unnecessary now. I'll help with the haggling if you spot something. How are you with German numbers?"

"I think I've mostly gotten them figured out, but the dialect here is hard to understand. Listening to you is helpful, though."

"And here I thought I'd eliminated my accent. Who'd you find to travel with? I'm surprised anyone at all was on the road, the way the weather's been."

"Getting from Antwerp to Cologne was no problem, but that was back in October. We were a great creaking procession of carts and gouty merchants, and I'm sure Uncle would have been pleased. Then I got stuck there for weeks and was almost ready to take off on my own when I found a group of people headed this way."

"Which group of people was that?"

"Actors, and their wives and children."

"Actors?"

"I was running out of money," Davyt replied, a shade defensively, "and they were very kind to me."

"I've kept stranger company and I'm disinclined to judge people based on their occupation. Could you tell whether or not they intended to stay in Mainz?"

"One or another of them made a rude noise every time I mentioned the name of the place. So I don't think so."

Ruarshi chuckled. "They know their audience."

"What did you mean by 'stranger company'?"

"Did you happen to pass through a leper colony on your way here?"

"No."

"You should spend some time in one. The general public likes lepers even less than it does actors, which in and of itself makes it worthwhile to talk to them."

"Is it possible to cure them?"

"After a fashion. We can't restore what they've already lost. And some don't want to be healed."

"Why not?"

"They'll feed you religious reasons, but the real difficulty is that they've given up. You can usually frustrate their arguments by reminding them that God can afflict them again later if he's really serious about their punishment."

"Ardan would call that manipulation."

"And I would call it clearing their heads of cobwebs. Care to lay a wager on which of us would win that argument?"

"No."

"Good for you. I'm not sure who'd win, either. But I wouldn't stop doing what I'm doing if I lost. Let me break off for a moment; I see an item that interests me."

When Etienne reappeared some time later Ruarshi had acquired a finely woven shawl for Charitas, a large Solingen knife for Kilian, and two toys for Peter. Davyt claimed not to be interested in anything, but

Ruarshi noted how his eyes lingered on some of the leatherwork and resolved to return to the market at a later date.

Etienne was carrying a small packet, a sure sign that he'd found what he wanted, brightly-colored or otherwise.

"Buttons?" Ruarshi asked.

"Not buttons. Is your nose running? Mine is. I'm ready to be somewhere warm."

"I think we're finished here. Davyt?"

The boy nodded and fell in beside them. "What was that hand puppet back there? The one that looks like the devil?"

Etienne glanced back at the booth they'd just passed and grinned broadly. "That's Krampus. He's an important cultural figure. German children receive gifts this time of year if they've been good, or a thrashing from Krampus if they haven't. Since the rules governing what 'good' means are none too clear, the poor kids have no way of knowing in advance which one they'll get. The arbitrariness of it all serves to instill dread in them from a young age, and gets them ready for the kind of leadership they'll have to endure for the entirety of—"

"Ruarshi!"

He looked up to see Isabel waving at him from the mouth of a side street. Ruarshi was relieved to see her. He hadn't been back to her place of business since the incident with the Naishanti, and on some largely unacknowledged level he'd become anxious about her welfare. He could have wished that his son weren't present for their reunion, but he knew Davyt would have learned about her eventually in any case.

Ruarshi swept her up in a broad embrace. Isabel had been running to catch up with him and was still breathing quickly when she broke away and stepped back.

"I'd have come knocking at your door if I hadn't thought it would embarrass you," she said, beaming up at him. "You've got no idea how worried I've been."

"There's no possible way you could embarrass me. I should have sent word that I was well. Isabel Amrhein, meet my student, Etienne Illyana, and my son, Davyt Illyana." He then translated the introduction for his son's sake.

A few breathless instants passed during which the three appraised each other. Etienne looked frankly appreciative, Davyt dubious. Isabel's reaction was harder to gauge.

Etienne ended the moment by sweeping off his hat and bowing elaborately. Davyt followed with a much stiffer rendition of the same gesture.

"Delighted to meet you," Etienne said.

"And I you. I had no idea your son was here. He *does* look like you."

"On my good days. How have you been? Is the tutor I found for you working out?"

"I am *wonderful*. I've got a long way to go yet, but you are now looking at a literate woman. The tutor's a polite and patient man. I didn't expect that. He hasn't tried to lecture me once about my sins."

"If he had, he wouldn't still be your tutor." Ruarshi found the whispered conversation going on between Davyt and Etienne to be entirely distracting, the more so as he was able to understand about one word in ten. He took a few steps away from them and Isabel followed. "Any new problems with the girls? Or Barbara?"

"No. Everyone's used to the situation now, or at least resigned to it." Isabel's smile faded. "Can you tell me what happened? The story Matti brought back didn't make any sense."

"I'm not sure. Neither is the magistrate's office. It must have been an accident of some kind, unless one of your admirers is trying to eliminate the competition."

"You shouldn't joke about it. You look exhausted."

"That's my son's fault. His arrival kept me up late."

"Why didn't you tell me he was coming?"

"Because I didn't know. He scared me half to death."

"He wasn't supposed to leave home?"

"Not alone, which is how he chose to do it. Think of him as a precocious fifteen-year-old European, and you'll understand why I feel like throttling him."

"I might believe that if you weren't so obviously proud of him. He looks... upset. I should probably go."

"People always end up looking that way when they become the sole focus of Etienne's attention. But I do need to get him home. I'll come see you this weekend. If the weather permits, we'll go riding."

"Riding?"

"The horses need exercise and I'm sick of being cooped up inside."

"But I'm afraid of horses."

"How afraid?"

Isabel considered the question. "Not so afraid that I can't try it."

"Look for me early Saturday."

"I will." She gave him a quick kiss on the mouth and hurried away.

Ruarshi turned back toward his son. Davyt had gone as red as a beet and was staring resolutely at the ground. Etienne, by way of contrast, seemed to be struggling to keep his face straight.

They left the market in silence. As soon as they reached a reasonably quiet street, Ruarshi spoke.

"Etienne explained my relationship with her?" he asked gently.

"Yes."

"If I'd thought we were going to run into Isabel, I'd have told you about her beforehand. Your mother and I haven't been together for fifty years. Surely you must know that."

His son nodded.

"If anyone's given you a different impression…"

"They haven't."

"Davyt." Ruarshi stopped, forcing the others to come to a halt as well. "I'm going to ask you to do something difficult. But it's important."

His son was clearly confused, as well he might be.

Ruarshi went on. "Everything you heard about me while you were growing up, good and bad—forget it. If you don't we're not going to get anywhere."

"I'm not sure what you mean."

"I mean that last night you told me you weren't angry. You should be. You must be. I've been no kind of father to you. The only thing that could be getting in your way is a lifetime's worth of useless stories, like the one Etienne told you about the epidemic. Pretend they're about somebody else. And then do something other than deny it or resort to monosyllables when you're disappointed."

"I'm not disappointed. Or angry. Why would you want me to be?"

"He hates it when someone gives him the benefit of the doubt," Etienne murmured in an aside to Davyt that he obviously intended to be overheard.

Ruarshi ignored him. "I don't want you to be anything other than honest, Son."

"Well, but that… but I am being honest."

"You were twelve when I left Miriyan. The number of times you've seen me since then could be counted on one hand."

"That hasn't bothered me for years."

Ruarshi flinched inwardly, though it was clear Davyt had meant the words to reassure rather than hurt. Finally they were making progress. "Good."

"There were plenty of times I wished I'd tested out as Nerthi, so I could have gone with you. But I gave up on the temper tantrums a while back. And being a healer isn't such a bad thing."

"No," Ruarshi conceded, "it isn't." He stood regarding his son, who held his gaze for a short time before looking away uncomfortably. "I'm not expressing myself very well. Let me ask you this: what could I do, Davyt, that you would not forgive?"

His son glanced back up at him, his expression cautious. "I don't know."

"I'll accept that answer for now, but only because I realize it's an unfair question. I would imagine you've spent far too much of your time defending me in one way or another, and I can't expect you to turn a lifetime's habit on its head in one afternoon. You should think about it, however, because I'll ask again."

Etienne was shaking his head. "I can help you out with this. You can begin the list of unforgiveables with 'asking his son impossible questions the day after said son makes it into town.' You could continue with 'being too uptight' or 'attempting to ruin a perfectly pleasant day' or—"

"Do you really believe," Ruarshi said, speaking so quietly that Etienne had to cut off his own flow of words in order to hear him, "that Davyt should hold me to a lower standard than he uses for everyone else? Because that's all I'm trying to avoid here."

Both Illyana were staring at him now, not saying a word, and the need for sleep was catching up with him. Ruarshi turned away and resumed the walk home, unhappy with himself and with the way the conversation had ended. It was a subject he'd have to broach again, later, when he and Davyt knew one another better.

$$\supset\bigcirc\subset$$

*Dear Slan,*

*Our son has arrived safely in Mainz. He is closemouthed about his journey, but he took no injury from it so I assume he encountered no more than the usual hazards of the road and was able to overcome them easily enough. He is up in our shared bedroom asleep at the moment, after having spent the better part of the day wandering through the holiday markets with myself and Etienne. His German remains rudimentary, but he approaches everyone with such obvious good will that I doubt he will have any*

*real difficulty settling in here as an honorary Mainzer for the rest
of the winter. He and my apprentice seem to be getting along
well, and he has already thoroughly charmed our cook.*

*I find myself wondering what set of circumstances could pos-
sibly have led our son to abandon his home at his age and travel
hundreds of miles in search of a father who is all but a stranger
to him. I know it was not for want of love, or of nearby places to
go after he was expelled from the circle. Perhaps he simply grew
tired of fighting my battles for me; perhaps a relationship ended
badly; perhaps he was seized with ill-timed youthful wanderlust. I
cannot even venture a good guess at this point, so little do I understand the boy. He does not seem inclined to indulge my curiosity
in the matter, either, though as you may imagine I am reluctant
to press him. He is too deferential toward me as it is, and I fear
that a direct question—no matter how delicately phrased—would
sound to his ears far too much like a demand for information. I
will force him neither to bare his soul nor to lie to me in order to
protect it.*

*He healed three patients this morning with hardly a stumble.
His abilities appear to have matured fully since my last visit to
Tomir, and what he yet lacks in dexterity he more than makes up
for in patience. It is a pleasure to watch him work, and I would
imagine that his instructors at the circle must be very proud of
him. I have agreed to take over as his teacher until he is rein-
stated there, and I plan to honor that promise regardless of*

Ruarshi broke off and set down his quill when the kitchen door
opened and Etienne emerged hesitantly into the front room.

"If you're busy," his student began, "I can—"

"No, no. Come in. I'm in no hurry with this letter, since I've got no
way of sending it off."

"I wanted to apologize to you."

"What for?"

"I should have kept my mouth shut today. You and he are going to
have a hard enough time of it, and you don't need me jumping in with
my opinions when things get serious. I understand what you were asking him to do, and I agree with it. In theory."

Ruarshi smiled wanly. "You've put your finger on the problem. The
more I think about what I said, the less sense it makes even to me. *I
can't do it.* I try to limit my impressions of Davyt to what I was able to

observe the few times I was home, and still the information I've gotten from other sources—Slan, Yael, Lorion, Ardan—colors everything I know about him. He picked a fight with a child from Casimir's clan after I left home that first time. He's never admitted it to me, but Slan told me about it in a letter. I also know he enjoys sketching, and has even become a talented portraitist, though I haven't seen a single example of his work...

"I can't imagine what ideas about me may have settled into his head by this time. Slan and Lorion can both be very blunt when necessary, but there's no possibility that they told a boy his age exactly what happened during the rebellion, or why I was in such a hurry to leave Miriyan twelve years later, or even the real story behind the rumors involving Casimir. Most of what he knows of those subjects he likely learned from unreliable or malicious sources, as I doubt he ever asked anyone in the family for clarification. Yet he trusts me anyway. This disturbs me." Ruarshi looked up then, met Etienne's concerned gaze, and sighed. "And now it's my turn to apologize. You are not my confessor and this isn't your responsibility."

"It's got you distracted as all hell, so I should at least try to be helpful."

"I'm not distracted so much as annoyed, but I can't change the decisions that landed me here. I'm on an unfamiliar stretch of coastline and I don't much care for it. Were you able to learn anything at the market? I didn't have much chance to eavesdrop."

Etienne's lips pursed as though he'd just bitten into something sour, but after a slight hesitation he went along with the change of subject. "There was a fracas last night involving some excitable young men. Injuries resulted, possibly a death. I heard no names mentioned. I think we can safely assume it was merchants' sons versus noblemen, but I can't be totally sure about that. People are nervous right now and they tend to squint in an unfriendly manner at strangers hovering in their vicinity."

"No hints regarding any planned repeat of the incident?"

"Not that I heard. Tobias would know what's going on. I should ask him tomorrow."

"I don't want you going out alone. Not yet. We'll probably hear the whole story soon enough from a talkative patient."

"I heard you tell Isabel you'd see her Saturday."

"Yes."

"The Naishanti attacked you the last time you were outside by yourself."

"I hadn't forgotten."

"So you're feeling up to a magical duel?"

"If he's stupid enough to start one in broad daylight, I suppose so. I plan to be back before sunset. I suspect I'll be safe enough."

"And while you're out having fun, I'll be helping Davyt with his shields?"

"You read my mind."

# The *Stillgericht*

After dinner the next day, while Charitas tidied up the kitchen and Kilian sat carving a gnomish face into a gnarled piece of wood, Ruarshi told his son why he and Etienne had decided to winter in Mainz. He also explained the events that had transpired since their arrival in the city, insofar as they were relevant to their hunt for the Naishanti. Davyt listened attentively, not interrupting at any point to comment or ask a question. Only when it was clear that his father had finished with his narration did the boy open his mouth to speak.

Ruarshi forestalled him.

"I'll answer any questions you have, but first I want you to answer one for me. There were two points in the story I just told you at which I left out something important. Can you tell me what they were?"

Davyt looked surprised and uncertain, but after a few moments he began nodding. "I can tell you what one of them was. You didn't say who sent the letter telling you where to look for the Naishanti."

"That's right. It was a Seer who told me to come here, as it happens. I would give you her name, but I don't think she'd deal with me again if she found out that I had."

"A Seer? Is she part of the same group that was trying to overthrow Casimir, back before I was born?"

"No. Her philosophy differs from his, but she's not a militarist like Shua. Neither of us would find the other's company congenial if that were the case. What else?"

"I don't know."

"Can I play?" Etienne asked, waving a hand laconically in the air.

"I suppose."

"You didn't tell him about paying the street urchin to tell you if he spots another Miriyanti in town."

"Well, no, I didn't, because I don't really expect the boy to be of much use. He didn't warn us that Davyt was here, did he?"

"You mean you gave him that money for *nothing?*"

Ruarshi responded with what he hoped was a quelling look and turned his attention back to Davyt, at the same time directing a quick surge of power toward the back left leg of Etienne's chair. It broke with a loud snap and spilled the Illyana onto the floor, where he landed with a startled yelp.

"It's okay," Ruarshi said over his shoulder in German, in response to an exclamation from Kilian. "I did that on purpose; the chair didn't just break."

"If you have a point to make," Etienne said, "you can probably make it without bruising up your apprentice. There are three unoccupied chairs sitting around this table, as you may have had opportunity to notice." He stood, his expression wounded, and began brushing the wrinkles out of his clothing.

"I'm sorry," Ruarshi replied unconvincingly. "You can sit back down now. I promise I won't do it again. The bruising was part of the point. The other thing I didn't explain, Davyt, was why my skull is still in one piece. That's all the warning you'll get when a Naishanti decides to attack you, and nobody's reflexes are fast enough to save them from that first blow. I got my arm up in time to protect my head only because I had a few seconds' warning."

"Did he say something to you?" Etienne asked, still standing and rubbing absently at his hip.

"No. I sensed he was there because I was monitoring the people around me."

"Your emotion-reading talent?" Davyt asked, earning a curious look from the older Illyana.

Ruarshi nodded. "But neither of you has that advantage. I've already scolded Etienne more than once about keeping a shield up whenever he's in public. Now it's your turn. When I'm out of the house this weekend, I don't want you to admit anyone for healing. You need to practice using your shields instead."

"And when that gets to be too exciting, we can start banging our heads against the cook pots," Etienne said. "Seriously, I have a deck of cards if we get too desperate."

"Was the Naishanti using a shield?" Davyt asked.

"I'm sure he was."

"How close did he get to you?"

"I'm not sure. He was across the street when I became aware of him. Why?"

"Is there anything made of wood around here that you're not too attached to?" the boy asked, glancing around the kitchen. "Mother taught me something that could be useful, and I've brought extra *tanan*. If you want them." He fiddled with his right sleeve and one of the small Miriyanti throwing knives appeared in his hand.

"Good lord," Ruarshi said. "Does everyone know about that modification to your clothes, or do you sew in the sheaths yourself?"

"I do it myself. I think I messed this one up; I should have been able to get the knife out one-handed."

"Did Slan ever tell you what an arm looks like after one of those things has been shattered against the skin?"

"She mentioned the problem," Davyt replied, standing. "But she also said that a warrior would have to know about it to shatter it, and that none of them would expect a healer to be carrying a weapon. Not the first time you met them, anyway."

"What'd she teach you to do with it?" Etienne asked.

"Get it through shields. It's hard, though."

"Ha. This I must see." Etienne disappeared into the pantry and emerged a moment later carrying Charitas' cutting board. "We're only going to dent it a bit," he told her in cheerful German on his way back toward the table, pausing to plant a kiss on the back of her hand as he edged by. He then retrieved his broken chair, propping it unsteadily against the back wall and setting the board face outward atop the seat.

"I use that every day, young man," Charitas said, "and it's the only one I've got. You give it back to me in pieces and your soup will be lumpier than you like it."

"You underestimate the appeal of your cooking," Etienne said, "as well as the extent of my determination when I'm presented with food. You're about to see yon young one hurl a weapon through his father's shields. Thereby proving some sort of point about the utility of wasting time on them."

Ruarshi eyed his student before turning his attention back to his son. "How often are you able to penetrate a shield with one of those?"

"If I'm lucky, about one time in five," Davyt said distractedly, holding the *tana* by its blade and looking at Etienne's target through slightly narrowed eyes. "Mother manages it once every two or three attempts."

"Thereby proving some sort of point about the wisdom of wasting time on shields," Ruarshi commented.

Etienne scowled at the floor. "I was only trying to save your son from a very tedious Saturday. Not to mention a pounding headache. And the possibility that before you can heal us of those, we'll be called upon to try putting you back together again. We should go with you. I'll only eavesdrop on the salacious parts of your conversation with Isabel, I promise."

Davyt was no longer squinting at the cutting board. "What?"

Ruarshi hadn't yet told Etienne about the unfortunate incident involving Davyt and his bond-shield, leaving his student with no way of understanding why he'd be safer going out alone than with them in tow. It was an oversight he would clearly have to remedy soon. "It's nothing, Son. My apprentice is a troublemaker with a low tolerance for repetitive exercises. I expect you to be a good influence on him in that regard."

"You said you thought the Naishanti had left town," his son said.

"Since I haven't seen or heard from him in weeks, I'm assuming that's true. I wouldn't be leaving you two here by yourselves if I had any reason to believe otherwise. As Etienne knows full well. Now show me what your mother taught you."

Davyt nodded and stepped back from the wall. "If you would, Father, weave a shield in front of the target for me."

"How far away from it?"

"Think of the target as your body, and put the shield where you normally would."

Ruarshi did as he'd been asked and then waited. Davyt did absolutely nothing to project his intentions, and when his arm finally moved the sequence of motions was almost too fast to follow. He sent the *tana* spinning toward its target with a powerful underhanded throw that Ruarshi knew couldn't have done his wrist or elbow any good, and they all watched as the little knife darted through the air, rebounded from the shield, and went skittering away across the floor.

"Rats." The boy bent over and retrieved his weapon, wiping each side of the blade on his sleeve in a gesture that looked to be completely unconscious. "Mind if I try again?"

"Not at all. Etienne, you put up the shield this time."

"Yes, Master," the Illyana replied, his tone making it clear that he was using the archaic title only half in jest. "Whatever you say."

Davyt tried again with the same result. It was only on his seventh try that he finally got the *tana* through. Ruarshi felt the blade pass through his weave point-first, much as an arrow would, right before its hilt smacked up against the target.

His son had his hands on his hips. He looked disgusted. "And that's the other problem with this idea. Just because the knife goes through doesn't mean it'll actually stab anything. You hold your shield farther away from your body than Mother does."

"I'm not sure that would matter so much if your target weren't expecting it," Ruarshi said. "He'd be so surprised to be hit with *any* kind of projectile in the absence of archers that he'd be vulnerable, at least for the time it would take you to throw another one or two of those. Has Slan taught this to any healers other than you?"

"No."

"Good."

"Why is that good?"

"Because if she was teaching this to everyone in the circle that she could get her hands on, it would mean she had a reason to think healers needed this skill," Etienne replied, scooping up the little blade and regarding it thoughtfully. "Which could easily presage another bloody disaster of the kind that nearly killed your father."

"Etienne—"

"Peace," the Illyana said, holding up a hand but not meeting Ruarshi's eyes. "I'm sorry. I won't say anything else about it." He turned back to Davyt. "May I try?"

"Uh, sure."

"If you would be so kind..." Etienne said.

Ruarshi couldn't tell if he was the one being addressed or if it was Davyt that his apprentice was talking to, but it didn't really matter. There was only one possible answer to the man's request when he was in a mood like this one.

"Do the honors, please, Son. That will give me a chance to get a good look at your shields." Not to mention the fact that if Ruarshi were the one behind the weaves, Etienne might sprain something in an overenthusiastic effort to punch a hole in them.

Davyt complied, and they watched along with Kilian and Charitas as Etienne's first several efforts ended in failure. His next attempt had a similar outcome, the only difference being that the *tana* rebounded straight toward Kilian. The man moved just in time to avoid a flesh wound to his bestockinged right foot, and the knife finally came to rest at the edge of the fireplace.

"I can't tell what the three of you suppose you're doing," Kilian said in his usual slow drawl, "but if you keep it up I'm going to go fetch the bandages. We'll be needing them."

"Sorry about that," Etienne said, again switching to German. "You're right. I'm done. Ruarshi?"

He had nothing to prove and he knew it, but he nevertheless found himself rising from his chair to retrieve the *tana*. Kilian bent over and picked it up for him, his expression mournful rather than reproachful. Ruarshi winked at him as he reached for the knife. "Just one try."

When he'd gotten himself in the right position and Etienne had woven a gratifyingly sturdy shield in front of the cutting board, Ruarshi flooded his body with warrior's magic and stopped thinking about what he was doing. He'd had years of training from both Lorion and Slan, and he knew that sometimes shutting off one's mind and letting muscle memory take over was the only way to accomplish a complicated physical feat. Still, he'd never attempted anything quite like this before, and there was no way in hell he was going to succeed at something that stymied Slan more than half the time.

But where was the harm in trying?

He threw the knife, and was as surprised as anyone to see it bury its tip in the target and hang there, quivering slightly.

### ))O((

"Midnight?" Isabel asked, gazing at the animal in ill-concealed trepidation. "This horse is light gray."

"Yes," Ruarshi said. "Etienne names all his horses Midnight, though he hasn't owned a black one since I've known him."

"That's odd. Why is it swinging its head around like that?"

"Because he doesn't like your looks, probably."

Isabel took a step back from the stall door and met his eyes. "You're not doing a very good job of convincing me to trust that beast. It's all teeth and hooves."

"He hasn't bitten Etienne often. Not above five or six times, I'm sure."

"Now you're laughing at me."

"Not really. This horse does bite. I'd never ask you to ride him."

She gestured toward the animal in exasperation. "Then why am I standing here?"

He couldn't give her an honest answer to that question, not without admitting to paranoia and explaining that the stable's proximity to his home allowed him to keep track of the individuals currently in the vicinity of his front door. He'd been distracted by worry all morning, and he was quite sure Isabel had become aware of that fact during the hour or so they'd spent talking in her room. She'd been too polite to ask him about it, however.

He decided to settle for a half-truth. "Stables are blessedly warm places on days like this one. I'm dragging my feet because I don't want to go back outside anytime soon."

"Isn't it much colder than this in Miriyan?"

"Sometimes. You become quite adept at finding reasons to remain inside on such days."

"We could have just stayed where we were."

He smiled. "I know. But I promised you a ride, and I'm willing if it's something you want to do."

Isabel eyed Midnight again. "I think I want to get more comfortable with horses first. Is your animal calmer than this one?"

"Yes. I don't like dodging horse teeth. Sophie's over here." Ruarshi led Isabel to the box across the aisle where his mare stood, head down and dozing. "Not exactly overjoyed to see me, is she? We'll see about that." He pulled a bag out of his pocket and entered the stall.

"What's in it?" Isabel asked, coming to stand at his shoulder. She held her skirts in both hands, ready for flight.

"Sugar. Horses like it and bribes are always a good idea."

Sophie perked up as he curled down the top edges of the bag, shuffling over and nudging at his shoulder with her nose until he offered her its contents. She lipped daintily at the sweets, regarding them both with a placid eye.

"She seems much nicer. I could ride her. When the weather warms up, I mean."

"Horses are handy to have around when it gets muddy. You'll find you can travel from one place to another without picking up five pounds of muck along the way. Here." He nudged Isabel gently forward and offered her the bag, which she took hesitantly. Sophie continued snuffling at it throughout the transition, not the least bit disturbed.

Isabel reached up to rub the animal between the eyes. "Good horse. If she tramples me, I'm going to be angry at you."

"Even if she was inclined, I wouldn't let her. You're safe."

"Do you mean you'd use magic on her or do something else?"

"Horses are generally controllable without resort to magic. If it were otherwise, I shudder to think what would have become of Europe. All your greatest kings and nobles, living in constant fear of marauding horse herds."

"Even if we hadn't tamed them, I don't think they'd *eat* us."

"Probably not. But they could if they wanted to. I once treated a man whose entire hand had been bitten off by a warhorse. They never did find it, either."

Isabel glared at him. "If you keep telling stories like that, I'm going to make you take this thing back."

"Sorry. It looks like Sophie's finished anyway." Ruarshi ran a hand up along the mare's jaw and peeked into the bag. Not a grain of sugar remained, as far as he could tell. "You're done, you great pig." He returned the sack to the pocket of his coat and stood regarding his companion. "I have an idea."

"What?"

"There's an inn not far from here I'd like to take you to. To eat. Etienne and I stayed there when we first came to town. Their sausage is only half gristle, and the proprietor tolerates my quirks."

"Including bringing a whore in with you?"

"Including that. One way or another. I can't promise he'll be gracious, but he will hold his tongue. And there won't be many people in the common room at this hour."

"I've got nothing to cover my hair with…"

"Between your scarf and my own, I'm sure we can come up with something workable. How shall I introduce you? Sister Celeste?"

"Don't you dare. I'll go. First, though," Isabel said, leaning out over the door of Sophie's stall and glancing up and down the length of the stable, "I have to ask you a question." She finished with her survey of the building's interior and moved away from the aisle, edging cautiously past Ruarshi's horse to lean against the stable's back wall.

The healer watched her, mystified. He diverted a wisp of the attention he was using to monitor the environs of his house and directed it toward Isabel, for just long enough to realize that she was nervous about something. Intensely so. She'd just been hiding it well.

"What is it?"

"Have you heard the term *Stillgericht*?"

"Is it anything like a *Vehmgericht*?"

"Sort of. But nobody on this one pretends that the Emperor approves of its existence. Or even knows about it. One of its members paid me a visit the other day."

"And this fellow's name would be…?"

"Raban Zweig. I'm sure he's not their leader, he's just a clerk."

"A prior acquaintance of yours?"

"No. But he'd been to the house before. We could never figure out how he afforded it. He must be stealing from his employer." Isabel stopped, frowned, and waved a hand impatiently before going on. "None of that matters. He wanted me to tell you that they know about your defense of the print shop, the night after the Archbishop died."

"Then they must also know that all Etienne and I did was sit in the cold eating pastries."

"They thought it meant you'd taken sides. They want to bring their injured members to you for healing, and they want you to promise you won't report them to the magistrate's office."

Ruarshi took a moment to think that through. "What are we talking about here? Brawling in the street? Assassinations? Arson? I don't suppose he outlined their plans."

"No. He just said that the *Stillgericht* had gotten back together and decided it was time to do something about what happened before."

"And in return for running the risk of being thrown out of town, how would I benefit from this arrangement?"

"I don't know. I'm sure they intend to pay you."

"He doesn't think much of me, does he? If their cause is as just as he must believe, they shouldn't have to pay me to help them with it. What did you tell him?"

"That I didn't know what you'd say, and would have to ask you about it."

Ruarshi crossed his arms and thought about Bebel. "What would you do, Isabel, if you were in my position?"

"... Help them."

"Why?"

"A lot of people were hurt and killed, and the ones responsible for it were never punished."

"The *Stillgericht* knows which of the nobles deserve punishment and which don't?"

"They must."

"I doubt it. If I say I'm willing to talk to them about this, what happens next?"

"I take that message back to Raban, he takes it to the *Gericht,* and they send someone to visit you."

"Then that's what you should tell him. You could also let them know that until I meet whoever's in charge of their secret court, I won't be inclined to agree to anything."

"I warned them you were stubborn."

Ruarshi snorted. "Stubbornness hasn't got anything to do with it. I've just learned to keep an eye on men who are capable of knifing people in dark alleys, especially when they say they're acting on principle. Oh, one more thing—your role in this has to end if they want my cooperation."

"Whether or not I want it to?"

"Especially if you don't want it to. A horse bite is nothing compared to what the strappado will do to you, Isabel."

"At least I'd finally have done something I could be proud of."

"That won't be much comfort to you once you've been arrested. If this clandestine street war of theirs goes sour, you've got no one to protect you. I can't do it; I'm a foreigner. You'll need one or two besotted noblemen at the very least."

"Maybe I could arrange that."

"As you wish. But like I said, to get me they'll have to give you up."

"They're not going to choose me over you."

"I'm counting on that," Ruarshi said. "If I end up turning them down, you'll have your chance. Just be sure to hide what you're doing from me, and decide in advance which route you'll take if you need to flee the city."

Isabel pushed herself away from the wall and approached him, still giving Sophie as wide a berth as she could. "I'll tell them what you said. I'm sorry if you think I'm a fool."

"I think you care. Sometimes it's the same thing, but I'd never hold it against you."

"Why not? I'm not that different from the others."

"There's a big difference between a weapon and the hand that wields it. It's the owner of the hand I'm most worried about."

"I'd love to know who that is. When you find out, will you tell me?"

"Absolutely not."

"I didn't think so. I'll be needing your scarf now, if you don't mind."

)O(

When he got home late that afternoon the book was lying on the kitchen table.

Wil's book. Last seen on Bebel's bookshelf between Aristotle's treatise on comedy and the natterings of St. Augustine.

Ruarshi paused when he saw it, his hands going still on the front of his coat.

Neither Davyt nor Etienne had responded to his greeting, though both of them were sitting in the kitchen. Davyt was staring at the floor, his face unreadable; Etienne had his arms crossed and was gazing into the air above Ruarshi's head, his expression mulish. The Bonnes were nowhere to be seen.

Ruarshi stepped forward and flipped back the book's cover, just to be certain he'd identified it correctly. He had.

"I trust one of you will tell me how this got here."

"I paid a visit to the doctor's house," Etienne said. "Davyt stayed here and did as he was told. I've already tended to his headache, for whatever it's worth."

"True?" He looked at his son.

"Yes."

Ruarshi turned back to Etienne. "How is Herr Bebel?"

"I don't know. He wasn't in. I talked to Helene."

"I thought I said something about you never going there alone."

"You did. You also said something about not minding if I act on my own initiative as long as I don't get caught. I didn't get caught. I spent an entirely proper hour with the lady of the house, retrieved the book, and came home."

"I see. Why did you do this?"

"I was bored."

"Bored?"

"Yes. How could I not be?"

Ruarshi gripped the edges of the table. He was breathing unevenly, he noticed. "I can tolerate a certain amount of disobedience. But not this. You're no longer my student, and I want you out of here by the middle of next week." He left the room and took the back stairs two at a time, hardly seeing them.

"Wait here for a few minutes, would you?" Etienne's voice. Ruarshi couldn't hear Davyt's reply.

He slammed the bedroom door, blocking out any further sound from downstairs, and started tearing at the buttons of his coat with hands gone clumsy and cold. He'd only gotten two or three undone when the door opened behind him. He spun, the task forgotten.

"How dare you leave him here alone?" Ruarshi kept his voice down, but it took effort. "He is a child."

"I trusted your judgment."

"What?"

"Since you decided it was safe to leave us here by ourselves, I thought it would be just as safe for me to leave him here by himself. I did talk to Kilian beforehand, in case we'd both guessed wrong."

"How are Kilian's shields these days?"

Etienne blinked. "Nonexistent."

"Do you really think he'd be as good at protecting Davyt as you would?"

"It's possible. He has very large arms and he owns an axe."

"Stop it. I trusted you to keep my son safe and instead you left."

"To do something useful."

"Get out."

"I didn't mean that what you—"

"Get *out*."

"No."

"Fine." Ruarshi brushed past the Illyana, went back down the stairs, and stormed through the kitchen. He flung a terse, "Going for a walk," over his shoulder to his son before pushing through the door into the front room. A moment later he was outside, striding quickly through the deep blue twilight.

He walked for some time without thinking, without even trying to. Instead he concentrated on the way the frigid air filled his lungs and bit at the back of his throat, and watched the stars as they made their nightly debut in the darkening sky, sometimes one by one and sometimes in great shining arcs that curved from one line of rooftops to another.

He finally came to a stop near one of the new university buildings and turned to look back the way he'd come. Only three figures moved in the darkness, none of them Miriyanti. Good.

Ruarshi leaned against a gray expanse of stone wall, just beyond a flickering square of light cast onto the dirty snow by a candle left burning in a window, and allowed himself to go back over what had happened. It was clear that Etienne had been wrong to disobey him. Ruarshi's instructions to him had been explicit, and there was no possible way the Illyana could have misunderstood the fact that he was being placed in a protective role.

On the other hand, hadn't he been justified in pointing out that his reasoning mirrored Ruarshi's own? He'd drawn a reasonable inference from his instructor's behavior and had acted on it. And in spite of all that nonsense about boredom, Ruarshi knew full well that Etienne had intended to do him a favor. He had even succeeded; Ruarshi was intensely gratified to have that book in his possession, though he still harbored significant qualms regarding exactly how that state of affairs had come about.

Which brought up another issue. The thought of Etienne alone in a room with Bebel made his skin crawl. What had the Illyana planned to do if Friedrich had been at home? Charm him? Probably. It would never have worked, and Etienne should have had sense enough to realize that.

Some sort of punishment was in order, but nothing so extreme as what he'd threatened earlier. He wouldn't turn Etienne out of the house, for reasons of selfishness as well as fairness. He'd come to consider the Illyana a friend, after all, and whatever disrespect for authority he displayed had almost certainly been learned from Ruarshi himself. The young healer had been remarkably malleable when they'd first met, for all his cockiness and swagger, and in many respects he still was. For Ruarshi to pretend he hadn't helped to create the person Etienne had become would be hypocritical, and to take no responsibility for the problems that inevitably resulted would be equally so.

And where did all this leave him?

Standing outside on a street corner, apparently, in the dark and cold, with the arm of his coat slowly freezing to the wall and enough adrenaline running through his system to fuel an all-night card game.

Ruarshi smiled to himself. He knew of a good way to burn off excess nervous energy, one that was ideally suited to nighttime work.

He started back south, pausing at intersections to check for the red stone house that would mark the street where he needed to turn. Color was difficult to discern at this hour, and it was only the presence of a magistrate's man hurrying along with a lantern that finally enabled him to spot the proper landmark.

Ruarshi turned right and went five more blocks, occasionally slipping on the refrozen slush, before emerging into a small square. On its opposite side stood the building he sought.

It was a church, a squat gothic pile named after one of the less illustrious saints in the Catholic pantheon, and it offended him.

He strode toward it, gratified to see that the area was deserted. As long as he could avoid making significant noise, no one would have cause to peek out their window and catch him in his act of beneficent vandalism.

Ruarshi ran his hands along the stonework to the right side of the church's front door until his fingers collided with a length of iron chain. He grasped it, running his fingers down the links to the heavy neck ring at one end and then upward to the spike that attached the entire apparatus to the church wall. It was a local variation on the pillory, meant to display criminals and unfortunates to the abuse of passersby, and it didn't belong on a building dedicated to religion. Didn't belong anywhere, really, but he had to start somewhere.

He settled himself as well as he could against the slight bulge of the church's foundation—in very much the same position the condemned would have to use, as the chain wasn't long enough to allow them to sit on the ground—and wrapped his hand around the spike.

Shattering a piece of iron as thick as this one wasn't even worth attempting. He'd have to chip away at the stone, reducing it slowly to sand until the ugly hunk of metal could finally be wrenched free. It was going to take a while, given how deeply into the wall the spike had been driven.

He took a moment to hope that Nerthu didn't have a sufficiently developed sense of irony to send the Naishanti to his home on this particular evening, and then he got busy.

Ruarshi poured power into weave after weave, tiny and finely constructed so that he could slip them into the gaps between the stone and the iron before blowing them apart with dissonance. These small detonations were accompanied by a steady trickle of powdered stone that increased almost imperceptibly in volume as the minutes ticked by. It was as painstaking a process as any healing. When the spike finally came free in Ruarshi's hand he stumbled forward, thrown off balance by the weight of the chain. The neck ring collided against the stone at his feet, as loud and out of place in that quiet courtyard as a shout.

Ruarshi ducked his head and stood still. His clothing was dark enough to conceal the outlines of his body, and though his hair might be visible to keen eyes he thought that his lack of motion would throw off any observers.

When he judged that he'd waited long enough, he carefully looped the chain around his hand and left the square. He saw only one other person on the way back to his house, a servant hurrying down a side street. The man didn't turn and probably didn't even know that Ruarshi was there.

)O(

"What is that?" Etienne was staring at the chain as though he thought it might be a snake.

Ruarshi had deposited the bulky iron contraption near the fireplace in the front room. The clatter it made against the flagstones had greatly increased the caution with which he'd been received by his son and his former student. He found their reactions gratifying.

"I believe the Germans call it a *Pranger*," Ruarshi said. He dropped onto the couch, hoping the motion appeared more controlled than it actually was.

"They sell those somewhere?" Etienne nudged at it with the toe of his boot. "This late at night? During the Christmas season?"

"Not exactly. It's for you. Consider it an early holiday present."

"A going-away gift?"

"No."

He had Etienne's full attention. Davyt was still hovering midway between the kitchen door and the cluster of chairs surrounding the fireplace. He waved his son forward.

"I can't have you gadding around Mainz on your own," Ruarshi said. "You'd be too vulnerable. You're welcome to stay here. I'd like you to stay here. But as you've chosen to defy my authority, our relationship has to change. You're now the junior healer in this household, and Davyt will take your place as my sole student. Understood?"

Etienne nodded slowly. The change in his status meant that he'd just gained a good measure of autonomy. It also meant, if they chose to follow tradition, that the level of intimacy between them would drop off sharply as Etienne took his place in the healers' hierarchy and began jostling for position. Ruarshi wondered which consideration mattered more to the man.

"That's... fine, Ruarshi. But if I have questions about, I don't know, the best way to tackle a disease, or the finer points of German etiquette, or... other things..."

Ruarshi smiled. "I still live here, too."

Etienne released a pent-up breath. "Okay. I need to apologize to you. Again. To both of you. I wasn't where I should have been today."

"And neither was I. I'm much more concerned about where you chose to go."

"Maybe you should mention the boy?" Davyt suggested. He was perched on the edge of one of the chairs and looked uncomfortable.

"I utilized your urchin," Etienne said. "Had him knock on the door and ask for Bebel, on behalf of a foreigner with suspect morals by the name of Señorita Embarazada. I didn't think he'd know any Spanish. It didn't matter, since he'd already gone out on another call anyway."

"So you intended to get him out of the house before you went in."

"Yes."

Ruarshi rubbed at his eyes. "And here I'd thought you were relying on your charisma. Thank you for clearing that up."

"Does this mean you'll stop threatening me with that thing?" Etienne leaned down for a closer look at the chain, fingering it in a gingerly fashion. He sat back up abruptly, holding the spike point upward. "You pulled this out of a wall."

"I find it a useful way of dealing with frustration. Careful, it's got dried blood on it."

"I see that. Yuck."

"What wall was it attached to?" Davyt asked. He'd moved over to examine the artifact from closer range.

"Some church. I suppose the only question I have left is how you got Helene to give you the book."

"I offered a trade. In your name, because I didn't think you'd mind. The book for a service."

"What service?"

"She wants you to use your connections in town to find another household for Wolter. Bebel's still after him."

"Beating him, you mean."

"I expect so."

"Is he still batting his eyes at Bebel's daughter?"

"That's not a question I asked and she didn't say."

"Did you get a look at him?"

"No."

"The sooner I get after it, the better," Ruarshi said. "How am I supposed to let Helene know that I've found something?"

"Send the urchin with another message about the señorita. Wolter will slip out the back door once night falls, all packed up and ready to go. If circumstances interfere, he'll try again the next night."

Ruarshi sat back. The two young Miriyanti in front of him returned his gaze solemnly. They'd put the chain back down on the floor, which was as good a place as any for it, at least overnight.

"You've been remarkably quiet, Davyt. What do you think of all this?"

The boy shrugged. "I'd like to see this Naishanti fall off a cliff. Aside from that, I'm satisfied."

Ruarshi had been right; the boy was very like his mother.

"I'll try to arrange it," he replied, and stood. "I'm going to bed. Don't you two stay up too late."

"Shouldn't you eat something?" Davyt asked.

He'd missed dinner, hadn't he? Just at present he was too tired to care. "Tomorrow," he said, and pushed open the door into the kitchen.

# Denizens of Asgard

They handled each other carefully during the days that followed, maintaining a deliberate domestic placidity as everyone adjusted to the changes Ruarshi had made. Etienne rejected the suggestion that he move onto the third floor, into a space of his own, muttering darkly that his former instructor was trying to freeze him to death before he had any kind of chance to challenge him for precedence. Davyt absorbed his father's brief lessons with eagerness and relative ease, and seemed altogether content with his circumstances. Ruarshi kept a close and possessive eye on them both, and soon came to realize that the feeling suffusing his chest each night when he went to bed was simple happiness, unmitigated by the sour tang of loneliness or regret.

Christmas came and went, accompanied by an intense flurry of social activity and the usual exchange of gifts. They ended the month of December stuffed full of sweets and very nearly swimming in spiced hard cider that Ruarshi for the most part avoided. Davyt, following his lead, did the same, and even Etienne restricted his intake and limited the amount of time he spent in taverns. The Illyana's friends took to showing up at the house more and more often, deferential and sober, and Ruarshi utilized the opportunity to become better acquainted with them. Davyt sat with them while they talked, steadily adding to his German vocabulary though rarely joining the conversation. Charitas contributed to the cheerfulness of the season by preparing ever more elaborate and inventive meals, while Kilian watched over the proceedings with avuncular approval.

Margaret had taken advantage of her holiday visit, after presenting the Miriyanti with a generous variety of fruit preserves and a small bag of raw sugar, to invite them all to a costume party. The event was set to take place on Epiphany at a nearby *Tanzhaus;* it would coincide with numerous other such celebrations being held across the city to inaugurate the liveliest part of the Karneval season.

Etienne, after glancing over his shoulder at his more hesitant housemates, had accepted Margaret's invitation with an enthusiasm that brought a blush of pleasure to her cheeks. He'd always been a fervent admirer of the Karneval spirit while in Italy, and he was clearly delighted to learn that the Germans were just as determined as their southern neighbors to misbehave in the weeks leading up to Lent.

Ruarshi had been less excited about the prospect of attending such a party, and for very good reasons. All of which were known to Etienne, who turned to face him as soon as Margaret said her goodbyes and left.

"You needn't look at me that way," the Illyana said.

"Why not?"

"Don't you want to go?"

"That depends." Ruarshi noticed his son's puzzled expression and snorted. "Sometimes Etienne hasn't got the sense Sotar gave a turnip. He caused us no end of trouble last year by going to one of these things dressed as a woman. That's not unheard of, especially at this time of year, but he played the role too well and had to spend the next several months disappointing lovesick Italian men. It was fortunate for us that Lorenzo has a well-developed sense of humor."

Davyt stared at the older Illyana.

"You never said anything about it at the time," Etienne muttered. "Why dwell on it now?"

"I had to tell Haarnan I'd approved of your costume to keep him from sending you home on the spot."

"Oh." Etienne had the good grace to look guilty. "That won't be a problem this time around. I'm going to this one as a demon. I won't stand out at all."

Ruarshi raised an eyebrow but didn't argue. Etienne was right about the prevalence of the devilish and demonic during Karneval, though he was of course lying when he said he wouldn't stand out. And he had to know it.

But backing out now would simply be rude, and with Etienne's promise in hand their attendance at the party couldn't do them any harm. It might even be a nice diversion, and it would further expose Davyt to some of the more colorful elements of European culture.

All that remained for them to do in the interim was get their cos-

tumes ready, in between attending to their never-ending stream of patients and meeting their remaining—and thankfully minor—social obligations.

Davyt and Etienne quickly agreed that the younger healer ought to
dress up as a fox, his pelt gone white for the winter, and they somehow
managed to convince Kilian to carve out a half-mask for the boy to
wear. He already owned a tunic of thick white wool, brought down in
his baggage from Miriyan. The fact that he owned no trousers that
matched hardly mattered, as the tunic was cut as long as Ruarshi's own
formal coat and would cover everything except Davyt's ankles and feet.

Ruarshi decided early on what his outfit would be and then, after
preparing one small part of it in advance, determinedly forgot about it
until the sixth of January. He was sure he could put the rest of the costume together in less than half an hour, using only what was already in
the house, and after having an unexpectedly busy day with patients he
realized he'd have to do just that.

Etienne ascended to the bedroom that evening with a collection of
soot in a battered earthenware mug to find his former instructor regarding his bed frame with a predatory eye. Ruarshi was wearing the
same clothing he'd had on all day, made of warm brown wool, the sole
addition to his outfit consisting of the ratty old cloak he'd thrown on
over his shoulders. It had once been black, but had over the years faded
to the color of ashes.

The Illyana, for his part, was dressed from head to toe in a black so
emphatic that it almost hurt the eyes. Two stubby horns protruded
from his hair.

"You're going as yourself?" Etienne asked. "That's... inventive."

"I thought so. Where's Davyt?"

"He and Kilian are down below running string through the holes in
his mask. You'll be impressed."

"I'm sure," Ruarshi remarked distractedly. He stepped to the head
of the bed, laid his hands on the post nearest the window, and dredged
up what power remained to him. A triangular piece of wood the length
of the post came away with a sharp crack several minutes later. He lowered its bottom end to the floor and leaned his weight against it until
he was certain the object was sturdy enough to serve its intended purpose. He needed it as a part of his costume and as an excuse not to
dance.

"You're very destructive lately," Etienne observed. "What's that
for?"

"Inflicting myself with splinters, I'm very much afraid." Ruarshi turned and watched the Illyana as he smeared soot expertly onto his chin and upper lip, creating the appearance of a mustache and diabolical goatee. When he paused and stepped back from the mirror, Ruarshi asked him, "Where's that Spanish hat of yours?"

"Stuffed in my trunk somewhere. You're welcome to dig around until you find it."

Ruarshi had the lid opened and the first layer of rumpled clothing turned back when Davyt appeared on the landing outside the door.

He smiled up at his son. "Very nice." Kilian had outdone himself, and the paint Charitas had added to her husband's handiwork made the mask look almost real. Ruarshi suspected, not for the first time, that the two of them were largely wasted on housework.

"Positively vulpine," Etienne added. "Can you see through that okay?" He'd gone on to outline his eyes with soot, making them look enormous in his thin Miriyanti face. He wiped his fingers on a rag and went over to sit on the foot of his bed.

"As long as I can keep it from slipping, I can see," Davyt replied. "The cloth Charitas stuck to the rough spots helps hold it in place. What are you searching for?" He crouched down next to his father.

"Etienne bought a ridiculous hat while we were in Florence. It resembles a cardinal's hat, only it's black. And I'm sure it's thoroughly crushed by this time."

Davyt spotted it first and snaked a hand into the trunk to pull it out. Its crown was flattened and its wide brim was both warped and slightly torn. As far as Ruarshi was concerned, it was perfect.

He extracted the eye patch from his pocket, slipped it over his right eye, and after restoring the hat to something like its intended shape clapped it onto his head. Then he stood and retrieved his improvised staff from its resting place against the wall.

"I'm ready if you two are."

"I think so," Davyt said.

Etienne was sitting with his arms crossed. He hadn't moved. "That's actually very good, Ruarshi. You're almost convincing as a Norse god. A bit on the small side, though."

"Thank you. You're entirely convincing as an incubus, but my son makes an even better fox."

"I'm just a run-of-the-mill demon. Not an incubus." Etienne pushed himself to his feet.

"We all know who'll be the judge of that. Try not to make enemies of too many husbands, would you? Let's go."

They paused downstairs to take their leave of the Bonnes, who seemed content to spend the evening at home, and then made their way to Margaret's. She appeared in her doorway at the center of a profusion of feathers, a snowy owl destined to spend the next few hours shedding plumage, with Johann at her shoulder. He wore a red and black harlequin's half-mask that he pushed up onto his forehead to greet them. After a brief exchange of compliments, and a few words of admonition from Margaret to her sullen and sleepy younger son, they walked together to the *Tanzhaus* a few streets away.

The party was in full swing when they arrived. Ruarshi gripped his staff and waded into the press and noise with Margaret on his arm, nodding and exchanging pleasantries and hating every minute of it. He would calm down soon enough, he knew. Somewhere along the way he lost track of Davyt and Etienne, which didn't worry him overmuch. The hall was big but not ridiculously so, and he managed to spot them both after a quick search. They had wandered away with Johann and were already dancing, Etienne with a tall woman dressed as a swan and Davyt with a short redhead. Ruarshi couldn't tell what she was supposed to be, unless perhaps all that red was meant to indicate that she was the element of fire. Or that she was on fire, possibly.

Because he knew it was the polite thing to do—indeed, that it was all but obligatory—he relinquished his staff and asked Margaret to dance with him when the instruments started up again after a short pause. She assented and they accompanied each other easily across the floor, gliding into the larger pattern of dancers while carrying on an inconsequential conversation about her business interests and his patients. Ruarshi was able to sustain his part in the exchange even after the back of his neck started prickling, but he progressively lost the thread of their chatter. He was completely unnerved by the time the music wheezed to a halt. Someone was watching him and he didn't know why. He bowed himself away from Margaret as gracefully as he could and retreated to the wall to pick up his stick.

Once there he flipped up the patch that covered his eye and scanned the crowd. Davyt was standing nearby, part of a small circle of young people that didn't include Etienne, and where had that idiot gotten himself off to—even if Davyt hadn't been so close to him, thinning his bond-shield would be of less use in a crowd like this than simply using his *eyes* to find the older Illyana, and why the hell—

There was a man in a long dark cloak moving determinedly in his direction. He had a cowl pulled forward over his head, and Ruarshi couldn't even begin to make out his facial features in the hall's inadequate lighting.

He headed toward the door, hoping to draw the stranger out into the night and away from all these people. Also hoping, as long as he was at it, that there was only one individual trailing him and that the Illyana wouldn't notice what was going on. At least not until Ruarshi himself had it sorted out.

He darted out of the door and around the corner, putting his shoulder to the wall. A moment later, he heard a cautious, "Hello?"

The man didn't sound hostile. Ruarshi confirmed his lack of ill intent with a flicker of magic and stepped forward to confront him.

No wonder he hadn't been able to get a decent look at the man. He had his face painted up in black and white, a skull superimposed on his skin. The effect was disconcerting.

"Did someone tell you to expect me?" the man asked.

"No. I don't know who you are." Though Ruarshi thought he might be able to venture a guess.

"That's a relief. Especially as I didn't decide until this afternoon whether or not I intended to meet you here."

"How did you know this is where I'd be?"

The man grinned behind the death's head. "Your black-haired apprentice likes to chat when he buys things." He held loosely balled fists up to either side of his forehead, his index fingers pointing toward the sky like horns.

Ruarshi sighed. "Is it even necessary for me to introduce—hold on, we're about to be interrupted."

He'd kept his bond-shield thinned and therefore knew that the other two Miriyanti at the party were currently barreling toward the door he'd just come out of. He held up a hand, asking the man to wait, and slipped back inside the *Tanzhaus*.

Davyt came to a halt immediately, his eyes searching his father's face for clues. Etienne had been moving somewhat faster than the boy; his boots slid on the wooden floor when he tried to stop, and he nearly ended up falling into Ruarshi's arms. He twisted sideways and collided with the wall instead.

"Son of a bitch," he muttered, rubbing his arm. "Who's the cloaked horror out there?"

The term *Stillgericht* didn't translate well into Miriyanti, but they'd heard the term from him before and understood what it meant. After they'd extracted a series of quick and exasperated promises from him, they agreed to return to the dancing. They stayed to watch him leave the hall, however, and he wasn't surprised when they peeked out a moment afterward. He gestured them emphatically back inside and they went.

The cloaked horror was chuckling. "Thus do the denizens of Asgard watch out for one another. The wolf is your son?"

"Yes. He's a fox."

"Not Fenrir?"

"No." Ruarshi frowned up at the man as the elements of the myth floated to the surface of his memory. Fenrir would kill Wotan at the end of time, he believed. Lovely. And that left Etienne in the role of...

Ruarshi pressed his lips together. He could see the parallels, and he might even tease the Illyana about the misunderstanding later, but just at the moment he didn't appreciate the slant of the stranger's sense of humor. "And Etienne isn't Loki. He's just a demon."

"I've mistaken you, then. I apologize. Shall we walk? I don't believe we're being observed, but if we are it would be better to move."

"No one's watching us," Ruarshi said, but he fell in beside the man and they started around the hall, walking slowly.

"You're sure of that?"

"Yes."

"Fascinating. And useful."

"But not to you. As I understand it, you're only interested in my healing abilities."

"True." Several silent heartbeats went by before the man continued. "My Christian name is Simon, and I'd like to leave it at that. I come from an old Mainzer family. My surname is relatively widespread in this region, and my throwing it around would do more harm than good."

"Many people must know it already."

"Many do. But not in this context."

"And what context is that?"

The death's head swung back toward him. "I don't knife people in alleys. That's not what the *Stillgericht* is for."

Ruarshi made a noncommittal noise. "A *Gericht* renders judgments. And punishments."

"We're interested in extortion, not blood."

This was unexpected. "Extortion?"

"Yes. Albrecht's supporters can afford it. Many of their victims have families who've been struggling to survive now for over a decade. They could use some financial help. We think of it as *wergeld,* long overdue."

"You're going to rob them?"

"No. We're going to explain the difference between *wergeld* and blood feud, and let them decide which they'd prefer. The two we've already approached have opted to pay with gold."

"How do you know which noblemen you should be talking to?"

"It isn't hard. Most of them were outspoken in their allegiance to Albrecht, and not shy about describing the reprisals they were involved in. When there's a question, we require three witnesses, at least one of whom has to be unknown to the other two."

Ruarshi glanced sideways at the man. He was telling the truth as he understood it. There would of course be members of the *Stillgericht* with a more bloody-minded disposition, but if Simon could keep them under control this scheme of his could work.

"You want me as an ally in case something goes wrong?"

"I take it for granted that something will go wrong. Probably many things before we're done. I want you on my side to help protect my people."

"You must know what you're asking. If Doctor Bebel were to find out, I'd be expelled from the city inside of a week."

"Friedrich Bebel happens to be one of the men we need to speak to. He won't trouble you."

"What are you going to do to the ones who refuse to hand over their gold?"

Simon shrugged, the movement barely discernible in the pale mix of moon- and torchlight. "Hurt them. This is a dishonorable struggle between dishonorable men, but it's not a war. That, we would lose. The nobles are better armed than we are and have no fear of consequences."

"If one of your people gets caught, what then?"

"We pray for him and get ready to run."

"That's not much of a plan."

"It's all we have. It's my occupation to move things in and out of Mainz, by land and by water. I can get dozens of people out in the time you've spent at this party."

"Dieter's adherents among the nobility won't help you?"

"Some have, mostly by testifying against individuals they personally dislike. We don't expect anything more than that from them. Nor do we want anything else."

"How much support do you have among the people?"

"Quite a bit. More since the cooper's boy was killed."

"He was the one murdered the night of the Archbishop's death." It wasn't really a question; he and Etienne had eventually succeeded in catching up with the rumors.

"Yes. He was fourteen years old."

"How old are you? You seem rather young to be in charge of all this."

"I'm thirty-eight. I inherited my role from my father; he helped create the original *Stillgericht* and was one of the more successful defenders of his neighbors' lives and property at the time of Albrecht's accession.

"I have a wife and three children at home and no personal axe to grind. I had cousins who were killed by Albrecht's partisans, along with an uncle, but I've put that behind me. I'll take none of the money we receive. I do well enough on my own. I hope that answers your remaining questions."

Ruarshi nodded. "All but one: how many women do you have carrying messages for you?"

"Only family. Talking to your leman wasn't one of Raban's better ideas. He's been given to know that if he tries anything like that again, someone's going to begin taking a hard look at his expenses."

"That sort of threat would deter anyone. I believe you've satisfied my curiosity."

"Excellent. Now I have a question for you."

"What is it?"

"Why were you in the print shop that night?"

"Etienne had made a promise to a friend."

"But you aren't Etienne."

"I'm responsible for his safety."

Simon's expression was pensive. "I have a theory. If I'm right, will you tell me so?"

"I might."

"I think you're here on Miriyanti business. I think one of your warriors lives around here somewhere, that he put that new scar on the side of your head, and that you're worried about what he'll do next. That's the reason you so rarely let the others out of your sight. If that's the case, we can help you. Assuming you'll help us."

Ruarshi should never, never have told that skinny little boy to watch for Miriyanti. "You've been talking to Udo, haven't you?"

"Not personally. But I'm aware of him."

It did no actual harm that Simon knew, not as far as Ruarshi could see, but he distrusted the situation. The man was frightfully well-in-formed. "Thank you for your offer, but I prefer to keep that part of my life here private. I'll consider my assistance amply repaid if you'll keep Bebel off my back. He's going to land there eventually. We don't get along."

"I'm glad to hear it. Bebel's a vicious man."

"I know."

"We'll be in touch if and when we need you. We won't bring anyone to your home for a healing; one of our men will guide you to us. I hope you won't take it personally when I say that I'd like our contact to re-main minimal."

"I feel exactly the same way," Ruarshi said, "but if I wanted to get a message to you, how would I go about it?"

"There's an old derelict named Olafsson, Olli for short, who can be found any hour of the day at The Sour Grape, south of the cathedral. Do you know it?"

"No, but I can find it."

"Just tell him you have something for the judge. He'll take care of it."

"I won't leave a message with a drunk."

"Good, because Olli isn't one." Simon came to a stop and grinned down at him. "I believe I'll be leaving now. We're still not being watched?"

"No."

"Thank you for chatting with me. Enjoy the party." He moved off into the darkness, heading toward the river.

"Don't mention it," Ruarshi murmured, looking after the man until he'd disappeared from sight. Then he turned to go back into the hall.

)O(

Ruarshi had made good use of his holiday social calendar, and it wasn't long after the party at the *Tanzhaus* that he received a message from Merten informing him that a position for Wolter had been found. A family from the minor nobility was seeking a male servant, and the old man knew them well enough to vouch for their collective character, in-sofar as it related to the treatment of the men and women in their em-ploy. Merten's reassurances in hand, Ruarshi put a remarkably agreeable Etienne in charge of overseeing Wolter's transfer from one household to another. He'd left the house just after dinner, Kilian in tow, both of them well dressed against the cold.

Ruarshi had chosen to remain in the kitchen, where he drowsed comfortably in the warmth while Charitas pulled out her sewing and Davyt bounded up the stairs to fetch an item of indeterminate nature from his belongings. He returned clutching a small collection of papers in one hand. He flipped through them as he approached the table, a distracted frown on his face, finally pulling one free and extending it in his father's direction.

"What do you think?"

Ruarshi leaned forward to take the paper, his breath catching as he got a look at what was on it. It was a sketch of his sister Yael, perfectly rendered in ink and charcoal, an expression of mild aggravation on her face that might possibly have been explained by the suggestion of Aethel's profile in the background. Only after he'd stared at it for several seconds did Ruarshi realize he was still stretched out over the table. He sat back down.

"You drew this?"

Davyt was grinning at him. "Yes. You like it?"

"It's incredible. You have more?"

His son chuckled and dropped into a chair. "These are just the ones I drew while I was traveling, plus two I did here the other day while you were out. There are a lot more at home." He chose another and slid it forward.

Lorion, caught in a rare serious moment. He looked tired, and the lines at the corners of his mouth were deeper than usual, hinting at anxiety or pain. This was followed in quick succession by a drawing of Ardan, her head tilted to one side in that exaggerated display of patience that her students found either endearing or irritating, and another of Etienne wearing a broad, brilliant smile that contained not even a hint of a smirk. More slowly, Davyt extended a sketch of a young European woman, her face mostly obscured by shadow and a pair of bedraggled wings rising behind her head, and finally a portrait of Slan. She seemed to be in motion, caught while turning to glance over her shoulder, perhaps. Her face was thinner than he remembered it. He felt the old, familiar constriction in his chest and looked up.

His son was watching him.

"These are beautiful," he managed. "The girl, she's one of the actors you came here with?"

"Yes. I did several of her, but her family kept them to use as advertisements for their performances. She was the right person for me to draw. Anybody else would have scared audiences away."

"How did you discover you could do this? Have you studied with anyone?" Unlike Italy, Miriyan had no art schools. The shapers and smiths might want to argue that point with him, but they used magic in their work, which put it in an entirely different category as far as he was concerned.

"I started out by smearing charcoal around on the bricks of the hearth. Mother got tired of that after a while and started supplying me with paper. There's a fellow named Maartos whose style is similar and he gave me some help, but mostly I learned this on my own. I just draw what I see."

"I wish we were still in Florence. Some of what's being done there..." His eyes strayed to Slan's face again, more or less against his will.

Davyt pushed a different sort of sketch toward him, distracting him. It depicted a man's bare shoulder, arm, and hand, all done in minute and lifelike detail. In its way it was even better than the faces. Ruarshi had seen plenty of arms in his career as a healer, and he couldn't find a thing wrong with it.

"This is perfect, Son. I never thought I'd say this to anyone, but I think healing might be a waste of your talents."

"That's... thank you. Since you like them, I guess I can show you this."

The final portrait was of Ruarshi himself, as he'd looked for a brief period of time right before leaving Miriyan when Davyt was still a young child. This would have been just after he'd been dragged back from the woods, and his face was painfully thin. Combine that with his absent facial expression and he looked like a starved half-wit.

Davyt seemed to feel a need to explain. "I know I've seen you since then, but that's what I had in my mind on my way down here. That's kind of how I've always thought of you, actually, which is stupid. I'll get rid of it if you want."

Nerthu, no *wonder* his efforts to get his son to treat him like a regular human being had never gotten them anywhere.

And Davyt had asked him a question, even if he didn't know it. Ruarshi needed to answer it.

"Keep it. I'm ashamed of this but you were right to show it to me. Give me just a minute." Ruarshi closed his eyes and carefully peeled away the layers of his bond-shield until it was thin as gossamer.

After an initial burst of startlement from Davyt, when the boy felt the first stirrings of their link humming back into existence, his son went quickly from caution to curiosity but made no move to extend his awareness through their connection. He would need some encouragement, Ruarshi supposed.

He opened his eyes and tapped the parchment. "That was a mistake," he said, "which I made because I thought I couldn't live without this kind of bond. I was wrong but it took me a while to figure that out. How much of this did you already know?"

"Mother explained what you did, later on when I was older, and why," Davyt replied. "And you told me what you'd replaced pair-bonding with when I got here. But why is this still...?" He gestured toward his head.

"I don't know. Back when you were born, my link with you persisted longer than it should have, but it did fade eventually. I'd thought it was gone for good until you arrived here and it came back. I don't mean this as an intrusion. I thought it would be the quickest way to let you know that I'm all right."

"This isn't necessary, Father."

Ruarshi smiled. "It's up to you, Son."

Davyt nodded and began a tentative exploration of their link. Ruarshi concentrated on paying as little attention as possible to his son's presence within his mind, so vivid in spite of all he could do, at that place where once Wil's spirit had meshed with his own. It was a feeling he missed so intensely that he found himself retreating from it, burying himself in the twilight of a shallow trance to avoid its pull. His son was after all a wholly inappropriate, not to mention unwilling, bond partner.

After a further interval of silence, Davyt nodded again and withdrew from the link. Ruarshi quickly reassembled his bond-shield while his son stared thoughtfully into the middle distance.

"You know," he said, "since you're able to bond with me you ought to be able to bond with anyone. I wasn't with Mecheta long enough to learn how to manipulate links, but maybe when you're back in Miriyan something could be done."

"Maybe so."

"I didn't mean to pressure you into letting me poke around in your head," Davyt continued quietly. "I hadn't realized it was still a possibility. I just thought showing you that," he jerked his chin toward the drawing, "would help somehow."

"And did it?"

"Yes. It helped me. I'm not sure it helped you."

"If it was of some use to you, I'm satisfied. It was little enough, provided your next sketch of me gets my weight right."

His son smiled. "It will. It'll probably show you holding a *tana* and looking smug."

"Smug?"

"Definitely."

Ruarshi laughed. "I'll be pleased to see it when you've finished. Would you like to go ice skating tomorrow?"

Davyt raised an eyebrow. "I play a mean game of *jhot*. Think you and Etienne would be up for a round or two?"

"There's a pond west of town we could use. The skates down here aren't what you're accustomed to—they use bone for blades rather than metal—but they serve their purpose. Full contact or touch-out?"

"Contact, of course."

"Hmmm. Etienne has the weight advantage if we take him on separately. Shall we team up and knock him out early?"

"Sounds good to me. For the honor of our clan and all that."

## An Arrow Shot through Dark Water

Early the next morning, a good several hours before dawn, a drunk collapsed on their front step. Ruarshi was made aware of this by a grumpy and rumpled Kilian, who'd come up the stairs to tell him about it.

"He thumped on the door a few times, or maybe that was just the noise he made falling over. I'd have sent him on his way but there's something wrong with his foot. What I can see of it is a purple mess, smells bad. He's not said anything coherent since I brought him in. He's on the couch by the fire. I think he's delirious."

"Thank you for coming to get me," Ruarshi said, already pulling a dark wool tunic over his head. His next words came out muffled. "I'll be right there."

"I'll see if he needs anything in the meantime," Kilian responded, heading back down to the kitchen and leaving the healer to finish his routine in the dim glow provided by what was left of the previous evening's fire. Not bothering to comb his hair, he threw a few small logs into the hearth and kicked the leg of Etienne's bed as he went by.

"I know you're awake. Go back to sleep. I can handle this." The Illyana moaned in reply and shifted beneath the blankets. He'd been sleeping with his head entirely covered, as was his habit on cold nights. Davyt, for his part, hadn't so much as stirred at Kilian's knock.

Ruarshi chuckled and shut the door, and then made his way groggily down to the ground floor, nodding to Charitas on his way through the kitchen. When he emerged into the front room, he observed Kilian leaning over a man-sized bundle of cloth on the couch. The stench of infection was indeed overwhelming, as was the smell of alcohol, though as with most Europeans both had to contend with the equally unpleasant odor of an unwashed body.

Kilian straightened. "He doesn't want water, nor anything else I've offered. Suppose if I'd mixed some wine with it I'd have gotten a different answer." The big man shook his head and left the room.

Grabbing a chair on his way by, Ruarshi set it beside the couch and then lowered himself into it, studying his patient's face. It was young but worn, narrow and sharp-featured with purple circles beneath the eyes and a well-tended mustache currently being overwhelmed by a profusion of untended stubble. His color was high, the result of a fever that had clearly been hollowing him out for weeks. His filthy wheat-colored hair hung past his shoulders. The healer glanced toward the man's foot, bundled up with rags to twice its normal size, with a single discolored toe protruding from the mass. No telling without a closer look if that was a result of the infection or frostbite.

The man's eyes opened. Bright blue, and surprisingly focused for someone he'd assumed to be staggering drunk.

"Karoli, clan Doshae. Pleased to meet you, Cousin. If he sent you here to kill me, now would be a good time."

Ruarshi was out of his chair and had his bond-shield down before he was even aware he'd moved. That would bring Davyt pelting down the stairs before long, but there was nothing he could do about it. He wove a tight little shield, not of the defensive kind, and waited.

"Sorry about the arm," the Naishanti went on, "but I always did think you were an arrogant little prick. Didn't believe I'd be able to mark you. Now I have to wonder if you deserve your reputation. What, nothing to say? If you are going to kill me, do it now; I don't want an audience."

Helpless fury rolled from the man in waves, almost overwhelming the desolation that underlay it. Beneath all that was something else Ruarshi couldn't read; the intensity of the Naishanti's physical pain acted as a barrier past which he could not reach.

"Use this, would you? I'd prefer a clean execution to that Nerthi bullshit." Karoli pulled a knife from his belt and extended it toward him hilt-first. Ruarshi took it and tossed it across the room, where after a bit of clatter it came to rest on the cabinet underneath the medicine rack.

The warrior stared after it for a moment before returning his gaze to Ruarshi's face. Dread rose beneath the anger, accompanied by a resignation so complete that it was indistinguishable from courage.

"I'm not here on Casimir's orders," Ruarshi said, resuming his seat but not yet letting go of the power he held. "Quite the opposite. Why did you assume otherwise?"

The man had started to shake. Ruarshi had to clamp down firmly on the urge to help him as the warrior wrestled with himself to bring the tremors under control.

"So you're not here to kill me," he said finally.

"No."

"It can't be a coincidence."

"It's not. I'm here for you, for reasons of my own."

"Are you going to tell—"

Davyt chose that moment to burst in, still in his nightshirt, followed by a half-naked Etienne. Ruarshi turned his head toward them without taking his eyes off the Naishanti.

"Etienne, Davyt, this is Karoli, clan Doshae. Not a close relation. For some reason we haven't yet gotten around to discussing, he thought I was here to kill him." He risked a direct look at his son, gesturing vaguely toward his temple. "Sorry."

Davyt shook his head and took a seat next to the fireplace. Etienne remained standing, arms crossed, looking curiously at the man on the couch.

"Do all the Naishanti that Casimir sent down here look like Europeans?" he asked.

The warrior's eyes flicked over each of them in turn before coming to rest on Ruarshi again. He didn't answer.

Sighing inwardly, Ruarshi allowed the weave he held to dissipate, replacing it with another that he used to cut off all sensation from the man's injured foot. Karoli's entire body sagged at that and he bit his lip, breaking the skin. A thin trickle of blood ran down the side of his face and into his hair.

"I assume you'd like your foot healed," Ruarshi said, moving his chair closer to the couch to see how the man would react. "What happened—"

Karoli surged upright and pushed himself to his feet. Ruarshi rose with him, grabbing his arm to restrain him when he would have started for the door.

"Let go of me."

They were face to face now. Incredibly, the man was trying to marshal what little magic remained to him in his weakened state. Ruarshi tightened his grip on the Naishanti while simultaneously letting go of his healer's weave.

Karoli collapsed to the floor as pain overwhelmed him again. "Fuck," he breathed, gasping for air. Ruarshi could tell how hard the man was struggling not to faint. His patience snapped.

"We can do this all day," he said tightly, once more blocking off the agony that burned upward from the warrior's injury, "but it would be easier on all of us if we didn't. Are you ready to talk to me?"

Behind him Etienne made a strangled noise, and Ruarshi looked down to see that the source of the faint pricking against his abdomen was the point of a *tana* held in the man's trembling fist.

"Go ahead," he murmured. "Either way you're going to have to go on living for a while."

After a brief hesitation, the man shuddered and the *tana* disappeared back up his sleeve. "By Sotar's left hand," he rasped, "I'll do nothing in future to harm you or yours, and I'll oppose all hands raised against you."

"That's better, if a bit excessive." Ruarshi gestured to Etienne, who was hovering right behind him holding the fire poker, and they helped the warrior to climb back onto the couch. Davyt was at his other shoulder, his face pinched and white.

"Can you read him through me?" he asked his son in a low voice.

"Yes."

"Then you know there was little reason to worry."

Ruarshi could tell that Davyt tried to smother the surge of disagreement that rose in him then, but his efforts were wholly inadequate. "As you say, Father," he replied stiffly.

"You have to trust me, Son," Ruarshi said, noticing only then that the kitchen door had cracked open again. "Kilian? Is there a problem?"

"We can hear you all speaking that *erl*-tongue of yours. Including the little man on the couch. Is he the one bloodied you up?"

"Yes, but we've just agreed there'll be no more of that. Please ask Charitas to fix enough breakfast for one more."

Kilian nodded and pulled the door shut.

Ruarshi turned back to his patient. "We can heal your foot first or we can talk first. Up to you. I take it you're left-handed?"

The warrior was dabbing at his lip with a filthy sleeve. He paused at that. "Why?"

"I imagine that badly healed shoulder blade gets in the way of your sword work. I can do something about that as well, if you're interested. At some later date."

"You'd have to break it to fix it."

"Yes."

"How would you do that? A maul?"

Ruarshi smiled down at him. "Nerthi bullshit would do just as well, with less risk of unintended injury."

Karoli returned his smile, his eyes glittering with fever. "Talk, Cousin. Why are you here?"

"Because I want to find out why you're here."

"Ask your boyfriend."

"Casimir and I aren't nearly as close as people suppose. I've spent the past six months wondering when he'll send his men down to arrest me."

Ruarshi heard an exasperated exhalation of breath from Etienne, but his focus on the warrior didn't waver.

"He's had plenty of time to do that if he wanted to," the warrior observed. "Why hasn't he?"

"I have no idea. There's still a slight possibility that his scrying has led him in the wrong direction. The Seers' talents are imprecise. They're fairly good with long-term likelihoods, but when it comes to specific events or the whereabouts of specific people, their power isn't always much use."

"You've observed them?"

"Every chance I got."

"He's not the one who told you I was here?"

"Hardly. But very few people in Miriyan know that you and the others are still alive. Casimir told your families that you were dead and your bodies were lost. There *was* a large fire right about that time at Mirror Lake…"

Karoli's expression froze. "I fucking knew it."

"Knew what?"

"That's why I thought you were an assassin. The old bastard never intended us to go home."

"He said it would be a temporary exile?"

"Yes. Do what he wanted for long enough and we'd be reprieved. That *fucking*—"

"And what did he want?"

"Mayhem."

Ruarshi waited but the man didn't continue. "Mayhem?" he prompted.

"Stir up the Europeans, get them killing each other over religion or politics or whatever else comes to hand. You've heard of Jan Hus? One of our early efforts."

"That doesn't make sense."

"Take it up with him."

"No, I mean… If one of you were captured, Casimir would have no reason to believe you'd keep his name out of the conversation. Unless that was part of the—"

"No, no, no. We've got European minders. The old bastard convinced them we're rooting out the troublemakers by way of a favor, so that trade won't be interrupted."

"The Europeans believe this?"

"Some of them. We've been kicked out of a few places. The high-ranking fuckers I've dealt with around here seem happy enough to have me."

"You're with the Drummer."

"Yes."

Ruarshi frowned. "I've lived among Europeans for a long time. I still don't understand why they would agree to this."

"When we're not doing what Casimir wants, we're doing what they want."

"Which is?"

"Typically it's killing people. Selectively."

"Has Casimir ever issued an order like that to you?" Etienne asked.

Karoli raised his chin and glanced over Ruarshi's shoulder. "A blanket instruction, right from the beginning. If another Miriyanti gets too close to one of us, kill him."

"And you were worried about *me?*" Ruarshi asked.

"As I said, I thought he'd sent you. Since my usefulness to him seemed to be at an end, I wasn't going to keep doing what he wanted."

"So what were you trying to accomplish that night? The same thing you just tried to do here?"

"I'm tired of Europe, Cousin. I want to go home."

"You didn't tell him I was here…?"

"No. I haven't written to him since last spring."

"Who's your minder?"

"One Herr Sprenger. Not an Inquisitor yet, but that's his goal. He'll get here in another month or so."

"Fuck," Etienne muttered.

Ruarshi stared at the Naishanti, incredulous. "An Inquisitor? Are you out of your mind?"

"He's no more dangerous to me than anyone else with authority.

Hard to hold onto your *reichsunmittelbar* status when only a handful of people know you're a Miriyanti."

"How many of you are left?"

"Seven."

Ruarshi had expected the number to be low, but nothing near as bad as that. His face must have reflected something of what he was thinking, because Karoli laughed, a breathy sound.

"He didn't bother to send a healer with us. We've been at the mercy of European doctors for the better part of a century. The results are predictable."

"You probably haven't heard. He's pulling Miriyanti out of Europe as fast as he can."

The warrior shrugged. "Maybe one of us is about to give him the big disaster he's been hoping for."

"Where are the others? No, never mind. Can they be here by summer?"

"… Probably."

"I think it's time all of us went home. Don't you?"

Karoli regarded him narrowly while Ruarshi did his best to ignore Davyt's anxiety, which was rushing through their link with the intensity of a tidal wave. The warrior, in contrast, had been all but impossible to read ever since his foot had ceased to trouble him.

"You're talking about fighting our way through to Miriyan?"

"If necessary."

"Oh, it'll be necessary. I want to know who told you to look for me."

Ruarshi shook his head. "No one who means you harm."

"It's an interesting idea you've got there. Five of us tried that very thing a while back. If they'd made it through to Miriyan alive we wouldn't be sitting here talking to one another."

Ruarshi hesitated and then shifted in his chair. Etienne jumped in before he could open his mouth.

"You're not sending us ahead if you decide to do this, Ruarshi."

He turned to glare at his erstwhile student. "*If* we do this, you two will stay well away from any fighting that occurs. Illyana *do not* assume front line positions in battle." He waited until Etienne broke eye contact to return his attention to the Naishanti. "Agree to let me heal your shoulder properly, and I'll keep considering it. That will be eight of us who can fight, with the possibility of reinforcements as we get closer to Miriyan."

"You want Casimir to fall?"

"It's time."

"Well past time, I'd say. Could I have a drink of something?"

Davyt rose from his chair and went into the kitchen, returning a moment later with a mug of wine. They sat in silence while Karoli finished it off. His hands were still shaking, Ruarshi noticed.

"I guess we'd best get to it," the Naishanti said. "You want me to lie down here?"

"It's either that or fall over in the middle of things."

The warrior stared at him as he set the mug aside and maneuvered himself down onto his back. "How long will this take?"

"Most of the morning. You've been walking around on that infection for at least two weeks and I don't know that I'll be able to save the whole foot."

"Just do what you can. I wouldn't want to stumble in the middle of a melee."

"How'd you injure yourself?"

"I stepped on a fucking chicken bone. A piece of it broke off somewhere inside. I tried to get it out myself. Twice. Then a barber-surgeon tried, and nearly hacked my foot in half. Fucking European doctors."

☽〇☾

Ruarshi had Davyt put the man to sleep and keep him unconscious while he worked on the injury, a vile mess that was already sending septic tendrils up as far as the Naishanti's thigh. It turned out that he wouldn't need to amputate part of the warrior's foot after all, but the damage was so great that he spent hours killing the infection and restoring proper blood flow to the area. When he finally finished the sun was past its midpoint and he felt like he could sleep for a week.

"Don't wake him up yet," he said hoarsely, blinking. Davyt was sitting on the hearth in front of a roaring fire with Etienne in a chair nearby. Kilian and Charitas were also present, dozing and sewing respectively. Kilian's axe was propped in the corner of the room near his hand. The house's entire center of gravity must have shifted while he'd been busy.

"Not until you say so, Father," Davyt replied, as Ruarshi stood and stretched. Then he paused, squinting at the scrap of cloth in Charitas' hands. It looked like a cap, a very small one, and the woman was radiating contentment like a purring cat. So was Kilian, which meant the man was only pretending to be asleep.

Ruarshi restored his bond-shield and waited for his head to stop spinning. He shouldn't have left the shield so thin during the healing; maybe that explained some of his fatigue. When he felt steadier he went over to Charitas and leaned against the back of her chair.

"May I?" He gestured toward the tiny hat.

"Yes, Ruarshi, of course," she said, flustered, and handed it over to him. Kilian had dropped his pretense and was watching him.

He examined it, smiling. "Congratulations, both of you. I should have noticed earlier. I can only plead distraction. We'll keep an eye on you, make sure things are progressing as they should, if you like."

"I'd be grateful, sir," Charitas said, ducking her head, her cheeks the color of strawberries.

Etienne appeared at his elbow. "I told you he'd pick up on it within the week. Since I won the bet, do I get an extra tart with dinner?"

"You knew? Someone should have told me."

"Don't fret about it," Kilian said. "The two of them overheard us talking about the mite, and then this one wanted to start wagering. That was only a few days ago."

Ruarshi extended a hand to the man, who shook it with enthusiasm. "You can take the axe back outside. Our guest won't be giving us any more trouble. I think." He looked over at the Naishanti and then at Davyt, who hadn't moved from the hearth.

"How long is it safe to hold him under?"

"Safe for whom?" Etienne muttered.

Davyt shrugged. "As long as need be. The worst that will come of it, even if I keep him asleep for hours yet, is a headache at the end of it. Well, that and a raging appetite. Mecheta recommends no more than eighteen hours of enforced sleep a day."

"Nothing so drastic should be necessary," Ruarshi said, mostly to himself. He returned Charitas' sewing to her and walked back over to the couch, where he stood watching the Naishanti for a minute or two before sitting down next to Davyt, thoroughly enjoying the heat against his back. The sun had slipped behind a layer of clouds, plunging the room into shades of gray and black where the fire- and lamplight didn't penetrate.

"All right," he said, rubbing a hand over his face. "Tell me your thoughts."

The two Illyana traded a glance before Etienne moved to sit on Ruarshi's other side. "We were talking about it while you were working," he began. "It seems to us that Casimir overreacts to threats. How many Diamyo do you think the eight of you can handle?"

"It depends on how far away they are and how quickly they're moving. And how good they are with bows. My range is only about twenty feet."

"Your range."

"Right. The maximum distance at which I can…" He waved a hand but didn't elaborate.

"I didn't know you'd been practicing that," Etienne said quietly.

"I've been working on stretching that distance. I can do that without inflicting any harm."

"I didn't mean to imply otherwise. Are you prepared to do that?"

"Yes."

"What if he sends members of your own clan against you?"

"Karoli is a Doshae. It would make no difference."

"And we're supposed to hang back and watch you be murdered, if need be?"

"Etienne, in a fight that's exactly what I'm *for*. I lost my status as a noncombatant a long time ago. Both of you know your role."

"It didn't take you long to throw in your lot with Karoli," Davyt observed.

"I suppose I've been looking for one more reason to go after Casimir. One that's not personal. But nothing's written in stone yet. Karoli might balk and decide his chances are better if he sneaks into Miriyan on his own."

"I couldn't tell very much about him."

"Funny, neither could I. He flattened right out once I blocked off the pain from his foot."

"Is that normal?"

"No."

"Do you trust him?"

"I believe his oath was sincere. He was within his rights to demand the same of me, but he didn't. That's an indirect way of admitting he made a mistake, but I think that's what he was trying to do."

"We could just carry their statements with us," Etienne said. "Those alone would cause Casimir no end of trouble."

"And if he knows we've got them? I'd rather have those additional seven swords to call on."

"Will it become easier for the Seers to find us, as more of us gather in one place?" Etienne asked.

"Yes. A healing does the same thing when it's performed on another Miriyanti."

Davyt blinked at him. "So you just…"

"I'm afraid so. If Casimir was waiting for us to kill each other, he knows better now."

"Would he send people to kill you? Or just take care of the others and bring you in alive?"

Ruarshi hissed in irritation. "I can't read his mind, Etienne. I know what you're asking. I can think of only one way he could manage that, which is why the two of you would need to be either right behind me or hidden at a distance." He glanced at his son. The boy looked intensely worried. Etienne seemed to be grinding his teeth.

Ruarshi sighed. "This situation is a bigger mess than I anticipated. What would you have me do?"

"It seems to me that these Naishanti have been wronged," Davyt said after a short pause. "If they need our help getting home, we can't refuse them."

"Yes we bloody well can," Etienne said. "Which observation has nothing to do with how we *should* behave. If you're not holding up a shield at the same time, does your range get any better?"

"I've never tried the one without the other."

"So start trying it. By the time any of this becomes relevant, your son and I are going to be able to put together a shield that a gnat can't get through."

Ruarshi's mouth quirked. "Thus ensuring that you'll need to be right there with me if the worst happens."

"I hadn't reasoned that far ahead yet."

"You're still a terrible liar. So it's unanimous? We keep talking to him about this?"

"We have to," Davyt said.

"Our offer stands," Etienne sighed. "Unless it turns out that these Naishanti trip over their own swords, in which case we'll have to rethink the whole thing."

## ☽◯☾

A little over an hour later, after the servants had been sent out on an errand and the three Miriyanti had finally eaten their breakfast, Ruarshi took a seat next to the head of the couch and nodded toward his son. Davyt took a deep breath and removed the weaves that had been keeping the Naishanti unconscious.

Karoli woke immediately. The blue eyes snapped open and the war-rior stared at the ceiling for a long moment, relief washing through him, tinged at the edges with more than a bit of bemusement. This was followed by something like disgust, and then… nothing. Again. Ruarshi blinked. If he hadn't been looking at the Naishanti, he'd have sworn the man was no longer there.

The warrior sat up carefully, his eyes resting on each member of his audience as he did so, and bent to look at his foot. Ruarshi had left it unwrapped, there being no further need for such measures, and Karoli began probing it with quick ungentle fingers. Though it was certainly still sore and his more aggressive explorations would only serve to make it more so, he kept it up for several silent minutes before raising his head.

"Thank you. I'll be out of here soon."

"Is there somewhere you need to be?"

"If you meant what you said earlier, I've got letters to write and couriers to hire. I think I can get the others here."

"Good."

"So you did mean it?"

"Yes."

"How handy are you in a fight?"

"Give me sufficient space and time and I can be useful. How are you?"

Karoli dropped his gaze to his lap. "I wouldn't be much good in a straight-on fight against another Miriyanti. But I'm quicker than I used to be and I have no fucking idea anymore about the rules of combat. That might give me an advantage depending on who we're up against."

"You've had to do a lot of fighting down here?"

"No," the warrior replied, shaking his head. "Some street brawling is about it. Nothing fancy. That would attract attention."

"What I do doesn't fall under the rules you were taught, either. Will that cause problems for the others?"

"Not if things get bad. I'll warn them when they get here."

"Not beforehand?"

"They can leave again if they don't like it."

Ruarshi thought about that. "You know them. I don't. Do what you think is necessary. But if you start lying to *me*, even by omission, this isn't going to work."

The Naishanti didn't raise his head, but Ruarshi thought he smiled at that. "They listen to me. That's what's important."

"Are you the eldest of them?" It seemed unlikely; Ruarshi didn't think the man was much older than he was.

"Not by a long shot."

"The strongest?"

"Probably, but I don't know. We never wasted our energy fighting each other."

There was one other factor that could give a young warrior precedence over his peers. "Who was your instructor?"

"Fuck. Finally," the Naishanti said. "At the time of Elyon's revolt, I had been apprenticed for eleven years to Aerik Diamyo."

The name sank slowly through the layers of Ruarshi's memory like an arrow shot through dark water. His chest felt tight. "What did you think of him?"

"Not a single fucking thing."

"What does that mean?"

"He pair-bonded me. He'd had some trouble with his prior apprentices and wanted to avoid more of the same."

That solved the mystery of Karoli's strange invisibility, Ruarshi supposed, but his reply raised more questions than it answered. "That's not allowed."

The Naishanti sighed and sat back, crossing his arms. "If I hadn't told you, one of the others would. You still interested in spending time in my company?"

"Why didn't you break the bond?" Ruarshi's bond-shield was becoming less substantial with each passing moment, a result of his current trouble concentrating, and at last there was *something* there…

"You did, didn't you? Was there no one willing to help?"

Whatever it had been, it was gone. The warrior's flat stare was as unrevealing as the water in a scryer's bowl after the magic had burned away.

"Ruarshi…" Etienne's voice.

He tilted his head but didn't break eye contact with the Naishanti. "Yes?"

"The man who cornered Aerik on his way out of Miriyan was named Karoli."

"Was he. I hadn't heard." Ruarshi had been in the infirmary at the time and had failed to keep up with events. This could certainly explain some of the warrior's older injuries. "So tell me why I shouldn't be thanking you."

"Too little, too late, Cousin."

"What's that?"

"Suppose you had a rabid dog on a leash, and you'd learned how to control it. Then suppose you let it go because you thought it had found a legitimate target."

Ruarshi's mind's eye yielded up an image of the lash they'd used, his blood being squeezed from it to spatter across the stone floor, the iron bar glowing red in the heat of the fire. And Aerik's face. Most of all, Aerik's face.

"You thought I deserved it."

"I thought you deserved something. You'd killed warriors and no one did anything about it."

"True. You were there?"

"Not in the room. But yes."

"What were you doing?"

"Getting fucking rip-roaring drunk. I think I also sent a message to your aunt."

Another memory flashed across Ruarshi's vision: Aerik stumbling, dropping the lash, and lurching from the room. Bonds could be made to work that way, though it wasn't easy. And the targeted partner wouldn't have any trouble figuring out what had been done.

"Did he go after you for that?"

"He'd gotten used to my hard-drinking ways. Never said a word about it. He liked making me work through the hangovers."

And now Ruarshi thought he knew just how an apprentice might try to control a sadistic instructor for over a decade, and what it would take to succeed. He attempted once more to get past the Naishanti's reserve and learn what the man thought of all this, and failed. He restored his bond-shield with some difficulty in the silence that followed the warrior's words. He wouldn't do that again, not with this one.

"Let's wipe the slate clean and call it even, shall we? Are you hungry?"

Karoli looked both taken aback and relieved at the sudden change of subject. "No."

"I believe I said something earlier about lying. Do you want your foot to start bleeding before you've gone half a mile? No? Then you'll eat as much as you can before you leave here."

"I won't eat in front of you."

"We can turn our backs, but that will make for an awkward conversation."

"For fuck's sake… All right. What have you got?"

"Bread, sausage, cheese, boiled eggs, milk. I recommend a little of each."

"If you're going to get it yourself, have a word with the black-haired one before you go. I don't want to have to hurt him."

Ruarshi, already halfway out of his chair, swung around to look at his former student. Etienne was smiling far too sweetly.

"Don't worry. I'm not going to mess with this Naishanti piece of dung."

"No, you're not, because you're coming to the kitchen with me. Davyt, you'll be okay on your own?"

His son nodded. As an unwilling witness to the turmoil inside his father's head over the past few minutes, he obviously had a better idea of what Ruarshi had just learned than Etienne did.

He'd have to take care of that now. "We'll be right back," he said over his shoulder, pulling the Illyana with him toward the kitchen. Karoli nodded and leaned back into the couch, his exhaustion becoming plain as some of the tension left his face.

"What the hell…?" Etienne asked, as soon as the door shut behind them. "Why'd you leave Davyt in there with him?"

"You missed it, because Karoli refused to say it and because you weren't there," Ruarshi began, taking a platter from the pantry and throwing the breakfast leftovers onto it, "so I'm not blaming you for what you just said. But that's the last time you'll address him that way. You know that physical distress can be transmitted through bonds, right? If one or the other partner makes it happen."

"Right." Etienne mulled that over. His expression changed from baffled resentment to skepticism between one breath and the next. "You're telling me that's why he got drunk?"

"Yes. That's why he got drunk. Go fill the milk jug, if you would."

Etienne did as he asked, clattering around by the door to the courtyard and returning with the jug filled nearly to the top. "Aerik had to have known he was being sabotaged, if that's true. Why would he put up with it?"

"I can't answer that. At a guess, he decided to tolerate it because his apprentice suffered far more than he did as a result."

"Okay, Ruarshi. No more name-calling, as long as he quits talking about what people deserve. As though he's in any fucking position to know."

"You take that," Ruarshi said, nodding toward the plate and relieving Etienne of the jug. He picked up a large earthenware cup from the table and led the way back into the front room.

"... more secure with the extra seam, but it's easier this way to..." Karoli trailed off as the door opened, but Davyt just glanced up at them and then continued examining the warrior's left sleeve with apparent keen interest.

"Don't you ever lose any?" he asked.

"Rarely," the Naishanti replied, his attention swinging back to the boy. "Just keep extras in your belt and boots."

"You don't have any boots."

"It's been a lean winter."

Ruarshi set the jug and cup on the cabinet and Etienne slid the plate in beside them. Karoli nodded and hobbled over in their direction, retrieved his dagger, and started in on the food without a word.

Ruarshi went to the fireplace and threw an extra log onto the flames, stirring at the arrangement until it was burning more vigorously. The short afternoon was almost over, and he could feel evening coming on in the slant of weak light through the front window.

"Tell me about Hans the Drummer."

"He's a fanatic," the Naishanti said, after pausing to swallow the piece of bread he'd stuffed into his mouth.

Ruarshi sat down on the hearthstones while the two Illyana resumed their seats. "I took that as a given. It's your job to encourage him and his followers, and then see to it that they get caught?"

"Caught or supplied with weapons," Karoli replied, pausing briefly to inhale more food. "The first option is always a lot simpler to arrange and it saves everyone time."

Etienne snorted at that but the warrior ignored him.

"You've been writing Sprenger about him?" Ruarshi asked.

"Yes."

"Are you planning to continue with that?"

"I can't very well stop. Not until I'm ready to be somewhere else."

"How accurate are your reports?'

"Fairly. I can't be the only spy in that camp."

"What are the churchmen going to do with him?"

"I send information to them, not the other way around."

"Execution?"

"I expect so."

"I heard he's got a Dominican advisor. Your outfit is all wrong."

"My outfit did exactly what it was supposed to. Nobody in town will remember I was here. I'll trade it out for the other one when I leave, so as not to get kicked around by the nobility."

"Does the boy listen to his advisors?"

"That depends on his mood. He seems to prefer the ones that natter all day about martyrdom."

"You're not one of those?"

"No."

"Then what do you tell him?"

"To go home to his mother."

"Any chance he'll do that?"

"None."

"How many followers does he have?"

"Maybe a hundred. He'll have more come summer after the spring harvest is in. That's probably when the archbishop will summon his knights."

Etienne was shaking his head. "Is that what you've always told him? To go home?"

"Yes, but it never seems to sink in. Maybe he can tell my heart's not in it. I don't care what he does."

"So you stir up this kind of thing and then wash your hands of it?" Etienne asked.

"That's what I'm supposed to do," Karoli said, pouring more milk into his cup, "but as long as I end up in the middle of whatever happens, Casimir has no way of knowing exactly what my role's been."

"So you're telling us you've spent all your time here trying to save them from themselves, out of the goodness of your heart?"

"No, just giving them my opinion."

"And lying to Casimir about what you're doing."

"Does he deserve anything else? We were talking about killing him a few hours ago, and now you're worried about some fibs?"

Karoli was clearly enjoying this and Etienne just as obviously wasn't, so Ruarshi decided he'd best step in. "We were talking about deposing him."

"It's the same thing."

"… Maybe."

The warrior mopped up the last of the food from his plate, finished off the milk, and then wiped his greasy fingers off on his threadbare tunic. "This will end with him dead or us dead, Cousin. Have a care for the youngsters and tell them the truth."

Etienne swore at him and Karoli responded with laughter, which just made the Illyana angrier. He surged up from his chair.

"Stop, Etienne," Ruarshi said, also rising and shooting a dark look at the warrior. "Is this necessary?"

"If the boy's going to be this picky about his allies, there'll be no end of trouble once the others arrive. Your son—he is your son?—is handling this much better. And here I thought the big one liked me, at least up until I suggested that murder ought to have consequences."

"Exactly," Etienne growled, launching himself at the man.

Ruarshi took a quick step toward them, not certain of what he intended to do, but the issue was decided for him an instant later when Karoli pinned the Illyana against the wall. The warrior whispered something into Etienne's ear and all the fight went out of the younger man. Karoli felt it happen and released him, stepping back.

Etienne turned away from the wall and raised his hands in a gesture of surrender. "Sorry," he said, first to the Naishanti and then to Ruarshi. "I'll be upstairs." He bowed to their guest and retreated swiftly through the kitchen, his footsteps fading as he ascended to the second floor.

"What did you say to him?" Ruarshi asked.

The warrior shrugged but didn't answer. "I think it's time I went. Thank you for the food and the healing. I know what's owed to someone who saves my life. You'll be hearing from me when I have news."

Ruarshi nodded. "At least take a pair of boots with you. I have a spare, and I burnt the wraps you were using."

"No. I'm a thief, not a beggar. I'll be fine. Anything I should know about the foot?"

"Forget about getting all the way back to the Drummer's camp, if that's where you're headed. Rest for a week or two or it'll start to split open along the lines of the injury. And eat, for Nerthu's sake. Not a peasant's diet, either; you need plenty of meat."

"Easy enough. I'll tend to it." The warrior turned toward Davyt. "You've been quiet. Anything you've been wanting to say to me?"

The Illyana paused before responding, considering his words. "You and my father share the same problem, and this isn't the first time that's happened. It's good that you're finally talking. Just remember that he let you get away from him the night you broke his arm and he didn't have to."

"I do know that. Dead men are careless." Karoli bowed and headed for the door, turning at the threshold. "For what it's worth, I'm sorry for baiting the boy. But I wouldn't bother telling him about the apology.

He won't believe you."

With a swirl of frigid air and a ray of pale golden sunlight, the warrior left. Ruarshi barred the door behind him and then returned to his son's side. "Feel like working on a sketch?"

☽○☾

While tidying up the medicine rack late that evening, Ruarshi learned what it was the Naishanti had said to Etienne after their short struggle. The Illyana's low murmur was occasionally audible through the kitchen door, and though the words were somewhat lacking in context it was easy enough to figure out what he was referring to.

"He said taking a swing at an ally was a poor strategy, but he'd let me do it if I didn't mind giving Ruarshi the extra work and wasting everyone's time. He had a point, unfortunately."

# Dreams of Fire and Blood

The next morning passed in a haze of fatigue, the result of getting to bed late and then spending far too much time fighting nightmares. Ruarshi stepped outside shortly after noon, Davyt's sketch of the warrior tucked inside his coat, and made his way through increasingly heavy snowfall to The Sour Grape. There he did in fact find Olli, as promised, a hairy Viking of enormous proportions and mild demeanor who listened carefully to what he had to say before tucking away the drawing and Ruarshi's five Mark coin with a thoughtful grunt. Ruarshi left the tavern with the fragile hope that if the warrior ever got himself into trouble, someone in Simon's network would learn of it and let him know.

That afternoon he did his best to keep his mouth shut and stay out of everyone's way without being too obvious about it. Dinner was a subdued affair involving very little conversation and entirely too much of Etienne and Davyt shooting dour looks at one another. The atmosphere was clearly affecting Charitas as well, and when she dropped the soup ladle with a tremendous clatter Ruarshi had to bite his tongue to keep himself from shouting at her. His temper, which he'd held rigidly in check all day, was about to slip away from him.

He set his spoon aside, pushed his chair back, and stood. After pausing by the fire to light an oil lamp he climbed the stairs to the second floor, where he promptly plunged the bedroom back into near darkness by hurling the lamp into the fireplace. He shook his head at his own stupidity and then went to sit cross-legged in the window seat, curling his hands into fists and pressing his knuckles as hard as he could against either side of the window frame. He gazed out into the darkness. It was snowing even harder now than it had been earlier.

Ruarshi closed his eyes and shoved his thoughts aside until he was left with an appealing inner blankness. Better. He wondered if a similar blankness was what Karoli had used to keep Aerik out of his head. It might be worth asking him about later, if he could figure out how to come at the topic from an innocuous angle.

He opened his eyes and looked out at the row of formidable icicles hanging from the roof of the house opposite. The ridge of ice that had formed at the roof's edge was holding back an accumulation of at least two feet of snow, a miniature avalanche in the making. Lights glowed in the building's windows but there was no one out front; nor did it seem likely, given the nonexistent foot traffic, that anyone would be passing by anytime soon.

Forming weaves when there was a physical barrier—in this case, thick panes of slightly warped glass—between oneself and one's target was so difficult as to be unworthy of the attempt, most of the time. As a complicated distraction, though, it would serve nicely.

Ruarshi was working on his third section of ice, the exertion of the task making him sweat in spite of the chill, when he heard the door open behind him. He continued with what he was doing. It wouldn't be safe for him to stop now, not with the dam of ice so close to giving way. There was enough weight to the snow behind it that it could hurt someone, falling from that distance, if he left off at this point and let it all come crashing down whenever it chose.

He saw the blanket of snow shift and sat up straighter, his latest weave half-finished, to watch as the entire mass paused for an instant and then continued on its descent, plunging to earth with a hiss followed by a low rumble. When it was all over, a pile of snow lay waist-deep in front of the house, partially blocking the entrance. The man who owned it, a reclusive and nondescript cloth merchant whose name Ruarshi couldn't remember, opened the door a moment later to peer out.

"Okay." Etienne's voice. "That looked fun."

"Go back downstairs," Ruarshi said, still staring straight ahead. He could feel blood welling from his knuckles and running down his fingers. "I'm just in a foul mood. There's nothing interesting about it and it will pass soon." His neighbor had the door all the way open now and was staring with a flummoxed expression at the frozen pile on his front porch.

"I'm going to be blunt about this, all right? Aerik's dead. So are all of his allies. You and yours survived. He—they—can't touch you or anyone else. You've got a son who loves you who is *right here*. You and Ardan and the others probably prevented several wars from getting started, which saved the lives of a lot of people on both sides. These things matter, even though I know you don't spend much time thinking about them."

"Etienne…" Ruarshi was caught somewhere between gratitude for what the Illyana was trying to do and anger at the presumption of it, and he had a horrible feeling that he knew which of those was going to win out.

"Quit fighting him, Ruarshi. Even in your dreams. You can't win a battle against a memory."

"No, but I can damn well win one against you," Ruarshi said. "Get out of here."

"What, and go trade more stares with your son and a couple of edgy Germans? No, thanks. Besides, I'm the one who drew the short straw."

Ruarshi hissed and turned to face the younger man. "*Please* go. I appreciate this, but now's not the time."

"When would be better? You'll refuse to talk about it no matter when I bring it up. What have you done to your hands?"

"It was either that or destroy our bedroom."

"By all means, spare the inanimate objects. You look like you've been in a fistfight. How about this instead? If you can tear apart one of my shields faster than I can put it back together, I'll leave."

"That's ridiculous."

"Is it? I've used almost no power today. If I can't hold my own against you under these circumstances, I'll die of embarrassment. It'll be a good test."

Ruarshi thought about it. "All right. Begin whenever you're ready."

It took him a brutal quarter of an hour to rip the entirety of Etienne's shield into useless shreds. If he hadn't had so much adrenaline surging through his veins, he wasn't sure he'd have managed it at all. The Illyana was on his knees, breathing heavily, by the time they'd finished.

"Shit," Etienne murmured. "I am going to stay the fuck away from warriors when we get back to Miriyan."

Ruarshi was also breathing quickly; he was just doing a better job of disguising it. "You're stronger than you think. You wouldn't have lasted half that time when we first arrived here."

"You feeling any calmer?"

"No."

"Then we're going to do this again. Give me five minutes."

Ruarshi considered the dark-haired healer. Having your shield slowly dismantled didn't cause pain, but there was nothing pleasant about the sensation either. It felt rather like having a knife blade scraped gently up and down your spine, and the few times it had been done to him in training he'd been left quivering for hours afterward.

"Oh for god's sake," he said. "Stand up. There's no chance we're doing this again, today or any other time."

"Afraid I'll get the better of you?" Etienne climbed to his feet and clutched the post at the foot of Ruarshi's bed.

"It's not impossible. But you did say you'd leave."

"If I go, you'll just have to deal with Davyt. He's tied to a chair downstairs."

"Now's really not—"

"Yes, I'm kidding. Has anyone who's better at this than I am ever said anything useful to you on this subject? That category would include everyone on earth, by the way."

In spite of himself, Ruarshi snorted a laugh. "Not that I remember. The nightmares get stirred up from time to time, but they always go away again. Give it a few days. In the meantime the less I talk about it the better off I'll be."

"You actually seem to believe that."

"When I have time to wallow, maybe I'll indulge. Not now."

"We shouldn't ignore the situation. This can't be good for you and you've given your son a fright."

"What do you mean? What did he say to you?"

The Illyana grimaced. "I'm not sure what he picked up yesterday through that bond you've got, but between that and the way you've been behaving today, the boy's as jumpy as a flea. He asked if you'd ever told me what happened. Then there were some nervous questions about Aerik, about whom I couldn't be the least bit reassuring. I'm not sure he's ever thought too hard about what was done to you, but now that it's hit him in the face I think he feels an... obligation to learn the worst so he can help you with it. That's a guess; I can't be certain."

"What did you tell him?"

"As little as possible. I suggested your privacy was the most important consideration and then I fled up the stairs."

"Did he elaborate on anything he's already heard?"

"Oh yes. He came at it sideways, but it's clear he was told in some detail about Aerik's reputation. He's not sure where the man drew the line, or if he drew one."

Ruarshi let his head fall back against the window glass. "This isn't something I'm going to talk to him about."

"I know. He won't ask you directly."

"No, he'll just worry about it. I wonder how often he wishes he had normal parents."

"Do you really suppose he'd trade you and Slan in on a boring couple of Tomirans who never look past the ends of their own noses? He's having the time of his life. He tumbled that actress, you know."

"Are you supposed to be telling me this?"

"He never asked me not to. I've been giving him advice. Not *that* kind. I'm trying to keep him safe. He hasn't taken anyone to bed since he got here."

Ruarshi held up a hand. "I trust you absolutely with my son, and I don't need to hear anything else. Knowing you're looking after him is enough."

For once in his life, Etienne appeared to have nothing to say. He'd lowered his head and was staring at the floor with determination.

Sighing, Ruarshi beckoned him closer. "Come here."

The Illyana glanced upward and raised a cautious eyebrow.

"You've still got the judders. I can fix that, if it's all right with you."

"They're not so bad," Etienne said, but he left his position by the bed and shuffled forward until he stood before his former teacher. "Then again, they're not enjoyable, either."

Ruarshi took his hand, lost himself in a brief trance, and then released him. "There'll be no more tackling of warriors in the front room. Understood?"

"So the kitchen's okay?"

"As long as you don't make a mess."

"Davyt suggested I let up on Karoli the next time we see him. Not that I'm any kind of threat to him. Did he introduce himself to you as Naishanti or Diamyo?"

"He didn't specify. Since he never finished his apprenticeship with Aerik, I'm assuming he wasn't elevated. But that tells us nothing about his strength."

"He impressed your son. Davyt doesn't care much for him, but he found something there to respect. He picks up a lot from that link."

"I need to get rid of it, and not only for that reason. Since I didn't create it I'm afraid to touch it. At least until all this is over."

"It's not a bad thing. Davyt seems to value it."

"We'll work on it later, once we're safely home. In the meantime why don't you go back to the kitchen and warm up? I'll be there shortly."

"Just one more thing: what did you think of the warrior?"

"I think he'd probably survive Armageddon. As long as our goals are the same, we'll be able to work together."

Etienne nodded. "I agree. Now, if you don't reappear after a reasonable interval, you should know that I'll be sending Kilian up to throw you over his shoulder and carry you out of here." He turned and slipped quietly out the door.

Ruarshi sat forward and propped his head against the heel of his hand. Nightmares or no, he had to do better than this. Neither of the Illyana needed the added strain of trying to nursemaid an erratic Nerthi through another self-pitying episode, not with everything else that was going on. Not ever, in fact. As he'd mentioned earlier to Etienne, this wasn't what he was for.

He stood, wiped the dried blood from his knuckles with his bedspread, and headed toward the stairway.

☽○☾

The second time the dreams of fire and blood woke him that night, Ruarshi stumbled downstairs and through the kitchen door to the well in their tiny courtyard. After breaking up the ice that had formed on the water's surface with the old scythe handle Kilian kept there, Ruarshi pulled up half a bucketful of near-freezing water and poured it over his head. He returned inside afterward, shuddering with the cold and wondering what he was doing.

☽○☾

Ruarshi stared blearily out at the man standing calf-deep in snow at his front door. A sword hung at the man's hip, a light helmet rested on his head over a frayed gray cowl, and an odd arrangement of leather straps and buckles covered his chest. He supposed it was meant to serve as armor, and he felt briefly sorry for the man. Whoever was outfitting the city's defenders was clearly an idiot.

"Are you Ruarshi Miriyanti, sir?" the man asked, not for the first time. He seemed to be a patient individual, which was fortunate, as Ruarshi wasn't at his sharpest after the nights he'd been having.

"Yes," he managed.

"I need you to come with me, sir. The magistrate is asking for you."

"Come with you? Right now?"

"That would be best, sir."

"Can you tell me why I should?"

"He just has some questions for you, sir. He didn't tell me what it was about."

Ruarshi frowned. "Give me a moment to fetch my coat. Would you like to step inside while I do?"

"No, thank you, sir," the man replied, peering nervously over Ruarshi's shoulder. "I'll be fine out here."

"As you will. I'll be right back."

Ruarshi pushed the door shut and turned to find Davyt and Etienne watching him, their card game momentarily forgotten. They'd had no patients come in that day, so Etienne had seized the opportunity to teach Davyt the rules of the more common European games, in preparation for some unspecified future need that Ruarshi didn't inquire about too closely. It was now past noon and they'd been at it for hours.

"Before you ask, I have no idea," Ruarshi said. He strode through the front room and kitchen and then jogged up the stairs for his coat, which he snatched off its hook and began buttoning on his way back down. The youngsters had both risen from their chairs by the time he reemerged into the main room.

"One of us should go with you," Etienne said.

"Go back to your game. If it were serious, they'd have sent more than one man. The magistrate is probably just following up on the night my arm was broken."

Etienne nodded. "Just in case there are twenty armed men hiding around the corner that you don't know about, we'll come looking for you if you're not back by dusk."

"If I have need of you, you'll know it. Davyt will be able to find me."

They walked with him to the door, where the man stood stamping his feet and blowing into cupped hands. He looked rather overwhelmed at the sudden appearance of all three of them.

"I'm ready," Ruarshi said, pulling on his gloves. "Herr...?"

"Markus Isener, sir."

"Herr Isener, Etienne and Davyt Illyana. Do you know how long this is likely to take?"

"I don't, sir. I'm sorry."

"Shall we?" They started off, Ruarshi following in the bigger man's footsteps to avoid the worst of the snow. "Be back soon," he called over his shoulder.

"We'll be here," Davyt replied. Ruarshi heard the door thump shut behind them.

"It's easier going toward the middle of the road, sir," Markus said, pausing to let Ruarshi catch up with him. "Not so much snow to wade through."

"It was a real mess last night, wasn't it?" he remarked amiably. "I hope you weren't out in it."

"No night watch for me, sir, not for years. They usually leave that to the younger men."

"Ah."

Their conversation lapsed at that point and Ruarshi was glad to let it go. The trudge through the cold wasn't making him feel any better, and when they finally stepped through a small door at the side of a building adjacent to city hall, he was annoyed but not surprised to discover it was hardly any warmer inside. A small brazier stood against the back wall of the dim inner room to which he was shown, right underneath a barred window. He went to stand next to it, hands held out over the meager warmth it provided. A worn desk took up most of the rest of the space, several writing implements and a bottle of ink arranged neatly along one side. There was no chair.

"There you are, sir. The magistrate's assistant is on his way."

"Thank you, Markus."

The man withdrew, leaving the door open. Ruarshi waited with what patience he could muster, listening to the tread of booted feet in the hall and weathering the occasional curious look from passersby. Eventually he bent to throw some additional wood onto the fire, for the limited good that would do. His breath misted the air in front of his face. He watched the little puffs of moisture sourly.

"Ruarshi Miriyanti?"

A tall, well-dressed man crossed the threshold into the room, clutching an irregularly shaped piece of paper in one hand and extending the other as he approached. Ruarshi shook it.

"Yes."

"Gottfried Hesse, assistant to the city magistrate. We have a peculiar situation on our hands, and I wanted to save everyone time and trouble by asking you about it directly. I can fetch a chair if you'd prefer to sit?"

"No, thank you. I can stand."

"Just as well. A cobbler's shop was broken into the other night. What can you tell me about this?" He handed Ruarshi the piece of paper.

He looked down at it.

*This shop was robbed by a fucking MIRIYANTI. Thanks for the good advice, Cousin.*

It required a tremendous effort on Ruarshi's part to keep his expression neutral, but even so he could tell he was about to lose the struggle. He raised his free hand and clapped it over the lower half of his face, hoping the gesture would be interpreted as the prelude to a thoughtful stroking of the chin.

"It's written in Miriyanti script," he managed in a strangled voice, "which is why I'm here, I would assume. But it's complete gibberish. Means nothing. I certainly didn't write it."

"It's nonsense?"

"Yes."

"Hmmm." Gottfried gestured at the paper and Ruarshi gave it back to him. "Do you have an enemy in town we should know about? First someone knocks you on the head and now this. I already talked to your tailor. He said you'd never asked for a recommendation regarding shoes, and those boots of yours don't look like they were made here."

"No enemies. I can't enlighten you about the incident last fall, as I can't remember it. This looks like something a cretin familiar with our alphabet must have scrawled just to waste everyone's time. Mine included. If that's all...?"

"Yes, that's all," Gottfried replied, glancing up from the note. "None of us has ever run into anything like this before. If you should happen to hear of anyone in town with an interest in your language, you'll let us know?"

"Of course. Whoever's behind this deserves to be punished."

"All right. Thanks for coming down. You can find your way out?"

"Yes."

"Good day to you, then."

"To you as well."

Ruarshi walked quickly and was able to make it three blocks before doubling over with laughter. Afterward he felt markedly better, and he smiled the rest of the way home.

If he ever saw the Naishanti again, he was going to wring his scrawny neck.

# Syrup of Poppy

Ruarshi took Isabel's hand as they stepped back through the door. Barbara's house was full of minor nobles and ambitious merchants chatting in the overloud voices of the moderately drunk, while the women whose company had drawn them there smiled indulgently and tried to look like they were having a good time. Some of them probably even were. A small musical ensemble situated in the back corner by the fireplace scratched out a sprightly dance tune, mostly wasted as there was no room left for dancing. The event was Barbara's lone concession to the Karneval season. Ruarshi had accepted Isabel's invitation to attend with some alacrity, and for more than one reason.

It had been almost three weeks since Karoli had stumbled into his front room, and the lack of news from or of him, though not unexpected, was beginning to annoy him. The nightmares had stopped troubling him several days earlier, which meant he'd been able to catch up on some sleep and might even succeed in accomplishing something useful here this evening. He'd left Etienne and Davyt with strict instructions that the two of them spend the evening enjoying themselves, not that either of them had required encouragement. It would be Davyt's first real introduction to the town's night life. The prospect made Ruarshi's stomach clench. His son couldn't be in better hands, though, and both youngsters badly needed the amusement, so he'd overridden his feebly protesting fatherly instincts.

He'd felt like a lout going out the door, but there was no help for that, either. There was no possible way he could tell Davyt that he hadn't slept with Isabel since the night the boy had arrived in Mainz, and that he had no plans to resume the activity. Isabel had understood when he'd explained his decision to her, along with his intention to keep seeing her regularly, both for the pleasure of her company and so that Barbara wouldn't think he'd abandoned their arrangement. His son would probably be pleased to learn of the change, but just the thought of having such a conversation with him made Ruarshi flush with embarrassment. It was something he'd tell the boy later, perhaps. In another decade or two.

In the meantime he needed to pay better attention to his surroundings. The tension that permeated the city of late was present at this gathering, as well, in spite of the copious amounts of alcohol being consumed and the mandatory jollity of the occasion. The *Stillgericht* was clearly doing its work well, leading to a certain nervousness if not outright paranoia among Albrecht's past supporters and an unhealthy glee among Dieter's. Ruarshi had no idea how well either side might be represented at this particular party, and hoped he wouldn't find out.

Isabel was tugging on his arm. She looked stunning in the red dress that had been his Christmas gift to her, and her color was still high after her first successful foray into the world of horse riding. They'd only taken Sophie out for a couple of circuits of the stable yard, but by the end of it Isabel was guiding the animal herself and having no trouble at all with keeping her seat. She still wore the modified underskirt he'd recommended she wear so that she could sit astride rather than sidesaddle, and the novel garment seemed to contribute to her ebullient mood. He wondered what she would think of Slan, and then frowned at the thought of the two of them crossing paths.

"Where are we headed?" he asked mildly, allowing her to steer him through the press.

"There's a man over here you need to meet. His name's Thomas Enngelhart. He's involved in the silk trade somehow. I'm sure you have at least one common interest."

"Still conspiring, are you. Just how widely are my interests known?"

"Don't worry. I knew you'd agree to help us. No one has so much as breathed your name."

"Then I can hardly chat with him about our 'common interest,' can I?"

"Not *that* one. He's our local magical expert."

Ruarshi stopped, pivoted, and headed back the way they'd come, pulling Isabel along with him in spite of her protests. "I just saved you from a tedious quarter hour, and the gentleman from quite a lot of ridicule that he'd never have recognized as such."

Isabel was giggling now. "That's horrible."

"It certainly could have been." He took a slight detour and snagged a glass of wine from atop a low cabinet at the side of the room. "For you."

She accepted the glass, taking a sip and then glancing at his empty hands. "Don't tell me you're planning on staying sober this evening."

"I'm not. But alcohol will only interfere with what I've got in mind. And I'd take it as a great favor if you'd limit yourself to the one, because I'm going to need your help."

"Of course. But what—"

He pressed a finger to his lips. "I'll tell you later."

"Magic?"

"Something like that. Nothing you couldn't tell your confessor about. If there are people here you need to talk to, please don't let me monopolize you."

"Are you asking me to go?"

"No."

"Good, because I've been trying to monopolize *you*. You've been my only client since you first visited this place."

Ruarshi looked at her, aghast. "What are you thinking, Isabel? When I leave—"

"I know what you're going to say. Only two men have asked for me since learning of your interest and they were both very easy to divert. I hardly had to say anything. They're very leery of gaining your unfavorable attention. I'm certain I'll become the most popular woman in the house once you go, but I won't gossip about you. If I decide to keep doing this at all."

"...You have a plan?"

"Not yet. But I don't think I can go back to being what I was."

Ruarshi gently lifted her braid, pulled it to his lips, and kissed it. "Good for you. Prostitutes have miserable life spans. You actually would be better off as a nun." He released her hair and ran his hand lightly across her cheek. "If you like, I'll glare at any man who looks at you for the remainder of the party."

Isabel smiled. "No, no, inscrutable is best. It leaves people wondering. There's an old man to your left who seems to be trying to get your attention."

Ruarshi turned to look and saw Merten heading toward them, moving slowly and using a cane.

"I met him at Doctor Bebel's. He's harmless. I would never have thought to run into him here. Shall we meet him halfway?"

Isabel rested her hand in the crook of his elbow and they intercepted Merten near one of the front windows. The old man sketched her a bow and clapped his hand against Ruarshi's upper arm.

"How are you, my boy? It's been a while. Who is the lovely lady?"

"Good to see you again, Merten. This is Isabel." She nodded to the old man, and Ruarshi went on. "Have you any news of Wolter?"

"Who? Oh, Wolter, yes, the servant. Haven't heard a thing. This is good news, as it happens, means he's doing well. We nobles only talk about the help when we've something to complain about. Servants ought never to trust their masters. Is the doctor giving you any trouble?"

"No. We haven't communicated since the dinner."

"Him I'd trust least of all. He's still got his eye on you. Plus he's not happy with the current climate in town."

"What do you mean?" Ruarshi asked.

Merten waved a hand impatiently. "Any explanation I gave you would be one more than you needed. Unfortunately, the youngsters have got wind of it. Heaven forbid their elders should have a quarrel going that they're not in on."

It occurred to Ruarshi that the old man was quite thoroughly drunk. He traded a glance with Isabel. "What about the youngsters?"

"The boat race! Don't tell me you haven't heard about the boat race; I won't believe you."

"I haven't heard about the boat race."

Merten peered at him. "Hmph. The Monday before Lent, the young bloods have it in their heads to race each other down the Rhine in whatever boats they can rent or steal. Only there's going to be a lot of cheating, mark my words. A hell of a lot of cheating. You should be there. Oh, and before I forget, funny thing about that book your friend wrote."

The old man started to wobble and Ruarshi reached out to steady him. "What about it?"

"Somebody took it, or somebody disarranged Bebel's library. That happens from time to time. But I went looking for it when I was over there last and it was gone. You know anything about that?"

"Not at all."

"Helene is in charge of that house but the doctor doesn't realize it. Good thing she is, too, since she's the one with all the brains. I'd only go to Bebel with a medical problem if I was tired of living. Which I'm not, though on cold days like this I sometimes wonder. Young lady, is

Petra here?"

"I think so. I saw her earlier by the base of the staircase, just over there." Isabel pointed, and Merten squinted in that direction.

"The two of you get your minds out of the gutter," the old man growled, adjusting his cane. "I'm too old for that nonsense. But it's pleasant to talk to a pretty girl with a lively mind, and if I have to pay to do it that's fair enough. I can hardly blame others for working to get what I've always had handed to me for nothing. It's all in choosing the right parents, you see."

"You sound like one of the Drummer's men," Ruarshi observed.

"He's a piker," Merten said, and started to move away. "If I was in charge of that little rebellion, we'd already be living in the Archbishop's palace, the hell with sleeping in the fields like a herd of cattle. They'll murder them in the end, you'll see. Have a nice evening."

With that, the old man turned his back on them and headed off through the crowd, leaving them blinking at one another.

"You know him?" Isabel asked.

"Not as well as I thought."

"If he was a friend of mine, you'd lecture me about staying away from him."

"Yes. I'd insist on it."

She took another drink of her wine. "Do you want to listen to some music? I'd like to sit in your lap by the fire for a while."

"Do you sing?"

"Not in public."

"Would you hum for me? Just enough to drown out that squeaky instrument the tall fellow is sawing at?"

"I'll try."

"Good enough."

)O(

Ruarshi removed his coat, hung it over the back of a chair, and took a deep breath before pulling the vial from his pocket and sitting down on the edge of Isabel's bed. He then pulled off his boots and set them neatly against the wall, unbuttoned his cuffs, and loosened the neck of his shirt. His limited preparations finished, he raised his head to look at the nervous young woman who shared the room with him.

"What's in the bottle?" Isabel asked.

"Syrup of poppy. A very small amount, just enough to help me with what I'm about to do."

"Which is what?"

"Try to find a man who showed up at my house a little while ago. It's rather important to me that he not be injured or dead."

"Find him? From here?"

"It might be possible. When I go into a trance with some poppy in my system, I can sometimes locate people I've healed recently. It's not very precise, but I may gain some notion of how far away he is and whether or not he's ill."

"You just healed him. Why would he be ill?"

"A healing done by a Miriyanti is hard on the patient when the wound is as serious as his, and he was malnourished going in. If he didn't follow my directions, he could still die. Though given what I know of him I wouldn't say that's likely."

Isabel sat down next to him. "How do you want me to help?"

"I could become disoriented while I'm in the trance. That's unpleasant. If I start breathing faster or twitching or doing anything that doesn't look right to you, I want you to slap me until I wake up."

She frowned at him. "So this is dangerous."

"It shouldn't be. Just a bit spooky, because I don't really know what I'm doing."

"Then why do it at all?"

"Because it's better than riding around Niklashausen in this weather."

"That's more than two days' journey from here by horse. Your trance can take you so far?"

"That's what I'm about to find out. If you'd rather that I went somewhere else to do this, Isabel, I'll understand. This is going to be rather tedious for you. I'd ask someone else to assist, but my son's presence would interfere with what I'm trying to accomplish and Etienne would probably refuse. You're the only other person in town I'd trust."

"I'll do it, Ruarshi. I'd just rather not have to slap you."

"And I'd rather not be slapped, so I'll do my best to avoid the necessity."

"How long will you be asleep?"

"Not more than half an hour. Either what I'm about to try will work or it won't. If it doesn't, I'll probably be awake within five minutes. Ready?"

Isabel shrugged. "Sure."

"Good." Ruarshi opened the vial, swallowed its contents, and settled back against the pillows. He patted the bed next to him. "You may as well lie down with me."

Isabel stretched out alongside him. He smiled at her and then shut his eyes, lowering himself slowly into the unnerving twilight world of a poppy-tinged trance.

He surveyed his surroundings with his mind's eye, struggling to suppress the mental equivalent of a shudder. He didn't care for this gray and nearly featureless place, and he thought again about cursing the dissolute, inquisitive Frenchman whose influence he had to thank for allowing him to discover it. It had proven useful once before, though, in his efforts to track down that troublesome Florentine, and there was no reason he couldn't wring some information from it this time. He hoped. His task was going to be more difficult this evening than it had been before, as his distance from the Naishanti in both space and time was considerably greater than anything he'd had to overcome previously.

The area beneath him was dotted with lights, glowing like candle flames in the murk. No more than two dozen or so were visible; so much snow had fallen of late that the usual stream of patients had nearly dried up, with only the residents of Mainz itself able to slog their way to his door. He skipped over them, heading east. There were no buildings or streets visible here, but he was still so close to his starting point that he was able to orient himself to the cardinal directions with no trouble. That would change as he went further afield.

He reached the river and paused, surveying the dim outlines of the barren expanse beyond it. The land itself was always visible in this place, but never the trees, grass, or other vegetation that one found in the real world, making it look as though an especially devastating fire had just swept through the area. He wondered, not for the first time, if such a thing were possible here.

Ruarshi shook himself and continued east over the slightly rolling terrain, doing his best to correlate his surroundings with the markings on the map he'd acquired earlier in the week. He knew better than to rely on a cartographer for anything like precision, but if the man's work was even roughly correct he thought he was still heading along the route he'd planned out earlier. Stars would have been enormously useful, had they been visible, but the sky above him was an endless expanse of swirling fog.

The flames that indicated the near presence of former patients had long since disappeared when he finally spotted another in the distance.

This one had a bluish tinge to it, which he'd never seen before. Another Miriyanti, perhaps? He arrowed toward it, slowing again as he came near and lowering his bond-shield so he could be certain of whom he'd found.

Instead of the prickly personality he'd expected, he discovered an amused malevolence that he also recognized. And it was aware of him.

Ruarshi tried to draw away but couldn't. He was wrapped in what looked to his frantic gaze like a fish net, and all his efforts to escape from it only served to entangle him further. The net seemed to be sinking into the murk. If true, he'd soon be face-to-face with that other presence.

He quit struggling physically and started to tear at the net with all the power he had, but this was nothing like destroying Etienne's shield. The space between strands was much wider and many of his weaves did little to no damage to the thing when he blew them apart. And now he was sure of his earlier impression: he was being pulled closer to his adversary with every second that went by, and he knew he wouldn't survive a direct confrontation. Not here, in a place with rules he didn't understand.

He shoved both hands through the small hole he'd created in the net and pulled. The gap widened and he redoubled his efforts.

Familiar pain stung him, lancing like fire through his skull. Ruarshi reached out toward that other consciousness and wrenched at it as only a Nerthi could, then did it a second time as pain flayed him again. The tension went out of the net all at once and it began to rip beneath his hands like rotten cloth. A moment later he was free but utterly lost. Even worse, his peripheral vision was fading. He shut his eyes and hoped Isabel had realized that something was wrong.

She had. Distant pain in his cheek pulled him back toward his body and he awoke coughing and shuddering in her bed.

Isabel was staring at him, her eyes enormous and one hand still raised.

"Oh thank god," she gasped. "You weren't breathing."

He started to check himself but stopped again at once, his head spinning. He was an hourglass whose chokepoint had been shattered, leaving the sand—his magic—to pour out of him in a rush that could prove lethal. And Davyt, who under normal circumstances would have been able to do something about it, was nowhere nearby and probably drunk.

So he had a dilemma. He couldn't try to heal himself, as that would merely accelerate the speed at which his power was draining from him. How long could he hold out? The poppy, still swirling through his veins, wasn't helping him any. He thought he might last the better part of a day, if he didn't do anything to aggravate his problem.

Isabel was saying something to him. He held up a hand and interrupted her flow of words. "Isabel, could you send a runner to fetch Davyt and Etienne? I think they're at the Cock and Bull. I need them here as quickly as possible. Please try not to alarm them."

"I'll send Matti. Are you all right?"

"No."

That one word seemed to galvanize her. Isabel jumped from the bed and rushed out, leaving Ruarshi to contemplate his idiocy in private.

## ☽〇☾

An hour or so later the sound of boots on the staircase heralded the arrival of the two Illyana. Isabel rose from her chair to open the door for them, but Davyt got to it first, bursting through it with Etienne right on his heels. Neither one of them seemed to be as inebriated as Ruarshi would have expected. Then he caught a whiff of the odor that underlay the alcohol and understood why.

"Been throwing up all the way over, have you?"

"Yes, but we're not sober yet," Davyt replied. "What happened?"

"It's complicated. The short version of the story is that Casimir just tried to kill me, and I need your help to prevent him from succeeding."

*"Casimir?"* Etienne asked incredulously, while Davyt placed his cold palms to either side of his father's face and closed his eyes. He jerked away a moment later.

"You're leaking power like a sieve."

"I know."

"Didn't this happen to you once before?"

"So I was told."

"Someday you're going to have to let me in on what you did to all Mecheta's careful work. We'll get to it later." Sweet Nerthu, the boy sounded just like him when he was angry. "Isabel," Davyt said, shifting his attention, "could you load up a plate for us with some of that food downstairs? It'll help clear our heads."

She was already nodding. "I'll be right back," she replied, slipping through the door.

"I don't suppose this is unrelated to your current predicament?" Etienne asked, picking up the vial from the nightstand. He pulled off the lid and took a cautious sniff.

Ruarshi shook his head, resigned. "I was in a trance. A deep one. You may remember my doing something similar back in Florence."

"The afternoon you stumbled out of your room with pupils looking exactly like yours do now, just before you cornered that sword-toting fop? Were you looking for someone?"

"Yes. I was concerned that Karoli hadn't done what I'd told him."

"Did you find him?"

"No."

"You're certain it was Casimir?" Davyt asked.

"Very. Unless I imagined the entire thing."

"And did that to yourself? I doubt it. So you were in the Seers' territory?"

"No. This place is nothing like what they describe. I don't know what it is."

Isabel reappeared then, carrying two full plates of food which she handed to the healers before subsiding into her chair, watching them in silence. The Illyana murmured their thanks and started picking at the offerings without enthusiasm.

Ruarshi didn't know he'd nodded off until Davyt appeared right in front of him, gripping his face hard enough to hurt.

"Stay. Awake."

"Sorry," he managed. He struggled to sit up straighter. Isabel joined him on the bed, rearranging pillows to help prop him up. His eyelids slid shut again and he forced them open, wondering why he felt so little concern about his current condition.

"Get him up."

Ruarshi couldn't tell whose voice that was, or who was maneuvering him toward the edge of the bed. He did his best to comply when the voice told him to stand up, but his legs wouldn't hold him. He didn't particularly want to end up on the floor...

A jolt went through him, bringing him back to full wakefulness. It felt rather like all his nerves had been set afire. His head jerked upward and he found himself looking straight at Etienne.

"That's the same thing I did to you on our way here and I'll repeat it as often as I have to, Ruarshi, to keep you conscious. Davyt tells me it can't do any additional harm, and he's got some distance to go before he can take this on. Do you understand?"

He nodded, and for the first time since the Illyana had entered the room he lowered his bond-shield to find out what was left to him.

The bond with his son was gone. The rest of it remained. He flinched away from the misery pouring from the man in front of him.

"It seems to me, Etienne, that you just did me a favor, so would you explain to me please why you're so fucking sorry about it?"

That startled a choked laugh from his former student. Davyt growled at them both, his fear and anger making a more coherent response impossible. Isabel, bless her, couldn't even follow their conversation. Ruarshi switched back to German.

"I am going to be *fine*. I'm not sure the same can be said for Casimir. I know this isn't how any of us planned to spend our night, but let's concede that it could have been worse and calm down a little."

That seemed to do some good. Isabel's distress waned and Davyt was no longer on the verge of putting holes in the walls. Etienne, though... Ruarshi would do something about him in a moment.

"When Mecheta healed me, Son, he went too far. Just do what's necessary and no more. I never believed I'd pair-bond again, but I don't want everyone else blocked out, too. We're not made to live in that kind of silence." He turned to Etienne and lowered his voice. "You have my permission to do whatever's necessary to keep me awake. Do you think I'm going to hold it against you?"

The healer shook his head tightly. "Is there anything else that might work?"

"We could try fresh air. If you'll help me to the window?" As Etienne moved to assist, Ruarshi glanced back at Isabel. "Is there any ginger in the house?"

"Yes."

"I promise this will be the last time I send you running down those stairs. Go get some ginger for these louts, and buttermilk if there's any available. They're not doing too well with their food. Feel free to steal from their plates when you return. Maybe competition will improve their appetites."

"Do you want anything, Ruarshi?"

"Not now. I'll make all this up to you later, but don't ask me how yet."

He propped himself against the window frame and breathed in the cold night air. It felt good on his feverish skin but it wasn't doing much to mitigate the fatigue that had him shaking again. He leaned his head against the wall and his surroundings faded for an uncertain span of time; when he looked up again Etienne was accepting a cup from Isabel and Davyt was staring at him.

"Eat," Ruarshi said, as emphatically as he could. Both of the young-sters did as he asked, while he tried to disguise the fact that he was leaning more heavily against the wall with every breath he took. He maintained the illusion of strength for as long as he was able—at least he'd given the boys time enough to get most of their food down—but finally had to admit that there was nothing left. He collapsed a heart-beat later.

He came to as a result of pain, unable now to block out anything coming from the others in the room or even, gods help him, from the revelers at the party downstairs. At least the excess of information made it almost possible for him to get the strands of emotion tangled, so he could tell himself that he didn't know exactly what effect his bad decisions were having on people he loved.

There was some conversation and movement and then rather sud-denly Ruarshi was back on the bed, Isabel's arms encircling him and her breath warm against his cheek. His head was pounding but he couldn't remember why. Isabel's breathing was uneven and the room seemed unusually dim.

She moved away just as Davyt's face swam into his line of vision. Ruarshi thought he felt something pressing against his temples, and then he lost everything to icy darkness.

)O(

He heard soft voices, speaking in the cadences of home. He struggled to reach them, but the weight on his chest pulled him back and away and the voices receded again until his world became silence and twilight and dread, and then even that winked out.

)O(

Daylight teased at the edges of Ruarshi's eyelids. They were too heavy to lift and in any case he wasn't ready to look at his son, or his student, or his lover. Unlike the last time he'd awakened, he now had access to that part of his consciousness that held memory. As had become his habit, he turned away from it. The pressure against his chest increased to the point of pain and he welcomed it, clutching it tightly to himself even as it blossomed into agony.

## ☽○☾

Candlelight flickered by the side of the bed. Ruarshi's entire body was heavy as a stone, but the anvil that had previously been resting against his rib cage seemed to have been removed. A wave of relief washed over him and he thought to check his bond-shield. Not a wisp of it remained. Ruarshi was glad to note that its absence wasn't causing him any pain, as it always had before, but neither was he getting much by way of information about the emotional states of the people who were there with him. The three he expected to find were still present, but they may as well have been half a mile away for all he could discern of them. He'd have to try a more straightforward method of learning what he wanted to know.

It required a ridiculous amount of effort to turn his head toward the room's sole source of light, but he managed it. His gaze fell first upon his son, sitting in a chair that had been pulled up to the edge of the bed with the upper half of his body sprawled across the mattress. The boy's head rested on one outstretched arm and his hand was wrapped around his father's forearm. Ruarshi hadn't been aware of the contact. He stared at Davyt's hand until he was sure he could feel its warmth.

His son was not asleep. "Father?"

Ruarshi blinked and tried to focus on Davyt's face.

"Shit, he's awake?" There was a rustling noise from the corner of the room and then the sound of someone stumbling and falling over. Etienne darted into the small circle of candlelight a moment later.

Both young men had driven themselves far past the point of exhaustion, so much was clear. It was time they got some rest and Ruarshi opened his mouth to say so.

"Hush," Davyt said, sitting up straighter but not letting him go. Instead, the boy shut his eyes in what was clearly a prelude to entering a healer's trance.

Ruarshi sighed in feeble exasperation but held his peace until his son was finished. When Davyt nodded and sat back, releasing him, he attempted to raise himself up onto his elbows. A single muscle in his arm twitched but that was all the response he got.

It seemed he was as thoroughly immobilized as he'd been for a brief time in Casimir's net. A jolt of panic went through him before he could calm himself. He'd lost a lot of power, and he thought his heart had stopped beating at least once. This recovery was going to take a while and he decided he might as well be patient about it.

"Thank you," he rasped. "Now get some sleep."

A gentle hand lifted his head from the pillow and a mug was set to his lips. Isabel held him as he took a few sips of heavily watered wine and then eased him back down onto the bed.

"You, too," he said to her. "Sleep."

She shook her head and smiled wanly, but her eyes were puffy with more than just fatigue. Watching her and the Illyana, Ruarshi felt a wave of anger and concern roll through and then over him.

Strong emotion was apparently a bad idea. He fell back into unconsciousness.

## ☽○☾

When he next awoke afternoon sunlight was streaming through the room's narrow window and Etienne, looking even worse than he had before, was standing in front of it with his arms crossed, staring down at the street below. Isabel was sleeping at his left side and Davyt was snoring softly in his chair. Ruarshi tried to take a deep breath and ended up coughing instead. He struggled to keep the noise to a minimum and neither of the sleepers stirred.

Etienne stepped to the side of the bed and looked down at him. "It would take a mallet to wake them up right now. Here." The Illyana offered him more of the watered wine and Ruarshi gratefully finished off the entire mug.

"I'll go get you some soup," Etienne said, setting the cup aside and heading toward the hall.

"Wait."

"It's been two days since you've eaten, Ruarshi."

"Then another five minutes won't matter."

"That's some very sketchy reasoning," the Illyana replied, but he took his hand from the door and returned to the foot of the bed. "What is it?"

"I'm sorry, Etienne. For this, and for the past several weeks."

The healer shook his head. "I'm not sure you've got anything to apologize for. Unless you knew that Casimir was going to be waiting for you in the murk."

"No."

"Didn't think so. We've had plenty of time to chat with Isabel. She didn't indicate that you were particularly wild-eyed going into this."

This conversation was going to wear him out even more quickly than he'd expected, that much was clear. "How are you? Have you slept at all?"

"Not for a while. The boy needed it more."

Ruarshi shot a glance at his son. "How is he?"

"Unsettled. Exhausted. A bit nauseous. I suspect the buttermilk."

Gravity seemed to be pulling Ruarshi deeper into the mattress. Even so he didn't need magic to interpret Etienne's mood. "You're angry at me for coming here to do this."

"You wanted a minder who wouldn't ask you too many questions, and you found one. She did say something about your being concerned that I'd refuse to help."

"She has an excellent memory."

The healer sighed. "I've been reading that book your Welsh friend wrote, you know. Being angry at you about this would be the same as being angry at you for existing. I'm annoyed but it'll pass. What happened with Casimir?"

"I don't really know."

"I mean, is he dead? Injured? Angrily disembodied?"

"Injured at the least. Beyond that I can't say."

"Injured enough to leave us be for a while? I have a creeping feeling that Karoli's friends aren't the only Naishanti who are going to be showing up here in the near future."

"Casimir will have suffered a massive stroke, and he tends to work alone."

Etienne considered that. "So it'll be a while before we can expect any response from the Seers. If anyone comes at all. Good. There's something else I've been wondering about. You said it was Davyt's well-informed Uncle Lorion who gave him permission to come down here, right?"

"…Yes."

"And he talks to the same faction of Seers who told you about Karoli."

Ruarshi nodded and then closed his eyes as the room started to spin.

"I'm thinking that Mecheta's decision to tutor your son wasn't his alone, and that Lorion probably had more to do with getting your son down here than Davyt realizes. Somebody's trying hard to keep you alive and it would be good of you to start cooperating a little.

"I'm going to go get that soup now. Be back up in a minute."

Ruarshi tried hazily to follow the Illyana's reasoning as Etienne disappeared out the door, but failed. He supposed he'd take it up later when he felt a little better.

He was dozing when his former student returned carrying a bowl of unappetizing liquid. Etienne insisted it was beef broth and kept after him until he'd swallowed most of it, after which the healer returned to his post by the window. Ruarshi fell asleep again as the sun slipped below the city's skyline and the street outside turned from gold to dirty gray.

)O(

At some point during the night Ruarshi awoke. The Illyana and Isabel were sleeping soundly, their breathing deep and regular. He thought cautiously back over the events of the past few days, wondering if his earlier embrace of that crushing pain in his chest had been real or was something he had dreamed. He hoped the latter was true, but had a feeling that was wishful thinking. Ever since Slan had given him his first lesson in warrior's magic, he'd approached the issue of his own identity in a slippery and dishonest way, and every time he took a good look at himself—intentionally or not—the result was a spasm of self-destructive behavior. The hell of it was that he'd never be able to mend the situation, to go back to being an Illyana rather than a Nerthi. Whenever and however he died, he would do so with blood on his hands.

Was refraining from self-harm in such circumstances a sign of maturity or cowardice? He'd had the nerve, once, to administer the punishment that no one else would, but he hadn't succeeded in his aim and afterward he'd gone back to insisting that he was a healer with a few extra and mostly irrelevant talents to call upon. This was nonsense, and if his strange little struggle with Casimir had been real the man was probably dead by now. Another corpse he was responsible for. Karoli had been closer in his estimation of what he deserved than Etienne had. The young Illyana had been around him too long, thought of him only as a healer, and had as a result become partisan. This wasn't the fault of the student, but of the teacher.

He couldn't abandon healing and stay sane. So much had become clear over the years. What he could do was embrace his proper title and every damn thing that went with it, and see what followed. Which meant turning away from the tasks of an Illyana and concentrating more on his other skills from now on. Fortunately it looked like this decision would mesh well with the likely requirements of the next few months.

And what if he couldn't reconcile himself to living this way, either? He'd make adjustments, he supposed. Eventually he was bound to hit upon a combination of honesty and willful blindness that he could tolerate, and with any luck it would hew closer to the truth than the mental sleight of hand he'd been using.

In the meantime it would probably be helpful if he stopped thinking about it, so he did. Or tried to. More than an hour passed before sleep rose to reclaim him.

)O(

Matti went to fetch their horses early the next day, and by mid-afternoon Ruarshi was more than ready to vacate Isabel's room. He felt as though he'd been trapped in it for weeks. He'd just managed to polish off half a plate of solid food, and though his son was still looking at him with a dubious air, he knew he could make it as far as their home with a little help.

He swung his legs off the edge of the bed and pulled himself to his feet, bracing himself against the nightstand until he felt a bit steadier. He donned his coat in silence and then turned to Isabel.

"Thank you again," he said. "I'll be back over soon, and we can try for a more pleasant evening."

She planted a kiss on his cheek and squeezed his hand. "I'll be looking forward to it. Send a message if you're not able to come yourself."

"I will."

Ruarshi made it through the door without incident but had to lean heavily against his son on the way down the stairs. Etienne went ahead of them, clearing their path of curious onlookers and offering their parting regards to Barbara, who was hovering nervously near the front door. Ruarshi nodded to everyone they passed without really seeing them. A few of the women shrank back from him as he went by, which didn't surprise him. Even though Isabel had put it about that he suffered from malaria, and therefore didn't pose a risk to anyone in the house or the city, some would still worry about the possibility of contagion.

He raised a hand to shield his eyes when they stepped outside into the glare of sunlight on snow. Etienne took the reins of their horses from Matti, sending the boy back inside with a few extra coins in his pocket, while Davyt steered his father toward his mount. Ruarshi clutched at Sophie's saddle, regarding the stirrup with resignation.

"That's what I thought," Etienne muttered, coming around beside him. "Up you go."

Ruarshi had been bundled onto the back of his horse like a gangly sack of potatoes before he was fully aware of what was happening. He blinked down at the animal's twitching ears while his feet settled in the stirrups, apparently of their own accord.

"I hope nobody saw that," he said.

"Of course somebody saw that," Etienne said cheerfully, still holding onto Sophie's reins as he swung himself onto his own mount. "I believe we have the undivided attention of everyone in the vicinity. Ready?"

Ruarshi nodded, and then concentrated on maintaining his balance as Sophie lurched into motion. Davyt rode alongside him.

"If you need to stop, just say so."

"I will, Son," he replied, although he had no intention of dragging this little journey out any longer than was necessary. "Do Charitas and Kilian know we're coming?"

"Yes. How's the headache?"

"Minimal."

"How's," Davyt waved a hand through the air, "everything else?"

Ruarshi applied as much attention to the question as he could. "There are dozens of people along this block right now. As far as I can tell none of them are experiencing strong emotion. Except for a fussy toddler."

"Are you using a bond-shield?"

"I don't need one yet. I probably will soon, to cut down on the noise. Are you picking up anything from me?"

"No."

"Good."

Davyt shrugged. "I expect I'll miss it. The bond wasn't intrusive, not the way you handled it. How long had you been feeling unusually tired?"

Ruarshi looked over at his son. The question wasn't a casual one. "Why do you ask?"

"Etienne told me that he thinks there's been something wrong with you since the backlash incident with Bebel. I'm wondering if that's really when it started."

"There's been nothing at all wrong with me. Between the broken arm and the cold weather..." Ruarshi paused, frowning. Was it possible that Etienne was correct? When, exactly, had battling fatigue become part of his daily routine? His attempt to follow the trail of memory back to the genesis of the problem went nowhere. Just at present he could hardly remember the route back to their house.

"You'd been losing power for a while, probably while you slept," Davyt went on. "I ran across some partially-healed but recent damage to Mecheta's work while I was in there. I'd never picked up on it, even though you were sleeping right next to me. A week or two of it wouldn't have hurt you, but over time... Eventually you'd have had trouble replacing what you lost."

Ruarshi's gaze strayed unwillingly to Etienne's profile as his mind's eye took him back to that frigid inn high in the Alps. At almost the same moment the younger man's face froze and he turned toward Davyt. "You didn't mention that before," the Illyana said, his voice tight.

Davyt opened his mouth to reply but Ruarshi was quicker. "Peace, Etienne. You were acting on Mecheta's instructions. You intended no harm. If there was a slate that needed cleaning, you've done that and more since we arrived here. Let it go."

His son looked a question at him but he shook his head, still watching his former student. The Illyana was once again facing forward, away from the two of them. As if turning his back would accomplish anything. Ruarshi nudged his horse to a faster pace and seized the back of Etienne's collar, along with quite a lot of his hair, as he came up beside him. The healer looked at him, startled, and pulled both their mounts to an uncertain halt.

Ruarshi didn't relinquish his grip on the man. Instead he tightened it, partly in aggravation and partly to help himself stay upright. "You're wallowing. I won't tolerate it. *Stop.*"

Etienne nodded. "I hear what you're saying. I'm just tired. Everything will be back to normal in a day or two."

As promises went, this one left a lot to be desired, but Ruarshi didn't have the strength to pursue the issue any further. He released the Illyana and dropped back. The bitter unhappiness blistering the air between them had begun to fade, just a little, by the time they made it home.

# Echoes of Violence

"What?"

There must have been something in his face or voice that he hadn't intended to be there, because Charitas took an unconscious half-step backward before replying. "Yes, sir. I should have told you earlier but they swore me to secrecy, and you've been so sick..."

"I had my eye on him," Kilian added. "If he'd gotten any worse, we'd have brought it to you anyway. I gave him a thorough once-over before letting him out the door tonight."

Ruarshi pulled the rough wool blanket more tightly around himself, wishing again that the heat from the oven would finally soak into his bones and put an end to these endless bouts of shivering. It had been over a week since they'd left Isabel's and he still couldn't get warm, no matter how determinedly he huddled. His power, by contrast, had come flooding back in a wave days before and his restored bond-shield was the only thing standing between him and the emotions of what seemed like every last soul in the city.

"What exactly did they tell you?"

"Your youngster says it's a minor lung infection Etienne was suffering from. He didn't want his coughing to disturb your sleep. I think he's good as new, now, but they still wanted to be careful."

Ruarshi stared at Kilian without really seeing him. So this was the reason Etienne had been dodging him, and sleeping downstairs, and taking his meals at odd times. It also explained Davyt's caginess when asked about his fellow Illyana. They didn't want to expose the resident invalid to disease, a disease that had no doubt gotten its hooks into Etienne while he was denying himself rest by said invalid's bedside...

And of course neither of them had been willing to let the situation interfere with *Weiberfastnacht*. He'd warned them both, through Davyt, to be home by midnight, but he'd forgotten to advise them that Merten was aware of his role with the *Stillgericht,* and that they should be careful when approached by women from noble families. He didn't really believe they'd run into that kind of trouble during this particular festival, but one could never be too paranoid.

"Thank you for telling me."

"I knew it was worrying you," Charitas said, settling next to her husband. "Since he's better, it didn't seem right to keep hiding it."

"Your judgment is clearly better than theirs," Ruarshi observed, "but I promise not to make more of it than it warrants. There'll be no shouting matches in your kitchen in the middle of the night. Go to bed, if you like. I won't be heading upstairs until they get here, but there's no reason that should cost you sleep."

They acquiesced gratefully to his suggestion; Charitas had also been exhausted of late and nauseous more often than not, though everything was progressing normally with her pregnancy. As Kilian pulled the curtain around their bed, Ruarshi settled deeper into his chair and let the sounds of distant revelry lull him into a light doze. A muted clattering at the front door several hours later propelled him out of the kitchen and into the front room in time to greet the Illyana as they stomped their way into the house, trying and mostly failing to knock the ice and mud from their boots.

"You're no longer my student, but you're still my charge," Ruarshi said once the door had been closed, "and your clan can and should hold me responsible for all injuries to your health. May I?"

Etienne exchanged a look with Davyt and nodded wordlessly. It took only moments for Ruarshi to ascertain that the Illyana was free of infection, if still a bit weakened from his bout with the illness. He withdrew from his inspection and turned toward his son. "Good work. The Bonnes are asleep. Shall we…?" He gestured toward the back stairs.

"… Sure," Davyt responded. They followed him up to their bedroom where they shed gloves, boots, and coats, after which Etienne busied himself with building up the fire while Davyt stood looking at his father uncertainly.

"I'm glad they told you," he said. "It was past time, I suppose. There was no way to reintroduce him to your company without explaining why he'd been avoiding you, so we were in kind of a bind."

"I appreciate your dilemma. I was certainly much better off thinking he was flaying himself with needless guilt on my account." Ruarshi shook his head. "Not important. I understand why you handled this the way you did, but you can't try it again in the future. For any reason. There's a good possibility we could find ourselves in a fight come summer, sooner if we're unlucky, and I have to know what's going on with the two of you. Speaking of which, no one tried to stab either of you this evening, did they?"

Etienne was frowning at him. "Do you have a fever?"

"No, I don't have a fever. I'm guessing the answer must be no. I should have told you before you left that my activities remain a poorly kept secret, and you need to be careful around nobles and authority figures."

"I'm always careful around authority figures," Etienne mumbled, working his way through what he'd just heard. "So everyone knows about the *Stillgericht?*"

"It's possible. Merten certainly knows. He's probably better informed than most, but given the way people talk, 'everyone' is the safest assumption to make."

"No one was talking politics tonight, to my vast relief. It was all about how nice and kissable we looked."

"The ladies lining up, were they?"

"You bet they were. A lot of them asked about you but settled for your son."

"The next time you get sick, you're on your own," Davyt said. "I didn't really believe it until we got out there. An evening devoted to a bunch of women kissing you for no reason?"

"They weren't kissing us for no reason, nitwit. They were kissing us because we're gorgeous and we bathe."

"Yes," Ruarshi muttered to himself, "that's what I missed."

Etienne looked back at him, his expression arch. "This is what I sound like when I'm guilt-free. There was also some chatter about religious processions. It seems we ought to stay close to home for the next few days, unless we want to be trampled by the devout."

"Are they worth watching?" Davyt asked.

"That depends entirely on your tolerance for boredom. Only old men participate, so there's not much of interest to look at."

Ruarshi smothered a grin and sat down on the foot of his bed, leaning against the post closest to the fire. "I'm glad you're back, and well. Your success at concealing Etienne's illness makes me wonder what else you're conspiring at."

Both Illyana focused on him immediately, their expressions deter-

minedly innocent. This time Ruarshi couldn't repress the smile. "That's
what I thought. Just stay out of the more obvious kinds of trouble,
would you? I'm going to bed." He was about to start shivering again,
and there was nothing either of the Illyana could do about it, so there
was no point in letting them notice. "Carry on with whatever it is you
two do when no one's paying attention. I'm sure I'll sleep right through
it."

)O(

Ruarshi felt the echoes of violence even through his bond-shield when
he woke before dawn the following Monday. He sat up and thinned the
shield at once, glancing toward the still-black window as he pushed
himself out of the bed. Pockets of distress and pain ringed their neighborhood, some of them no more than a few streets away. He grabbed
his clothes from the back of a chair and started pulling them on.

"Up," he said, walking over to yank the covers from Etienne's inert
form. Davyt was already stirring. "Trouble."

"What kind of trouble?" Davyt began groping clumsily for his own
clothing.

"I'm not sure. People are being injured."

"How?" That was Etienne.

"It's too widely spread to be a fire."

"Someone's gone on a rampage, then?"

"That's my guess."

"Well, shit."

Both of the younger men were ready to go before Ruarshi had finished pulling on his boots. He swore quietly at himself. He'd be back to
normal soon, he was certain.

"Which way?" Etienne asked as they clattered down the stairs.

"Any direction will serve," Ruarshi said. "The worst of it seems to
be just to our west. Don't worry about a lamp." As they were passing
through the kitchen he raised his voice. "Kilian, Charitas, we'll be
back." Then they were out of the house and running as quickly as
could be managed through the ice and snow that still clogged the city's
streets.

Ruarshi slowed and then stopped before they'd gone two blocks.
They could hear a woman's angry screams coming from nearby, and
lights were being kindled in the homes across the street.

"What are we doing?" Etienne whispered.

Ruarshi held a finger to his lips and peered around the corner. Three men in what passed for the uniform of the city guard were standing in the flickering light coming through the open doorway of the second house to their right, watching what was transpiring within. One aimed an opportunistic kick at something. It was clear that none of them were concerned about attack from the rear.

"They're in there beating up a woman?" Davyt was just behind him, a restless silhouette in the dim light of the crescent moon.

"No. Two men are getting the worst of it. The woman is watching, I think."

"How many of the guard are in there?" Etienne asked.

"Counting the ones at the door? Five. I'm going to have to break things. You two wait here. I mean it." Ruarshi approached the men, wishing it were as simple to put people to sleep as it was to kill them. But the world wasn't made that way, which meant this was going to be complicated and might have adverse consequences down the line. If he had any sense, he'd have stayed in bed.

Two of the three men at the door had swords, and all of them were carrying truncheons. Since those were ready for wielding and the blades were still in their sheaths, deciding where to start was easy.

He shattered all three of the clubs, one after the other, and didn't concern himself much with where the splinters went. The man in the center whirled and reached for his sword, but was hampered by the man to his right. The fellow on the end had no such difficulty, and his sword was halfway out of its sheath before Ruarshi managed to snap it at the hilt. The remaining sword he took care of next.

Now the one in the center was shouting something and lunging at him. Ruarshi took a quick breath and broke two of the bones in the man's ankle just as he came down on it. He shouted and collapsed, which gave the other guards pause. They wavered at the bottom of the stairs, watching as the injured man cursed and tried to rise.

Ruarshi snapped another bone, this time in his wrist. "You're fine where you are. You two, in the house?" The guardsmen in the entry hall also appeared to have truncheons. One of them was stained with blood. Ruarshi turned both of those to kindling, as well, before their wielders were properly aware that the situation had changed. "Come out here, if you would."

"What the fuck do you think you're doing?" He of the bloody club stormed outside, glaring. "What did you do to my man?"

"Very little. Shut up and listen to me." He had their undivided attention now, which was an improvement, and the woman's voice from the house was quieter than it had been. "Go home. This," he waved a hand toward the doorway, "is stupid, and I'm not going to let you continue with it. Leave. *Now.*" His negotiating tactic, such as it was, resulted in a moment of silence during which the men had time to realize they were mostly unarmed and facing a sorcerer of unknown capabilities. For all the damn good that did.

Two of them surged forward with another following close behind. He took the first down with a shattered kneecap and then the second slammed into him. The guardsman shouted in surprise as his collarbones snapped. They hit the ice together, Ruarshi already twisting away from him to avoid being trapped by his weight. A dagger flashed in his peripheral vision and he reached out blindly to snap arm bones. They gave with a meaty crunch that suggested a messy break, and the slash of silver metal fell into the snow a few inches from his head.

He sat up immediately, scooting back and away from the guardsmen. The one he'd gone after first hadn't joined in the attack, nor had the mouthy one. The violence hadn't rendered him speechless, however.

"What kind of devil are you?" he asked, regarding his men in horror. They were moaning in pain, and were only going to get louder as time went on.

Ruarshi pushed to his feet and stepped clear of the patch of ice where he'd fallen. "I can't very well leave you whole while your men suffer, can I?" he asked.

The guardsman raised his hands. "I'm going to have to get them help."

"There are people inside who need medical attention, as well," Ruarshi observed. "Why don't you fetch a doctor?"

"I'd rather not leave them here with you."

"You can go now, or you can join them on the ground." Ruarshi heard movement behind him and glanced over his shoulder. People had begun to emerge from nearby houses. He wondered how much of what had just happened had been observed by someone other than his son and former student. Speaking of whom… there they were, standing at the edge of the pool of light, their faces blank.

"You'll not harm them further?"

"No. Go."

The man finally did so and Ruarshi climbed the steps to the door. Three women and a man crouched over two more men lying on the floor, one of whom looked to be still in his teens. They had a handful of fractures and nasty bruises between them, but no hurts that ought to prove fatal.

"You," Ruarshi said, too preoccupied to worry about being rude, "do your people know how to set broken bones?"

The woman he was addressing, the oldest there and presumably the lady of the house, raised her head. "Yes."

"Good. Do that. If you need our help later, send a message. Your neighbors are gathering outside; I don't think the guard will give you any more trouble." He waited just long enough to be sure that she understood him before turning away and descending the steps to rejoin the Illyana. They moved away from the growing crowd, Ruarshi still leading them west.

"You cannot be planning on doing that again," Etienne said mildly a block or so later.

"I wasn't planning on doing that at all."

"Are you all right?" Davyt asked. "You hit the ground pretty hard."

"I'll be sore for a while, I expect. Thank you for staying out of it."

"That wasn't by choice, Ruarshi." Etienne's voice slid into a growl as he continued, "Once you got started, we didn't have *time.*"

"Thank you anyway. If you'd been involved, I could have hurt you."

"We're headed toward another scene like that one?" Davyt asked.

"Let's hope not. There's something bigger going on ahead of us. I'd like to know how many people Simon is likely to be sending our way over the next few days."

"You think this is retaliation for all that blackmail?"

Ruarshi glanced at his son and shrugged. "It could be that, if they actually know who sits on Simon's court, but I would expect straightforward arrests if that were true. This is more likely an attempt to soften up his support among the merchant class by beating people at random."

"That's not going to work," Davyt said. "It'll just make people angrier."

"And then we'll be out here defending nobles from enraged candle makers. I don't like it," Etienne said, "and it sounds an awful lot like we're approaching a mob."

"It does, doesn't it?" Ruarshi took a left at the next intersection and they could see the reflection of torchlight off ice and brick where the street opened into a large square. The shouting from up ahead was mostly an incoherent roar, though he was occasionally able to pick out the word 'murder'. He thought 'justice' might also have been mixed in there, as well as the name of the guard commander, Georg Schramm.

A small group of young men emerged from the plaza and made to go around them. Ruarshi grabbed the nearest by the arm. "Where are they taking the wounded? Do you know?"

The youngster shook his head and Ruarshi released him. He stepped cautiously past the building at the end of the street and looked into the square.

It wasn't as bad as he'd feared it would be. The townspeople had cornered a group of guardsmen and were obviously enraged, but only one rock flew in the direction of the armed men while Ruarshi watched. The guards, for their part, seemed to be staying in one position, either standing their ground with a purpose in mind or simply refusing to be chased through town. Someone was keeping a lid on the situation, just barely.

"This is… tense," Etienne said.

Ruarshi didn't know whether they should remain there or not. He had no intention of intervening one way or the other; whoever was in marginal control of the crowd wouldn't thank him for the interference. He did need to know if there was a central location to which the injured would be taken, however, and someone here might be able to tell him. Without that consideration to hold him in place, he'd feel obligated to seek out another of those bright pinpoints of pain nearby, and he could easily end up in another disastrous fight. He wasn't remotely ready to mutilate anyone else.

"Stay behind me," he said, and headed toward the statue at the center of the square. There were already a few people standing on its base, trying to get a better view of events, but sufficient room remained for the three of them. If they hung back but at the same time made themselves as obvious as possible, maybe someone would approach them with the information he wanted.

He waited while the Illyana climbed up ahead of him and then jumped up himself, clinging to the neck of the life-size bronze horse with which they were sharing the platform. Nothing about the standoff taking place in front of them had changed. He pushed his hood back so his hair would be visible and waited.

Eventually the guardsmen began to move slowly toward the north, weapons still sheathed, hands held out away from their sides. The noise from the crowd increased but the bulk of it didn't move to follow. Two or three rocks flew toward the retreating men. They neither sped up nor slowed down, and then suddenly it was over. The last of the guards disappeared into the mouth of the narrow alley at the square's north-west corner, and the mob lost its cohesion as individuals and then groups began to move away.

Ruarshi glanced sideways at Davyt and Etienne, who looked back at him wordlessly. When he turned to face forward again he saw a shadow detach itself from what remained of the crowd and head in their direction. He recognized the man more by his height than his face, which on this morning wasn't covered by paint.

"So it wasn't you they murdered? I wondered," Ruarshi said, by way of greeting.

"No. We're going to need all three of you. Can you come?" Simon asked.

### )O(

Simon led them to a small guild hall not far from the square. Blazes roared in the two oversize fireplaces, centered along the building's north and south walls, but it was clear they'd been only recently lit; Ruarshi could still see his breath misting before him in the gloom. Cots and pallets were being brought in through another door, and seven victims of the night's activities lay in a rough line down one side of the vaulted room. Three of them appeared unconscious and one was a child.

"Were the guards after anyone in particular?" Ruarshi asked.

"The families of the boys who showed up by the river for that idiotic boat race," Simon replied, "as near as I can tell. The noble lads they let off with a warning. The others… it's as you see. We've got surgeons on the way to assist you with the more easily treated wounds, but please, if there's anything you can do in the meantime…"

"We'll get started. Bring some food when you can."

Simon nodded and disappeared through a door that opened onto a stairway. Ruarshi turned his attention to the Illyana.

"I can probably handle two or three of these, unless there's something unusual to be dealt with that I'm not picking up from here. Etienne, you know what to do. Davyt, can you pace yourself?"

The boy watched as another man was brought in, carried by wailing relatives and bleeding profusely from the head. "Yes, Father."

"When you start to feel light-headed, you sit down and eat. If you faint I'll have you carted back to the house."

"No fainting," Davyt said, nodding. "Right."

Ruarshi waited until they'd chosen their patients, and Etienne had commenced demanding stools for them with an imperiousness that he could only admire, before settling down on a pallet next to an older man. The fellow had a compound fracture to his lower left leg and a tally of cracked ribs that made Ruarshi wonder if he had fallen from a height. The man was watching him, and Ruarshi was completely out of patience with formalities.

"You know who I am. I can heal you or you can wait for the local bonesetter. Which will it be?"

The man chuckled, which was a bad idea as one of his lungs had been punctured. "I'll take you, wizard."

"All right. Close your eyes."

For the next several hours Ruarshi was mostly unaware of the activity taking place around him. He managed to heal four of the morning's victims before a stumble upon rising warned him that he needed to heed his own advice. After looking over the room to make sure that the Illyana were still there and doing well, he made his way toward a bench that had been pushed up against the wall next to one of the fireplaces. Once there he lowered himself onto it, shutting his eyes and enjoying the warmth. When he opened them again, Simon was standing in front of him, holding out a piece of dark brown bread wrapped around a steaming sausage.

"Hungry?"

"Yes." Ruarshi accepted the offering and started nibbling at it. How long had he been dozing?

Simon sat down next to him. "There are rooms upstairs you and your boys can sleep in, if you'd care to stay here for a few days. Karneval is tomorrow. I can try to minimize the mayhem that's coming, but I won't be able to squelch all of it, not after this. We'll have further need of you. I also think you should stay away from that house of yours for the present."

Ruarshi kept chewing, so Simon went on. "I'm not saying they'll arrest you for assaulting four of the city guard and scaring the piss out of the fifth, but they might get a little sloppy with the legalities until they calm down. So it is possible. The man you saved is a friend of mine. Thank you."

"I assume I'll be asked to leave, sooner rather than later."

"That may or may not happen. The authorities are going to be too busy for the next little while to worry about you specifically, unless you give them more reason to. Stay here, lay low, heal people. I'll use my influence on your behalf if you still need more time for whatever it is you're really doing here."

"Another month or two would be welcome."

"I'll see what I can do. When you or the youngsters need something, tell that sour-faced fellow by the door, yes? He'll see you get it."

"My servants need to be told what's happened. If you could send someone when things calm down, I'd appreciate it. I'd also appreciate knowing if anyone starts harassing them."

A smile ghosted across Simon's face. "I expect they'll be safe, but I'll drop a warning into a few ears. You're going to start seeing patients from the opposite side of the battlefield soon."

"The guard?" Ruarshi asked, startled. His stomach commenced a slow roll and he suddenly regretted the little he'd eaten.

"Uh, no," Simon replied, chuckling. "There've been nobles injured, too, mostly because they went looking for trouble and found it. But offering them assistance is important."

Ruarshi nodded. "We'll need men here to make sure their families don't try to kill each other."

"There are a dozen or so waiting outside. Women, too, including Oma Agnes. You should talk to her when you get a chance. She has a most amazing talent for knocking the belligerence out of young men. Verbally, of course." Simon rose. "Thank you again for your help. I'll take up a collection for you and your boys; no one expects you to do this work for free. I'll be back this evening."

Ruarshi watched him go and finished eating his sausage. He then went in search of watered wine and eventually found some in a small room off to one side, along with quite a lot of food that people had begun bringing in for the swelling number of townsfolk who'd shown up to tend the injured.

It was time for Etienne and Davyt to eat something, if they hadn't already. Ruarshi returned to the hall and spotted his son sitting at the bedside of an old man, in the middle of a healing; it would be a good half hour or so before he finished. Locating his former student proved more difficult, as the Illyana had retreated to a murky corner of the hall where he was in close conversation with a woman Ruarshi hadn't met before.

He had a clear view of Etienne's profile as he approached the two of them, and what he saw in the young man's face was so unexpected that he considered reversing course, leaving them to it, and pretending that he hadn't noticed anything. Instead he kept walking, hoping he didn't look quite as grim as he felt.

Etienne spotted him when he was still about a dozen paces distant and visibly flinched away from the woman, who turned at once to look at him. Ruarshi guessed she was in her upper twenties, with a face and bearing that reminded him of home.

He came to a stop in front of her and inclined his head respectfully. "I'm Ruarshi, as you probably know. You are?" It wasn't the way Europeans handled introductions, but he thought they'd all be best served here with a little Miriyanti directness.

"I'm Jonata," she replied, her chin going up. It didn't have to go up far, as he had at best two inches on her.

Ruarshi took in her clothing, the way she was standing, her lack of a ring. "Noble house. Widow?"

"Oh, for god's sake," Etienne interrupted. "You don't have to answer that. Could you be a little less rude, Ruarshi?"

"Not at the moment. I'm tired and cranky. I'm very pleased to meet you, Jonata, not to mention surprised. Excuse me." He turned to the Illyana. "Have you eaten?"

"No."

"I suggest you do. This lull can't last forever. Our friend has decided to bring us some nobles, which probably won't double our work but will certainly have an effect. There's a lot of food over there," he pointed toward the room he'd just vacated, "and I'd like a minute or two with Jonata if neither of you has an objection."

"None at all," she replied.

"Can this wait for a less fraught occasion?" Etienne asked, looking back and forth between the two of them, though not hopefully.

"I suppose it could. Would you like to invite her to our house?"

The Illyana sighed. "I'll be right back, Jonata. If he gets to be too obnoxious, just swat him on the ass. No one will notice and he'll leave you alone afterward." Etienne moved off, not looking back.

Ruarshi found he was smiling after the younger man, very much in spite of himself. "How long have you two been seeing each other?"

"I was visiting Helene when he came to fetch a book for you."

"That was right before Christmas, so… two and a half months. What an idiot."

"He is far from being an idiot."

Ruarshi turned the smile on her. "That is correct. How well can you protect him from your family if they find out?"

"We are a matriarchy at the present time. I anticipate no problems."

"Any brothers, first cousins…?"

"A number of cousins. I think you overestimate their protectiveness."

"I'm mostly wondering about their theories regarding property, and how those might affect their behavior around female family members. Europeans can be strange that way." She blinked at him. "Have you considered returning with us to Miriyan?"

"What? I… no. Etienne has said nothing about it."

"He probably won't. I don't suppose he's mentioned being in love with you, either?"

Jonata shook her head. "This isn't such a relationship. It is agreeable to us both, but—"

"You're wrong, my dear. Be careful, please."

She opened her mouth to speak but slowly shut it again, looking now in the direction Etienne had gone. "You're sure?" she asked finally.

"Yes. Keep in mind, if you would, that he'll outlive you by quite a number of years. Decide what it is you want. And if you ever need my help, find me."

She nodded. He bowed in reply and went to see how his son was progressing with his latest patient.

# A Friendly Game of *Jhot*

"I'm still not going to talk about it," Etienne said, trudging along at Ruarshi's side. He was carrying his new ice skates by their laces, and they swung around dangerously as he gestured in aggravation. "Though I might be a tiny bit more forthcoming if you'd tell me what you said to her. I've caught her staring at me three times over the past week like I'm some kind of prize pig."

"Isn't it nice that you can see her so often?" Ruarshi asked. "All the sneaking wasn't necessary, you know."

Etienne snorted. "It's still necessary. Helene's our only go-between. I may not have to creep around on your account anymore, but Bebel's still a concern. A loud, nosy concern."

"So exchange notes in the market instead."

"Ruarshi, Jonata can't read."

"So draw her pictures."

"That would be rather crude of me, wouldn't it?"

Ruarshi swatted the Illyana on the back of the head as Davyt tried and failed to swallow a laugh. "I mean draw her a picture of where you want to meet and a clock face. Not pornography."

"Oh. I guess I could do that."

"Are you sure you want to play *jhot* today?" Ruarshi asked, glancing down at his own set of skates. He'd had a pair made for each of them, the kind with metal blades rather than the older bone version. "Because I'm feeling sort of annoyed with you, and I wouldn't want to bruise the prize pig."

"You don't need to worry about that. Look to your own pig."

With another ten minutes of walking they reached the frozen pond southwest of the city that was their goal. It was an overcast day a week and a half into Lent, and it looked like they would have the place to themselves. A few children were shouting and throwing snowballs at one another along the far bank, but no one was out on the ice.

They needed the break. They'd spent the better part of a week in the guild hall, and the amount of blood spilled on Karneval and during the days immediately following had been even worse than Simon had predicted. Eight people had died, three of those in the hall itself. One, a young man with a stab wound to the upper leg, had expired of blood loss practically in Davyt's lap; afterward Ruarshi had been much more careful about getting to the serious cases before either of the Illyana could.

The crisis had finally passed, a result of general exhaustion and even more widespread disgust, and no city officials had yet shown up at their door. When the cobbler had sent word that their skates were ready, Ruarshi had jumped at the chance to get all of them out of the house. The Illyana appeared to be every bit as eager as he was to leave the city behind for the space of an afternoon.

By the time the three of them had laced up their skates and stepped out onto the ice, the children had abandoned their game and were heading back toward town. The silence was welcome, as was the faint hint of late winter warmth that blew past them on the breeze.

Ruarshi fished in his pocket for the palm-sized, nearly flat stone he'd picked up at the base of the city wall where the recent spate of sunny days had melted the snow from a patch of ground. He dropped it at his feet where it landed with a solid thunk. As pucks went, it was heavy, but he'd selected for that intentionally. His shields were still a good bit sturdier than those the Illyana could produce, so he had to handicap himself in some way to prevent the game from turning into a rout. Not that he intended to point that out to them. It was likely they'd notice on their own anyway.

He wove a small shield and used it to push the puck back and forth in front of him, then around in a circle. Getting the rock from one side of the pond to the other was going to be difficult, and would of course only be made more so by the need to prevent the youngsters from doing the same with theirs, while also fending off whatever sort of physical attacks they intended to launch at him. If they'd chosen light stones, he might be able to shatter one or both of them, which would be a tidy way of winning the game. Dropping their pucks through the ice was out of the question, as it had to be at least two feet thick and there was no possibility he could punch a hole in it.

Since they couldn't break things with their magic, as he could, Ruarshi expected the Illyana to be fairly aggressive with their shields. The only rule governing their use in full-contact *jhot* forbade players from tripping their opponents backward from a standing position, due to the high risk of head injury. Everything else was permitted.

He looked up at the younger men, wondering how creative they'd be. He couldn't really picture Davyt body-slamming him, though Etienne might try it. For his part, he'd attempt to avoid that sort of nonsense. The most intense game of *jhot* he'd ever witnessed had been between two Chamani, and they'd never even touched each other.

Ruarshi began gliding slowly forward over the ice. It was in good condition, not too badly scored by other skaters or roughened by frozen snow. He picked up speed and swung around to the south in a wide arc, pivoting on his blades and continuing backwards. He didn't much like skating that way, so he turned around again.

There was movement to his left. Glancing in that direction, he saw Karoli top the slight rise about thirty yards from the pond's edge. Ruarshi came to an immediate stop, relieved that the man was alive but both irritated and apprehensive that the Naishanti had chosen to approach them in that manner. He'd clearly gone to quite a bit of trouble to make sure he wouldn't be spotted until he was almost on top of them.

And he seemed to be carrying skates.

Etienne ground to a stop right beside him and Davyt wasn't far behind. Karoli was watching them. He'd put on some weight since their first meeting, cleaned himself up, and found a new set of clothes of a style and quality that wouldn't have been out of place on an Elector.

"Greetings, Cousin," Karoli said, lowering himself to sit in the snow where he began strapping on his own skates, probably rented in town. He must have moved fast to get here so soon after they'd arrived. "And to you, *marchid,* and you, *barai.*"

He'd addressed Etienne as 'worthy foe' and Davyt as 'honored son,' so he clearly hadn't sought them out in order to strengthen friendships. Ruarshi didn't see much point in continuing with the pleasantries.

"How's the foot?" he asked.

"Good as new," Karoli replied, finishing up with his straps and then standing and launching himself out onto the ice. He came to a halt an arm's length from Ruarshi, who hadn't moved, and regarded him critically. "There is no fucking way you have malaria," he said after a pause, "since I'm sure you could cure that in your sleep. Remember, *I* don't go home without *you*. So what have you been fucking around with?"

"Should I be touched?" Ruarshi asked blandly.

"I'm in town because Sprenger's due to arrive in a few days. Didn't hear the rumor until I got here. Now answer my question."

"Casimir."

Ruarshi was enormously gratified to see a wave of profound confusion roll across the Naishanti's face.

"What?"

"He might be dead, although that's probably too much to hope for. Have you gathered in the other exiles yet?"

Karoli visibly calmed himself. "No. How is it that Casimir might be dead?"

"I'm not sure of that myself. It was all very mysterious. Even if he is, that doesn't necessarily mean we'll be able to just walk back into Miriyan. His cronies, whoever they are, must still be kicking."

"Or you've set off another round of murder, and he has no cronies left. We need to be heading north now. Fuck." Karoli took another deep breath. "I'm still waiting for three of them. The other three are already here, staying with me at the Drummer's camp."

"When will they get here?"

"I don't know."

"A month? Three?"

"I said I don't know."

"All right," Ruarshi said, holding up a placating hand, "then there's nothing we can do yet, no matter what's happening in Miriyan. Unless you think we should leave them behind."

"No."

"Right. Ready to have your shoulder broken?"

Karoli smiled. "That oath I swore to you earlier. Is a friendly game of *jhot* considered harm?"

Ruarshi thought about it. "No."

"Give me a run for my money and I'll consider it."

"And how should we team up?" Etienne asked.

The Naishanti regarded him. "No matter what we decide, it's going to end up three against one. That being the case, I should warm up with my cousin first."

Ruarshi suspected he ought to be alarmed. Then again, Karoli had made it plain that his plan to return home hinged on Ruarshi's continued existence, so maybe his current case of nerves was an overreaction. He supposed he'd find out.

"Fair enough," he said. "You two mind refereeing for us?"

Davyt and Etienne exchanged a tight-lipped glance but didn't voice any objection.

"Good. Do you have a puck?"

"I thought I'd borrow one," Karoli said. "Where's yours?"

"It's over here."

They spent the next several minutes getting ready to start, Karoli having declined to try out his rented skates on the ice before beginning the game. When everything was in place, Ruarshi crouched down, his left knee and gloved hand against the frozen surface of the pond. He didn't relish the idea of having his legs knocked out from under him as part of Karoli's opening salvo, and the notion had to be on the Naishanti's mind after what Ruarshi had done to him that night in town.

Etienne, standing unhappily at the pond's northern edge, gave the signal to begin. Ruarshi tensed, flooding his body with warrior's magic while at the same time using a shield to shove his puck up under the south bank, out of sight. He expected this game to become very physical very quickly, and his only real hope of winning involved shattering Karoli's puck as fast as he could. It might be workable; the warrior had chosen to use Davyt's stone, which seemed scarcely heavier than limestone. Whether the Naishanti could do the same to his was an open question.

Karoli barreled toward him. He waited until the man was close before rising from his position and surging forward. Much to his surprise, he managed to knock the warrior's right leg out from under him and he sprawled on the ice, sliding several yards before friction brought him to a halt. The Naishanti rose, laughing, before Ruarshi was half finished with the weave he intended to throw at the man's puck. The stone in question was now skittering over the ice toward Ruarshi's side of the pond. If it hit the bank, Ruarshi lost the game in the most straightforward and embarrassing manner possible.

He threw out a shield to block his opponent's stone while bringing his own into play, hoping to distract the warrior. Instead he felt his legs going out from under him, a problem that was compounded when Karoli jumped on his back as he went down.

His face hit the ice. Mercifully he neither broke his nose nor lost any teeth, but his upper lip was thoroughly split and he spat blood while he struggled to elbow his way out from under the warrior's weight.

An arm went around his throat. "You haven't got a fucking chance."

"Only because I'm not breaking every goddamn bone in your body, out of the goodness of my heart."

"I'm counting on that. Up with you."

The weight disappeared from his back and he looked over his shoulder to see the warrior extending a hand to him. Meanwhile both pucks were moving, and not in directions that made him happy.

He countered that, ignoring the proffered hand, and lashed out at Karoli's nearer calf with the blade of his skate. The warrior dodged that easily but ran into the shield Ruarshi had placed on his opposite side, down near the ice, and almost fell himself before twisting away to put some distance between them.

Ruarshi rose to a crouch, concentrating again on his opponent's puck. The man could tell what he was doing and kept sliding the stone around, making the task impossible, so he abandoned that line of attack for the time being and gave his own puck a tremendous shove toward Karoli's bank.

That won him a moment's inattention from the Naishanti, and he shot forward directly toward the man, pivoting at the last instant to speed off on a tangent. That left Karoli bracing himself for a hit that never came, and Ruarshi was able to scoot his stone about a yard closer to his goal before his opponent recovered.

Karoli slammed into him from the side and he felt himself falling. He seized a handful of the man's coat and they both ended up going down, somehow with the warrior on the bottom. Ruarshi tumbled off him and aimed the warrior's weave he'd been working on since the game started at Karoli's puck; he shattered it with everything he had but the rock remained intact, resulting in an entirely predictable spike of pain through his temples. He stumbled as he stood, going back to shoving at his own stone with a sloppy shield that the Naishanti then destroyed with a weave of his own, compounding the throbbing in his head.

He wavered and ended up back on his knees. That last move of Karoli's had been unnecessary, as Ruarshi's latest shield hadn't pushed his puck so much as an inch. The warrior had intended to hurt him and nothing else. Ruarshi wove a small, nasty shield, focused in on the Naishanti, and put it where it needed to be.

It was one of the dirtiest of his dirty tricks. He'd just blinded the man. The effect would last only as long as the shield did, but Karoli couldn't know that.

The Naishanti froze, which was exactly the reaction Ruarshi had expected. He went back to moving his puck toward the warrior's bank, and there was really nothing Karoli could do about it.

The ice next to him exploded upward as though a cannonball had been shot into it, showering him with freezing water. He pushed away from it, but the next explosion was half underneath him and it sent him tumbling across the surface of the pond. Ruarshi wrapped his arms around his head and waited for the world to stop spinning. When it did, both the Illyana were right there with him and he was close enough to Karoli that he could hear his words, though he spoke at a volume barely above a whisper.

"Get this fucking thing off me."

Ruarshi removed the shield and watched the warrior blink his eyes into focus. He didn't know what sort of expression he had on his face, somewhere between stunned and incredulous at a guess, but Karoli took a look at him and grinned.

"Scared one another, did we?" he asked.

"*You* did that?" It was a stupid question.

"Well it wasn't the fucking fish."

"I've never seen anyone do that before," Davyt said. "And what did you do to him?"

"Blinded him. You're Diamyo."

"Not officially."

Ruarshi sat up carefully. He was going to have bruises.

"You're averse to hurting people," Karoli went on. "You only hit me once, and it was defensive. That explains a lot."

"This is a game," Ruarshi said.

"True. We'll work on it. Can you do that blindness thing at a distance?"

"I suppose. You've ruined the ice."

Karoli glanced over at the damage he'd done. Each jagged hole was at least a yard in diameter. "People can skate around it. The ice won't last more than another month anyway."

"I'm going to have to sit out any further games. Do you two want to go a round? I can referee from a sitting position."

"With two enormous hazards in the middle of the pond? I'm not enthusiastic." Etienne looked at Davyt. "What do you think?"

"We'll just end up trying to push each other in and then feeling sorry if we succeed. I don't see the point."

Etienne gave the other Illyana a flat stare. "I outweigh you. We both know how that contest would end."

"I'm not conceding. If you insist we can try it."

"Oh, yes?"

Ruarshi watched bemusedly as the two Illyana began grappling with each other, a struggle involving an occasional elbow to the gut and a lot of cursing. They were staying well away from the breaks in the ice, however, so after a short while he turned to the warrior. "I'll need to get out of these damp clothes and catch an hour's rest before I go to work on your shoulder. You can come with us back to the house or meet us there later. What's your preference?"

"You're like a damn hunting dog circling a burrow."

"What kind of rodent would that make you?"

Karoli snorted. "The kind the dog doesn't actually want to catch. I'll meet you there later."

"See that you do."

)O(

"I'm tired of spending time on this couch of yours. How long will it be sore?" Karoli stretched his left arm out to the side, moving it forward and backward in tight circles, and then raised it above his head.

"A few weeks." Ruarshi sat several feet away, watching him. Breaking the warrior's shoulder blade along the lines of the old injury had been no easy task, and he'd been glad to turn the healing over to Davyt once he was done. Etienne had assisted them by throwing out cynical observations regarding the merit, or lack thereof, involved in what they were doing.

"Is sword work safe?"

"You should wait at least a week before going through drills with anything heavy in your hand. How are you going to explain that, incidentally? A Dominican with a sword?"

"I'll make up some nonsense about warrior monks."

"And they'll believe you?"

"That hardly matters as long as it gets them out of my hair."

"And if it doesn't you can always stab them to death," Etienne said.

Karoli glanced at the Illyana. "I thought you'd gotten that out of your system."

"Not yet. Don't rush me."

"Take all the time you need," the Diamyo said, lowering his arm. "Thank you, again. If you ever need your woodpile turned to kindling or the roof collapsed on that one's head, let me know." He stood to go.

"You're staying in town until Sprenger gets here?" Ruarshi asked.

"Yes."

"Are you at The White Stag or The Piper?" He was fairly sure it had to be one or the other.

Karoli narrowed his eyes. "The Piper. How do you know that? You had me followed?"

"Not necessary. Those are the only two inns in town where someone dressed like that would stay."

The warrior glanced down at his clothes and shrugged. "You and the children should come visit me some evening. We can sit out front and shout curses at passersby."

"Is that what you have planned?" Etienne asked.

"Yes. I'm a crazed Russian nobleman, as far as anyone around here knows, and I'm going to act the part."

"Russian," Ruarshi repeated.

"What else?" Karoli replied. "I don't trust Sprenger. If I make myself as obvious and foreign and heretical as possible, he might not insist on a face-to-face meeting. Hence my advice to you: come join me sometime. He's completely obsessed with magic and will likely be a nuisance otherwise."

"So you think Orthodoxy will put him off?"

"It might. It was either that or try to pass myself off as a Turk, which would be difficult and ridiculous. More ridiculous. One thing I won't be doing is getting into flashy magical fights in town, and I hope it takes him a while to hear that story." The warrior paused on his way to the door. "Did you really take on six of the locals at once?"

Ruarshi felt himself flushing and discovered he didn't want to answer. The silence stretched and Karoli smiled.

"What, shy?"

"There were five of them," Davyt said finally. "All armed."

The Diamyo's smile widened. "Well done." He put a fist to his chest in a warrior's salute. "You'll hear from me before I leave town, unless you come visiting first. It really is a very nice inn." Karoli nodded once, pulled on his hat, and let himself out. Pale golden light spilled into the front room before Etienne pushed the door shut and dropped the bar into place.

"Traveling with him is going to be a lot of fun, I can tell," he said.

"I'm kind of starting to enjoy his company." While Etienne glared at him, Davyt went on. "Can Sprenger do anything to us?"

"He can waste our time," Ruarshi said. "That's about it. Avoidance is probably our best strategy. There's nothing we need from him and

I've never found the company of Inquisitors to be congenial."

"How many have you met?" Davyt asked.

"Three. Two Italian, one French. The thought of listening to some-one natter away about heresy in German holds even less appeal; I don't like being barked at."

"So we'll be leaving here when the other exiles show up?"

Etienne's question sounded casual, but Ruarshi wasn't buying it. "Yes. Jonata shouldn't come with us, but there's no reason she can't fol-low with a chaperone and a reliable man or two to act as bodyguard. You can meet up with her once we're safely home."

"I wasn't going to invite her along," Etienne said.

"Why not?"

"I...uh..." The healer shook his head. "I'm still not going to talk about it."

"Suit yourself," Ruarshi said, a smile playing at the corners of his mouth.

"What?" Etienne asked, looking at him suspiciously.

"She never did slap me on the ass, you know," Ruarshi said. "It was rather disappointing."

# Chains

Ruarshi dropped his third armful of wood into the box by the upstairs fireplace. Kilian had spent the better part of the afternoon reducing a sizeable pile of man-sized logs to manageable proportions, was currently dozing in the kitchen, and didn't need to be troubled to perform a chore that Ruarshi could just as easily take care of himself. The youngsters had gone out with friends, so for the time being he had the bedroom to himself. He intended to work on his never-ending letter to Slan, although he wasn't sure at this point why he bothered.

As had become his habit, he thinned his bond-shield and scanned to the south, looking for the Illyana. His hands stilled their rummaging as he realized he was picking up on four Miriyanti, not two, and that one of them was in pain. He shut his eyes and concentrated more closely.

Etienne.

Davyt was with him, as yet uninjured.

The other two…

Ruarshi was outside in the darkness, running south with no memory of having left the house, dodging past the few others out at this hour without really seeing them. He slipped on a thin patch of ice as he rounded a corner, caught himself on one hand, and kept going. The consciousness that was Etienne's went dark as he watched and began to move quickly away along with the two strangers. Davyt didn't seem to be following them; if anything, he was heading slowly to the north. Ruarshi changed course to intercept him.

He spotted his son a few minutes later. The boy was jogging in his direction, his gaze focused on the ground, one hand trailing along the wall next to him. Ruarshi called out to him while he was still several yards distant and Davyt came to a startled halt.

"Father." The boy paused and swallowed, struggling to speak. He was shaking violently. "Two warriors came in and found us. They said you were to return to Miriyan right away. They took Etienne with them to make sure you'd comply. He tried to fight them off but couldn't, and it happened so fast, I just stood there—"

Ruarshi slipped an arm around his son's waist and pulled him back into motion. "So he's a hostage." The warriors were outside the city walls and headed west. Their speed made it clear they were mounted and in a hurry.

"He's going to be a bad one," Davyt said, and barked a laugh that ended as a sob. "He wouldn't stop fighting. One of them hit him so hard…"

"I know. We'll get him back. Tonight. We'll need our horses."

"They said you weren't to try to catch up with them, that they'll hurt him more severely if you do. They'll send a man to meet us at the southern gate at dawn."

"Sounds like a waste of time to me. Wait here." Ruarshi darted through an open doorway to his right and found himself in a small, shabby tavern. He grabbed a dented lamp off the bar and turned to face the portly man who rose to confront him.

"I need this. Send a man to my house tomorrow and I'll pay you for it."

The man must have recognized him by this time; he raised his hands in a pacifying gesture and said only, "Take it."

Ruarshi nodded to him and hurried back out. He and Davyt continued north, moving more swiftly now.

"I'm not sure I understand this."

Ruarshi glanced at his son. "Someone in Miriyan dislikes my alliance with Karoli, at a guess. Their decision to take Etienne and leave you out of it is likely meant to keep the situation from turning into something they can't control."

"Casimir?"

"Possibly. It's the kind of thing he would do."

A short while later they reached the stable. When no one responded to his knock, he splintered the wood around the latch and forced the door open. They went inside and began saddling Sophie and Midnight.

"You'll be okay with him?" Ruarshi asked, nodding toward Etienne's horse. "He can be aggressive."

"I'll be fine. Mother likes temperamental animals."

They worked quickly in the dim light. When they were both ready to go, Ruarshi snuffed the lamp and left it in a pile of dirty snow outside the stable door. Once they were mounted he turned Sophie's head toward the center of town.

"Shouldn't we be going the other way?" Davyt asked.

"There's one more stop we have to make. It won't take long." Ruarshi urged his mare into a trot and his son followed his lead. After another silent interval, they pulled up in front of The Piper.

"You think we need Karoli."

"I think his people need him. I'll be right back."

Ruarshi slid from his saddle and pushed his way through the inn's front door into the sparsely populated common room. He made no effort to be quiet as he ran up the stairs. Startling the man would most likely be a bad idea. The warrior remained as invisible to his senses as ever, but he thought that could be dealt with easily enough.

Eight rooms, four to a side, lined the hallway. Five of these were clearly occupied. A sixth seemed to be empty, but faint firelight shone through the gap between door and floorboards. Ruarshi stepped forward and knocked, rattling the door in its frame.

"Karoli."

The warrior pulled it open. He was still fully dressed. "What's happened?"

Ruarshi gestured for permission to enter. Karoli moved back and he followed him inside. In as normal a voice as he could manage, he explained the situation. Before he was halfway through, Karoli was moving: first to his desk, where he picked up a piece of parchment covered in fine, dense writing and tossed it into the fire, and then over to the wardrobe in the corner of the room. He pulled two coats from inside and tossed one to Ruarshi as soon as he finished speaking.

"I'm coming with you. Put that on before you freeze."

"You should go back to your camp. I'd be willing to wager there are others looking for your exiles right now, and I doubt they have kidnapping in mind."

"I understand that. They're too far ahead of me. If I want to turn them around, I need to go after the warriors we can reach tonight."

Ruarshi felt a chill as he realized what Karoli was saying. He hadn't been thinking straight. Slan had explained to him once that a band of warriors, if confronted with the need to split up, would always try to make sure that at least one bonded pair was similarly split between the two resulting groups. This took care of a large part of the communication problem that generally arose in such circumstances: if something went wrong with one group, the other would know about it instantly.

He nodded. "All right. Davyt and I will wait out front while you get your horse. We'll be leaving through the western gate."

Ruarshi clattered back down the stairs in Karoli's company, explained the change of plans to Davyt, and waited for the warrior to appear. Only now that he was wearing the borrowed coat did he notice how cold it had become. He watched the breath plume in front of his face in the dim moonlight and tried not to think about the passage of time.

He glanced over at his son, wishing he had something reassuring to say. The boy was probably terrified, though the only emotion Ruarshi could read in his expression at the moment was anger. He trusted him to stay out of the way of the coming violence, and that was all he could ask of him for now.

The sound of hoof beats heralded Karoli's arrival. They followed in his wake and the three of them rode toward the western edge of the city at a brisk trot. When the gate finally came into view, the warrior pulled up to wait for them.

"I'm going to break that as quietly as I can, which is to say there's a small chance I won't wake the entire neighborhood. If your horses dislike loud noises, be ready."

Karoli rode ahead, leaned sideways in his saddle, and put his hand to the wood. Moments later the bar holding the massive doors shut split vertically down the center with a tremendous crack. This was followed by incoherent shouting from the gatehouse, and frantic, dimly silhouetted movement within that Ruarshi barely glimpsed as he followed Davyt through the gap. Karoli shoved the gate shut once they'd made it out and they headed toward the line of trees about a half mile distant. Once there, with no sign of pursuit from the city, the warrior reined in again.

"I'm no tracker. Do you know where they went?"

"Wait." Ruarshi closed his eyes, removed his bond-shield completely, and cast his senses as far as he could to the west. He ran across wildlife… a small group of cottages, their occupants European and deeply asleep, their few animals clustered nearby against the cold… and nothing. He lowered his head and began again, this time skipping more swiftly across the landscape in the hope that he could reach farther before his momentum failed him. There would be an outer limit to what he could sense, but he didn't know yet what that was and thought his current state of desperation would help rather than hinder him in his efforts.

Still nothing. And nothing again. He shook his head and made another attempt, and there, just at the edge of his perception, was someone he knew.

He opened his eyes and discovered that the world was spinning. Davyt had a hand clamped around his right arm, no doubt to keep him from falling out of the saddle.

Ruarshi sat up straight and took a few deep breaths, then nodded at his son. "I found him. This way." He pointed just north of west and put his heels to his horse, weaving a thin bond-shield back into place as his companions fell in behind him.

He set as fast a pace as he felt was safe, but even so over an hour went by before they came to a halt several hundred yards from the warriors' camp. It was difficult to be sure at this distance, but it appeared to him that the Miriyanti had settled into an abandoned manor house, partially collapsed and being gradually swallowed by the forest on its southern and western sides. The flickering light of a fire issued from a small window in the eastern wall, barely visible through the trees.

"There are two sentries outside and three Miriyanti inside with Etienne."

"I see the one there on the northern side of the place," Karoli said. "Where's the other?"

"To the south, in amongst the brush. There." Ruarshi pointed.

"I see him. Later I'm going to want to know how you're doing that. They've set up tethers; can you feel them?"

"Tethers?"

"Thin ground-level weaves around their perimeter. Shields, basically. If anyone blunders through one our friends will know they're not alone. They've set them in concentric circles starting just beyond their walls and extending out as far as that half-dead tree with the pile of rocks next to it."

Ruarshi was able to locate them all, now that he knew enough to look.

"That's going to make it hard to sneak in there," Davyt said.

Karoli breathed a laugh. "I'll trigger all their tethers at once so they won't know which way to run. Unless one of you has a better idea?"

"They might respond to that by killing my apprentice," Ruarshi said.

"Yes," the warrior conceded. "You want to try diplomacy instead?"

Ruarshi didn't even have to think about it. "No."

"Let's leave our horses here and get a bit closer," Karoli said, dismounting. Ruarshi and Davyt followed suit and soon they were all standing a few feet away from the outermost tether. Neither of the sentries gave any indication of being aware of their presence.

"Ready?" Karoli asked.

"Yes," Ruarshi replied. Davyt nodded.

"Here we go."

Six, seven... *eight* of Karoli's own weaves began converging on the house from all points of the compass, kicking up trails of powdered snow as they sliced through each tether in turn. The response from the Miriyanti was silent but immediate. First the sentries darted for the woods, followed closely by those who'd been inside with Etienne. No two ran in the same direction.

Karoli was laughing softly. "They are scared as fuck of you. That's one of the funniest things I've ever seen. Shit."

Ruarshi noticed the increase in the intensity of the firelight at the same moment the warrior did. They were burning the building down with Etienne inside it.

It was a trap, yes, but that hardly mattered. Ruarshi ran flat out toward a dark space in the ruin of the outer wall, which was rapidly filling with light as the fire grew. He reached it and plunged inside, blinking through the smoke until he spotted Etienne by the northern wall, to which he seemed to be chained. Half of his face was covered in blood.

Ruarshi darted forward and went to his knees by the younger man's side.

"Good to see you," the Illyana said, his feet braced against the wall as he pulled with all his strength against the iron staple that prevented his escape. "Can't get my wrists out of these so I thought I'd try this instead." His arms were bloody to the elbows.

Ruarshi was so angry that he was shaking. "Get down." Etienne obeyed without question and he covered the man with his own body as he readied the weave he was going to need.

A loud cracking noise issued from above them and the ceiling collapsed with a roar. Something heavy struck Ruarshi in the back, knocking the wind out of him before sliding off to one side. He took a careful breath and raised his head to assess their situation.

Their position by the wall had saved them from serious injury, but the fire was growing, feeding on its new fuel, and both he and Etienne were half buried under a pile of shattered timber.

He filled his body with warrior's magic and pushed upward against the weight of wood. After several moments of fruitless effort he had to concede that this tactic wasn't going to work. Ruarshi started on his weaving again, doing his best to ignore the growing heat of the flames, and split the crossbeam that was responsible for most of the pressure pinning them to the floor.

That was better. He moved to the side and concentrated on the wood surrounding the iron staple, reducing it to splinters with weave after methodical weave and hoping that he didn't bring that part of the building down on them as well. He started pushing at it with his shoulder and Etienne joined him. It had just begun to crumble when something struck it from the outside and then hands were reaching through a hole in the wall and dragging the Illyana out by his chains.

Another pair of hands came for Ruarshi, seizing him by the hair and collar and yanking him sideways through the wall and into the snow.

Etienne was there, a warrior standing just behind him pressing a knife to his throat. Blood was already slipping down his neck from the line of contact. Ruarshi realized at the same moment that there was a dagger point being held to his left eye, just as the limit of his peripheral vision.

Ruarshi snapped the blade that threatened him and simultaneously shattered a weave inside the skull of Etienne's captor. She spasmed and fell, still twitching and making a repetitive bleating noise. A line of fire traced its way across his ribcage and arm as he twisted free of the other warrior's grip. Etienne slammed into the man from the side and Ruarshi snapped his spine. He went still and silent, his weapon slipping from his limp fingers just before it could plunge into the Illyana's back.

Ruarshi stood catching his breath while looking over the scene before him. All of it was clearly visible in the light of the burning building.

"Etienne?" he asked.

"I'll be fine as soon as I can get these fucking things off. Please make her stop."

Ruarshi stumbled over to the warrior, who was still in terrible pain in spite of the ruin he'd made of her mind. He knelt next to her and wrapped her heart in a healer's weave, pressing against it until it stopped beating. When he looked up again, Davyt was there and Etienne, free of his manacles, was holding the other warrior's bloody knife. He wondered why until he saw that the man's throat had been cut.

He'd botched both attacks, then. Of course he had.

He shook his head and switched his focus to the Illyana, checking quickly over the two of them. Davyt was untouched. Etienne was recovering well from his concussion, but he had three broken ribs and a nasty gash along one hip, in addition to the shallower cuts on his cheek and neck and the mess he'd made of his wrists.

"Thank you," Ruarshi murmured, with a nod toward the dead man. "Hold a moment." He stood and turned his attention back to his mind's eye. He found Karoli off to their northeast, concealed by the darkness of the forest and engaged in a fight with another of the warriors. He had been injured, but not badly. A second stranger was lurking at the southern edge of the clearing. The third individual he had expected to see was nowhere in evidence, which meant he or she was already dead.

"Did they have a healer with them?" Ruarshi asked.

"They did," Etienne replied.

"Davyt, don't start working on him yet. I need to make sure you won't be interrupted."

Ruarshi rounded the corner of the manor house and approached the stranger, keeping part of his attention on Karoli and the remaining warrior. When the healer started to slink away, Ruarshi called out to him.

"I know exactly where you are. Stand still." He could feel the man's indecision, and had no intention of doing any more running this evening. "I'm already as close to you as I need to be." That did the trick. The healer stopped fidgeting and didn't even open his mouth when Ruarshi grabbed him by the front of his coat and pulled him into the light.

The man looked familiar. "Who are you?"

"Baltasar Illyana, clan Veris." His eyes were flat black in the firelight and his stare didn't waver.

Ruarshi thought he had met the healer a time or two, but as Baltasar was at least twice his age and came from an eastern clan, they'd never had much cause or opportunity to socialize. He continued yanking the man along until the burning house no longer obstructed their view of the bloody mess on the building's north side.

Baltasar made a choked noise and Ruarshi threw him to his knees.

"When your friends get here," he said, "you make sure they understand. If anyone touches my apprentice or my son, the same will happen to them."

The healer didn't respond. Ruarshi seriously considered repeating what he'd done to the warrior who'd threatened Etienne. The temptation was so strong that he looked away, which didn't help.

"Why didn't you heal him?" Ruarshi realized in a detached way that the man's life depended on his answer.

"Lukas was an ass and a dangerous man to cross. I was waiting until he fell asleep."

"Lukas?"

"The Diamyo in charge of this disaster."

"So you defer to warriors in matters of healing?"

"Not at all. But the boy wasn't going to die."

That was the wrong thing to say. Ruarshi was face-to-face with the man, his knees sinking into the snow, his fist bundled in the cloth below Baltasar's chin. "You—"

"Casimir's doing this for your own good," the healer cut in, lifting his head to take some of the pressure off his throat. "If his enemies get their way, neither of those boys will be safe because of their association with you."

"Do you think I can't protect them?"

"Now you're being stupid. Whatever else Casimir may have done, and I'm beginning to think he's done plenty, he's right about this. He's barely holding the traditionalists at bay as it is. If they get the upper hand—which they might, if your stunt here succeeds—you can forget about staying in Miriyan. And you won't be left alone down here, either. They have strong feelings about Nerthii."

Baltasar was leaving out a lot but Ruarshi followed him well enough. A few things he hadn't understood suddenly clicked into place, leaving a familiar sour taste in his mouth. He clearly knew Casimir much too well.

"You think he didn't lie to you, too?" he asked, shoving the man away from him and getting back to his feet. "He's not nearly so opposed to that pack of malcontents as you might wish." So Casimir's attack on him probably hadn't been a murder attempt, after all. An injured Nerthi, rushed back to Miriyan for treatment, would be of more use to him than a simple dead body.

"Don't move," he said, and blinded the healer before turning back toward the two youngsters. A soft moan followed him as he made his way across the clearing.

He'd just started searching the woods again for Karoli when the warrior appeared at the edge of the firelight, walking rapidly with his opponent in tow. He'd wrapped the man's arms in shields so strong that the warrior couldn't fight free, and it seemed he'd gagged the new-

comer as well. The stranger collapsed to his knees a few yards from the
manor house, and it was only when Karoli forced him to stand that Ruarshi understood what he intended to do.

Karoli shoved the man into the flames, and as he began to burn the
silence of the scene was broken by the man's desperate screams. The
noise and the rising smell of searing flesh knocked Ruarshi backward a
step before he could collect himself and intercede, taking the few moments he needed to kill the man cleanly and with no additional pain.
The agony he'd been in was more than sufficient, he thought.

He circled around to approach Karoli from the right, with some
vague notion of putting himself between the Diamyo and the healers.
The man was staring at the blackening corpse expressionlessly.

"I thought you might do that," Karoli said, not removing his gaze
from the dead man. "He was pair-bonded to someone in the other
group. They sent another four warriors and a healer south before taking your youngster. I want them turning around now, if they haven't
yet, and I want them terrified." The Diamyo smiled thinly. "You'll let
me know if and when your scruples get the better of you and we have
to part ways."

"Yes, I'll let you know." Ruarshi realized, as he made his way toward
the two Illyana, that he was exhausted, that his back hurt badly where
the ceiling had landed on it, and that he was still bleeding from his confrontation with Lukas. He drifted to a stop and watched his son work
on Etienne, wondering when he'd started with the healing. If he knew
anything at all about Davyt, he'd bet the boy had seen and heard just
about everything before diving into his magic.

He waited for his son to finish, not paying much attention to his
surroundings until a sharp pop from the burning house caused him to
startle and collide with Karoli. He stepped away from the man, annoyed that the Diamyo had gotten so close to him without him knowing about it. Then he noticed something odd about Karoli's right hand,
and squinted more closely at it.

"One of the warriors cut your hand? And you thought to bring bandages?"

"No. I did this myself back at the inn."

"...You're pair-bonded."

Karoli nodded. "So now my fellow exiles know there's something
wrong, and they should be well away from the Drummer's people. That
quivering pile there, I assume he's a healer?"

"Not much of one."

The Diamyo laughed. "I see you got the better of Lukas. I don't rec-ognize the woman. Unlucky for her and the others that they ended up under his command. Lukas was known for being strong as an ox and just as smart. Although their plan for catching you wasn't too bad, which leads me to wonder who was giving him advice."

"So the roof didn't come down on its own."

"No. And I should have been more use with these two here, even though the others got in my way. As I said, I'm not much good in a straight fight anymore. Aerik's maggoty corpse is probably laughing at me."

Ruarshi shook his head. "If you hadn't been here, this would have ended differently. I couldn't have dealt with four at once."

"Would you have tried?"

"I don't know. Maybe."

Karoli shot him a sidelong look. "You know you're bleeding, right?"

"Yes."

"You get hit on the head?"

"No. Why?"

"Because I feel like I'm talking to a sleepwalker."

"I'm just tired." Ruarshi was grateful that he hadn't started to shake yet, and hoped those days were over.

"You think we should stay here and set up a nice little ambush for the others?"

"No, I don't."

"Why not?"

"Because Etienne is injured and needs a warm place to sleep, and because I don't want to spend one instant longer than necessary in this place."

Karoli shrugged. "I'm persuaded."

Metal flashed in Ruarshi's peripheral vision and he stumbled back-ward, alarmed. Karoli caught him by the arm.

"That was me." He pointed to the hilt of his sword, now sheathed, by way of explanation. "Sorry. You're really out of it. How much longer until your cub is finished?"

"It'll be a little while yet." Ruarshi's eyes skittered across the bodies of the two warriors and away again. It was his responsibility to consign them to the flames, and he should ask Karoli to do the same to the one he'd killed and left lying somewhere out in the woods. Otherwise they risked the possibility of a local stumbling onto the scene and mutilating the bodies. The powdered bones of his countrymen were popular with self-styled European magicians, or so he'd been told on more than one occasion.

He knew he couldn't do it. He hoped it wouldn't matter, that the dead warriors' friends would find them before anyone else happened along. The thought of touching either of them—even for a relatively benevolent purpose—caused a blackness he couldn't name to fill his chest. It was a sensation so much worse than simple dread that all he could do was shy away from it, so he did, and hoped that Karoli wouldn't mention the subject.

He looked at the Diamyo. The man was staring out into the darkness but he seemed aware of Ruarshi's regard.

"It'll be hours yet before we can get back into the city," Karoli said. "I'm not breaking any more gates. Fortunately I know of a place where we can go to ground."

Ruarshi wasn't ready to deal with more guardsmen, or possibly worse if anyone had seen Karoli use magic on their way out. "Where would that be?" he asked.

"There's an old ruined monastery north and east of here. We'll have to start our own fire and make do with some disgusting food originally intended for sailors, but it'll shelter us for a few hours."

"Sounds fine."

They lapsed back into silence. Ruarshi listened idly to the crackle of the fire and the rising rasp of Baltasar's panicked breathing. He glanced at the healer and away again, uninterested. The man wasn't going to die.

"What's wrong with him?" Karoli asked.

"Blind."

"Ah," the warrior replied, amused. "What are you planning on doing with him?"

"Nothing. He can stay here and wait for the others."

"What if a wolf eats him?"

"It would be doing Miriyan a favor."

The subtle sound of movement brought Ruarshi's attention back to the Illyana, and he turned to see that Davyt was sitting back, rubbing at his eyes with the heels of his hands.

"Search him before we go," Etienne said, struggling to raise himself on an elbow.

"For what?" Ruarshi asked.

"*Schaal.* They were going to make sure you got a nice big dose after you surrendered."

Karoli hissed. His entire posture had changed. "He's carrying

*schaal?"* Without waiting for an answer, he stalked toward the huddled
healer and threw the man onto his side, rifling through his clothes with
quick, rough hands. He came up with a fist-sized leather pouch which
he yanked open, sniffing cautiously at the contents. The warrior closed
it again carefully, set it aside, and then plunged a dagger into Baltasar's
throat.

Davyt gasped. Ruarshi just watched, chiding himself for not having
seen that coming but unable to work up any real dismay on the healer's
behalf. He'd never run across *schaal* before, but there was a good reason
its name was derived from the Miriyanti word for death. Ingesting the
stuff made it next to impossible to wield magic, but it was almost never
used because the difference between a debilitating dose and a fatal one
couldn't be reliably determined even by a Chamani. Which Baltasar definitely wasn't.

He looked back at the youngsters, who were both still staring at
Karoli. The warrior's lips were moving, but Ruarshi wasn't the least bit
curious about what he was saying to the dying man. And the Illyana
needed to focus on something else.

"Can you stand, Etienne?" he asked. "We need to go."

## )O(

Davyt insisted on patching Ruarshi up before they left the clearing, a
procedure that didn't take long as the cut he'd suffered was shallow and
the injury to his back involved a bad bruise but no broken bones.
Karoli refused to allow either of them to heal his hand just yet, so after
they'd commandeered one of the dead Miriyanti's horses for Etienne's
use, they mounted up and rode east with the warrior in the lead.

No one spoke. Ruarshi drifted in the silence, keeping an eye on the
Illyana while the greater part of his awareness blanketed the surrounding area. Now that the danger was past he felt light-headed and distant,
a sensation he welcomed. He wondered how far behind them the other
group of warriors might be, but didn't dwell on the question. There
was no point to it.

It wasn't until the small hours of the morning that they finally
reached Karoli's monastery. Some time before that Ruarshi had shifted
from his own saddle to Etienne's, where he sat with an arm around the
younger man's chest to keep him from toppling off his horse. He'd
been concerned about the healer's concussion, but a quick check told
him that all was basically well: aside from exhaustion and lingering pain,

Etienne wasn't suffering physically and would recover without complication, barring any further injury.

After guiding them through a collapsed section of the monastery's overgrown and crumbling outer wall, Karoli dismounted and motioned for the rest of them to do the same.

"The horses can stay here. The abbot's cell is this way. We can sleep there."

Twenty minutes later they were settled in a profusion of blankets on a stone floor in front of a small but vigorous fire, nibbling with varying degrees of interest at rock-hard pieces of bread and sipping at sour wine. Karoli had explained, while pulling these and other supplies out of a niche in the far corner of the room, that he always set up bolt holes like this one when he moved into a new area. There might have been a hint of smugness in his manner, but Ruarshi wasn't paying much attention, didn't particularly care, and was in any case asleep before he could take his second bite.

# The Monastery

Ruarshi woke with an elbow in his ribs and a curl of black hair in his mouth. This sort of thing had happened before, so he lay still for a while longer, enjoying the warmth of their improvised sleeping arrangement if not the hardness of the stone beneath his cheek. Then he noticed that the hair tasted of blood and sat up abruptly, wiping at his mouth with the back of his hand.

Sunlight was streaming in through the empty doorway of the chamber and the large hole in the far corner of the ceiling, rendering the interior bright enough that he could see Davyt and Etienne sprawled in front of the cold fireplace, still asleep. Of Karoli there was no sign. More encouragingly, a brief thinning of his bond-shield told him that there was no one else in their vicinity, either, and Mainz was far enough to their southeast that it registered as no more than a distant hum to his senses.

He stood and went out the door, found a remote part of the monastery in which to take care of his morning necessities, and went looking for the warrior. He found him in the courtyard with the horses, sitting on a low stone wall and unwrapping the bandage from his hand. Ruarshi considered the stab wound in his palm, then reached down to turn Karoli's hand over.

After a short interval of silence, he said, "I'm fairly certain that you could have gotten your bond partner's attention with something less drastic."

The Diamyo squinted up at him. "It's how our code works. A serious situation calls for a serious injury. Anything less she attributes to clumsiness or bad luck."

"So what's your code for imminent death?"

Karoli made a fist and a trickle of blood ran down the back of his hand and into his cuff. "That's what this is."

"It's good to know your signals don't get any more extreme. I assume she's on her way and you'd like it healed now?"

"Yes."

Ruarshi sat down next to the warrior and took his hand again, looking carefully at both the entrance and exit wounds. "You've kept it relatively clean, but this will go more quickly if I can wash it out first. Did you store any lye here?"

"No. I've been spending the last century blending in with Europeans, Cousin, and you can't do that if you appear overfond of soap. People get suspicious."

"I just figured out why you and Etienne don't get along. Hold still."

Ruarshi descended into a healing trance, reached out for the magic that would allow him to start knitting torn flesh back together, and found that it dissipated like smoke when he tried to wield it. The power was still there, but that just made his inability to bend it to his will that much more aggravating. He could spend hours struggling with it and get no further than any novice healer in Miriyan, he knew, because he'd gone down this road before.

He'd regain control over this aspect of his magic with time, or he wouldn't. There was nothing he could do about it for now.

He released Karoli's hand and stood. "I'll go wake Davyt."

"Why?"

Ruarshi was already headed back inside. "Because he's the only functional healer we've got at the moment."

"What? Wait."

Ruarshi chose not to comply with the request, instead quickening his pace and returning to the cell where they'd spent the night. To his relief, both the Illyana were stirring when he entered the room.

"Good morning," he said. "Davyt, could you see to Karoli's hand? There's something I have to do. It will only take a few minutes." His son responded with a bemused nod and he left the room, heading along the ruined cloister away from Karoli and darting through a hole in the north wall. He pressed his back up against a pile of stone, shut his eyes, and told himself to stop being ridiculous. He'd gotten through this before, it was survivable, and there wasn't time for him to tie himself in knots just at present.

Even if his ability to heal never came back, it couldn't matter. He couldn't *let* it matter.

He took another deep breath and exhaled slowly. He opened his eyes. It was a beautiful day, already past noon, and he had an errand to run.

)O(

The others had argued against his plan, but not with any real conviction and not for long. It was clear to all of them that staying on in Mainz was no longer an option. After the events of the previous night, city authorities would have to take a more active interest in them, assuming they didn't just order them to leave. Karoli's position was particularly untenable; they had to assume he was now known to be an undeclared Miriyanti, a status that would endear him to no one and could potentially lead to his arrest. Kilian and Charitas needed to be warned to get out of Mainz before the Inquisitor could arrive, and given the means to do so. The same went for Isabel, though Ruarshi didn't mention her specifically. Even if Sprenger turned out to be unusually benign for an aspiring Inquisitor, which Karoli thought unlikely, it would be better for those three if they simply vanished for a while.

Davyt had wanted to come along, an idea Ruarshi had quelled with a mild glare and a promise to be back by nightfall. He climbed into Sophie's saddle shortly thereafter and headed toward town.

There were two guards stationed at the northern gate when he passed through it the better part of an hour later. Both of them looked at him sharply, but neither spoke to him or tried to impede his progress. He returned their scrutiny in as unfriendly a manner as possible and hoped he could get his business finished before anyone tried to interfere with him, more for their sake than his own. His mood wasn't improving as the day went on.

He stopped by his banker's office first, emerging from the dimness within carrying three small but heavy sacks of coin. Then he turned toward his home, slowing Sophie's steps as he neared it before finally pulling her to a halt three blocks away. There was a Miriyanti loitering in the vicinity, probably positioned to keep an eye on his front door. He couldn't tell if it was a man or woman, but he picked up on the stranger's mild anxiety and boredom with no trouble at all. It wasn't a combination that promised imminent violence, which was encouraging. He nudged his horse back into motion and advanced carefully, wondering if this was one of Casimir's minions or Karoli's exiles.

When he turned to make his way up the street where the stranger was standing, he got his answer to that question: the individual's hair was Miriyanti white. He or she had to be Casimir's. He considered readying a weave, but in the end simply rode forward and reined in be-side... her. She was an older woman, probably about twice Slan's age. When she caught sight of him, she took one surprised step backward before catching herself and bowing slightly.

"I am Britt Naishanti, clan Avorae, former second in command of the troop Casimir sent out to bring you home. First in command, now."

Ruarshi dismounted. Whatever kind of conversation they were about to have, he doubted it would be the sort that he'd want them shouting back and forth in the middle of the lane.

"So you've found the others. Good. They're being tended to?"

"They are."

"It's my understanding that one member of that group was pair-bonded to someone in your contingent. Will this be a problem?"

"If it becomes one, you have my promise that I'll deal with it."

A fair answer. Warriors who'd just lost their bond partners were no-toriously volatile, and the best commander in Miriyan couldn't control one who decided to go his or her own way. A good percentage of the classical tragedies performed in Tomir every summer centered around just this issue.

Ruarshi nodded. "Come inside."

He led her across the street, looped Sophie's reins through the small iron ring set in the stones next to the front window, and knocked on the door before pushing it open. A pair of arms emerged from the gloom and wrapped him in a warm and breathless hug before he could take a second step into the room.

"Ruarshi!" Charitas let him go and beamed up at him, belatedly noticing that he wasn't alone. She gave Britt a narrow look and turned back to him. "We didn't know what had become of you. Have you eaten?"

"I'm fine. We're all fine. I'll want to talk to you in a few minutes. Is Kilian home?"

"No, but he should be back soon."

"I'll see you in the kitchen once I'm finished with my guest."

Charitas glanced toward the warrior again, nodded uncertainly, and left them alone. Ruarshi gestured toward the chairs in front of the fire-place and took one himself, while Britt surveyed the furniture arrange-ment and decided to remain standing. He gave a mental shrug and bent forward to warm his hands over the low fire.

The silence stretched. Ruarshi watched the warrior and felt her mood shift from slight bemusement to impatience, at which point he sat up and crossed his arms, leaning back in his chair.

"You got here quickly."

"I have something for you." She reached into her vest and pulled out a roll of vellum tied with deep blue ribbon, stepping forward to hand it to him.

Ruarshi accepted it, pulled the ribbon away, and unrolled the scroll. It had been mangled in transit and he took the time to flatten it out before beginning to read.

*Ruarshi,*

> *I am on balance not displeased that you are in receipt of this letter. In your recent confrontations with myself and my agents I was careful to give you even odds, as I find that I am rather fond of you still. I do wish, however, that you had put your crusading nature to nobler purposes than could ever be served by your current endeavor.*
>
> *I trust you understand what you are now.*
>
> *I am, as I hope is obvious, very much alive. Yes, in escaping me you did some damage, but one of your old friends from the circle was with me at the time so I suffered no permanent harm.*
>
> *Though circumstances dictate that I cannot remain your ally, I would like you to understand that what I have done has been in the service of political necessity. You know better than most that the common weal demands sacrifices from those upon whom the Norns' gaze comes to rest.*
>
> *Enjoy the remainder of your sojourn in Europe. The waters tell me that I may yet share a drink with you before the winter solstice.*

> *Casimir*

Ruarshi shook his head and extended the scroll toward the Naishanti, who reached out to take it with eyebrows raised. Her eyebrows continued to climb as she scanned the text, but her face was composed when she gave it back to him.

"Is that what he told you? That you'd be riding into 'even odds'?"

Britt paused as though considering her answer, but only said, "He didn't instruct me to ask for a reply. Would you like to send one?"

"No. This is pure horseshit. I must have very nearly killed him. There is no way the man I remember would willingly get into a fair fight with anyone."

Her lips quirked. "That's the part of the letter that irritates you?"

"All of it irritates me. He defines 'political necessity' as whatever best serves his own interests, which he furthers by cheating. Generally while under the influence of an appalling amount of opium. That's not an occupation I feel inclined to respect."

"I could take that comment back to him."

"Please do. Did he explain why he thought the *schaal* was a remotely good idea?"

Britt eyed him. "He did not."

"Have you done anything like this for him in the past?"

"I should go," she said, turning away.

"Are you going to shadow us on our way back to Miriyan or does Casimir trust us to find it on our own?"

Still nothing from her, though she did at least stop moving and was looking at him again. Finally she sighed. "*Tai* Nerthi, we have nothing useful to say to each other. In a more forgiving time, we wouldn't have met in circumstances like these. We probably never would have met at all. I regret the outcome of last night's battle, but I had no friends among the dead. I appreciate the fact that you seem to bear me no ill will. Now I need to get back to my people. We must prepare for our journey north. So if I may...?" She gestured toward the door.

Ruarshi smiled. So this was Naishanti professionalism, a rare thing in his experience. "Meeting you has been... uninformative."

"Maybe you'll get your answers from Casimir," she said, responding to his smile with a ghost of her own. "Good day."

"Goodbye."

She was out the door and gone even as he spoke. He glanced over his shoulder toward the kitchen, waiting to hear Kilian's heavy footsteps so he could go in and take permanent leave of the couple he'd shared his home with for so many months.

☽○☾

Extricating himself from Kilian's and Charitas' presence had been difficult enough—he'd ended up packing several pounds of food into his saddlebags, along with what he could carry of his own, Davyt's, and

Etienne's belongings—but saying goodbye to Isabel was quite a bit worse.

The prospect of having to leave town for a while didn't disturb her; she had an aunt in the countryside who she thought would take her in, now that she had the resources to pay for her own keep, and she had no desire to come to the attention of an Inquisitor. She even listened patiently to his rambling advice, delivered at unnecessary length, without chiding him for fussing over her as though she were a child. Their conversation was going remarkably well, in fact, until Ruarshi set his wine glass aside and got ready to exit the room.

She stopped him with a hand on his arm. "Surely there'd be no harm in…" she trailed off, glancing significantly toward her bed, "… one more time?"

He hadn't really believed she'd ask. And in spite of the fact that he was running on nothing more substantial than adrenaline and nerves, his desire to do exactly what she suggested was almost overwhelming. But he couldn't say yes. Without access to his healer's talents, he'd be no different than any other man who'd paid for the use of her body, and he didn't want her to remember him in that way. Pride came with a price. For both of them, since he didn't know how to explain his refusal.

"I can't, Isabel. I'm sorry."

"Your son won't find out."

"Because there won't be anything for him to find out about. But don't blame this on him." He took her hand and kissed the palm, then spent several silent moments tracing its lines with the tip of a finger. "I've valued our time together, Isabel, and I apologize for having turned you into my nursemaid. Please take care of yourself."

She didn't reply right away, instead curling her fingers around his and leaning toward him until her forehead rested against his. "You've been so peculiar about all this that you might not believe me, but I'll say it anyway: I'm going to miss you. I'm going to miss all of it. I don't think I'd deny you anything, and you're the only person on earth I can say that to."

Ruarshi slid his hand from hers, kissed her fiercely on the brow, and left the room without another word.

)O(

Olli was at The Sour Grape when Ruarshi stopped by a short while later, rooted in the same chair as before, nursing an enormous mug of beer. He wasn't alone, but Ruarshi was too anxious to be gone to wait for a better time. He spoke in a low voice, directly into the big man's ear, leaving a final thank you and farewell for Simon. Olli blinked once at him and nodded, and Ruarshi pivoted on his heel and left the tavern.

He was done. He climbed into Sophie's saddle and rode back to the monastery.

$$\text{)O(}$$

The feathery clouds in the western sky had just shifted from lilac to purple when Ruarshi rode through the gap in the wall and noticed the extra horse. This wasn't a surprise, as it happened; he'd known they had a visitor almost since he'd left the distracting mental noise of the city behind him. It was another Miriyanti, not hostile but with lingering traces of anxiety that she—he was fairly sure it was a woman—hadn't managed to quell just yet. Karoli's bond partner, he was sure.

He dismounted with a tired exhalation and led Sophie over to the shallow basin that the warrior had filled with water the night before. The well behind the kitchen was still functional, a fact for which Karoli had refused to take any credit, pointing out that they probably weren't the only travelers to seek shelter here in recent years. Ruarshi was just pulling the saddle from Sophie's back when Davyt emerged from the rubble of the monastery's southeast corner, picking his way carefully among the stones.

"Did you have any trouble in town?" his son asked.

"No. Quiet here?"

"More or less. Etienne and Karoli haven't killed one another."

"I've brought food, there in the saddlebags. Help yourself. When did Karoli's partner get here?"

"That's... I mean, she's, uh..."

Ruarshi, busy rubbing the sweat from Sophie's hide as well as he could with the saddle blanket, paused to glance over his shoulder at Davyt. "Yes?"

"It's Jonata."

He stared at the healer, his task momentarily forgotten. His first thought was that his senses and his son were telling him two different things. When he realized that this wasn't necessarily so, he felt a flash of both amusement and irritation.

"How long have you known?"

"Since this afternoon."

"And how long has Etienne known?"

"A lot longer than that."

Ruarshi smiled at the hint of asperity in his son's tone. "One would hope so." He folded the blanket and set it aside, leading Sophie into the meager shelter provided by what was left of the old chapel. The other horses eyeballed them briefly before going back to their drowsing, showing little interest in the fodder he and Davyt pulled from another of Karoli's stashes. He didn't blame them. Though thankfully not moldy, the food was of poor quality and he wished he had something better to feed his mare.

"She came alone?"

"Yes. I get the sense that she was in a hurry and her household staff doesn't argue with her. She's suggested that we stay at her home outside of town for the next few weeks."

Ruarshi left the chapel, motioning for Davyt to follow him. He bent to retrieve his saddlebags on his way across the courtyard. "This was her own idea?"

"Yes. Why?"

"Nothing. Dealing with Casimir tends to make people crazy in a very particular way. I won't let it get the better of me."

"You don't think she's...?"

"No. Not seriously. How is Etienne recovering?"

"Quickly. He and Karoli spent most of the afternoon critiquing the fight in the tavern. 'Fight' isn't even the right word for it. Etienne's being harder on himself than he should be, and Karoli's helpful suggestions are sharper than I like. Fortunately they both shut up about it when Jonata got here."

"And since then you've all been smiling uncomfortably at each other?"

"It hasn't been that bad, no..." Davyt's voice trailed off as they stepped through the doorway into the abbot's chamber.

Karoli, who was poking idly at the fire with an old pot hook, stopped to look up at them, while Etienne stared with fanatical concentration at the brilliant red rose in his hand. The presence of the flower answered an as-yet unasked question about the third member of the little tableau, who jumped to her feet when they entered the room.

"*Tai* Nerthi," Jonata began, "I feel I should apologize for—"

"Please, stop there," Ruarshi interrupted. He set his baggage aside and bowed to her. "We're all going to be sleeping on the floor together

in a few hours, so there's no point to formalities. Apologies aren't necessary in any case. You've been looking after our patient?"

She turned to regard Etienne, who was now watching them from his
makeshift bed of blankets. He appeared placid enough but his grip on
the rose was still rather tight, Ruarshi thought.

"After a fashion," Jonata said. "He's been restless since I arrived
here."

"He's been 'restless' since he woke up," Karoli said. He tilted his
head toward Ruarshi's bags. "Is there any food in there? Yes? Good.
For a man who got cracked on the head, he remembers more about
what happened to him than I would have expected. The cub did a good
job on him." The warrior leaned sideways to snag the saddlebags with
the hook and began pulling them in his direction.

"Cub?" Davyt muttered.

"You try lying on this floor all day," Etienne said mildly. "You'd
come off as restless, too."

"This floor isn't that bad—" Karoli began.

"What happened in town?" Jonata asked, overriding him. "Are you
still in danger?"

"Your second question I can't answer." Ruarshi pulled Casimir's letter from his tunic, unfolded it, and handed it to Etienne. He had spent
most of his ride back to the monastery becoming more and more suspicious of Britt's behavior. Casimir never gave up, not in his experience, and given what Karoli had told him the previous night he'd be
willing to bet that she'd been in charge of the warriors' mission from
the beginning, regardless of what Lukas might have thought. "As to
your first, Karoli, have you ever met Britt of the Avorae?"

"No, but I've heard of her. Why?"

"What the hell is this?" Etienne was holding the letter as though it
were a snake, his face flushed. Davyt pried it from his grip and began
reading, while Karoli got to his feet and went to peer at it over his
shoulder.

Ruarshi knelt beside the younger man. "It's Casimir at his most
charming. I read it as a threat, so I thought all of you should see it. I
wouldn't get too worked up about it. May I?" He gestured toward the
rose and Etienne's flush deepened. The healer glanced toward Jonata
and handed it over without a word.

Ruarshi examined it, smiling. It even smelled like a fresh bloom.
"Do you always carry seeds with you, or only on special occasions?"

"Always."

When Jonata didn't say anything more, he turned to look at her. She was regarding him thoughtfully, her head tilted to one side and a slight frown on her face.

"So Britt is here?" Karoli had returned to the saddlebags and was slicing a piece of sausage with a dagger Ruarshi hadn't seen before. "She gave that to you?"

"She did. They'd found the clearing. She wasn't the least bit perturbed about what had happened. She implied they'd be leaving for Miriyan once that message was delivered."

"And you don't believe that."

"I don't know whether I do or not. Her disinterest was genuine." He returned the rose to Etienne and sat down next to him. "But she's not here of her own will, is she? It's not like Casimir to let things lie."

"Have you figured out what he's trying to do?" Davyt asked.

Ruarshi grimaced. It was the one question he didn't want to answer, but evading it would be worse than useless. "I think he wants to mollify the traditionalists by selling out the Nerthii. I can only hope he's starting with me."

"That could work," Etienne said quietly. His was staring off into the middle distance. "And he wants you breathing when he hands you over, but just barely."

"It would make his job easier."

Karoli snorted. "There are a lot of senior Naishanti and Diamyo among the traditionalists. But I expect you know that."

"Yes."

"So all of this really has nothing to do with the exiles?" Etienne asked, gesturing in Karoli's direction with his free hand.

"I wouldn't go that far. Casimir's never been averse to killing two or more birds with one stone."

Etienne's gaze shifted to his fellow healer. "So *Casimir* might have had Davyt sent down here to keep you alive? I thought it was the other side...?" The Illyana trailed off unhappily.

"This is why it's not a good idea to keep company with Seers. Sometimes the factions work together to get something done, because it's important to all of them for different reasons. Sometimes they trip each other up with their plots. It's an impossible tangle and it's best not to get caught up in it. And I might be wrong about his purpose."

Karoli chuckled nastily. "If you're right, it means your enemies carve you up no matter who wins."

"You're assuming our only two choices are Casimir or his loudest, most obnoxious opponents."

"You want to put the Sotarii back in charge?"

The warrior had begun handing around pieces of bread piled high with sausage and cheese, and Ruarshi leaned forward to take one. "I don't want to put anyone anywhere. And I'm not going to let anyone use me, either."

"Good luck avoiding that. Anyone want wine?"

Ruarshi glanced over at Jonata. They'd been speaking German by unspoken consent, but that didn't mean their conversation had been an easy one to follow.

"Sorry about this. We do talk about pleasant things sometimes."

She gave him a distracted smile and stepped forward to retrieve three cups from Karoli, handing one to Etienne and another to Ruarshi before settling onto a low stool. Silence descended on the little group as everyone turned their attention to their food, but soon Jonata set her cup aside and turned to face him.

"So what do you think these people will do next?" she asked. "There are five still here that you know of. Four fighters against two. Are you enough to hold them off if they come for you?"

Ruarshi was sufficiently startled at having been placed in the same category as Karoli that he found himself unable to answer right away. Fortunately he didn't need to.

"We'll number five fighters by midnight," the warrior said. "Not that he and I ought to need the help."

"The others are so close?" Davyt asked.

"They're nearby but still on the other side of the river. Right now they're probably stealing a boat or threatening a ferryman."

"If they are arriving tonight, we should head to my family home tomorrow," Jonata said. "We can reach it in less than a day. It will be somewhat warmer than this ruin and much easier to defend."

"Who's living there now?" Ruarshi was uneasy at the thought of immuring himself behind unfamiliar walls, but had to admit it was a vastly better option than remaining where they were or heading for the nearest village. And as the woman was a Sotari in firm control of her talents, there was no likelihood that they would strain her family's food supply.

"A cousin and her husband, along with their younger children. This won't be the first time I've shown up there unannounced. My existence is an open secret within the family."

"I expect we will overburden your servants."

Jonata smiled at him. "They will manage. There are more of them than you may imagine."

"How big is this place?" Karoli asked.

"It used to be more extensive than it is now. Only a keep, a few out-buildings, and a single wall remain. We shall cause little disruption in the yearly routine."

Ruarshi looked at Etienne, who was clearly trying to force himself to attend to the conversation and just as clearly losing to an over-whelming need for sleep now that his stomach was full. A day-long ride would do him no good at all, but then neither would yet another turn of the sun spent on a cold stone floor. He pushed a tendril of power toward the younger man, a weave of the sort he would normally use to augment his own strength and speed, to see if he could use the magic left to him for some positive purpose. To his mild gratification the weave took. Etienne opened his eyes and blinked blearily up at him.

"Will you be able to ride tomorrow?" Ruarshi asked.

"Of course." The Illyana sounded slightly offended. "You know I can sleep in the saddle."

"Yes, and you know I've seen you fall out of it, too."

"One time, and I was drunk, not asleep."

"I rather thought you were both." Ruarshi turned to the warrior. "He shouldn't stay here any longer than he has to. If your exiles are de-layed, will you wait for them or come with us?"

"If they can't get across a river between now and morning, they de-serve the extra trouble. I'll go with you."

Ruarshi nodded. "Thank you."

"Don't thank me. I have entirely selfish reasons for not letting you out of my sight."

)O(

Ruarshi volunteered to take the first watch and spent the next several hours alternating between keeping a mental eye on the surrounding landscape and watching the others sleep. He wanted to ask Etienne when he'd pair-bonded with Jonata, and why, but the healer had dropped into an exhausted slumber shortly after finishing his wine and in any case it wasn't the sort of thing he could bring up while the woman in question was in the room. Nor did he want to go into it while Karoli was present. The warrior was a light sleeper, stirring every time Davyt twitched or muttered, which happened often enough that

Ruarshi wondered if he ought to wake his son. He'd just decided to do so when the boy took a deeper breath and settled into stillness, leaving the nightmare behind.

He didn't know what he could say to soothe his son's fears, not when his main strategy for dealing with his own involved ignoring them. He thought again about sending the healers away, back to Miriyan where they could claim the protection of clan and family, and again rejected the idea as too risky. The likelihood that they would run into enemies while in his presence was unacceptably high, but he and the Diamyo could bring quite a lot of power to bear in their defense; on their own they would be too vulnerable. The incident of the night before had made that painfully obvious.

Then there was the strictly emotional side of things to consider. The prospect of watching them ride off without him filled him with a sense of foreboding so strong it made it difficult to think. They might very well make it safely to Miriyan's border, but once there he didn't trust that no one would be lying in wait for them, and Nerthu knew what Casimir would do to them if they ended up at Mirror Lake.

Ruarshi shook his head, refusing to let his imagination lead him down that particular path, and went to put more wood on the fire and wake Karoli. His watch had ended some time earlier, but he had decided to let the warrior rest a bit longer since he was in no danger of falling asleep anyway. He returned to his previous position with his back propped against the cold stone of the wall next to the fireplace. Their silent vigil stretched deeper into the night, his drowsy deliberations helping to pass the time but getting him nowhere.

A light hand on his shoulder, shaking him gently, brought Ruarshi back to wakefulness and he realized that he'd somehow worried himself into a light doze. There were Miriyanti outside the monastery, not a quarter mile away.

He surged to his feet. The hand shifted from his shoulder to his arm and tightened, holding him in place, and he found himself looking at Karoli through the fading image in his mind's eye of three blue flames, drawing nearer in the darkness.

"No need to be so jumpy. Those are friends. I'm going outside."

Karoli released him and disappeared through the doorway. Ruarshi followed, still rubbing sleep from his eyes, and trailed him through a maze of scrubby growth and tumbled stone to what had once been the monastery's east wall.

As the riders drew near, the warrior stepped out from the ruin's shadow and raised a hand in greeting. The foremost rider slid from the saddle and jogged forward to wrap Karoli in an exhausted but enthusiastic embrace. When it became apparent that it wasn't going to end in the immediate future, Ruarshi switched his attention to the others.

Second off her mount was an older woman, probably about the age of Ruarshi's mother, wrapped in what looked like a coat of rabbit fur and considering him in the moonlight. She extended a hand and he took it.

"I'm Atali, clan Corvis. That," she continued, pointing toward the shadowy form of Karoli and his bond partner, "is Saoirse, clan Annorae, and the third of our party is Elin, her sister." She nodded toward the woman riding up behind her. To Ruarshi's eye Elin appeared to be the youngest of the three, but it was hard for him to tell as a thin leather mask obscured the entire left half of her face. All three women wore trousers. Slan would have approved.

"I take it you're Ruarshi?" Atali asked.

"I am. We don't have much to offer by way of hospitality at present, but there's food and wine, along with a roof that's mostly intact and some blankets to sleep on."

"It'll do. Saoirse, leave off with that and get over here."

After lingering to exchange some soft words with Karoli, the new arrival appeared in front of him. "Glad to meet you. Sorry about the hour, but this one had me convinced he was being murdered. We went through three sets of horses to get here."

Ruarshi shook her hand, then turned to the taciturn Elin and exchanged a brief clasp. He studied the horses as well as he could in the wan light. "These don't appear to be blown. Will they and you be up for a ride tomorrow? This isn't a good place to stay."

"We only have to freeze here for one night?" Atali asked. "That's good news. I never expect much by way of accommodation when Karoli's involved. You have a fire?"

"Of course there's a fire," Karoli said. "And a stranger you're not expecting, a Sotari who was born and raised here. She's bonded to the crabby one and will be traveling with us."

"The crabby one," Ruarshi repeated, with a quelling look at the Diamyo, "is injured. If he sleeps through your arrival he's not to blame and he'll probably benefit from the extra rest come morning."

"Understood," Saoirse said. "We'll be quiet. We don't need to eat and I'm sure I'll be asleep as soon as I lie down."

They led the newcomers onto the monastery grounds, helped them settle their mounts, and then preceded them back to the chamber where the others were still sleeping. Everyone awoke when they arrived, though Etienne seemed only vaguely aware of what was happening and started snoring again before the warriors had their blankets spread. Ruarshi settled to the floor next to Etienne, listening with half an ear as the warriors set up a watch schedule for the remainder of the night.

Ruarshi's eyes drifted shut of their own accord and Saoirse's quiet murmuring faded gradually into silence.

# The Keep

Ruarshi was awakened early the next morning by a drop of water striking his forehead and trickling slowly toward his hairline. He wiped it away and squinted up at the ruined ceiling, aware of the faint patter of rain and an unexpectedly mild breeze wafting through the chamber. He pushed himself to his feet, throwing a worried glance at Etienne on his way out the door. It was entirely too likely that the healer would end up ill again if he had to ride through wet weather all day.

When he stepped into the chapel a bit later to check on the horses, he found Elin already there. He nodded to her and went to wrap an arm around Sophie's neck, soaking up the mare's warmth as she nuzzled at his shoulder.

"*Tai* Nerthi."

Elin's words were soft and somewhat distorted, and when he turned to face her he got a good look at the scar tissue that was making it difficult for her to speak. She had removed her mask and stood watching him, unmoving.

"Yes?"

"I've learned it's a good idea to get this out of the way shortly after meeting someone, if there's a chance I'll be in their company for more than a few days. I prefer to take this off while eating. I know you can sense the injury through the mask anyway."

"Was it the result of an accident or intentional?"

"It was intentional. Very much so. I was too angry to be cautious when I first arrived in Europe."

Ruarshi considered his next words. "I would say that I wish there had been healers among you to tend to such things, but that wouldn't be true."

"You feel that what Casimir has done to us is just? Why have you agreed to travel with us, if that's the case?"

Ruarshi shook his head. "There's nothing to like about what Casimir has done to you, beyond the fact that he let you live. I seem to recall that Elyon's adherents were less merciful."

"You're wondering what role my sister and I played in the revolt."

"I'm more interested in how you feel about it now."

"My opinion hasn't changed. I regretted it then and I still do." When Ruarshi didn't respond, she went on. "Are you aware that Clan Annorae is a sept of the Sylvae?"

It had been years since he'd heard that particular clan name. "The Sylvae lost a tenth of their number fighting the rebels."

"The Annorae lost even more. They—we—regarded Seggita and the rest of the Nerthii very highly. Saoirse and I were training in Tomir that summer. We decided to stay on as long as we could, gathering information, before leaving the warriors' enclave and offering our services to your allies. We waited too long."

"You could have surrendered."

"Not with the enclave surrounded. We broke our swords in secret, along with a few others who felt as we did. It was an empty gesture. When the standoff ended we were rounded up with all the others."

"Your clan didn't step forward to speak for you?"

"Our clan had no settled leadership at the time. I don't blame them. I only hope they received the message we sent. Whether we make it home or not, I do not wish to be known as a traitor to my own family."

"Karoli has told you about the fire at Mirror Lake?"

"Yes. We're believed to be dead." The unscarred corner of Elin's mouth quirked upward. "I might come to regret not remaining that way if our letter didn't get through. The Annorae use the old form of the Rite of Atonement when warriors are involved. I would prefer to avoid that."

Ruarshi nodded absently. That particular rite varied from clan to clan, but he knew that prolonged starvation and the lash were common elements of the ritual. It would be a lot to require of someone just returned from exile, but that consideration wouldn't mean much if Elin's people believed she had betrayed them.

"How did you meet Karoli?" he asked.

"He came looking for us about fifteen years ago. There were... fourteen, I think... of us left by that time. He knew our numbers were dwindling and wanted to keep us as close together as he could."

"And Atali?"

Elin lifted her mask and began tying it back into place with a frayed black ribbon. "He gathered her in more recently. She'll break from our group the instant we reach Miriyanti soil. She's a true believer. She thinks that Miriyan has been ruined by too much time spent under the rule of the Sotarii. Please don't mention Casimir's name in her presence."

"She did shake my hand."

"She'll shake anyone's hand. Don't worry, she won't do you or the healers any harm, but you might not care for everything she has to say. It can be hard to tell when she's serious."

"I'm not following you. A true believer of the kind you describe would just kill us in our sleep and be done with it."

"No. She would never do that to another Miriyanti. If you were European, I'd advise you to stay away from her."

Ruarshi watched as Elin made a final adjustment to her mask. "If the Annorae decide that you and Saoirse have to atone, come visit me beforehand. I can give you some things that will ease your way through the ritual."

"That's hardly the point of the rite."

"If they feel about the Nerthii as you say they do, they can't really object to my meddling, can they?"

"Maybe not. Will you be returning to your clan rather than to Tomir?"

"I hope to avoid the capital entirely."

"I doubt you'll get your wish," Karoli said, striding through what remained of the chapel doorway. The hood on his coat was pulled up and rain dripped from its edge. "Is Etienne good to travel? Judging by the looks of things, the weather's only going to get worse."

"He needs several more days of rest," Ruarshi replied. "But staying here wouldn't be good for him, either. We should leave as soon as everyone is ready."

$$\supset O \subset$$

The rain continued throughout the day, sometimes as a heavy downpour but more often as a light drizzle that was less troublesome but still far from pleasant. The snow and ice underfoot had turned into a heavy slush that sucked at the horses' hooves with every step. Ruarshi and Jonata rode at the front, followed closely by Davyt and Etienne. Elin,

Atali, Karoli, and Saoirse brought up the rear in an ill-defined formation that seemed to have shifted every time Ruarshi glanced back at them.

The third time he reined in to check on Etienne, who was riding silently but doggedly with his eyes mostly focused on the ground, Davyt asked, "What are you doing, Father?"

"Tending to my stubborn former apprentice."

"Yes, but what are you actually doing? I can tell you're using a weave, but I can't make heads or tails of it."

"You are?" Etienne looked at him blearily. "I do feel better. I thought it was just the warmth of your attention."

"Well then, that's what we'll call it."

"No, it isn't. Father?"

Ruarshi sighed. "It's something I've never heard of before, but I'm sure I didn't invent it. You know that warriors can use their power to strengthen themselves physically. That's what I'm using on him."

Etienne looked down at himself as though he thought the magic should have changed his appearance. "Really?" he asked dubiously.

"That's clever," Davyt remarked. "I can't help noticing, though, that you're already yawning. It's, what, noon? We could run into Britt's people. Are you sure you should be doing this?"

Davyt was right. Ruarshi was still thinking like a healer, even though that's not what he was or what their little group needed most right now.

"Point taken. I won't push it."

Jonata had turned in her saddle to watch them. "Is everything all right?" They had been speaking Miriyanti.

Etienne smiled at her. "I'm being well tended to. Possibly too well. It's embarrassing."

She frowned at him. "I have known men to die from blows to the head. Why should they not be paying close attention?"

Ruarshi sat back in his saddle and watched Etienne struggle to come up with an answer to that. "It's just more than I need," he mumbled.

"Is it? Perhaps they're in a better position to judge." Jonata inclined her head toward Ruarshi with a rather alarming wink and continued, "Besides, they are your friends and they worry, so you cannot blame them."

Etienne didn't respond. Ruarshi clapped him on the shoulder, lending him a little extra strength in spite of his promise, and then urged his mare forward until he was once again riding next to Jonata.

"His concussion was serious, but Davyt was able to heal him only

hours after he was struck. Etienne should suffer no long-term consequences, and in the short-term, only the fatigue you're seeing today."

"So you really are miracle workers."

"It can look that way."

"I was in France when you came through Mainz earlier. I was disappointed not to have met you, although I would not have had the
courage to approach you then. Nor the freedom, I fear."

Wondering if he were stepping into waters deeper than he wanted
to deal with, Ruarshi asked, "Have you ever thought about visiting
Miriyan? I don't know what arrangements you've made with your family here, but there you would be considered a—hmm, it would translate
as 'lost child'—and you would be welcome to stay with your clan if you
wanted to. It wouldn't be obligatory."

"I don't know which clan I belong to."

"There are Miriyanti called Adepts who may be able to shed some
light on that. They specialize in finding things that have been misplaced."

Jonata nodded in response, but her expression remained pensive.
Ruarshi took a deep breath and plunged onward. "Etienne hasn't been
forthcoming. Nor do I have any right to ask, but –"

"You want to know what is going on between us."

"Yes."

"I have asked him to remain here with me but I know he will not. I
may visit him in Miriyan one day, but I have no wish to permanently
leave my home. He has also indicated that he has difficulties with his
family that would be made worse by my presence. He did not phrase it
in this way, but that was his meaning."

Jonata wasn't answering the question he was really asking, a consideration that would have to wait. "What difficulties?"

"I am not certain. He talks around the subject. I believe there was a
scandal involving his mother. She was not Miriyanti, and his clan did
not approve of this? Is this possible?"

Ruarshi tried to remember everything he'd ever been told about Etienne's clan, the Jinnae. He came up with nothing. Ruarshi seldom
spoke of his own clan or family, but Etienne was considerably more
voluble; why had he never noticed that the younger man intentionally
avoided the topic of his home life, and had done so ever since they'd
met?

Ruarshi was overwhelmingly tired all of a sudden, and felt an almost
irresistible urge to turn around and give the younger man a suffocating

hug. Which would do no good at all.

"Yes, it's possible," he said. "Some of Miriyan's clans are populated by backward, small-minded, cretinous bigots who would make the most provincial European look like Maimonides." He now had a very good idea of what Etienne's childhood must have been like. As a boy he would have been allowed few friends, and during lean times he and his father would have been the first to go hungry. The Doshae clan didn't practice shunning but he knew well enough what it involved. Even during the best of times, there were aspects of life in Miriyan he hated and always had. Did he even *want* to go back?

"Thank you for telling me that, but what I really want to know is why he pair-bonded you."

"Please don't be angry with him. He described what it would involve and asked for my assent. It is wonderful. I would like to keep it when you leave and he has agreed."

This wasn't the response he was hoping for, either, but it seemed that Jonata wasn't the type to bare her soul to a near-stranger. He couldn't very well hold that against her, now could he?

He nodded in reply but was spared the need to continue the conversation by the arrival of a sudden and intense downpour. It lasted for the better part of an hour and left them all out of temper and shivering in its wake. It also left Etienne feverish again.

Ruarshi poured as much of his power as he could spare into the healer, ignoring Davyt's dark looks, and hoped they would arrive soon at Jonata's keep. He was so distracted by what he was doing that he almost missed the flickering presence at the edge of his range, there and gone, of a consciousness that was most definitely Miriyanti. Farther south than the ruined manor house to which the warriors had taken Etienne, and therefore farther south than a Miriyanti had any reason to be if Britt had intended to take the survivors home. As she'd never actually said she meant to do.

Ruarshi rode through the remaining daylight hours in tense silence, concentrating on the woods to their west and finding nothing. When they finally passed through the primitive gatehouse of Jonata's ancestral home in the purple and gray of twilight, it was all he could do to climb the rough wooden stairs to the main floor of the keep, and later he wouldn't even remember ascending another level and being pointed toward a narrow bed in a cramped chamber. He did have enough presence of mind to remove his boots before collapsing onto the mattress,

and he considered this small feat something of a victory as he fell into
sleep.

)O(

Ruarshi awoke to gray stone walls, pale ambient light somehow suggestive of late afternoon, and ravenous hunger. His clothes and hair,
though dry, still felt sticky and rolling onto his back only made the sensation worse. Before he did anything else, he needed to take a bath.

He stood carefully, waiting until a surge of dizziness had passed before sidling his way toward the door and pulling it open. He found
himself looking into a circular central room furnished with two threadbare tapestries, a small wooden table and benches, and a disordered pile
of blankets on the floor in front of the glowing fireplace. A flicker of
magic confirmed that the occupant of the blankets was Karoli, and
that both Davyt and Etienne were asleep in the bedchamber along the
south wall. Others stirred on the floor above, and about a dozen people were moving about the keep's great hall below them.

After a quick visit to the garderobe, Ruarshi went to the table and
helped himself to a mug of buttermilk and generous slices of cold
sausage and cheese. His efforts to keep the noise to a minimum were
apparently unsuccessful, as when he looked up from his third bite he
discovered that Karoli was propped up on an elbow, watching him.

"Still among the living?"

"It looks that way. What time is it?"

"Almost night. Again. You slept through the entire day."

The news wasn't welcome, but Ruarshi had to admit it was what
he'd expected. He'd drained himself much more thoroughly than he
should have. Understanding why he'd done it didn't justify or excuse it.

"What is it you were trying to tell us about Britt?"

"I...." Ruarshi didn't remember mentioning that momentary contact.
"What did I say?"

"That there was at least one Miriyanti out there and someone
should keep watch. You went on afterward but I think you were speaking Welsh."

Ruarshi sighed. "That's all I know. Sorry."

"Out *where?*"

"In the woods. Hours north of here. I seem to recall that the outer
wall of this place is a good twenty feet thick at the base."

"It is."

"Then we should be safe enough."

"I know that," Karoli growled, rising. "You only spotted the one? Could you tell if it was a Naishanti?"

"That's not how it works."

"Then explain it to me."

"Sometimes I can tell the difference between a Miriyanti and a European, sometimes I can't. The same is true for whether it's a man or woman, adult or child."

"It doesn't sound like you have much control over this ability of yours."

"Why would I? It's the result of an injury."

"An injury? Aerik?"

"No." Ruarshi gestured toward the table. "Have you eaten?"

"Yes, I've eaten."

"I have too, but I could eat a little more," Etienne said, slipping through the door of his bedchamber. "Good morning? Good night? Why aren't there any windows in here?"

"Because we'd just be looking at the staircase if there were," Ruarshi replied, cutting the Illyana generous slices of the available fare and handing them over as Etienne lowered himself to sit on the opposite bench, his back to the fire and the Diamyo. "How's the fever?"

"Gone. I feel better than I have in... hours. How about you?"

"I'm well."

Etienne was studying him closely, Ruarshi noticed. "You could use some fattening."

"Couldn't we all."

Karoli made his way to the outer door. "I've been informed that there's a small pocket of rock under the floor of the keep that houses a natural hot spring. We're welcome to bathe in it. I'm going to go visit it now. The women have already come and gone, so you'll be spared any awkward situations if you make your way down later."

"They're staying on the floor above us?" Ruarshi asked.

"Sadly, yes. The Sotari insisted on a segregated sleeping arrangement. Sorry, cub." Karoli left the room and the sound of his boots against the stone staircase dwindled and disappeared.

Ruarshi watched the healer eat in silence for a few minutes, then decided there was no point in delaying the conversation. Quite the opposite, as private time might be hard to come by over the next weeks and months.

"Why didn't you ever say anything about your family?"

The healer froze. "What do you mean?"

"You saw me talking to Jonata yesterday. She told me your clan disapproved of your mother."

"They did."

"Etienne. Do you suppose I don't know what that means?"

The younger man shrugged. "My father was the bright spot. He died before I turned ten. I don't enjoy thinking or talking about the years before I went to the healers' circle, but Jonata needed to know."

"Who had custody of you in the interim?"

"Does it matter? I'm sure you've never met him."

"It matters to me if he didn't treat you decently."

Etienne shook his head and his mouth curved upward in an expression that wasn't quite a smile. "He worked me hard, as one would expect. There was the occasional beating. Nothing so bad that anyone else had to step in."

"When we get back, I could step in."

"And do what, Ruarshi? Knock him around? Would that change anything? Would it make you feel better?"

"It might. I don't think you understand just how intolerant I intend to be of people who hurt you."

"No. I do understand. I've had all the rescuing any one person should need in a lifetime. Nerthu, I never even thanked you, did I?"

"You did, on the ride to the monastery."

"Good. Did I thank Davyt and Karoli, too?"

"Yes."

"Well, that's a relief." Etienne had stopped eating and was staring abstractedly at nothing. "I should not... That should not have gone the way it did."

"I agree. I was careless. If I'd been as cautious as the situation warranted, they would never—"

"That's not what I meant. The fight should have ended differently. I should have been able to get both of us out of there safely."

"Are you saying you should have outfought two Naishanti?" Ruarshi asked gently.

"Not outfought. Evaded. I was good at that, once. You don't need to worry about anything like that happening again. I've decided I don't like being used as bait."

"Meaning what?"

"I'll either move faster next time or make sure they hit me harder."

"Do you really believe I'd rather be burying you than talking to you?"

"No," the healer said, "but it's what I intend to do if we're in that situation again. Your preference doesn't enter into it."

Ruarshi was trying not to give in to his growing anger, and failing. "The man whose throat you cut? I'd already killed him. You just ended his suffering. I hope you're not carrying any guilt on his account."

"If I hadn't been there, you wouldn't have needed to do that. How can you be so dense?"

"Perhaps you'd be so kind as to explain whatever it is I'm missing."

"Karoli told Davyt you can't heal, and Davyt told me. It's pretty clear from that letter of Casimir's that he wanted this to happen. That makes me his accomplice, doesn't it? Or his puppet. Just another tool he can use against you."

"Etienne…" Ruarshi's anger had already faded. "You know this isn't the first time my ability to heal has deserted me. You can't blame yourself for something that happened decades ago, that you had no part in."

"No, but I can take blame where it's warranted for something that happened a few days ago. I don't need to be the weak link in this chain. I won't be. There's nothing else I can do to make this right."

"Some things can never be made right. I'm hoping that my cavalier attitude toward Naishanti, which has resulted in this damage being done to you, doesn't end up falling into that category. I'm sorry, Etienne. I knew better, and I allowed you and Davyt to go out anyway. I was riding along in your head when the warrior hit you. I would have given… quite a lot to have been there in your place."

"Trying to imprison us in that house would never have worked," Etienne said, looking at him with an expression he couldn't begin to read. "I might as well admit to it."

"Admit to what?"

The Illyana leaned over the table, seized the front of Ruarshi's shirt in his fist, and planted a hard kiss on his mouth.

"I won't do that again, but I'll never apologize for it, either. I should have done it months ago." Etienne moved away from the table. "I'm going to fetch some clean clothes and head down to this hot spring. When I woke up earlier I heard rumors of dinner, to be served a little while after sundown. We're all expected to be there."

The healer left the room a few minutes later, fresh clothes bundled in one hand. Ruarshi stared at the door through which he'd gone, both flattered and worried, and not as surprised as he should have been.

### ☽○☾

Ruarshi ended up availing himself of the hot water after everyone else had finished. His son had yet to catch a glimpse of his back and he wanted to maintain that state of affairs for as long as possible, even though he knew it was likely the boy had gotten more than one good look at his scars while still a child. Afterward he pulled on a rumpled white shirt, a pair of black trousers, and his long green healer's coat, all a little the worse for wear. By the time he made it to the great hall where the others were gathered, food was already being brought up from the kitchen.

He hurried to the table, offering hasty apologies to Jonata and the couple who called the keep their home. He was quickly introduced to them and just as quickly forgot their names when he noticed that the only space remaining at the table was located between Etienne and Davyt. He took a deep breath and sat down, being careful not to touch his former apprentice as he did so and deeply unsettled at how aware he suddenly was of the young man's physical presence at his side.

Because he wasn't made of stone he had to concede he was curious, but in a mostly abstract way; he thought of Etienne as a family member and in any case one didn't mess about with one's apprentice even after he'd been promoted. If the Illyana could tell he was flustered, he gave no sign, behaving with perfect normality until Ruarshi was able to calm down and attend to the general conversation. Which was, as he expected, polite and excruciatingly banal and entirely unsuited to taking his mind off his current preoccupation. He spent most of the meal worrying, uselessly and in retrospect, about what Etienne might have gotten up to while they were in Italy, and how badly that could have ended. Even more alarming was the thought that he might have done something similar in Mainz. Ruarshi had legal standing to protect the healer from the local authorities, but the outraged prejudices of the mob were another matter.

Damn him, anyway. He didn't need anything else to fret about.

As they rose from the table, Etienne put a hand on his shoulder. "It's okay, Ruarshi. It's okay. Nothing has changed."

"And it won't. You know this?"

"*Of course* I know it. Are you disappointed in me?"

"Sweet Nerthu, no." For the first time, Ruarshi considered the situation from Etienne's point of view. Certainly the healer must have known he wouldn't react with distaste, but if so, why the question?

And Ruarshi had been careful not to touch him, for reasons that could just possibly have been misinterpreted.

He looped an arm around the back of Etienne's neck and pulled him closer. "I'm distracted, not disappointed. There are some kinds of prejudice I have never understood; this is one. I would only ask you to be careful." As Ruarshi pulled away from the younger man to follow the others toward the stairs, he saw the tension leave Etienne's shoulders, and a little later watched him rub a hand over his face when he thought no one was looking.

By unspoken agreement—or perhaps it had been spoken and Ruarshi had simply missed it—all the Miriyanti crowded into the chamber one level up from the hall and found places to sit, either at the table or on the blankets next to the sputtering fire. Etienne disappeared into his bedchamber and Ruarshi took up a position next to his closed door, determined that the healer would remain undisturbed until he reemerged in his own time.

)O(

"How long do we need to stay here?"

That was Karoli, and the question was meant for him. "Two weeks," Ruarshi replied.

"That long?" the Diamyo asked.

"Yes."

"All right." Karoli turned to the Naishanti. "Had you heard anything from the others before you left Niklashausen?"

"Just a note from Valentin, saying he'd be there as soon as he could get away," Atali replied. "Which, knowing him, only means he doesn't want it to look like he's too eager to follow your orders."

"It wasn't an order. Nothing at all from Klas or Alexandra?"

The warriors shook their heads.

"That's not reassuring."

"We don't need to go back there," Saoirse said. "We shouldn't. We can leave a message asking the others to meet up with us somewhere else. There are too many people, too much idleness, too much... fanaticism. It's as unsafe a group as I've ever been a part of."

"Oh, I don't know," Atali said. "It might be interesting to see how it all ends."

"We're done currying favor with Casimir," Elin remarked. "Why should we care how it ends?"

"I'm in no rush to get back to the camp, either," Karoli said, "but leaving a message that the others may or may not get seems a bit careless to me."

"There may be safety in numbers," Jonata said. "Ruarshi believes the other warriors are still here. Might it not be wise to stay amongst a larger group, where Miriyanti strangers will be immediately noticed? These others have Ruarshi and Davyt's coloring, correct?"

"We don't know that except in Britt's case, but it's likely," Atali said.

"What's your opinion?" Karoli was looking at Davyt, who seemed surprised to be asked.

"It depends on how many Europeans we're willing to endanger," he said. "If we were to be attacked by the others while staying here, or while holed up in another isolated spot, there's only a limited amount of damage they could do. If they came for us while we were surrounded by hundreds of people who had no idea what was happening…"

Karoli turned to Ruarshi. "Do you agree?"

Ruarshi shook his head. "We cannot leave Britt's people out there. If they are out there. I may have been mistaken the other day."

"What would you have us do?" the Diamyo asked sharply.

Ruarshi returned his regard, certain the man had understood his intention perfectly well. "They have four warriors. There are five of us. I don't like being hunted."

"They receive their instructions from a Seer," Saoirse said. "Might that not give them an advantage we can't overcome?"

"It might," Ruarshi conceded, "but if we get close to them, I'll know it. That's our advantage."

"Unless they've somehow already accounted for that," Etienne said, emerging from his bedroom and taking in the tableau with a quick glance. "We don't know what weapons they have. What if they've brought guns?"

"In this weather they'll have a hard time keeping their powder dry," Atali said.

Etienne shrugged. "My point stands. There was a moment the other night when they could have killed us both. They'd obviously been ordered not to. When are those orders going to change?"

"I'm with you," Saoirse said, nodding to Ruarshi. "We can't have them trailing us. We'd be looking over our shoulders all the way to Miriyan."

"Atali? Elin?" Karoli asked, and was answered with a pair of nods.

"So we go out tomorrow, aiming for the last spot where you sensed one of them," the Diamyo continued, meeting Ruarshi's eyes, "and you follow our lead. We're used to working together. You okay with that?"

"Yes."

Etienne's expression was pensive. "You'd better set the ground rules now. Ruarshi, you know you're not going out there to talk to them?"

Of course he knew that. He was determinedly not thinking about it, but he knew it. "I don't see any other way to handle this. They're a threat to all of us."

"They're a potential threat that you have to treat as mortal enemies. No chatting, not even with their healer."

"It's not necessary that we harm their healer."

"Can you tell the difference from a distance? What if their healer is armed? That's not impossible."

"Peace, Etienne. If we find them it will be as you say."

"Good," Karoli said, "and as much as I'd like to take you cubs with us, you'll have to stay here."

"Naturally." That was Etienne at his blandest. Ruarshi didn't trust it, but since he'd be aware of any attempt on the part of the Illyana to follow them, he decided he wasn't going to worry about it.

"Afterward any survivors will head to the Drummer's camp to pick up our stragglers, and then back to Miriyan we'll go. Probably killing people right and left the entire journey."

Karoli was looking at Etienne as he spoke. The healer responded with a flat, unwavering stare that Ruarshi appreciated. He appreciated it even more when the Diamyo continued.

"Any purification rituals you need to carry out beforehand, Nerthi? Immersion in still waters? Self-flagellation? A wild orgy?"

"If so, that's my own business and you're not invited."

Karoli laughed. Elin tilted her head at him and said, "Not all of us like what the world has made of us. It's your great good fortune that you're more than content to be an ass."

The Diamyo rolled his eyes and Saoirse tried unsuccessfully to smother a chuckle.

"Still waters sound like a good idea to me," Atali said, standing up from the table and stretching. "If I'm going to get killed tomorrow I will do so in a state of physical cleanliness. I'm not particular so if any of you care to join me, feel free."

"I'm with her," Saoirse said, following her out of the room. Elin trailed them wordlessly a heartbeat later.

Karoli sat up straighter. "The Valkyries aren't wrong. A wash before a fight is part of *our* ritual. You may not know this, Ruarshi, but warriors are superstitious. If you're one of us for long enough, you'll end up just as bad. I'm going with them. It will be no wild orgy, and you're all welcome to come."

With that he was gone as well, and Ruarshi was in danger of liking him again. Even Etienne looked mollified. No one stood to follow, though, and a few minutes later a timid young man appeared at the outer door to offer them two large jugs of mulled wine.

# Visitors

The next day dawned gray and blustery, and a cold rain started to fall while everyone was still picking at the breakfast that had been brought up from the kitchen. Karoli slammed through the door into the bedchamber Ruarshi had been using, yanked aside the shutter to take a look out the tiny window, and muttered, "Fuck this," before returning to the central chamber and throwing himself back down onto the bench next to Etienne.

The Illyana looked at him, grinning, but continued chewing. Ruarshi was feeling less tactful. "Don't tell me you're going to let a little bit of rain get in your way?"

Karoli eyed him. "I'm absolutely going to let it get in the way. The others are welcome to come attack us if that's their inclination."

"How would you go about it?" Ruarshi asked.

"Go about what?"

"Attacking this place."

"I'd dress up as a peasant who'd come to speak with the lord of the manor," Karoli replied without hesitation, "and when no one was looking I'd poison the well."

Davyt stared at the Diamyo. Etienne considered the plan and said, "Seems risky. How could you be sure you'd killed everyone?"

"I couldn't, not right away, but eliminating the only source of clean water would force everyone out. Murdering them on the road would be easier and safer than murdering them in the keep. People tend to hide in situations like that, and it can be difficult to find them all. Especially the children."

"Please stop talking, Karoli." Atali had appeared in the doorway. She looked irritated. "We finally have access to healers again and you spend your time trying to convince them we're not worth the trouble? Just admit to Etienne what you told us last night and be done with it."

Karoli was clearly aggravated by this but Ruarshi thought he hid it well. "And what would that be?"

She grinned at him. "Shall I quote it for you?"

"You shall not." Karoli shrugged and addressed the empty air in front of Etienne's nose. "I may have conceded that you were a better fighter than average, for an Illyana. It is not common for a healer to knock a warrior over with a chair."

Etienne's expression went blank before shifting toward embarrassment. "Uh, thank you?"

"Not necessary," the Diamyo said stiffly. "If you're really interested in fighting people with furniture, there are a few things I could show you. Some other time. I plan to spend the day resting and possibly getting drunk. Who's our watcher this round?" That last was addressed to Atali.

"Elin. So we're postponing the wild goose chase?"

Saoirse came in behind her. "We are?" Her glance swept around the room before coming to rest on Ruarshi.

"Seems likely," he said. "I can do some searching from here. Is there access to the roof of the keep from farther up?" He assumed there was but hadn't gotten around to doing any exploring yet.

"There's a ladder," Saoirse said. "It's not very sturdy. The hatch at the top is padlocked."

"You can't mean to sit up there in the rain," Etienne said.

"I don't, but the higher vantage point might be useful if it clears up."

"I'm sure we can find something better to do than drink," Atali said.

Karoli shifted to straddle the bench and leaned back against the wall. "Such as?"

"Literally anything else."

"I disagree. And since when have you objected to indolence?"

"Never, as you know, but this is the first time we might have to face Naishanti together."

"If you intend that we should practice, we'll have to go to the hall to do it," Karoli said. "We'll scare our hosts and won't get much benefit out of it." Atali's smile widened and he shook his head. "For fuck's sake, Atali. No."

"The people here don't know us. They're probably curious. We should give them something to talk about."

Ruarshi had been keeping an eye on Atali, and he was beginning to understand Elin's warning. "I'd prefer that we not leave them with stories about how a group of Miriyanti guests abused Jonata's hospitality by wrecking her home. Even if it means enduring a day or two of boredom."

"You could watch, as well. You might learn something."

"I'm sure I would."

"If you're that desperate for something to do," Elin said, slipping into the room to stand next to her sister, "you could take a walk to the nearest village market and buy some ribbons."

Atali rolled her eyes. "It's been months since we've drilled properly and you know it. How about this: if it stops raining, we put in an hour of practice out in the bailey? The healers can tend to anyone who faints."

Karoli considered the suggestion and nodded once. "*If* the rain stops and *if* we're all agreed that it's what we want to do. And we use only defensive magic."

Ruarshi watched the Naishanti accede to this decision and wondered where he would fit into the warriors' power hierarchy, before realizing that he didn't care at all.

The Diamyo glanced over at him. "Suppose we do find ourselves in a fight with the others, Cousin. What would you need from us?"

Ruarshi had been worrying at the question for some time, so he had an answer ready. "Shields. Distractions. Speed. Break their bows, break their guns if they have any. Don't waste time on their swords. The more quickly we close with them, the less opportunity they'll have to hurt us. It would also make things much simpler if I were in front."

"We just take a run at them?" Saoirse asked.

"Yes."

"It does have the virtue of simplicity," Karoli said. "I'm less concerned about them shooting at you than I am about them tying you up in shields and dropping you where you stand. They know better than to let you get near them."

"I'd be obliged if you'd help me shatter any shields they send my way."

"If we all wore hats," Elin said, "they wouldn't know which one of us to target. Not right away."

"Maybe I could borrow one?" Ruarshi said, glancing at Etienne. "Nothing I brought from Mainz is intended to cover the hair."

"I'll ask Jonata," the Illyana replied. "They probably have something here you could use."

"So that's settled," Karoli said. "With the proper headgear and an hour's practice, I'm sure we'll be unstoppable."

☽〇☾

Watery spring sunlight broke through the clouds late that afternoon as a short procession of Miriyanti and interested Europeans made their way down the stairs from the keep and into the bailey. The warriors chose a relatively untrodden patch of ground near the southeastern curve of the wall for their practice while everyone else settled in to watch. Ruarshi, Davyt, Etienne, and Jonata leaned against an empty wagon a short distance away and waited for them to start.

At first there was nothing to see, though the air began to hum softly to Miriyanti senses as each of the warriors wove a shield. Only Karoli's was comparable in strength to the kind of shield an experienced healer could put together, but then they began to overlap and tie the weaves together until they had created a wall of power that no dagger, no matter how well thrown, would ever be able to penetrate. Afterward they lined up, drew their swords, and began flowing through a series of different formations and stances that had to be rehearsed, because no one was giving any signals to the others regarding what to do next...

Ruarshi watched them a little longer and then closed his eyes. There was just enough occasional roughness to the transitions between one position and another that he finally realized they were in fact exchanging information somehow and he was simply missing it. When he figured it out his eyes shot open again.

They were using their intertwined shields to communicate. Saoirse had just told them, using some obscure pattern of vibrations through the weave, that they needed to pivot to their left and drop into a crouch, and now Elin was evidently warning them about danger coming from above. They shifted their shield, angling it toward the top of the castle wall, while at the same time rising to their feet and lifting their swords to parry an attack from their imaginary opponents. They continued like this for a good while before bringing the exercise to a close with all of them standing in a straight line, swords sheathed, facing out into the bailey. They were breathing quickly but no one was winded.

Ruarshi smiled in appreciation. "Did you notice what they were doing with that shield?"

Davyt nodded. "I think I might have worked out the code for 'turn left' and 'turn right,' but that's about it."

"If they ever get tired of being warriors, they could switch to burglary for a living," Etienne said. "The first person in would be the only one barking their shins."

Karoli approached them. "This kind of thing isn't useful during an actual battle. If more than one of us tries to talk to the others at once, we end up turning each other's signals into gibberish. Now we're going to do something else." He jerked his chin in Ruarshi's direction. "Come stand over here."

As the afternoon deepened toward dusk, Ruarshi and the warriors learned that he'd have to stand within ten feet of them to enjoy the protection of their shield if they were in close formation, but that he could extend his forward distance to almost fifty feet if they spread out. They might be able to push this range even farther; they were constrained in their experimentation by the size of the bailey. They had all expected a result of this nature, given the tendency of shields to become weaker as their degree of curvature increased. Only novice healers and warriors tried cocooning themselves in weaves.

Ruarshi was gratified to discover that the European part of their audience had found other things to do while they were working. As spectacles went, he was sure the latter part of that one had been quite dull.

"Did you learn what you needed to know?" Jonata asked.

"Some of it," Karoli said. "Which is good, because I'm not doing that again. Is there any chance we could get some hot soup? Or hot anything?"

"Of course. All of you come with me to the kitchen. And Etienne was asking me about hats?"

## )O(

Karoli did end up getting slightly drunk that evening, along with Saoirse and Atali. Ruarshi matched their pace for the first two glasses of wine before the initial glimmerings of a headache had him bowing out of their company, along with both Illyana. He spent the next several hours tossing restlessly in his bed until he heard Karoli return to their floor and the entire keep descended into silence.

Some time later he rolled onto his back and sighed into the darkness. As he knew all too well, his choices were to remain lying there in boredom until he finally fell asleep or the sun came up, or to wander the castle grounds like a ghost and run the risk of startling people. Either way the next day was likely to be a grim slog of muddled thinking and sore bones that would make him feel like he was three times his actual age. He wasn't looking forward to it.

Ruarshi sat up in his bed, intending to visit the garderobe before deciding what to do. As he moved toward the door, a flicker of movement in his mind's eye caught his attention: outside the castle walls to the north, someone else was awake. A Miriyanti.

He waited, breathless, and checked again.

He wasn't mistaken.

Ruarshi threw on his pants, his warmest shirt, his green coat, and his boots. Upon leaving his room he saw that the fire in the central chamber had burned down to one skeletal log, flickering dimly, but it provided enough light for him to make out Karoli's sleeping form. He bent down and set a hand on the man's shoulder. The warrior woke at once and sat up so rapidly that Ruarshi had to take a step back to avoid a collision.

"They're here," he said. "Get dressed and go downstairs."

"What are they doing?"

"I don't know." He moved on to the healers' room. Pushing open the door, he said, "Get up. Follow Karoli. I'll tell you more when I know more." Then, to the Diamyo again, "I'll warn your Valkyries. Rouse everyone."

He was up the stairs and knocking on the women's door moments later. When Atali opened it, he repeated the same warning he'd given Karoli. Once he was sure the message had penetrated the remnants of her inebriation, he took the remaining steps to the landing where the ladder to the roof was located. He continued around the curve of the wall until the light spilling through the doorway below illuminated a small door on its north side. Unless he was very much mistaken, it led to the short bridge that would take him to the wall walk.

This door was also locked, but the wood from which it was made was so old and so swollen by recent rains that he was able to split it down the middle with minimal effort. He shoved the remains out of his way and ran across the partially covered bridge to the outer wall, where he leaned into an embrasure and looked down. The moon was up but obscured by clouds, and all he could see were the indistinct dark shapes of trees and the low gleam of standing water in a small clearing. Another Miriyanti had joined the first seemingly out of nowhere. A third appeared shortly afterward.

He wondered if there were tunnels under the castle that Jonata hadn't told them about. Certainly not, but it was either that or someone on Casimir's side had learned of a way to appear out of thin air, which was absurd…

A series of muffled but tremendous cracks rent the stillness and Ruarshi whirled, horrified to see that the ground on the east side of the keep had started to sink. The ominous grinding of stone against stone followed as the enormous tower began to tilt. The sound vibrated in his chest, making it difficult to breathe.

Footsteps and a low curse brought his attention back around as Elin tumbled off the bridge and onto the walk next to him. He spared her a nod and raced south, relying on her to follow. When he reached the gatehouse door he blasted it off its hinges and stumbled down the stairway to ground level.

Before turning his attention to the main castle doors, he paused to glance again at the keep. It was listing even further as the sodden ground beneath it continued to collapse. The stairs to the main hall had twisted and broken beneath the building's weight, and several dark figures were clinging to it. Some of the keep's inhabitants had already reached the ground and were gesturing at those above.

He spun back toward the gate to the accompaniment of a renewed rumbling and terrified screams. If he were a healer there'd be reason for him to stay, but he wasn't. The most useful thing he could do was waiting for him outside the castle.

The bar on the doors was short and not heavy, intended to deter passersby rather than invaders. Elin had already freed it from its brackets and lowered it to the ground.

"Where are we going?" she asked, her voice barely loud enough to be heard over the now constant growl of shifting stone.

"The warriors are on the north side of the wall. I need your help with shields."

Some small part of Ruarshi's mind recognized the fact that he wasn't thinking all that clearly. An even smaller part was willing to acknowledge the reason for that, but he had to ignore it because it was shouting at him to go back, as though he had anything meaningful to contribute to a rescue effort. He was evidently making some sense, because Elin shoved the gate open and stepped back so he could precede her through it.

He ran west and then north, having no particular desire to be crushed by the east wall when the keep fell into it. Before plunging into the shadow of the trees, he scooped up two handfuls of mud and coated his face and hair as well as he could. He hoped it would make him harder to see.

Ruarshi felt Elin's shield take shape in front of him as he considered whether to go after the most distant or the nearest Miriyanti first. He didn't want to end up chasing the warriors through the forest, but neither did he want to risk losing his chance at the two standing closest to him. Once his opponents realized they weren't alone the situation could become complicated.

He slowed down and took a deep breath. He could hear their voices. He would have to silence both of them at the same time. Could he?

He could. Killing them was almost effortless.

The rumbling from the castle had become a roar, drowning out whatever noise the Miriyanti made as they fell. Ruarshi held his position until the ground stopped trembling beneath him, then focused on his next adversary. This one was standing a little to his left and about twenty feet farther out. He started cautiously in that direction, Elin a silent presence at his side. She—he was fairly sure this one was a woman—died quietly, but one of the two remaining Miriyanti must have seen or heard something.

"Britt?" a voice asked sharply.

Had he just killed Britt? Did it matter?

They knew he was there now, so there was no purpose to be served by continuing to hide. He ran straight for the man who'd spoken and killed him as he was pivoting to flee. His magic was precise and instantly lethal, much better than the clumsy blows he'd landed against Etienne's abductors.

The last one was too far away for him to reach and had already started running. He darted through the trees after his quarry and Elin kept pace with him. He appreciated that even as he wondered if he really needed a shield at this point. The Miriyanti in front of him was terrified and he didn't think there was any chance that the man would turn to fight him.

Ruarshi's foot collided with an unseen object on the forest floor and he fell forward, pain shooting upward from his ankle. He shoved himself up onto his knees but realized very quickly that his odds of catching the warrior had just dropped to zero. He'd have to finish his task off from here.

The distance between them was too great. He prepared a weave anyway and reached toward his prey with all the power left at his disposal, wishing it were possible to wrench the man backward and make him stand still.

His magic caught at the edge of something he couldn't see and pulled it aside. He released it, disoriented, and the Miriyanti gave a startled cry and collapsed like a puppet whose strings had been cut. In the silence that followed, Ruarshi was able to reassure himself that the man was definitely dead though he had no idea what had caused it. He allowed his weave to dissipate into the air and counted off the number of his victims to make absolutely sure he was finished. Five. That's all there had been, right? Just five.

He lost consciousness.

## )O(

Elin was crouched over him in the dim moonlight when Ruarshi woke.

"We need to go back," she said.

He started to rise and she offered him a hand to help him up. Once on his feet, he tottered sideways and caught himself against a tree. He'd injured his ankle badly enough that he shouldn't be putting any weight on it. Oddly, it didn't hurt.

"One moment."

He limped toward the body of the last Miriyanti who had died. He felt distinctly strange. He didn't think there was anything wrong with his memory, and yet what he recalled of the final seconds of the fight couldn't be accurate because it made no sense.

The corpse was lying in deep shadow, and it took a short while for his eyes to adjust. When they did he had cause to wish they hadn't.

The man's head was missing. A sharp sword could inflict that kind of wound, but there was nothing else on earth that could account for it as far as he knew. The hair on the back of his neck began to rise and he stepped away from the body.

Elin had followed him and was looking queasily at the dead man.

"I'm sorry. If I'd believed... You shouldn't have had to see that."

"You shouldn't have had to do that. Let's get back to the castle and find out who's still alive."

Ruarshi nodded and set off after her. His ankle still didn't hurt, although he could feel it throbbing against his boot, and his perception of time was slipping in unexpected ways. One moment he was slogging his way back through the forest and the next he was heading around the south side of the castle, with nothing in between.

The survivors were gathered in the clearing there, far enough away
from what remained of the walls that a further collapse wouldn't endanger them. As they neared he found Davyt first, healing Karoli. The
Diamyo had two breaks in his lower right leg but was in no real danger.
Davyt, damn the boy, had a broken collarbone. Had no one ever
warned him against trying to heal someone while dealing with an un-
treated injury of his own?

Etienne was also there, working on Saoirse's broken ribs and damaged hip joint. His former apprentice had a bruised shoulder and side
but was otherwise unharmed. Atali was sitting some distance from all
of them, her injuries limited to a pair of sprained wrists. Jonata was
well, and their hosts, and their hosts' children. Two people he only
vaguely recognized were holding torches near a still form that had been
covered by a blanket, and a group of three suffering from a handful of
scrapes and bruises huddled at the edge of the firelight.

All the damage he saw could be accounted for by a fall. There were
no crush injuries, with the possible exception of whatever had killed
the dead man. Which meant they'd almost all had time to get out and
Casimir's trap, set however many years or decades ago, had largely
failed.

Ruarshi realized that he'd lost another indeterminate span of time
and that he was on his knees with tears tracing ragged tracks through
the dried mud on his face. He scrubbed at his cheeks with the heel of
one hand but made no effort to stop crying. He knew it would be a
good while yet before he'd be able to.

### ☽○☾

He awakened to find Karoli scowling at him, Davyt cutting at his boot,
and a hint of light in the eastern sky. He was very cold.

He tried to sit up but a hand on his shoulder restrained him. He followed the arm up and discovered that it belonged to Etienne, who
seemed taken aback when Ruarshi met his eyes.

"Sotar's nuts, Ruarshi, what…"

Now Davyt was staring at him, too. "Your eyes are bloodshot. Really bloodshot. There's no white at all; everything's red."

"That must look terrible," Ruarshi said.

"Did one of them try to strangle you?" Etienne asked.

"No."

"Elin told me you killed all of them." That was Karoli.

"Yes," Ruarshi replied, not looking at the Diamyo. He was more in-terested in what Davyt was doing with his foot.

"Leave it, Son. It doesn't hurt. I am relieved to see you got Etienne to heal your collarbone. I'll save the lecture for some other time."

"I'll leave it when I'm ready to. You were walking on this."

That observation didn't seem to call for comment, so Ruarshi let his eyes drift shut. The day was much brighter when he opened them again, and he was fairly certain he was in the wagon he'd been leaning against the day before. His son and former apprentice were in there with him, deeply asleep, and the other two had to be Saoirse and Karoli. Somewhere above them Elin and Atali were talking quietly. That was all right, then. There was nothing that needed seeing to. He drifted off once more.

# Nor Rises the Moon

"We're here." Davyt had a hand on his arm and was shaking him gently. "Jonata's house in Mainz. We need to go inside."

"Mainz?" Ruarshi mumbled, struggling to get his legs untangled from the folds of a dark woolen blanket. He grimaced at it, unable to remember if it had been there when he'd awoken earlier. "Is that wise?"

"Wiser than camping out in a muddy field or overwhelming a village," his son replied, but Ruarshi hardly heard him. The events of the night before had started replaying themselves in his mind's eye, drowning him in dread so intense that he thought he might be sick.

"We need to bury those Miriyanti," he said. "The local authorities will have to take an interest in what happened, and we can't be tied to—"

"It's already done, Father." Davyt helped him out the back of the wagon and propelled him firmly toward the front door of a large, unfamiliar house. "Elin and Atali took care of it this morning. They put them far enough from the mouth of the tunnel that they won't be discovered."

Ruarshi had finally woken up sufficiently to realize what he'd just said, out loud on a public street. No one was there besides Jonata's family and their little group, and they'd been speaking in Miriyanti, but that hardly excused his outburst. He clamped his jaw shut and followed his son through the door, down a hall, and into a warm room where a large amount of food was being set out on a table.

He was both very hungry and reluctant to try putting anything on his stomach. Instead he sought out a chair in a shadowy corner of the room and was just about to lower himself into it when he caught a glimpse of the front of his coat. He ran the fingers of his right hand through his hair, touched his face. He was filthy. There was no possibility he was going to sit on that nice chair in his current state.

Ruarshi knew he was close to breaking down again. This would embarrass everyone and accomplish nothing, so he considered smashing things instead.

Elin interrupted his musings before they could go any further. "Drink this." She handed him a cup of something and he took a sniff. Cider. He thought that might be safe and essayed a small sip.

"Thank you."

"Now sit down. No one cares about the dirt."

He shook his head and she sighed. "There might or might not be a bath available tonight. There are a lot of us and the household didn't receive much advance notice that we were coming. So unless you're ready to stand there all night, you're going to have to make the best of what's available, when it's available. Sit."

Ruarshi smiled. He knew what she was doing. He'd done the same often enough with seriously injured patients, when they awoke to a world that was permanently changed from the one they'd been living in before. He placed the cider on a small end table and sat, noticing only then that his ankle had finally begun to hurt. It seemed that Davyt had thoroughly demolished his right boot, though someone had thoughtfully taken the time to tie it back into some semblance of order with a strip of cloth.

"Eat when you're ready. Not until then. I mean it."

Elin patted him on the shoulder and headed toward the table. This was probably the first food that any of them had been offered all day. Ruarshi was glad to see that Etienne and his son were filling their plates, along with most of the others. Jonata was keeping an eye on the situation but had touched nothing, and Saoirse was standing just inside the doorway with her arms crossed.

He thought he should say something to all of them. Then again, he couldn't guarantee that this place wouldn't go sliding into a hole in the earth like the last one had, so how reassuring could he honestly be?

There was an arm wrapped loosely across his chest and a fall of black hair hanging over his face, obscuring his vision. This unusual circumstance turned out to have Etienne as its cause: the Illyana was leaning over the back of the chair and giving him a hug. Ruarshi didn't know if he'd slipped through time again or just fallen asleep.

Etienne sat down next to him and resumed eating. "Leave a note next time before you go running off like that."

"Sorry. I had no paper."

"Excuses."

"How many did we lose?"

The healer swallowed, paused, and then went back to his meal. "Just the one you saw. That was kind of his own fault. He stopped to look back as the keep went over while the rest of us were running. A stone —well, several stones—hit him. We should talk about this tomorrow. Or never."

"I agree."

Davyt drifted over and Ruarshi checked the boy's collarbone again. Etienne had done a good job, not that he'd been expecting anything less.

"Was there any trouble getting into the city?" Ruarshi asked.

"No. A little bit of bribery and two wagon loads of exhausted, wounded people eased the process quite nicely," Etienne said. "The story of the disaster didn't hurt, either. I think the guards at the gate were reluctant to get too close to us once they heard what had happened."

"Were we recognized?"

"Jonata was," Davyt replied. "As for the rest of us, I'm not sure."

"That's encouraging." Ruarshi thought he might try eating something now. There was a loaf of bread on the table that looked edible, with a bowl of butter beside it. He stood. "I'll be right back."

Saoirse intercepted him on the way across the room, somewhat to his surprise. He hadn't exchanged more than a handful of words with her since they'd met.

"Thank you for keeping my sister safe."

He shook his head. "It was the other way around."

"I had been... concerned that you would try to negotiate with them and endanger us all."

Ruarshi looked at her, nonplussed. Had they not all been endangered, to quite a ridiculous degree, by his feud with Casimir? But he knew what she was saying, and had no idea whether to be relieved or offended by her opinion of him.

"Talking to them never even crossed my mind. I thought they had killed my son."

"After the tower fell, I couldn't find Elin and felt much the same way. Which was why I wanted to say something to you."

Ruarshi had no notion of how to respond to that, so he didn't. Instead he bowed to her and turned back toward the table, where he helped himself to some bread and cold meat without paying a great deal of attention to what he was doing. By the time he was seated again he was certain he wanted none of it but he attempted to eat anyway. Etienne and Davyt were keeping an eye on him, just as he was with them, and he didn't want to give them any additional cause to worry.

$$☽◯☾$$

Space considerations saw the men in their party allotted two rooms between the four of them, and without need for discussion Ruarshi, Davyt, and Etienne took one while Karoli disappeared into the other. The bed wasn't made to accommodate three but they all squeezed in anyway, unwilling to let much space come between them until their nerves had settled. None of them had cleaned up yet and none of them cared. That was a concern that could be addressed later, after the sun had come up and they got back to living their lives as normally as they could.

Late the following day, having eaten, bathed, and dressed in borrowed but freshly laundered clothes that were quite a bit too big for him, Ruarshi sat with the other Miriyanti in the first-floor room that had hosted them the night before. The Europeans had tactfully withdrawn to the front part of the house for their own discussions, or possibly just to escape the pall that had settled over the foreigners. Ruarshi couldn't blame them either way.

"We need to leave here," Etienne said, with a nod that encompassed his fellow Illyana, Ruarshi, and Karoli. "For a few days our wounded and pathetic state will keep the neighbors from talking, but much longer than that and they'll convince themselves that Jonata's hosting an orgy. We have to be gone by then."

"I rented my room at The Piper for a full month," Karoli said. "We can stay there. Once we've all stopped limping and groaning I intend for us to head to Niklashausen, pick up our strays, and leave."

That seemed like a reasonable plan. Ruarshi turned his attention to the Diamyo's injured leg. Karoli was going to be limping for some time yet, he thought; it was harder to predict how long he'd be groaning, as that had more to do with the man's disposition than the pain itself. He had a feeling that Karoli would try for stoicism but would end up struggling with bad temper instead, which would not make him particularly good company.

Time started to slip sideways again as it had twice before that day, but in this instance Ruarshi was able to recognize the peculiar inner hush that preceded the phenomenon and prepare himself for it. Gently he reached out and arrested the slide, using intent alone rather than a weave, and then paused to make sure that the internal pressure had subsided before releasing his breath and turning his attention back to the conversation. Fortunately it seemed he hadn't been distracted for very long. Unfortunately he was going to have to tell the Illyana about this little problem one day soon if it continued to trouble him.

"... coats sent to my tailor," Karoli was saying. "None of us would even be allowed into The Piper dressed as we are now. Nor do I have any desire to be mistaken for a peasant. You don't either, *marchid*. Trust me on this."

"I wasn't objecting to the clothes," Etienne said mildly. "I was objecting to you calling Midnight a nag."

"Our horses were saved?" Ruarshi asked. He'd assumed they were lost, for what he now understood was no good reason; the stables at Jonata's family home had been situated along the wall to the west of the keep.

"Yes," Davyt said, looking at him critically, and Ruarshi realized his question had come just a little bit too late in the conversation to make sense.

"Sorry," he said, "I lost the thread for a minute."

"They're stabled nearby," Elin said, "none the worse for wear."

"Unless your tailor works miracles, we'll be waiting for weeks yet," Atali remarked.

"He was already putting together a few new outfits for me," Karoli said. "I asked him to modify what he already has to fit these three. We should be ready to go in a few days." The warrior noticed the appalled expression on Etienne's face and smirked. Ruarshi's own reaction was much the same as the Illyana's. He remembered how Karoli had been dressed when he'd shown up at the frozen pond for a friendly game of *jhot*.

"If we're going to be traveling in these clothes, the tailor will need to tone it down."

The warrior sighed. "I know what's required, Cousin."

"We'll be ready whenever you are," Saoirse said. "When we get to Niklashausen, Karoli and I will set out for the Drummer's camp while the rest of you stay in town. We'll either find the others or leave them a message."

Ruarshi was already shaking his head. "You two are the most severely injured. If you have no objections, Elin, you and I should go.
You've also met the other Naishanti, I assume?"

"Yes. I'll recognize them."

"Fine," Karoli said, "but I'm going, too." When Ruarshi opened his
mouth to object, the warrior held up his scarred palm. "Pair bond, remember?"

Saoirse's face settled into discontented lines but Ruarshi spoke before she could. "Your hip will need rest after that many miles in the
saddle."

She accepted that argument but was clearly unhappy about it. Ruarshi looked from her to the unoccupied couch against the room's far
wall in a pointed manner. She was already in pain as a result of sitting
up in that chair for too long and he thought she should probably lie
down. She ignored him.

Ruarshi glanced toward the Illyana. Neither of them appeared satisfied with the plan, but if they had complaints they'd evidently decided
to air them at some other time.

Karoli rose and began pouring wine into glasses. The women stood
as well and arranged themselves in a half-circle as he handed them out.
Ruarshi, unsure of what he was seeing, remained seated until the Diamyo looked over at him. "All of you were part of it," he said, by way
of explanation. "It'll be bad luck if you don't participate."

Still mystified, Ruarshi rose and helped to complete the circle, the
two Illyana trailing him. When Karoli offered him a glass he accepted
it.

The warriors bowed their heads and started reciting a poem or a
prayer. The form of the language they were using was so old that he
was unable to pick out many of the words. He recognized the term for
battle and the name of the war god Tir, but the meaning of the whole
was largely lost on him. When it was over the warriors drank their wine
and Ruarshi did his best to follow suit.

The Diamyo smiled at them. "And now we get drunk."

)O(

Three days of enforced inactivity had passed since they'd all woken up
with hangovers, little had changed beyond a slight improvement in the
condition of the wounded, and Ruarshi thought it probable that he
would die of impatience sometime in the next several hours if he

didn't get out of this room. Even the musicians sitting in the corner by the fire, playing one sprightly spring tune after another at the behest of one of Jonata's well-meaning friends, weren't helping. He checked to be sure the other Miriyanti were safely occupied and then headed up to the top floor of the house.

If anyone showed up unexpectedly and asked what he was doing there, he intended to tell them he was going to bed early. Sleep was the last thing on his mind just at present, however. He was still puzzled by the way the fight had ended the other night, he needed to explore the issue, and he felt he had waited long enough. It was a harmless obsession in comparison to the other matter vying for his attention, after all. There was no possibility, now or at any time in the future, that he was going to spend time dwelling on what he had done before that strange door swung open onto nothing. To do so would be pointless.

He had already decided that the door wasn't something he'd just stumbled onto in the forest, fortuitously positioned to inflict fatal injuries upon his enemies. Therefore it had to be something that he had called into existence, and if he could do it under those conditions, recreating the event in a quiet hallway shouldn't be much of a problem. His memory of how he'd accomplished it was a bit hazy, but he thought with a little work he could pin it down.

Ruarshi crossed his arms and stared down the dark hallway. The window at the end admitted faint moonlight through the thin white curtain hanging there, and he reached toward that piece of fabric with his mind, wondering if he could just peel it back...

There it was. A door had opened in the middle of the hall and he approached it with caution. No light burned beyond its threshold, yet he could still see it perfectly well. In some way he could not explain it seemed to his eyes to be illuminating the entire floor. Yes, it was; he could now make out the doorknob to his bedroom, a detail that had previously been lost in shadow. The air coming through it was somewhat cooler than that in the house, but wasn't the kind of freezing draft he had inexplicably been expecting.

Ruarshi wondered what he would see if he stepped through it. The temptation to do so was strong, but he remembered the body outside Jonata's keep and extended his left hand across the threshold instead.

*That* was cold. His instinct hadn't been as far off as he'd thought. He withdrew his hand and looked at his fingers, rubbing them together. They tingled a bit but were otherwise fine. He took a step away from the door and was suddenly flung backwards and against the wall, pinned in place with an iron hand against his shoulder.

Elin had arrived in the hallway and was using her magic to keep him immobile while she regarded the doorway warily. Eventually she looked back at him.

"You didn't step through?"

"No."

"Thank Nerthu. Get rid of it, please."

He did so and waited for her to release him, which she did a moment later.

"I knew I should have talked to you before this. I didn't because I wasn't sure that you would listen to me."

"What do you know about it?"

"That's a doorway to the Halls."

"The Halls." He hadn't thought Elin the type to believe in myth, yet here they were. "I suppose the Great Dragon, Mother of the Miriyanti, is waiting there to meet me?"

"There is no dragon. Everything you've heard about the Halls is allegory. Give me a minute."

She disappeared down the stairs and Ruarshi allowed himself to slide down the wall until he was sitting on the floor. His hand had started to hurt. He made a fist with it but this did nothing to lessen the pain. It still looked fine.

When Elin returned she seemed calmer, with a wry smile turning up the corner of her mouth. She was carrying a candle in one hand and a small mirror in the other.

"If I hadn't believed there were Seers on both sides of this disagreement before, I do now. Two Annorae just happen to meet up with the first real Nerthi that Miriyan has produced in over ten generations. That's quite a coincidence."

Ruarshi thought about that. "Pretend that I didn't understand anything you just said, and start from there."

She laughed and sat down next to him. "There's a very old poem that begins, 'Nor do the stars shine there, nor rises the moon; nor shall fire light your way.' It's describing what you'll find on the other side of that door. Nerthii are shamans, Ruarshi. You can walk the Halls. Seers can only access them with magic and mirrors. Quit scoffing. I'm telling you the truth. The people you've dealt with over the years haven't known what the truth is, which is why the explanations they've offered you have never made sense."

Ruarshi just shook his head. He still wasn't following her but he was trying hard to give her the benefit of the doubt. He liked Elin and would prefer it if she weren't actually out of her mind.

"You've been told that warriors dislike Nerthii because you're more skilled with violence than they are, though you're not one of them. If this were the real problem, the enclave would simply insist on raising all children who show proficiency in both the healers' and warriors' arts. And they would be allowed to, because the circle doesn't like you, either. You taint their holy healing abilities with destructive magic, which makes you impure in their eyes. The healers' excuse for washing their hands of you is the more believable of the two, though one wonders why they would reject out of hand the only type of talent that allows someone to lend strength to others, or to heal himself. Neither group has ever been averse to power."

This was a line of reasoning he could understand, though he didn't like it at all. "What are you telling me? That the Seers thought of the Nerthii as rivals and wiped them out, and then kept them from coming back for thousands of years by nurturing the prejudices of our leadership? People have memories, Elin. And I stumbled onto… this," he gestured toward the spot where the doorway had appeared, "by accident."

"I don't know much about your recent history, just what Karoli has told us, but I suspect Casimir and his people have intervened on more than one occasion to try to prevent you from discovering what you can do. If any of the Nerthii in Miriyan are aware of this, it will only be because they, too, slipped from his control. As to your other point, yes, people have memories. The Annorae are a small, insular clan. We maintain our own library. Removing certain books and scrolls from our possession must not have been a priority for the Seers at any point in their history, but perhaps it should have been. Though they may have been concerned that any attempt to seize those writings would only draw attention to the history that they're trying to keep hidden."

"So you've read some of these books and scrolls."

"Yes. One other thing." She gestured for him to take the candle and mirror from her, which he did. Reluctantly.

"Look at your eyes."

He glanced at his reflection in the mirror. His eyes were normal, the whites having returned to their usual hue two days earlier. "What? They're no different than they've ever been."

"Really? Hold the candle closer to your face and look again."

Oh, Nerthu. The irises had gone dark red, dark enough that they

couldn't be distinguished from black in low light but red enough that
the change would be obvious in daylight. "I look like a demon."

"You look like a shaman. I can answer some of your questions, but
my mother would be more help to you. You should visit us once we get
back to Miriyan."

Ruarshi thought of Lorion, Mara, and Aurel, the only other Nerthii
with whom he was personally acquainted. The likelihood that his earlier
notion had been correct, that Casimir intended to sell them all out to
the traditionalists, seemed higher than ever. He felt a sudden urgency to
be gone and couldn't help wondering if they were already dead.

"My good-brother is in danger."

"Lorion? He may be. Or he may not. One of our oldest words for
'shaman' translates to 'master of life and death.' Or 'mistress,' actually,
since most shamans are women. But unless the old initiation methods
have been reconstituted while we've been away, which I judge to be *very*
unlikely, none of them are opening that door without killing someone
first."

Ruarshi stared at her. "*That's* why that happened?"

Elin shrugged, as though this were the most obvious deduction in
the world. "Of course. The earliest shamans killed enemies in battle or
doubled as clan executioners. If the situation were desperate and a clan
felt it needed a shaman right away, a volunteer would be asked to step
forward to act as a sacrifice. Later they began to substitute animals for
humans and turned the entire procedure into a ritual that was generally
followed by a clan feast. Some elders opposed animal sacrifice right up
until the end because they thought it led to the creation of weak
shamans. They may have been right."

"Wait. To retain access to 'the Halls' it's necessary for a shaman to
continue killing people? Or animals?"

"No. Once you open your first door that part of the process is
done. You are as powerful a shaman as you'll ever be. Now you need to
be taught how to use whatever power is available to you, which is why
you should spend time with my clan."

Ruarshi's thoughts edged dangerously close to consideration of the
trail of corpses he'd left behind in the forest before he forced them
away again.

"How long is my hand going to hurt?"

She grabbed him by the wrist and proceeded to inspect his fingers.
The jostling made his entire arm throb and he hissed at her.

"Idiot," she concluded, though she set his arm back down more gently than she'd lifted it. "You'll be fine but don't play around with that place until you know more about it. Agreed?"

"Agreed."

They sat in silence for a while, neither of them eager to end the conversation. Finally Elin spoke.

"Something else you should know about the Halls. When you open that door, many people can sense its presence even though they have no idea what it is. It tends to frighten people. Saoirse and I seem to be mostly immune but the others aren't. Jonata's friends and the musicians have left. The others are still here but jittery and Saoirse's calming them down. How much do you want us to tell them?"

"If you'd explain it to Karoli and Atali, I'd appreciate it. I'll take care of my son and apprentice."

☽○☾

Predictably, once Ruarshi had finished explaining the situation the next day, Etienne insisted on positioning him next to a window and taking a good close look at his eyes. Davyt absorbed the news in thoughtful silence. Karoli's tailor had arrived with a delivery earlier that morning and they were getting ready to go downstairs to say their farewells to Jonata and her household. Ruarshi had chosen this moment to talk to them for exactly that reason. He didn't want the discussion to go on for long because there wasn't much to say and the information, interesting though it was, had no practical ramifications as of yet.

Ruarshi was pleased with his outfit, although this wasn't something he intended to convey to Karoli. The clothes were soft, nicely made, and cut well for horse-riding, his in a pleasant forest green that he would continue to wear by preference until the day he died and to hell with the Miriyanti inclination to color code their more powerful magic users by occupation. Etienne was in a subdued blue and Davyt in light gray.

He left the bedroom and went to knock on Karoli's door, where they had a short conference on the subject of Jonata's wrecked ancestral home. They had decided some time earlier to offer her help to rebuild, perhaps a nice manor house to replace the drafty centuries-old castle she had inherited, and planned to make funds available to her in town should she ever need them. Both Karoli and Ruarshi lived frugal enough lives that they'd been able to parlay their rare and sought-after skills into small fortunes over the course of several decades. Karoli made no secret of the fact that he'd liberally supplemented his more usual sources of income with the spoils of banditry, most likely to see if Ruarshi would say anything about it, but he let it pass. He was more interested in the logistics of highway robbery than he was in attempting to defend European wealth distribution in any case.

A short while later Karoli, Davyt, and Ruarshi were gathered in a restless group in the entryway to Jonata's home, waiting for Etienne to finish his conversation with the lady of the house. The Illyana still declined to discuss his relationship with her and Ruarshi had stopped pressing him about it. He didn't know what sort of emotional damage Etienne's impending separation from her would do, but decided the matter was none of his business unless the healer chose to make it so. In the meantime he should probably mention the financial arrangement they'd made with Jonata sooner rather than later. It might make Etienne feel marginally better about the timing of their departure.

A knock on the door interrupted Ruarshi's musings and he stepped back to allow one of Jonata's servants to squeeze by and answer it. He was startled to see Helene standing on the front step with a diminutive serving girl as chaperone until he recalled that Bebel's wife was in fact a close friend of Jonata's, and the entire reason that Etienne had met her in the first place.

Ruarshi was glad to see her regardless. He returned her smile and swept her a deep bow.

"Frau Bebel. It has been some time. You look well." And she did, which wasn't something Ruarshi would have taken for granted when it came to any member of Doctor Bebel's household.

"As do you, *Tai* Nerthi. I am delighted to run into you again," she said, stepping through the doorway and chivvying her companion along with a light hand on her forearm. The girl did not look pleased to see them was only too happy to accompany Jonata's man farther into the house. "I didn't believe I would have the opportunity. When I came by earlier I was told you were resting. I am sure there was much healing to be done after the catastrophe at Jonata's home."

Ruarshi chose not to correct her misapprehension, instead moving on to introductions. Once those had been completed, Helene asked him to follow her into the small parlor that opened off the front hallway. He did so after gesturing a request to his companions to give him a moment. Davyt dipped his head in assent and Karoli began tapping his foot impatiently.

When they could talk without being overheard, Helene said bluntly,

"Thank you for Wolter."

Ruarshi nodded. "Do you have any recent news of him?"

"I have not inquired too closely but I hear he's doing well. That friend of yours who recommended the placement knew what he was about. And since we're speaking of your associates, I should let you know that some other of your friends here in town have brought Friedrich to understand the importance of philanthropy, and assisting one's less fortunate neighbors. It is a transformation that is unlikely to endure for long but it is doing him a world of good while it lasts."

Ruarshi smiled, but the expression faded as he spoke. "I regret to tell you that the book you passed on to us was most likely destroyed. I believe Etienne read it but I never had the chance." Which was of course a lie. He'd had plenty of time to get through it if he'd wanted to.

"I am sorry to hear that. Perhaps you will find another copy during your travels."

"It's possible. I appreciate what you did for Etienne. Once I learned of his relationship with Jonata, I was concerned that he would suffer for it. That he has not must in large part be credited to your efforts."

"I was glad to assist. Etienne is a good boy, and I think he has made her happy. It looks as though you are leaving?"

"Soon, yes. It's warm enough to head north now."

"Our city will be poorer for your absence. Here, you must take this with you." Helene unclasped a thin silver bracelet from her wrist and held it out to him. "The medal, it depicts Saint Christopher. I will be more content knowing you have it." She grasped his hand and pressed the bracelet into it, folding his fingers over it. "You may not refuse."

Ruarshi was touched by her concern and he wished he'd had the opportunity to get to know her better. "Thank you."

# Exodus

Three mornings after they'd moved into The Piper, the Valkyries showed up at the door to their room wearing new riding dresses and ready to be gone. Ruarshi tried to argue with Saoirse about the timing —it would be a week or more before he'd be comfortable with the idea of her sitting on a horse all day—but she insisted she would be fine and eventually he surrendered.

They'd had no trouble while staying in Mainz, the local authorities either not having had sufficient time to decide what to do about them or simply uninterested in acknowledging their continued existence as long as they did nothing else to draw attention to themselves. Nor did they run into any problems on the road. They'd agreed to travel in easy stages and by early evening of their second day out they'd come to a minor crossroads. The unexpectedly large inn there showed signs of extensive recent construction and was at least half full, a festive crowd of what Ruarshi thought were most likely pilgrims on their way to join the Drummer.

He dismounted near the front entrance and had started to head inside when he felt the presence of a Miriyanti among the group gathered near an open fire just to the east. He returned to his horse and rested one hand on his saddle, suddenly short of breath. When he thought he'd picked out the individual in question, he seized a startled Karoli by the arm and propelled him in that direction.

He spoke into the warrior's ear as they walked. "The man with the dark brown hair and short beard, standing next to the one turning the spit. Do you know him?"

Karoli understood at once and slowed, squinting. Then he smiled. "It's Klas. Come with me."

Ruarshi very nearly stumbled, his relief so complete that he actually felt dizzy as they crossed the well-trodden ground toward the knot of people waiting for their turn at a slice of roasted meat.

Klas spotted them while they were still a short distance away and came bounding forward to greet them.

"Karoli!" What began with clasped forearms morphed quickly into a bear hug. The Diamyo seemed uncomfortable and Ruarshi thought he should probably be amused.

"This is my cousin, Ruarshi," Karoli said once he'd extricated himself. "He doesn't always look that blank. I believe he was preparing himself to kill you."

That earned him a befuddled look from the Naishanti, who rallied a moment later and held out his hand. Ruarshi took it.

"Greetings, Cousin Ruarshi."

The others caught up to them then and more hugging ensued. Ruarshi withdrew and took a seat on a nearby bench, learning in short order that Klas had set out the day before to try to track Karoli down while the remaining two Miriyanti, Alexandra and Valentin, stayed behind in a tent on the outskirts of Niklashausen. The town itself had been completely overrun by Hans' followers and more were arriving every day.

They were well into their chatter before Klas thought to mention that a Dominican friar was present at the inn, and to explain that he had in fact been following the man. Rumor had it that he'd mentioned Karoli's name on more than one occasion, so it had seemed sensible to Klas to keep tabs on the friar as part of his search for his fellow Miriyanti.

Karoli glanced over at Ruarshi, grimacing eloquently, and the former healer pushed himself to his feet and returned to the inn. Once there he negotiated with the owner for two adjacent rooms at the end of the hall on the ground floor. The innkeeper tried to insist that they take rooms upstairs, which was evidently where he preferred to accommodate presumed nobles, but Ruarshi refused. It was likely the Dominican and his party would be staying on the second floor and he had no desire to make it even more probable than it already was that they would run into the man.

Together with Etienne and Davyt he saw to the stabling of their horses and the transfer of their limited baggage to their rooms. By the time that task was accomplished twilight had set in. They went back outside where they found Saoirse sitting alone near the fire. The rowdy crowd that had been gathered there earlier had mostly drifted off, with the exception of a handful of very drunk individuals who were acting out scenes from the lives of various saints, with heavy emphasis on their methods of martyrdom. He wasn't sure what the man currently rolling around on the ground was meant to be dying of and had no intention of finding out.

"Where are the others?" Etienne asked, signaling the young man by the outdoor tap for drinks as he settled onto the bench next to the Naishanti.

"Sprenger's room."

Ruarshi had started to sit down but at that he jumped back to his feet, glancing with some alarm toward the inn. "Doing what?"

"Bleeding them."

They struggled to process that information. "What?" Davyt asked eventually.

"It sounds dreadful, I know, but it's the safest method we've found for taking care of possible troublemakers. Hitting people over the head is faster, but they sometimes die. Though to be fair," she added reluctantly, "we've had one person die of this, too."

Their beer arrived and Ruarshi sat on the bench across from Saoirse, still watching the inn. "So you bleed them until they pass out and then... tie them up? Gag them? No, you'd have to gag them first or they'd be shouting the entire time... I had hoped we could simply avoid them."

"None of us much likes leaving things to chance. I'm sorry if I sounded flip earlier. They're doing this on my behalf, since I'm too delicate to ride farther tonight, and I'm not helping."

"What do you do with all the blood?" Etienne asked.

Ruarshi shot him a sour look but Saoirse answered readily enough. "If we really dislike the people we're dealing with, we tell them we're going to drink it. It's not often that we have bowls available, though. Usually we soak it up with cloth. Either way it ends up in the privy afterward. If you're worrying about them dying later of infection, don't. We soak the cuts with the strongest alcohol we can find and splash the rest on their clothes. This has the additional virtue of making them look like raving drunks if they do slip out of their bonds before we're safely away."

"And how often does this strategy go wrong?" Ruarshi asked.

"Just the once, so far," she replied, "which is why we favor it."

Ruarshi took a sip of beer, wondering if this was what keeping company with warriors was going to be like. He wasn't irritated at Karoli and the others, not exactly. He was no more eager to spend time talking to a meddlesome friar than anyone else, and this course of action suggested that the Diamyo considered the man more dangerous than Ruarshi would have guessed, a judgment call he had no interest in challenging. He would have appreciated some warning of their plans beforehand, however. If a hue and cry had gone up before he'd known what was happening, he could have reacted in all the wrong ways.

He considered intruding on the assault while it was still in progress but decided against it. The scene upstairs was likely to be both messy and ridiculous, and an ill-timed knock on the door might cause knives to slip, resulting in a general massacre.

Ruarshi took another drink. It was possible he was angrier about this than he was admitting to himself. Although Saoirse made a good point about blows to the head leading to unintended consequences, he wasn't sure he'd ever heard of a more harebrained way of dealing with one's adversaries. Then again, if he'd been abandoned in Europe with no reliable access to poisons and no healer, and he didn't want to kill people unnecessarily but had to protect himself and the other members of his group...

He wasn't sure he'd have come up with anything better. The easiest solution would always be to put distance between oneself and one's enemies, but as in this case that wasn't always practical. Was avoiding an outrage of this sort worth what it would cost Saoirse, and Karoli for that matter, in extra pain if they were to continue down the road this evening? He wasn't the best person to answer that question. Nor was he in charge of the warriors' actions.

Nor did he want to be.

He drank and waited along with the others until the rest of their party came wandering nonchalantly out of the inn and they all ate dinner. No one looked alarmed so he assumed everything had gone well and listened with half an ear to the warriors' reminiscences on past European misadventures. By the time the meal was over he was more than ready to go to bed, but he couldn't resist pulling Karoli aside as they made their way to their rooms.

"It would have been easier to put them to sleep," he said, keeping his voice low even though they were speaking Miriyanti. "In the future let's try that instead."

Karoli shook his head. "What you don't understand, Cousin, is that every once in a while I enjoy watching my enemies bleed. If we're going to travel together, you're going to have to get used to that. As we're still getting used to you."

They had reached the door to the men's bedroom, and as they went inside the Diamyo turned his attention to the others. "The spot closest to the fire is mine, because my fucking leg hurts. The rest of you are free to fight amongst yourselves for what's left."

## )O(

Their group was subdued as they rode away from the crossroads the following morning, heading south and east for the final leg of the journey to Niklashausen. Ruarshi hadn't slept well, concerned over the possibility that the friar and his men would be discovered, but they had left the inn without incident and now the sun was peeking over the horizon in a wash of yellow and pink, melting the last vestiges of frost from the new grass by the side of the road.

As the day wore on and they grew closer to their goal, they overtook an ever-increasing number of small groups of peasants, composed variously of the religiously inspired, the curious, and those just along for the trip. Much of the conversation that Ruarshi overheard had less to do with the Drummer's spiritual opinions than his economic ones; evidently the idea that God wanted the mass of mankind to live in poverty while the lucky few reveled in idleness and luxury had never caught on to the extent the nobility might have preferred. Ruarshi grimaced, wondering not for the first time what was wrong with Europeans in general. Miriyanti were raised to understand that equality was the natural state of sentient beings, and he had never quite figured out why it was that so many of his southern neighbors brought up their children to believe exactly the opposite, even against their own interests.

By mid-afternoon the press of people had become so thick that their progress slowed to a crawl. They moved off the road and into the sparse stand of trees that lined its route, where they ate a cold lunch and waited for the crowd to inch its way past. In spite of the crush no disagreements broke out, and the festive atmosphere that had prevailed at the inn persisted even here.

"What's going to happen to these people?" Davyt asked. He sounded as though he wasn't eager to hear the answer.

"Nothing good," Ruarshi said.

"Best case scenario, they'll be chased off," Etienne said. "Worst case, they'll be killed. At the crucial moment, their fates will be decided on

the basis of how fast they can run." The younger Illyana stared at him
flatly and he shrugged. "It's true. Either that, or the local nobility starts
giving away their jewels and brocades. You tell me which you think is
more likely."

Davyt turned to Klas. "How far are we from your friends?"

As it turned out, less than ten miles separated them from the Naishanti they sought but it took the rest of the day to reach their tent.
When they did, Klas staggered inside without ceremony.

"Thank Sotar you're here. It's madness out there. I'd like to suggest
that we pack up now and head directly west. I'd prefer getting lost in
the wilderness to dealing with that road again. Where's Valentin?"

The woman inside the tent, presumably Alexandra, was regarding
the Miriyanti gathered outside with a pensive air. She had black hair
threaded with gray and was easily twice Atali's age. Her eyes lingered on
Ruarshi when her gaze met his.

"Out getting us something to eat. I see you found the others."

Klas was already flat on his back on a blanket. "They found me.
Mayhem ensued. Now we're here and it would be better if we were
somewhere else."

"Soon. Mayhem? There was trouble?" This question was directed
toward Saoirse.

"None to speak of. Is it always like this now?"

"The number of pilgrims coming in, you mean? It's picked up over
the past few days, but even before that you'd have been justified in giving this place a name and starting in on building a city wall. You're all
welcome to come in and take a seat. No one will touch your horses.
Valentin hasn't been quiet about our origins and our neighbors are
leery of us."

The warriors went inside but Ruarshi stayed where he was, surveying the plain to the south. He was no expert at estimating numbers but
if he had to guess he'd say the camp held at least two thousand people.
The amount of food required to sustain a group of that size had to be
incredible, and he supposed that the local farmers were pleased by the
chance to earn some extra income. That was assuming they could protect their fields from being trampled by all the foot traffic or, more
likely, from being raided by people who'd arrived with nothing to barter
and insufficient copper. He could smell something spicy cooking
nearby and a constant stream of pilgrims came and went from the
Tauber River at their backs.

He'd had an idea. He needed to talk to Elin about it, but there was no particular hurry and he could wait to get her attention until the combination of food and alcohol left most of their party dozing in what was sure to be an uncomfortable heap inside the tent.

## ) O (

Elin was unable to answer his questions and expressed some reservations about his plan, most of which had already occurred to him, but she seemed to think it was worth a try. The last light of the long spring evening saw Ruarshi, the two Illyana, Elin, and Saoirse standing up to their calves in the startlingly cold water of the river, fishing out as many pebbles as they could find. Some of the pilgrims watched them curiously for a while, but most went on about their business without giving them a second glance.

When Ruarshi thought they'd gathered enough he handed his collection off to his son and went looking for a quiet spot. After five minutes of walking he decided his criteria were too stringent and he'd have to settle for an area that wasn't overrun, or constantly under threat of being overrun, by the Drummer's people and eventually he found what he was looking for. It was a small pocket of space at the river's edge enclosed by three trees with branches low and profuse enough to discourage idle intrusion. Even so, he would need Elin there in case someone happened along at an inopportune time.

Back at the tent the rest of the Miriyanti had been told about what he intended and were absorbing the information with apparent perplexity, on the part of the Naishanti he'd just met, and tolerance on the part of Karoli and Atali. In truth Atali seemed less tolerant than simply resigned to the idea, but by the time they'd hashed out the details everyone had agreed to assist. Even if their cooperation was only meant to speed things along in the morning and see them out of the camp more quickly, he was surprised and gratified by the unanimity.

As they settled down to sleep that night, Valentin elbowed him in the ribs, less gently than he might have. He was unusually big for a Miriyanti and clearly chafed under Karoli's leadership, though he was pragmatic enough to realize there was nothing he could do to change that particular situation. For all his size, he'd never be as strong as the Diamyo.

"Is Elin having pipe dreams? Tell me she's having pipe dreams. You're no shaman and this whole notion is the result of eating the wrong sort of mushrooms. Right?"

"We'll all find out in a few hours," Ruarshi replied. Valentin snorted in dissatisfaction but rolled over without further protest and went to sleep. It took Ruarshi quite some time to nod off, as he was unaccustomed to resting among a jumble of other people as though they were a litter of puppies, but after a while he managed it and when he next opened his eyes his internal clock warned him it was time to get up though no light yet shone in the sky.

He rose, quietly waking the others and then waiting at the tent's entrance until Elin joined him. Feeling his way along in the dim moonlight, he led her to the area next to the riverbank that he'd identified the evening before. Once equipped with a sturdy branch broken off one of the trees hemming them in, he hooked the bag of pebbles from one end to make sure the stick could support the weight. It could. He set it down on the ground at his feet, backed up against the tree farthest from the river's edge, and opened a doorway. Lifting the sack, he approached it carefully and deposited the pebbles on the other side of the threshold.

The stirring among those who'd bedded down nearest to his current position began almost immediately. Low cries of uncertain alarm spread out in ever-widening rings that soon jumped the river and made their way into the main body of the camp. Still Ruarshi held the doorway open, determined that this effort should work if what he was attempting was possible at all. Several minutes later Elin hissed at him, urgently requesting that he retrieve the bag and let the door swing shut. People had started to move about and she was concerned that someone would stumble onto them.

Ruarshi did as she asked, using the stick once again to bring the stones back through the doorway and then grabbing the bag in his gloved hands, and they headed back the way they'd come. The others were ready for them, or as ready as they were likely to be; several of them flinched when Elin pushed the tent flap back and they stepped inside. Their reaction confirmed that whatever it was about the doorway that caused such fear could in fact be transferred to other objects, and Ruarshi allowed himself to feel the first faint glimmerings of hope.

Pausing only to make sure that everyone had covered their hands, Ruarshi divvied up the stones among the Miriyanti and they left the tent, each of them heading to the sector of the camp they'd been assigned. They were all moving quickly, whether due to the morning chill or a desire to be shed of the pebbles with as much speed as possible he couldn't say.

When he reached what he judged to be his patch of ground, Ruarshi began salting the earth with the stones. He took his time and pressed them into the ground with the heel of his boot, as he didn't want careless feet kicking them aside later. A growing disturbance among the pilgrims followed the path of his footsteps, and he was encouraged to see a similar uproar spreading outward from various other points about the camp. Now they really did have to hurry, as the reaction among the Drummer's people would be decidedly negative, and potentially even lethal, if they were able to trace the cause of their disquiet to the actions of the Miriyanti.

Ruarshi let his last stone fall and turned back toward the north, keeping his head down and threading his way around the occasional knots of pilgrims gathering in the early morning light. They were anxious but not panicked, and some had begun striking their tents and readying their wagons.

His path converged with Etienne's well before they'd reached their campsite, and they walked together as the sky continued to brighten.

"If this works, I'm going to be disappointed," the Illyana said.

"Why?"

"I bet Davyt that it wouldn't. Not because I lack faith in you, mind, but I'm a pessimist by nature and this struck me as too good to be true."

"No one has left the camp yet. Let's wait and see what develops."

Yet it soon became clear that an exodus was well and truly underway. They stood in the placid company of Sophie and Midnight, who had not been bothered in the slightest by the pebbles, and looked out over the camp as the rest of the conspirators returned to the tent and the Drummer's followers abandoned him in droves. The Miriyanti ate an unhurried breakfast even though most of them looked as ready to bolt as the pilgrims did, and Ruarshi wondered how far away they'd need to be before the stones' effect wore off. He made a mental note to keep an eye on the others and come up with an estimate of the distance when the time came.

When they left they went straight north across the river, eschewing the busy roadways. They hadn't gone far before Valentin reined in next to Ruarshi.

"I guess I was wrong about the mushrooms. And about you. I don't know if that little stunt of ours will end up making a difference or not but I'm glad we tried. Think the drummer boy will give up and go home?"

Karoli was riding close enough to overhear their conversation. "No."

Valentin shrugged. "That's too bad."

The Diamyo snorted.

"What kind of odds do you give us on getting home in one piece?" Valentin asked.

"Those," Karoli said without hesitation, "are much higher."

Ruarshi meant to see to that personally. He nodded in agreement and the big Naishanti turned his face once more toward the north, evidently satisfied with that answer.

# Nor Shall Fire Light Your Way

# Homecoming

*Believe me when I tell you I know exactly what's about to happen, because I made sure it would. The alternatives were worse. You'll understand eventually.*

Ruarshi woke with Seggita's last words to him echoing in his head. He sat up in his tiny bunk on the Hanseatic cog they'd boarded in Lübeck several days before and swung his legs over the side. The touch of his bare feet against the oak planking steadied him against the slight roll of the ship. He sat listening to the darkness. Judging by the regularity of his bunkmates' breathing, they were all still asleep. That was good. The journey overland from Mainz had been more difficult than they'd anticipated due to a heavy late-season snowstorm, and his traveling companions needed all the rest they could get.

If the winds remained favorable, they'd be in Tomir in less than a week.

For just under half of their party, that would mark the end of their travels. Klas, Alexandra, Atali, and Valentin would go straight from the harbor to their Tomiran clan circles, in the hope that they'd be safely back with their families before Casimir or his allies could interfere. The rest of their group would stop by the Maelae circle before heading out to Ruarshi's clan home. If all went well, they would proceed from there to the far northern territory of the Annorae.

Ruarshi was not altogether satisfied with this plan, even though he'd helped come up with it. Their initial idea had involved putting in to shore south of Tomir and traveling stealthily overland to their respective clan homes, but they'd had to abandon that notion for two reasons: they couldn't find a ship's captain willing to take time out of their schedules for the detour, and Miriyan's small navy was showing an unusual level of interest in trading vessels this season. Their captain had insisted the Miriyanti ships would both notice and investigate any unexpected behavior on the part of their small convoy, and as this was exactly the sort of attention they wanted to avoid, Ruarshi had seen no point in arguing about it further. The fact that a stop in Tomir could be turned to good purpose had also helped reconcile him to the change in strategy. Now he was left to wait and hope that they would all reach their destinations without being taken into custody, a possibility he could not rule out.

He stood and edged sideways toward the door, intending to step out on deck for a breath of fresh air. He couldn't remember the dream that had ended with Seggita's final words, for which he was grateful, but what they implied was disturbing enough on its own. He hadn't thought about that night in years. He wished he weren't thinking about it now, but it seemed his unconscious mind had other ideas.

Ruarshi left the cabin and went down the short hallway of the sterncastle. A moment later he emerged on deck. He could see clearly in spite of the late hour, as it was now early June and true night had abandoned them in favor of a silvery twilight that would brighten further as they continued north. A crewman nodded to him as he made his way to the starboard rail, where he stood to watch the coast of Finland slide slowly past in the distance.

Elin had almost certainly been wrong when she'd asserted that he was the first Miriyanti shaman to come along in ten generations. Seggita must have been one, too. The man had stepped across that strange threshold one fateful day and resolved upon the time and place of his own death, because to his way of thinking *the alternatives were worse*. Seers didn't speak with that level of confidence. Their discourse and decisions hinged on probabilities, on images dimly perceived through ripples in water, and they knew better than anyone that they couldn't ensure any particular outcome. When it came right down to it, they rolled the dice like everyone else.

Seggita had been referring to something very different. Ruarshi shivered. He'd been trying hard not to get ahead of himself ever since his fraught conversation with Elin, as fretting about what the future might hold would be pointless until he knew what a shaman could and couldn't do. And if he didn't like the answers he received to his many, many questions, he was free to turn his back on the role whenever he chose. Abjuring such a responsibility wouldn't come easily to him, but it would be vastly preferable to putting himself in a position to decide the fates of others. He was no Norn. His own life he could do with as he wished; no one else's would he touch except by conventional means. He wanted to resolve upon that now. The temptation to make a different decision could arise at any time and he needed to be ready for it. Otherwise he risked becoming a more dangerous and arrogant version of Casimir, an outcome he would gladly go to great lengths to avoid.

He considered backing out of his commitment and telling Elin that he wasn't coming to her clan home to study after all. Then he sighed, because he knew himself better than that. He'd never be able to let the situation rest until he'd looked at it from all sides and probably made a series of grave mistakes on top of it. That had been the story of his entire adult life, distilled down to its essentials.

That last thought had come to him in Wil's voice. He could almost see the Welshman shaking his head in that tolerant manner he'd had. His *pir* had done the best he could with him, and it wasn't the man's fault that Ruarshi had ended up so far from the kind of life he'd intended to lead.

It was a night for ghosts, it seemed.

He turned and leaned back against the ship's rail, crossing his arms and wondering if he should go see his clan's Skeltari once he got home. He wasn't sure how much good a blood oath would really do if he felt he had a compelling reason to break it, but he couldn't reject the notion of taking such a step out of hand. He'd keep it in the back of his mind, he supposed, continue talking to Elin to find out what more she knew, and come to a decision later. And if he dithered too long, he could always consult the Skeltari at the Annorae clan home. They almost certainly had one, as it was thought to be tremendous bad luck for a clan to leave the position unoccupied.

Karoli emerged from the sterncastle's door and came toward him, still rubbing sleep from his eyes. "Something going on?"

"Not as far as I can tell."

"Couldn't sleep?"

"I had a dream I didn't like. I plan on going back to bed."

"I don't much care for this mode of travel," the warrior said. "Nothing to do but sit on your ass and hope the captain doesn't run us aground." Karoli was staring intently at the Finnish shoreline. Ruarshi turned to look as well before realizing there was nothing untoward to see there and the man was simply homesick. Finland hadn't yet been visible when they'd all gone to bed the night before, and this was the first the warrior had seen of it in close to a century.

Ruarshi went back to watching the cog's sail billow in the breeze and pretended he hadn't noticed anything out of the ordinary.

"I am not looking forward to the turnips," Karoli said.

"But think of all the berries."

"Hmm. Yes. Those are good. I can't even remember what *keth* tastes like."

"It's better than beer."

"I am aware. The crushing disappointment I felt the first time I drank it stands out very vividly among my memories of arriving in Europe."

"Sorry I woke you."

"Don't worry about it. I don't like my berth any better than you do yours."

They lapsed into a silence that was companionable rather than awkward. It still felt strange to Ruarshi that he had a Diamyo as a close ally, and was even relying on the man to help keep his son and former apprentice safe while they traveled together. That was an unanticipated development in a year that had seen more than its share of those.

Karoli moved off toward the bow of the ship and Ruarshi turned back toward the coast, watching as a line of dark trees gave way to rockier ground. He thought he'd probably calmed down sufficiently to get some more sleep and was ready to go back inside when the warrior returned, carrying a small pouch in one hand.

"I'd almost forgotten I had this," he said, and tossed it over the side.

Ruarshi regarded the spot where it had vanished beneath the waves. "What was it?"

"*Schaal.* What was left of it. I pulled some out of the bag that healer was carrying and kept it close to hand, but there's no chance I'm getting caught with it in Miriyan."

"I had no idea you'd kept any."

"Yes, well. It wasn't something you needed to know. The stuff is even more poisonous to Europeans than it is to us and I hate to waste resources."

"Did you use it on anyone when I wasn't looking?" The question wasn't entirely casual.

"No. I'd have offered you and the youngsters a pinch if I thought it would do any good."

Now that was an obscure and alarming statement, far too obscure and alarming for this hour of the morning. "What?" Ruarshi asked.

"*Schaal* doesn't taste like anything. Exceptionally weak honey, maybe? I can't teach you how to recognize it if it shows up in your food or drink, because nothing about the flavor gives it away."

"Casimir won't try that again. Not within Miriyan itself, for the same reason you just threw that overboard. He'd be hounded out of the country."

Karoli made a noncommittal sound in reply. "There's something else I should mention."

"Yes?"

"You needn't concern yourself about being arrested. Many things could happen when we go ashore, but that isn't one of them."

"I see."

"I doubt you do," the warrior responded. "Between the seven of us, we could level the Council Hall. We've discussed it."

Ruarshi had no good memories involving that particular building. "You would risk killing anyone being held in the cells below. And servants are quartered there."

Karoli chuckled. "That's all you've got to say about it?"

"Begin as you mean to continue," Ruarshi replied, as mildly as he could. He wanted to say more but decided against it.

The Diamyo didn't respond right away, but the mischief gradually faded from his expression and Ruarshi felt the tension in his body ease a fraction.

"In our defense, we exiles do tend to daydream a lot. But we're not the fools you seem to think we are."

Now the man was just needling him. "You have every right to defend yourselves. I've never said otherwise. I would ask only that you don't do anything I'd have to take notice of."

Karoli smiled and clapped him on the shoulder.

"There they are."

"There *what* are?"

"Your claws, Cousin. I needed to be sure you hadn't done away with them in a fit of poorly timed guilt. If we come up against opposition, I can't have you showing them your belly."

Ruarshi was no longer anywhere near sleep. "A few minutes ago I was thinking of you as an ally," he said, deeply irked. "Have I been too optimistic?"

"Our little war band is a wolf with two heads, Cousin. This can't continue. I'm trying to figure out whether to yield or not."

Ruarshi just stared at the other man, completely flummoxed and still having trouble controlling his irritation. "This is how warriors handle power struggles? I would have thought you'd be more inclined to beat each other bloody and then share a drink afterward."

"That's one way to do it," Karoli said. "A wise woman once told me that a true leader is the one who isn't even aware that a challenge to their authority is possible. Did you really not understand that this was coming?"

"No. Nor do I think it's necessary. I expect all of us to cooperate. It's very simple."

"We'll cooperate, Cousin. Until we part ways or you lose your nerve. Good night."

The warrior disappeared back into the sterncastle, leaving Ruarshi alone to deal with the memory of dead Miriyanti that Karoli's words had called to mind. Guilt wasn't the problem. What he felt in its stead was horror at his methods and the human wreckage they'd left behind, and disappointment in himself for not having prevented the entire disaster from unfolding as it had. Though how exactly he could have accomplished that, he wasn't sure.

He *was* sure that he needed to act more wisely in the future. If he could.

Ruarshi tried to settle more comfortably against a crate of Italian brocade down in the ship's lower hold, only to discover that no configuration of back, arms, and legs was any better than his initial position. He sighed in aggravation and looked over at the dim outline of his son, who appeared to be crouching on his haunches.

"How are you doing over there?"

"This isn't too bad," Davyt replied, struggling to get a small tarp arranged to cover his head. "It could smell a lot worse than it does."

The youngster made a good point. If the hold had been packed with ambergris or tallow, Ruarshi would have insisted upon finding a different place to conceal himself.

"How long will we have to stay down here?" his son asked.

"Probably not long. At a guess, the harbor officials assigned to search inbound ships will have been given the extra duty without any very clear explanation of why the work is necessary. I don't believe they'll go about the task with particular zeal."

"I'm concerned that Karoli will start something with them."

"He won't." The Diamyo, along with the other former exiles and Etienne, had remained on deck as the small boat from Tomir had swung alongside their ship. They were all indistinguishable from Europeans and therefore had no reason to hide. "Which is not to say that one of the inspectors might not take a swing at *him* if he opens his mouth one too many times. I think we're all ready to get off of this thing."

Davyt had stopped his rustling and they could hear the sound of boots and indistinct speech up on deck. Ruarshi unfolded the piece of sailcloth he'd been given and burrowed underneath it. They waited in silence and listened as the inspectors made their way into the upper hold and, eventually, down the short ladder into the lower hold. The trade goods stored there didn't leave the Tomirans with a lot of room to maneuver—Ruarshi and Davyt had found it necessary to crawl over several rows of crates in order to reach their current location—and their muttered conversation sounded tired. This convoy of four was evidently not the first to have arrived in Tomir today, and as it was now early evening they were ready to finish off this last set of tasks and head home.

After a few minutes of what sounded to Ruarshi like fairly listless prodding at various shadowy objects, the inspectors returned to the deck. He pulled the cloth to one side and took a deep breath of the stale air. About a quarter hour later more footsteps clattered down the ladder and Etienne's voice drifted through the hatchway.

"They've gone."

Ruarshi stood, stretched out on top of the crate against which he'd wedged himself earlier, and awkwardly rolled his way from box to box toward the exit. Davyt saw him and laughed, and then began crawling in the same direction.

When Ruarshi reached a gap between crates and was able to get his feet back under himself, he looked up at his former apprentice.

"Did they give you any trouble?"

"No." The young healer was dressed in the outfit that Karoli had gifted him in Mainz and looked every inch the respectable and prosperous merchant. The other Miriyanti had adopted the same strategy, and the only thing the inspectors might have noted as being a bit out of the ordinary was the presence of four women among the ship's passengers.

Ruarshi knocked the dust from his shirt and trousers while he waited for Davyt to join them. When he did, they headed back to their cabin and got ready to go ashore. As Ruarshi pulled on his dark green coat, it occurred to him that he'd never gotten around to having his hair cut, though he'd been intending to do that for at least the last six

months. Its current length no longer suggested a mere disregard for social preferences; he'd long since crossed a line and now looked more
like a wild forest dweller than anything else.

He grinned at the thought and told himself to stop worrying over
nonsense. Let people think whatever they liked about him. They tended
to do that in any case.

They remained in their cabin for a while longer, occasionally attempting conversation but more often sitting in silence. A quiet knock
at the door finally roused them.

Elin waited outside. "Are you ready?" she asked.

Ruarshi nodded as the two healers jumped off their bunks and
crowded in behind him. He followed her out onto the deck where the
exiles had gathered. They were watching him expectantly.

He slowed and came to a stop. Did they want him to... say something? Why? Their plan, such as it was, had been worked out days before.

He settled for stepping forward and bowing to the group, and then
nodding toward each member of their party who'd be heading off on
trajectories different than his own. "It has been an honor. Please be
careful."

Atali returned the bow on their behalf. "We will. If anyone gets in
your way, give them hell."

A few members of their party chuckled at that and they all strode
down the ramp to the docks.

There was no use in trying for stealth. The hour was now late
enough that most Tomirans would be off the streets, but anyone they
passed might recognize any number of them. In the case of the exiles
this would cause an immediate stir, since they were all believed to be
long dead. In his own case he wasn't sure what the result would be. He
thinned his bond-shield, wincing at the sudden onslaught of emotional
noise, and led the way into Miriyan's capital.

No one in the lower part of the city paid them much attention.
They were mostly dockworkers, and as far as they were concerned the
traffic to and from the ships at harbor didn't warrant so much as a second glance. One woman recognized Alexandra as they walked up the
shallow switchbacks toward the bluffs above, and the group paused
with nervous good humor to allow the reunion some time. Alexandra
didn't try to explain the situation to her excited cousin, instead indicating that she'd meet her later at their circle so everyone there could hear
her story at the same time. The woman kissed her lightly on the cheek

before nodding and hurrying off, running back the way she'd come.

A few minutes later the street they were on took a sharp right and leveled out as they entered Tomir proper. The city lay in a slight depression and from this vantage point they could see it in its entirety, drowsing in the low sunlight.

The Maelae clan circle lay somewhat south of Tomir's central square and Ruarshi turned in that direction. Soon Atali, then Valentin, then Alexandra and Klas peeled away from the larger group, taking their leave silently with a simple warrior's salute. Ruarshi watched them go but kept most of his focus on what the Miriyanti around them were feeling, searching for signs of alarm, hostility, or violent intent.

By far the most common reaction they elicited as they moved farther into town was curiosity. A spike of wariness here and there probably meant that either he had been recognized or Karoli had, though he had no way of knowing for certain. The sudden surge of joy he perceived as they crossed another intersection was no mystery at all, as its source came bounding toward them a moment later.

"Etienne!" The young man threw an arm around the grinning healer's shoulders and gave him a light squeeze. His smile faltered. "What happened to you?"

Which meant the stranger was also a healer, and a nosy one. Ruarshi looked to his former apprentice for any indication that he might welcome intervention but found none. In the meantime the man's gaze drifted to Ruarshi and stayed there.

"Adventures, Tiko. Many adventures. This is Ruarshi Nerthi, whom you will know by reputation, and his frighteningly competent son Davyt. These two are Elin and Saoirse, Naishanti with nerves of steel from the clan of the Annorae, and this disagreeable-looking fellow is Karoli Diamyo, who once fought and defeated Aerik of the Anemoi."

Etienne had not been speaking quietly and everyone within earshot had turned to stare. Ruarshi smiled, oddly delighted by the entire tableau. The healer had just ensured that news of the exiles' return would spread far and wide, likely before bedtime and with the correct names attached to all the members of their group.

Tiko looked a bit overwhelmed. "Where are you headed?"

"That I cannot tell you. Don't follow us, Tiko. The warriors here were illegally exiled by Casimir and we may run into trouble."

"If you need help..."

"Unlikely."

The man's eyes skipped over them again and he exhaled noisily. "I'll

let the Chamani at the healers' circle know you're here. Unless you're
heading that way yourselves?"

Etienne shook his head.

"All right. Can I come see you later?"

"I don't see why not. We won't be far. Rumor will tell you where to
look." Etienne mimed tipping a hat at the man and they continued
down the street.

"'Nerves of steel'?" Saoirse asked.

"That's been my observation. Running into Tiko was a stroke of
good luck. He's Aesir clan and knows everyone."

Ruarshi took a left at the next cross street. Not far to go now. "I'd
like to be out of here before he stirs up the entire city. This isn't a criticism, mind. That was well done."

"Not entirely," Karoli said. Etienne just grinned at the warrior over
his shoulder until the older man gave up on him and went back to
scanning the shadows for possible trouble.

After another short interval the buildings lining the sides of street
gave way to an open area, a sure sign that they'd reached their goal. Ruarshi wanted to quicken his pace but forced himself not to.

The Maelae circle hadn't changed since he'd last seen it. The gate
stood open, as one would expect, and the yard was deserted when they
entered it.

"Is Lorion still in the same rooms?" Ruarshi asked.

"That's where he was when I left," Davyt replied.

Ruarshi headed up the worn wooden stairs to the second level of
the circle's living quarters. Once inside, he counted the doors he passed
until he reached the fifth. He took a deep breath and knocked.

"Lorion?"

The door flew open and Ruarshi stood face to face with his fellow
Nerthi, who looked back at him incredulously. Then Lorion smiled and
pulled him into a rough hug. "Brother!"

Ruarshi's sense of relief at seeing the man alive and well was so
overwhelming that his knees went weak. He returned the embrace with
what strength he could muster as Lorion went on. "And Nephew!
Come here." Ruarshi stepped to the side when the former warrior
shifted his attention to Davyt, and he could now see past the door to
the fireplace along the western wall. Slan was there, frozen in place
where she had half-risen from a chair.

He had wasted so, so much time that would have been better spent
with her. With her and Davyt both. He studied her face in the firelight

and found something there he'd desperately needed to see. It wasn't forgiveness, which he did not deserve in any case. But it was enough.

Ruarshi went forward and wrapped his arms around her. She moved to meet him, returning the embrace with a fierceness that surprised him. After an indeterminate period of time a small commotion at the door impinged upon his awareness, and he turned unwillingly to find that Lorion had shifted to block the threshold.

"Brother, why is he here?" Lorion was glaring at Karoli, who appeared bored with the situation.

"He's an ally, Lorion. It's all right."

"He was Aerik's!" His good-brother wasn't quite shouting, but a real potential for violence lay beneath his words. If Ruarshi could perceive that, he was certain Karoli could.

"I know," he said quietly.

"You... know." Lorion was squinting at him and Slan stepped back, releasing him. Cool air flowed over his skin, leaving him chilled in spite of the fire.

"I'll tell you what's happened, but right now we don't have time. I believe you and any other known Nerthii may be in danger and I'm here to ask you to come with us."

"Come with you where?"

The fact that Lorion didn't immediately scoff at the notion that he might not be safe made Ruarshi's skin prickle. "To my clan home, and then north to visit the Annorae." He nodded toward Elin and Saoirse, still waiting outside in the hall with Karoli and a harried-looking Etienne.

"I can't leave Tomir," Lorion said.

"Yes, you can," Slan said. "Let them in."

Lorion scowled but did as she asked, and Ruarshi handled introductions while Davyt crossed the room to embrace his mother. Once everyone was inside, Lorion closed the door and leaned back against it, crossing his arms.

Ruarshi ran an agitated hand through his hair. He was well enough acquainted with the siblings to understand that some explanation would be necessary if he wanted either of them to budge from this room, but he hardly knew where to start.

He took a breath. "Casimir sent warriors south with orders to kill us. I was a target, as were these three. You remember that some of those involved in the rebellion supposedly died in the fire at Mirror Lake? They were warriors who could pass as Europeans. Casimir exiled them in secret. Seven of them are back now.

"Has Casimir been spending a lot of time lately talking to the old guard?"

Slan and Lorion exchanged the kind of glance that left him without the need for a verbal answer. "Where are Mara and Aurel? Have any other Nerthii come forward?"

"Mara died two years ago, Ruarshi," Slan said. "She never really recovered from her injuries. Aurel has disappeared. We know of three others. They're not in Tomir. Lorion thought it wise to avoid bringing them all together. Is Casimir aware that you're here?"

"I don't know," Ruarshi said. "If not, he will be soon. Aurel is missing?"

"No one has seen her for more than a decade," Lorion said. "She was... she's probably dead."

Ruarshi was considering that when he noticed that Slan was staring at him strangely. "What's wrong with your eyes?"

"Nothing. We should go."

"They're red."

"Yes."

"Is the explanation for that something we should hear sooner rather than later?" Slan asked.

"Probably," Etienne muttered.

Karoli opened his mouth but Elin laid a hand on his arm, forestalling him. She turned to face Lorion. "Most of the tale is Ruarshi's to tell but you need to know that he opened a doorway onto the Halls. You can do this as well. You are a shaman. There is much that both of you need to learn, and my clan can teach you."

Ruarshi saw out of the corner of his eye that Lorion's jaw had fallen open. He was very careful not to let his gaze stray to Slan, who likely thought they were all delusional. He spoke into the silence.

"We've been busy, but as I said you'll get the whole story later. We're leaving and you're coming with us, even if Karoli and I have to bind you in weaves and carry you out of here."

The Diamyo was the only one smiling now and Ruarshi was afraid he would have to make good on his threat. More wordless communication passed between Slan and Lorion and his *chesida's* lips quirked. "I would like to see you try that, but it can wait. We'll come."

"Good. Thank you. We'll need to borrow some horses. The Doshae will see to it that they're returned to your clan."

"How many days' ride will it be?" Lorion asked. "Do we need supplies as well?"

"Three days, and yes, we should raid your kitchen."

"Wait." Lorion paused, staring distractedly off into the distance. "We should swing a bit south to pick up Tuomi on the way. She's an Alvae."

A flurry of activity followed, which unfortunately included answering some questions from a handful of concerned Maelae who'd been drawn by the raised voices. The siblings were well-regarded and the news that they were leaving was met with regret and some agitation, which slowed their preparations further. Though everyone moved quickly it took more time than Ruarshi liked before they were all mounted and on their way, and he rode out of the clan circle's gate with the uncomfortable feeling that they'd squandered their advantage by dallying too long.

He rode in front with his *chesida* and good-brother, with Davyt and Etienne immediately behind and Saoirse, Elin, and Karoli bringing up the rear. Fewer Tomirans were out now and some of those whose paths they crossed seemed dubious or appreciative of their little procession rather than puzzled by it, which had to mean they'd already heard some of the rumors that must be floating through the evening air. A rowdy group of young men and women emerged from a side street and shouted inebriated greetings at them as they neared the city's outskirts, but no one moved to intercept them and the foot traffic gradually dwindled to almost nothing.

It was then that Ruarshi became aware of a group of nine mounted Miriyanti approaching from the south and east. They were full and drowsy and clearly not looking to cause trouble, but he reined his horse in anyway and motioned for the others to stop. Otherwise they'd all have ended up out in the middle of the next intersection at the same time, and he deemed it wiser to allow this other party to pass ahead of them. There was no need for them to interact at all.

Someone in this other group had different ideas. One of the men saw them waiting in the shadows and leaned back in his saddle to speak with the rider behind him, after which they all turned their horses and began a cautious approach.

Ruarshi had not been keeping a figurative eye on his own party, but a sudden wash of anger from Lorion nevertheless caught his attention. His good-brother glanced over at him, a tight smile on his face.

"Sorry, Brother, but I've exercised all the restraint this evening that I intend to." He kicked his horse into motion and hurtled toward the other group, where he seized one of the men by the front of his tunic and threw him to the ground. The Nerthi followed his quarry down and was lost to sight among the press of men and horses.

Ruarshi was already moving, forcing his mount through the mass of milling, shouting Miriyanti toward the spot where his good-brother had disappeared. He found him crouched over an older man, speaking to him in a low, intense voice. Ruarshi couldn't make out any of the words, distracted as he was by the semicircle of bared swords to his left and Slan's sudden appearance on Lorion's other side, where she faced a similar predicament. Karoli and the Valkyries were also nearby, though they had remained outside the ring of steel.

Ruarshi raised his hands, gesturing for calm. This didn't have the effect he'd been hoping for on the Naishanti that surrounded him. He glanced over his shoulder again and finally recognized the man lying in the dirt as Liam, chief of the Taanor clan. That would make these warriors his honor guard, and would also explain what was wrong with Lorion.

His good-brother had risen to his feet and taken in the situation at a glance. "Put up your swords. I needed a word with your chief. You can see he is unharmed."

The warriors didn't move to comply until Liam sat up and repeated the command. Even so, one of the Naishanti on Ruarshi's side was slow to obey and nicked him on the cheek with his blade as he returned it to its sheath. Ruarshi threw together a quick warrior's weave and snapped the man's sword at the hilt. He leaned forward in his saddle.

"If you want to make this personal, we can do that."

The warrior attempted a scowl, eyes darting toward his broken weapon, but Ruarshi could feel the fear that lay behind his expression. "Well?" he prompted.

The man shook his head and looked away. Satisfied, Ruarshi turned his attention to Liam. The Taanor chief was watching him sourly.

"You *are* back. What a wonderful day for Miriyan." The older man stood, moving stiffly. "I was merely going to ask if you had any knowledge of my clanswoman Aurel Illyana. This one's misplaced outrage on her behalf would suggest that the answer is 'no'."

"If she is dead, the fault is yours," Lorion said, "and you would do well to use her proper title."

"I will not be lectured by an ill-mannered child. In recognition of our shared concern for my clanswoman, however, I will let this incident pass without making more if it than the circumstances warrant."

Which only meant that he wasn't eager to spread the story of how he'd ended up flat on his back while a full complement of guards stood by and did nothing.

Ruarshi smiled at him and then, because he remembered their last meeting very well indeed, he blew the clan chief a kiss. Even in the deepening twilight he could see Liam's face darken in anger and embarrassment.

"Good evening, Liam."

Lorion climbed back onto his horse and their group rode away from the small knot of Naishanti, resuming their previous formation on the far side of the intersection. As they continued eastward Slan swung her mount over until their knees were almost touching.

"What was that about?" she asked.

"I was just reminding Liam that I don't like him, either," Ruarshi said.

# A New Healer for the Clan

When Slan started moving determinedly in his direction, Etienne thought about pretending that he needed to relieve himself and darting into the trees that surrounded their camp. This approach wasn't one that could easily be sustained over time, though, so instead he took a deep breath and waited. As she neared, he bowed. "Slan Naishanti."

She returned a bow of equal depth, which was not at all required by the polite conventions that covered such behavior. She was both a good deal older than him and vastly more experienced. He'd been a full-fledged Illyana for less than a year.

"Etienne Illyana. There is a question or two I would like to ask you."

He'd known this was coming. Ruarshi's skill at wriggling out of the way of an unwelcome inquiry was unparalleled in Etienne's experience, and Slan was hardly going to interrogate her son about his own father. Nor would she want to interact with the other warriors any more than necessary until she'd figured them out. Naishanti were funny that way. All of which left him as the obvious and only choice.

"I'll do my best to answer."

Slan shot him a tentative smile. "Thank you." The expression faded. "I would like to know how long Ruarshi has been unable to heal, and why a Diamyo has agreed to follow him."

Etienne let go of the breath he'd been holding in a drawn-out exhalation that he made no effort to hide. She was observant. "You're wondering why he hasn't healed that cut under his eye. Right. He's been this way for about two months. Both Davyt and I offered to help with it but he waved us off."

She absorbed this information with an apparent placidity that Etienne didn't believe for an instant. "Not quite as bad as I feared, then. And the other?"

Ruarshi had alluded in passing to a strange conversation he'd had with Karoli while they'd still been aboard ship. It had sounded to Etienne like the most awkward clash of antlers in history, involving as it had just the one contender and a puzzled bystander. He wished he'd been there to witness it.

"Because the likelihood of Ruarshi following someone else's direction for any prolonged period of time is approximately zero?"

That won another smile from her, but she was shaking her head. "You're not wrong, but neither is that a real answer."

"I think you should ask him that question."

"I did. He insisted that you're all just traveling companions, headed toward the same clan home and staying together for purposes of mutual defense. But Karoli is consciously following his lead. Diamyo don't do that, so I'm looking for an explanation."

Etienne found that he'd crossed his arms defensively and made a mostly successful effort to lower them to his sides. "I'd like to say it's because Ruarshi saved our lives when Casimir's people tried to crush us with a castle. I suppose Davyt has mentioned that? But that's not the reason you're looking for. Ruarshi killed five people that night, one of them a healer. Elin was with him and helped bury them later. She hasn't said much about it either, but she gets a queasy look on her face when the subject comes up. I think Ruarshi may have hit them with a lot more power than he really needed to. At the time he didn't know if any of us had survived the collapse, so I'm unlikely to hold it against him. Karoli admires him for it."

"Elin. She's the one who claims he's a shaman."

"Yes. That doorway she mentioned is real. And eerie. It's given him something else to think about, at least."

Slan was staring distractedly off into the forest. After a while her gaze returned to his face.

"He told me that he feels very much in your debt."

Etienne couldn't tell if that was intended as an indirect question or not. He shifted uneasily.

"I'm not trying to make you uncomfortable. I think you know more about me than I do about you and I'd like to catch up a little, since it seems likely that our acquaintance will extend beyond the next few days."

He purposely hadn't been thinking about that. The odds that the

Jinnae clan would allow so much as a week to pass without demanding his presence were slim. They had no use for his parentage but his skills were a different matter, and he was many years away from having the kind of seniority that would enable him to evade that particular obligation.

"I'm honored by your interest, but I'll be wanted at home."

An expression composed of one part mortification and three parts exasperation drifted across Slan's face. "It seems I have already said too much, but now that I have it would be unkind not to continue. I assumed Ruarshi had already asked you if you'd like to join the Doshae clan."

"… No."

"I have no idea why he was waiting to bring this up. Is this something you would like to do?"

Etienne was going to kill him. If he had to guess, he'd say that Ruarshi had put off the conversation because he was concerned that Etienne would regard it as another attempt to manipulate him into staying by his side. Or even worse, he was worried that Etienne would mistake the gesture for some kind of… invitation. He thought that issue had been resolved.

"I'd like it very much. Thank you for letting me know. Would you excuse me for a minute?" Slan nodded, bemused, and Etienne bowed again and turned on his heel.

The last time he'd seen Ruarshi, the man had been on his way down to the creek near their campsite to wash up before they resumed their journey. Clearly they needed to talk, and if Ruarshi happened to be near-naked while they did it then that was just the way things sometimes went.

He didn't hurry and was careful to thrash through the brush with all the grace and delicacy of an angry bear, in spite of the fact that Ruarshi wouldn't need the noise to know that he was coming. He didn't want his former instructor to think he was trying to ambush him at his ablutions. Any such suspicion would make him irritable, and that was no part of Etienne's purpose.

When he caught a glimpse of flowing water through the undergrowth, he called, "Ruarshi! You down there?"

"Yes, Etienne. I'm dressed. You can stop lurking in the bushes."

"I'm not lurking," he said, pushing past the last line of vegetation separating him from the creek. "I just got here."

"So I see. What is it?"

Etienne tried to look stern but the muscles around his mouth kept turning the scowl into a grin. "What do I call you? Uncle Ruarshi?"

Ruarshi stopped wringing water out of his hair and rose to his feet. "I'm sorry," he said, not quite meeting Etienne's eyes. "I must have dropped a hint I didn't mean to while I was talking with Slan. I would never..." He trailed off and cleared his throat. "What do you think of the idea? Your clan will complain, I'm sure, but there's nothing they can do to prevent you from shifting clans if that's what you want. Ciarn will agree to it."

"The sooner the better, Ruarshi. Thank you." Etienne strongly considered crossing the last five feet that separated them and giving the man a hug.

"I'm curious about why you didn't just ask me to do this," Ruarshi went on. "You had to have known what my answer would be."

"I never thought of it," Etienne admitted. "I was too mesmerized by my approaching doom. This kind of thing isn't common."

Ruarshi finally returned his smile. "Don't call me 'Uncle'. It would make me nervous."

"Maybe 'Grandfather' would be better?"

"That's much better, yes." Ruarshi paused, considering. "We'll make a place for you in my family's hall, if that sounds all right to you. The Doshae are conservative when it comes to architecture and use the traditional layout. I've never known ours to be full, and unless my cousins have been producing children at an alarming rate, finding a room will be no trouble."

The reality of the abrupt change in Etienne's circumstances finally sank in and he felt a little dizzy. He took a few seconds to collect himself before responding. "That would be fine, Ruarshi. Whatever you think."

His former instructor turned to gesture toward the creek at his back. "You should take off that coat and get in the water. You could use a wash."

Etienne rolled his eyes. "Is this how it's going to be now? I intend to get in there. It just wasn't the first thing on my list today."

"Good. Otherwise I suppose I'd have to throw you in."

"You can't throw me anywhere. I'm bigger."

"You're also uphill from me. I might have to trip you, but I'd get you in the water."

A glint had appeared in Ruarshi's eye and Etienne backed away a step. "Looks shallow. And there are rocks. Best not."

The Nerthi's smile shaded toward a smirk and Etienne shook his head. He pulled off his coat and laid it carefully on a moss-covered rock by the creek's edge. "Since I'm down here anyway I'll go ahead and get it done, before someone starts demanding I get on a horse. You people are bossy. If you spot anyone else on their way down, you might warn them that I'm a big believer in bathing while fully nude."

"I'll pass that on," Ruarshi said. He clapped Etienne on the shoulder as he went by and leaned in to murmur, "Welcome to the family."

The healer listened to his fading footsteps until they were lost beneath the faint susurrus of the breeze wending its way through the trees. Then he pulled off his clothes and slid into the water.

On their way out of Tomir they had ridden through the few hours of twilight that passed for night at this time of year, stopping to get some sleep only when the sun appeared on the horizon. Slan and Lorion stood watch while everyone else rested because, as Slan put it, they were the only ones who didn't look like they'd spent the past month being dragged back and forth across a washboard. Etienne didn't find that characterization to be entirely fair, but he had to concede that their little party had arrived in Miriyan looking a bit worn around the edges. The various injuries they'd suffered outside Mainz had all healed by this time, with the sole exception of Saoirse's hip. He still caught her limping once in a while, but she got defensive when he mentioned it so he'd quit bringing it up.

It was still early in the day when Etienne, much cleaner than he'd been before, returned to their campsite and they resumed their travel. He wasn't concerned about pursuit, since Ruarshi would be keeping a mental eye on their surroundings and would give them plenty of warning if anyone showed up in their vicinity. He tried to observe the man's interactions with Slan without being too obvious about it. Ruarshi was still in love with her, whether he was interested in admitting to it or not, and the prospect that things might go sideways between them again made him anxious. He needed to let Slan know about the stash of her letters that Ruarshi had retained. That would be manipulative and cheeky of him, but Ruarshi hadn't hesitated to interfere in his relationship with Jonata so he really couldn't object to a little helpful meddling on Etienne's part.

He dove into his link with her, checking to make sure that she was well. It appeared that she was, though she felt a tad melancholy. Missing him, maybe? He couldn't rule it out. He'd pushed to retain their link mostly because he enjoyed their bond, but also because he was trying to draw Jonata to Miriyan. He wasn't sure how she'd survived as long as she had in Europe without competent healers around and he wanted her here. If he felt a pang of his own at her absence, he tried not to let it bother him. He still cared for her and always would, but people had a way of coming into his life and then disappearing again before he was remotely ready to let them go, and he'd long since stopped telling himself that the world could ever work any other way. It looked like he might actually be able to hang onto Ruarshi, against all expectation, but that remained to be seen and he wouldn't get his hopes up.

And he couldn't keep thinking about this kind of thing or he'd be morose in no time. Clearly he needed a distraction. He urged his horse forward. When he came up alongside Davyt, he leaned over and tugged on the younger healer's stubby braid.

"So how much trouble are you in?" he asked.

Davyt's smile grew wry. "Not much. Mother wasn't pleased about my sneaking out of Miriyan, but Uncle told her that it had been necessary. I..." He trailed off and then said in a lower voice, "I don't think she knows what happened to Father in Mainz. Lorion seems to have an inkling. I'm not going to be the first one to tell her."

"That's probably wise of you. I notice we haven't been attacked yet. I was half expecting to be set upon the instant we left the ship."

"If Casimir could have gotten to us in a remote area before anyone knew we were back, I'm afraid he would have tried that," Davyt said. "But coming after us with a big group of warriors in the middle of Tomir or chasing us now would be a bad idea. I'm not good at politics but even I know that no one wants to see a repeat of what happened when I was a baby. I think Father was right about the risk of arrest, though. If just a few Naishanti had shown up to bar our way... He'd have been worried about people getting hurt. I'm not sure he would have resisted."

Etienne glanced at Ruarshi's back. He was riding just ahead of them, in close conversation with Slan. "He would have. Not that it would have mattered one way or the other. Karoli and the Valkyries would have killed anyone who came at us with manacles."

"True. How did you get used to this?"

"'This'?"

"Living in mortal terror all the time." Davyt shot him a weak grin.

"And wondering when someone you cared about was going to be killed. I'm not handling it that well, to be honest."

"I'm not going to be of much help to you there. Since we're home now, we should be able to do something about the problem."

"But we don't know why exactly these people are our enemies. Not really. Do we?"

"I know that the group of superannuated horrors Ruarshi calls 'traditionalists' oppose anything that smells like change, and Ruarshi has been doing nothing but changing things since the turn of the century. Casimir? He's jealous of Ruarshi's power, and threatened by it, and he definitely didn't want those exiles making it back here. That's as close as I can come."

"There were promises made. The Nerthii were meant to be protected. That's one of the things Father won for Miriyan. How dare *anyone* break those promises."

Davyt's hands were shaking and Etienne realized he'd never seen the younger man truly angry before. He wanted to assist but wasn't sure how best to go about it.

"To answer your earlier question, I try to imagine that someone I respect is watching me." He tilted his head in Ruarshi's direction. "It steadies me. A little."

"When we made it out of Tomir without trouble—well, mostly without trouble—I almost fell out of my saddle in relief," Davyt said. "I don't want to do that in front of everyone."

Etienne had seen the tears running down Davyt's face the evening before and he'd had to struggle with himself to keep from doing the same. They'd all been under too much strain for too long and he wouldn't have blamed anyone for a display of emotion at that point. "It would have been all right if you had. We'd have picked you up."

"I know."

They lapsed into silence until Etienne reached out to give Davyt a gentle punch on the arm. "Would you like to be roommates? The Doshae are adopting me but I'm not sure how many spare beds they have."

Davyt brightened. "We are?"

"That's what I was told."

They grinned at each other.

"Our *saal* is a big one, eighty rooms," Davyt said. "They'll probably put us in the northern end somewhere. My cousins can be a little overwhelming. Let me know if you need help and I'll chase them away for you."

"Overwhelming in what way?"

"They tend to run in packs, and they're going to find you fascinating."

Etienne looked doubtfully at the younger man. "Why?"

"They're starved for novelty, for one thing. For another, since you won't technically be a Doshae yet, my family is going to want a story from you our first night back. I don't know that all the clans still do that, but that's how we ask guests to repay our hospitality. Tales from foreign lands are always appreciated and a certain amount of exaggeration is expected. By which I mean lying. I'm sure your story will be a good one. You'll pick up admirers."

On the infrequent occasions when the Jinnae actually hosted guests, storytelling was no part of the routine. Etienne sighed. "Thanks for the warning. I need some time to think about this."

"Not really. We're not that particular an audience."

"I want to make a good first impression."

"And you will. I mean it. Don't fret about it."

Etienne sat back in his saddle and started reviewing the events of the past several years. This was not something he did very often and it felt strange, but inside of a few minutes he thought he'd found what he needed. He smiled absently at Ruarshi's back even as he decided that he'd hurl himself onto the nearest sword before he'd do anything to screw this up.

Mid-evening two days later they arrived at the Alvae clan home. It was a tiny place, consisting of only five *saele* and a guest house that was going to be filled to capacity by the time all eight of them had settled in. Slan and Lorion dropped their packs by the fireplace and left again even before food and drink had arrived in order to track down Tuomi and her clan chief. They were anxious to arrange for the young woman's protection overnight, and to get whatever thorny conversations would be necessary beforehand out of the way as soon as possible. Etienne gathered that Tuomi hadn't yet told anyone in her family about her unusual talents, and depending on the clan's temper that could mean that the two of them were in for an unpleasant couple of hours. At the very least the situation would be uncomfortable. Etienne was glad to be able to sit down on one of the low stools in the guest house's central room and devour a slice of salmon pie while the re-quired discussions went on without him.

Ruarshi was less satisfied, he could tell. The man had argued that he should go along to meet Tuomi, but had conceded after a terse ex-change with Lorion that he would be more of a distraction than any-thing else. He was currently standing in the eastern doorway of the guest house, looking toward the Alvae's largest *saal* and probably fret-ting. Two curious familiars, a mink and a grey owl, had appeared out-side and were monitoring him from a cautious distance. Davyt was also watching his father, frowning. The other three members of their party had already eaten, and the sisters were now busy rustling around in one of the guest rooms while Karoli went for a walk.

After a while Etienne decided that he should say something.

"I don't hear any shouting yet, Ruarshi. Everything is likely going as well as could be expected. Sit down. Eat."

Ruarshi turned to face him. "We've made some people very un-happy, but I think you're right. They're controlling themselves and seem disinclined to resort to violence." He sat down next to his son. "How's the cooking?"

"A bit soggy but familiar," Etienne answered. "Our exiles did not fa-vor the cabbage so I haven't touched it. This clan seems rather small to have its own chief."

"They're an offshoot of the Vrochi, who live some miles south of here," Ruarshi said, cutting off a slice of pie and attempting to convey it to his wooden trencher before it could fall to pieces. He was mostly successful. "Some feud back at the dawn of time led a few families to split away and settle here. They've always been prickly neighbors." He finally started eating, which seemed to remind Davyt that he, too, had food sitting in front of him that was in need of attention.

That was better. Etienne rotated on his stool and began poking idly at the fire. A log shifted and a shower of sparks swirled upward, draw-ing his gaze toward the fireplace itself. The stone from which it was made had been crafted by a long-ago Shaper into the form of a tree trunk, which wasn't terribly original but which, now that he was taking a closer look at it, he had to concede reflected an unusually high level of skill. Those were meant to be ladybugs on that leaf there, weren't they? His estimation of the clan and its guest house rose a notch.

"What do we do if Tuomi decides she'd rather not spend the winter in the frozen wasteland the Annorae call home?" Etienne asked.

"I heard that," Elin called, though she didn't emerge from the room she and Saoirse would be sharing that evening.

"So tell me what part of what I just said was untrue."

"You've never even been there." Elin again.

"And I hoped never to go. Life is cruel." When this pronouncement was met with silence, he shifted his regard back to his former instructor.

"I'll make sure she's assigned a pair of guards so persistent and intrusive that she'll follow us north just to get away from them," Ruarshi said.

Which was both a joke and not a joke at the same time. "Can you do that?" Etienne asked.

"I have no authority over warriors, if that's what you're asking. But if I were to relay a request through Ardan, it would be done. I'm sure the Alvae would love having heavily armed Doshae in their midst for months on end."

"Lorion does intend to verify her claims, I assume."

"I believe that was the first thing he did when he found her," Ruarshi said. "The mood over there shifted from offense to something like mourning rather abruptly."

"Mourning?"

"Yes."

"Oh, fuck them all, then." Etienne's opinion of his hosts shifted again, this time to disgust. He really did know better than to give strangers the benefit of the doubt.

"I don't think we'll have much trouble convincing her to come with us," Ruarshi said. "There's an upside to everything."

Etienne snorted at that but decided to leave it alone. "Maybe the Vrochi will end up with a shaman while Tuomi's people continue mourning whatever it is they think they've lost."

"That's a good thought, but it doesn't work like that," Saoirse said, coming to join them. She'd changed out of her trousers and was wearing a loose skirt, which would be her one and only concession to the pain in her hip. "The power of shamans to accurately read and shape the future is limited to the people they're most closely related to. Their clan, as a rule. It sounds like the Alvae split off so long ago that her ties to the Vrochi will have faded."

Etienne wondered what would happen if a clan found itself saddled with a hostile shaman. He thought the Alvae might have a chance to find out one day soon, and that they were unlikely to enjoy it.

"So shamans don't travel much?" Davyt asked. He'd been eyeing the pudding but hadn't touched it yet. Etienne nudged the bowl in his direction.

"No," Saoirse replied. "Though I don't know that distance from one's clan would make it any harder for a shaman to look after her people. Or his people. I think it's more a matter of having one's Skeltari around."

"Why is that important?" Davyt was no longer interested in his pudding, and Ruarshi had that blank look on his face that meant he knew what Saoirse was going to say and wished she wouldn't.

"The Skeltari takes care of the shaman. If they're doing their job properly, they spend a lot of time bedridden."

"Goodness, that doesn't sound like fun." Etienne was quite sure he was glaring at Ruarshi as he spoke, and equally certain he wasn't going to stop. "Why do they do that?"

"Coaxing the future onto paths it wasn't inclined to take is exhausting. The blood loss doesn't help."

"Saoirse, what are you doing?" Elin emerged from the dimness of her bedroom, her mask off. Etienne was used to the burn scars that marred the left side of her face, but he understood why she kept them covered. He hoped some of their hosts would wander in and take a fright. "They don't need to know all this."

"Since they're coming with us, they're going to *see* all this. There's no harm in letting them know what to prepare for."

"Blood loss?" Etienne prompted.

"Blood is evidently necessary when one is bending the future," Ruarshi cut in. "Quit worrying. I have *no* intention of doing that."

Now Etienne was confused. As was Elin, if the expression on her face was any indication. "So you intend to learn how to be a shaman, but not to become one?" he asked. "Can we skip the trip north, then?"

"No. Tuomi and the others need to go there and learn what they can, and they need protection while they do. I can help with that." Ruarshi glanced at the sisters. "I'm sorry."

Etienne was caught between relief and skepticism. He understood that Ruarshi felt responsible for looking after the others, but the notion that he would restrict himself to a protective role, and would forever refrain from fiddling with his abilities to find out what exactly they encompassed, didn't line up with what Etienne had learned to expect from him. Not at all.

"So if there were some kind of disaster coming and you knew you could avert it, you wouldn't?" Elin asked, apparently after having read

Etienne's mind.

"Of course I'd try to avert it. But not that way." Ruarshi had flushed, just a little. "That sort of behind-the-scenes maneuvering is what almost brought a keep down on our heads. I'd much rather have faced a straightforward ambush on the road. Wouldn't you?"

"You find shamanism dishonorable?" Elin asked.

"I can't answer that without sounding like a judgmental ass."

"You may change your mind, if you're willing to listen to your teachers," Saoirse said. "Foreknowledge can be used in selfish and destructive ways. None among the Annorae would contest that. But there are better and gentler uses for your skills. I would ask that you don't turn your back on your inheritance before you learn more."

"I'll admit to curiosity, but I plan to watch while the others do the work."

"That will present its own challenges," Elin said.

"I won't be a burden to your clan," Ruarshi said. "I'll earn my keep one way or another."

"That's not what she meant. We're not ogres, Ruarshi," Saoirse said. "They'd shelter you indefinitely for saving our lives."

Ruarshi opened his mouth, closed it again, and then said, "That wasn't my doing. I just gave you some time."

Karoli chose that moment to return, took in the stares being aimed at the former healer, and asked, "What did I miss, Cousin?"

Ruarshi shook his head in reply. "Any luck?"

"No. We won't be picking up any swords here. The Alvae armory might conceivably provide the means to ward off an attack by a small child, but not much else. We're going to have to wait until we get home to arm ourselves properly. I believe our friends are on their way back."

Etienne was annoyed at the change of topic, as he'd hoped to avail himself of Saoirse's expansive mood to learn more, but resigned himself to picking up the thread again later on. Hopefully when Ruarshi wasn't around to stifle the conversation. He tapped his fingers idly against the table and waited for Slan and Lorion to appear, which they did a short time later. They looked tired but grimly satisfied.

"How is she?" Ruarshi asked, as Slan took a seat next to him and examined the food spread out on the table before her without enthusiasm.

"Disappointed in people she trusted. It was difficult to watch and even harder not to react to. I want you with us when we go to fetch her in the morning. Perhaps her family will behave with a little more restraint if there are two of you standing there."

"Doubtful," Lorion said. "They recognized my name but it hardly slowed them down. She seems resilient. She'll be all right once she's away from here."

"I could go talk to her now if you think it would help," Ruarshi offered.

"She shares a room with an older sister who isn't terrible," Slan said, "and our sudden arrival came as a shock to her, even though she understood why we couldn't send ahead. I say we leave her to a last night with her family, for better or worse."

"Is her room shielded?"

"Our meeting didn't go well, Ruarshi, but it wasn't so bad as that," Lorion said. "No one is going to sneak into her room and attack her."

Ruarshi tilted his head in acknowledgment and warned Slan about the cabbage. Afterward he ceded his stool to his fellow Nerthi and excused himself. Etienne followed him outside, as did Saoirse. That was unexpected and the healer watched her curiously.

"A word, if I may," she said. "I need to know how Karoli will be received by your clan. He is too stubborn to ask you himself."

Ruarshi thought about it. "The Doshae lost a number of clan members during Elyon's revolt, on both sides. If he doesn't bring it up it's unlikely that anyone else will. Which is not to say no one there harbors a personal grudge. Given the role he played, that kind of thing could come from either faction."

"I know he told you about the problems he had with Aerik. In this context I should mention that once he realized he'd get no help from the warriors, he asked Ciarn for assistance and was denied."

"Why?" Ruarshi asked. Etienne was equally shocked.

"Karoli was involved with Ciarn's daughter for many years. I take it they grew up together and were inseparable throughout their early youth. Then he went to Tomir for training, and did what young people often do when their family isn't there to look over their shoulder any longer. Karoli has been evasive when I've asked about any vows they might have exchanged, so I've come to the conclusion that the woman had a legitimate complaint."

Etienne felt a pang of sympathy for the warrior, the first time he'd been troubled by such an emotion on Karoli's behalf. He didn't like it, but he also couldn't deny that he'd made similar decisions at the same tender point in his life.

Ruarshi's eyebrows were approaching his hairline but his answer was deliberate. "Regardless of their personal history, Ciarn was wrong not to intercede. I'll be meeting with him soon after we get there, and I'll make it clear that Karoli is a member of my party. That should deter our leadership from harassing him."

"That would be well. I should also warn you…" Saoirse trailed off, looked over her shoulder toward the guest house, took a breath, and continued. "He may challenge Ciarn's First. The situation could become messy."

Etienne wanted to laugh but restrained himself. Karoli was certain to defeat the head of Ciarn's bodyguard, since Diamyo didn't accept subordinate positions of that sort, and in so doing he'd thoroughly humiliate his clan chief. This would have no legal effect on Ciarn's power within the clan, but it might leave him with no choice but to step down. As long as this happened *after* Etienne's adoption was approved, he had no objections.

"That would be inconvenient," Ruarshi said. He glanced at Etienne. "I'd like to get into and back out of my clan home without incident. Should I suggest that he not pick fights while we're there?"

"No. Definitely not," Saoirse said. "He can be a difficult person. I'll try to see to it that he stays within the bosom of his family. I hope that their *saal* isn't too close to your chief's. If he lays eyes on the man there's not much I'll be able to do."

"If Karoli's really accepted your authority as he claims, you can always rescind the challenge whether he likes it or not," Etienne pointed out.

"If he were a child sticking his head into a bear's den, I'd do that," Ruarshi said, "but he's not and his grievance is serious. I'm going to let the Norns handle this one. And now we've come full circle. This is exactly why I've got no interest in becoming the Doshae's pet shaman."

Saoirse shot him a pensive look. "That's just as well in this instance, since there's nothing any shaman in history could do to prevent Karoli from getting himself into trouble if he's determined to do it. But give it time." She offered them a quick warrior's salute and disappeared back into the guest house.

"I hadn't thought the adoption thing all the way through," Etienne said. "'Uncle Karoli' it is." Ruarshi didn't comment, and he went on. "In case you're wondering, I came out here after you to help you shield Tuomi's room. I can handle the outer door and window for you, if you'll take care of the inner door." The shields wouldn't stop an intruder, but they'd slow him or her down and hopefully lead to the kind of startled flailing that would give Tuomi all the warning she needed.

Ruarshi smiled. "Was I that obvious?"

"Not really. You have considered the fact that if her family finds these, they'll be insulted."

"That's part of my purpose."

"Understood. Shall we?"

# Nemesis

Ruarshi helped shepherd Tuomi out of her family's *saal* and clan home the next morning. She was even younger than Davyt, wrapped in a cocoon of silence that he thought it wise not to disturb, and obviously exhausted. He doubted she'd slept well the night before. She gravitated toward Davyt as they rode north, possibly because of his age, and he was content to let his son look after her if that was her preference. Davyt seemed embarrassed at first by her attention, but after a while they were chatting amiably and the stiffness had gone out of his shoulders.

That day and half of the next passed peaceably as the terrain through which they rode grew more and more familiar to him. When the bridge over the river just south of the Doshae clan home finally came into sight, he was both glad to have arrived and not quite ready to be there. He and Slan still hadn't managed to resolve anything, having instead become bogged down time after time in catching each other up on their recent history while shying away from more serious discussions. She now had as good a picture as he could paint of his past few years, and he knew more about the English civil war than he wanted to. He also better understood the role that Lorion had assigned himself in Tomir: he'd taken on the thankless and dangerous task of representing the interests of the Nerthii as publicly, loudly, and frequently as he could, ensuring that no one in a position of authority could forget about the pledges that had been made regarding their status. And guaranteeing that any assault on their safety would most likely begin with an attack on him. That was also why Ruarshi had found Slan staying in Tomir with her brother. It was something she did whenever her clan obligations allowed for it, which didn't happen as often as she would have liked.

He sat up straighter in his saddle as a strange shiver passed over and then through him. They had just crossed the bridge into Doshae territory. He'd never before reacted physically to a homecoming and thought perhaps he'd missed the place more than he'd been willing to admit. He shook off the odd sensation and started searching among the passersby for a familiar face. Before he did anything else, he needed to escort the sisters, the Maelae, and their new Nerthi to the guest house. After that he intended to find Ardan. His clan chief wasn't one of the people he needed to speak to today, but she was, and the sooner he attended to that the better.

Ruarshi swung off his horse when a small group of the curious and idle, along with a handful of familiars, began to gather to watch them. He had limited patience for extended welcomes. Fortunately he soon spotted his cousin Larssi in the crowd, hurrying along with a covered basket. He called out to the man, greeting him with every evidence of cheerfulness and asking him to fetch one of the clan stewards. Larssi soon hastened away, smiling, and the rest of their group dismounted to be engulfed in a sea of hugs. Ruarshi did what he could to maintain a position at the edge of that particular interaction without being too obvious about it. There was a fine line to be walked between the necessity of not appearing rude while at the same time not permitting himself to be sucked into the middle of that kind of whirlpool. He exchanged a glance with a large wolf who had wandered over. He got the distinct impression, before he looked away again, that the familiar both understood his discomfort and was amused by it.

Ruarshi was afraid the strain had begun to show by the time Larssi finally returned with Valda in tow. He knew her well. His smile became genuine and he returned her embrace without hesitation.

"Welcome home, Cousin. We have missed you." She shifted her attention to Davyt and gave him a smothering hug in turn. "You will be wanting a bit of food and some time to rest? And these others will need accommodation?" She visibly startled when she set eyes on Karoli and didn't attempt to embrace him, though she listened with interest to the brief and mostly true tale he offered to account for his continued presence among the living.

Once everyone had been sorted out a short while later—a task which mostly involved clarifying Etienne's ambiguous clan status and explaining that he'd be staying in Ruarshi's *saal* rather than the guest quarters—they were able to proceed without further delay. Ruarshi ac-

companied the rest of the party to the guest house and nodded to
Karoli when the man peeled off northward toward his own hall, where
he would probably spend the rest of the afternoon fending off offers
of *keth*. It wasn't every day that someone returned from the dead. Valda
left Ruarshi, Davyt, and Etienne just outside his family hall after
promising to stop by later that evening.

They swung around the south side of the large building so that they
could enter by the centermost eastern door. Ruarshi didn't lend any
credence to the superstition that asserted it was bad luck to step into
one's hall through a westward-facing doorway, but other people did and
he didn't want anyone starting a rumor that their return was ill-omened.
Once inside he hailed the first youngster he spotted and asked her to
fetch the *sperra*, who was in charge of assigning rooms and, when necessary, dealing with minor family disputes. When Jolanthe appeared after a brief search, he requested that she allot him and the Illyana adjacent rooms. He then ascertained that his parents were out in the fields,
his brother and sister had recently left on a visit to another clan home
in anticipation of the summer solstice, and Ardan was in fact alive and
well—which he'd never seriously doubted—and was spending the afternoon in her rooms.

He left the healers to get their minimal baggage unpacked and
crossed the hall to his great aunt's door. She was quartered in the
southwest corner of the *saal*, three rooms away from the enormous
fireplace that dominated the southern wall. He rapped on the door and
waited.

When she opened it a moment later, she gasped to see him there
and then beamed up into his face. "Ruarshi!" He hadn't anticipated
quite this level of enthusiasm from her and watched, nonplussed, as
she seized his hand and clasped it in both of hers. She disengaged just
long enough to ask a young woman whose name Ruarshi couldn't recall to have the kitchens bring them some food and blueberry wine,
and then grabbed him again, pulling him into her quarters and closing
the door behind them.

"Davyt is also well?" She led him into her outer room and released
him. The top half of the split door was open wide, as were the shutters
on her two small windows. The air that wafted in smelled of greenery
and damp. Ruarshi took a deep breath of it before answering.

"He is, Aunt. He's showing my former apprentice around the hall.
The Doshae are about to acquire a new healer."

She looked a question at him as she settled into her padded chair, and Ruarshi was briefly distracted by the presence of a cane at her left hand. He shook himself and replied. "Etienne of the Jinnae. He was in Italy with me. He deserves a better family than the one he was born into."

"He is very welcome to join us," Ardan said, and dismissed the matter. "Tell me why you have come to see me so soon after your return."

If she didn't already know, Ruarshi would be surprised to the point of catatonia. That letter Casimir had written him had, he was almost certain, been partially intended to push him in Ardan's direction. He had a good number of 'old friends from the circle,' true, but he hadn't seen most of them for so long that he'd settled on his great aunt as the one most likely to have healed the Seer.

"I received correspondence from Casimir while I was in Mainz. It made reference to you. I have been concerned about your well-being ever since. It's not generally a good thing to draw his attention."

"I prefer not to speak of him, so I will be brief," Ardan said. "I presume he told you that I came to his aid after he'd attacked you. All I can offer in my defense is ignorance of what he was doing. Casimir collapsed in front of me and my only thought was that he required healing. Weeks later he told me what I had abetted. I have been terrified that I saved your murderer. To see you standing before me is a gift I have in no way earned."

Ruarshi shifted, unsure of how best to respond to that. To say that Ardan did not tend to be demonstrative in either word or deed was something of an understatement. "He is manipulative. I never thought you were working with him."

Tears sprang to his aunt's eyes and he almost fell back a step. He quietly checked on her health, wondering if she might indeed be ailing but trying to keep it a secret. He found nothing amiss.

"Once upon a time, as I'm sure you will recall, I scolded you for pursuing magical skills that I claimed did not belong to you," Ardan said. "That was rubbish and I should have admitted to it long ago. The truth is that I was trying to come up with an argument that would convince you to abandon the path you'd chosen. Quite without the assistance of a Seer, I foresaw the likelihood that it would cause you nothing but trouble. You had already met your Slan by that time. I didn't believe I was telling you to give up anything you couldn't live without. And before you ask—yes, putting down Elyon's revolt would have been more difficult had you heeded my words, but you may perhaps have been spared all the ugliness that you were subjected to. The risk to

Miriyan would have been worth it. *You* were worth it."

If there had ever been anything to what she was saying, it was true no longer. The man she remembered wasn't the one who stood in front of her. "I'm not proud of a number of my decisions, but I still derive some satisfaction from my role in getting my *chesida* out of that cell. The unpleasantness that came before is something I've learned to live with."

"I am selfish, Nephew. I would rather have seen you whole than have used you as I did. Are you happy?"

The question irritated him. He didn't know if she was asking out of genuine concern, or as part of some belated attempt to remake him as a proper healer. "I am content. That's more reliable than happiness."

She met his eyes. "You've never been good at lying to me."

"It's not a lie."

"Content but troubled, then. I would like to help you if I can, to make up for my failings in the past."

He sighed. This was very much Ardan's way: even in the middle of an attempt at reconciliation, she made demands of him. He tried deflection. "When have you known me to be otherwise?"

"You used to possess a purity of purpose that your instructors at the circle couldn't help but admire, even when you were at your most obstreperous. Don't despair if you feel you've lost that purity over time. We all do. It's the price of outliving your youth. If your concerns are more specific... well. I do not know why you stayed in Europe so long after being summoned home, though I gather you were working against Casimir's interests. I am aware that he sent some warriors south not long ago. If there is something weighing on your mind, I am one of the more discreet confidants you could hope for."

A knock on the door interrupted them before their conversation could proceed any further, and a cheery young man brought in a platter of food and a jug of what had to be the wine Ardan had requested. After a murmured back-and-forth with his aunt, the man left again.

"Will there be any legal consequences if those warriors don't return?" Ruarshi asked.

"That depends on what they were there to do," Ardan said. "Casimir would have had to go through Jair to get them, but he may not have been honest about why they were required."

Ruarshi thought of the exiles. Word of their presence would have reached the warriors' enclave the same evening they'd arrived in Tomir, he was sure. "Jair and Casimir are about to have a falling-out, if they haven't already. The Naishanti you refer to went to Europe to murder the victims of a prior crime. The warriors who died in the fire at Mirror Lake didn't die at all, at least not in Miriyan. Casimir sent them south to act as agitators and assassins for the past seven decades."

"Given those facts, I don't understand the problem."

"Casimir can be persuasive. I'm cautious about matters he's had a hand in. Britt of the Avorae was among them, as was a man named Lukas. Baltasar of clan Veris was there as well. Can you inquire as to the identities of the others? Their families should be notified."

"They should. I'll send a note to Jair. Tell me: did they comprehend the role they were playing?"

"Yes. I spoke to Baltasar briefly. He was quite convinced that Casimir's actions were justified."

The question Ardan wasn't asking hung in the air between them. The weight of it was almost tangible. "In this context, it might be appropriate for you to point out that you warned me about this," Ruarshi said finally. "The ability to do a particular thing will eventually, under the right circumstances, lead to a desire to do it."

"Are you worried that you may have overreacted to these circumstances?"

"What I did was akin to shutting the barn door long after the horses had left. I suppose they were still a threat at the time, though probably not to me. If I'm awake and sober, *nothing* is a threat to me. Nerthii are aberrations. We shouldn't exist."

"You do exist. Any other consideration is useless noise. I had to wrestle with myself to accept that, but accept it I did."

"The plague exists. Famine exists. That's not much of a defense."

"I will not say you should be eradicated from the earth. Is that what you would like to hear?"

Ruarshi considered the question. "I have found myself wondering in quite unexpected ways about the wisdom of our ancestors. Perhaps they were right to eliminate us."

"We have traded positions on this issue," Ardan said, an absent smile tugging at the corners of her mouth. "Do you feel that one day you will go berserk and lay waste to the surrounding countryside?"

There was a dash of humor he couldn't appreciate. "It would be difficult for anyone to stop me if I felt so inclined. That's the problem. Can you imagine what would happen if someone like Elyon turned out to be a Nerthi?"

"I know that you have a friendly acquaintance among the Seers,"

Ardan said, "and that this individual—I don't know who it is, no—has been active for some time. Maybe there is a reason you came into your talents in advance of everyone else."

Rely on Ardan to come up with a horrifying idea he hadn't yet considered. Before he could shape his reaction into any kind of coherent sentence, she spoke again. "You are their guardian in all senses, Ruarshi. If an ill-intentioned Nerthi were to surface, you would step forward and you would handle the situation. I have no doubt of this."

"Aunt, I don't think... I'm not..." Ruarshi took a breath. Was he really going to ask her for help? It was clear she was no longer angry with him, if she ever had been, but even so he was reluctant to drop this problem in her lap. He'd proven over the years to be an unusually troublesome family member, she was now clearly infirm, and he didn't feel he had the right to add to her burdens. But he was getting desperate and there was no one else he could turn to.

"I haven't been able to heal for months," he said. "Until this passes, it would be best not to consider me reliable." His aunt knew that this had happened to him in the past, though he'd never told her directly.

He looked up after an interval of silence to find Ardan regarding him steadily. "You needn't be embarrassed, Nephew. The origin of this difficulty, if I have understood it correctly, speaks rather well of you. Though I'm sure that's no comfort. I will set aside an hour every morning after breakfast. You will visit me here at that time and we'll go through simple drills together. We will continue to do this for as long as it takes."

It couldn't be as easy as that, but he resolved to try it because he had no other options and wrestling with it alone was getting him nowhere.

"Thank you. Please don't tell anyone about this. Those I've been traveling with already know but no one else needs to."

"I won't. Any requests for healing that arise before you are well will be routed to someone else."

Her easy assumption that he *would* recover was almost reassuring. The temptation to start in at once with the drills was overwhelming, but he had Illyana to look after and formal greetings to see to. "Can we begin tomorrow?"

"Of course. Now please sit down and share this with me. You have been gone for years; the others can wait an extra ten or fifteen minutes. I promise I'll trouble you with no further questions once you tell me how you and Davyt are getting on."

By the time Ruarshi had checked on the healers and finished with the initial round of visits considered obligatory upon one's return from an extended absence, he had to hurry to make it to the bath house and back before the impromptu homecoming feast at his family's *saal* could begin. Once he was clean he had no choice but to don the same set of clothes he'd been wearing, an unfortunate situation that prompted him to add another item to the list of tasks requiring his attention. At least the coat wasn't terribly worn yet. He didn't want to show up at the celebration looking like he'd slouched in after a nap. The hair he also couldn't do anything to remedy at the present time, but he'd get to it.

He stepped through the door to find the trestle tables already half-full. Small fires burned in the fireplaces at each end of the hall, and someone had brought out the enormous feasting candles. They were almost a foot in diameter and when new stood over six feet tall. A dozen of them burned in iron tripods spaced evenly down the length of the *saal,* adding to the warm yellow glow that brightened the dark wooden walls and illuminated the gathering.

Etienne and Davyt were holding a seat for him next to Slan, with Lorion and Tuomi sitting across from them. His parents were at a table farther north, and he nodded to them respectfully before moving away from the hall's entrance. They'd been openly relieved to see him when he'd sought them out earlier, leading him to wonder how many people Ardan might have spoken with about his confrontation with Casimir. If Ardan had been sufficiently angry with the Seer, and now that he was thinking about it he realized that she must have been furious, she might have gone to Ciarn and turned the entire clan against the man. He should probably ask her about it later. He didn't want to raise the subject with anyone else.

Ruarshi settled in and helped himself to a little bit of each of the dinner offerings, all of it reassuringly familiar. He soon discovered that he was in fact ravenous, and he listened to the chatter ebb and flow around him as he ate, satisfied to drop all his concerns for a few hours and perhaps even get moderately drunk. The *saal* was soon almost full and a quick look around confirmed that small groups from neighboring halls had chosen to join his more immediate family for the evening. If he'd been in a less generous mood, he might have marveled at the way the reputation of the clan's lone Nerthi had evidently restored itself while he'd been gone, or considered putting everyone off their feed by sharing stories about a few of the things he'd gotten up to recently. Instead he reached for the jug of *keth* and refilled his mug, intending to drown his capacity for coherent thought for a while.

Fortunately it looked like he would have plenty of company in his inebriation. Lorion was also on his second mug, Slan wasn't far behind, and even Davyt was making an effort, the first time he'd done so while in his father's presence. Ruarshi had no intention of allowing the boy to drink to excess, but Davyt needed to feel it was safe to relax in his own hall. Only Etienne and Tuomi remained abstemious, which Ruarshi would have been concerned about if he hadn't been able to venture a good guess as to why. Eventually he elbowed his former apprentice and jerked his chin at his mug, pitching his voice to carry across the table to the silent young woman as well. His words were meant for both of them.

'You're not on watch tonight."

"Yes, thank you, I know," Etienne replied.

"He must be pining for Karoli," Lorion said, winking at the healer. It hadn't taken his good-brother long to pick up on the mutual antipathy between the two, though Ruarshi suspected they were keeping it up for show at this point.

"I'll drink you all under the table once this dinner's over," the Illyana said grimly. "Davyt will heal me in the morning and we'll leave the rest of you to suffer."

Lorion grinned and raised his mug. "Doshae versus Maelae? You're on."

Ruarshi had no idea who would win that contest. Slan looked amused. "I will leave you here on the floor, Brother."

The warrior stamped the wooden boards a couple of times with his boot. "Nice and soft. It'll be fine."

Etienne regarded the older man warily, possibly gauging his weight and considering the odds. "I wouldn't want to embarrass a grizzled older fellow like you. Out of respect."

Lorion laughed. Ruarshi supposed he should have anticipated this kind of thing. He leaned in toward Etienne and spoke quietly. "Please don't feel obliged. I'd like you to have fun on your first night here, not make yourself sick."

"Don't worry," the younger man murmured. "I'm just talking because I'm nervous."

"Let me help you put that behind you, then." Getting the next phase of the gathering started wasn't his role to play, but Ruarshi had never been a stickler about rules and he wasn't going to change that now. He stood, called the room to attention, said a few brief and largely scripted words about his joy at returning home, and then surrendered the floor to Davyt. His son continued in the same vein and formally introduced their companions, after which it was their turn to regale the assemblage with stories for as long as they cared to. Slan led with a tale of an English pageant gone wrong, resulting in a baffling scene during which a number of actors dressed as rocks ended up kicking in frustration at the actors outfitted—for reasons that remained obscure to her—as belfries. Lorion followed with a recounting of a Welsh border raid that Ruarshi remembered well. It had netted the Welsh a grand total of three head of scrawny cattle, a collection of bruises, and one broken bone.

Etienne traded a glance with Tuomi and went next. Ruarshi listened as he described an incident one night in Florence during which they'd been pursued by footpads. Their assumption at the time, which had turned out to be correct, was that the men hadn't recognized them as Miriyanti since Ruarshi's hair was hidden under a hat. The Illyana added more drama to the chase than it had actually entailed and rolled it together with an unrelated (but true) tale involving a well-known magistrate who'd been caught emerging from the front door of a house of prostitution by the city guard. The pursuit had ended with Ruarshi throwing all three of the would-be thieves off a bridge into the Arno, after which he'd removed his headgear and had a few quiet, terrifying words with them as they emerged onto the riverbank. Tuomi concluded the recital by telling a startlingly earthy story about a practical joke at the healers' circle, involving the sort of shenanigans that the instructors knew went on but went to great lengths to avoid hearing about. Clearly there were depths to the young woman that her continued shyness around him had prevented him from detecting.

The Doshae raised their mugs and cheered the storytellers, a handful of Elders rose to conclude the formal welcome, and the ceremonial part of the evening was over. Ruarshi told the others he'd be right back and stepped outside, feeling oddly overheated. The crowd and the alcohol must have gotten to him. He wiped a trickle of sweat from his forehead with his sleeve and stretched in the open air, enjoying the smell of the place. It called to some of his earliest, happiest memories, and he decided to stay out there until he felt a little better.

A moment later he was on his knees, a breathtaking pain in his gut doubling him over. He checked himself for signs of food poisoning, found none, and rose slowly. Another cramp followed the first but he was able to remain standing until it passed.

He moved back toward the *saal* and leaned against its outer wall, giving himself a more thorough once-over. There was still nothing discernible wrong with him, which made him intensely uneasy. He closed his eyes and reached for calm. He might have to rethink his plans in relation to *keth* but there was no reason to inconvenience the others over what was probably an inconsequential bit of discomfort. Ruarshi straightened slowly and stood motionless for a minute or two. The pain did not return and he exhaled in relief, turning to go back inside. He would have fun this evening if it killed him.

An hour later Ruarshi had to concede that his earlier resolve wasn't holding and that he needed to disappear into his rooms before any of his companions took too close a look at his face. He bade them goodnight, pleading fatigue, and then stopped by the kitchen to fetch a jug of water and a cup. Once his door was closed he pulled off his coat and shirt, throwing them aside onto the nearest chair, and then sank down onto his narrow bed to remove his boots. When he'd recovered from that round of exertions he drank half the contents of the jug and lay back.

That was a mistake. As soon as his head hit the pillow a wave of nausea rolled upward from his sore midriff and he barely made it through his outer door into the evening light before vomiting into the grass. He considered putting his clothes back on and seeking Ardan out, but dismissed the idea as a bad one. He might not be able to heal at present but that didn't mean there was anything wrong with his ability to diagnose, and she would be just as baffled as he was. No matter how he felt he knew it was impossible to die of nothing, so he was going to end up riding this out on his own one way or another. No need to drag anyone else into it.

Ruarshi staggered into his quarters again and seized the cushions from all the chairs, creating a small nest in his bed so he could rest upright. He fell asleep in that position to the soothing murmur of low voices from the hall but the respite didn't last. When he awoke several hours later he was shivering, bathed in sweat, and ridiculously thirsty. Several more overnight trips to the kitchen in search of water ensued, and by morning he was exhausted and dreading the day's obligations.

That didn't mean he could shirk more than a handful of them, however. He found Ardan at breakfast, the smell of the food bringing back the full force of his nausea, and made his excuses. There was no reason for him to struggle through drills while he was in this state. He must have been convincing because she allowed him to go on his way afterward without peppering him with questions or demanding to examine him, as he had half expected.

Next came his visit to Ciarn. If he delayed it much longer his chief would be insulted. Later he was able to remember very little of that conversation, but he was certain that the man had approved Etienne's adoption and he thought he might even have persuaded his chief to offer Karoli an apology for what had passed between them prior to the revolt. He was concerned that he might have said more than he'd meant to about Aerik during the course of their discussion, but if he had that couldn't be helped. He stopped at the bath house on the way back to his hall. His tossing and turning the night before had left him filthy again and he thought a brisk scrub might perk him up a little.

That decision proved to be his undoing. He passed out while in the water and awoke to see Valda's anxious face hovering over him, and to hear the unwelcome news that she'd sent to his *saal* for help. At least whoever had dragged him out of the bath had covered him with a towel. Somehow his inability to convince himself to move resulted in another period of unconsciousness, and when he next bobbed to the surface Davyt, Etienne, and Ardan were all there.

"Oh dammit," he said.

"Quite," Etienne agreed. "What's wrong with you?"

"If I knew I wouldn't be lying here like a shipwreck."

"You're dehydrated," Ardan said.

"A little, yes. I've been drinking as much water as I can hold and it's not helping. I'll be glad to get dressed and come with you, but I'd prefer not to pull on my pants in front of an audience." He was trying not to let his frustration bleed into his voice and failing, he knew. Everything about this situation vexed him. When he was once more settled in his bed he chased Ardan away, reassured Etienne about his place with the clan, and resolved to sleep until he recovered.

Fortunately he didn't wake again until late evening, when a diffident knock on his outer door roused him. Slan was the only one currently in the room with him and she went to answer it, returning with a rolled piece of paper that she held out to him, a dubious expression on her face.

"I'm not sure you need this just now, but it's from your Skeltari so I don't dare withhold it. What's happening?"

Satu had sent him something? She'd been a frightening old woman since before he was born and the number of times she'd interacted with him in any capacity whatsoever was zero. He was still thinking about paying her a visit, but he'd never expected her to initiate contact.

"I have no idea," he said, reaching forward to take the missive from her. His entire body ached but the cramping had let up somewhat. "The fuss has been mortifying. I didn't mean to worry any of you."

"The current best guess is that you had a violent reaction to something you ate yesterday."

"Maybe," he said, though he didn't believe it. He unrolled Satu's letter and its first line jolted all other thoughts from his mind.

*Cousin,*

*The Seer Casimir has come to me and requested a meeting with you. I have agreed to be present as a witness. He is alone and carries no weapons. Please attend.*

*Satu*

"It's a summons," he said. "I have to go. Please don't trouble the others."

"Are you well enough?"

"Yes. Even if I weren't, it would still be necessary." It was difficult to keep his voice even, but he managed it. If Slan or anyone else learned why his presence was required, they wouldn't allow him to go alone and he didn't want them there. What the Seer planned to say and why he'd traveled to the Doshae clan home to say it were mysteries to him, but he knew how the conversation was going to end. He didn't want anyone he cared about to see it.

He'd nodded off while still clothed so it was only a matter of pulling on his coat and boots and he was out the door. The Skeltari's *kiva,* the only round dwelling known to Miriyanti builders, was located a bit north of the Doshae clan halls, near the edge of the forest where the sacred well had been dug when the settlement was in its infancy. It was the kind of place that children dared each other to approach. He hadn't been near it since he'd first left for the healers' circle and he'd never caught a glimpse inside. He hoped, after all was said and done, that Satu wouldn't be too upset with him.

As he approached the Skeltari's home another cramp tore through him and he stumbled to a halt, waiting for it to pass. There were indeed two people inside, waiting for him, one of them almost dismissive and the other calm. Far too calm. That wouldn't last.

He pushed on the door—unlatched, what luck—and crossed the room in four strides, seizing Casimir by the neck with one hand, yanking him from his chair, and slamming him to the cold dirt floor.

"Why are you here?" he demanded. The warriors' magic he was using was more than adequate to keep the man pinned, in spite of his efforts to pry Ruarshi's fingers from his throat.

"*Tai* Nerthi, please control yourself," the Skeltari said quietly from behind him. He glanced over his shoulder at her and noted with some amusement that she hadn't moved. He'd barely taken note of her on his way in. "The man came to talk, not fight. Or so he says."

Ruarshi released the Seer and put some distance between them, dragging a chair over next to Satu so that Casimir would be left sitting in front of them, like a petitioner.

"So talk." He sat down while the other man picked himself up off the ground with a display of equanimity at odds with the anger rising inside him. "Quit with the act, Casimir. Or have you forgotten that it doesn't work with me?"

"I forget little," the Seer said, resuming his seat. "You ought to be satisfied with the harm you've already done, rather than seeking to inflict more."

Ruarshi didn't respond. This discussion was going to be remarkably short unless Casimir's manner changed. The Seer had to believe that his utter lack of defenses would somehow protect him. There was a time when it would have.

"You've won, Ruarshi. I stepped down from my position at Mirror Lake two days before your ship arrived in our harbor, as I found resignation preferable to being removed from office. There will be no more centralized power in Miriyan. I do hope that's what you were trying to achieve."

"My recent goals have been more modest than that. Lately they've been focused on keeping everyone alive. *You almost killed my son.*" In spite of his best efforts, his voice went hoarse before he could finish.

"I'd like to know how all of you escaped."

Satu's hand was on his arm, holding him in place with surprising strength. He could have broken her grip easily but subsided instead.

"I'd rather describe for you how your people died." He wouldn't, actually, but if he didn't strike back verbally this was going to turn into a brawl.

Casimir grimaced. "No need, Ruarshi. My imagination suffices."

"I doubt it." Something the Seer had said earlier finally made it past the fog of renewed pain. "You overestimate your own importance. I'm sure someone else will pick up the reins now that you're gone."

"Someone will, and then another someone and another. They won't last. The return of shamans to Miriyan marks the return to ascendancy of individual clans. The Doshae will be better off than most, but there will come a time when a central authority will be needed, and we won't have it."

Ruarshi's attention had sharpened at mention of the word 'shamans', as had Satu's. What did Casimir think he knew about it? It was a question he'd have to come at sideways if he wanted an answer, but before he jumped for the bait there was something else he wanted to ask.

"What *is* the punishment for sending dozens of Miriyanti into exile without the knowledge or approval of their clan chiefs?"

"I am not running from the consequences of my actions," Casimir said stiffly. "Jair's people will find me in due time. It's vital that I speak with you before they do, however."

"We're speaking."

"So we are." The Seer paused. "You intend to go north with the Annorae warriors?"

"Yes."

"They will be of great assistance to you, but you may find that the contents of their library are insufficient to explain the cause of the shamans' disappearance."

"Whereas you know the story, and are willing to trade it. What is it you want?"

"We'll come to that. I am not entirely mercenary, Ruarshi, regardless of what you may think of me. Many of Mirror Lake's older records are all but unintelligible, and the parts we can decipher wander into the realm of mysticism too often to be entirely useful, but one fact is very clear and stands out from the rest of it because of the panicked tone of much of the writing: all the shamans, every last one, died within a span of weeks as the result of a threat emanating from the Halls themselves. They were not murdered by their fellows."

"Seggita believed otherwise."

If Casimir was at all discomfited by the name, he didn't show it. "Our research has progressed since he last lived among us. The Seers are what Miriyan was left with after the demise of our shamans, and a poor substitute we have been. No one wanted to lose the power you now represent. It happened anyway. I suggest you approach the Halls very carefully and one at a time."

"You don't know what the threat was."

"We do not."

"Who's leading this research? I might like to talk with them."

"Ilias is his name. He is brilliant with runic script but can be a bit obsessive about his books."

"So I'll be allowed into the library now?"

"We relaxed our rules about that some time ago. There were complaints of undue secrecy."

"Anything else I should know?"

Casimir shook his head. "The warning is all I have for you."

"So now you want us to survive."

"I would prefer it. Retaliation won't mend the damage you've done and there are indications that you and the other shamans may prove useful in the future."

Ruarshi considered the man. This conversation had been so straightforward that he not only disliked Casimir's message, he distrusted it even more than he would have otherwise. The Seer had never been possessed of the kind of generous spirit that could accept defeat and move on. He intended to gain some advantage by coming here today. Perhaps he meant to slow them down by spreading a false tale, in the hope that he could resume his position at Mirror Lake before they'd learned enough to outweigh his influence? That didn't sound quite right. Jair would be howling for Casimir's blood by now, and the Diamyo First could extract as much of it as he wanted, whenever he wanted.

Which might just mean that the Seer had already found some way to defang the warrior, one Ruarshi wouldn't even hear about until Casimir had been set loose to continue wreaking his particular brand of havoc.

Ruarshi gritted his teeth through another spasm, waiting for it to pass before he said, "I have been warned. What is it you plan to leave with in return?"

"My life, and a promise."

"Oh?"

The Seer clearly didn't care for Ruarshi's tone of voice. For the first time he looked uneasy. "How have you been feeling recently?"

"Fine. Why do you ask?"

Casimir smiled at him. "You can hardly sit still. This means my experiment was successful. I honestly didn't think it would work, but since it did, I now have an entire arsenal I can turn against you and the other Nerthii. Cross me and I will."

"Would you care to tell me what you've done? Diagnosis has been a problem."

"She'll be able to tell you," the Seer said, glancing toward the Skeltari, "so that's one method I can't use again. But there are others that I suspect are much more effective. Now. I will have your word that you will leave me be, and that you will advise your allies to do likewise."

Ruarshi stared off into the middle distance as though he were considering Casimir's ultimatum. Instead he extended a weave and broke the Seer's neck, while at the same time smothering his consciousness under a blanket of malign magic that he didn't lift until the man was dead. His passing had been painless, and he'd never realized it was coming. Casimir's body slumped over in the chair and fell bonelessly to the floor.

Ruarshi met Satu's eyes. "I apologize. I accept whatever punishment I'm due."

The old woman was watching him dubiously. "Are you our shaman, young man?"

Opening his mouth to answer her question seemed to be momentarily beyond his capabilities. He wondered if he was going to faint again. When he could speak, he said, "There are two Annorae in our guest house who think so. It would be more accurate to say I am a walking disaster."

"The one doesn't preclude the other," she said. "Come with me."

He stood and trailed her to the wall of her dwelling, where she crouched down to throw a rug aside, revealing a trap door beneath. She raised it, grabbed a flickering candle off a nearby shelf, and turned to descend the ladder that led into the darkness below. He followed her downward and a few seconds later his feet met another floor, this one also of dirt and, it seemed to him, terribly cold. He clung to the ladder for support, breathless, while she went to the edge of the Doshae's sacred well and bent to dip a finger into the water, an expression of distaste on her face.

"Sometime late yesterday he dumped several pounds of salt in here. Enough to make you sick," she said, "but not enough to kill an adult.

Had you been a child still, you would likely be in much worse condition."

Her words were perfectly clear, but Ruarshi couldn't understand what she meant. "What?" The only way to make a person ill with saltwater would be to force them to drink it.

Satu laughed at him. "Let's find out if the Annorae and that dead fool upstairs are right before this goes any further. For all I know you're suffering from a summer fever. Can you cleanse the water, young shaman? Or must we wait for it to cleanse itself?"

"I wouldn't know how to go about cleaning it," he said, approaching the well slowly and kneeling next to the old woman. "But I should be able to drain the water." He didn't believe that doing so would make him feel any better, because the notion was idiotic, but he'd just murdered a man in her home and the least he could do was try to tidy up the mess Casimir had left behind.

Ruarshi kept his mind on the task at hand and refused to consider the wisdom of it. He grasped a corner of the door-into-nothing, shifted it into a horizontal position, and shoved it downward through the well's lightless depths until he thought he'd come up against soil. Then he pulled the door wide. It was harder to do in water than it was in air—finally, one aspect of this peculiar magic that behaved as he thought it should—but when he had it fully open the water rushed out of the well so rapidly that the air swirling in to replace it lifted the hair around his face and set it to brushing against his cheeks.

He dropped his hold on the door a moment later when he realized he couldn't breathe. He closed his eyes and fought to draw in air, struggling for what felt like an eternity but couldn't have been more than a few seconds before his chest opened up again and he was able to pull in a lungful. And another. Another.

When Ruarshi looked up, Satu was standing above him and to his left, her hand bleeding freely into the well from a cut across her palm, her face shadowed and remote in the candlelight. He was lying on his back at the well's edge. He tried to sit up, abandoned the effort, and shifted a few inches away from it instead.

"If you had told me in greater detail what you meant to do," the Skeltari said testily, "I would have advised against it."

Ruarshi badly wanted to start swearing, but that wasn't something one did in front of an elder. Other than a pervasive weakness in his bones, he was very nearly back to normal already. The pain in his gut was gone, the aches had faded to a dim memory, and the sweat that had beaded his hairline earlier had disappeared.

Satu pressed her bleeding hand into a corner of her shawl and scowled at him. "I suppose I have my answer."

"Could you please explain what just happened?" Ruarshi managed.

"You're our shaman, whether we're ready for you or not. How long have you known?"

"A few weeks. And 'known' is far too strong a word. I don't believe half of what I've been told."

The Skeltari snorted. "To answer your question, you are now bound to your clan home in ways that may prove to be inconvenient to you. If the well is fouled again, you will know it. If insects ravage our fields or illness lays low our people or our herds, you will suffer. But there are compensations. The blood," she nodded toward the well, now rapidly filling back up with water, "will restore you. You should leave my home today feeling uncommonly hale. If you find that you're hungrier than usual, take that as a warning and fill your stomach."

Ruarshi raised his hand to his forehead and rubbed at it in vexation. If this continued, he was going to be trading out his earlier ailments for a pounding headache. It wasn't that he'd never heard of anything like this before—it was that he *had,* from Slan. Quaint English nonsense having to do with a mythical king. He had no patience for this.

He shoved himself up into a sitting position and from there was able to push himself to his feet. "I will see that someone is sent to remove Casimir's body."

"And I will warn the other Skeltari to be alert for miscreants." Satu extended her injured hand toward him. "Heal this before you go."

"I cannot."

"Is that so? I did say there were compensations. Give it a try."

He looked away from the Skeltari, ashamed to exhibit his debility in front of her, and reached for his healer's weaves. When they responded at once to his guidance, he drew back from them, startled beyond words, and then ever so carefully began introducing them into her self-inflicted wound. He knitted the flesh back together without difficulty, as though the past months had been nothing more substantial than a bad dream, and when he was done he studied the faint pink scar with a mixture of gratitude and bafflement that left him dizzy.

"Thank you," he said.

"You're welcome." Satu bowed deeply to him. Ruarshi had expected neither the gesture nor its depth. He mirrored her and then fled up the ladder and away, not stopping to glance at Casimir's body on the way out.

It didn't take Ruarshi long to locate a member of the Doshae's burial society and to explain the reason for his intrusion. The man quickly gathered up the necessary supplies and two more society members, both women, and Ruarshi led them wordlessly northward past the clan halls. Satu responded at once to his knock, inviting them in, and he held the door for the others before following them inside. When they'd finished wrapping the Seer's body in a temporary shroud, he trailed them back out into the twilight and watched them carry it away. In mere moments they'd disappeared from view behind a *saal.*

Some time afterward he discovered that he was sitting in the grass outside the Skeltari's home, his back resting against the slight convexity of the outer wall and his gaze focused on his hands, which rested loosely in his lap. He should return to his family's hall now, he thought.

He was still there when Satu emerged from her home, five minutes or an hour later, responding to what prompt he couldn't imagine. He hadn't made a sound or otherwise betrayed his continued presence. She saw him but didn't speak, instead shuffling over to him and laying her palm against the top of his head. She left it there, whether in benediction or condemnation he could not say, for several long minutes before returning indoors. He rose when he heard her throw the latch. It was past time he left her in peace.

# Blood Magic

"Shit! Are you sure?"

When Slan had called Etienne into Ruarshi's room the night before to check on his health, the man had been deeply asleep and in mystifyingly good physical condition. She'd mentioned his visit with the clan Skeltari in passing but had attributed no particular importance to it, and Etienne hadn't thought twice about it before heading to bed. If this rumor he was hearing about a certain dead Aesir Seer were true, he expected Slan would be back in his new family's *saal* in no time, and that she'd be every bit as upset as he was.

The young man who'd given him the news was watching him warily. "I can't imagine that Maija would have made up such a thing. Did you know him?"

"No. Sorry. Thanks for the information." Etienne abandoned what was left of his breakfast and pivoted away from the table. He very nearly collided with Davyt and had to grab the younger man to avoid a startled fall backward. Davyt reciprocated, seizing and holding onto his arm until he'd regained his balance.

"You heard that?" Etienne asked, though he didn't really need to. Unlike his father, Davyt was fairly easy to read.

"Yes."

"Is he up yet, could you tell?"

"I don't know. I didn't hear any noise from his room."

"Oh fuck." Etienne's roving gaze came to rest on a small group of warriors that had just come into the hall. They had paused near the door, uncertain. He'd be willing to bet quite a lot of money that they'd been sent by Ciarn, who had no doubt also heard the rumor and would be wanting some answers about now.

He strode over to them. "Is it Ruarshi you're after?" Several of the Naishanti nodded in reply. "Is he under arrest?" If he didn't like what he heard next, he was going to help get Ruarshi out of there even if it meant he'd end up back among the Jinnae.

A tall woman standing slightly in advance of the others answered him. "No. Should he be? Ciarn would like a word with him."

Etienne gestured for them to wait and went to Ruarshi's door, Davyt on his heels. When he'd gotten up that morning he hadn't been at all prepared for a cascading disaster, yet here they were. He hoped the man was already awake.

He knocked once and tried the latch. When the door proved to be unlocked, he pushed his way inside.

Ruarshi was up, dressed, and tying his hair back in a ragged ponytail when they entered. He glanced over at them in mild curiosity. "Ciarn?"

"Yes. What the *fuck,* Ruarshi?"

"Satu—that's our Skeltari—seemed disinclined to object, and if I remember correctly Ciarn doesn't have jurisdiction over matters that concern her. He's just nosy. You can come along if you like."

Which was the kind of cheeky nonsense that one got from Ruarshi on occasion, but which he was disinclined to tolerate this time. "That's not what I was asking."

"I know."

"Is that a grin? Because if that's a grin, Ruarshi, I'm going to stab you."

"Please don't. Besides, it's your fault. You look like you're ready to square off with a lion."

Etienne narrowed his eyes. "I'm prepared to talk them to death if you need the time to get away."

That brought Ruarshi up short. He stopped fiddling with his clothes and stepped forward to squeeze Etienne's shoulder. "Thank you," he said, "but that shouldn't be necessary." Then he moved to open the door, mussing Davyt's hair as he went past and leaving the two of them to exchange a long-suffering glance in his wake.

By the time their little procession had made its way to the clan chief's modest audience chamber, every last one of their recent traveling companions had joined it, along with a small assemblage of curious Doshae youngsters. Slan, Lorion, and Tuomi intercepted them right outside the *saal,* while Karoli and the Valkyries caught up with them just after they'd passed the guest house. Etienne shot the Diamyo a quelling look, which was ignored, and Ruarshi slipped sideways through the press to engage the man in a low-voiced conversation. Shortly afterward a grimace and a few placating hand gestures on the warrior's part left Etienne feeling somewhat reassured about his intentions.

When they reached the chamber's threshold, the children were turned away while the rest of them were allowed inside to find a place among the several semicircles of benches facing the clan chief's chair. The only strangers left in the room were two of the Naishanti who'd come to fetch them, Ciarn himself, and a solemn old woman. Etienne blinked when he realized she had to be the clan's Skeltari. She wasn't at all what he'd been expecting.

"I am aware that any observations I might make about what happened last night carry little weight," Ciarn began, his gaze snagging on Karoli's face before moving smoothly onward, "but I do need to understand the sequence of events. The Aesir have a right to an explanation, and I do not want to set off a feud between our two clans. *Tai* Skeltari, can you tell us what took place?"

"The Seer fouled our sacred well," Satu said without hesitation. "It was an unprovoked assault upon our entire clan. If any formal apologies need to be made, they should come from the Aesir."

Ciarn looked like he had just bitten into something sour. "How did he foul it?"

"By the introduction of foreign matter. The young one there," she lifted her chin in Ruarshi's direction, "fixed the problem for me."

"And how exactly did Casimir die?"

The old woman shrugged. "He fell over in his chair in the middle of our conversation. I really don't know. Perhaps a heart attack?"

"I was told he had a broken neck."

"That could easily have happened when he fell."

Etienne bit his lip so hard he feared that he might have drawn blood. Ciarn, for his part, was doing an admirable job of maintaining his equanimity, though he didn't sound happy.

"I am sure the Aesir will also want to know why our Nerthi was present."

"His presence was neither here nor there, but I take it the two of them didn't get along," the Skeltari said. "The Seer had just threatened to kill the young one when he had his attack."

"Could you discern the motive behind the threat?"

"The Aesir was afraid of the young one, I think."

"Did he have on his person any means of harming 'the young one'?"

"He had no weapons. I would not have allowed him into my home if he had."

"So the threat was something he intended to act on in the future, but not during the course of your discussion."

"I could not read his mind, Ciarn. Men have been known to murder one another with their bare hands."

Etienne thought he might be falling in love with the Skeltari. He'd have to take her a gift of apples later.

"So you're telling me that the Seer came to our clan home, polluted our well, asked to meet with our kinsman in order to threaten him, and then dropped dead?"

"Yes," Satu said, unsmiling.

The clan chief shifted in his chair. "Do you have anything to add to that account, Ruarshi?"

"I do not."

Ciarn scowled at him. Ruarshi returned his regard equably and the silence stretched. Before it could quite cross the line from uncomfortable into unbearable, the clan chief released his breath in an explosive sigh and sat back. "I will prepare a letter to accompany the body back to the Aesir clan home," he said. "Both will be gone by late afternoon. If anyone would like to add any additional detail before that time, please come find me. Thanks to all of you for attending."

And just like that the inquiry was over. Such as it was. As their group started back toward the hall, Ruarshi addressed them in an undertone. "I'm sorry I didn't warn you last night."

"You seemed barely capable of making it into your bed," Slan said. "You will let us know what happened." It wasn't a question.

"I'll try," Ruarshi said. "Just don't ask for explanations when I come to the stranger parts, because I have none to offer."

"Did the subject of shamanism come up?" Lorion asked.

"It did. Maybe you can help me make some sense of it."

"Maybe," Elin said. "Did you bring it up first, or did Casimir?"

"Casimir."

"That's not good news," Elin said. "Mirror Lake shouldn't have any of those old writings. Several of our ancestors died to get them out of that place."

Ruarshi waited for her to go on. When she didn't, he said, "If he was telling the truth, the bits and pieces they retained are rather unnerving. Satu knows a lot about it, too."

"Did she accept you as the clan shaman? Is that why she was protecting you?" Etienne asked.

"It was either that, or she just took a liking to me. We should have a long talk with her soon."

There was another question Etienne wanted to ask, this one about Ruarshi's sudden recovery, but he decided it could wait. Unless he missed his guess it was tied up with the mysterious events of the night before, and he didn't think those were best discussed out in the open air on an otherwise beautiful morning. That was the sort of conversation you had indoors with a mug of *keth* to hand, a fire flickering dimly at the corners of your vision, and thick walls standing between you and the rest of the world.

Etienne emerged from Ruarshi's rooms an hour or so later with a sick feeling in his stomach and wishing he'd somehow contrived to miss the entire discussion. The strange shaman-Skeltari relationship that lay behind the particulars of what had happened at Satu's house was unsettling enough on its own, and his former instructor's sanguine acceptance of his newly discovered vulnerability to harm at the hands of anyone with a grudge, a little bit of knowledge, and access to the clan's sacred well only made it worse. Etienne would even go so far as to say that Ruarshi had been relieved to learn of the dangers inherent in his situation. He'd had no trouble grasping why the man might feel that way, and Ruarshi's spare but merciless description of what had passed between him and Casimir had only confirmed his suspicions. The Seer was satisfactorily dead, which meant they had one less hazard to contend with, but the manner of his demise was certain to cause trouble and he had no idea where it would show up first, or what form it would take. And he needed a better plan than keeping an eye on Ruarshi and hoping for the best.

Elin had lingered inside but when she appeared in the doorway he pounced. "Do you have a minute?" Saoirse was giving him a borderline disapproving look, but he was too preoccupied to care.

"Certainly," Elin replied, and they moved away from the *saal* until they could speak without being overheard.

"How much of that was news to you?"

"Almost all of it," she said, "which annoys me to no end. I knew a bit about the role of the Skeltari, of course, but as to the rest of it… We need to go to Mirror Lake, I think."

As ideas went, that definitely qualified as one. Etienne gave it some
consideration. "How hard would it be to find anything useful in their library?"

"At a guess, very. But we can't send anyone into the Halls without
knowing if they harbor some kind of threat, and the Seers mustn't be
left in possession of information telling them how to murder Nerthii. I
hope Casimir was the secretive sort."

"I'm certain he was," Etienne said. "Any guesses as to *how* the
Skeltari guard the clan wells? Beyond controlling access to them. It
didn't sound to me like Satu took any great pains to keep Casimir from
doing whatever he wanted with ours. What if he'd gone straight for
something fatal?"

"Surely this is a concern Ruarshi has already addressed with her,"
Elin said.

"I can almost guarantee he hasn't."

"Why wouldn't he?"

"It's complicated and not really my place to say." Etienne knew it
was an inadequate answer, but he didn't have anything better for her.

"Saoirse and I will pay her a visit," Elin said. "Today. It's a question
worth asking and perhaps we can compare notes while we're there. It
would be useful for introductory purposes if a Doshae went with us."

"I'm at your disposal."

"Hold on." Elin went over to confer with her sister, and after a
short exchange she returned with Saoirse in tow.

"No time like the present," she said.

Etienne ducked out of the hall early the next morning before breakfast,
determined to seize the opportunity to take a walk in relative silence.
He needed to clear his head, and as much as he already cared for his
new family—every last member of it living in that particular *saal*, without exception—he felt a short break from the near-constant clamor
within its walls might do him some good.

He'd left Satu's *kiva* the day before feeling even more anxious than
he had after the session with Ruarshi, and the uneasiness had yet to
loosen its hold on him. One the one hand, the horrible old woman had
assuaged his worst fears by making it clear that she and her fellow
Skeltari had matters well in hand. Without quite coming out and saying
so, she'd given him to understand that Casimir's pollution of the well

would not have gone unanswered, had the man lived long enough to try to walk back out her door. Something about her manner had made him wonder if Ruarshi's decision to murder the Seer had actually been a merciful alternative to whatever she'd had planned. On the other hand, Satu had then launched into a discourse on magic that had gradually made the hair on the back of Etienne's neck stand on end.

All Miriyanti thought of the working of magic as weaving, so there was nothing particularly novel about the Skeltari's words so far as that concept went, but she'd taken the metaphor further. Etienne supposed it was his own fault that he'd never thought about the nature of the loom that supported their weaves. Assuming such a thing even existed, and the old woman wasn't pulling their legs for the hell of it.

Satu had explained, without prompting, that warriors' weaves were the weakest and least consequential type of magic known to Miriyanti. They affected only the immediate moment and then dissipated, though they could be impressive while they lasted, whereas the Wood- and Stoneshapers could change the essence of a thing now and for many hundreds or thousands of years into the future. What healers did fell somewhere in between, and Satu seemed to think that the Nerthii's ability to manipulate weaves from two entirely different parts of the loom accounted for the fact that the natural world could, in some sense, 'see' them. The shadow they cast on the loom was... larger? Heavier? Etienne still had no notion of how that translated into salt in a well having made Ruarshi so sick, but evidently the same principle enabled Nerthii to choose among the futures once they reached the Halls. They cast a sizable shadow there, as well.

None of this very interesting information was responsible for his current mood, however. That had set in at about the time Satu had mentioned blood and some of the uses thereof. He didn't object to the notion of utilizing blood for magical purposes, as long as it led to some good outcome, but he seriously disliked the Skeltari's assertion that the loom itself had been created in the distant past by means of massive bloodshed. That was disturbing on several levels. One, it implied that some ancestral lunatic or set of lunatics had gone on some kind of ritualized rampage. Satu hadn't made any such claim, but if a straightforward bloody melee could give rise to magic, there wasn't a civilization on earth that would be without it at this point. Since Miriyanti remained the only magic users Etienne had ever heard of, this meant someone had committed mass murder with specific intent.

Which brought him to point two: somehow the murderers had

known exactly what they were doing. Where they would have come by such knowledge Etienne couldn't imagine, and speculating about it was both useless and frightening. Three, Satu's account raised the possibility that magic itself was basically malign. Etienne had always thought of it as a neutral and more or less rational force, adhering as it did to certain rules and regulated as it was by means of law and custom. And maybe it didn't even matter if magic arose as a result of some nightmare series of events. But, if true, Satu's tale meant that unspoken assumptions Etienne had relied upon his entire life had been upended, and the talent he'd always been most proud of was just a raft afloat upon an ancient ocean of blood and pain.

Which was an unwelcome visual, and Etienne thought sourly that he now understood why Skeltari led solitary lives, visited only by their apprentices and an occasional intrepid family member. It was possible that he and the warriors had deserved to leave Satu's *kiva* in a jittery state, since their whole purpose in going there had been to question her competence, but he hadn't mistaken the subtle antipathy underlying her remarks. Satu had gotten her apples, but that was the last basket of anything he'd be taking her.

Etienne's feet had brought him to the bridge over the river. The breeze off the water was refreshing and he walked out onto the short span, stopping when he reached the midpoint to look over the edge at the ripples below. He leaned against the chest-high stone and allowed his worries to ebb away, certain that they'd still be there waiting for him when he took up that fruitless line of thought again in the future.

When people began moving about in his peripheral vision he turned away, unwilling to allow the day's bustle to interrupt his moment of peace just yet. He was startled when a light hand landed on his shoulder a few minutes later. He pivoted to find Ruarshi standing next to him, a smile on his face and a faint puzzled crease just visible between his eyebrows.

"Good morning, Etienne. I can leave if I'm intruding."

"Good to see you. You're not intruding." Etienne watched as his former instructor walked a little farther along the bridge and then retraced his steps, the crease deepening as his abstracted air grew more pronounced. He thought he might take a guess at what was troubling the man. "There's a difference, isn't there? Between one side of the bridge and the other."

Ruarshi nodded. "It's... strange. The closer I get to the far bank, the more I feel like an unwelcome stone that's lodged itself in someone's shoe. I hope it's a sensation that fades with time." He shook his head as though to clear it, and his smile grew focused. "But that's not why I'm here." He reached into the pocket of his light summer vest and withdrew a small object that he extended toward Etienne. "Some of the others argued for an elaborate ceremony, but I thought you might prefer something simpler. Once you accept our totem, you're one of us and no power on earth can make it otherwise."

Etienne studied the object: a snow fox made of silver and plated with white enamel, its tail curled up behind its head to form an elegant circle. The tip of a pin extended from its right side. He felt himself in some danger of starting to sniffle, but then he noticed that the fox's eyes had been rendered with tiny faceted rubies. They glinted up at him. He laughed, startled, and accepted the pin.

"Red eyes? Really?"

Ruarshi, the irises of his eyes almost equally red in the morning sunlight, looked embarrassed. "I asked my mother if she could obtain one of these for me. She hasn't noticed the eyes yet. It's a coincidence."

"Thank you, Ruarshi," Etienne said, his voice reduced to a near-whisper by the lump in his throat. The man didn't reply, instead moving to stand beside him, close enough that their shoulders touched. They gazed westward in silence until Ruarshi spoke again.

"How are you settling in?"

"No complaints. Everyone has been very welcoming. Three young women and one young man have tried flirting with me."

Ruarshi chuckled. "That's as it should be. Do you lack for anything? I want you to be comfortable here."

"I am comfortable. I'm a little concerned that one of the Jinnae will show up someday and make trouble."

"I'll send them away with whatever level of force is required. Unless it's someone you want to talk to. Is there anyone who belongs in that category?"

"There are a handful I wouldn't mind having a chat with, but they're unlikely to send a clan member from my generation over here to complain. They'll send someone older. I can't imagine that I'd want to spend time with any of them."

"Noted."

Etienne seized upon the lull in conversation to pose a question of his own. "Are you all right?"

"I was about to ask the same of you."

"When I have complaints, you'll hear about them. At length and in great detail."

"You're not nearly as forthcoming as you pretend."

"Trying to change the subject. Tsk."

Ruarshi shrugged uncomfortably. "I can't seem to dredge up any honest remorse about what I did. Murdering Casimir made me feel better. Eventually. It seemed unjust that I should have killed all those countrymen in Europe, while allowing the man who'd sent them there to go on his merry way. It's possible that I have always been this person and just didn't realize it."

"Good."

"Good?"

"If you were self-flagellating over this, I was going to take your whip and break it over my knee."

"Impertinent."

"Yes."

"You've had your question answered," Ruarshi said. "Now it's time for mine."

"It's okay. I'm okay. Davyt is less okay."

"I am aware. And now you're doing it."

"Doing what?"

Ruarshi looked at him blandly. "Changing the subject."

Etienne raised his hands in a defensive gesture. "I grew up doing awful things to my elders because they deserved it. People are terrible. Nothing about what's happened over the past few months surprised me. Well, the particulars surprised me, but not the overall unpleasantness. I'm doing well."

"Wait. What? But you like everyone."

"For a while, I do. I live in hope. It's the great tragedy of my existence."

Ruarshi shook his head. "Etienne. I appreciate your bravery and resilience, and most of the time I even appreciate your sense of humor. But it's safe to be more forthcoming now, if that would help. All this stoicism is beginning to concern me."

"It's not stoicism so much as it is putting it out of my mind. Dwelling on what happened certainly won't help. I haven't had a terrifying dream for at least a month. And I don't know what to do for Davyt."

"I don't, either. I've asked Ardan to speak with him. She has a way of keeping her distance that makes it easier to talk." Ruarshi ran a hand through his hair, the only indication of his agitation. "I made a lot of mistakes while we were in Mainz. I am so sorry, Etienne."

"Didn't we already have this conversation? At least twice?" Etienne asked, annoyed. "Quit apologizing." He glanced over at the man, and the bleakness in his expression was suddenly more than Etienne was willing to put up with. "Why do you want me to help flay you for the decisions you've made? You don't appear to need any assistance. It's encouraging that you're distressed on behalf of the living rather than the dead, but when we offer you anything that smells like absolution you reject it out of hand. You forgive others everything, and yourself nothing. It's frustrating."

"I can see why it would be, but I think you've misread me. I *will* let it go. Once I'm persuaded that the rest of you really are on the mend."

Though the prospect terrified him, Etienne decided to bull ahead with the subject that had floated to the forefront of his mind. "If you're serious about clearing the air, there is one incident I fault you for."

"That would be...?"

"I had to lie to Davyt on your behalf. I hated doing it but I didn't have a choice." The day was fully upon them now, and a small group from the southernmost *saal* was headed for the bridge. Etienne lowered his voice. "I know what you tried to do while you were laid up in that bed in Mainz. I tried to persuade myself that you were in pain and your power got away from you, but I never believed it. If it had just been me there and you had succeeded, that would have been one thing. But your son was in the room and you knew it. I don't even remember what I told him."

"For what it's worth, I wasn't in my right mind at the time," Ruarshi said quietly. His eyes were closed and his face seemed to have lost its color. "I would not do that to either of you."

"Except you did. I was very angry with you afterward. I still am. A little."

*'That's* why you were avoiding me."

"I was sick, if you recall. But that had less to do with my behavior than the other."

"Thank you for the lie. Whatever it was."

"You're welcome."

"He was convinced?"

"As far as I could tell."

The man had gone slightly gray and Etienne wondered if he was going to faint.

"Ruarshi?"

"I'm here." He opened his eyes but didn't look up. "I wish I'd had you around instead of Aethel while I was growing up. Don't tell him I said so."

"He would probably be offended."

"It's likely. You've stabbed yourself."

Etienne glanced down and swore under his breath. A half inch of fox pin had embedded itself in his palm and he hadn't even noticed. He extracted the gleaming metal and started patting his pockets with his left hand, looking for a scrap of cloth or something else he could use to absorb the blood before it ended up all over his clothes. He had nothing.

"Dammit." He hurried off the bridge and made his way to the river's edge, where he kneeled to submerge the wound in the water. Ruarshi trailed him and sat down on the bank at his side, extending a hand in a wordless offer of healing. Etienne acquiesced and Ruarshi cleaned and closed the small puncture with careful haste.

"I've botched your formal acceptance into the clan pretty thoroughly, haven't I?" Ruarshi asked. He held the pin now and was turning it over in his fingers. "Our totem has injured you and our conversation has upset you. Perhaps our river spirit will now prove to be real and attack you, so we'll have a full triad of mishaps to look back on one day."

"Your river spirit sounds unusually belligerent."

"She's placid most of the time. Let me pin this to something other than your skin." Ruarshi chose a spot on Etienne's upper chest and pushed the point through his shirt, then made sure it was safely clasped before leaning back on his elbows in the grass. "There. You're ours now. You needn't wear that all the time, in case you're wondering."

"It's impressively heavy."

"What's the Jinnae's totem?" Ruarshi asked.

"Magpie."

Ruarshi laughed, and Etienne raised an eyebrow. "Why is that funny?"

"Because it suits you."

"I remind you of a bad-tempered bird?"

"The other way around, maybe. If birds could talk, I'm certain the similarities would become even clearer."

"You're going to be a troublesome adoptive family, I can tell."

Ruarshi smiled at him. "You'll win everyone over in no time. If you haven't already."

"Your Skeltari seems immune to my charms. Maybe I shouldn't have shown up at her house in the company of warriors. She liked them even less. Just as well you started out a healer."

"Just as well," Ruarshi murmured, before rousing himself and sitting up. "Have you had breakfast?"

"No."

"I haven't either. Should we fix that?"

"We could, but I'm feeling dizzy. Blood loss."

"I'll fetch a sled and drag you home."

"That sounds undignified."

"Count on it."

Etienne found that he was mirroring Ruarshi's grin, and what remained of his earlier unease melted away in the time it took him to draw his next breath. The man's close presence, as it had for years now, made him feel that pessimism was unjustified and anything was possible.

"What with my being the newest member of the clan and all, I suppose I ought to aim for 'impressive' instead. For at least a week or two. I don't want people to get the wrong idea."

"They'll mark your general indolence soon enough, anyway."

"I am offended."

"I apologize," Ruarshi said, rising and offering him a hand up. Etienne took it and the smaller man pulled him to his feet. "You could enter our solstice strength contests if you're inclined to try showing off. Though your efforts would be a lot more effective if you actually managed to win something."

Etienne chuckled as they started back toward their hall. "No need to sound so doubtful. There are always ways to bend the odds in one's favor."

# The Halls

Lorion stood unmoving, staring at the open doorway. "I have misgivings," he said.

"We don't have to do this now. Or at all, if you don't want to." Ruarshi was closer than his good-brother to the strange gap into apparent nothingness, and he could feel the cold radiating outward from it. If he believed what Elin had been telling him—and at this point he'd decided to give her the benefit of the doubt, though with certain reservations—the temperature would only become a threat if one of them tried straddling the threshold rather than moving on through. The Halls themselves were not inimical to life. Or at least they hadn't been ten generations earlier, or no one would ever have explored them in the first place.

Elin's other two warnings were only slightly less peculiar: shedding blood was to be avoided until one was ready to start having visions, and falling asleep was similarly discouraged, unless one wanted to become untethered from time and emerge from the Halls days or even years after entering them. While the first of these might conceivably prove to be a challenge, as the possibility of blundering into a sharp object or tripping and falling couldn't be ruled out, Ruarshi didn't think either of them would settle in for a nap until they'd finished with this little adventure. He personally felt very far from sleep at the moment.

"If I back out, you'll just explore the place alone," Lorion said.

"Yes, if by 'explore' you mean take a quick look around and then come running back here. I'm not in the mood to contemplate the future."

"Can't say that I am either. I don't even like thinking about the next five minutes."

They had discussed this at some length the night before. It was now the afternoon of the summer solstice, Ruarshi's entire clan was fully engaged in the attendant celebrations, they'd walked a mile through sparse forest so no one would stumble upon them by accident, and there would never be a better time for them to do this. Especially since their little group was about to split up for a while.

"No purpose to hatching a conspiracy if we're not going to follow through," Lorion said. "Are you ready?"

"Yes. One modification to the plan. I'm going to step through and let the door close. Then I'm going to try to reopen it from the other side while you wait for me."

That elicited exactly the frown he'd expected. "I can't open one of these to get you out."

"Not yet. But if we were both to end up trapped in there, no one would know that we needed help."

"You could have mentioned this idea yesterday. It will fall on me to rescue you if something goes wrong."

"Better you than Tuomi or someone else."

Lorion's scowl had turned into a glare. "So if you don't reemerge, I go back to your clan home, use magic to murder the first person I come across, return to this spot, and then figure out how to open a door? *Don't* tell me you've explained the process more than once. Every attempt you make is more incoherent than the last."

"I wouldn't recommend exactly that approach to the problem, no. But if we can't get back out once we're in there, better that only one of us has to learn this the hard way. I don't believe that will happen. Doors generally operate from either direction; it's one of their greatest virtues. I'm just being cautious."

"I'm sure you are, Ruarshi. If I have to pull you back through that door, Slan will be with me when I do. You can explain yourself to her." Lorion rubbed a hand over his face. "Assuming you don't return instantly, how long should I give you before raising the hue and cry?"

"A few minutes should do. I don't intend to dawdle."

Lorion nodded in response but said nothing more. Ruarshi, hoping that he appeared as sanguine as he'd sounded, tightened his grip on the small and probably useless torch he held, took a deep breath, and plunged through the doorway. At the last moment he remembered to close his eyes to protect them from the cold.

After a frigid instant that knocked the wind out of his lungs, he was falling.

Gasping, he opened his eyes. His gaze landed on a dark stone wall, dimly illuminated by murky gray light. He blinked. Nothing in his field of vision changed.

Finally he thought to look down. His feet rested firmly on sandy soil, though the sensation of hurtling downward at great speed continued to knot his gut. The mismatch between what his different senses were telling him very nearly doubled him over with the urge to vomit, so he closed his eyes again and concentrated on steadying his breathing until the sensation passed. He briefly rested a hand against the wall through which he'd come in an effort to keep his balance, but yanked it back with a low oath. It had felt worse, much worse, than spreading one's palm against a frozen waterfall. He didn't understand why the entire surface wasn't coated in ice.

When he'd mostly regained his equilibrium, he squared his shoulders and looked around. He was in a narrow corridor, its floor unremarkable, the opposite wall neither warm nor cold to his touch. Both walls disappeared into the darkness directly above him, but several yards to his left a shaft of dim light spilled through a roughly rectangular hole in the ceiling, suggesting a gap into open atmosphere. Far down the corridor to his right he could see another such shaft. His torch had gone out, as Elin had warned them would happen, and he glanced down at it in mild aggravation before letting it fall. The air tasted of dryness and dust and nothing else, and seemed thin, as though he stood on top of a mountain.

Ruarshi shook himself and turned back the way he'd come. He was certain he'd been standing there longer than he'd intended to, and he was glad he'd resolved before coming through the door that he'd need to relinquish his hold on it for this test to mean anything. He'd never have been able to maintain his grip on it in any case, not in the rush of fear he'd felt when he'd believed himself to be plunging to his death. Its absence was all part of the plan, and no cause for panic. None at all.

Doing his best to ignore the trembling in his hands, he reached for the doorway, found it, opened it, and hurried back through.

Lorion was exactly where Ruarshi had left him. He slumped to the grass and sat staring at the trees without really seeing them, waiting for his shakes to subside.

"Are you all right?" Lorion asked, kneeling beside him.

The falling sensation hadn't returned. "I'm well. It's good to see you. The Halls seem very dull."

"Nothing lurking in the shadows?"

"I'm… not sure there were any shadows."

"No shadows?"

"I suppose there must have been. I wasn't attending and my torch went out. I doubt there's anything alive in there. Elin was right about the temperature drop at the doorway, but that's not the real problem. Stepping through feels like falling off a cliff. Odd that the shamans of old didn't mention that."

"Maybe they all had a wicked sense of humor. Or maybe that didn't happen to them. It has been a while."

"Maybe." Ruarshi looked up. "How'd your last meal settle?"

"I'm as steady as I'm ever going to be. We can delay this if you need more time."

"No. I don't want to have to sneak back out here tomorrow." He rose and gestured toward the door, which he'd kept open. "Brace yourself. You should go first. I'll probably drop the doorway again."

Lorion stared at the blackness in the air before him for a moment, visibly centering himself, and then strode across the threshold.

Ruarshi followed right behind him. The falling sensation returned and he stumbled forward, narrowly avoiding a collision with his good-brother before fetching up against the inner wall. He swallowed several times, waiting until he was sure he had control over himself before allowing the doorway to close. When he glanced over at Lorion, the man was watching him curiously.

"Don't tell me. You didn't feel that?" Ruarshi asked.

"The cold, yes. The falling, no. It looks like my torch didn't fare any better than yours."

Lorion dropped the still-smoking bit of pine and pitch and pulled a small square of white cloth from his vest. He bent and spread it on the ground to mark the spot where they'd come through. Though both Annorae sisters claimed that this realm wasn't much concerned with matters of distance, and that they'd emerge where they entered regardless, neither Ruarshi nor Lorion had been content to trust to precedent in this case. They wanted to make sure they left the Halls in the right place.

Lorion moved a few steps away. "Murky, isn't it?" he observed. "If there's anything living in here that can move much faster than a turtle, my sword will be useless."

The reminder was helpful, in that it distracted Ruarshi from his ongoing struggle to convince himself that he was standing on solid ground. He located his own discarded torch, focused a weave on it for a heartbeat or two, and snapped it in half.

"Our magic still works. We should be able to handle any monsters that jump out at us."

"Unless there are too many of them. I would swear that this floor is level, but I'm upslope from you now."

Ruarshi swallowed one last time and looked at his companion. If asked, he'd have insisted that Lorion was now standing on a surface a foot or so below *him,* leading him to wonder if a sword fight would even be possible here. They couldn't both be downhill from each other at the same time, could they?

It was a mystery that would have to wait. They had some exploring to do, and then they could leave, and with any luck neither of them would ever find a reason to return.

"I'm steadier now. Shall we?" Ruarshi asked.

Lorion led the way down the hall, heading rightward from their point of entry. They'd been assured that going left would sooner or later leave them staring at a tremendous rockfall that blocked their way forward, and though that didn't necessarily mean there was nothing to be learned in that direction, it did give them a more practical option to pursue.

Ruarshi stretched his senses as far as he could both before and behind them and encountered nothing. Not that this meant much, since he couldn't estimate the extent of his reach here. It felt like he was covering a vast distance, but this realm had already proven to be unreliable and for all he knew his ability to sense another living thing extended no farther than he could see.

He continued in his good-brother's wake as the hallway turned to the left and bent back on itself. A short while later it bent rightward and did the same.

"Let me know if you spot any side passages," Lorion murmured. "She promised us a labyrinth, not a maze, but an unwelcome surprise or two would be in keeping with the rest of it."

"The stroll to the center is supposed to have a calming effect."

"I don't feel any calmer than I was when I got here. Do you? You've noticed that our voices sound muffled?"

"I have. Another oddity to add to the list."

"I am anxious that this is going to turn out to have been a waste of time. And a number of people will be furious about this."

"It's not something I'm going to bring up at dinner."

"Smart."

They kept walking, as they had no real alternative, and after a mile or so Lorion growled and came to a halt.

"Did Elin ever happen to mention how long this goes on?"

The dead silence of the hallway was getting to Ruarshi, too, and he was carefully not thinking about claustrophobia or the possibility that the irregularly spaced holes in the roof might peter out at some point, leaving them to decide between turning back or fumbling through absolute darkness. "She didn't. I'm not sure distance and time are the same here for everyone."

"The idiots who built these walls damn sure knew how many rocks they stacked up."

"You would think. Maybe one of us will find a count in an old scroll."

Lorion eyed him. "What a discovery that would be. If you don't mind, I'd like to pick up the pace."

"I'll be right behind you."

Lorion set off at a steady jog and Ruarshi matched his speed. Three switchbacks later, Ruarshi spotted a ground-level source of illumination ahead, in the shape of a low doorway with a bowed lintel. His good-brother sped up, only to shy away from something that lay partially across the floor of the corridor a few feet from the exit. Then the man came to an abrupt halt.

"Is that what I think it is?" Lorion asked.

Ruarshi glanced down at what he initially took to be a pile of cloth, only to realize that it was an eerily well-preserved but ancient corpse. He crouched in the sandy soil to take a closer look.

"A dead woman," he said. "I wonder how long she's been here."

"A fair span, by the look of her," Lorion said. "Why would they leave her here?"

"Perhaps she was the last of them. The old shamans. No one left who could come in to bring her out."

"Hmm. Maybe. I suppose the task will fall to us, then. We can't leave her behind."

Ruarshi had been searching for an obvious cause of death, but the woman's head appeared intact and the rest of her body was swathed in two or possibly three layers of clothing. Another unknown to add to the day's tally.

"So much for not telling the others what we did with our afternoon."

"That idea was doomed from the start," Lorion said, grimacing.

"Well, we're here. Hooray. Come on."

The former warrior mumbled a blessing over the woman and covered the remaining distance to the doorway in a few quick strides. He ducked through and Ruarshi trailed him out.

Once outside, he straightened and surveyed his surroundings. They stood at the edge of a sizable clearing which was completely encircled by the inner wall of the labyrinth they had just left. A low stone rim bounded a lightless area at its center. A well?

Beside him, Lorion exhaled explosively and pointed upward. Ruarshi raised his head.

The cloud cover made it difficult to see in its precise outlines, but he could tell what had disturbed the man: the sun was the wrong shape, an hourglass rather than a sphere. And it loomed much too large in the sky. It occurred to him to be thankful for the overcast, as he couldn't imagine how unbearably bright it would be here on a clear day.

"I had half expected to land in China. Or India," Lorion said. "I don't care for this at all. Let's take a look at that and leave." He gestured toward the well with a nervous shooing motion and moved toward it, only to stop again after going two or three yards.

Ruarshi had pivoted to look back the way they'd come, on the off chance that some hazard might have emerged from the labyrinth behind them, but he could still see his good-brother out of the corner of his eye. He turned back around. "What is it?"

"The well shifted. Didn't it?"

Ruarshi considered it. "I don't think so...?"

Lorion drew his sword and continued cautiously forward, pausing before each step to prod the ground in front of him. The man was still a short distance from the edge of the well when the tip of his blade seemed to disappear into the soil. After a slight pause, he started swearing.

"How far away from it do I look to you?" Lorion asked.

"About five feet."

"Close your eyes for a few seconds. When you reopen them, tell me what you see."

Ruarshi did as Lorion asked, didn't like the result, and tried it again. The outcome was the same. "You're right at the well's edge."

"I know. I shouldn't be. A few minutes ago, the clearing was larger than it is now."

Ruarshi had never been particularly good at estimating distances, but he thought his good-brother might be correct. "I'm coming up be-

hind you." Retracing Lorion's path should be safe, he reasoned, but as
he had no weapon with which to test the ground, he moved slowly.

Even so, he flinched when Lorion suddenly shouted at him to stop.
He closed his eyes, opened them, and discovered that he was now at
the near edge of the well, with his good-brother standing along the rim
opposite. He cast a quick glance over his shoulder. The door through
which they'd entered the labyrinth's heart was still behind him, right
where it should be.

Ruarshi smiled at Lorion, who was looking a little wild-eyed, and
shrugged a shoulder as nonchalantly as he could. "That was disconcerting," he remarked. "Can you try walking around this thing until you're
back over here with me? I don't like having it between us."

Still using his sword as a prod, Lorion started around the well's
perimeter. When he arrived at Ruarshi's side, he lowered himself carefully to sit on the rim. He shoved the weapon's point into the dirt and
rested his forehead against the hilt, letting out a long sigh.

"If I ever do this again, I'm coming blindfolded."

"I don't see any water down there."

"Squint," Lorion suggested. "I'm not sure it's water, but there's
something. I swear to you I heard a splash when the well moved to
meet you."

Ruarshi took another look but still saw nothing. Closing his eyes
again, he crouched with his knees against worn stone and leaned forward. His hand wasn't half a foot below the surface of the ground
when he felt an unpleasant prickling followed by wetness against his
fingers. He raised his arm and discovered that his hand was covered
with what appeared to be blood.

Lorion seized his wrist. "What did you just do?" he demanded.

Ruarshi opened his mouth to deny he'd done anything stupid, but
then he felt a wave of heat rush up his arm and decided he'd need to
revise his opinion on that. His vision swam.

Fortunately he'd had a good bit of practice over the years at keeping
unwanted intrusions out of his head, and although he didn't think that
merely allowing the onslaught of images to play themselves out before
his mind's eye would harm him or anyone else, he was disinclined to let
the process unfold without his consent.

He set his mental feet and resisted, and for a while was able to hold
off the tidal wave of color and motion, but in the end he proved unable to prevent one sequence from slipping through: *He was standing on
an unfamiliar shore and holding an odd obsidian dagger. He drew his arm back*

M J McBride

*and threw the weapon as hard as he could, and it spun end over end against the backdrop of a starry purple sky before disappearing without a sound into the water...*

When Ruarshi fell back into his body some indeterminate time later, he found Lorion staring at him in alarm for the second time that day. "Having visions?"

"Just the one. I hope I wasn't sitting here long."

"No, but I'm about done with this place. There are no wounds on your hand or arm, or anywhere else."

Ruarshi glanced down at his torso, legs, and feet, then sighed and rubbed his still-wet hand against his pants to clean it. "I think the well pulled the blood through my skin. Don't fall in. Tell me you didn't look everywhere."

The corner of Lorion's mouth quirked upward. "I gave you a very thorough examination. You'll be interested to know that someone else has been here. When I set my hand down a minute ago, this was right under my palm." He dangled a leather strap in Ruarshi's face. It took him a moment to notice the small stone token of a bear that hung from it. "I couldn't see it until I touched it. This belonged to Aurel. She didn't just wander off to die. She came here."

Ruarshi nodded distractedly in acknowledgment. Without quite having made up his mind to do so, he'd begun delving down into the well as far as his power would take him, looking for something that could account for the vision and the rest of it. How could anything other than a conscious awareness respond to his presence here, and where would it reside other than the well, the apparent focus of this place...?

There was nothing to be found. Nothing at all, and Lorion was talking to him again.

"Did you hear what I said?"

"Yes. If Aurel is alive, we'll find her."

"She wouldn't have gone to her clan home, but someone must know where she is." Lorion rose and waited, fidgeting, while Ruarshi climbed to his feet. They were both more than ready to leave.

The well showed no further inclination to shift position, and after returning to the labyrinth they paused in their journey home only long enough for Ruarshi to lift the dead woman from the floor of the hallway. Lorion went before him, keeping one hand on his sword hilt and setting a brisk pace. At one point the woman's body shifted alarmingly beneath its clothes, leading Ruarshi to fear that she would disintegrate in his arms, but after the one fright there were no others and soon afterward he was able to lower her gently to the grass of a friendlier realm, under a more familiar sun. Lorion agreed to go back to the Doshae clan home to fetch a horse and litter, while Ruarshi waited at her side.

As soon as the former warrior had disappeared among the trees, Ruarshi raised the obsidian dagger from beneath the fringe of the woman's skirts to examine it more closely. It had practically fallen into his hand when he'd picked her up. The unusual double crossguard was made of bronze, as was the hilt, and altogether the object was in amazingly good condition for its age. He couldn't help wondering about the possible future in which he'd apparently taken possession of it.

*Begin as you mean to continue,* he'd told someone once.

Smiling to himself, Ruarshi tucked the dagger into the woman's clothes and left it there. He would talk to Satu to make sure that it was interred with the body, along with whatever clues it might hold about her identity. He was no plunderer of the dead and no vision could make him one. If the potential series of events he erased today turned out to have been important, or even vital, then he supposed that was unfortunate. He also supposed he could deal with it, since he would have no other choice.

"This is *exactly* the same thing," Slan said, not bothering to lower her voice in the slightest.

"No, it isn't," Ruarshi said, trying and failing to keep the heat out of his reply. "I rode into the warriors' enclave that day relying on other people to protect me, because that was their duty. That's not a mistake I would make again."

"Do you plan never to sleep once we reach Mirror Lake?" she asked. "Yes, you'll be a guest in their home, but that won't matter to Casimir's friends if they decide something has to be done."

"If someone storms our quarters, for god's sake wake me up."

That, at least, had the desired effect: Slan smiled at him. "That is not nearly good enough, Ruarshi."

She had a point but it made no difference. He'd insisted on accompanying the party traveling to Mirror Lake for a very good reason—his presence would keep the Seers agitated and focused on him, which should allow the others the opportunity to get into the library with minimal interference, get what they needed, and get out in a few days' time. It wasn't a role he would enjoy, but he was determined that no one would step over that place's threshold without him. Slan was the obvious second choice, as she'd come to have considerable influence in Miriyan and could get in touch with his mysterious benefactor among the Seers if that became necessary. Elin had to go along because she was the only one who was reasonably fluent in ancient Miriyanti, and Etienne was to be their fortunate fourth, the party's healer. He would have been impossible to shake in any case, having observed with ill-concealed satisfaction that since the only other candidate to fill that role was Davyt, and since Ruarshi could hardly take both his *chesida* and his son into a nest of potential enemies, they were stuck with him whether they liked it or not.

The rest of their group would head north to the Annorae clan home, where Saoirse would find a place for them all, Lorion and Tuomi would learn what they could, Karoli would deter any troublemakers, and Davyt would hopefully shake the ghosts he'd picked up in Mainz. Ardan had agreed to join that contingent, for his son's sake, and Ruarshi had been so grateful to hear it that he'd actually hugged his great aunt in spite of her protestations.

They were all riding out in the morning, so naturally Slan had chosen this evening to come to his quarters and argue with him about it.

He had neither the energy nor the heart for a protracted battle, so he conceded. "I know it isn't. But Seers are cautious by nature, alliances will be shifting in the wake of Casimir's death, and we should be finished there long before anyone has time to work themselves up to the point of violence. I'd never have gone along with Elin's suggestion if Satu hadn't agreed to mine."

"Does she really have the authority on her own to name you the Skeltari's emissary?"

"She didn't do it on her own. The Skeltari use something like a pair-bond to communicate with each other, but it's not a reciprocal bond; she sends a message to a Skeltari living nearby, and that one relays it on until they've all gotten word. And they're able to convey ideas this way, agreement and disagreement, not just emotions. I don't understand it, but it works. Satu graciously let me know that the first vote on the matter was a close one, but they eventually reached a consensus."

"Interesting," Slan said. "But I'm still not convinced that Casimir's closest allies will let the prospect of antagonizing the Skeltari deter them from going after you. You haven't forgotten that Seers are notoriously unstable?"

"No."

"And it's occurred to you that Casimir might have left a nasty surprise behind? He all but told you to go pelting off to Mirror Lake."

"I'm not pelting, and he could have left a nasty surprise for me anywhere, including right here in my family's hall. There's nothing to be gained by worrying about it."

The warrior snorted and shifted where she sat against the windowsill. The low evening light glinted in her hair and along one sharp cheekbone, while the rest of her face was softened by shadow. "You're as reckless as ever. It's just as well that you'll have a real bodyguard this time."

She didn't explain, but Ruarshi thought he understood her. "So while Elin has her nose buried in scrolls, she'll be protected by Etienne? No, Slan. I don't require a bodyguard."

"Those two will be accompanied everywhere they go by whichever warriors the Maelae circle in Tomir can spare. I sent ahead. They'll probably get there before we do."

Ruarshi sat back in astonishment. It had never occurred to him to call in reinforcements, since the whole trip to the Seers' fortress was more of a raid on the archives than anything else, but there was nothing about the notion that was objectionable. Quite the opposite, in fact. "So word of our intentions is out. How much of a busybody is your clan chief? Is he likely to decide that he needs to show up there, too?"

"Ciarn is going, so I imagine so."

"What?"

Slan was definitely smirking at him now. "Don't worry, he won't be traveling with us. But he won't be far behind, either. The Skeltari haven't meddled in politics within living memory, so their decision to do so now has turned this whole thing into an event. Even the High Sotarii will probably join in before it's all over. You've thrown off the balance of power yet again, and these people need to sit down and talk to each other, now rather than later."

The silence stretched as Ruarshi considered what she'd said. "How long have you had this in mind?" he asked mildly.

"Since it became clear to me that you wouldn't be dissuaded. I intend to keep our party safe in spite of you."

Now that was just offensive. But also, he realized slowly, true. What had he planned to do if the Seers were to turn their scanty force of warriors against them? Kill them all? Persuade them to disobey orders? Run away? And if an attack was directed against the others while he was off doing something else? What then?

Ruarshi hadn't protected his people in Europe, and he wasn't behaving any differently now that he was home. Mainz had taught him nothing.

"Thank you," he said. He could hardly hear his own voice, and he wasn't sure if that was because he was whispering or because all sound in the room was being drowned out by the remembered roar of stone grinding against stone. He blinked to clear his vision and found Slan watching him.

"What are you thinking?" she asked.

He sighed and decided not to dodge the question. "I'm disappointed. In myself. I rarely think to ask for help. You've also seen to it, I assume, that a handful of warriors will accompany the other group?"

"Yes, though I'm sure Karoli won't appreciate the implication."

"That doesn't matter. He hasn't been home in decades. Threats might arise where he wouldn't anticipate them. He'll understand the need for caution until the situation settles."

"Let's hope so." Slan crossed her arms and leaned back, her posture so deliberately casual that Ruarshi was instantly wary. "What exactly is wrong with Davyt?"

He had avoided talking with her about their son because he'd had no reassuring answers to give her. He still didn't. If anything, his selection of possible responses to her question was worse now than it had been before, thanks to his conversation with Etienne.

Ruarshi wasn't going to mention that exchange to Slan or anyone else. His feelings about what he'd tried to do to himself in Mainz went so far beyond shame that he wouldn't even know how to put them into words.

"He wants to protect everyone. He's learned he can't and it doesn't sit well."

"That's a cause for annoyance, Ruarshi, not nightmares. Are you sure you're not oversimplifying his concerns?"

He raised an eyebrow at her. "I probably am, but I can only go by what he's willing to tell me. He almost died, and he didn't know where I was at the time. He saw one man get crushed to death and watched another one burn. He's not doing too badly considering what he's been through."

"Do you believe that separating him from us will help?"

"His spending some time away from *me* will help. He finally got a chance to become acquainted with his father and then his life was overtaken by one horrible event after another. Those things are part of what he sees when he looks at me. You could go with him."

"Nice try, love. No. If he had wanted to confide in me, he'd have done so by now."

*Love?* Was the word significant, or was she just lapsing into old patterns?

"I might say the same of you," she went on. "You've never been one for bad dreams, but there are other signs. You've dropped weight. You avoid touching people without even being aware that you're doing it. Should I wait to see where this leads, or should we talk?"

Ruarshi watched her cautiously, unsure of what she expected him to say. Slan knew he didn't like to dwell on unpleasant memories, preferring instead to let the rougher edges erode with time until they no longer troubled him.

She rolled her eyes. "Or we can skip the part where we try to take care of each other, and just move right on to having sex."

Ruarshi smiled. "If we were to do that, would a jealous lover come bursting through the door?" His expression faltered. "That's a serious question. I expected you to move on."

"Have you moved on?"

He shook his head.

"I didn't think so. Are you still concerned about pair bonds? You shouldn't be. You're necessary. The bond isn't."

"That's harder to answer. Not being able to bond is... a problem. It's never gotten any easier, and I've stopped hoping that it will. Are you telling me it's not a problem for you?"

"It might be by this time if I hadn't taken care of it, but Lorion and I have been bonded for years. It started as a way of looking out for each other, but we're comfortable with it now."

Ruarshi blinked. "That explains a comment Lorion made the other day, I suppose. It's also incredibly awkward."

Slan's smile returned. "Both of us are very good about guarding our privacy. I have been faithful, Ruarshi, but not abstinent."

"That's a good way of putting it." He leaned forward, rested his forearms on his thighs, and directed his gaze at the floor before continuing. "I know what you think of the warriors' oaths, particularly where they touch on the matter of honor. I agree that they're mostly useless and far too easy to skirt, but recent events have led me to reconsider. The Nerthii need something like them, and they need to be binding, and I'm not even talking about what we may or may not be able to do with the Halls."

"When you say 'binding,' I assume you mean blood oaths," Slan said. "Some warriors choose to add those to their formal elevation ceremony, more often because of the prestige involved than because they're smart enough to be anxious about what they might do with their power. Elyon was one such. I think Aerik was, too."

"You're telling me I'm an idiot."

"I'm telling you that people who are afraid of everything will always find justifications for violence, while people who fear very little will always waste time second-guessing themselves. Oaths are of no use in helping someone distinguish between a valid fear of harm and an imagined one, so they do nothing to constrain the worst of us. Warriors-in-training—the thoughtful ones—spend a lot of time talking about this." Slan paused, and Ruarshi felt her eyes on him though he didn't look up. "How exactly does all this relate to the conversation we were having?"

"You should know that I fight like a gutter rat."

"You learned some of that from me. I'm still not sure what any of this has to do with sex."

Ruarshi met her eyes, exasperated. "Nothing. Nothing at all."

"If you're not in the mood, you could just say so."

"I'm trying to be honest here."

"So you are in the mood? Going off on a tangent about honor isn't very seductive."

"You did ask me if we should talk. That's what I was doing. Talking. About the things that have been on my mind."

"And I'm providing a helpful distraction because it's clear you're getting nowhere. You won't, either, because you can't save the other Nerthii from themselves. Stop trying. I'm not saying that they should be allowed to run amok, but I'm sure the Skeltari would intervene if they did. Which leads me to ask: have you spoken with Satu about any of this?"

"Yes. She was terse. She reminded me that I'm supposed to be looking after the Doshae now, and told me to quit searching for shortcuts where they don't exist."

"So your minder isn't displeased with you."

"If she's my minder, we're all in trouble. She didn't even blink when I murdered a man in her front room."

"Do you trust her?"

"I don't know."

"I dislike the power she wields. If she tries to interfere with you, be assured that I'll interfere with *her.*"

"Now I'm thinking about sex again."

"Really." Slan rose and approached him, swaying her hips as she moved. When she was close enough Ruarshi reached out and gathered her in, pressing his face against the warmth of her body. She gently cupped his jaw in her right hand while running the fingers of her left through his hair and over his scalp. He shivered.

"I'm sorry, Slan," Ruarshi said. "For running away. For the self-pity masquerading as concern. You didn't deserve to be tied to me, but not for the reasons I thought. I regret every year I spent in company other than yours. I don't expect forgiveness, but your companionship would be welcome."

"My companionship you shall have. Let's see what we can make of it."

Slan knelt before him. He took her head in his hands and kissed her.

# A Fistfight

When someone started knocking on his outer door in the middle of the night, Etienne abandoned the unsatisfactory half-sleep that had dogged him for the past hour and rolled to his feet. Davyt had left the *saal* with a number of cousins just after dinner and hadn't returned to their room yet, which accounted for both Etienne's restlessness and his sudden sharp fear that all this racket meant the youngster had gotten himself into some kind of trouble. He didn't blame Davyt for avoiding sleep, but worried that weeks of fatigue had started to impair his judgment.

His bleary momentum very nearly sent him careening into the corner of the wash stand, but he jerked sideways at the last moment, bounced gently off the jamb of the interior doorway, and navigated the outer room without incident. He pulled open the door and blinked in surprise.

What was Karoli doing here?

"Yes?" he said. It sounded more belligerent than he'd meant it to.

The warrior was looking past him, into the room's murky interior. "Just you? Where's the cub?"

"Davyt's not here. Is something wrong?"

"What kind of question is that? There's always something wrong. With the world in general, I mean. Tonight is no different."

"You're drunk."

"I am *slightly* inebriated. Which is going to make this even more humiliating for Ciarn."

Etienne understood that his anxiety had been entirely justified, if misdirected. "You're not. The night before we leave?"

"I didn't want to ruin the solstice for everyone. And I don't want to be here for all the fucking dithering that will come afterward. I need you with me for this."

"Why?"

"Because they won't let me fight the chief's First if I don't have a healer standing by to patch me up. Which won't be necessary. But rules are rules."

"You came to me for this?"

Karoli gestured vaguely toward the room just south of Etienne's. "That one would argue with me. Just as well that I don't have to deal with the cub, either. You don't intend to tattle, do you?"

Etienne didn't think Slan had left the hall that evening. He wouldn't disturb Ruarshi for the world, not unless the building caught fire. "He wouldn't try to stop you."

"No?"

"No. And you're not wearing a sword."

"Because I won't need one. Are you coming or not?"

On the one hand, Etienne was gratified that the warrior thought enough of his skills to ask him to do this. On the other, he didn't really want to be responsible for healing the man if he did get himself hurt. On the third hand, he understood Karoli's grievance, sympathized with it, and didn't want to miss whatever was about to happen.

"I'm coming. Let me put some clothes on." Because of course he'd made it all the way to the door without remembering that all he was wearing was his hip-wrap and a pair of socks. "Come in if you want."

As Etienne dressed, Karoli leaned against the doorway, silent, his eyes downcast. If he'd been sober, the healer might have thought him pensive, but odds were that he was fully in the grip of the alcohol and just wasn't paying attention to his surroundings.

That would have to change. Etienne wanted Karoli to win.

"Wake up," he said sharply. He couldn't find his boots. Where had he left them?

"I am not a horse. I don't sleep in this position."

There his boots were, wedged under the corner of his bed. Etienne lunged forward to grab them and started pulling them on. "You should wait until you're sober. Ciarn's not going to like this whether it happens now or later."

"You're not listening to me. As I said, my current state is not a coincidence. I do regret the embarrassment this will cause Geir."

"That's his First?"

"Poor fool."

"Save it. You're enjoying this."

"Maybe. I'd rather be sleeping."

Etienne gestured for Karoli to precede him out into the night air and followed in his wake, closing the door quietly behind them.

When a few intervening buildings had blocked his *saal* from view, Etienne spoke again. "So do you just hammer on Geir's door and tackle him when he opens it?"

Karoli shot him an amused glance. "I sent a rude note earlier this evening. I'm sure he's already at the clan's audience chamber, limbering up and cursing my name. The forms will be proper, even if the fight itself is not."

Etienne waited for the warrior to go on. When the man gave no sign that he intended to do so, the healer growled in aggravation. "So what's your plan?"

"We have a fight. I win. I go to bed."

"Will Ciarn be there?"

"That's up to him, but I expect so. He's a very conventional man."

"Who do you suppose will replace him?"

"Someone better, I hope."

"Define 'better.'"

"You're asking me to think. I'm not in the mood."

Etienne snorted. "Does Saoirse know about this?"

"How is that any business of yours?"

"It isn't. But I'm curious."

"She knows."

They lapsed into silence for a handful of strides before Etienne said, "I thought you had decided to let this lie."

"I had. I changed my mind."

"Why?"

"This is an itch that's needed scratching for a long, long time."

"That doesn't really answer my question."

"Call it a whim, then."

"I don't believe that, either."

Karoli was examining him in the dim light. "Are you trying to find a *good* reason for this? How unlike you."

"Oh, stow it. There's a chance you're doing this because you think the clan will be better off without Ciarn as its chief. A small chance. I'd like to know for sure."

"You have found me out. My motives are pure as the driven snow."

"You are such an ass, Karoli. All the time. It must be exhausting."

The warrior opened his mouth to reply, then shook his head and closed it again. "Thank you for coming with me," he said eventually, his tone remote. "Don't feel obligated to talk if you're not enjoying the conversation."

Etienne pressed his lips together in annoyance and left them that way. Before too long they rounded a corner and he could see the glow of torchlight ahead. A few moments more saw them entering the clearing in front of the chamber where Ruarshi's peculiar trial had been held, and they both slowed their steps as they neared the small group assembled there.

The first face he recognized was Ciarn's. The Doshae chief was standing off to one side, expressionless. A bulky man with a sword Etienne identified as Geir by a quick process of elimination, while the rest were likely friends or allies of the pair judging by their general air of agitation and the glares they were shooting in Karoli's direction. The warrior stopped just at the edge of the pool of light and bowed.

"I apologize for the lateness of the hour," he said, "but as I am heading north tomorrow, I was left with the choice of acting now or putting this off indefinitely. I thought this might be a question we would all like to have resolved."

Geir had approached them as Karoli spoke, and his face twisted in disgust when he got within range of the man's breath. "You've been drinking."

"It's possible."

"I'm not obliged to fight you 'til you're sober."

"I'm sure that's true. It's also true that you're not obliged to fight me at all, given the difference in our rank."

"You were never raised to Diamyo, Karoli."

"No. Because I had to apprehend the man who should have nominated me. In case you'd forgotten."

"No one's forgotten," Geir said. "There's no chance I'm backing away from this fight." Unexpectedly, the man turned to Etienne. "You're his healer? Is he sufficiently clearheaded for this?"

His first instinct was to try to evade the question, but he did in fact know Karoli well enough to judge. "He had no trouble arguing with me all the way over here. He's capable."

Karoli was smiling unpleasantly. "Are we done? Can we get on with it?"

"Challenger chooses the weapon," Geir said. "I don't see a weapon."

"These were all I brought," Karoli said, raising his hands and waggling his fingers. "They will suffice."

Ciarn's First narrowed his eyes at his opponent before shrugging and stepping away. "A fistfight it'll be, then." He unbuckled his sword belt and tossed it to one of the men standing behind him.

A woman Etienne thought he might have run into a time or two at the healers' circle scowled at him from the other side of the clearing. Should he wave? He wasn't sure. This confrontation was turning out to be even more awkward than he'd feared.

Ciarn moved then, stiff as a marionette, until he stood at the center of the ring of light. "You're set upon this, Karoli Naishanti?"

"Yes."

"And you accept the challenge on my behalf, Geir Naishanti, First of Clan Doshae?"

"Yes."

"If Karoli wins, I will resign my position as clan chief and the Doshae will be free to choose another. If Geir wins, the challenge is extinguished and Karoli forfeits any right to issue another such challenge against me in future. The contest will continue until one of the combatants yields. Are these terms acceptable?"

A nod from Karoli, and another muttered 'yes' from the other man.

"You may start whenever you're ready." Ciarn stepped away, casting one more sharp glance at Karoli before settling into a chair near the door of the chamber.

Karoli, his arms crossed, strode forward until he was about ten feet from the larger man, who crouched and raised his fists. When Karoli didn't adjust his own stance in response, Geir straightened and lowered his arms. "Come on, man. You can't fight me like that."

"Yes, I can." And Geir toppled backward.

Karoli had taken him down with an ankle-level shield, whipped forward with such speed and force that Etienne had barely been aware of its existence before the man started falling. Karoli leapt toward his opponent and what followed was the most systematic dismantling of another human being that Etienne had ever seen. It was also the dirtiest fighting he hoped ever to witness.

Karoli used his shields like an artist, pushing and pulling at Geir, keeping the man off balance and open to his blows and then dancing back out of range whenever the other warrior found his feet. Judging by Geir's inadequate responses to this technique and his all-too-evident anger, this was not a standard fighting style among Miriyanti warriors.

Before five minutes had passed, Geir was a bloody, staggering mess while Karoli didn't have a mark on him.

The fight continued in much the same vein in spite of the rising chorus of hisses and shouts coming from Geir's supporters. The First was visibly slowing, one of his eyes was swollen shut, and a sheet of blood from a cut above his eyebrow had covered the left side of his face. Another blow to the body sent the man to his knees, and Karoli stepped back.

"Do you yield?"

Geir shook his head and forced himself back to his feet, charging forward with single-minded determination and catching Karoli just before he could slide out of the way. Karoli went down beneath him, hitting the ground so hard that Etienne began to worry about broken ribs, and the man lifted his fist to deliver the type of blow that tended to bring fights to a quick end. Karoli caught Geir's wrist before his arm started its descent, slipped a shield between them, and—unbelievably—used it as leverage to flip the man over onto his back and pin him there. The smaller man straddled the First's chest, hitting him as hard as he could in the side of the head, over and over. Blood spattered Karoli's shirt and the ground next to Geir's head. Etienne backed a few steps away from the fight. He felt ill.

"Yield," Karoli demanded.

Geir, barely conscious at this point, shook his head.

"If I knock you out, you lose anyway. End this. Yield."

"Knockout won't matter," the First said, his words barely intelligible through his swollen lips. Etienne couldn't guess at the number of teeth he'd lost. "Must yield. I won't. Have to kill me."

Karoli's expression shifted from incredulity to outrage, and he struck the man again, this time square in the face. Geir's nose broke with an audible crack.

"Yield!"

"Won't."

Karoli sat back, momentarily at a loss, before leaning forward to whisper something in his opponent's ear. Etienne thought it might have been a question. Geir's lips moved in reply. Karoli nodded and laid his palm gently against his opponent's battered forehead before rising to his feet, turning to face Ciarn, and raising his bloody hands, palms out.

"I yield," Karoli said.

The warrior spun, strode blindly past Etienne, and stopped a few feet away. He stared out into the twilight, his back rigid, while a flurry of activity erupted among those gathered in the torchlight behind him.

Etienne was so shocked that he froze in place. He watched the man as Karoli's soft litany of curses came to an end and he started ripping at his shirt, not sparing the buttons in his haste to get it off. He was wiping his hands on the untidy wad that resulted when Etienne finally got his legs working again. He approached the warrior with caution and addressed him in a low voice.

"What happened?"

"I'm not going to kill a man for loyalty. Fuck him. Fuck all of them. Let's go." He started off without waiting to see if Etienne would follow, and the healer had to hurry to catch up.

"You have three broken fingers, and if I don't do something about your back you'll be sorry by morning."

"What?"

"Karoli. Stop. *Stop.* You brought me along to heal you, remember?"

The warrior came to a halt, but he didn't turn around. Instead he flexed his right hand and rolled his shoulders. "I'll be fine."

"If I don't heal you tonight, it'll be Davyt doing it tomorrow." When Karoli didn't respond, Etienne went on. "For fuck's sake, I know it hurts. *Let me do something about it.*"

Karoli sighed impatiently but didn't charge off again, which Etienne chose to interpret as assent. Before he could get started, though, he heard footsteps approaching from behind. He took a look over his shoulder and saw that it was Ciarn, and moved quickly to interpose himself between Karoli and the chief.

Ciarn noticed and shook his head slightly. "I'm not here to cause trouble, Etienne."

"What do you want?" Karoli snarled.

"I don't know if you want to hear it, coming from me, but thank you. Geir is a good man and my friend. I am sorry for what I did—and what I failed to do—all those years ago."

"Do you think that matters now?"

"No. I don't. It needed to be said, all the same."

"Glad to help you salve your conscience. Now leave us be."

"As you will." Ciarn bowed to Karoli, deliberately and very deep, and nodded to Etienne before turning to rejoin his people.

Karoli's uninjured hand landed on Etienne's shoulder and he almost jumped out of his skin. "Let's go back to your hall."

"Okay. *Quit* balling up your fist like that. I can almost feel the bones grinding together."

Neither of them spoke on the way to the *saal.* When they arrived at Etienne's quarters, the place was still empty and he directed Karoli toward a chair before picking up a lamp and going to his small fireplace to kindle it. He returned to the outer room to find the warrior perched uncomfortably on the chair's arm, a bemused expression on his face.

Etienne set the lamp on a nearby table, mustered up what patience he could, and asked, "What?"

"I never expected to number you among my few defenders."

Etienne flushed. He'd acted without thinking earlier. Obviously Karoli didn't need him to take his part against Ciarn or anyone else. "I respect what you did. I'm dangerously close to respecting you. Don't spoil it."

"So the evening wasn't a complete loss."

"That's *exactly* what I just asked you not to do."

"It would have been if I didn't mean it. You're all right, for a healer."

Etienne studied the man, and decided he was being sincere. How odd. "Well. Thank you. I guess. Sit in the chair properly, if you would, though you probably don't want to lean back just yet."

Karoli moved to comply and Etienne got on with tending to the reason he'd been rousted from his bed in the first place.

Etienne began the next morning with a quiet but frantic search for Davyt that ended abruptly when he discovered that the young man in question was sitting at one of the tables in the family *saal,* picking listlessly at his breakfast. He didn't bother with questions or recriminations, but kept a close eye on the younger man while he put some food in his own stomach. When Ruarshi emerged from his room a short time later, Etienne pushed his plate aside, engaged in a brief internal debate on the ethics of ratting out a friend, and adjusted his route to make sure he'd intercept his former instructor on his way back to his quarters.

Ruarshi's gaze had already come to rest on his son's exhausted face by the time they were close enough together to talk quietly. The distracted smile he'd been wearing a few seconds earlier was long gone.

"He didn't come back to our room last night," Etienne murmured. "I don't think he even tried to sleep."

"Did you speak to him?"

Etienne shook his head.

"Thank you for letting me know." Ruarshi continued in Davyt's direction, leaving Etienne wondering if he should have said something about Karoli. Probably not. That had worked itself out satisfactorily and was no kind of priority at the moment.

Once he'd returned to his room, Etienne stuffed his meager collection of clothing and the blankets off his bed into his saddlebags and headed outside. He took a few deep breaths and started around the hall, intending to make his way to the stables to gather up their mounts, but Elin and Saoirse had evidently had the same thought some time earlier. They were less than fifty yards away, with fourteen horses in tow—ten bearing saddles and four others laden with what appeared to be food. They were being trailed closely by half a dozen hopeful familiars. Etienne felt both lazy for not having gotten up in time to help them and relieved about the pack animals. The fact that he'd had little appetite this morning just meant he'd be extra hungry later, and since they didn't intend to stop at either of the clan homes that lay between them and their destination, there wouldn't be much opportunity to provision themselves along the way.

Etienne went to meet them, exchanging greetings and then taking the reins of a friendly brown mare he'd already dubbed Midnight. He moved off a bit while the others gathered. The horse lipped at his fingers and he rubbed the animal's muzzle affectionately, leaning into its warmth. When Slan, Lorion, and Tuomi arrived, he caught Slan's eye and pointed toward the hall. Her brows drew down in puzzlement but she went inside, and a few minutes later Karoli sauntered up, looking none the worse for wear. He nodded toward Etienne and went to join Saoirse, who didn't appear to be as annoyed with him as she might have been.

Everyone was where they were supposed to be, at least. Etienne had taken part in expeditions with less auspicious beginnings, and depending on how things were going inside the hall, he thought he might be able to ride away from his new clan home in a spirit of cautious optimism.

While the rest of the group was still sorting itself out and getting bags and packs strapped to saddles, Davyt came out of the *saal's* nearest door arm in arm with Ardan, with his parents following close behind. He still looked like he could use a week's worth of uninterrupted sleep, but there was something stubborn in his expression that hadn't been there earlier. Which could mean almost anything, really.

Etienne had just coaxed Midnight into motion, hoping he could get his roommate to drop some clues about what had been said before everyone shifted to goodbyes, when he heard the hoof beats. Quite a lot of hoof beats, and he thought that maybe he should just start swearing now to get it out of the way, and that he was probably jumpier than he ought to be, and that there was every possibility that whatever was going on had nothing to do with them. A hope that became harder and harder to maintain as the noise grew louder.

When the band of eight riders finally swung into view around the northeast corner of the hall, they found themselves confronted by an unbroken line of ten tense people and an even greater number of edgy horses. Etienne would have been entertained by how quickly the newcomers scrambled to a halt if he hadn't been so nervous.

The tension ebbed somewhat when the lead rider called out Slan's name in greeting and Slan stepped forward to meet her, and then everyone calmed down completely when it became evident that these were Ciarn's reinforcements. He'd sent more than they'd agreed upon, four warriors for each party, but Etienne couldn't see anything wrong with that and his companions seemed willing to go along with it.

He sidled over to Davyt as the others began mounting up. "Okay?"

The healer nodded wearily. "It's okay. They offered to scrap the trip to Mirror Lake on my account. It was embarrassing." Davyt read the astonishment on Etienne's face and laughed. "I know. They were trying to help, but... how awful, for me to be the reason they don't get the information they need. Anything but that. I'll manage."

"I have no doubt of it. You'll be careful?"

"Of course. You?"

"Same. I'm guessing we'll be bored most of the time. We'll catch up with the rest of you before too long."

They exchanged a grin and a hug, and then Etienne was clasping hands with those who were heading north and watching as they rode out of sight. Soon just the four of them were left, along with the four Naishanti they'd acquired. The one who had spoken with Slan was named Mona, and the others were Mads, Kennet, and Solvi. Etienne looked them over as he swung into his saddle, decided they would do, and chivvied Midnight forward when everyone started moving.

They left the Doshae clan home in their wake and turned west, keeping the river to their left and riding steadily over gently rolling terrain and through the occasional stand of trees. The trip to the Seers' seat of power was going to take a full week, so Etienne settled in to enjoy it as well as he could. As long as they got their traveling done before autumn weather set in, he'd be satisfied. There would be no more riding through blizzards if he could help it.

Their Naishanti escort proved to be amiable company, so much so that one evening, after watching in amusement as Slan gave Ruarshi a much-needed haircut, he found himself sitting up with Kennet through the first watch. He was a sharp-eyed man with a mordant sense of humor who was somewhere between Ruarshi's age and Etienne's, and the two of them had fallen into the habit of bantering with one another as they rode.

After ribbing him yet again about the warriors' insistence on setting watches even though they were out in the middle of nowhere—which admittedly did make him feel better, though he would never say so out loud—Etienne asked him, "So what do you think of our errand?"

Kennet eyed him. "Generals should never ask the opinion of foot soldiers."

Etienne chuckled. "I'm not the general. Though I've been around the general for years now, and this may have affected my thinking, and so I'm wondering how all this," he gestured toward their small campsite, "looks to everyone else."

"If Seers were known for physical courage and an inclination to take risks, I'd laugh at the lot of you. Fortunately they're not, so I'd say the odds are good that you'll get in and out of there in one piece. If anything has changed recently, by which I mean if the Seers have persuaded someone to increase the size of their garrison beyond the score of warriors they're supposed to have, you should all turn around and leave the instant this becomes clear."

That was a more intense answer than he'd bargained for. "Why do you say so?"

"Ciarn didn't choose us for this duty because we're bad at what we do, but there are limits. Say we were all in an open area, with no choke points to take advantage of or walls to back up against, and twenty warriors came for us at once. They would wipe us out. Even a Nerthi couldn't prevail against more than four or five warriors at most—and I'm giving Ruarshi a lot of credit here—if they were already in close proximity when the attack started."

"Congratulations, now you've got me feeling like someone just walked over my grave. Is this how warriors spend their time, thinking about how to kill everyone they keep company with?"

"The smart ones do."

"There should be a word for 'driven mad by paranoia.' Do we have a word like that?"

"Not that I know of."

"I'll invent one and use it until it catches on."

"It's good to have goals."

"Sometimes you need small goals to keep your mind off the big ones."

"Speaking of which... Ciarn wasn't exactly a fount of information. What's your aim here, anyway?" Kennet asked. "Other than waving Casimir's murderer under the Seers' noses to see if they've got the nerve to do anything about it. That is, incidentally, an excellent way of undermining whatever influence they've got left. Ruarshi is one hell of a bad enemy."

Etienne shifted against the tree trunk at his back, disturbed. "That's not the reason for our visit. We have shamans now, but the shamans don't know what they're supposed to be doing, or how any of it really works. We're trying to fix that."

"Ruarshi could have gone with the other group if he'd wanted to. It would have made the whole endeavor less risky."

"He leads from the front."

"So I see. Not always the best place for a general."

"That's not how he thinks of himself, you know. Unless you happen to be his apprentice."

"You're telling me nobody's in charge here?"

"In the sense of 'barking orders at everyone else,' no."

"If things get dicey, a free-for-all isn't going to work."

"I'm sure Ruarshi trusts you and the other Naishanti to do what you've been trained for. I'm equally sure that if it comes to tactics, Slan will have some ideas. Don't make it more complicated than it is."

"I can picture it now: absent instruction, the four of us all rush off independently to do what seems best, collide while trying to get through a narrow doorway, and end up in a pile on the floor."

"Well, if you really think that will help..."

Kennet laughed and nudged him. "I actually can't wait to see what happens when we get there. I've been mouldering at the clan home for too long."

"Hopefully the worst we'll have to deal with will be some rudeness and sour *keth.*"

"The way my luck is running, you'll probably turn out to be right."

"Don't underestimate the virtues of mouldering. That's how I'd prefer to spend the entire winter."

"Liar."

"What do you mean by that?"

"That you're lying. I know your sort."

"Do you?" Etienne asked. "What sort is that?"

"You love being in the middle of the biggest mess on offer. You were there for your friend's fight with Geir, and you're with this bunch now. Tell me Europe was any different."

"Europe was fairly placid, right up until our last year there. But it may be that you're onto something. I did enjoy some of it." When he wasn't too terrified to enjoy anything at all. Etienne rubbed at his eyes, his good mood evaporating with the last of his energy. "Thanks for keeping watch. Let me know if a badger shows up and you need help fighting it off. I'm heading to bed."

"Etienne, did I say something I shouldn't have? I'm sorry."

"You didn't. I'm just tired. See you in the morning."

Etienne left the warrior to a contemplative silence and returned to their camp, where he skirted the dying fire and lay down in his blankets, using his saddlebags as a stiff and unsatisfactory pillow. He fell asleep after only a brief interval of staring up at the endless nighttime sky, and the next day everyone got up and did the same thing all over again. And again, and again, until their party emerged from a small copse of birch trees late one afternoon and Etienne got his first look at the massive ancient fortress that had become the Seers' home.

Even at a distance he didn't care for it. He'd seen less attractive stone piles, such as the one that had fallen down around their ears outside Mainz, but this one seemed to be actively louring down at them from its perch. The massive gates in its featureless eastern wall were open, and through it he could see what he supposed was the fortress' main building, made of the same slate gray rock as the rest of it and easily big enough to contain the entirety of Tomir's central square. North and south galleries climbed the rising terrain to its west, terminating a mile or so short of the cliffs that overlooked the bay beyond. The south gallery extended farther than the one on the north, giving the entire structure a lopsided appearance, and what he could see of the interior walls hinted at the presence of open walkways interspersed with enclosed stairways. A few small wooden buildings clustered in the area between the galleries, and the shallow bowl midway between the edifice's westernmost point and the cliffs had to be the location of the lake that gave the place its name.

For all its hideousness, the fortress was completely indefensible. It seemed to Etienne that any stone structure that big might be forgiven for having one or the other of those flaws but not both, and he scowled up at it in instinctive dislike.

"That's where we're going, I take it?" he asked.

"Yes," Ruarshi replied, looking up at it with a resigned expression. "That's where we're going."

# The Shrine of the Ancestors

Ruarshi sat staring up at the imposing main doors of the fortress. They were hardly less massive than the gates that stood open behind them, and he didn't know if a knock on the wicket gate would even be audible to those inside. When he'd come to Mirror Lake in the past on one bit of business or another, his arrival had always been anticipated, with people gathered on the steps to receive him. He wasn't sure what he would do if the Seers decided to deal with their unexpected visitors by leaving them locked outside all night. That wouldn't reflect well on their hospitality, no, but they hardly had a reputation as gracious hosts to uphold and they might consider the embarrassment worth it to keep him waiting.

The stables, a long, low wooden building situated against the wall to their north, were dark and silent. He considered shouting for a stable hand, but in the end he just shrugged, dismounted, and wrapped his horse's reins loosely around one of the iron rings set into the fortress' front wall. He ascended the shallow steps at a jog, aware that the others were close behind him but with most of his attention focused forward, in case there was trouble waiting for them on the other side of that door.

Ruarshi raised his hand to try a knock, but the wicket swung open before he could touch it. A woman of middle years stood facing them, backlit by an oil lamp resting on a trestle table a few feet away, and even if she hadn't had a sword strapped to her hip he'd have identified her as a warrior with no trouble. It was something about the set of her shoulders.

"Well, hello," she said, swinging the door wide and gesturing for them to enter. The greeting was a bit unorthodox; perhaps she was new to door duty? She bowed to them as they filed by. "More guests. Please be welcome. I'm Nairna, clan Drys, nice to meet you, whoever you are. Mads!"

"Good to see you," the warrior said, moving forward to clasp her arm. She drew him into a brief embrace before stepping away, closing the door behind them, and giving them all a thorough once-over now that she could see them properly. She raised her eyebrows, waiting.

"Thank you," Ruarshi said, returning her bow. "I am Ruarshi, clan Doshae, and these are Etienne, Solvi, Mads, Mona, and Kennet, also of the Doshae. This is Slan of the Maelae, and our eighth is Elin of the Annorae. Is Ilmatar available? And a groom to tend to our horses?"

Nairna paused a moment before answering, still studying them. "That's an interesting list. A groom I can get you, but Ilmatar will be harder. He's in Tomir."

Ilmatar had been Casimir's second-in-command for as long as Ruarshi could remember, and he wouldn't willingly have abandoned his post at a time like this. "Why is he in the capital?"

"Where to start. Jair is in a snit and sent a delegation up a while back to fetch Casimir. He wasn't available, having resigned without warning and ridden away on a visit to his clan home, so Ilmatar and a few others went in his stead. They also took half our garrison. Then word arrived that Casimir had died. Is that true?" She was looking right at Ruarshi when she asked it.

He sighed inwardly. "Yes."

Nairna absorbed that and went on. "So. A few days ago a group of Maelae Naishanti showed up, and we thought they were partial replacements for those who'd left but that turned out not to be the case. They've been close-mouthed about their reason for coming here so I can't explain it. Neither can the Seers, which is a little strange. You probably know more about it than we do. And now you've arrived. The Seers are disturbed, and the garrison, well, we're mostly confused. If you could tell us why you're here, that would be helpful."

A handful of people had come into the fortress' great hall while she spoke, lingering in the gloom outside the range of the lamplight. Some had the facial tattoos that marked them as Seers and some did not. Servants or Naishanti, then. Ruarshi pivoted slightly to address them all. "I'm here as an emissary of the Skeltari. My clan chief will be arriving soon, as will the chiefs of some of the other clans. I don't know how many. They intend an impromptu meeting to discuss the... disruption among the Seers, and how the governance of Miriyan may need to change."

This announcement was met with some murmuring, and more residents of the fortress drifted in. Ruarshi was concerned that if this went on much longer, they'd have the full attention of everyone living there, which possibility he'd just as soon avoid.

"I apologize for our late arrival," he said, "but we knew our advent was going to be inconvenient regardless of when it happened, and decided to get on with it. There's no need to trouble the kitchens on our behalf, but we will need rooms."

An older man stepped forward and bowed. "Rafal of the Aesir, senior steward of Mirror Lake. Your rooms have already been prepared. Four sets of adjoining quarters, since we didn't know your preferred arrangement. South gallery, of course."

Ruarshi knew they'd been observed during their approach, so this wasn't actually surprising though it did come as a bit of a relief. No need to stand around waiting in this cavernous dark space. Like most large stone structures he was acquainted with, it somehow managed to remain a good deal cooler than the outside air at all times, and its current temperature bordered on the uncomfortable. Not only that, but he'd never before been at Mirror Lake so late in the evening and the hall had a hushed, heavy quality to it that was making him twitchy.

A voice boomed out of the darkness to their left and he flinched. "Ruarshi! Slan! Elin! Etienne! My friends!"

A large form hove into view and Ruarshi squinted into the murk. "Valentin?"

"None other." He came to a stop before them, grinning widely. "I came up with the Maelae when I heard there was something brewing. It is good to see you again!"

"It's been, what, a whole month?" Etienne asked wryly.

"And already so much to talk about!"

Ruarshi was smiling, too. The man had been slow to warm to them when they'd first met, but he'd ended as a stalwart ally on their trip home. Making it back to Miriyan would have been much harder without him.

"Sometime tomorrow, perhaps?" he suggested. "We've been on the road a while."

"Yes, yes. Follow me. I know where they have put you."

With a final thanks to Nairna and trailed at a short distance by the steward, they left the great hall in Valentin's wake and headed down the central corridor of the building's south wing. This was where the Seers lived and ate, if Ruarshi remembered correctly, while the north wing housed the garrison and the workrooms. The servants' quarters were located in the north gallery. Those individuals rotated in and out of service in clan groups, and Ruarshi wondered—not for the first time—if Mirror Lake was considered a good posting. He suspected not.

Irregularly spaced lamps lit their way down the corridor. Soft voices could be heard behind some of the doors to either side as they passed, and about half of them had light spilling across their thresholds. The hallway's far end, where it merged with the south gallery and took a sharp right, was lost in shadow but Valentin didn't slow. They turned west, went through an open doorway, and climbed a short flight of stairs illuminated by reflected evening sunlight. Once they'd reached the top, the wall to their right yielded abruptly to a series of open archways, giving them a view of the outbuildings, the north gallery, and the clear blue sky beyond. The archways continued onward for fifty yards or so, terminating at a closed door that concealed another enclosed stairway. Exploring what lay ahead would have to wait, though, as Valentin had begun pushing open the doors on the south side of the walkway and gesturing toward the rooms that lay within.

"You see? The fires have been started, nice and warm, shared fireplaces. One bed in each room, more than big enough for two with all of you so scrawny. Now that you are here, the Maelae warriors and I will move from the north wing to be near you." He turned to Slan, who had leaned into the first room in the row to take a look around. "The Maelae clan chief will be coming?"

"Probably," she replied.

The Doshae warriors were also investigating the arrangements, and none of them looked happy. Mona had opened the shutters in the second room's south wall and was muttering to herself. Solvi, by far the quietest member of their party, finished with her inspection and spoke. "At least we've got a door between each pair. The first room will be mine and Mona's, with Slan and Elin in the one adjoining. The next goes to Ruarshi and Etienne, with Mads and Kennet to their west." No one was startled that she had been the one to decide upon their disposition, and no one disputed her word. Naishanti were ferocious about maintaining their pecking order and even the two non-warriors in their group had, over the past week, figured out which one of them had seniority.

Rafal was still with them. "I will call the grooms and have your baggage brought. Please settle in and let us know if you require anything further. The kitchens are along the west wall of the south wing, and you can always find staff there. Some of our Seers work through the night." He bowed to them again and headed back down the stairway toward the main building.

Elin was staring through an archway in the direction of the north gallery, and something in the quality of her stillness caught Ruarshi's attention. He approached her carefully.

"What is it?"

"They didn't rebuild it. The barracks where we were kept before Casimir sent us off. The foundations are overgrown now and I can hardly make them out." She pointed toward a grassy patch of ground near a tidy outbuilding of uncertain purpose. "I hadn't been in the main hall before," she went on, "so I never made the connection. This was the Autumn King's fortress, wasn't it? I'd thought his castle had fallen to ruin."

"Most of it did. The hall is all that's left." The Autumn King, so named because his reign had lasted barely a season, was a legendary figure in Miriyan for all the wrong reasons. He'd been their nation's one and only monarch, self-declared, and no one else had tried it since.

"There are likely to be some interesting old artifacts here," Elin said. "Keep an eye out. I'm going to be buried in too many dusty books to do much exploring."

"I envy you. I'm going to be trapped in meetings I'm unqualified to take part in. How is an emissary even supposed to behave, when his principal couldn't care less about what's being discussed? Please finish your research quickly."

She smiled at him. "I'm not so fond of this place that I'll be searching for excuses to stay. I should have a good idea of what's here to be found within a few days, assuming the archivist is cooperative."

"I promise I'll let you know if I find anything of interest," Ruarshi said. "Everyone seems to be crowding into your room, hopefully not for a meeting. Shall we join them?"

"Go ahead. I'll only be a minute."

Ruarshi nodded and left her to her thoughts. He feared that her time line would prove to be far too optimistic, but that would depend on how much relevant material the Seers' library actually contained. As this was a topic about which he knew exactly nothing, he decided not to speculate and went to see what the others were up to.

It turned out that they were all watching Kennet, who had taken it upon himself to demonstrate how easy it was to climb through the window from the outside. The distance from the bottom of the sill to the ground was a good twelve feet, but he was up the wall and through the opening in the same amount of time it took Ruarshi to cross the room, his point being that they could be attacked from any direction save through the floor or ceiling. Ruarshi was certain they'd all been aware of this already, but Kennet evidently thought it was part of his duty as bodyguard to make them all as nervous as possible.

When their bags arrived a few minutes later, everyone said their good nights and paired off to head to bed. Ruarshi hoped the warriors weren't going to bother with setting watches but he didn't ask. He didn't think the risk of someone coming after them here was particularly high, especially not with most of Casimir's close associates down in Tomir, but they'd have come to their own conclusions about potential hazards and it wasn't his place to second-guess them.

Etienne was undressed and snoring in no time and Ruarshi wasn't far behind. He woke to early morning sunshine, feeling more rested than he had since leaving his clan home.

Meals at Mirror Lake were generally communal and held in the large, low-ceilinged refectory between the great hall and the kitchens. Ruarshi entered with the rest of his group in some trepidation, fearing that he would be cornered by someone who either assumed that his presence here meant he had important things to say or who wanted to ask pointed questions about Casimir, but they managed to get through their breakfast without difficulty. Their arrival did cause a small stir, and several Seers and Naishanti came forward to introduce themselves and bid them welcome, but other than that they were left alone to discuss their day.

Elin had by far the most important task: track down Ilias and convince him to show her around the library. Her low-voiced inquiry to one of the servants as they finished their meal would hopefully set that part of their plan in motion. Since Slan had assumed the role of Ruarshi's bodyguard, Elin would have both Solvi and Mads trailing her as she embarked on her research. Etienne sighed but didn't comment when he was assigned Kennet and Mona.

"I'll find out who's nominally in charge of the place and see if they'll meet with me over lunch," Ruarshi said. He wasn't enthusiastic about the prospect and was sure the others could tell. "I'm guessing that's where I'd start if I had an actual job to do." One of Mirror

Lake's many cats had approached him while he ate, and he was now scratching the little creature tentatively behind the ears. Several of his companions were similarly occupied.

"Sounds reasonable," Mona said.

"Will the Seers get nervous if I take a look around?" Etienne asked.

"I have no idea. Perhaps you could request a guide?" Ruarshi hadn't been taken on any tours during his previous visits, but that might have had something to do with the fact that he was usually focused on getting back out of the fortress as quickly as he could.

"The Seers seem a little standoffish," Kennet said. "Maybe Nairna would do it?"

"She might," Mads remarked. "Ask her. She'd be less disruptive than your friend Valentin."

"If that doesn't keep you busy, go outside for a while," Ruarshi said. "They might steer you away from their workrooms, but no one can object to a hike along the cliffs."

"Workrooms," Slan repeated, and snorted softly. "They don't seem to be doing much work. They weren't even sure their leader was dead."

"A Seer told me once that they have a hard time keeping track of Nerthii. That might account for the blind spots," Ruarshi said.

"There she is now," Mads said, pointing toward the doorway. He gestured Nairna over.

In short order Ruarshi had arranged to meet with Photius, who'd inherited the unenviable task of keeping Mirror Lake running in the absence of its senior leadership, and Nairna had agreed to act as Etienne's tour guide when she finished with whatever duties the garrison tended to in the mornings. They had just started back toward their rooms when a small, nervous man hurried up to them.

He bowed. "I am Ilias, archivist of Mirror Lake. I was told one of you wished to speak with me?"

Elin stepped forward, returned the bow, smiled widely at the man, and linked her arm in his without asking. "Call me Elin. My family have long been the historians of Clan Annorae. Would you mind showing me your collection?" Their voices trailed off as they moved away, Solvi and Mads following her like heavily armed ducklings.

Ruarshi had never seen Elin behave in quite that way before, but he trusted that she knew what she was doing. He wished her luck.

His conversation with Photius was about as entertaining as he'd expected. The man was humorless, suspicious, unsure of the limits of his temporary authority, and openly reluctant to take Ruarshi's words at face value. Ruarshi ran out of ways to phrase 'defending the interests of the Skeltari' about ten minutes into their meeting, and as those interests began and ended with being left alone by whatever power structure emerged from the upcoming talks, he wasn't able to elaborate convincingly on his preferred outcomes. The result was that he ended up sounding evasive and untrustworthy, which hadn't been his intent at all. He wasn't much of a diplomat.

The one bright spot during their discussion came when Photius brought up the subject of the traditionalists. Ruarshi thought he'd been able to convince the man that the Nerthii would no longer be the target of that faction's particular ire, not now that they'd been revealed as the long-lost partners of the Skeltari. The old guard practically worshiped the keepers of the wells, whom they viewed as the sole remaining exemplar of the mythical golden age for which they so noisily longed. He couldn't imagine them turning against the Skeltari for any reason, but just in case their ideology had developed a new wrinkle he hadn't anticipated, he intended to spread the rumor of their change of heart as widely as he could. Expectations could be persuasive if they were held by a sufficient number of people, especially if those people were in positions of power, and he was happy to use his influence to try pushing his old foes in the right direction.

He'd attempted something similar back before the rebellion, of course. His efforts then hadn't met with notable success. Ruarshi could only hope that adding Satu and the others into the mix this time around would make a difference.

When he returned to his room that afternoon, he was both aggravated and restless. Slan had waited outside Photius' chambers with two of the garrison's warriors while he'd talked with the Seer, and though she sympathized with his frustration she didn't share it. Her attempts to settle his nerves weren't helping him much, either, though he appreciated the effort.

He rose suddenly from the windowsill where he'd been sitting and tossed his formal coat over the back of a chair. It was time, he decided, for them to go on a short expedition.

"Follow me," he said, and headed left when they emerged onto the walkway.

Ruarshi was prepared to blast through any locks that might get in his way, and was a little disappointed to discover that a gentle push was all that was needed to open the doors that stood between them and the far end of the south gallery. He slowed his pace as they ascended the third and final set of stairs, glancing over his shoulder at Slan.

"Have you ever been to the Shrine of the Ancestors in Tomir?" he asked.

"Once or twice."

"This is the oldest one in the country," Ruarshi said. They reached the landing and passed through one more door, this one sturdier than the others and elaborately carved with the totem of every clan that had existed at the time of its creation. "I was here once before, but wasn't able to stay very long."

Slan's mouth fell open when they went inside and Ruarshi smiled at her before turning his attention to the reason he'd brought her here.

Every inch of the walls was covered in glass mosaics, the most beautiful example of the art he'd ever seen. Rich blues, reds, silvers, greens, golds, and purples glinted in the sunlight spilling through the row of small clerestory windows set just below the vaulted ceiling. Clan totems rioted across the stone expanse, interspersed with greenery, rivers, stretches of coastline, and the occasional mountain, all arranged according to no scheme Ruarshi was able to perceive beyond the whim of the artist who'd fashioned them. The ancestral shrine in Tomir was quite different: it grouped totems according to clan alliances, each with its separate niche, and while this made it easier to decide where to set one's candle, Ruarshi much preferred this glorious chaos.

They were alone in the shrine so he felt free to wander. There was Slan's lynx, slinking out from behind a tree, and there his fox, one front foot raised. He searched for the magpie and was unaccountably gratified to find it only a handspan from his totem's bushy tail. He continued picking out animals as he went, still amazed at how hard some of them could be to discern at first glance but, once located, how impossible they were to miss afterward.

His gaze swung around to the western wall and he paused, unsure of what he was looking at. On his prior visit he hadn't made it so far into the shrine. Blue and green scales, a sinuous body, and no clan in all of Miriyan's history had chosen a snake for a totem. Finally he found the head, tinted red and purple, was briefly mystified to discover that it looked more leonine than anything else, and then realized he was looking at a depiction of the Great Dragon. An unsettling depiction, as the expression on the creature's face was malicious in the extreme. He scowled and turned his back to it, watching Slan as she slowly made her way in his direction. She hadn't said a word since they'd entered the place.

"I saw art in Europe that made me despair for my country," she said finally. "This is all very reassuring. Thank you."

"I thought you would like it."

"I do, very much. What is that?" She squinted past him.

"The Dragon, I think."

"How... lovely."

"Isn't it."

"Would you like me to go fetch a candle for you?" she asked. "I don't see any in here."

He was going to say no, to spare her the trouble, but she forestalled him.

"I want a candle, so I'll get you one, too. You, sit. Your day has been more challenging than mine and I suspect you could use a few minutes to yourself."

She wasn't wrong. Ruarshi sat obediently on one of the low stone benches and tried to think about nothing while she was gone.

He wasn't having much luck. The Dragon continued to glare at his back, and his eyes seemed to settle of their own accord on Casimir's owl or Britt's dolphin every time he glanced upward. He didn't even know which other totems he needed to ask forgiveness of, there were so many now.

Ruarshi rose to his feet and went to the door. He had come to the shrine to show Slan something beautiful, not to wallow in old emotions and pretend that regret mattered. He wavered for a moment, then unleashed a string of halfhearted curses and went to stand before Britt's totem. She wasn't the first or only person he'd killed, but she was the only one besides Casimir he'd spoken with beforehand. And Casimir didn't deserve his remorse.

The dolphin returned his regard serenely. He lifted a hand and placed it just under the creature's placid eye, not sure why he was doing it but unable to resist the urge. They had been so busy since the night the tower fell, and it had been so easy to concentrate on other matters because Davyt and Etienne and the rest of them had been his responsibility and his primary concern had been to shepherd them safely home. Now they were out of danger, as much so as anyone ever could be, and maybe he needed to think about what he'd done.

He closed his eyes and permitted the memories to flood in, every

ugly image that had been waiting in the murk for him to let his guard
down. It wasn't that he'd forgotten them—they'd been a constant
ghostly presence at the back of his mind, the dissonant music underlying every hour of every day—but now he focused in on them rather
than allowing his thoughts to slip away on whatever likely tangent offered itself.

Ruarshi shuddered, as cold as he'd been when he woke the morning
after the disaster, wondering if this was helping, if anything would. He
rather thought he already knew the answer to that, and his shaky equanimity gave way to sudden fury. It was fury with nowhere to go.

He opened his eyes and took his hand from the wall, afraid he'd
shatter the artwork if he remained where he was. Ruarshi backed toward the bench he'd occupied earlier and sat down again, his mind and
face as blank as he could make them.

When Slan returned with the candles and taper a little while afterward, he was able to greet her with a smile. He lit his candle mechani-
cally and placed it on the floor beneath the Dragon, an odd choice that
elicited a small frown from her when she noticed it. Ruarshi's manner
must not have been encouraging, because she didn't ask him about it,
but he knew she would later.

Perhaps by that time he'd have an answer for her.

They gathered again in Slan and Elin's room after dinner. The evening
meal had been a raucous affair, with two tables full of young Seers taking turns singing the most ribald songs Ruarshi had ever heard, some
of which he was already familiar with and some not. He supposed it
was an instance of the mice playing while the cats were away, or perhaps it was more of an attempt to scandalize the newcomers, but in
any case the noise made it impossible for them to carry on a conversation while they ate. This was fine with him, as he was still in no mood
to talk.

He nevertheless did his best to recount his conversation with
Photius for the others, and listened with interest to Elin's summation
of what she had gleaned from Ilias during the course of the day. He'd
taken her to the library on the ground floor of the north wing first, but
as those shelves contained texts primarily of interest to practicing Seers
with very few old works mixed in, they'd soon moved on to the basement that lay beneath it. This was the first Ruarshi had heard of the ex-

istence of an underground chamber. When she told them that there were upward of five hundred books, scrolls, and other oddments down there waiting to be sorted, he'd groaned inwardly and wondered what the librarians had been doing with their time. Her eyes twinkling, she'd gone on to add that over five times that number of texts had already been cataloged by topic, age, and sometimes author as well, and Ruarshi decided that he could forgive her for saving the good news for last.

Etienne's description of his explorations was subdued, as there hadn't been much of interest for him to see. Most of the rooms currently in use were living quarters, and the workrooms, as Ruarshi knew, were spartan affairs that typically contained nothing more than a water bowl and some cushions. The healer barely touched on his visit to the shrine, and had already moved on to an uncharitable description of the lake when they were interrupted by the arrival of Valentin and the Maelae warriors.

Slan's clan chief had sent four of them northward, a number that had initially struck her as a bit stingy but which, when added to their own forces, meant that the Naishanti in their party now outnumbered the Seers' entire garrison. They introduced themselves in passing as they hauled their sparse baggage into the next two rooms along the gallery, while both Valentin and Rafal hovered in the background. Once they were settled and the steward had drifted away again, the big warrior crossed his arms and leaned against the wall by the fireplace.

"I mislike this place," he observed, without preamble.

"It could use a garden," Mona said.

"Tapestries would also help," Elin remarked.

"Fewer geese," Etienne suggested. "The geese up by the lake are belligerent."

Valentin huffed a laugh. "I would not disagree, but that's not what I meant. The people are strange. There are no familiars! Dozens of cats, but they are all unattached. This is not normal."

"There's a lot of opium floating around," Ruarshi said. "It's necessary to their work, and not really compatible with bonding a familiar. Or a *pir.*"

"This… is not reassuring to me."

"Talented Seers are able to get by with very little of it. The others do have problems, especially over time."

"And why is this tolerated?"

"Because people are scared to death of the future, probably," Etienne said.

"I ask a simple question, I get philosophy."

"I'm not defending their practices, but some of the weaker Seers can experience breakthroughs," Ruarshi said. "After they've been here a while, their talents increase and they can cut down on the amount of opium they use."

"The first night I was here, I heard howling from one of the bed-rooms."

"Hallucinations are a possibility."

"Did you kill their leader?" Valentin asked.

Ruarshi, taken aback by the abruptness of the question, didn't an-swer.

The warrior read his silence correctly and threw his hands in the air. "Then why are you here?"

Several of the others chuckled in response, leaving Ruarshi feeling rather aggrieved. "We need information, and it will be easier for us to get it if it's not widely known that this is our only reason for coming. So I'm here to caper around in front of everyone while the real work is done elsewhere."

"This is a very stupid idea."

"Thank you," Ruarshi said dryly. "What rumor did you hear?"

"That Casimir went to visit you, hoping for reconciliation, and you killed him."

Ruarshi sighed, his aggravation deepening. "Did anyone explain why a reconciliation would have been necessary? We were on amicable terms when I left Miriyan."

"No. I thought maybe you had an argument."

"Please enlighten them, if you're so inclined."

"So you are not holding back word of the Mainz murder attempt?"

"No."

"There is a Seer who has helped us in the past," Slan said. "I've sent them a message, through the usual intermediary, asking if they know of any specific threats. I should receive a reply soon."

"You are being careful with the food?" Valentin asked.

"We are being careful with the food," Solvi said patiently. Ruarshi considered this to be a waste of effort, given that everyone at Mirror Lake ate from the same bowl, as it were, and trying to poison his din-ner would be much more complicated than just shooting him from am-bush.

"What was happening in Tomir when you left?" Mads asked.

"Great agitation," Valentin replied with relish. "Family and friends returning from the dead! My clan circle held a feast in my honor. Klas and I went to see Jair, who welcomed us as though we were his own sons. When I leave this place, I will return to my clan home and lie in the bath house for a week."

"Any notion of what Jair is planning to do?" Mads persisted.

"No. Politics are a curse."

"What? How does that relate to my question?"

"Paying attention to what the higher-ups are doing leads only to sadness. If I do not know what is happening, I cannot make bad decisions."

Etienne choked and burst out laughing. Valentin, who wasn't actually an idiot, smiled.

"Jair flays Ilmatar alive, Jair doesn't flay Ilmatar alive," Kennet said. "Do we care either way? We'll be long gone by the time any of the leadership gets back here, right?"

"That depends on how thorough we want to be," Elin said.

"You're going to have some extra help," Etienne said. "As of tomorrow morning, Mona, Kennet, and I will be down there with you. I can't read the old script, but I—we—can assist with the newer documents. Be thinking about how best to use us. And don't look at me like that. I'm not illiterate, and I can't just sit around twiddling my thumbs."

"No, sorry. Thank you for the offer. I've already put Solvi and Mads to work, but doubling our numbers will certainly help."

"I will come, too," Valentin said. "And until the Maelae chief arrives, maybe those warriors can also help?"

Elin was shaking her head. "I think I can get Ilias to agree to three more, but not eight. He's a little skittish. Maybe talk to the garrison, see if they know anything we ought to be aware of?"

Valentin appeared to think about this, tilting his head slightly from side to side. "I will spar with them. Afterward we will drink, and I will ask questions."

"Don't say that," Etienne groaned. "Now I'm tempted to go watch, in preference to burying myself in moldy paper all day."

"Too late," Elin said. "You made the offer and I'm not letting you back out of it."

"Perhaps I could put a melon on a stick, tell everyone it was me, and join you," Ruarshi mused.

"Do you have a melon?" Etienne asked.

"No, I don't have a melon."

"That's really the only impediment, but it's a big one."

Solvi was pinching the bridge of her nose, either because she already had a headache or wanted them to believe they were giving her one. "In between bouts, I'd take it kindly if you and the others could keep an eye on Ruarshi and Slan. While we're guarding the library."

Valentin drew himself up. "Of course. And in the evening, when the studying is over, you and I could go for a walk along the cliffs. To be sure there is no threat from the sea."

Now this was an interesting development. Ruarshi struggled to keep his expression neutral.

"We could," Solvi said. "What kind of seafaring enemies are you worried about?"

"Giant squid. Very dangerous."

"Unlikely to be interested in us, however."

"Still. It is better to verify this."

"Hmm," Solvi said. "You may be right. Find me tomorrow after lunch and I'll let you know whether or not I'll have time."

"This is a good plan," Valentin said. He left shortly thereafter, looking pleased with himself, and then Solvi and Mona excused themselves and disappeared into the adjoining room. The rest of them remained where they were for a bit longer, chatting about nothing in particular, but when Elin started yawning Ruarshi rose and ushered the men out.

When he and Etienne were back in their quarters with the door latched, Ruarshi asked, "Not a good day, I take it?"

"It was fine," Etienne said, shrugging out of his coat and hanging it from one of the pegs that jutted from the wall next to the wardrobe. "But I realized halfway through that I was going to end up helping with the research, which put a real damper on my mood. There's nothing here to explore."

"What were you hoping for?"

"A secret passage or two, a spooky cave. I don't know. This place has a resident healer, whom I met this afternoon by accident, so I can't even roam around looking for people with physical complaints."

"You don't want to be a healer here. Opium tears up the Seers' bodies. There's specialized training attached to this posting."

"Yuck." Etienne took off his shirt and trousers, pulled the blankets down on the bed, and sort of fell backward onto his side of the mattress.

"This place never reports suicides," Ruarshi said. "Not because no one here ever kills themselves, but because you usually can't tell the difference between that and an unintentional overdose."

"Sotar's balls, Ruarshi. Your day must have been a lot worse than mine."

And just like that he was back in the shrine. He should have kept his damn mouth shut.

"No."

"I'm detecting a falsehood here."

Ruarshi lowered himself into a chair. Eventually he spoke. "The shrine made me angry. It's my own fault for going in there. It's not as though I was unaware of what I would see."

Etienne sat up. "That fucking shrine," he said, with real heat. "It's beautiful and I hate it."

"That's... yes. Maybe those of us who've done terrible things are supposed to hate it. That doesn't explain why it had a similar effect on you."

Etienne exhaled slowly. "It's a lie. The animals it depicts, half of them eat the other half, and Miriyanti are no better. I'm sure I'll appreciate it more when we all learn to get along."

"Isn't art intended to show us what we should aspire to?"

"Keep talking like that and I'll pull all the covers off you in the middle of the night."

"Oh no."

The healer lay back in the bed again. "I'll bet that artist was an exhausting person. I'll 'aspire' to live in harmony with everyone provided that they go first. And that's the whole problem, isn't it. Are you planning to sit up long?"

"Not really, no."

"Good. I can practically hear it when you brood. It's a tedious sort of grinding noise."

"I had no idea."

"Well, now you know. Get in here and go to sleep."

# A Little Research

Etienne woke sometime after dawn to find Ruarshi snoring softly next to him, cocooned in the bedding. He smiled to himself and tended to the morning's ablutions, and as he'd expected, the other man was stirring before he'd even had time to splash water on his face. Ruarshi had always been a light sleeper.

The various members of their party met up again for breakfast. Etienne slipped a few morsels under the table and ended up with a purring cat on his lap for most of the meal, and afterward they split up into two separate groups to tend to the day's assignments. Ruarshi intended to meet with a handful of senior Seers to ask some questions about the Halls, but he harbored no real hope that they'd have anything useful to tell him. He was much more interested in continuing to spread the word that Nerthii and shamans were the same thing. This seemed to Etienne a worthy goal, which would probably be made easier if they could also explain what it was shamans were supposed to do. Ruarshi was still working out the arrangements with Rafal when Etienne headed out to the north wing with Elin, trailing their Naishanti escort.

She pushed open a coffin-shaped door that he somehow hadn't noticed the day before and preceded them down a long, dark flight of stairs. As they descended, Elin said, "We're going to need more lamps, but first I want to clear our new plan with Ilias. I was afraid if we came prepared that he might be offended."

"He's territorial, I take it?" Solvi asked.

"'Protective' might be more accurate. I can hardly blame him. They've got some treasures down here."

They emerged from the stairwell into a cool, dry, high-ceilinged chamber, stuffed with cluttered shelving and illuminated by half a dozen lamps. Two of these rested on a table near the entrance, where the little man Etienne remembered from yesterday's breakfast was sitting, and the others were located at random intervals farther back in the room. Shadowy figures could be seen moving about in their vicinity, presumably Ilias' assistants.

"Elin Naishanti," the man said, rising and coming forward. His expression went from welcoming to dubious as he surveyed the small crowd standing behind her. "Good morning, good to see you again, Solvi, Mads, hello. Who are these others?"

Elin handled the introductions while Etienne concentrated on looking as agreeable as he could at this hour of the morning. For some reason he had pictured the library as a bright and cheery place, which was of course ridiculous since it was situated underground, and he could already feel his soul curdling in dismay. Working down here for hours at a time was going to be a challenge, and he was afraid he'd emerge in the evening blind as a mole.

Ilias seemed inclined to accept their presence, at least on a provisional basis, and after warning all of them twice not to attempt to return anything to the shelves—there was a basket on his desk where all materials were to be left for his later attention—he went back to his work. Elin sent Mads back up to the main level to retrieve a lamp for each of them, and then led them to the sections she'd identified as the most likely to contain the types of texts they wanted. This part of the library held only those documents written in modern script, which would be more or less accessible to all of them, whereas the area farther from the entrance contained the writings that hadn't yet been translated from the ancient runic alphabet. She would be concentrating most of her attention there. She was rattling off a list of terms for them to look for when Mads reappeared and starting lighting lamps.

After Elin had gone and her Naishanti had picked out some thin volumes and moved away, Etienne gestured Mona and Kennet closer.

"There are a few more words I'd like to add to those that Elin just gave us. Don't ask why right now, please. There's no way I'm going to try explaining it in this crypt of a library, but I'm serious. Look for anything related to ritual sacrifices or mass murder. Anything about looms or dragons or Skeltari. Or blood magic. Information about shamanism is more important, yes, but if you run across something that sounds unlikely and makes your skin crawl, I want to know about it."

"That's quite a collection of interests you've got there," Kennet observed.

"I know. And if that old woman was lying to me and wasting our time, I'm going to have things to say to her later." And with that, they all got busy.

Etienne proceeded to lose himself in study in a way he hadn't managed since his intermediate years at the healers' circle, and lunch came as an unwelcome interruption. Afterward he couldn't have told anyone what he'd put into his mouth, and he dragged his bodyguards back downstairs with him before they were entirely finished eating. By the end of the day his head was swimming with random bits of history, odd magical theories, bizarre and impractical sexual advice, love poetry, rather suspect suggestions for communicating with angels, a concise refutation of monotheism, and a weird allegorical tale that involved various embodied virtues and vices wandering around in a garden and having tedious conversations with one another. He couldn't imagine that gluttony and lust, in particular, wouldn't have more interesting things to say.

He'd found nothing that shed any light on the Halls or the history that Satu had described. On the other hand, he'd picked up a lot of trivia and would probably be a fascinating conversationalist until he forgot all of it again, which might be useful if he was really going to try talking Kennet into bed. He still wasn't sure how he felt about that idea. His bond with Jonata was in no way intended as a pledge of sexual fidelity on the part of either one of them, but that didn't mean he was prepared to resume his prior habits. It was a bit of a dilemma, and he decided he'd think about it later.

Etienne emerged from the library, blinking, to find that the sunlight was spilling through the windows of the fortress at a low angle and the refectory was half full, which was about as close to capacity as he'd ever seen it. Ruarshi, Slan, and their warriors were already there, but Elin and her crew were still downstairs. He dragged himself toward their table, sat down, and leaned forward to rest his head on the wooden surface in preference to going to the trouble of filling a plate.

Ruarshi observed this for a moment and said, "Tell me what you want and I'll put something together for you."

Etienne raised his head, waved a hand toward a few items that smelled good, and went back to resting. Something clanked down near his ear and his former instructor nudged him with a shoulder.

"Eat. What did you learn?"

"Too much and not enough. You?" Etienne levered himself upward and began picking at his food.

"Nothing whatsoever from the Seers I talked to. Slan heard back from our mysterious friend, and it appears that no one is inclined to menace us for the time being. I met your friendly geese."

"You went to the lake?"

"I had some spare time, and my wanderings seem to put people on edge, which keeps them focused on me, which is what I want. And it was a nice day. How was the weather in the basement?"

"I hate you."

"I know." Ruarshi talked past him, to his bodyguards. "Is he over-working you?"

"Yes," Kennet said.

"It was restful," Mona said, "and I found a detailed description of a mass grave that was discovered here while they were building the north gallery."

"You did?" Etienne asked.

She nodded. "It sounded ghastly. None of the bodies showed evidence of injury, so the best guess was that some kind of epidemic swept through the area. They had to drop the idea of reburying them in separate graves, or even relocating them, because there were just too many. Hundreds at least. Its position explains why that gallery is shorter than the other, if anyone was curious about that."

"Maybe they should have abandoned this place," Kennet said. "Seems unlucky."

"If the grave was the first thing they'd unearthed, that might have been an option," Mona said, "but they'd already built the rest of it. That would have been a lot of work for nothing."

"Still," Kennet said. "What if there are ghosts?"

"Ghosts?" Etienne asked.

"Yes. The unquiet dead? Spirits of the deceased? You must have heard of them."

"You're kidding, right?"

"Not at all. I've seen one."

"Oh." Etienne had heard similar claims before. He decided to let the matter lie, as his attempts to gather information about such things in the past had usually ended with the other person getting defensive. For no good reason.

"Less talking, more eating," Ruarshi suggested. "You need to keep your strength up."

Etienne turned his attention back to his food, but he had even less appetite now than he'd had before. When Elin, Solvi, and Mads arrived a few minutes later, they didn't have much progress to report, either. This wasn't what anyone had hoped for but wasn't too discouraging, he supposed. They had, after all, just gotten started.

And so the work continued. After four more days in the underground library and several whispered consultations with Ilias, Elin had put together what she thought was a thorough list of allegedly effective ways to attack Nerthii, the methods that Casimir had referred to during his final conversation. She read them off that evening with only Slan, Ruarshi, and Etienne in the room.

"Salt in the clan well, as we know, will sicken a shaman. These assaults on the well only work if the shaman has already bonded to the land. No description of how or why this bonding occurs, or fails to, beyond the need for the shaman to open a doorway onto the Halls before it can happen. Putting poison in the well does nothing. Drowning the clan totem in the well will kill a shaman, and any other kind of dead creature left in the well will cause sickness. If a Stoneshaper plugs the well, the shaman dies. If the well dries up, same result. If the Skeltari does not 'renew the well by blood' from time to time, the shaman and the clan will sicken until the situation is rectified. Wounding a shaman with a weapon that contains silver will create an injury that's unusually painful, bloody, slow to heal, and inclined to fester. Oak also seems to be especially bad for you if you're stabbed with it. That's all I've found."

"As a rule, I try to avoid being stabbed with anything," Ruarshi said. He leaned back in his chair. "I feared the list would be much worse. I didn't want to die because of a bad harvest."

Etienne was beyond glad to know that Elin, at least, was getting somewhere. He and his Naishanti hadn't run across anything interesting since Mona's discovery on the first day. "Any other word on the Halls?"

"Nothing yet," Elin said. "Casimir's information… Assuming he didn't just invent all of that, it is of course possible that he removed items from the library without telling anyone. Ilias looked offended at the suggestion, but a few hours later he told me he was going to have Casimir's rooms checked. Just in case."

"How much more do you have to get through?" Ruarshi asked. The clan chiefs had begun arriving at Mirror Lake two days previously, and though attending meetings didn't sound as horrible as what Etienne was doing, he could tell Ruarshi was eager to be gone. Etienne would have felt the same way had there been any chance the Jinnae chief would show up, but he knew the odds of that happening were minuscule.

"Give me one more day to pursue a few tangential possibilities. There may be a lot more material down there, but if so it could take months to locate it all. I'll come back another time and try again."

"How about you?" Ruarshi asked, turning to Etienne. "Any more racy monographs?"

"I've run across too much of that, as it happens, and after a while it's just torture to read. The ones with illustrations are even worse. I found a line in a poem describing the future as a stream that flows from a dragon's maw, some old lunatic ranting about wells because he thought he'd seen a demon swimming in one once—I have no idea what he meant by 'demon' because he didn't define the term—and a mystic who contended that building labyrinths for everyone to wander around in would somehow strengthen magic in general. That's it."

"You can't find what's not here," Ruarshi said. "Thank you both. I know there are other things you would rather be doing. Now help me come up with a good excuse to stay in my room tomorrow. Liam arrived today."

"Did you have to interact with him?" Slan asked.

"No. But he certainly knew I was there."

"Is he likely to set his warriors on you?" Etienne inquired. "What's your history with him, anyway?"

"Sparse, and most of it predates the rebellion. He fancies himself a leader among the traditionalists, which was never helpful, and he convinced himself that I was sleeping with Seggita, which he used to bolster his dislike."

"If all or most of his good friends decide you're acceptable, he'll leave you alone," Slan said. "Lorion never seemed very concerned about him. If you can avoid antagonizing him, it will probably help your cause."

"The problem with that being that the sight of me antagonizes him. Hence my question."

"We could tell everyone that you're spending the day meditating," Etienne suggested. "Doing shaman things. Talking to animals."

"You could."

"It might make more sense for you to ignore him," Slan said. "Or, failing that, to try for icy politeness."

"I've been wielding politeness all week like a cudgel. I have almost run out."

"That's clearly a skill that needs strengthening, then. You can manage for one more day."

"We'll find out, I suppose. I—"

A soft rap on the door interrupted him. Elin rose and swung it open, revealing a heavily tattooed Seer carrying a thick folio in one hand. The man bowed to them before speaking. "My name is Amadan, clan Rossae. May I come in?" Elin bowed to him in turn, looked back toward the rest of them and, receiving only blank stares in response, waved the man forward and shut the door.

Etienne went to sit on the bed, gesturing their visitor toward his vacated chair. The man sat slowly, obviously ill at ease. "I should have come days ago. I apologize for not having done so. I know you are trying to learn what you can about shamanism, and I have something for you." He patted the cover of the book, which rested on his lap. "This was written many years ago by our last known Delver, Alcina. Casimir thought it was quite important. He kept it in his quarters under lock and key." He handed it to Ruarshi, who—after exchanging a quick glance with Elin—took it and let it fall open in his hands.

He examined the page that had been revealed and shook his head, passing the volume to the Annorae warrior. "I have heard of her. Thank you for entrusting this to us, but not only is it written in old script, it appears to be practically illegible."

Etienne was watching Elin, who was paging through the book in consternation. He was quite interested in what it might have to say; Delvers, the obverse of Seers and rare as hens' teeth, were able to scry out events that had happened in the past. "I've never run across anything written in this way before," she said. "She seems to have combined runes in some kind of idiosyncratic shorthand. I don't know whether I'll be able to figure out what it says or not."

"Casimir was having similar problems, but he found it worthwhile to try," Amadan said. "You will see that he wrote some of his translations in the margins."

Elin continued turning pages, frowning, as Ruarshi returned his attention to the Seer. "You were working closely with him?"

"From time to time, yes. You deserve to know that I was eventually made aware of what he'd done to the exiles," he paused to nod at Elin,

who stopped what she was doing to look at him, "as well as what he more recently attempted to do to you. I am sorry."

"A word of warning would have been appreciated," Ruarshi said mildly.

"I would very much have liked to send you one, but I fear that any missive I might have written would not have reached you in time."

"Pardon the question, but why are you helping us?" Ruarshi asked.

"Two reasons. Mirror Lake has wronged many people of late, and I would like to begin making amends while I can. Were Ilmatar here, I have no doubt he would prevent it. The second reason: with shamans having returned to Miriyan, I would prefer them to know what they are doing. They are too powerful to be allowed to flail about in ignorance."

Ruarshi chuckled. "I agree with that." Etienne was observing his former instructor closely, certain that he was using that weird ability of his to tell if someone was lying to him. He looked thoughtful, which probably meant he accepted what Amadan was saying. "Yet I'm sure you've heard the rumors. There are other Nerthii you could have sought out. Why bring the book to me?"

"Because you are the one who is here. I am a practical man."

"Did Casimir ever suggest that I should have it?"

"Ah, I see. You are concerned that this may be another of his traps. It is wise to be wary, but no. He could be a subtle man when he wanted to be, but I do not believe I am being used in this way. When he left, I would not say that the possibility of his own demise was uppermost in his mind. Therefore, he saw no need to prepare for it."

"You don't resent what happened to him?"

"When a man attempts to kill you, he cannot complain if you return the favor and meet with greater success."

"Is that sentiment widespread among the Seers?" Slan asked.

"Everyone knows now about Casimir's deception and illegal behavior with regard to the exiled warriors. Very few would excuse that. His more recent endeavors are less well known, but even so he was never interested in inspiring personal loyalty. There are not many among us who genuinely mourn his passing."

"That's a grim epitaph," Etienne muttered.

"Yes," Amadan said. "Now. There is something else I would show you, if you are willing to accompany me to the chamber beneath the shrine."

"What is it?" Slan asked.

"I do not know, and I would prefer not to attempt a description.

Perhaps one of you, seeing it for the first time, will have some insight. Casimir was certain that it relates in some way to the Halls."

Ruarshi looked toward Slan, who shrugged her assent. Etienne grabbed the lamp off the room's side table and hurried to the fireplace to light it. By the time he'd gotten a small flame burning, the others were outside, waiting for him. He joined them and handed the lamp off to Amadan, who led them west along the gallery through the quiet evening air.

When they reached the final landing, the Seer continued past the entrance to the shrine and ducked into a low wooden antechamber. Once inside, Etienne saw that it enclosed a small basin of ritual purification water. Amadan shut the door firmly behind them and went to the opposite wall, where he shoved aside a narrow, faded tapestry to reveal another door, this one set in solid stone.

As Amadan unlocked it and pulled it open, the hinges squealing softly, he said, "The existence of this room is not widely known, and I would request that you not mention it in conversation with others. It is used as a storage area for items of undetermined purpose, most of them magical in nature, and it were better for it to remain a secret. The stairway is steep. Please be careful."

With that Amadan started down the steps into the darkness, holding the lamp out before him. Slan swung in behind him, with Ruarshi and Etienne following and Elin bringing up the rear. The staircase was only about half as long as the one leading to the library, and when they reached the bottom the Seer ushered them over to one of the large cupboards lining the wall on the far side of the room. He pulled a key from inside his tunic and unlocked it, throwing the doors wide and bringing the lamp forward to illuminate an object sitting on a shelf at about hip level.

"Do not touch it," he said. "There was an unfortunate incident some time ago that resulted in the death of a young Seer. He cut himself on a blade that Casimir later came to believe had been chipped from its edge and bled to death, in spite of the best efforts of the healer."

Etienne had no idea what he was looking at. It appeared to be a shallow, narrow bowl with a smooth finish, tapering to a sharp point at one end and with a squared-off rim at the other. The bottom of the vessel was curved like the hull of a ship, and it rested on the shelf with its inner surface tilting away from them. It was black in the lamplight and measured a little over a foot long. A few tarnished silver rings lay within it, along with what might have been an ancient belt buckle, and the long edge nearest to them looked like it had been chewed upon by rats.

The Seer was watching them hopefully.

"If it's meant to serve as a bowl, it's a bad design," Etienne observed.

"What is it made of?" Elin asked. "Obsidian?"

"For a certainty, no," Amadan said. "We suspect some type of metal." He struck the key against the base of the object and it emitted an odd clanging noise.

Ruarshi took a step backward and Etienne frowned at him. "Is something wrong?"

"No. That was just louder than I expected."

Which was a strange sort of answer. If anything, Etienne had thought the sound was muffled. He turned back toward the cupboard but kept his former instructor in the corner of his eye.

"I've never seen anything like it," Elin said. "I don't know much about how Stoneshapers operate. Could it be some type of mold?"

"I don't believe so," Amadan said.

"Has anyone made a suggestion that seems likely?" Slan asked.

"Not to my knowledge," the Seer replied.

"How much does it weigh?" Etienne asked.

"I… have no idea. Nor am I going to attempt to pick it up."

"I don't think we're going to be much help," Ruarshi said. "Was it something Casimir found in Alcina's book that led him to tie this to the Halls?"

"I am not sure, but I suspect so."

Slan blew out a breath in mild frustration. "Thank you for the book, and for showing this to us. If one of us has an epiphany, we'll find you and let you know."

The Seer nodded in acknowledgment and they took their leave of him. Etienne cast a final, curious glance around the room, quite possibly the only secret chamber that Mirror Lake had to offer, and followed the others up the stairs. When they'd made it back to the quarters he and Ruarshi shared, Elin returned to the book and flipped it open, her expression guarded.

"Wasn't that a funny sort of coincidence. Should I mistrust it?"

Slan stood just behind her, looking over her shoulder at the closely-written pages. "Even if Amadan meant us ill, it's just a book. I'm not sure how it could harm us."

"What if he intended it as misdirection?" Elin asked. "But then again, why would he care if I waste my time on useless translations?"

Slan pondered the question and looked over at Ruarshi, who was staring into their small fire with a distracted air. "Ruarshi? What do you think?"

He shook himself and answered her. "I dislike coincidences involving Seers, but I'd wager that's what we're dealing with here. Unless you really believe Amadan was listening in at our window. I can't quite picture that, but he'd have had no other means of spying on us."

"Maybe Ilias' search of Casimir's quarters prodded him into action," Elin mused. She closed the book and rapped her knuckles gently against the cover. "This is going to be a real challenge. This thing runs at least a hundred pages. Rather than extending our stay here to see how far I can get with it, I think we should take it to my clan home. The work will go much more quickly if half a dozen of us are poring over it at once."

"That's an excellent idea," Ruarshi said.

Etienne sat down on the bed and smiled up at his former instructor. "You should come with us to the library tomorrow. Take a break from all that sitting in comfortable chairs, in rooms with windows, and listening to other people talk. That way we can all suffer from neck cramp and eye strain together."

"Only if you're willing to take my place in those meetings and pay attention to what's being said. They do request my input from time to time."

"About what?"

Ruarshi shot him a look. "Questions pertaining to Europe, for the most part. My role isn't entirely decorative."

"But they can't make any decisions until everyone gets here, can they?"

"They can't take any action that would be considered binding until at least half the chiefs arrive. I don't think they're going to hit that number, but they might reach a third as early as tomorrow, which would make it possible for them to get some preliminary work done. Ciarn should be here any day. If one more chief were to wander in, they'd have the eighteen they need.

"Speaking of which, word is that they're planning a formal dinner in the great hall tomorrow evening, to declare the convocation officially begun."

"Even if they don't have the numbers required to do anything?"

Elin asked.

"Some of the chiefs are already getting bored," Slan said. "They need reassurance that their presence here is recognized and appreciated."

"Hard on the larders," Etienne observed.

"And the servants," Slan said. "Fortunately, the nearby clan homes have offered to assist, and a few of the chiefs thought to bring extra provisions."

"Will there be music?" Etienne asked.

"Maybe?" Ruarshi ventured.

"Do you dance?" Elin asked.

"Of course," Etienne said. "I'm quite good."

"He actually is," Ruarshi said.

Etienne flushed a little. "There you have it. May I partner with you for the first dance? Assuming someone in this awful place knows how to play an instrument."

"Certainly," Elin said.

"I'm trying to imagine the clan chiefs hopping around on a dance floor," Slan said.

"Get a large volume of *keth* into them," Ruarshi said, "and it could happen."

"Better that than a brawl," Elin said. She picked up Alcina's book and went to the door. "I'm going to sit down with this before I start nodding off. Even if I only decipher one or two runes, I'll feel better. Puzzles like this drive me to distraction."

"Do you need anything from the kitchens?" Slan asked.

"No, thank you. I won't be working very long. Good night. Sleep well." She disappeared out the door.

The rest of them sat up a while longer, unwilling to call it a night just yet. The evening's peace was interrupted when a group of warriors attached to one of the clan chiefs began an impromptu game of ninepins in the gallery, but they skulked back into their rooms without complaint after their neighbors poured out onto the walkway to hurl verbal abuse at them. Once the fortress had descended into silence once more, Slan took her leave, and Etienne and Ruarshi settled into bed.

Etienne felt so well, and safe, and happy that he spent the next half hour lying awake, wondering what sort of terrible surprise was going to come along and spoil it all.

When he woke up the next morning and saw Ruarshi standing in the doorway, bathed in early sunlight, he didn't get his answer, not precisely. But he did begin to understand what its outlines were going to look like.

He sprang to his feet. "Ruarshi."

His former instructor, who had been gazing up toward the lake, turned in his direction. "What?"

Etienne wanted to be certain he was right about this before he opened his mouth. He paused to pull on his trousers and went to the door. With a quick shrug of apology he grabbed Ruarshi's chin and turned his face back toward the light.

"Your eyes are a lot redder than they were yesterday. And before you ask, it's not an illusion caused by the angle of the sun." Etienne frowned and put his palm against the man's forehead. "Damn it. You also have a fever." He let his hand fall.

"Do I?" Ruarshi's brow creased. "Hmm. You're right." He met Etienne's eyes and concern flashed across his face. "How do you feel?"

"I don't think changes in eye color are contagious, Ruarshi. Why would you—" He broke off as the real significance of the question became clear to him. "This is about that stupid bowl, isn't it? Did you know it was dangerous?"

Ruarshi looked at him reproachfully. "I'm not sure that it *was*. It may be that Satu has taken some kind of action and this," he waved vaguely at his face, "is the result. But there was definitely something off about it. Your eyes and temperature are normal, which is reassuring."

"What do you mean by 'off'?"

"It was unnerving. It's difficult to describe."

"Did you want to run away from it for no good reason?"

"… Yes."

"That's how those doorways of yours affect everyone else. And you stood in a room with it and didn't say anything?"

"Amadan had obviously been down there a number of times and suffered no ill effects. If I'd thought it posed a risk to anyone, I'd have said so. Are we seriously considering the possibility that it was emitting some kind of magic that none of us could sense, and that only I was susceptible to? That's a bizarre idea."

"Everything about shamanism and the Halls is bizarre. When Amadan hit it with his key, what did that sound like to you? You backed away."

"Like a church bell. A big one."

"To me, it sounded more like a cowbell someone dropped on the floor. I think you should follow your own instincts when it comes to anything Hall-related. The rest of us might not be seeing what you're seeing."

Ruarshi growled quietly in exasperation. "This is without a doubt what I like least about my new role. Rules are nonexistent, oddities crop up everywhere, and I might drag a bystander into a bad situation out of sheer ignorance."

"Well, I'm fine. We can check on the women on the way to breakfast, but I bet they will be, too. Should we ask Amadan if a local Skeltari could be brought it to try to identify the thing?"

"I'd rather see it locked away and thrown in the ocean. Failing that, the fewer people who are exposed to it, the better. I'll describe it to Satu the next time I talk to her. In the meantime, I'll request that Amadan refrain from taking anyone else down there.

"The eyes," Ruarshi went on after a short pause. "Are they very obvious?"

"I'm afraid so."

"I'll try to keep to shadowy indoor areas today. Maybe they'll fade over time."

"Maybe. I should warn you now that I'm going to be monitoring that fever of yours until it goes away."

"Fair enough."

"It's a good thing that we were already planning on leaving tomorrow. I'm not even sure we should stay here another night. What if the bowl is putting off some kind of magic waves that can soak through the walls and ceiling and end up—"

Mads and Kennet emerged from their room and Etienne cut himself off in mid-sentence, to Ruarshi's obvious relief. It was a short-lived reprieve; Kennet startled at the sight of him and Mads' stride faltered as he went by.

When they'd moved out of earshot, Ruarshi said, "That wasn't promising, was it?"

"They'll get used to it. So will everyone else. Though I suppose this will lead to more wild rumors."

"Probably."

Once Etienne finished dressing, they gathered up the others and made their way to the refectory. As he had predicted, there was nothing wrong with Elin or Slan, and he continued to pretend that he wasn't concerned about Ruarshi's fever even though he most definitely was. He spent two or three fruitless hours in the library, looking at the words on the page without really seeing them, before giving up on the effort and heading outside for a breath of fresh air. He fell asleep leaning against the west wall of the main building, observed but unmolested by the great variety of horses currently being pastured in the area between the galleries, and didn't stir until Kennet jostled his leg with the toe of his boot.

"Up. Unless you want to miss lunch."

"I never miss a meal on purpose."

He rose and went inside, looked around for his former instructor, and excused himself when he realized neither Ruarshi nor Slan was there. The warriors tried to follow him to his room, but Etienne found their constant attendance faintly ridiculous at this point, and he persuaded them to go ahead and start eating by promising that he would return before they were done.

When Etienne burst into his quarters a few seconds later, he found Ruarshi sitting on the windowsill across from an unfamiliar Miriyanti woman. She rose from her chair as he came in.

"Etienne," Ruarshi said, "I'd like to introduce you to Aurel Nerthi, clan Taanor. She traveled through the Halls to find me here. Aurel, this is Etienne Illyana of clan Doshae, my former apprentice."

He bowed politely and she mirrored the gesture. As she straightened, he studied her more closely. Her eyes were indeed red, but they were the deep red he'd grown accustomed to while Ruarshi's were still the alarming shade he'd first seen that morning. And the man was still running a fever.

Etienne schooled himself to patience and apologized for interrupting them. They'd been in close conversation when he'd entered the room and he didn't want to interfere with whatever it was they were saying to each other. He'd catch up on what he'd missed later, during the long ride north if not before.

He left them to their discussion and returned to the refectory, where he sat down to eat some lunch.

# Red Eyes

Ruarshi yanked his formal coat off its peg and tugged it on with a series of swift, ungraceful movements, still out of sorts and fighting a headache that was only growing worse as the day progressed. Etienne, also getting ready for the evening's formal dinner, was silent behind him. Ruarshi had no doubt that the younger man had picked up on his sour mood and was doing his best to become invisible. He wanted to reassure Etienne that all was well, or that all would be well soon, but the words wouldn't come.

Slan was annoyed with him again, in a very familiar way. Ruarshi wondered for possibly the tenth time that day just how much of their life together had been marred by one or another of his inconvenient physical complaints, of which the eye situation and the fever were just the latest examples. He was keeping a close watch on the others and so far they remained healthy, which was a great if provisional relief, but this also left him unsure about the true cause of his problem. He wouldn't know anything for certain until he was able to pay a call on Satu.

He buttoned his coat, pushed open the shutters, and stood with his palms pressed flat against the windowsill, breathing in great gulps of the mild air and trying to calm down. Even Aurel's unanticipated but welcome arrival hadn't made him feel any better. In a perverse twist that was in no way her fault, the extraordinary news she'd brought about the Halls had only served to unsettle him further. He was now more than half convinced, based on little more than paranoia, unpleasant dreams, and his current physical discomfort, that he was engaged in the opening maneuvers of a battle that he was unlikely to win. He didn't even know what the stakes were.

After Aurel had left his quarters to have a much overdue chat with her clan chief, Ruarshi had done his best to explain what she'd told him to Slan and Etienne. It still seemed incredible to him, the equivalent of making a wish and watching it come true, but apparently the Halls could be used to travel almost instantaneously between locations, no matter how far removed they were from each other. She claimed—and he had no reason to doubt her word—that she'd stepped into the Halls in Tomir that morning and had stepped out just beyond the walls of Mirror Lake. She'd been able to do so because he was there. Nerthii, she said, could always locate others of their kind via the Halls, assuming their target had opened a doorway of their own at least once. He could use the same ability to travel to his clan home whenever the urge struck him, or to visit close blood relations regardless of where they happened to be staying at any given time, or even to track down friends and acquaintances as long as he was in possession of a personal item of theirs.

Aurel's description of how these wonders were accomplished amounted to nothing more complicated than entering the Halls, concentrating on your goal, and then opening another doorway. Ruarshi had done his best to keep his face immobile as she relayed this to him, but some slight change in his expression must have given him away because she'd laughed, shrugged, and told him to try it for himself before deciding it couldn't be done. He was sure this was solid advice and he did intend to give it a go once he had the opportunity, but after a few tentative questions on his part she'd diverted their conversation to the subject of the Taanor clan chief Liam, whom she very badly wanted to see, and he hadn't asked her anything else about it.

He wasn't sure he wanted more answers right now in any case. While Aurel had been talking he'd found his thoughts circling around the figure of the wish-granting djinn of Islamic mythology, and decided that was how he was going to think about the intelligence inhabiting the Halls until he had cause to call it by a different name. Because something like that *had* to exist; the vision he'd been granted, all unwilling, hadn't emanated from the stones or the soil. The fact that he hadn't found a consciousness in the well when he'd searched for it only meant he'd been looking in the wrong place, or it had stepped away for a time. Or it was something so foreign to him that he wouldn't recognize it if he saw it.

Ruarshi hadn't shared these particular speculations with his small audience, as he didn't want either of them to start thinking he'd gone delirious with fever. If he were ever able to learn something about his quarry, he'd pass it on, but until then he thought he'd be best served by keeping his odder notions to himself.

He'd rounded out his afternoon by taking another stroll up toward the lake, hoping that stretching his legs would make him feel better. It hadn't, but Etienne had perked up somewhat at the sight of the geese and Slan had enjoyed herself, so the effort hadn't been wasted. Now all that was left to get through was the dinner, after which he could return to his room, hide his aching head in the pillow, and ignore the world for a few hours.

Ruarshi could almost feel Etienne's eyes on his back. The man was probably wondering how long he planned to stand there, and whether or not he should say something.

Ruarshi smiled and turned. "Ready?"

"Whenever you are."

They went out onto the walkway, where they proceeded to knock on doors and wait while the other members of their small party gathered. Once they'd all emerged from their rooms, they headed for the main building as a group and by unspoken agreement remained together upon their arrival at the massive entrance hall. Dozens of lamps and candles illuminated the thirty or so trestle tables that had been set out for the meal. Most of the clan chiefs and their retinues were already seated, so after a brief stop to exchange pleasantries with Ciarn, they ended up at one of the tables closer to the eastern wall.

Slan excused herself as they were settling in and made her way over to the Maelae chief, and while she was gone, Ruarshi sought out and located Aurel in the crowd. She was sitting at Liam's right hand, which startled him a little given the chief's open hostility toward her a few weeks prior, but evidently their conversation that afternoon had led to a shift in their relationship. He could almost wish he'd been there to see it. However it had gone, he hoped that their apparent truce was genuine, and that Aurel would be able to live openly at her clan home now. She'd been reluctant to talk about her personal history, but he'd gotten the impression that her last few years had been spent in unhappy self-isolation. She'd certainly been under some type of strain, and seemed physically fragile in a way more appropriate to a woman twice her age.

Amadan, he noted in passing, was not present.

As expected, the dinner started with several brief speeches from the clan chiefs, none of which would be remembered by anyone there after they'd swallowed a mug or two of *keth*. Ruarshi listened with half an ear, most of his attention focused on the small Mirror Lake staff as they struggled to feed almost three times the number of people they were accustomed to looking after. This reflection led him to do a little bit of math and he frowned, looking out over the gathering again. Solvi caught his eye as his gaze returned to their table.

"Most of the older Seers aren't here," she said. "I don't actually know what they do with their time, for the most part, but that seems strange."

"All the chiefs are in attendance," Slan said, "along with their warriors and hangers-on. Maybe the Seers went to bed early."

"More food for us," Kennet said. "I think I'm going to need an extra serving of the soup."

The warrior wasn't wrong; the main ingredient was salmon and it was, indeed, very good. Ruarshi toyed with his spoon, wondering with tired exasperation what had happened to his appetite.

"Let's just assume they're plotting something we won't like and try to enjoy our dinner in the meantime," he said. "It will save us some effort."

"I would like to draw your attention to the fact that all of Mirror Lake's Naishanti are sitting right there," Mads said, nodding toward a nearby table. "If the elder Seers are hip-deep in plots at the moment, they're not telling their warriors about it."

"Everyone who cares to know is aware that we're leaving tomorrow," Elin said, between bites, "but they'd have to be fools to try anything while surrounded by this many clan chiefs."

Ruarshi inclined his head. "This is true. How much by way of provisions will we be able to wring from the kitchens in the morning, do you think?"

As intended, this shifted their conversation toward more cheerful topics and the rest of the meal went so smoothly that he was able to tune most of it out without feeling that he was being negligent. Once the sparse remains of the meal had been cleared away and half the tables, including theirs, had been disassembled and stacked against the walls, a young Seer produced a hurdy-gurdy and began to play. Ruarshi had seen only one of those during the entire time he'd spent in Europe and he moved in to get a closer look, fascinated, while Etienne took Elin's hand and whirled her out into the open area. By the time the instrument had wheezed its way back into a state of quiescence, the evening was well advanced, the entire assembly appeared to be in good humor, and every member of their little group had made it out onto

the dance floor at least once. Ruarshi had even remembered, after very
nearly colliding with Valentin in the wake of a particularly lively reel, to
ask the warrior to keep an eye on Aurel once they'd gone. He didn't
think she'd stay at Mirror Lake long, but that was no reason to be careless, and if she thought it high-handed of him he was prepared to
weather her wrath the next time they met. The warrior cheerfully
agreed before disappearing into the press again.

When some of the older chiefs began trickling back to their quarters, Solvi gathered up her charges and ushered them toward the south
gallery. She didn't quite go so far as to remind them all that they had an
early morning to look forward to and needed their rest, but Ruarshi
thought it was a close thing. He was satisfied to let himself be herded
off, and he fell into bed shortly thereafter, boneless. What his attempts
to settle his nerves through sheer determination hadn't succeeded in
doing, exhaustion had, and he nodded off almost immediately.

He awoke from yet another dream he didn't like with a hand on his
shoulder and Etienne peering down into his face, muttering under his
breath. Ruarshi sat up, still sodden with sleep, and realized that quite a
lot of light was coming into the room through the gaps in the shutters.

"What time is it?"

"Late enough that I've had to chase Solvi away a couple of times."

"Damn. Why didn't you get me up?"

"Because I thought you could use the rest. We're not in a hurry, are
we? Your fever is gone, by the way."

"Good." He checked on Etienne as he dressed and was relieved to
find that the healer was still healthy as a horse. After tending to his
morning routine he went to the wardrobe, intending to pack his saddlebags with the few items of clothing he'd brought along, only to discover that the task had already been done. He stood for a moment with
his hands on his hips, staring at their baggage where it rested against
the wall.

"Thank you. I think. I'm not sure you should be facilitating my lazi-
ness."

"The others have already eaten and Mads is saddling the horses.
Let's get some breakfast while we still have the chance."

As they made their way toward the main building, Ruarshi studied
the sky. The sun was about to disappear behind a heavy bank of

clouds, meaning they were probably in for a wet day. That wasn't ideal, but they were overdue for this kind of weather and as long as the temperature remained mild, traveling through some rain wouldn't be too much of a burden. He did ask about tents, though, once he and Etienne had joined the rest of their group in the temporary paddock. As expected, that detail had already been seen to. Everything had already been seen to, in fact, including a substantial sack of food that would last them until they reached the Eirenae clan home about two and a half days' ride to the northeast. Since they were planning to stop at most of the clans that lay between Mirror Lake and the Annorae, they could travel light, and had decided to leave their pack horses behind. The animals would be returning home later with Ciarn's party.

Which reminded Ruarshi that he hadn't taken leave of his clan chief yet. It was a formality he'd just as soon have skipped, but people were watching, and it never did any good to antagonize one's chief for no reason. He turned to go back inside just as Ciarn emerged from the south wing and headed in their direction. It was a mark of respect that the chief should come outside to see them off, rather than wait for them to seek him out, and Ruarshi wondered which of them the gesture was meant for. The obvious answer was that he intended this public display of regard to bolster the reputation of the Nerthii, but Ruarshi wasn't so sure, and a quick glance at Etienne revealed that the healer was currently hiding behind his horse. There'd been some kind of interaction between the two of them on the night Karoli had challenged Ciarn's First, but Etienne had never told him exactly what had happened. Ruarshi thought the healer had probably done something impressive, and was embarrassed by it, and he'd have the truth out of the man sooner or later if he had to wring his neck to get it. Or he could just ask Karoli, he supposed.

He and Ciarn made their way through the required forms, and the chief ended by wishing them good fortune. Ruarshi responded with a few polite noises, they clasped hands, and then he and the others mounted up and rode away from Mirror Lake. He was glad to leave it behind.

It started raining on them about ten minutes out and kept it up for most of the day. It was a light, steady rain rather than a deluge, and it wouldn't have been any kind of problem if Ruarshi's fever hadn't returned about noon, leaving him shivering and miserable. He tried to prevent his distress from becoming obvious, but it wasn't long before Etienne broke off his conversation with Elin and appeared at his right stirrup.

"Do you need to stop?" the healer asked, his voice conversational.

"No. It will pass."

"Oh? So you know what's causing it?" Etienne's tone remained light.

Ruarshi shot him a glare.

"That's what I thought. If I have to overrule you and call a halt, I will."

Ruarshi didn't reply and Etienne stayed at his side from that moment onward, riding silently for the most part. When Solvi reined in that evening Ruarshi slid from the saddle and helped set up camp, though he would have preferred to dive into one of their two small tents as soon as they were ready and collapse. He forced himself to eat more than he wanted to, because his day wasn't over yet.

First he had to win an argument, and then he had to go get some answers while he still felt sturdy enough to manage it.

Slan and Etienne didn't approve of his idea, and they were vocal about it. Elin seemed supportive but didn't say much, and the warriors mostly stayed out of the discussion. Fortunately Ruarshi had a solid line of reasoning on his side. His questionable condition was actually of some use to him here, as it helped underline the urgency of the situation, and eventually his position prevailed.

"What should we do if you don't return?" Slan asked, jabbing viciously at their small campfire with a stick. It had finally stopped raining.

"Continue riding, of course, but that's not going to happen. Speaking of which, do you have a small token I could borrow? I'll need it to get back here."

She tugged up her left sleeve and rolled a braided leather bracelet off her wrist. "Will this do?" she asked, holding it out to him.

"Take this, too," Etienne said. His fox pin lay in the palm of his hand.

Elin dug in the pouch at her belt and extracted a black ribbon, of the kind she used to tie her mask in place. "I always keep a spare. Here."

"Thank you," Ruarshi said. He accepted their offerings, using the pin to affix the bracelet and ribbon to the inside of his tunic. If all those items combined didn't prove sufficient to enable his return, he couldn't imagine what would.

"Tell Satu to cheer up," Etienne said. "She might even try a smile sometime."

"I'll suggest it," Ruarshi said, rising. He nodded to his companions
and strode away to the north, where the ground rose slightly and was
clear of all vegetation save for a few sparse tufts of grass. He needed to
put enough distance between himself and the others to ensure that his
doorway wouldn't alarm them too badly, but at the same time he knew
they'd want him to stay in their line of sight, so he couldn't very well go
traipsing off into the copse of trees that bordered their campsite to the
south and east. When he'd gone what he judged to be about an eighth
of a mile, he came to a halt, opened a door, and stepped through.

He'd braced himself for the sensation of plunging to his death and
was relieved when his transit from one realm to another felt no different than crossing the threshold of any other doorway. His relief turned
to uneasiness when he saw that the wall in front of him was a light rose
color, rather than the gray he'd been expecting, and he realized that the
entire place was both brighter and warmer than he remembered. He allowed the doorway to close behind him and spun slowly, taking note of
the changes.

The hall looked to be the same width as it had been on his first visit,
but everything else was different. The walls were smooth to the touch
and appeared to be faced with marble, and when he looked upward he
could see that at a height of about fifteen feet they began angling inward toward a rectangular opening. Sunlight poured through it and
threw a patch of almost blindingly white light onto the floor just to Ruarshi's left. The stone beneath his boots was of the same rose color as
the walls, woven through with thin lines of red, blue, and purple in an
intricate geometric pattern. The air seemed slightly damp. And he'd be
willing to swear that the Halls were now inhabited.

He froze, breathless. Whatever was in there with him, it wasn't human. But he'd already known that would be the case, hadn't he? He
prodded gently at the edges of this other awareness, but was unable to
discern anything about it beyond the fact of its presence. If it experienced emotions of any kind, he couldn't make sense of them.

The air seemed to be growing thicker around him, possibly as a result of his rising terror. He struggled to suppress it, but its origin was
instinctive and no matter how insistently he told himself that his reaction was irrational and worse than useless, the feeling only increased in
intensity. It was many times worse than it had been in the chamber beneath Mirror Lake's shrine. He was beginning to find it difficult to
breathe, and soon he wouldn't be able to think at all.

Ruarshi closed his eyes and concentrated on his family's hall until it dominated his thoughts to the exclusion of all else. When he believed he could safely attempt to leave, he opened his eyes again, waved another doorway into existence, and hurried through it.

A soft rain was falling but otherwise the landscape was still under a blanket of low gray clouds. He was standing on a rocky patch of ground, with a scatter of neat wooden buildings spread out over the rolling terrain before him and the yellow glow of firelight outlining a window here and there. An owl hooted in a bush somewhere behind him as he tried to make sense of the scene. When he finally succeeded, he took a deep, relieved breath and stumbled forward, heading toward the small round building off to his right.

He pushed Satu's door open without pausing to knock first because he didn't know how much longer he'd be able to remain upright. It swung shut behind him and he leaned back against it, sliding slowly downward until he was sitting on the ground. Only then did he begin paying close attention to his surroundings. The Skeltari was standing in front of him, a displeased expression on her face, and a younger woman sat at the table behind her. He'd known Satu had an apprentice, but this was the first time he'd seen her. He was sure he was making a wonderful first impression. A small fire burned in the fireplace and the room smelled of berries and honey.

"Young one. What have you been up to?"

Ruarshi stifled a sudden and inappropriate urge to laugh. "Why do you ask?"

"The water in the clan well's gone cloudy. And there's something in the wind that I mislike."

He thought he already had the answer he'd come for, but decided to ask the question anyway since he'd gone to so much trouble to get here. "I don't suppose anything you've done could have caused this change in my eyes?"

Satu's frown intensified. She snatched a candle from the table and crouched down in front of him. He rather disliked having a light source shoved into his face, thanks to an incident a while back involving some Seers, but he tolerated her examination for the sake of getting it over with.

The Skeltari rose and chewed briefly on her lower lip. "That is not good, young one."

"What makes you say that?"

"It's too much." She shook her head emphatically. "Too much."

"Too much what?"

"The Halls, they are an alien place. Your place is here."

Ruarshi agreed with that, but didn't find her cryptic comments to be terribly helpful. "Is there any way to reverse it?"

Satu had commenced staring at the wall and didn't reply. He tried again. "Or, if there isn't, can my tie to the clan be broken?"

The question seemed to startle her and she looked back at him, but still didn't answer. Her apprentice chose that moment to rise from her chair. She was carrying a mug of something warm and aromatic, and she handed it to him with a small smile. "I'm Mira. I'm honored to meet you at last."

"Likewise, and thank you." Ruarshi accepted the cup and took a swallow. It was a sweetened tisane, and the source of the comforting smell he'd noticed when he came in. "I'm Ruarshi."

"I know. Why would you want to break your bond with the clan?"

He didn't want to, but suspected it might be necessary. "If what happens to the clan can make me ill, I have to assume that the reverse is also true. Something is badly wrong and I don't want it to affect anyone else."

"Tell me what you mean by 'badly wrong,'" Satu said, so he did. He told her about all of it, including the appalling dreams and the dizziness and the shuddering weakness in his chest that sometimes made him wonder if he was going to topple over without warning. When he finished, she asked him about Amadan's artifact and he did his best to describe it. She heard him out and shook her head.

"I do not know what that is, but it has strengthened your connection to the Halls beyond your capacity to tolerate it. I fear I may be unable to help you. None of my attempts to cleanse the well has succeeded. We will keep trying. If you stay away from this object, time may heal you."

"And if it doesn't?"

"Your supposition is correct. What harms you may harm the clan, though I cannot know if the damage will extend beyond the well. If it does... I cannot allow the entire clan to be sickened."

Ruarshi's stomach tightened, though it was no more than he'd expected. "It may be less distressing, as I suggested earlier, to sever my tie to the clan."

"Even if I knew how to do this thing, I would not. That tie is keeping you alive."

Ruarshi drew up his right knee, rested his elbow on it, and propped his aching forehead against the heel of his hand. Why that hadn't occurred to him, he didn't know. It hardly seemed fair that he hadn't been pessimistic *enough*.

"I see." So now his next move was—what? Hope for a miraculous recovery? Keep going until he collapsed? Lie to everyone in the meantime? As though that strategy had any chance of success, with Slan and Etienne watching him like hawks and neither one of them a fool. "If my condition improves, I'm sure you'll know. If it doesn't, I'll return here from time to time and you can tell me about the well. I'm in the middle of something and I don't feel I can abandon it. Not yet."

"I will consult again with the other Skeltari. Perhaps we can find a way to draw you back. You will become a fine shaman for us one day."

"It's something to aspire to. I wasn't much of an emissary."

"Did you defend our prerogatives?"

"I didn't have to. As you very well knew was going to be the case."

"Not with you watching them, certainly."

Ruarshi felt a smile tugging at the corners of his mouth. "You should know that Aurel took over that role when I left Mirror Lake this morning. She seemed interested in learning what the chiefs were talking about, and I thought that would be the best way to get her in the door."

"This is acceptable. You are on your way north?"

"Yes." Another salient consideration finally penetrated the dense fog that inhabited his brain of late. "You knew our plan. Why weren't you surprised to see me here?"

"I expect shamans to work wonders. It is their entire reason for existence."

His first thought was that she was trying to cheer him up by telling jokes, but he quickly realized that she was serious. He snorted. "Maybe you should be talking to Aurel instead of me. She knows a lot more than I do."

"And yet her Skeltari has never met her. Let us hope she will address this."

"I'm sorry for coming in here the way I did. And for getting your floor wet."

"Young one. There is something I think you have failed to understand. It is our task, yours, mine, and Mira's, to protect this clan. All else is foam on the surface of the sea. If you wish to come through my door in a state of drunkenness at midnight, you are welcome. I only request that you do not make too much noise."

Ruarshi's eyes stung. That wasn't what he needed to hear. He rose hastily, set his mug on the table, and bowed.

"Thank you for your time. I need to get back before the others decide I've gotten lost."

"You should allow your healer to help you, in whatever way he can," Satu said.

He shook his head. There was one approach that he thought might be of some benefit to him, but unfortunately Etienne wouldn't be able to attempt it. "I'd rather not have him poking around to no purpose. It would only upset him." How Satu had known he hadn't asked for assistance was an interesting issue that he'd have to pursue at a later date.

"Stubbornness is both a virtue and a vice. It may be that someday you'll learn when it's better to yield."

That sounded more like the Skeltari he knew, and restored some of his steadiness. "Unlikely, but it's a good thought. I'll swing by for another visit when I can."

"Nerthu watch over you, young one."

Ruarshi left the warmth of Satu's small home behind and headed back in the direction from which he'd come. When he'd gone an adequate distance he stepped into the Halls and paused for a moment, waiting. His sense of the djinn told him it was still there, but possibly… farther away? Asleep? Uninterested? It hardly mattered, and he took advantage of its inattention to see if he might be able to use the news Aurel had brought him in another way. He wasn't eager to try what he was now considering, but if his health continued to deteriorate he might have to resort to it as part of a last-ditch effort to save himself. He was grateful that Satu's comment had reminded him of it.

He sat down on the floor, unwilling to risk a fall, and pictured the location of his camp as though it were a small, glowing point on a map. He then backed out and away from it until he was far enough up in the air, figuratively speaking, that Mirror Lake and Miriyan's coastline were visible to the west. He had no idea whether or not this was how Aurel had found him, because he hadn't inquired, but it was the same technique he'd utilized in Mainz to try to locate Karoli so at least it had the advantage of familiarity. He allowed his focus to go fuzzy around the edges. If he gave the process sufficient time, Aurel's presence might spring to life on his map with a glow of its own, and that might in turn enable him to figure out how he could reach her. Not that he intended to seek her out anytime soon. He had a different target in mind.

After a while he became aware that he was leaning against the hall's outer wall, and that the stone was warm against his back. That was new, and soothing, and if he didn't want to fall asleep and become un-moored in time, this effort was going to have to yield some results in the next few minutes or he'd be forced to break it off.

Ruarshi continued to float in the mental space he'd created, while keeping half an eye out for any threatening changes in the atmosphere. He pulled back further until he was looking at a rough outline of the entire country. He was no cartographer and was sure the borders he'd drawn would elicit only scorn from a professional mapmaker, but something about the shift had prodded an inner sense into wakeful-ness. And there she was. Or if it wasn't Aurel, it was another Miriyanti in the vicinity of Mirror Lake whom he could perceive from his posi-tion within the Halls. He kept looking, and two more small sparks of light burst into visibility to his north, with yet another to his east. He studied that one, wondering if it meant that Lorion or Tuomi had opened a doorway. No answers were forthcoming and he decided he'd have to try this again later, when he had more time and energy to de-vote to it.

He climbed back to his feet and reached inside his tunic, where the tokens he'd borrowed rested against his shirt. He enfolded them in his hand and thought about the people to whom they belonged, and dis-covered he had no trouble at all in finding them. After sending an ironic thanks to the djinn, he opened a final doorway and returned to camp.

Someone was shouting.

No, that wasn't correct. Several people were shouting, or had been.

Ruarshi shoved himself upright in the tent he shared with the other men and tried to figure out what was happening. It was the second morning since he'd returned from his chat with Satu, and the day be-fore had been a good one involving no fever, minimal rain, and consid-erable progress on their journey. The night just past, assuming it was now morning, hadn't gone quite so well. His bad dreams were back, and he was still attempting to emerge fully from the latest one when he saw two pairs of eyes staring up at him in the dimness. Mads was still asleep, but if his tossing and turning continued he probably wouldn't be for much longer.

"What's wrong?" Ruarshi asked.

"Nightmare," Etienne whispered. "Very strange nightmare."

Ruarshi glanced at Kennet. "You too?"

"Yes."

Suddenly the fear that still clung to him, the last persistent remnant of his own dreams, seemed inadequate to the situation. Mads jerked awake and gasped, half rising.

"Could you describe it, please?" Ruarshi said.

"There's not much to describe," Etienne said. "I can't even tell you why it scared me. A half naked man in a chair? Looking at me? Was it a man? The lighting was bad…"

"Not a man," Mads said. "Built wrong. Too many joints. You're saying we all had the same nightmare?"

Ruarshi stood and stumbled from the tent. He came to a disheveled halt in front of the other one, where the women slept. "Slan?" he said, his voice pitched to carry. "Are you and the others all right?"

Solvi joined him outside, and there was some murmuring from within as Mona followed her.

"What is it?" Slan asked. She emerged next, her eyes raking their campsite before returning to his face. "Has something happened?"

"Did any of you have an odd dream?"

Mona and Solvi both replied that they had, but Slan just looked puzzled. Elin poked her head through the tent flap. "No dreams for me, odd or otherwise. Would you please tell us what's going on?"

"Shit," Ruarshi murmured. He went to sit next to the remains of their campfire, staring out at nothing. His nightmare had spilled over onto every one of the Doshae. What did that mean?

At a minimum, it meant he had to separate himself from them as fast as he could. Otherwise they might all be at risk of waking up with red eyes.

Everyone was fully alert now and had come outside. Etienne sat down next to him and scrubbed a hand over his face. The twilight was only just beginning to brighten in the east.

"I need to leave. Alone, before this gets any worse," he said. The healer looked mutinous, but Ruarshi had no patience for it. "Don't even think about arguing with me. What good will it do if I spread this to all of you?"

"Slan and I weren't affected," Elin said. "I take it that everyone else was?" When no one contradicted her, she went on. "I'm coming with you."

"As am I. Where are we going?" Slan asked.

"I'm willing to take the risk," Etienne said.

"I know. But *I* am not." Ruarshi tried to consider the situation rationally. "Slan, Elin, you may be right. I'm not your shaman. It's possible that you're not in any danger."

"I promise to let you know if I start sharing your dreams," Slan said. "What did the nightmare involve?"

"It was some kind of monster," Mona said, "and a sense of dread all out of proportion to what was actually going on. Which was nothing."

Mads looked over at Ruarshi. "Do you know what this was? Have you seen it or something like it in the Halls?"

"No and no."

"But you've had dreams like this before?" Elin asked.

"Yes. They started right after Amadan had us take a look at that bowl."

"You could have said something about it," Etienne said.

"The meanderings of my subconscious aren't usually worth mentioning. I very much regret that I didn't anticipate this."

"I'm not sure how you could have," the healer said. "We're all tapping in the dark here, and Satu was no help."

Ruarshi had summarized his conversation with the Skeltari for the rest of them the day before, though he'd edited out some of what he'd learned. He didn't want any of them getting angry with her for doing what was necessary, if it came to that.

"Why don't you just go into the Halls," Kennet said tentatively, "and, you know... fix it? Isn't that within your power to do?"

"It may be," Ruarshi said, "but I guarantee you don't want me to try. I wouldn't attempt to alter so much as a dinner menu unless certain calamity would result otherwise. There are unintended consequences to consider. What's best for me may be disastrous for someone else."

The warrior frowned but seemed willing to accept that answer. Mads started rummaging in their sack of supplies. "So, we split into two parties," he said, "and we'll continue on our way to the Annorae while you go where?" He pulled out some bread, cheese, and apples and went to work preparing a cold breakfast.

Ruarshi was reluctant to talk about his intended destination, which was just silly. Of the two preoccupations that dominated much of his thinking these days, this was by far the less absurd.

"I'll head north via the Halls. Slan, Elin, you're welcome to come, though if you don't want to travel that way I'll understand. Aurel told me it would be safe for you but not pleasant. I think Seggita is alive."

This assertion was met with the incredulity it deserved. He shrugged. "I know how that sounds. But if Casimir, using a Seer's resources, can bring down a tower from three decades and over a thousand miles away, shouldn't a Nerthi be able to survive a few arrows? I doubt he was even injured."

"That's an interesting idea," Slan said. "I wouldn't mind meeting him."

"Wasn't there a funeral?" Solvi asked. "A large, elaborate, well attended one?"

"There was. I'm assuming that if he could successfully fake his own death, he could also refrain from sneezing for an hour or two while lying on a bier. He would have needed a lot of help to carry it off."

"Wouldn't Casimir, at least, have known?" Elin asked.

"I've wondered the same thing," Ruarshi said. "Seggita is still among the living or he's not, but either way there's a Nerthi somewhere in the far north that I should be able to reach. He or she isn't far from your clan. We can get Alcina's book to them in a matter of days, if you don't mind returning home before your sister gets there."

"That... well. I can do that."

Ruarshi could almost see Elin steeling herself for a potentially unhappy reunion. "I promised to help you with your clan Elders, if it turns out they're in an unforgiving mood," he said. "I meant it."

She aimed a fleeting smile at him and returned to her tent to finish dressing for the day. The others did the same and then they all settled in to eat. By the time the sun appeared over the thin line of trees on the horizon, the tents had been packed away and most of the horses were saddled and ready to go.

"I trust I'll see all of you again at the Annorae clan home," Ruarshi said, throwing his saddle bags over his shoulder. "Travel safely. Take good care of my horse." He clasped hands with each of the warriors in turn, and enfolded Etienne in a hug. The healer had hardly spoken during breakfast.

"You've still got the pin," Etienne said into his shoulder. "Feel free to visit anytime."

Ruarshi released him and stepped back. "Stay out of trouble. Yes, that's an order. Student."

He left the camp shortly thereafter with Slan and Elin, opened a doorway, and led them through. As he crossed the threshold, he was already checking to see if the djinn was anywhere in evidence. It was not, so he started in at once on recreating the mental map he'd first envisioned two days previously. The task went more quickly this time, and as he worked, a stray thought occurred to him.

"What color do the walls look to you?" he asked.

"They're gray," Slan replied. "This place is a ruin."

That was not what he'd expected to hear. To his eyes, the walls were the same rose color they'd been the last time he was there.

Ruarshi faced the outer wall and began concentrating in earnest, and he'd soon located the glowing point in Miriyan's far northern reaches that he sought. He spun down toward it. A slight shift in his awareness told him when it was time to open another doorway. He did so and they left the Halls behind, emerging onto a low rise in the middle of a heavily treed landscape. A clan home of moderate size lay in a shallow depression to their west about a quarter mile distant, the roofs of a few of its larger structures rising above the surrounding forest, and a large lake dominated the view in the opposite direction. The air was cooler here, but not uncomfortable.

Ruarshi allowed the doorway to dissolve and turned his attention to his companions. Elin seemed unaffected by the transition but Slan had gone to her knees in the grass. He crouched down beside her.

It was nausea, nothing more, and he breathed a small sigh of relief. "Shall I?" he asked.

Slan nodded and he descended into a light trance, just deep enough to steady and strengthen her a bit before returning to full wakefulness. Then he sat down next to her to wait. The local Nerthi, whoever it turned out to be, would have been aware of his doorway just as he'd sensed Aurel's. Someone would be along presently.

When a lone figure came into view among the trees below them, Ruarshi rose to his feet and the three of them made their way down the hill, angling their route to intercept the newcomer. The dapple of light and shadow made it difficult to discern facial features, but as the distance between them lessened he could see that their visitor was a man, and a familiar one.

Ruarshi stopped and bowed, as did Slan and Elin. The man had recognized him and was smiling broadly as he returned the gesture.

"Seggita," Ruarshi said, after a short interval of silence. "It's good to see you again."

# The Raid

"You want to steal a magical artifact from the Seers?" Kennet asked, as though he had suddenly gone hard of hearing and needed to repeat everything Etienne said.

"I don't *want* to steal the artifact. I'm *going* to steal the artifact. The only question is whether or not I'll have any help."

All the warriors were looking at him dubiously and he didn't have time for it. "Fine," he said, and wheeled his horse around.

"Hold on, hold on," Kennet said, riding up beside him. "We're coming with you, but I for one would like to know why you want this thing."

"I would also find this information helpful," Solvi said, swinging her horse around on Etienne's other side.

"Ruarshi was exposed to it and it made him sick. We might need it to cure him, if he's curable, and it would be nice if we had it to hand. The round trip to fetch it from the Annorae clan would take over a month."

Kennet digested that. "Are we sure it won't make us sick, too?"

"No. But it hasn't made any of the Seers sick, so there's probably nothing to worry about."

"That's reassuring," Kennet muttered. "I feel very confident and safe now."

"Where is this item located?" Mads asked.

"Under the shrine."

"Under it?"

"There's a hidden chamber. It's likely to be shielded, but unfortunately I don't know exactly where we'll run into trouble. I wasn't paying attention."

"So we're going to be caught," Mona said. "Won't this make it difficult to get the artifact out of there?"

"I'm open to ideas. I'm guessing the clan chiefs won't have left yet,
meaning the place will still be crowded with unfamiliar faces and people going in unpredictable directions. If we can draw a lot of them out
onto the walkway by banging on pots or something, maybe we can
confuse the issue and slow down any response."

"That's quite a plan," Mads observed neutrally.

"As I said, I'm open to ideas. If we move fast, a distraction might
not even be necessary."

"Or the Seers might know this is coming and have their Naishanti
lying in wait for us," Solvi said.

"Could be," Etienne conceded.

"What's the punishment for stealing artifacts?" Mona asked.

"I don't know."

"If this doesn't work, are you prepared to be caught up in a legal
wrangle that could keep you here for months?" Solvi asked.

Etienne hated that question intensely. "I want to be of use in this
situation. This may be useful, and I have nothing better to do. Look, if
the three of you want to ride up to the front door, whooping and carrying on to draw everyone in that direction, I'll go in alone. No need
for you to risk capture with me. But I'll want a small axe to get through
a couple of locks."

"I think we can do better than that," Mads said. "We could bar the
doors from the main building, or stir up the horses…"

They spent the next few hours discussing tactics, alternating their
pace between a walk and a canter as they made their way back toward
Mirror Lake. They needed to get there by sundown the next day, which
wouldn't be difficult, but Etienne felt a little anxious about what would
happen then. They'd have to wait for twilight to descend before approaching the fortress, so that they'd have some hope of arriving unde-
tected, and that meant it would be past midnight when they finally
reached the place. This was later than he would have preferred. But, he
reasoned, with the convocation in session it was probable that at least a
few of the inhabitants would still be awake and active at that time. This
was important, as Etienne didn't like their chances were they to attempt
the burglary after everyone else had gone to bed. If they were the only
ones moving, they'd be too easy for the Naishanti defenders to focus
on.

When they stopped for the evening Etienne found himself wandering aimlessly in and out of their campsite, unable to settle and feeling absurdly bereft. He knew he really ought to take it as a good sign that he hadn't been able to accompany Ruarshi northward, since this confirmed that something fundamental had shifted and he was definitely a Doshae now, but the thought failed to console him. The man needed a healer, and though Etienne supposed whatever Nerthi they'd turned up could fill that role for a week or two, the task was properly his and he wouldn't be happy until it was back in his hands. By which time, if they were all very lucky, Ruarshi wouldn't require the help because he'd have worked out the problem on his own.

Etienne didn't think he should count on that.

The warriors kept throwing surreptitious glances in his direction, but they left him alone to work the restlessness out of his system in his own way, and he appreciated them all the more for that. He was still amazed they'd agreed to come with him on this harebrained mission of his. Retrieving the object was a fine idea, Etienne had no doubt of that, but he suspected if he examined his motives too closely he'd find they were rooted in something other than common sense. Which was a very good reason to go to bed before his thoughts could make it that far, so that's what he did, and when he woke up the next morning his earlier troubles no longer seemed so pressing.

The weather remained mostly dry as they continued west and they made good time, arriving downslope from Mirror Lake with hours of daylight to spare. In the end, Solvi had decided that stealth and speed would be more conducive to their success than chaos, so their plan had become less convoluted as it evolved. They intended to stay together—with the exception of Mona, who would hide out at the far end of the south gallery with their horses—and Etienne and Kennet would break into the chamber while Solvi and Mads remained outside to fend off any response from the Naishanti. They would then creep back along the gallery wall, hopefully still unnoticed, meet up with Mona and ride away. If things started to go sour, Mads planned to pull down the rickety fence at the edge of the paddock and see if he could persuade the horses to bolt. They weren't interested in being pursued, as that could result in actual fighting and none of them were prepared to take it that far. If the situation threatened to turn truly ugly, they would simply surrender.

Just before sunset another heavy layer of clouds rolled in, a bit of good luck that transformed the deepening twilight into something closer to true night. They stripped the gear from the horses Ruarshi and the others had been riding, stacked it in a neat pile, and set the animals loose among the trees. Keeping the extra mounts with them on the raid would only slow them down, and given the number of people traveling into and out of Mirror Lake lately, it was likely that someone would find them and take them in hand before too long. Assuming they didn't just wander back up to the fortress on their own. Etienne didn't like breaking their promise to look after Ruarshi's horse, but he knew they didn't have much choice. He gave each of the animals a last nibble of turnip and then returned his attention to the task at hand.

Once Solvi was satisfied that conditions were as murky as they were likely to become, they mounted up again and headed for the grim stone edifice that the Seers called home. They approached it from the south, where a slight rise in the terrain between the tree line and the cliffs offered them a bit of cover. Etienne felt a flutter of concern from Jonata and realized he might be more apprehensive about what they were doing than he'd yet admitted to himself. He sent soothing thoughts back in her direction but wasn't sure they were all that persuasive, mostly because it was impossible to lie when communicating through a bond. A surge of skepticism from her end startled him and he twitched in his saddle. He smiled and she faded gradually from his awareness.

As they drew closer to their destination, they could hear low voices and occasional quiet laughter through a few open windows in the south gallery. Fortunately no one looked out and spotted them, and a few minutes later they made it to the far end of the shrine. Etienne dismounted along with the others and reached up behind Midnight's saddle to retrieve the sturdy leather bag in which he planned to carry the artifact. He'd tucked a ragged scrap of woolen blanket inside it earlier in the day. Given what Amadan had said about the thing, Etienne wanted at least two layers of material between him and it at all times. Nicking himself on its edge and bleeding to death as they made their escape wasn't among his goals for the evening.

Solvi led them east along the inner wall of the gallery, walking normally. The moon hadn't risen yet, and once they squeezed past the fence into the paddock their indistinct dark shapes blended in with those of the horses loitering at that end of the enclosure. A handful of people stood on the walkway near the main building, conversing softly, but no one else appeared to be out and about. Etienne checked the deeper shadows for lurking Naishanti, but the same conditions that were helping to conceal their party made it impossible for him to tell if anyone waited for them there. He gave a mental shrug and continued onward.

They came to a stop at the bottom end of the stairway leading up to the shrine, where the walkway ran at shoulder height to the ground. Mads gave Kennet and Etienne a boost up onto the stone and the two of them ran lightly up the stairs. Once they'd made it to the top, Etienne hurried into the antechamber and the warrior followed him inside, where the man dug a fire steel, a small tinderbox, and a candle out of a bag attached to his belt. Etienne closed the outer door behind them when Kennet had gotten the candle lit, inclining his head toward the next obstacle in their path.

"Breaking through that lock might or might not bring down the shielding," he whispered. "Like I said, I wasn't paying close attention and Amadan would have waved it aside like a cobweb. I think it's further in, somewhere along the stairwell."

Kennet nodded in response and stepped up to the door, handing the candle off to Etienne. He studied the lock for a moment and then closed his eyes, and shortly thereafter a series of dull popping noises began to issue from the wood. After an impressively brief interval of this, Kennet reached forward and pushed on the door. It swung inward, leaving the metal mechanism dangling from the frame. The warrior moved forward carefully and Etienne followed, both of them pausing again at the head of the staircase.

"There it is," Kennet said, "three steps down. It's all about speed now. Are you ready?"

Etienne handed back the candle and grabbed the leather bag off his shoulder. "The cabinet they keep it in is flimsy. Just break it open when we get down there and I'll do the rest."

They smiled nervously at one another and Kennet plunged down the stairs with Etienne close behind. When they reached the floor of the chamber, Etienne pointed toward the piece of furniture in question and was rewarded a second later with a sharp crack. Both cabinet doors sagged open a few inches and he elbowed them back the rest of the way, pulling the blanket free of the bag. He grabbed the artifact with one swaddled hand, happy to discover that it was lighter than he had expected, dumped out the odd silver detritus that had accumulated in it, and wrapped it up. He tied the bundle together using a narrow strip of leather and eased it into the bag. Then they darted back up the stairway and out into the night.

The first thing Etienne noticed was that the paddock fence was down, and the second was that there were a good number of human figures moving about in the darkness where before there had been none.

He considered jumping to the ground from where he stood, decided a broken leg or two wouldn't be helpful, and instead ran down the stairs to the walkway. Kennet shadowed him, and both Solvi and Mads were still waiting for them in the paddock. Solvi took a breath to say something, but before she could utter a word the door to the room behind them swung open, bathing Etienne in a wash of lamplight, and a voice bellowed, "It's the black-haired healer! By the shrine!"

Etienne found that extremely worrisome for all sorts of reasons. He shoved the bag into Kennet's arms and hissed, "Get that away from here while I draw them off. I'll meet back up with you in a few minutes. *Go.*"

He ran east along the walkway, hoping that whoever had been yelling was following his movements rather than tracking the others, and took a chance with the drop to the ground about halfway to the next staircase. He landed without hurting himself and began to weave his way among the horses, some of whom looked as spooked as he felt. When he reached the first of the wooden outbuildings he dropped into a crouch beside it and tried to figure out what was happening.

More shouting. They were definitely looking for him in particular, and he could only surmise that 'they' were the local Naishanti. He glanced back toward the shrine and was relieved to see that his companions were no longer there. It was time for him to vacate the place, as well, and possibly to chase off some of the horses in the process.

Etienne stood, dodged around a couple of the agitated animals, and started to sprint. Someone on his right moved to intercept him. He jinked to the left and continued running. He had less luck avoiding his second pursuer, who lunged out from behind a building and tackled him. Etienne lashed out with elbows and boots on his way down, and had just managed to break free when another warrior appeared in his peripheral vision and a fist slammed into his torso.

He went to his knees, unable to breathe, and was seized from behind and pulled to his feet.

"Stop it, Illyana. The Seers just want to talk to you."

Etienne swung an elbow at the source of the voice as hard as he could, and was rewarded with a grunt and a slackening of the grip on his other arm. He darted away but was brought up short when yet another figure materialized out of the darkness and landed a blow to his jaw. He fell. The warrior who dragged him upright this time did something with his hands that Etienne couldn't quite follow, wrenching his shoulder out of its socket. He screamed in pain and fury and his vision went dim. There was more shouting in the middle distance, Solvi's voice this time, and Etienne's heart sank.

"—is a member of my clan and you *will* tell me what this is about."

An indistinct murmur answered her and Etienne raised his head. There was a clear path between him and the downed fence, and if he was going to get out of this mess he needed to do it soon. His condition wasn't optimal but that didn't mean the situation was hopeless. The man holding him started to drag him toward the main building, and Etienne stumbled and went down. His captor jerked him upright by his bad arm and he fell again, though this time it wasn't intentional. He ended up on his back in a damp patch of grass. When the man went to raise him once more, Etienne held up a hand.

"Wait. Please. I just need a minute."

The warrior relented and Etienne took a few deep breaths, looking around in a renewed attempt to get his bearings. His eyes landed on a familiar large figure standing in the south gallery. Almost every door along that wing of the fortress was open now, spilling light out into the night.

"Valentin!" Etienne yelled. Nothing wrong with his lungs, he was pleased to note. "Tell Ciarn! I—"

The toe of a boot collided with his temple and the world went hazy.

When Etienne was next able to take stock of his surroundings, he was mildly interested to observe that he was lying in perfect darkness with what seemed like half his body throbbing in pain. He was positioned on his side, on a stone surface, his hands tied behind his back. An attempt to shift his weight off his right shoulder made it clear that his ankles had also been lashed together, which seemed excessive given his current capabilities. He rolled onto his back, suppressing a groan, and tried to think.

Why the hell did the Seers care about him one way or another? What did they want to talk about? Something he hadn't even done yet? That was sure to be a great conversation, assuming it ever happened. Ciarn would intervene soon if he hadn't already, and put a stop to this whole thing before it could go much further. Solvi was also likely to be around somewhere, dammit, and would be doing her part, but where were the others? Etienne fervently hoped they were miles away by now, with the artifact still in their possession.

Since Mirror Lake didn't have a dungeon, as far as he knew, he had to be in some part of the fortress that was more or less populated. Perhaps shouting would help. But what to shout? Rather than calling for aid, which he thought would get rather tedious after about the tenth iteration, he started singing at the top of his lungs. This he could do for hours, or at least until his throat became too sore to continue. He'd moved on to his third tune, a child's song about goblins that he'd always favored, when the door opened and a Seer came in.

Still singing, Etienne squinted up at her in the light of her lamp. She was both ancient and wizened, and he was clearly not meant to perceive her as any kind of threat. She was carrying a jug and a cup and appeared sympathetic, even mournful as she stood there staring at him, but she was quick to kick the door shut behind her, cutting him off once more from the outside world.

He relented and went silent. The truth was that he didn't feel very good.

"Etienne, isn't it?" she asked. "I apologize for your treatment. Some of the Seers need to talk to you, but we didn't intend for you to be injured. Do you require a healer?"

What kind of question was that? One of his eyes was practically swollen shut. "Yes."

She nodded, still mournful. "I'll send for her. In the meanwhile, I'd like to release you from your bonds and offer you some wine. I'll have food brought up as well."

Etienne rolled wordlessly back onto his side and she did as she'd promised, which had the unfortunate effect of actually increasing the amount of pain he was in. Moving his right arm was a bad idea just at present. He considered trying to force the bone back into its socket—he'd done the same for a number of patients over the years, after all—but concluded that he'd have to leave the effort for another time. Once he was sitting up with his back against the wall, the Seer offered him the wine.

He took the cup from her, sniffed it, and almost gagged. Somebody had mixed opium in there, sure enough. Was it meant to make him easier to interrogate? More inclined to talk? Would that even work? He was much less familiar with the drug than Ruarshi was, but he thought he might take the Seers up on their offer. It would certainly help with the pain, there was nothing much he could tell them in any case, and they couldn't really mean to poison him. That would be even less for-givable than what they'd already done. Inflicting this kind of brutality on someone in response to theft wasn't normal, and he couldn't imag-ine any of this was going to go over well with the clan chiefs still in res-idence at Mirror Lake.

Etienne took a sip. "Thank you."

The Seer smiled at him, a dimple appearing in the dried apple ter-rain of her face. "You're welcome. I will go for the healer and the food now."

"Or you could just let me out of here."

"The Naishanti would bring you back, child. You'll be free to go once you've spoken with the Elders."

"Are you an Elder?"

She paused in the doorway. "Yes."

"Can't I just talk to you?"

"I'm not the one who had the vision. It would serve no purpose. You just wait here, and we will have this resolved before the day is out."

She left him then, thoughtfully setting her lamp on the floor by the door before disappearing. Etienne heard her turn a key in the lock.

He stayed where he was and drank his wine. It didn't take long for the spiky edges of his pain to begin flattening out, and though he struggled for a while with the urge to vomit, he was feeling quite a bit better by the time an hour or so had passed. He wasn't disappointed to note that neither the healer nor the food was yet in evidence. That cute little old woman wasn't on his side in this, in spite of all the friendly noises she'd made, and he hadn't expected any better from her.

Etienne realized that Jonata was once again present at the back of his mind, and had in fact been there for some time. His eyes slid shut and he turned all his attention toward her, sending his love along on a warm gentle wave of drug-induced euphoria and then ruthlessly squeezing their bond down to almost nothing. This whole interlude had been unpleasant, it might yet get worse before it improved, and there was no reason for her to be subjected to it. He dozed.

When he awakened, a man and a woman were in the room with him. They were standing on the wall, arguing.

Etienne blinked. No, that was wrong. He had tilted over while he slept—onto his left side, fortunately—and they were located on the floor where they belonged. He'd been right about their disagreement, though.

"... whose authority he was given this."

"What's done is done and we haven't got much time. We need to—" The woman drifted closer. Etienne examined the embroidery on her slippers, gold and silver lines wending their way through a dark blue background. "He's awake."

"Then I suggest you ask him your questions now, while you have the chance. Maybe you can salvage something. But I doubt it."

A face appeared in Etienne's line of vision and something struck his cheek. He thought it possible that the blow had been intended to sting.

"Do you understand me?"

He didn't reply and the woman hit him again.

"Do. You. Understand. Me."

Etienne didn't respond to that, either, though this time it was more about the principle of the thing than his lingering befuddlement. The Seer would mend her ways or this would be an entirely one-sided conversation. And what sense did it make for them to give him opium and then try slapping him around? He was beginning to think that the Seers, taken as a group, didn't know what they were doing.

Something passed between his two visitors that resulted in the woman moving away from him and the man lowering himself to sit on the stone by Etienne's side. The Seer laid a hand on his shoulder. Despite the opium, Etienne flinched.

The man was leaning in closer to him now, and he might have been swearing. Etienne heard the name of the in-house healer, and the next time he opened his eyes, the woman had gone.

"Can you hear me? I am sorry, so very sorry. Can you follow what I'm saying?"

"Yes," Etienne murmured. It sounded to his ears more like 'yeth,' but apparently it had been intelligible.

"Good. I will tell you what's happening, because I'm sure you're curious. Stop me if I start talking too fast. One of our Seers had a vision that suggested you would be involved in some kind of cataclysmic event that would do irreparable harm to Miriyan. Please don't ask me for details; I have none. As is always the case with such visions, it wasn't clear whether you were doing this on purpose or unknowingly. I choose to believe that you're not ill-intentioned and a simple warning will suffice to avert this disaster. Are you still listening to me?"

"Yes."

"You and your friends need to return the object you stole from Mirror Lake tonight. We don't know what it's for. If you do, please enlighten us before you go. But what truly matters is that you *leave it alone.*

If you will agree to do that, the Seers will stop panicking. This potential future event also involves the Nerthii in some way, but of course we cannot tell which one. Or ones. Only you were recognizable. Hence the... zeal with which you were apprehended."

Etienne suspected that all of this would have been difficult to follow even if he'd been sober. It seemed that the rest of his party had gotten away, with the likely exception of Solvi, which was good. It also looked like he was going to wreck his country soon, which was presumably bad, but he couldn't help wondering why this Etienne-of-the-future would think that was a fine idea to begin with. He couldn't imagine he would do something like that by accident, even on his worst day. For one thing, it would probably take a lot of effort.

"Is Ciarn here?" he asked.

The Seer chuckled, but not as though he found the question funny. "He is very much here, and has been insisting all night that he be allowed to see you. As is his right. I will retrieve him as soon as I am persuaded that you will be safe if I leave. Right now there are some among the Seers who are too terrified to be sensible."

"You're not terrified?"

"No."

"Why not?"

The man shrugged. "Getting worked up about dire visions is a waste of energy. Usually they don't come to pass, without our having to lift a finger to prevent them."

Etienne thought he could actually come to like this particular Seer, given time and assuming that this show of friendliness wasn't a ruse meant to persuade him to let his guard down.

Some time later it became clear to him that he'd drifted off again. The healer was in the room now and was frowning at his shoulder, while the man he'd been speaking with earlier watched her from a position near the door. Etienne wanted to tell her to get it over with, but his mouth was so dry that he couldn't. He pushed himself laboriously upright instead and nodded down toward his arm.

"You're prepared for this?" she asked him.

He nodded again. She gripped him and forced the joint back into its proper configuration while Etienne concentrated on his breathing and his unsteady stomach. It didn't take long for the opium in his system to overcome the brief surge of pain, and soon he felt even more relaxed and distant than he had before.

"Drink this," she said, and handed him a cup of water. When he was done with it, she went on. "I'm going to heal the rest of it now. Is that okay?"

He slept while she worked, and when he woke he was in a narrow bed and dim reflected sunlight was spilling through a partially opened shutter. Solvi sat on a chair next to the headboard, her arms crossed and her chin resting on her chest.

Etienne tried to say something but only succeeded in croaking at her. She leapt to her feet and bent down over him, while he gestured somewhat desperately toward the table a few feet away. There was a jug sitting on it and if it didn't contain water he thought he could probably still drink whatever was in it, provided it was in liquid form and generally considered to be fit for human consumption.

She poured some of it—yes, it was water, thank the stars—into a large mug and helped him sit up so he could drink it. He downed about half of it in a single swallow and his stomach rebelled instantly. He lunged forward to lean over the edge of the bed, where he hung coughing and choking until he felt as weak as a kitten. When the spasms finally subsided he wanted to crawl into a dark, quiet hole and never come out of it.

"Let's try this again, but more slowly." Solvi peeled him up off the edge of the mattress and returned him to his prior position, and then sat down on the bed next to him. She lifted the mug and he essayed a tentative sip. A little while later he tried another, and they continued like that until his mouth, at least, felt better. His head was a different story, and he feared it would be days before he could think clearly. He needed to ask her about what had happened the night before but decided to hold his tongue. He didn't trust his judgment at the moment. What if someone was listening in at their door, and he was misjudging the likelihood of that kind of thing because he was still addled by opium? After casting about hazily for a few seconds, he decided on a safer question.

"Are they going to let us go?"

"Yes. We'll be leaving sometime today with Ciarn. Once he's finished berating them about your condition."

"I'm fine. Mostly. Aren't I?"

"The healer says so, but you look terrible and that's not a question people who are doing well usually have to ask."

"No one forced me to drink the opium."

"Would you have felt the need if you hadn't been hurt?"

"Well, no. They could have brought the healer instead."

"That's what I thought. Did they question you?"

Etienne had to struggle a bit to remember. "No. One of the Seers told me I was going to do something awful, and asked me not to. It was a strange conversation."

"'Something awful'?"

"Yes. He said he couldn't be more specific."

"But he was confident you'd know it when you saw it?"

"I suppose. Otherwise I'm not sure I'd be sitting here."

Solvi's expression sharpened. "You were threatened?"

"He sent another Seer away, and told me he'd be staying with me until he was certain I'd be safe."

"Did you get his name?"

"I don't think he ever told me what it was."

"Was he wearing a light blue tunic? High-collared shirt? Taller than average?"

"I think so?"

"I met him. I can find him again if I need to. I should warn you that Ciarn's not too pleased with us, either."

"You told him why we did it?"

"He understood our reasoning, but I don't believe he was persuaded by it. He seems a little ambivalent about our shaman."

"Damn," Etienne muttered. He'd been right not to trust his current ability to think. "We need to head north."

"And we will. But we're going back to our clan home first."

"No! I can't. I've got to—"

"You've got to recover fully, and we need supplies so we can skip the socializing on the trip up and make better time. We'll get there, Etienne."

The healer subsided. He knew she was right, but that didn't make him any happier about the situation. "I should eat something. I feel like my head is going to fall off."

"I'll see to it."

Solvi arranged to have food brought up without ever leaving Etienne's room, by the simple expedient of going to the door and speaking with the Doshae guards who'd been posted there. His meal was suitably bland, but he was unable to get more than about half of it eaten. As he set it aside, he noticed that he was still wearing yesterday's clothes, because of course he was, and that he was a mess of dried mud, sweat, and blood. He fingered the healed but still swollen cut next to his left eye, where he'd been kicked, and asked Solvi if she could have their hosts supply him with a small basin of water and a cloth.

He'd just finished cleaning himself up, a procedure during which Solvi had kindly absented herself for a few minutes, when Ciarn burst through the door. He was trailing at least half a dozen warriors and appeared to be displeased. He looked Etienne up and down.

"You take care of your own, I'll give you that," the chief said. "I'm sure one day you'll become a real asset to our clan, but for the next little while I'm going to make it my business to keep an eye on you. Is there anything you need to tell me?"

Etienne felt a bit overwhelmed. He shook his head.

"All right then. Be ready to leave in half an hour. Meet us out front. You'll be able to sit a horse?"

Etienne drew himself up. There was no mirror in the room so he had no idea how his face looked, but he was sure that question had been intended as a challenge. "For as long as I need to, yes."

"Hmm. Okay. See you then." With a brisk nod, Ciarn exited the room, followed by his small army.

Solvi moved to stand at Etienne's side, smiling a little. "He likes you."

"How can you tell?"

"I've never known him to be overgenerous with his compliments. Keep on the way you've been going and he'll make you an advisor."

"I'll stick to healing. What did he mean by keeping an eye on me? He won't try to stop us from heading north, will he?"

Solvi considered the question. "Probably not. It might smooth our path a little if you can persuade him that you're not always so wild and impulsive."

Etienne thought about defending himself against this accusation—their raid on the fortress had been neither wild nor impulsive, as she well knew—but he decided instead to save his strength for the ride ahead. As it turned out, he was fighting exhaustion within an hour of their departure and in a vicious mood, either as a result of coming off the opium or simply because he'd botched everything and was now obliged to waste valuable time. He took care to let none of it show, an effort that was somewhat undermined when he collapsed after dismounting that evening. His legs just went out from under him.

After sitting there for a few moments he raised an arm and made a grab for his stirrup, but his horse rolled its eyes at him and sidled out of reach. He glared at it and was about to let his arm fall when Ciarn appeared and pulled him to his feet. The chief led him away from the bustle of the campsite and threw some bedding down on a loamy patch of soil. He pointed at it.

"You're excused from duty. We'll bring you some food when it's ready. In the meantime, get some rest."

Etienne remained standing. He'd heard what the man said, and even understood the words, but couldn't connect them to any necessary response on his part. Ciarn didn't move, either, and the healer eventually managed to shake off his stupor, mumble his thanks, and lower himself to the ground. He was half unconscious before he was fully horizontal, and woke up later only long enough to tend to his needs and eat a few bites before plunging back into a deep and dreamless sleep.

# The Light Within Him

Seggita proved to be a considerate host, but there was only so much he could do to overcome the awkwardness of their reunion.

Ruarshi realized belatedly that he wasn't prepared for this, partly because he'd been only half convinced that it would happen and partly because he'd expended a lot of mental energy over the years in avoiding the memories tied to his two brief interactions with the man. It had been a nightmarish span, with the one shining exception of the birth of his son, and circumstances hadn't allowed them to develop anything like a friendship. As a result, although there were a great many things they could have talked about, their lack of familiarity with one another made them both reluctant to bring up their shared past. Thus their conversation meandered uncomfortably between topics like the weather, Slan's and Elin's clan affiliations, and generalities pertaining to Seggita's family and the Sylvae clan as a whole. Ruarshi remained mostly silent and kept his eyes down. As their small group passed through the clan home's periphery, a few people called out greetings. Seggita waved to them in return.

It wasn't until they'd entered the guest house that the older Nerthi asked them why they'd come. Elin answered for them. "I'm taking a book to my clan. It needs deciphering." She set her bag down on the table in front of the cold fireplace and pulled out the folio. "It was written by the Delver Alcina and parts of it, we were told, relate to shamans and the Halls."

"Your method of travel suggests you already know quite a bit about those subjects," Seggita observed, propping the building's main door open to let in some sunlight and fresh air.

"You might be surprised," Ruarshi said. "I ran into Aurel at Mirror

Lake, and she told me how to use the Halls to get from one place to another. Beyond that, I know basically nothing."

"I haven't opened a doorway in decades. You were at Mirror Lake?"

Ruarshi braced himself. He couldn't very well fail to mention what he'd done. Seggita had saved his life all those years ago and honesty was the least he was owed. "You should know. Casimir came to visit me at my clan home. I killed him."

Seggita had been moving restlessly around the room, but at that he went still. "Why?"

"He tried to kill me and my son, and a good number of other people, outside Mainz. I was concerned that he would try it again. It's a long story."

"I would like to hear it."

So Ruarshi told him what had happened, beginning with the letter from the mysterious Seer and continuing up to the present moment. Some of what he said was news to both Slan and Elin, and there were a few details he chose to leave out for the sake of future harmony. A description of his first encounter with Karoli, for instance, would add nothing important to the tale.

When he was done, Seggita looked over at him thoughtfully. "I wasn't aware of any of that," he said. "This was by design; I spent most of the years since you saw me last in Sweden. If you were worried about my reaction to this news, please don't be. There's no need.

"Tell me something," he went on. "Aurel was livid with me when she learned that I had survived, and I could hardly fault her for it. She thought I should have remained in Tomir, that I could have helped the rest of you ride out the rebellion. She wasn't exactly wrong. What's your feeling on the matter?"

"You *did* help me survive it," Ruarshi answered slowly, "so it may be that I'm not the best person to ask. Elyon had hundreds of supporters. I'm not sure how you could have changed the outcome."

Seggita grimaced. "Had I known what fate awaited so many of the Nerthii, I would have stayed. My reasoning at the time was based on what the Halls were showing me. Or rather, on what I was focusing my attention on, but it amounts to the same thing. The steps I'd have had to take to save my own skin in that situation would have made life in Miriyan impossible for the rest of you for a very long time afterward. It seemed wiser for me to bow out than to frighten everyone. None of which would be any consolation to the dead, I'm sure." His scowl deepened. "I'm sorry. I didn't mean to turn this into an exercise in self-exoneration. I just wanted your opinion."

"I'm not in the habit of judging people for decisions they make while under stress," Ruarshi said. "Unless I don't like them, of course. Did any of those arrows actually hit you? I wasn't going to ask, but now that I'm here my curiosity is getting the better of me."

"One of them, yes. In the leg. I was wearing an armor chestplate and thought I'd be safe, but the archers' aim turned out to be worse than I anticipated. I was so busy deflecting the arrows coming at my head that the one got away from me."

"I missed your funeral," Ruarshi said. "I heard it was quite an event."

"I heard the same, but personally I thought it was tedious."

"How long have you been back in Miriyan?" Elin asked. She was still looking at Seggita as though he were a ghost, but she'd settled somewhat since their initial meeting.

"A few years. I returned under an assumed name. I suppose I can drop that now with Casimir gone."

"Even so," Ruarshi said, "I'd have expected word of your presence to spread. Are you living in a hermit's hut?"

Seggita responded in a heavy northern dialect that Ruarshi found impenetrable. Elin translated for them. "He said that the sophisticated south long ago decided it didn't need to pay any attention to the barbarians in the north."

"Regional prejudices aside, if you could tell Ruarshi whatever you know about the Halls, we'd be appreciative," Slan said.

"The most important thing for you to know about them is that they have nothing at all to do with your real task as a shaman."

"They don't?" Ruarshi asked. "Then what is my real task?"

"To be a source of strength to your land and people. I mean that literally," Seggita said. "You've figured out how to transfer power to someone who's ailing? Beyond the healing itself, I mean."

"Yes."

"Do that for your kinsmen when they get a little frayed around the edges. It doesn't matter if they're actually ill or not. You'll learn to recognize this sort of thing when you run across it. Intervening with a handful of people can sometimes lift a weight from an entire hall. Do the same for your orchards and fields when they start to droop, even if the Sotarii have already been by. You can't solve all your clan's problems, but you can ensure everyone feels protected and that alone makes a big difference."

"Given what you told us earlier," Ruarshi said, "I understand why you might dislike the Halls."

"They're mostly useless. Trying to control the future is a dicey and exhausting business. You said you've seen Aurel?"

"Yes."

"Did she look well to you?"

"Not really."

"She's still trying to recover from her initial burst of enthusiasm," Seggita said. "It may be something we all do: we discover we have the power to change the future for the better, so we feel that it's our responsibility to do so. We push past our limits, we become more ambitious over time, we harm ourselves in the process, eventually we make a mistake. I would advise you to avoid the temptation. Once you get started it becomes addictive."

Ruarshi had to make a conscious effort not to look at Elin. "Are there any other Nerthii living here in Miriyan?"

"There are two you haven't met, both returned exiles. Older than me. The next time I talk to them, I'll tell them that you inquired. They may contact you and they may not. May I ask what's happened to your eyes? I can't help thinking they shouldn't look that way, and along with the rest of it..."

"The rest of what?" Slan asked.

Ruarshi knew what he was referring to, but this wasn't a conversation he wanted to have in front of her. "I don't know. There's an artifact at Mirror Lake that a Seer named Amadan showed us—"

"Amadan?" Seggita asked.

His tone brought Ruarshi up short and set the hair at the back of his neck to prickling in alarm. "Yes, Amadan."

"Casimir must have been worried about going to visit you, after all, if not quite worried enough. He always did carry a sting in his tail."

Ruarshi rubbed at the space between his eyebrows, trying to stave off a headache. He wasn't going to like what he was about to hear, but he couldn't stop himself from asking for the details. "So it was revenge."

"No question. I knew Amadan as a relentlessly jealous person, always ready to aid and abet Casimir's worst impulses. He'd have knifed me in my sleep if he thought he could get away with it."

Ruarshi was remonstrating with himself for missing the man's lies, but he'd known for a while that there was a small subset of people whose honesty or lack thereof he couldn't judge no matter how hard he tried. It seemed Amadan was among their number.

"Better to know than otherwise," he muttered.

"Then why did he give us the book?" Elin asked, staring down at it with renewed disfavor. "To gain our trust? Or is it also some kind of trick? If it's a forgery…"

"A forgery it would have taken Casimir months to create? No," Seggita said. "It's probably genuine. The price Amadan was willing to pay to convince you he was on your side."

"Ruarshi's been ill," Slan said. "Can you do anything to help him? His Skeltari couldn't."

Seggita studied him and Ruarshi tried not to fidget under the scrutiny. Eventually the man shook his head, clearly baffled. "You're out of balance in some way, but I can't find a cause for it. There's nothing for me to heal."

Ruarshi glanced at Slan. "I'll ride it out, whatever it is."

She returned his gaze unhappily but nodded, willing to let the matter drop for the time being. Meanwhile Elin had begun describing the artifact to Seggita, on the off chance that he would have better luck identifying it than they'd had, but he proved similarly unable to venture a guess as to its nature. Their conversation stuttered to a halt a few minutes later, and Seggita suggested that they make themselves comfortable while he tracked down the clan steward and had some food and drink brought over.

Slan was the first to break the silence after he had gone. "I am concerned, Ruarshi. Very concerned."

"As am I," Elin said.

"That makes three of us," Ruarshi said. "We will figure it out, and we will deal with it when we do. But please let's not waste time talking about it in the interim. I'd like to take a look around after the steward has been by. I've never been in this part of the country before. Would either of you like to come along?"

It was evening. They had gone for a leisurely stroll in the forest, chatted for a while with a group of curious Sylvae, eaten a light lunch, visited the bath house, and then returned to their temporary accommodations to find Seggita waiting for them. He invited them to dinner at his family's hall, which offer they politely declined, preferring the peace and quiet of the guest house to the bustle of a communal meal. They had already decided to leave for the Annorae clan home the following morning, and the older Nerthi had offered to go with them. Ruarshi thought there was some motivation beyond simple friendliness lurking behind the proposal that Seggita wasn't admitting to, but he had no objection to the man's company and neither did the warriors. They agreed to meet again after breakfast.

He and Slan had a room to themselves, the only real privacy they'd enjoyed for weeks. Judging by her response to his overtures, she'd been anticipating the opportunity as eagerly as he had, and they nearly knocked over the furniture in their hurry to divest one another of their clothing. Slan had fallen into a doze afterward, and Ruarshi lay next to her, studying her face in the light of their single candle.

There were things he wanted to say to her that he couldn't say, because the words he needed didn't exist and the ones available to him were inadequate to the task, ungraceful tools in the hands of a man disinclined to attempt poetry. How to tell her that she had kindled a light within him that had been burning steadily ever since the first moment of their first meeting? That this light had been a constant comfort to him during their long years apart, and that even now it illuminated every step he took? That in the absence of this small but brilliant flame he would be quite lost?

Poet or no, he supposed he could say that much and so he did. Slan's eyelids fluttered open midway through and she smiled up at him. "I don't think I ever told you. The night after we met I dreamed of you."

"In a good way?"

"We were walking together, talking. Outdoors somewhere. There were trees. I noticed right away that you had one of the most expressive faces I'd ever seen."

"I thought I had my serious face on the first time we talked. Stoic. Opaque, even."

"I'm sure that's what you were trying for. After you left I very much wanted another chance to look at you. Did you know that whenever you get emotional, your voice deepens? It gives me the shivers."

"You mean like this?" he asked, deliberately parodying what he thought she was referring to.

She laughed and threw a leg up over his hip, and conversation ceased for another little while. When their breathing had returned to normal, Ruarshi mumbled, "And all this time I thought you just wanted a pliable young man for your bed."

"I would have wanted you no matter what body you'd shown up in. Though I appreciate my good fortune in that regard."

Ruarshi grinned into the dimness. The candle had burned itself out while they'd been occupied but he hadn't taken note of it until now. Thanks to a small gap between two of the logs on the outer wall of the guest house, and the fact that the sun didn't set at all this time of year so far north, they could still see each other with some clarity. "Stop, you'll embarrass me. Shall I retaliate by listing your charms? For starters you've got very nice hair. Silky. Or should I begin with your feet and work my way up?"

"You have nice things to say about my feet?"

"They're endearingly... wide. And flat. Like a duck's, sort of, except..." Speech dissolved again as wrestling and tickling became the primary focus of their attention. They froze when they heard a sharp noise from the main room, quickly identified it as the arrival of dinner, and went back to what they'd been doing. They laughed themselves into a state of comfortable exhaustion and when they finally settled down, Slan was draped sideways over Ruarshi's torso, rather like a beached whale. He mentioned the similarity and she pinched him but didn't move.

He reached up and ran his fingers gently through the shining waves of her hair where they rested against his chest. She turned her head to watch him. "I was afraid at first to enter your tent," he said, returning to their earlier conversation. "When I did, I found you to be both lovely and terrifying. I hadn't interacted much with warriors prior to that, beyond those at my clan home."

"I was dirty, tired, and irritable. I can't imagine what you found lovely about that. And I'm not fishing for compliments."

"Your poise. You had made a place for yourself, alone, among a horde of mercenaries. I'm not sure that's something I would try even now."

"It seemed like a good idea at the time. In retrospect, my decisions are harder to defend. European squabbles aren't all that interesting." She sat up and then snuggled in at his side, pausing at one point to kiss the tip of his nose.

He responded in kind and she lowered her head to rest it against his collarbone. He wrapped her in his arms and held her while she played idly with the hair on his chest. She began to hum softly, a sad but soothing old lullaby, and he hugged her more tightly, fighting the inclination to nod off. Neither one of them wanted to move from the bed.

It seemed to Ruarshi that time would resume its forward motion if they did.

"I want to ask Davyt to draw a portrait of you," Slan said eventually. "Would you mind?"

"I... no, I wouldn't mind. What in Nerthu's name will you do with it? Can we have him draw one of you as well?"

"I will treasure it, you lout. If you must have one of me, I'll sit for it. Your portrait should be done at night, so your face is illuminated by both candle- and moonlight."

"You've been thinking about this. Why that setup in particular?"

"The candlelight because it suits you and the moonlight because you've always been, and will always be, just a little bit feral."

"So says my ferocious *chesida*. I'm going to need time to think about yours. Setting you down in a field of flowers wouldn't be quite right, but a halo made of swords doesn't work, either."

"Don't you dare give me a halo of any kind."

Ruarshi chuckled. "Tired, dirty, and irritable then. Sitting on a camp stool by lamplight."

"Is that how you think of me?"

"Sometimes. More often I think of you naked. It's a male weakness."

"I wouldn't call that a weakness, exactly." She kissed the hollow of his throat. "It's more of a tendency and it's quite charming in the right context."

He lifted her hand to his lips and kissed the palm. "Do you ever think of me naked?"

"All the damn time. Every hour of the day. Stop laughing at me."

"I can't help it. What did you expect."

Slan pulled the blankets up to cover them and they drowsed for a time. When she shifted in her sleep and a lock of her hair began tickling his shoulder, Ruarshi groggily wrapped it around his fingers. He awoke fully a little while later to discover that she was looking at him.

"I love you," she whispered.

"I love you, too," he said.

"We should eat something now."

"We should."

He followed her out of the bed and moved slowly around the room, picking up clothing as he went and draping it in two piles across their rumpled sheets. Once they'd gotten themselves back in order, they opened their door and found Elin sitting in a chair next to the fire, the

Delver's book open in her lap. A small collection of dishes had been set out on the table. Whatever they contained, it smelled delicious.

Elin smiled up at them. "I've already eaten. I hope you don't mind. The food is very northern—I think the cook must be trying to make a statement of some kind—but you'll probably like it."

They resumed their journey to the Annorae clan home early the next morning, riding southeast along the edge of Lake Riani. According to Seggita, the trip would require two long days of travel or three short ones, and Ruarshi was uncomfortably aware that he was the reason they hadn't been able to commit themselves to the faster option. His uncertain health was causing them trouble even though he felt fairly normal at the moment. It was true that he'd been fighting queasiness ever since he awoke, but he thought that could be blamed on the excessive saltiness of the prior evening's meal rather than anything related to their adventures among the Seers.

Ruarshi was carefully not dwelling on the fact that learning of Casimir's involvement in his current predicament had led him to revise drastically downward the likelihood that he would emerge from the situation unscathed. The only question that remained was how bad it would get.

Fortunately the landscape through which they rode held his attention, and Seggita was more than willing to act as their guide. He answered Slan's occasional questions and regaled them with tales of local events, including a possibly apocryphal story of a weeklong battle between ice trolls, said to explain an unusual pile of rocks they passed shortly before noon. The surface of the lake was clear as glass in the sunlight, mirroring the many small islands that dotted its expanse, as well as the trees that lined the shore and the sparse sprinkling of clouds that drifted through the pale blue sky overhead. The entire scene was idyllic and Ruarshi did his best to appreciate it properly.

He was sunk in a blank reverie, riding side by side with Slan, when Elin broke off her conversation with Seggita to join them.

"I need to tell Seggita what kind of reception we're likely to receive at my clan home," she said without preamble, "and why. They'll listen to you, but they're going to look to him for counsel first. Since he's one of us."

"Of course," Ruarshi said after a brief and slightly puzzled pause.

"This is your family. We'll handle it however you see fit."

"I didn't want you to think that I doubted your promise to speak for me, and had gone looking for reinforcements."

"That's not an assumption I would have made. He needs to understand what's happening."

Elin smiled at him. "You don't get touchy over nothing. I like that. Thank you." She kicked her horse into a canter and returned to her earlier position.

Ruarshi watched her go, still somewhat bemused. "I hope I've never given her cause to think otherwise," he said.

"While she's explaining the situation to him, I'm going to need you to explain it to me," Slan said. "You alluded to this before but didn't elaborate. Will there be trouble?"

"Maybe. She was nominally on Elyon's side during the revolt, as you know. She's concerned that her clan might hold that against her. They may even demand a Rite of Atonement."

"Surely they'll spend a few days celebrating her return first? They've thought her dead for the better part of a century."

"I hope so. But I don't know."

"Was she telling the truth?" Slan asked. "When she told you she and her sister broke their swords before the fighting started?"

"I believe her. Even if I thought she'd lied to me, I'd still ask her Elders to let it go. Elyon's bad judgment has caused enough suffering already."

"You could tell them that she's restored the clan's honor by means of her ongoing assistance to you, if that's their chief concern. She can't help translate that damn book if she's fasting in a cave."

"Also true. One way or another I think we'll prevail. They know Seggita. I can't imagine that they'll insist on punishing her if he opposes it."

The subject of Elin's doubtful welcome at her clan home came up again after they'd stopped for the night, and Ruarshi learned that he'd have to abandon part of his argument in her defense. Seggita mentioned it with some reluctance while arranging his blankets on the opposite side of their small fire.

"You're going to need to downplay Elin's role in teaching you about the capabilities of the Nerthii. I would recommend not bringing it up at all."

"Why is that?" Ruarshi asked.

"Your eyes. Someone is certain to start shouting 'sova' at you shortly after we arrive. Be ready. It's an old northern word for 'owl' that can also mean 'demon'. I can keep you out of the clutches of the more superstitious Annorae, but it won't help Elin's case at all if they think she corrupted your power."

Ruarshi was taken aback. "Corrupted my power?"

"I'll tell them—or you can tell them, if you prefer—the truth about Amadan and that object he showed you. The Annorae, like most northern clans, aren't fond of the Seers and your wrangle with them will gain you some sympathy. But it's still advisable that we dissociate Elin entirely from your current condition."

"I can't lie to my family," Elin said sharply.

"Of course not," Seggita replied. "I'm just suggesting that the two of you keep each other at arm's length until the Elders have made their decision. Once you've been there a while, you can be more forthcoming."

"I've never heard of Miriyanti taking the idea of demons seriously," Slan said. "If they mean it, we'll be in danger."

"Yes. A little."

"Ruarshi and I can go somewhere else."

"It's not so bad as all that," Seggita said. "Their Skeltari may shriek at us a bit, but half of that will be because she dislikes me personally. Noora seems to believe that I'm responsible for the fact that her clan lacks a shaman. She has some strange ideas."

Ruarshi traded a glance with Elin. "This is going to be more complicated than I thought. I apologize in advance in case it turns out I'm not much use to you."

"Please don't," she said. "You might see a few warding gestures aimed in your direction but that will be it. Seggita's giving you the wrong impression. The Annorae are not a band of raving, unkempt forest dwellers."

Seggita sighed. "Under the right circumstances, everyone is a raving, unkempt forest dweller. I'd be the first to admit that the Sylvae can be just as superstitious as your people. The difference being that I'm one of them, they trust me, and our Skeltari doesn't spit every time she sees me."

"Is their guest house arranged in the usual way?" Slan asked.

"Yes, but it doesn't matter," Elin said. "I'm inviting you into my family hall. No one will trouble you there. You too, Seggita."

He inclined his head toward her and stood. "Thank you, but your chief will want me to stay with him. It's customary and no reflection on your family. Now if you'll excuse me, it's my habit to roam a bit before going to bed. It helps me situate myself in space. It's a shaman thing." He winked at Ruarshi. "I won't be long, but don't wait up for me." He headed northwest along the shore of the lake, clearly visible until his form was lost among a stand of trees.

Slan rose and stretched. "I could use a tent about now. Preferably made of black cloth."

"The sun up here takes some getting used to," Elin said. "It's hard to believe that I'm almost home. After all this time."

She was jittery and Ruarshi didn't think she'd be getting much sleep that night. "In my experience homecomings are difficult, but worth the strain. Whatever your clan's mood, remember that you're among friends."

Elin smiled at him, and in the angled light he could see that the eye not lost in the shadows of her mask was brimming with tears. She mumbled something about the call of nature and darted off into the pines.

"Do we need to post a watch for bears?" Ruarshi asked a short time afterward, musing aloud.

"I have no idea. When Elin gets back, we'll ask her." Slan sat down next to him. They leaned against each other, shoulder to shoulder, and stared out over the gently rippling water of the lake while they waited.

Ruarshi was lost in bad dreams for most of the night and got up the next morning feeling groggy, out of temper, and even more nauseous than he'd been the day before. For Elin's sake he was determined that they should reach the Annorae that evening, and he kept his complaints to himself though he was sure that Slan knew something was wrong. A little while after they stopped for the midday meal he found himself on his knees among the trees, vomiting it all back up again, and the same thing happened after dinner. Despite his request for privacy, Slan had followed him on this foray into the woods and she shouted for Seggita when she registered his distress.

The old shaman came at a run along with Elin, so all of them got a good look at him in the midst of his misery. He wanted very badly to snap at them until they backed off and left him alone, but he quelled the urge.

"Can you do something?" Slan asked.

"There's only one thing I can think of to try," Seggita replied.

"Then try it. Please."

The man kneeled next to him on the damp earth. "I'd like to lend you some power. It may do some good."

Ruarshi considered refusing the offer, more because he feared it wouldn't help than because he had any pride left to maintain. He'd concluded some time ago that what Seggita was suggesting was his only hope as far as healing went. If this failed he'd have to pin all his prospects for salvation on Satu, and he wasn't optimistic about her chances of finding him a cure.

In the end he assented, and Seggita laid a palm lightly against the back of his head. When the surge of power came a few moments later, it did strengthen him somewhat and lift his nausea, but it soon became apparent that the magic was flowing through and then back out of him again as though being lost to the air. When Seggita realized there was a problem and discontinued his weaving, Ruarshi felt every bit as bad as he had before. Maybe even worse.

"That went straight into the Halls, didn't it?" Seggita asked.

"I think so."

"There's no doorway here. How is that possible?"

Ruarshi shook his head and then wished he hadn't. "Satu thinks I'm connected too strongly to them, but I can't tell you what that means." He took a swig of water from his flask, spat, and drank a few swallows. When he was reasonably certain they would stay down, he put a hand against the tree next to him and started to rise. Slan helped him up.

"We're stopping here for the night," she said.

"Let's not," Ruarshi said. "It can't be that much farther and I'm already tired of the place."

She was studying his face and he could feel her decision to accede to his request before she spoke, in the shift of her body against his. "If that's what you want, we'll continue, but I won't tolerate any delays on the way to Elin's hall. Any discussions about demons or treason will have to wait until tomorrow."

Elin and Seggita agreed with that and they returned to their horses. It was late in the day when Seggita turned their course toward the south, away from the lake shore, and a quarter hour later they arrived at a vast, gently rolling meadow dotted with about two dozen wooden structures of various sizes. They could see a number of people moving about among them, and as they drew nearer a goshawk landed in the grass in front of them and took three hopping steps sideways, tilting its head for a better look at the visitors.

"Our arrival has been noted," Seggita said.

Elin took a deep breath and pointed. "My hall is along the southern perimeter. They're not going to recognize me."

"They will," Slan said. "Give them time. They were told you had died."

Elin led the way and they swung around the long, low hall at the clan home's southwest corner and headed east. When she came to the third building along she reined in and dismounted, and the rest of them followed suit. A few of the Annorae had stopped what they were doing to watch them, while a few more emerged from nearby doorways and a curious lynx trailed them at a distance.

Smoothing her tunic and trousers as she went, Elin approached the east entrance to the building and almost collided with a woman on her way out. They both stopped at the same moment and regarded each other warily.

"Aunt?" Elin said, her voice thin and tentative in the quiet air. "Rada? It's Elin. I'm sorry about my face. Are my mother and father here?"

The woman's eyes widened as the warrior spoke, and she glanced over at the rest of them as though seeking reassurance that they truly existed. Her face was still expressionless when she looked back at Elin, who had taken a cautious step forward, and then her hands flew to her mouth.

"Elin?" She rushed toward her niece and seized her by the shoulders, examining her face closely as tears began slipping down her cheeks. "How do you come here? Where have you been?"

"I've been in Europe," Elin replied. She was about to go on when her aunt pulled her into a hug. She wrapped her arms around the older woman and held onto her tightly. "There's a lot to tell. Saoirse is also alive and should be here soon."

More family members had begun crowding through the doorway behind the two women and the growing volume of their chatter drowned out the next part of their conversation. Ruarshi leaned against his horse's shoulder and watched it all, feeling like an intruder but glad that he was finally able to witness the reunion of an exile with her kin. Elin disappeared for a time into the press of people around her and then into the hall itself, to emerge a bit later with her eyes red and swollen and her mask somewhat askew. She led a small group of her kinsfolk in their direction.

"… with us from the Sylvae, and these are Ruarshi Nerthi, clan Doshae, and Slan Naishanti, clan Maelae. Ruarshi took it upon himself to redeem the honor of the exiles, but the Seers retaliated and now he's ill. Is there a place he can rest?"

Ruarshi looked at her in astonishment, wondering when she'd come up with that little gem. There was no time to dwell on the question as they were soon engulfed in a celebratory, weeping crowd, being welcomed and embraced on all sides at once. Since he had little choice in the matter he surrendered to happy disorientation, and allowed himself to be swept into the hall where food and drink were already being set out on a sideboard while tables and benches were cleared away. Seggita headed off on his own after a short while, wading with determination against the general flow to have a word with someone, and a stout little woman soon appeared at Ruarshi's side and gestured him and Slan toward the southern end of the building. When they were mostly free of the throng, she spoke.

"I am Tille, the *sperra* of this hall. You will be staying with us for a time?"

Slan nodded on their behalf and the woman gestured again, urging them along. "Follow me, please. Sleep may be difficult for the next little while, but you will be able to lie down. Seek me out anytime if there is something you need."

Tille led them to a room near the massive fireplace along the south wall and threw open the door. She then raised her eyebrows in brief inquiry and, when neither Ruarshi nor Slan responded with additional requests, bowed and took her leave.

Ruarshi slipped inside the room as the crowd in the hall's central area continued to grow. It appeared that the neighbors were coming over to find out what the fuss was about.

"The reunion seems to be going well," Slan observed. She was looking out over the boisterous mass of Annorae, and unless Ruarshi missed his guess she was searching for potential threats. Ruarshi had seen a few warding gestures on his way in, as Elin had predicted, but nothing that he considered worrisome. He glanced over his shoulder toward the bed. The urge to pull off his boots and lie down was overwhelming. He didn't think the noise would be a problem.

Slan noticed the direction of his gaze and her face softened. "Bed or food?" she asked.

"Bed. Definitely. I'll feel better tomorrow."

She joined him in the room and closed the door. Within minutes,

and despite the raised voices and laughter from the hall, Ruarshi was
asleep.

The next few days were a blur of introductions mixed with a light
sprinkling of social obligations. Elin and Seggita went to some trouble
to keep those to a minimum, which Ruarshi appreciated while at the
same time chafing at the knowledge he was being treated like an invalid.
For the most part he felt fine, if a little fatigued and occasionally feverish, and he was capable of doing much more than was being asked of
him.

He met early on with the Annorae chief and the Elders at a relaxed
meeting during which he was hardly called upon to speak at all, went
riding a little later with Seggita and some of Elin's male cousins, who
did in fact carry axes everywhere they went, and conferred from time
to time with the group Elin had put together to work on Alcina's book.
He watched one afternoon as an older man clipped the bindings apart
and divvied the pages up among the eight of them, hoping that
Amadan had unwittingly undercut his own attempt at vengeance by
handing the folio over.

They were an unlikely band of scholars to find in such a remote
place, and they made short work of the Delver's peculiar shorthand.
Ruarshi took to wandering over to keep company with them whenever
he had nothing better to do, reading through the translated passages as
they became available. He learned quite a bit about Miriyan's history in
the process, usually unpleasant facts such as who had betrayed, poisoned, or stabbed whom, and for what inexcusably feeble reason, but
more often he set the pages aside in mild impatience. He could follow
the substitution of clan totems for proper names, but trying to decipher Alcina's symbolism and elliptical style was usually more trouble
than it could possibly be worth. Was the 'frigid wind from the east' a
Russian border raid or an unusual weather event, and did it matter to
him either way at the moment?

The gradual acceptance of his presence by Elin's kin proceeded as
well as could be expected, with no one coming forward to raise any serious objections to his owlish, potentially demonic nature. He had yet
to meet the Skeltari and assumed that she, like Satu, didn't get out very
often.

He was visiting with the scholars again one evening when he was drawn outside by a growing hubbub of uncertain origin. He spotted the riders at once, recognized the man in the lead as Lorion, and hurried over to Elin's hall to fetch Slan. They had discussed this, and she'd agreed to wade in among the new arrivals first to explain why Ruarshi couldn't mingle too closely just now with any of the Doshae. Knowing that he couldn't embrace his son left a bitter taste in his mouth, but to behave otherwise would be wildly irresponsible of him.

There was nothing to prevent him from watching their reactions to Slan's unexpected appearance, however. Surely that bit of joy would make up for the news she brought.

Slan leapt up at his soft touch on her shoulder and read the tidings in his face. She ran ahead of him out into the sunlight and across the clearing until she stood at her brother's stirrup, where she raised one hand to shield her eyes as she lifted her head to speak with him.

## Alcina's Vision

Etienne almost couldn't believe it. Of all the people they could have chosen, they'd sent Lohcca.

It was late afternoon and he'd already swallowed two mugs of *keth* before she showed up in the doorway of Ruarshi's family hall, where he'd been leading a restless and discontented existence for three interminable days. He'd spent the time since their return from Mirror Lake trying not to die of impatience and drinking more than he should, as well as avoiding Ruarshi's siblings and plotting ways to steal a horse without getting caught. It wasn't that Aethel and Yael weren't friendly, because they were, but Etienne had no idea what to say to them or even how to act when he was in their vicinity. He sort of wanted to punch Aethel on general principle, based on what little Ruarshi had said about him over the years, but giving in to the urge would hardly improve his situation. They probably thought him taciturn or even surly by nature, which was almost funny in a way, but it wasn't a problem he could focus on right now. The horse issue was much more pressing, and he might have attempted to make off with one already were it not for a note he'd received from Satu the day after they'd gotten back. She'd let him know that Ruarshi had promised to call on her every once in a while, and that he should wait for the man's next visit if he was anxious to rejoin his company. Which was all well and good, but what if Ruarshi was no longer able to travel through the Halls for some reason? How long did he intend to wait around before taking matters into his own hands?

It was all very vexing and Etienne stared up at Lohcca with mixed feelings. Her arrival meant he could stop thinking in circles for a little while, which was a relief, and he had to concede that he'd have been offended if the Jinnae hadn't sent anyone at all to ask after him. Less happily, she was one of an exceedingly small number of his close relations whose good opinion mattered to him, so he was going to have to handle this tactfully. He wasn't sure he was quite sober enough to manage that.

He stood and waved to her, and she wove her way through the tables and benches to join him. It would be hours yet until the evening meal and he'd been sitting alone, so they had all the privacy they could want.

Etienne studied her as she approached. She was his second cousin, a century or so older than him, and her round, pleasant face hadn't changed a bit since the last time he'd seen her. She was frowning at the moment, probably having noticed that the area around his left eye was still a little discolored and puffy, but he'd come up with some harmless explanation if he had to.

He bowed to her, smiling. She returned the gesture and then embraced him.

"Cousin." She let him go and stepped back to look him over again. "I've missed you."

"Same. I hope you had a good ride over." Etienne waved a hand in invitation toward the bench he'd been sitting on and they both took a seat. "Would you like something to eat or drink?"

"No, thank you. I overnighted with the Chioni and they fed me too much."

"How is everyone at home?"

"No deaths or serious illnesses since you were last with us. Livli had a baby. Morale is good among the sheep and goats."

His smile widened. She'd always had a strange sense of humor. "What brings you?" He knew very well what brought her, but he was anxious to get this part of the conversation over with as quickly as he could.

"You do."

"Were you sent to yell at me or bid me good riddance?"

"Neither." She looked mildly reproachful. "There are those among us who were saddened by the news. Not surprised, but saddened."

Which, Etienne thought, summed up his birth clan's reaction to the entirety of his existence. He shrugged. "Then what were you sent to do?"

"You're aware that the Jinnae aren't overblessed with healers. Grigore would like you to rotate in for three months per year to look after us."

Now there was an unwelcome request from his former clan chief. He suddenly understood how Persephone would have felt if she'd been asked to spend time in the underworld without Hades at hand to console her. "Sounds awful," he said.

"What's your task list here? Would there be a conflict? He's willing to be flexible about the timing."

"Generous of him. You may tell him that I refused."

"Etienne. He's trying hard to be reasonable. You could meet him halfway."

"What, offer him a month and a half? No. I'm sure this sounds reasonable from his point of view, but from mine it's an insult. Once I receive an actual assignment from the Doshae, I'll consider it. I think slowly so I may not have anything to add for several years."

"That's your final word?"

"It is."

Lohcca grinned and leaned back against the table. "I'll tell him. I'll get some satisfaction out of doing it, too. But I'd still like you to visit whenever you can. You're more direct than you used to be. How was Europe?"

"That's a big question. Noisy?"

"That's it? Noisy?"

Etienne considered her, wondering if she would object to some bluntness on his part. He decided to try it out. "Since coming back, I've noticed that your question can be meant in one of two ways. Most often it's just a stand-in for the usual chatter about the weather and the person asking isn't interested in a real answer. Rarely, someone wants actual information. This usually happens when whoever it is I'm talking to has thought about heading south themselves. I can go on about it for hours if you're inclined to listen, but I don't want to bore you."

"I'm ahead of schedule. And I *have* missed you. I can think of no better way to spend the afternoon."

"Really?"

"Yes, really. I won't return from this quest victorious, but at least I'll have learned something."

Etienne launched into an account of his travels, starting at the beginning in Italy and continuing up through the day they'd clambered onto a ship in Lübeck. Since Lohcca knew him better than most and had always shown herself disinclined to judge him, he included a few amusing anecdotes relating to his adventures in Florence that he would have edited out for a different audience. On the whole he'd found the Florentines to be delightful people and he wanted to give them their due in his retelling. He was charier with the details once his tale wound its way north to Mainz, and in the interest of not saying too much he ended up saying so little that his cousin noticed.

"You should know," she said slowly, as though choosing her words with care, "that there is genuine concern for you at the clan home. We've been hearing some worrying rumors."

"I'm sure they're nonsense. I'm well and happy here. You don't need to tell me what's being said, either. It would probably make me angry."

Lohcca studied his face and Etienne, annoyed, crossed his eyes at her. She laughed. "If there's no genuine scandal on offer, people do have a tendency to invent one. I'm glad this place agrees with you. I shouldn't admit to this, but a lot of the concern I mentioned is rooted in the notion that you haven't got any sense."

Etienne snorted but didn't otherwise respond.

"You have to admit you went to considerable trouble to create that impression."

"It never fooled you."

"Well, but I'm uncommonly perceptive. You can't hold everybody to that kind of standard." She hesitated before continuing in a more serious tone. "Your new clan here, the Doshae, are they likely to end up in a feud with the Aesir? If that kind of thing is starting up again, I'd just as soon not see you in the middle of it."

"It'll depend on whatever mood the Aesir leadership is in, but I doubt it. If they were to retaliate, it would upset their Skeltari. Our Skeltari, Satu, took responsibility for Casimir's death. I can't imagine her counterpart would want a clan chief meddling with that. Those women are a law unto themselves."

Etienne waited patiently as his cousin tried to reconcile what he was telling her with what she knew of Cosmina, the unassuming Skeltari of the Jinnae. He'd only spoken with her a few times, but he couldn't recall that she'd ever gotten into so much as a minor disagreement with anyone. "Their Skeltari's opinion will matter that much to them?" Lohcca asked.

"It should. They're not all like Cosmina. Satu scares me." Etienne told her a little bit about his interactions with the horrible old woman, and some of the things she had said to him, and how her talents meshed with Ruarshi's. "The Aesir must be wondering by now if they have a shaman of their own hiding in plain sight somewhere. It would be a bad time for them to start trampling around in their Skeltari's territory."

"I would like to meet your friend Ruarshi someday," Lohcca said. "Every time he comes home he throws the hierarchy into an uproar."

"Yes, he does. So you've had my news. Is there anything in particular going on at my former clan home that I should know about?"

Lohcca obligingly caught him up on the events of the past six years or so. Her recitation was nothing out of the ordinary, just a description of the usual cycle of seasons and the customary unwinding of life events, most of it involving people who'd never had much interest in the lonely black-haired child growing up in their midst. Her words nevertheless left Etienne with a growing ache in his chest that he could neither explain to himself nor dislodge. He didn't have many questions for her, and when she finally wound down she asked him if he could possibly fetch her a drink. By that time he needed another one himself.

He passed all the way through the kitchens to the southern door, which stood open to the balmy afternoon air, and stopped there to gaze outward at nothing. A few inquiries from the cooks followed him through the wide room and he assured them without turning that all was well. When he felt a little better, he went to the row of barrels along the wall and poured himself two mugs of *keth* before returning to the main room and Lohcca's voluble company. He handed one off to her. She saluted him with it and took a long swallow.

"Hmm. This is better than ours," she said. "I suddenly have a much clearer understanding of your decision."

"You've discovered my secret," he murmured.

"Now that I've faithfully discharged my official duties, I'm free to do as I please. My first priority is letting you know that Narcis gave me a letter for you, which I immediately burned to ash to save you the trouble. I hope you don't mind."

And there was yet another disagreeable name from the depths of his personal history. What a disastrous relationship that had been. Etienne just barely avoided choking on his *keth*. "I don't mind. Thank you. What is he doing these days?"

"Rendering the very ground upon which he walks unhappy. He may have a trace of the Stoneshaper spark, but he's still struggling to figure out what to do with it. I would swear rock formations try to get out of his way when they see him coming."

"How unfortunate."

"Yes. Would you like to go for a walk? A ride? A swim in the river?"

"All three? It's been a hell of a week. You'll eat dinner here with us?"

"I'd be delighted to. I should run by the stables and guest house before we do anything else. You'll show me the way?"

"Of course."

When Mira appeared at his door late one evening to let him know that Ruarshi had arrived, Etienne was half dressed and alternating between staring morosely at his small fire and paging through a short treatise on Doshae clan history. He pulled on his shirt, tunic, and boots with frantic speed while she watched him in amusement and then grabbed his saddlebags from the corner of his room. He'd left them packed in the hope that this would happen, and he was ready to go in less time than he would have thought possible. It might have been the fastest he'd ever moved in his life.

Solvi's hall was north of his own and they went to fetch her next. He chafed at the delay even though Mira assured him that Ruarshi was going to be there for a while. Evidently he and Satu had a lot to talk about, which sounded ominous to Etienne but that might have been his anxiety talking. He'd been keyed up about everything in the wake of Lohcca's visit and trusted that being back where he belonged would settle him down, even if some or all of the news from the north was bad.

The warrior was still struggling to get an arm into her coat when she joined them, and Etienne wondered how much colder it would be where they were headed. Not that it mattered, really, since he didn't currently own a coat. He would manage.

After a perfunctory knock at Satu's door, the three of them burst into her home in a breathless rush. The Skeltari was sitting in her chair near the fire with Ruarshi standing in front of her. They'd caught him in mid-sentence. The man looked drawn, as twitchy as Etienne had ever seen him, and vastly surprised.

"What the devil are you two doing here?" he demanded.

"It's a story of middling length with a disappointing ending," Etienne said. He turned to Satu and bowed. "Thank you for sending Mira for us."

The Skeltari nodded at him, unperturbed by the interruption. Solvi bowed as well and studied her surroundings with interest.

"You split from the other Naishanti?" Ruarshi asked. His eyes narrowed. "Where did you get that scar?"

Etienne rubbed at it self-consciously. It was unfortunate that his former instructor had been able to spot it so quickly in the firelight. He hoped Ruarshi's eyesight wasn't getting sharper, as that would be just one more weird thing piled atop a hill of strangeness that he judged to be of adequate size already.

"It's all the same story. I'll catch you up later, I promise. If you and Satu have more you need to talk about, we can disappear for a while. I just wanted to make sure you didn't leave without us."

"Stay where you are." Ruarshi looked back at the Skeltari. "I think we're done here?"

"It was the best we could do, young one," Satu said, her voice subdued. "I'll give you a day's warning if it comes to that."

"Thank you," Ruarshi said briskly, wrapping up an exchange that Etienne didn't care for at all. The man inclined his head to Mira as he passed her and gestured for the two of them to follow him out, which they did. There was something in his manner that discouraged talk and Etienne was more than content to keep his mouth shut for the time being. They'd gone a short distance up the low rise to the east when Ruarshi spoke again. "Can I get a quick summary? From either one of you?"

Solvi glanced over at Etienne and answered him. "Etienne thought we should go back for Amadan's artifact, so we did. We succeeded in removing it from the premises—the others should have it halfway to the Annorae by now—but his attempt to draw off the pursuit didn't go well. One of the Seers had spotted Etienne in some kind of apocalyptic vision and their warriors were rough with him. I tried to intervene but it was too little, too late."

Ruarshi's steps had slowed as the warrior talked and he came to a complete halt when she finished. Etienne shifted uncomfortably from foot to foot, caught between the man's glare on one side and Solvi's rueful look on the other. He hadn't known she'd taken the blame for his mistakes upon herself, and he needed to say something about that, but there was also his irate former instructor to deal with. Etienne didn't know which problem to address first.

"Do you remember how angry I was with you for going to Bebel's house after that copy of Wil's book?" Ruarshi asked.

Etienne met his eyes and glanced away again. "I seem to remember the incident."

"That doesn't even… stealing from the Seers, of all the godfor-saken… *why* did you do that?"

"Instinct." It was an inadequate reply, but a true one.

"Instinct?" Ruarshi wielded the word like a whiplash.

"Yes, instinct," Etienne said, bristling a bit. "There was a little voice in the back of my mind telling me we'd need the thing if we ever wanted to get that red tint out of your eyes, and the idea of waiting around for someone to go get it didn't appeal to me. And what would we have done if the Seers had decided to move it?"

A strange expression flashed across Ruarshi's face and Etienne stepped forward, alarmed, some unconscious impulse warning him of impending disaster. The man raised a hand, palm out, and backed away.

"I'm not sure it's safe for anyone in my clan to touch me right now," Ruarshi said. He paused and Etienne could hear him taking one deep breath after another. "Thank you for looking out for me. Maybe it will turn out that you were right. Did the Seers tell you much about the vision?"

"One of them told me I was going to harm Miriyan. The artifact was definitely involved. That's all I remember."

Ruarshi shook his head. "They'll never change."

"Ciarn subsequently took this one under his wing," Solvi said, "and brought us home. I'd say he has a bright future ahead of him if he can avoid destroying the country."

"About what you said earlier. The way all that turned out wasn't your fault," Etienne said, trying to sound reasonable rather than mulish.

"I'll forgive you for that, but only because you're not Naishanti. A warrior would know better than to make that argument."

"That makes no sense. It was my idea."

"With which I, and all the others, went along. At which time it became our mission, too. You might want to stop now. You can't win this."

Etienne couldn't think of any good way to respond to that. He quashed the impulse to look to Ruarshi for help. "Then I should apologize. For improvising and getting myself caught."

"You should *not* apologize," Solvi said placidly. "It was important, and we knew going in that the odds weren't on our side." She looked at Ruarshi. "I take it you've reached the Annorae clan home? Did you find Seggita?"

"He found us. The others are there now, too."

"It sounds like quite a gathering," the warrior said after a short pause, her voice slightly strangled.

"I'll be glad to take you to join them."

"Thank you. I can't wait. Any chance we'll run into that creature from your dream?"

"Let's hope not. But I don't know."

"It must be the Dragon," Solvi said. "It's real after all."

Etienne was fairly sure this thought had occurred to every single one of them by now, but he remained resistant to it. "It doesn't look anything like a dragon."

"And you don't look like a fox," Solvi pointed out. "There's no reason that thing can't have its own totem."

That was an idea Etienne hadn't considered. "Have you seen it?" he asked Ruarshi. "Outside of a dream, I mean."

"No. But I've been staying out of the Halls. Tonight's the first time I've gone back in since heading north. Speaking of which." Ruarshi resumed walking and they fell in to either side of him. "When I go through the doorway, wait for a count of twenty before you follow. I'll want to make sure it's not there before bringing you in."

"If it is?" Solvi asked.

"I'll come running back out and we'll wait a while, or spend the night here, before trying again."

"Say it's standing around waiting for you," Solvi said. "Does it want to talk to you? Kill you? Play a game of cards?"

Ruarshi glanced at her sidelong. "If it speaks to me in a language I can understand, I'll pass on whatever it says." He stopped after a few more strides and turned slowly in place. "This is as good a location as any. Please don't flee in terror when I open the door. Remember to close your eyes when you cross through." He winked at them and a black rectangle shimmered into existence in the air before him. He disappeared into it as Etienne watched in apprehension, trying and failing to suppress a shiver.

"I don't want to get any closer to that," he said.

"I would also prefer to be several miles away," Solvi agreed. "Hold hands?"

She moved around to his right side and he took her left hand, leaving her sword arm free to do something warlike but probably ineffectual should they find themselves in the presence of an otherworldly monster. He tried to smile at her and she reciprocated.

Ruarshi did not reappear.

"Ready?" she asked. He nodded and she stepped forward, pulling him along. He shut his eyes and when he reopened them, he was in a warm, bright hallway that smelled like roses, still clinging to Solvi. Ruarshi stood a few feet away.

"Before I get started on our exit, tell me what you see," he said.

"Nice hallway. Marble? Interesting pattern in the floor," Etienne replied. "I thought you said it was cold in here."

"The first time I visited, it was. Slan and Elin perceived it that same way when I brought them through. You see it as I do now. Solvi?"

"Same as Etienne. Is this significant?"

"Maybe. Give me a few minutes and I'll have us out of here." Ruarshi pivoted to face the outer wall and closed his eyes. Etienne continued with his examination of the place, still terrified to be there but willing to stifle the effects of his ongoing adrenaline rush until they'd arrived somewhere safer.

Ruarshi staggered backward with a wordless cry of protest just as Etienne was engulfed by a wave of dread. There was a flicker of motion to his right and he turned toward it, unsure of what he was looking at. It was a tall, emaciated human figure, possibly the creature he'd seen in Ruarshi's dream, but oddly obscured as though he were viewing it through a raging waterfall. He couldn't discern any facial features at all, which was probably just as well, and there was indeed an extra joint near the monster's shoulder, the presence of which somehow deepened his horror and revulsion. It seemed to have something wrong with its legs, too; its stride was off. He had no way of knowing for certain whether or not he was right about that, as it was wearing some kind of wrap or skirt that covered its body from the waist down. The creature was advancing on them rapidly in spite of its strange gait, not a surprise given that its height was easily twice that of the largest man Etienne had ever seen.

Ruarshi was swearing frantically. "It knows I'm here. It's interfering with my ability to make a doorway."

Solvi drew her sword and stepped toward the creature. Etienne followed, unsure of what he could do to help but willing to try anything.

"Solvi," Ruarshi said urgently, "keep moving. Not toward it. Wave your sword or your arms." She began swinging her sword from side to side in slow, deliberate arcs. Ruarshi closed his eyes again. "It's working. The motion is distracting it. Don't stop. You too, Etienne. Get ready to run."

Etienne waved his arms for all he was worth. It was a long hallway but the monster was closing the distance that separated them with appalling speed. The thing was about twenty yards away from them when Ruarshi seized Etienne by his flailing forearm and threw him through another doorway. He stumbled forward into a green and sunny landscape and Solvi emerged just behind him. Ruarshi followed a moment later and all three of them ended up on the ground, gasping and shuddering. Etienne threw up without any advance warning and surrendered to the shakes that ensued. A little while later Ruarshi knelt next to him, and when his nausea finally let up Etienne slid out from under the man's hand to sit cross-legged in the grass. Solvi was lying on her back off to one side, a stunned expression on her face.

"I'm sorry," Ruarshi said. "I had thought... it doesn't matter. I shouldn't have taken you in there."

"I wouldn't have let you leave without me." Etienne felt like he'd become detached from most of his body, and if he told it to do something it likely wouldn't comply. He hoped the sensation would pass soon.

"It was wise of you to avoid the Halls," Solvi said. "You should go back to doing that."

"Yes," Ruarshi said.

"Do you think all our talk about it beforehand summoned the thing?" the warrior asked.

"How could it have heard us?" Etienne asked. "And all the ritual magicians I met in Europe told me you had to know the name of a monster to summon it. What's the use in getting around that by calling it 'the Dragon' if it's going to come after you anyway?"

"You met ritual magicians in Europe?"

"A few," Etienne said. "Could you tell what it wanted?"

Ruarshi shook his head. "There's nothing in its mind I can relate to. I'd be better off trying to read the emotions of a shark."

"Maybe they're similar. Maybe it's just hungry." Etienne's thoughts wandered uneasily back to his first conversation with Satu, and Mona's mass grave. "What if it makes a doorway of its own and shows up here?"

"What a horrible idea," Ruarshi said.

"I'm going to put a gag on you, Etienne, if you open your mouth one more time," Solvi said.

"Not lying there like that, you're not," he replied, but decided to change the subject for the sake of his sanity. "The Annorae don't know we're coming. Is our arrival going to cause problems?"

"No. The Doshae are staying in two different halls on the north side of the clan home. Davyt has a room to himself and is waiting for you. Solvi, I'm sure you'll find a bed among the warriors."

"So that means you're at the south end somewhere," Etienne said.

"That's exactly what it means. I shouldn't be this close to the two of you right now."

Ruarshi stood and managed to remain upright, so Etienne thought he might also give it a try. He succeeded on his second attempt, though his legs continued to shake. He gave Solvi a hand up. She bent to retrieve her sword while Ruarshi waited for them at a distance.

"This standoffishness of yours is going to get old fast," Etienne said.

"You're right. I'm already tired of it. Follow me and they'll get you settled. I should warn you that the *keth* here is stronger than what you're used to."

Etienne and the rest of the original crew from Mainz, along with Slan and Lorion, went for a picnic along the lake shore the next afternoon. The others were variously occupied, with Ardan and Tuomi having wandered off somewhere, Elin and Saoirse busy with the book, and the Naishanti carrying on a raucous mock battle with some Annorae warriors while Seggita regaled them all with bad advice.

They'd explained his and Solvi's unanticipated arrival by telling everyone that he'd taken a bad fall outside Mirror Lake and been subsequently hauled back to the Doshae clan home to see a healer, where Ruarshi had found them. No one had inquired too closely into the details, which was a relief, but Davyt had looked at him strangely when he'd first heard the story. The Illyana would have questions for him sooner or later, which Etienne would deflect as necessary. Until they knew what if anything should be done with the artifact, they intended to keep its whereabouts a secret.

It was a nice day, if a bit overcast, and the pleasant weather was cited as the official reason for their collective decision to lug food, blankets, and several jugs of *keth* northward come lunchtime. Everyone was carefully not saying that moving the meal outside was the only way they could convince Ruarshi to eat with them, but Etienne knew that was the real impetus behind all of the activity. Ruarshi knew it too, and seemed to be caught somewhere between embarrassment and gratitude. He went along with the consensus without comment. When they arrived at their destination, he settled down a few yards from the rest of their little group and leaned back against a tree.

Etienne didn't like what he saw when he looked at him. It had been just over two weeks since they'd parted ways, and he was appalled by the deterioration in the man's condition that had taken place during that time. Ruarshi's face was haggard and he was unsteady on his feet. Sometimes his hands shook. From a healer's perspective the view was even worse. Whatever was wrong with him had caused his entire body to stop functioning in harmony with itself, to slow down in some ways while speeding up in others. He was running a fever again. Etienne noticed that he didn't try to eat much, and was careful to monitor what happened with each bite of food before attempting the next. Even so, he held up his end of the conversation without apparent trouble and might almost appear normal to someone who wasn't watching him too closely. Etienne was so distraught that he thought he might cry. If he did, he'd blame it on the northern food. As an excuse, it was plausible enough.

They had all finished eating and were dawdling around, none of them eager to be the first to stand and start gathering baskets, when Elin arrived and ended the interlude for them. She had a section of Alcina's book in her hand and a ghastly expression on her face. She hurried to Ruarshi's side and dropped down to speak with him in low tones for a few minutes, while Etienne looked on and tried to brace himself for whatever he was about to hear. He spared a glance for Davyt, who appeared petrified.

Ruarshi took the pages from Elin's hand, read a short passage, and gave them back to her with a slight nod. His features reflected no emotion whatsoever, and Etienne felt the bottom drop out of his stomach.

Elin rose to her feet. "We finally found something," she said. "Prior context makes it clear that the 'they' in what you're about to hear refers to shamans. Here's the part that matters: 'They were poisoned by the claw of the Dragon and became as claws themselves. Their lands and their people sickened and died. Some among them were lost to self-murder, some to the hands of their kin, and some to the maw of the Dragon itself. The claw was buried and lost. May it remain so.'"

Etienne swallowed, fighting down bile. His mind skittered back to memories of the night before, and he tried to picture the creature's hands. He gave up when he realized that he *would* be sick if he continued with the effort.

"You're saying that Amadan's artifact was a claw," Slan said, her voice flat.

"The shape was right," Etienne said. "Does the book tell you what the Dragon actually is?"

"No," Elin replied.

"The Dragon exists?" Karoli's face was blank with shock. "Are you serious?"

"It's not really a dragon," Ruarshi said. "It's more of a tall man who wasn't put together properly."

"You know this because of your dream?" Slan asked.

So Ruarshi hadn't told her about the prior evening's incident. Etienne couldn't blame the man, as he and Solvi hadn't spoken of it afterward, either, but he thought maybe everyone should hear about it now. "No. The thing came charging toward us in the Halls yesterday. It looks sort of human but it lurches when it moves. I couldn't see its face and I don't remember its hands."

Etienne looked up to see they were all staring at him and he flushed. All of them but Slan, that is, who was watching Ruarshi.

"There was no harm done, Slan," the man said. "Your token, and Elin's, got us back here safe and sound."

She responded impatiently to that but Etienne was no longer listening. Ruarshi's mention of tokens had set off a cascade in his mind, as the various bits of information he'd been collecting finally came together to form a coherent whole.

He sat for a while in silence, examining the picture he'd put together, searching it for flaws. There were a handful of intuitive leaps involved, yes, but he believed his guess would prove to be correct. His suppositions and what he planned to do about them would, after all, explain why some of the Seers had been prepared to murder him. Their hostility was actually another important clue.

And they were right to be worried.

When Etienne turned his attention back to the ongoing conversation, the group was speculating about the creature's nature and intent. Etienne kept his thoughts to himself and glanced over at his former instructor.

Ruarshi met his eyes and smiled. The expression had a fierce edge to it, a hint that the man was looking for his own way out of the trap. Etienne returned the smile. This was all going to work out, and Ruarshi would be alive and well at the end of it. He would see to it.

# The Well

Ruarshi shut the door quietly behind him and walked south, heading for the tree line ahead. He was far from certain that his errand would meet with success but he had to make the attempt. His only other option was to lie down and die, and he hadn't quite resigned himself to surrender. Not yet.

He stopped halfway to his destination to take a look around and catch his breath. It was a beautiful night, with the midnight sun shining through a bank of low clouds on the horizon, its light limning the meadow and forest with a faint lilac tint. A cool breeze stirred his hair against his cheek, chasing a shiver through his failing frame. At his current rate of decline, he thought he'd be dead in a week, possibly less. And that was assuming his Skeltari didn't take steps before then in order to protect the clan. He hadn't told Slan how dire his situation had become—that was a task he would undertake only if tonight's effort failed—but Davyt and Etienne already knew. He had no idea what to say to either of them, or even how to ask what was behind the flinty look that had recently appeared in the eyes of his former apprentice. It was good that they had each other to lean on, and Slan had her brother. If the worst came to pass, none of them would have to face it alone.

Satu's proposed solution to his dilemma wasn't one he favored. It was the kind of suggestion that only a non-healer or a European physician would make. Bleeding him nearly dry in the hope that the Halls would lose their hold on him might have had a very slim chance of succeeding in the days right after his exposure to the creature's claw, but it had none now. He was too weak. Even if that approach worked as intended, the best healer in Miriyan wouldn't be able to keep him alive afterward.

Ruarshi started to cough and stifling it was a chore that left a smear of blood on his palm. Grimacing, he wiped it clean on a scrap of cloth he'd taken to carrying with him and trudged onward until he was within the shelter of the trees. Once there he waved a doorway into existence and stepped through.

Nothing waited for him on the other side. That was a relief. Disappearing into the ether wasn't his goal. Seggita would be sure to come after him, for all the good that would do, and he still wasn't quite sure the man believed him about the djinn. The Dragon. Whatever it was.

Because he was curious and not in any kind of hurry, he turned left first. The pile of rubble that Elin claimed lay in that direction didn't seem consistent with the well-ordered environment of the Halls as he knew them now, and he wanted to see what he might find there. The corridor continued unchanged, curving slightly to the left, for perhaps half a mile before he came to an arched doorway that opened onto the landing of a huge spiral staircase. The stairway led downward only, and Ruarshi stood considering it for a time in the wash of sunlight spilling in from overhead. The stairs were both broader and deeper than any he'd seen before, suited to the use of giants rather than humans. If he explored them for any distance he was afraid he'd never make his way back to the top.

He turned away and retraced his steps, and soon he'd returned to the twisting passages of the labyrinth. The low doorway into its heart hadn't changed, and he dropped onto his hands and knees to crawl through it. On the other side loomed a riot of greenery, none of which he could identify, and in the center of it all lay the well. A bit of experimentation reassured him that it was disinclined to shift position this time around. He sat down on its low rim. The water level within was so high that all but the slightest disturbance would send some of it spilling over the edge. He avoided looking at his reflection and lowered his hand into the water. When he brought it out again, it was bloody. That was the result he'd been counting on and he lay back in the grass, settled his hands on his stomach, and waited.

Given that his alleged ability to manipulate the future represented his last chance at survival, it was a shame that he had no real notion of how to go about this. Repeated attempts to clarify what Elin had been telling him had left him with the impression that he would intuitively know what to do when the time came. He hoped that would turn out to be true.

After a short interval, most of which he spent studying the disturbingly asymmetrical leaves on one of the trees growing near the well, a riot of images burst into his mind and obliterated all other awareness. He floated among them, trying not to panic, struggling to resist the temptation to impose order on what he was seeing. Eventually the whirling kaleidoscope slowed and stilled, and he was looking out over a vast array of twinkling color, a complex web spun by a crazed spider.

Ruarshi focused on a single strand and attempted to reel it in. It slipped away from him. He tried again and found himself watching a domestic scene involving a number of people he didn't know. If he understood the rules correctly, they would be Doshae and currently living. He nudged at the image and a family's morning routine played out before him. He returned the sequence to its beginning and pushed it backward in time, past the initial scene, and observed them as they rose from their beds. There was no sound.

Backing up and away from the image, he searched for branches in the time line and discovered that a dauntingly large number of them split away from the original progression of events. Was it safe to assume that the straighter a particular sequence of images appeared to his mind's eye, the more likely it was to occur? Some of the paths ribboning off to each side intersected with other strands in the web that the original line didn't touch anywhere in his field of vision, or touched only much further along in time. Those entanglements led to more and more divergent paths, some of them so faint against the black depths beyond that he wasn't sure he could focus in on them if he wanted to.

Making sense of it all was every bit the nightmare he'd imagined. But in spite of the fact that he was still fumbling with his environment like a child with a new toy, at least this strange place seemed to understand what he wanted and appeared willing to comply with his wishes.

How to go about finding himself in all of this?

Ruarshi closed his inner eye, shutting himself off from the web that lay before him. He thought of his son, and Slan, and Etienne, and reminded himself to go slowly. He had both very little time left and all the time in the world. As long as there was no risk that he would fall asleep, which he found it difficult to do these days even in the most comfortable of surroundings, he was free to unravel the well's mysteries at his leisure.

When he opened himself up to the array of futures again, Davyt was there. This was a more mature Davyt than the one he knew, and Ruarshi drew back in fear lest he touch something he shouldn't and send his son's life careening off in an unintended direction. He closed his mind's eye again and remembered the evening just past, with Slan sitting next to him and the murmur of voices floating into their room from the clan hall.

And there he was, his arm around her, relaxed if not exactly at peace with the world. Did he really look so bad as that? Probably. He backed away from the scene, watching as his potential futures swam into view before him.

What he saw wasn't encouraging. A distressing number of the strands in that particular section of the web simply disappeared into darkness before they'd gone very far. But over at the edge of the array there were a few that showed some promise...

A sudden sharp pain between his eyebrows shattered his concentration and the web slipped from his grasp. It lost its cohesion instantly, dissolving into a chaotic jumble of disconnected strands and falling away into the distance. His eyes snapped open. He knew what that pain signified because he'd felt the same sensation two nights earlier, right before the creature had appeared in the Halls. Evidently it had returned.

He sat up stiffly and swung around to look back the way he'd come, frowning. If the monster was trying to reach him, it was going to have some trouble covering those last few yards unless there was a second, larger door somewhere that Ruarshi hadn't found yet. That thought spurred another: if this place had been built to house that ghastly thing, why was there an area the creature couldn't access?

He was getting ahead of himself. He rose and retraced his steps until he stood by the low doorway into the labyrinth. No shadow darkened the floor on the other side, meaning that the monster was further afield somewhere. He turned to the right and began to make his way along the wall, checking for openings, both because he didn't want the creature sneaking up on him and because confirming the absence of another entrance could have important implications.

Ruarshi moved at a deliberate pace, occasionally pushing branches aside or swinging away from the wall when a particularly dense bramble grew up along its base. He paused once to stare for a bemused interval at a bush bearing leaves that looked exactly like human hands, before shaking himself and resuming his search. Once he'd made the full circuit he leaned back against the stone, thinking.

The answer to his earlier question was clear. The labyrinth had been built to protect or imprison something other than the creature they'd encountered. That dreadful thing might be the Dragon, as they'd assumed, but it was also possible that it was more of a minotaur, set there to guard the place.

Ruarshi's eyes returned to the well, just visible through the vegetation that surrounded it. It had been uninhabited on his first visit, but was it still?

A breathy snort from the other side of the doorway made Ruarshi jump. He backed away from the wall and examined the stone around the opening closely, until he was sure that any attempt on the monster's part to get through it would take a considerable amount of time and generate sufficient noise to jolt him from a trance. Turning his back on the creature wasn't easy but he did it, and with measured steps he returned to the well.

He sat down where he'd rested before and propped an elbow on the rim. It wasn't necessary that he look at the water in order to take the next step, but he found the reflected greenery calming and therefore helpful. When he was ready he sent his thoughts arrowing downward, too tired now to be cautious.

His awareness brushed up at once against a foreign consciousness and he drew back, gasping. It was vast and strange and for an instant he was looking at an impassive feminine profile, somehow familiar, before an enormous force slammed into him. He tumbled through darkness and landed on grassy soil with a doorway dissolving behind him and an imposing Miriyanti woman standing nearby, hands on hips. Ruarshi lay where he'd landed, his palms pressed against the earth, trying to get his bearings.

"I'm Noora, Skeltari of the Annorae. You're the Doshae shaman?"

Ruarshi swallowed. "I am."

"Come with me." She turned and headed away, and Ruarshi saw that a large man had been waiting behind her. He recognized the fellow and thought he was one of the clan's warriors.

The man stepped forward as he struggled to rise. "Up you go." He wrapped an arm around Ruarshi's shoulders and pulled him upright, brushing his clothes back into order with a few quick swipes before releasing him again.

"Who are you?" Ruarshi asked, still disoriented and unsettled by the attention.

"Her brother. I do her lifting. Name's Simion."

"Nice to meet you. Where are we going?"

"Her house," the man replied, nodding toward his sister's straight-backed figure. She hadn't looked back to see if they followed. They started walking.

"How did she know I'd be here?"

"No clue."

"Why is she having me over for a visit?"

The man shrugged. "You just came from the Halls?"

"Yes."

"Do you always exit them like that?"

"Like what?"

"By falling through the door sideways?"

"Not usually, no."

"Just trying something new this evening, then."

Ruarshi looked up at the man. "I was pushed."

"And what did the pushing?"

He found that he was unwilling to talk about what had just happened. "I'm not sure."

"Well, you did hit your head pretty hard when you fell."

"I did?" Ruarshi hadn't noticed, but then again he hurt all over and could hardly be expected to register a new source of pain right away. He glanced toward the sun and saw that it had scarcely moved while he'd been absent. That was another one of his questions answered. "There hasn't been any hue and cry tonight from the south side of your clan home, has there?"

"It's quiet as the grave, as usual. We're a somber, humorless lot."

"I'm sure you could liven it up."

"Nah. Too much trouble. We're here."

They had arrived at a small round building, outwardly similar in every way to Satu's home with the exception of the door, which was located on its south side rather than the north. It stood open and Simion gestured him toward it.

Ruarshi strode up to the threshold and discovered that he could go no farther. A gentle pressure with no discernible origin resisted him when he tried. He backed off a step, equal parts confused and wary, and Simion walked through the gap and went inside.

"What's wrong? Come on in." The man reached out, grabbed his forearm, and pulled him through the door.

It felt as though he had been hurled into a roaring fire. Ruarshi fell to his knees. Simion crouched beside him, concern plain on his face, and said something to him.

Ruarshi couldn't hear the words. His entire world was pain and nothing else.

He fainted.

When Ruarshi awoke he was lying on bare ground. Someone had thrown a blanket over him and shoved a pillow under his head. The heat and unbearable pain had disappeared. He was now too cold, in fact. Tugging the blanket more tightly up under his chin, he surveyed his surroundings.

The first thing he noticed was the books. Noora was apparently bookish in a way that Satu was not; they were strewn across a majority of the flat surfaces in her home, and curved bookcases covered most of the wall. He registered the presence of a table on one side of the fireplace and a bed on the other, upon which a dim figure sat, unmoving. The fire had burned low and wasn't much help to him as he tried to make out facial features, but he knew who it had to be. A soft creaking noise behind him, as of a chair being gently rocked, hinted at the continued presence of her brother.

"What happened?" he asked.

Noora rose and moved into the firelight. She tapped her temple. "You had a wicked spirit riding behind your eyes. Couldn't you feel it?"

Was *that* what the creature had been up to? Forcing its way into his mind? Why?

"Is it gone?"

"Yes."

"What was it?"

"I couldn't tell you. Would you like some *keth?*"

"Yes. Please." She lifted a mug off the table and brought it to him, but his hands were shaking too hard for him to take it from her. Simion came to his rescue again, kneeling next to him to prop him up and hold the cup while he drank. When he'd had enough he nodded in gratitude and the man withdrew.

"You're dying," Noora said.

"I am aware." Ruarshi didn't want to dwell on it. "Why were you out there waiting for me?"

"The wind told me to keep an eye out. I had no idea what or whom I was waiting for. I've been standing in that spot every night for the better part of three years."

He hadn't really expected a response that would make sense to him. "Thank you. And convey my thanks to the wind, as well. I should leave so you can get some rest." He very much wanted to make it back to his hall before Slan woke up and discovered that she was alone in their room.

"You need to stay here for a few hours."

"I do?"

"Yes. The spirit wasn't a strong one, but it could still pose a danger to you. Wait a while and the sunlight will destroy whatever is left of it."

"You've dealt with something like this before?"

"No. Call it a hunch." She relented and smiled at him. "This is how our magic works. Surely you've learned that much from Satu."

"I suppose so," he murmured.

"While you remain, you shall have my bed. Simion, if you would?"

Ruarshi protested and tried to stand up, but there was little he could do in his current state other than comply with her wishes. Simion scooped him off the ground and deposited him in the Skeltari's bed while he fought back tears of pure frustration. When he was arranged to the man's satisfaction—he didn't even have the strength to take off his own boots, and had to watch while this was done for him—he said, "Please send word to Slan, in Elin's hall, and tell her where I am. It will save us all some trouble come morning."

"Don't be concerned. It will be done. Now get some sleep."

He was so exhausted he'd started to wheeze. Ruarshi closed his eyes and did as she suggested.

Slan and Lorion were both sitting by his bedside when he woke up some time later. The hour was still ridiculously early, but Ruarshi was anxious to return to his room before the rest of the clan was up and about. He had a feeling that he wasn't going to be too steady on his feet this morning, and didn't want to totter his way across the clan grounds with the entire Annorae population watching him.

He was able to cover the distance without help, as it turned out, though he wasn't moving very quickly. The two Maelae watched him like hawks in case he stumbled, which he didn't, and as they went he explained what he'd been doing—attempting to do—the night before. He omitted the part about the woman in the well, leaving them with the impression that he'd returned from the Halls under his own power, and by the time he came to the end of the story he was back in his quarters. He subsided into a chair with a sigh of relief.

Grasping what was left of his courage in both hands, he concluded with, "I won't be going back. I can't risk letting that creature into my head again. I'm sorry. There's nothing else left for me to try. Casimir is going to win this round after all."

Slan stared at him, her face blank, and then her expression changed. She whirled and left the room. Lorion sat down heavily in the chair across from him.

"This is going to be fatal?"

"Barring a miracle, yes."

Lorion looked downward and shook his head sharply once. "I'll take care of Amadan for you. I promise."

"Please don't."

"Why not?"

"Revenge is a never-ending spiral. Best not to get caught up in it. How is Yael? I missed her on my way through."

His good-brother flushed, which was an interesting reaction. Lorion and Ruarshi's sister had been conducting an on-again, off-again relationship for the better part of a century.

"We'd been spending some time together in Tomir before you got back. She's pregnant."

"You're kidding."

"I'm not."

Ruarshi had to blink to clear his vision. "And you didn't think to mention this earlier? That's wonderful. Congratulations. Give her my regards when you see her next. Surely you're not staying up here all winter?"

"No. I'll head south soon." Lorion's mouth thinned to a tight line. "You seem to me the type for letter-writing. Would you like to write some letters?"

Ruarshi hadn't thought of that, but it might not be a bad idea. "I'll give it a try."

"I'll have some paper and whatnot sent over."

"How is Tuomi holding up?"

"She's going to be fine. Seggita offered to take her to the Sylvae clan home for a while and she accepted his invitation. I think a few years away from her family will help straighten things out."

Lorion left soon afterward to see to his sister and Ruarshi dozed off. When he next returned to the waking world, he was lying in his bed looking through the inner doorway of his quarters at Etienne's back. It occurred to him that he was already quite sick of being tossed around like a sack of oats and he resolved to put a stop to the practice before it could take hold.

His former apprentice was staring out the window into the sunlight, his arms wrapped tightly around his chest, still as a statue.

"Good morning," Ruarshi said.

Etienne turned toward him and Ruarshi got a glimpse of his expression before he could cover it up with a weak smile. It was bleak and heartbroken and much older than his years, and Ruarshi couldn't tolerate the thought that he was the cause of it.

There was going to be more of that over the next few days, he knew. He wondered if it was even possible to brace oneself for such a thing.

"It's after noon," Etienne said, abandoning the window to come stand by the bed. "You must be hungry by now?"

"Actually I am."

"I'll go fetch something."

"Thank you."

Etienne hurried out of the room. While waiting for him to return, Ruarshi noticed that a neat stack of paper now lay on the table near the outer door, along with a quill and a small jar. There was probably a pen knife in there somewhere that he couldn't see from his current angle. Lorion had always been an efficient person, even when pretending to be drunk.

When Etienne bustled back in a few minutes later, Ruarshi was the one standing at the window. The healer squawked in dismay, left the tray he'd been carrying on the bed, and joined him, searching his face for… what? Signs and portents of his imminent demise?

"Moving around won't hurt me," he said. He tried to keep the asperity out of his tone but didn't quite succeed.

"So long as you don't go running off into the Halls again." Etienne seemed to be on the verge of saying something else but instead he grimaced and subsided.

"I had to try it."

"I know you did."

"I wish you wouldn't come in here."

"You grabbed me by the arm the other day. No harm done. You're being paranoid."

"Probably."

"What's the paper for?"

"Lorion thought I should write some letters."

"Did he?" Etienne said. "You should eat."

Ruarshi shuffled over and gazed down at the tray. The berry pie and cheese looked appealing, the bread stuffed with fish less so. "So much salt," he murmured.

Etienne chuckled and dragged a chair closer to the bed while Ruarshi sat and began picking at the offerings. The pie was good and it disappeared in short order, followed by the cheese. They carried on an inconsequential conversation while he chewed and by the time he was done, Ruarshi was almost content. There was little point in his feeling any other way at this juncture.

He would keep telling himself that and see how well it worked.

"I've been meaning to return this to you," Ruarshi said, reaching inside his tunic. He fussed with the clasp on the fox pin until it came loose, and caught Slan's wristband and Elin's ribbon as they fell away. Setting them aside, he leaned forward and dropped the little fox into Etienne's outstretched hand.

The healer sat back and gazed down at it. "I forgot to mention. One of my cousins came by while I was waiting for you to show up. The Jinnae chief wants me in residence for three months per year."

"What did you say?"

"That I'd think about it. Then we got drunk and ended up in the river."

"Do you miss your family?"

"Less my family than certain others, but I'm not anxious for a reunion." Etienne held up a finger. "One moment."

His eyes lost their focus and Ruarshi realized that he had to be in contact with Jonata. He'd had no idea whether or not that bond still existed and hadn't wanted to ask, seeing as how it was none of his business. The healer emerged from his trance with a lopsided grin that faded quickly.

"Jonata and I have been communing a lot lately," Etienne said. "I'm afraid she's getting the wrong impression of Miriyan. She thinks it's all anxiety and aggravation." He attempted another smile but abandoned the effort halfway through. "I'm not sure she'll ever come north. I'd like her to. Though my eye strayed in Kennet's direction on our way to Mirror Lake. I'm sure you noticed."

"He certainly had his eye on you. What was your understanding with her?"

"We both find the bond comforting. That's it."

"Really?"

"What, you're my matchmaker now?" the healer asked.

Ruarshi chuckled. "Not at all. But I would like you to be happy."

The hard gleam returned to Etienne's eyes. "I'm working on that."

This was a genuinely mystifying statement. Ruarshi rested his chin against his drawn-up knees, watching the younger man closely. "Meaning what?"

Etienne returned his regard steadily, saying nothing, and then gasped and looked away. It was clear that some unwelcome thought had just occurred to him, and Ruarshi was beginning to feel a bit distressed at being shut out.

"What?" he demanded.

"Nothing," the healer said, struggling for air. "I just realized that resisting temptation is a bad idea. I wish I'd known that sooner."

"You're not making much sense."

"That's all right." To Ruarshi's considerable alarm, a single silent tear streaked its way down Etienne's cheek. "The situation is no worse than it was before. I'm sorry." He scrubbed a hand over his face, wiping away the wetness.

"Are you still trying to…? Etienne. What do you think can be done?"

The healer widened his eyes, feigning innocence in a manner that could best be described as completely unconvincing. "What do you mean?"

Ruarshi growled at him but Etienne only said, "Feel free to ignore my more obscure pronouncements."

"You leave me with little choice if you won't explain them."

"Weren't you on the verge of giving me relationship advice? I'm all ears."

Ruarshi understood he was being diverted and decided to allow it. Adding to Etienne's misery was something he'd very much like to avoid. "Actually I wasn't. I have no skill to speak of in that domain."

"You seem to be doing well with Slan."

"Because she has a forbearing nature. Not because I have any idea what I'm doing."

"Maybe I'll stumble into some good luck, too."

"Say you get involved with Kennet and then Jonata shows up. What then?"

"A delightful threesome?"

Ruarshi raised an eyebrow. "This isn't Europe, but the Doshae do have their limits. Don't tell anyone."

"I've never actually done that, you know. Though I have day-dreamed about it."

"Sounds like a mess of elbows to me."

That startled a laugh out of the healer, which was an improvement. "And knees. You'd have to be careful."

"I know you always try to live up to what others expect of you," Ruarshi said. "Or what you think they expect. You're also permitted to protect yourself, in case no one's mentioned that to you before."

"I'm an expert at protecting myself."

"Are you?" They were no longer just talking about potential love triangles.

"Some risks are worth taking. I'm pretty good at identifying them. Are you sure you're qualified to be giving this lecture?"

"Maybe not, but I'm the one sitting here."

"So you are. Would you rather not be? We could go for a ride."

Ruarshi had been mostly sedentary of late, which was what came of being both tired all the time and surrounded by people who insisted on treating him as though he were made of glass, and the notion was appealing. But was he up to it? He checked in with himself and decided he was.

"I'd like that."

No sooner had he spoken than Etienne was on his feet and out the door to go retrieve a pair of horses from the stables. Ruarshi tidied himself up while he was gone, taking a quick and partial sponge bath, brushing the dirt off his tunic, and combing out his hair. As a result of Slan's recent haircut it fell to just past his shoulders and was slightly lopsided, a little longer on the right side than the left. Somehow he'd never gotten around to saying anything to her about it.

When Etienne came jangling up to his outer door, Ruarshi was waiting for him. He climbed into the horse's saddle and they rode away south, skirting the edge of what he'd been given to understand was a vast forest stretching for over fifty miles in that direction. They passed a number of game trails that wended their way through the undergrowth and then disappeared into the shadows of the trees, but spotted no wildlife.

Neither of them was inclined to talk. There was plenty that Ruarshi wanted to say to his former apprentice, but he knew he'd never get through a fraction of it without becoming incoherent. He'd write it all down that evening, and would do the same for Slan and Davyt. He'd leave missives for a handful of others, as well, but he thought those three would be adequate for his initial session. Nothing about the task was going to be easy.

Etienne was leading the way and it soon became apparent that the man was searching for something. He was painfully tense and his gaze returned time and again to the southwest, which probably meant that Ruarshi's earlier guess was accurate and Etienne was waiting for the warriors and the artifact to arrive. This preoccupation of his worried Ruarshi quite a lot. In circumstances like these, hope could become a terrible thing. He thought about asking the man a direct question about his intentions but decided against it. He had no appetite for another strained conversation just now.

After what felt to him like an hour-long excursion but was likely closer to half that, Ruarshi was ready to lie down again. Fortunately Etienne had judged his stamina correctly and turned their course back toward the clan home a while earlier. His grip on the reins tightened convulsively when his vision wavered and darkened for the space of several shuddering breaths, but it returned to normal before he could decide whether or not to say something about the problem. He understood then that if his fragile sense of equanimity were ever to slip entirely from his grasp, he would need to remove himself from the company of others as quickly as he could. Because what he really wanted to do was howl until his throat bled.

*Not yet.*

*Not yet.*

*Not yet.*

When they arrived back within sight of the halls, there were a handful of people gathered outside Elin's *saal*. Ruarshi couldn't quite tell who it was at this distance, but it looked like they were waiting for him.

"They've found us," Etienne said. "I'm in trouble now."

Ruarshi snorted. "No, you're not. This wasn't an abduction."

"Don't tell *me* that. Tell them."

"No need. They know me fairly well." Ruarshi kicked his horse into a canter. Etienne did the same and they rode forward side by side as Slan and Davyt broke from the group and came out to meet them.

# The Darkness Beyond

Three days later, Ruarshi collapsed shortly after rising from his bed. Etienne, Ardan, and Davyt all confirmed that he hadn't suffered a concussion when he fell, but repeated attempts to wake him had proven futile. It was now early evening and Etienne was sitting next to Elin in the main room of her family's hall, which was where he'd been all day. He was mired in a state of such deep misery that time had ceased to have any meaning and normal activities were all but incomprehensible to him. He knew his eyes were swollen and he didn't care.

He thought again about riding out to find Kennet and the others. The problem with that idea was that there were no choke points in the terrain to the southwest, so any particular path he chose was likely to be the wrong one. It would be just perfect if the warriors showed up while he got himself lost in the forest, and he missed his last chance to save Ruarshi's life. If that happened, he'd never recover.

Had he remained the impulsive young man he once was, he'd have thrown caution to the wind back at Mirror Lake and pulled Kennet into his bed. They'd have exchanged buttons or locks of hair or something, and Ruarshi could have used that to locate the Naishanti days ago. Etienne would have had to tell Ruarshi a number of outrageous lies to accomplish what he intended, but that would have been among the least of his concerns. The waiting would already be over, one way or another. He wouldn't have to sit here with his head on the table and try to smile at everyone who paused to lay a hand on his shoulder or offer him a drink.

Word of Ruarshi's decline had cast a pall over the entire clan. The man would be startled to see how much the Annorae cared for him and for those around him. Nor would he accept it easily, Etienne knew. Ruarshi had been deeply involved in some of the worst violence in Miriyan's recent history, and somewhere along the line he'd stopped believing in the kindness of strangers. He could have relearned that sort of trust, given time.

And if Etienne didn't find some way to distract himself from all this, he'd soon be unable to function at all.

He stood and stretched, and began walking in circles around the perimeter of the room. He concentrated ferociously on nothing. He was so successful at blocking out the rest of the world that he almost didn't hear it when someone shouted that riders were approaching.

Etienne dashed outside, squinted into the distance, and then ran back into the hall. He seized Davyt by the front of his tunic and pulled him to his feet.

"Go find Seggita," Etienne said, low and rushed. "Bring him back here and tell him that Ruarshi needs him to open a doorway, as close to Elin's hall as he dares. Tell him it's an emergency."

Davyt didn't budge. Etienne wasn't sure the healer had understood him. "Why?" he asked finally.

"Because I may be able to save your father's life and if you don't go *now*, I'm going to miss my chance."

"Etienne—"

*"Do you trust me?"*

Davyt searched his face and nodded.

"Then do it. Go."

The healer gathered himself and ran. Etienne followed him out and saw him sprinting northward while he hurried to intercept the riders. They weren't moving quickly and as he neared them, he saw that both warriors and horses looked exhausted.

Etienne raised a hand in greeting and started talking as soon as he was within earshot. "I can't tell you how glad I am to see you. Do you have the artifact?"

They'd reined their mounts to a halt and Mads nodded toward Midnight, who was serving as a pack animal. "The bag on her right side. What's wrong?"

Etienne dashed forward and began untying the knots that bound the sack to the rest of their gear. "Everything. Everything is wrong. I can't dawdle; Ruarshi is ill. You made good time." He let the bag fall to the ground and plunged a hand into it, feeling along the object's edges through the layers of wrapping to make sure he really had it. He did.

"The Seers sent Naishanti after us. Two of them." Mona was scowling at him. "They were aggressive and we ended up killing one. The other we haven't seen in a while, and the past week has been a race. Talk to us, Etienne."

Her request for an explanation was addressed to his back.

"Later," he said.

He'd already spotted Seggita and Davyt, who'd stopped about midway between the hall at the southwest corner of the clan home and the line of trees that bordered the clearing. He wedged the bag up under his right arm and jogged toward them, waving his left hand, trying to catch their attention.

"Open the doorway!" he yelled. He kept yelling until he was sure that the man had heard him. Seggita complied, though he looked puzzled, and several things happened at once.

Out of the corner of his eye, Etienne saw someone moving among the trees. A quick glance revealed it to be a man with a bow. He couldn't tell if the weapon had been raised yet, or an arrow nocked, or even who the intended target was.

Behind him the Doshae warriors were shouting. At least one of them was racing northward, toward the archer.

Seggita pivoted to look behind him. Davyt, standing off to his side, pointed at the tree line, and the Nerthi began running in that direction. The doorway wobbled but didn't disappear. Seggita was at least twenty feet away from it now, possibly far enough that the claw's malign aura wouldn't touch him, and Etienne knew he'd never get a better opportunity.

He took the sack out from under his arm and sped up. The part of his mind not completely focused on his task noted a sharp crack off to his left followed by a low cry. He didn't turn to find out what was going on. When he was near enough to the doorway that he couldn't miss, he gave the bag an underhanded toss and watched it sail over the threshold and disappear into the darkness beyond.

For the duration of an indrawn breath, nothing happened. Then the doorway abruptly vanished, his ears popped, the world spun, and Etienne found himself sprawled on the ground several yards away from the spot where he'd been standing.

He'd done it. Now it all came down to finding out what, if anything, that meant.

Etienne rolled over onto his belly and waited for a wave of dizziness to pass. When he raised his head a little later he saw Davyt sitting in the grass a few feet in front of him.

"That man tried to shoot you," Davyt said. He sounded dazed.

"Did he?" Etienne didn't care one way or the other but he took a look around regardless. Part of an arrow lay on the ground behind him. One of the warriors must have broken it into pieces for him. He doubted he'd ever been in any real danger.

"Are you well, Etienne?" Seggita approached and crouched down beside him. Off in the middle distance he could see Mona, Mads, and Kennet gathered around a crumpled form lying just at the edge of the clearing.

"I'm fine."

"Hmm. You seem sound enough, but I'll still want to have a healer take a closer look at you while we sort this out. You, too," he said, turning a critical eye on Davyt. "I'm sure someone is on the way. In the meantime, could you tell me what you just did?"

"I'm not sure yet."

"Then let me rephrase it: what were you trying to do?"

Etienne could continue being difficult, or he could admit to the worst of it and commence dealing with the consequences. He knew the latter option would ultimately prove to be easier, but even so he found it necessary to come at his answer indirectly.

He sat up. "Can you still open a doorway?"

Seggita's frown deepened and then all expression disappeared from his face. "No."

Etienne felt a tremor run through his body. "I was trying to save Ruarshi's life," he said. "The Halls were poisoning him, so I cut off our access to them. I hope." He might have cut off their access to a lot more than that. He reached for a small healer's weave and flinched slightly when the magic responded to his call. He surged to his feet and would have fallen if Seggita hadn't caught him.

"You should sit back down."

Etienne sidled closer to the older man and took a good look at his eyes. The red tint was gone. His shakes intensified.

"How is Father?" Davyt asked. He was talking to Slan, who'd just arrived on the scene. Etienne glanced toward the clan home and saw that about a dozen people were approaching their little group, while the entire western edge of the place was lined with curious Annorae. They hadn't started edging their way forward yet, which was a relief, as he wasn't sure he could handle a crowd right now.

"Davyt, you know—" Slan began.

Her son rose and pelted off toward Elin's hall. Slan watched him until he'd gone inside and then shifted her attention to Etienne.

"Explain that, please."

He nodded. It was time for him to stop being cruel to these people. In Davyt's case, it had been unavoidable; *someone* had to convince Seggita to open that doorway in Ruarshi's name, and Davyt had been his best option. But he wouldn't raise Slan's hopes until he was sure he had cause.

"I will. Let's go back to the hall first. Davyt should hear it, too."

She looked unhappy but gestured her assent, and Etienne preceded her and Seggita across the open space and through the press of on-lookers. By the time he made it indoors, he'd almost stopped trembling. It was only after he'd taken a seat that he remembered the newly arrived warriors. Someone should look after them.

Etienne stood up again, bracing himself against the table. "I need to show Kennet and the others where to go," he said.

"Solvi is taking care of them," Seggita said. "Please sit."

So he did. His gaze slid to the door of Ruarshi's room, through which Davyt had presumably disappeared earlier. Ardan had been watching over the man for the last several hours, and she should know by now whether or not there had been any change in his condition.

"Okay, Etienne," Slan said. "We can catch Davyt up later. I'm waiting."

How to begin with his explanation? Satu's story would be an unappealing start and its relevance not immediately apparent; nattering about tokens would be of no help in getting to the real heart of the matter; she'd been at the picnic and knew about the creature's claw...

Slan didn't know what had been in the bag, though. He'd lead with that.

Before he could open his mouth, Ruarshi's door swung open. Slan read his face and turned around to look just as Davyt stumbled through it, his face wet. He located them without difficulty among the small sea of faces and beckoned them over.

Etienne and Slan exchanged a glance, rose together, and hurried across the hall. She paused in the doorway and gathered Davyt to her side before continuing within, where all three of them came to a halt.

Ruarshi was sitting up against the headboard of his bed and talking to Ardan, who was perched on the mattress beside him. But that wasn't what made Etienne feel so lightheaded that he feared he was in some danger of floating away. His healer's senses gave him the information he really needed.

The man was still very weak, and he would be for some time yet, but his body was functioning normally again. It would repair itself with no trouble if they could convince him to eat like a horse and refrain from all but the mildest activity for the next fortnight or so.

Etienne would persuade him at knifepoint if he had to.

He stumbled into the outer room of Ruarshi's quarters, deaf to the low commotion rising at the man's bedside, and leaned against the wall by one of the windows. He slid slowly down to the floor and from there a few minor adjustments had him lying on his back, blinking up at the ceiling without seeing it at all. The hard knot in his chest would take days to dissipate, and there was nothing he could do about the renewed shivers running through his body or his sudden and complete exhaustion, but the release of tension felt good on the whole. He suspected he was going to be useless for a little while.

Karoli wandered in later and found him still on the floor. The warrior sat down, stretched his legs out in front of him, crossed his ankles, and said, "I understand you're responsible for his recovery?"

"Yes," Etienne said. His voice was hoarse.

Karoli rose and left the room, returning a moment later with a mug. He set it down next to Etienne's shoulder and resumed his earlier position, while Etienne raised himself on an elbow and took a sip. The floorboards were hard and a little rough but he wasn't ready to get up yet.

"We're all anxious to know how you did it."

Etienne couldn't concentrate worth a damn and could only hope that his reply would make sense. "I gave the creature its claw back. That cut off our connection to the Halls. I think. The link probably worked both ways, you know, which means that monster could have come *here* anytime it wanted to, but really that's just an excuse. I did it to help Ruarshi. I expected our magic to stop working."

"You... what?" Karoli's tone was determinedly neutral.

"Satu told me we bought our power with blood. A lot of it. Allowing Ruarshi to become the latest sacrifice in a long line of them didn't sit right with me. Don't get me wrong, I enjoy healing and it's the only thing I've ever been any good at, but eventually you've got to stop feeding the Dragon. This was never going to end well."

An explosive sigh issued from the threshold to the inner room. Etienne turned his head and saw Elin standing there. It was probably safe to assume that she'd heard most or all of that, which was fine with him. They knew what he'd done now, and would respond however they chose.

It was out of his hands.

In the silence that followed Etienne could hear the murmur of low voices behind her, though he couldn't make out the words. He closed his eyes.

Eventually Elin spoke. "That was quite a gamble, Etienne. Our magic may yet be in jeopardy. It could take some time for all the ripples caused by that stone you threw to reach us."

"I sympathize with your reasoning," Karoli said, "but I'm not going to be terribly happy with you if I end up as just another idiot with a sword."

There were a number of ways Etienne could respond to that, ranging from the unwise to the suicidal. In the end he just said, "I'd do it again."

"Of course you would. Now tell me what you think Ruarshi will say if he and every other healer in Miriyan—including you—loses their abilities overnight."

"I'm sure he wouldn't be pleased."

"It's much worse than that, Etienne," Karoli said. "He'll feel guilty about it. He'll know he's the cause of it."

*"I'm* the cause of it. Obviously I didn't tell him what I was going to do. He'd have stopped me."

"You want him alive even if it means he suffers, is that it?"

Etienne glanced up at the warrior. If the man kept talking like that, they were going to have a problem. "I'd be willing to bet that you're a lot less concerned about his suffering than you are about your own. Quit crying before you've been bitten, Karoli. Do you realize how you sound? *'Alas, I'll be no better off than any other human on earth'?* That's what comes of spending your entire time in Europe looking down your nose at everyone."

Elin stepped between them before Karoli could reply. "Enough for now. We don't know what's going to happen, and until we do there's no reason to fight about it."

"We're not fighting about it," Karoli said on a long exhale, sitting back in his chair and rubbing tiredly at his eyes. "What's done is done. I am extremely glad that Ruarshi is going to recover. I'll keep my fingers crossed about the rest of it. For what it's worth, I'm not convinced we owe our magic to a hideous monster. The Dragon is our Mother. This other thing you've described…"

"No one will be more relieved than I am if we keep our magic."

"The Nerthii, at least, are going to feel the effects of this," Elin said. "Maybe not Ruarshi or Seggita, who've already formed a bond with their clan, but I know of no way the others can forge that link that doesn't involve the Halls. Opening a doorway has always been the catalyst."

"Those two might think of something," Karoli said.

"Aurel's case might prove instructive if she hasn't gone back to her clan home yet. And we, the Annorae that is, still have our books," Elin said. "Another project. When you're asked to explain today's events, I think you should say only that Ruarshi was being poisoned by a magical artifact and you got rid of it. The rest is unnecessary detail."

"I'm sure a Seer will show up sooner or later to contradict me," Etienne said, "but I'll go along with that for now. Not with the others in our group, though."

"That should do," Elin said. "I originally came in here, Etienne, to tell you that Ruarshi is asking for you. He's also having a late meal and I think you should join him. I watched you put nothing in your mouth all day."

"I'm not hungry," he said. When she tried to protest, he waved it away. "Speaking as a healer, let me reassure you that I know what I'm talking about. I'll need at least another hour before I'm ready to eat."

"Speaking as a person with common sense, I'll remind you that *keth* on an empty stomach is a bad idea. Don't let it go too long. I'm sure I'll see you again presently." Elin gave them both a last, long look and left the room.

"She's right about the *keth,*" Karoli said.

"You're the one who brought it to me," Etienne observed. "And if you start mothering me, I'm going to jump off a cliff."

"There aren't any cliffs around here."

"I'm sure I can find one on our way south."

Karoli, who'd been staring out the window, looked down at him. "When will Ruarshi be able to travel?"

"Three to four weeks from now. Probably."

"So we'll be heading home before the snow starts to fly."

That was a welcome thought. Etienne had been prepared to suffer through an entire winter in this frozen place, but now they wouldn't have to. The knot in his chest loosened a little more.

"Yes. We will be."

Etienne had been waiting for it, and he knew that the moment had finally arrived when Ruarshi came around the corner of the hall and crooked a finger at him. The man had just returned from a short walk with Slan, and had found Etienne lounging in the sunshine after doing some light healing work: an Annorae youngster had sprained his ankle while tending to his chores that morning and he'd stepped in to help. The resident healers didn't seem territorial but he wouldn't have responded to the situation any differently if he'd thought them likely to object. Etienne wondered, not with any particular urgency, if he was completely out of control at this point.

He was sure Ruarshi would let him know if that was the case.

He followed his former instructor around to the south side of the hall, where the man was sitting cross-legged in the grass, propped against the wall. Ruarshi patted the ground at his side and Etienne sat down next to him.

"I have questions," Ruarshi said.

Which meant he'd put Etienne's partial explanation together with everything else he knew and taken a hard look at the picture that resulted. As promised, Etienne hadn't lied to anyone in his immediate orbit about what he'd done, but he had gone easy on the details in order to delay exactly what was happening now. A week had passed since he'd disposed of the artifact and Ruarshi was strong enough to support a certain measure of agitation, but Etienne feared his feelings on the matter might be more intense than that. If he had to shut down the conversation, he would. Ruarshi was already upset, he could tell, and about all he could do was withdraw if he started to make it worse.

Unless the withdrawal itself would cause more trouble than just giving the man the information he wanted. This could get complicated.

"I'll answer them," Etienne said.

"How did you know what the result would be when you returned the artifact to the Halls?"

"I didn't. I expected it to be impossible for you and Seggita to open a doorway afterward, but even that was a guess. That was the only outcome I was really interested in."

"I remember what you said about your conversation with Satu."

"It was a memorable discussion."

"The implication was that the Miriyanti had made a bargain with some strange being. Magic in exchange for blood. Right?"

"She never mentioned a being, but as you say, it's hard to negotiate with an inanimate object."

"And we've been assuming that creature we saw in the Halls was the Dragon."

"Karoli doesn't like that idea. I don't like it, either, but it seems likely."

"So what did you think cutting off our connection to the Dragon would do?"

Ruarshi, who'd been staring off into space, was now watching him. Etienne leaned his head back against the wall with a feeling of resignation. The man had followed the trail of crumbs all the way back to the pie. "I thought we'd lose our magic."

"And you did it anyway?"

"The Dragon should have known better than to take a run at you. If it helps, I was offended on behalf of all the others, too. The ones who went before. It wasn't an arrangement that could continue forever."

"You might be the only person in Miriyan with the courage to act on that," Ruarshi said in a breathless voice. "What were you planning to do with your life, if you'd come through all this without the power to heal?"

"I don't know. Farm? It seemed unlucky to think that far ahead."

"The Seers tried to prevent this. Twice. Karoli let slip that they sent a warrior here to kill you."

"That arrow never got anywhere near me. I don't know if Seggita diverted it, or if it was one of the Doshae warriors who did it. That Naishanti was either incompetent or just didn't have adequate time to plan."

Ruarshi was looking at him again. Etienne tried not to let it unnerve him.

"Karoli didn't tell me that the man had actually gotten a shot off. But I was leading up to my next question: is our magic still in jeopardy? Can anyone answer that?"

Etienne shook his head. "The Skeltari might know something. Elin's looking into it."

"So we'll have to wait and see?"

"Yes."

"Do you have any sense of whether or not the Seers will come after you again?"

"No. It might depend on what happens with our magic."

"You're going to need an ongoing bodyguard. I'll arrange it."

They fell silent. Etienne would have been happy to let the conversation lapse its way into oblivion, but after a while Ruarshi went on. "I admire what you've done. I'm also appalled by it. Not to mention grateful. I'm in your debt."

"No, you're not. You must have a terrible memory. And our friendship doesn't belong on a scale." Etienne remembered something he'd been meaning to ask about for the past little while. "Where's my letter?"

"What?"

"My letter. Lorion's suggestion, the pile of paper…?"

"Oh." Ruarshi paused, clearly uncomfortable. "I threw them all in the fire."

"Why would you do that?"

"They were awful."

"I'm sure they weren't."

"Only because you didn't read them. Once I sat down to work on them, I discovered that there was nothing I could say that you didn't already know. Nor was I in the mood to hand out advice."

"It would have been perfectly safe to hand out advice. None of us would have followed it anyway."

Ruarshi bumped him with an elbow. "What do you want to do when we get home?"

"What do you mean? Eat dinner and go to bed?"

"That will do for a start, but I was referring to your longer-term plans. I probably have sufficient influence by now to get you whatever assignment you want. Healing only? Healing plus field work? Shepherding? I presume hunting wouldn't be among your preferences."

"Do they need someone to loll around the bath house? Keep an eye on things?"

"I don't think so."

"I always liked being out among the cattle and sheep when I was growing up. That and healing, maybe? It doesn't really matter. I'll do whatever needs to be done."

"That's certainly true. We'll begin there and see what develops."

"Sounds good to me."

Another interval of silence followed, this one less fraught than the last. Ruarshi was asleep within minutes and Etienne was content to remain where he was for as long as the man continued to doze, his shoulder serving as a bony and somewhat doubtful cushion for his head. He listened unmoving to the bustle of the Annorae around them and enjoyed the damp green smell of the forest in the morning sunlight. For the first time in a long time he wasn't worried about the future. For now, all was well.

# Epilogue

They began to hear rumors of disarray among the Seers about midway through their journey south. The Ostrae clan home, where they stopped one evening to spend the night, was buzzing with them. No one was able to say exactly what was wrong at Mirror Lake, but Ruarshi suspected he knew. His magic and that of the other members of his party remained unchanged; he doubted the same was true for the Seers. The ultimate source of their visions had to have been the well at the labyrinth's center, and when the Halls had been lost to the Miriyanti, the well had gone with them. Mirror Lake's power, both magical and political, was at an end. Ruarshi couldn't bring himself to regret this outcome.

Five of their number had chosen to remain behind at the Annorae clan home. Ruarshi didn't expect to see Seggita, Tuomi, or Elin again anytime soon. Seggita would be returning to the Sylvae before long with Tuomi in tow, and Elin seemed content to remain with her family for the foreseeable future. Saoirse planned to winter there, and Karoli with her, but whether they would stay in the north beyond the next spring was an open question. Karoli had grumbled as they rode away and he would certainly return to live among the Doshae one day, but he was probably wise to maintain some distance between himself and Ciarn for the next little while. Elin promised to write to them with the results of her investigations, and they pledged to write back with their news. Ruarshi hoped that any missives they sent northward would be conventional in their content, possibly even boring.

He'd gone to see Noora before they'd departed, and had made his bows and thanked her for her help. She'd smiled at him and wished him luck with Satu.

When they arrived at the Doshae clan home late one September afternoon, Ruarshi had scarcely dismounted from his horse when he found himself holding an armful of Yael. Aethel and his parents appeared among the welcoming crowd shortly thereafter, and he passed the remainder of the day in a state of mild and pleasant inebriation. He was tired after the long trip, but not excessively so. He fell asleep that night in his own bed with Slan in his arms.

A few days later he went to the clan cemetery. He stopped beforehand at the small garden behind his hall to obtain a sprig of tarragon. It was a drab and unassuming sort of plant, its bright yellow flowers having long since faded and fallen, but as its nickname was 'the little dragon' he thought it might be an appropriate offering.

Before stepping through the gap in the waist-high fence that encircled the burial ground, he stooped to gather a handful of soil. He went first to the graves of his grandparents, where he paused and scattered a bit of earth on each one in the customary gesture of respect, and then headed to the burial site of his great-grandfather, where he did the same. Brushing the last of the soil from his hands, he proceeded to the place where they'd interred the woman he and Lorion had found in the Halls. Only a handful of non-Doshae had ever been laid to rest in their cemetery and she was among them.

It had taken him weeks to realize that the face he'd seen in the well matched that of the woman he'd carried from the labyrinth. He didn't know whether or not the resemblance meant anything, and he supposed he never would. He'd nonetheless decided to leave her something, in case offerings such as this one turned out to have some significance after all.

Standing at the foot of her grave, he bowed formally to her small headstone and laid the sprig at the center of the mounded soil. It looked forlorn lying there, as though blown to the spot by an errant breeze, but it was a remembrance all the same.

Ruarshi turned and left, rejoining the living as they engaged in their day-to-day activities and profoundly thankful that he was able to do so. He went first to check on Etienne, who if he remembered correctly would be found among the livestock at that hour. The man had been caught singing to the cattle a few days previously, and the animals had taken to him like iron to a lodestone.

Half a week passed before he returned to the cemetery, in response to an impulse he couldn't name. It was a blustery day, autumn beginning to make itself felt, and he expected to see only bare earth above the woman's grave. But that wasn't what he found.

The sprig was still there, impervious to the force of the wind whipping at Ruarshi's hair and cloak. He stared at it, unsure of what to think.

It was in bloom.

www.ingramcontent.com/pod-product-compliance
Lightning Source LLC
Chambersburg PA
CBHW020240030726
47499CB00001B/3

* 9 7 9 8 2 1 8 2 7 9 3 7 0 *